By the Author of

NOEL BARBER'S

A FAREWELL TO FRANCE

A NOEL BARBER
FAREWELL TO FRANCE

AVON
PUBLISHERS OF BARD, CAMELOT, DISCUS AND FLARE BOOKS

AVON BOOKS
A division of
The Hearst Corporation
1790 Broadway
New York, New York 10019

    Library of Congress Cataloging in Publication Data
    Barber, Noël
      A farewell to France.
      1. World War, 1939–1945—Fiction.   I. Title.
    PR6052.A623F37   1983   823'.914   82-22917

First Avon Printing, August, 1984

Printed in the U. S. A.

WFH 10 9 8 7 6 5 4 3 2 1

*For
Denise Kilmarnock
with love*

Contents

Acknowledgments

My most grateful thanks to Anthony Davis for his pains-taking help with research in both France and England; and to Jean Riddell for her patience in typing out the many versions of this book.

NB, London, 1982

Prologue

FOR ALL OUR YOUTH the Astell family had lived in and out of Douzy, the small château named after the village, hidden by vineyards lining the gentle, sloping hills of Champagne. My American father and mother, his father's father, my French grandma, my brother and his twin sister, our friends, our lovers—all had made up a patchwork of happiness that none believed would ever end.

Douzy in those days was the warm and friendly heart not only of our home, but of the village, the orchard where we stole apples, the lake on which we rowed, the fields in which we picked wild flowers, the vineyards, the cellars, the Home Farm with its smell of freshly baked bread, the horses, the cows, the cars. Though never gasping with opulence, we were never poor, and it seemed to us, in those far-off days of peace, when it all started, when I first fell in love with Sonia, as we began to grow up in the thirties, impossible that our secure world would ever disintegrate.

Why should it? Even after 1939 Douzy remained unique, an American enclave in a war that gave every indication of petering out through boredom. And if we caught glimpses of gun emplacements in the Champagne area, or read about the Maginot Line, we hardly noticed them in a French world guarded by an army unsurpassed in valor and fighting skills. To us—to thousands like us—we regarded all this with an aloof air, almost flaunting our unconcern as though Americans, even in France, would always remain neutral, closing a collective eye to the dangers surrounding them.

That was before. But then the serenity of Douzy was exchanged for lives that tore us apart, of death and torture for some, despite neutrality, and eventually, after America entered the war, for me a life spent in ditches and barns, hunting the enemy or being hunted—to protect or to kill.

For though I was an American, I was also as French as the Resistance leaders with whom I worked. Most of my life had been spent a few hundred yards from the ditches into which I slid hiding from the Germans, from the house where my father had vanished, and which had been turned into an officers' mess for the Wehrmacht. Only my French grandmother had been permitted on sufferance to occupy a couple of rooms apart from the rest of the house, while I learned, too, that my father, more French in many ways than American, had remained in Reims.

Then, after we had blown up the tunnel in 1944, and the lethal cargo inside it, Patton's armor—drinking four hundred thousand gallons of gas a day—had thundered in, past Le Mans, Chartres, past Paris itself, scything eastward in terrifying sweeps, brushing aside the enemy Germans like maggots. By the end of August Patton himself drove into Reims, and for the first time in months we walked freely in the streets, surrounded by thousands of exulting American GIs thronging the cafés, the sidewalks, stopping the traffic in the streets itself.

No wonder that at first it was impossible to realize that the nightmare was over—that the sunny skies of the summer of 1944 really did exist, that the air was free to breathe. I remember that moment so well. A Frenchman in the Resistance had joined me for a celebration drink—a beer first in the Bar Central in the rue de Chanzy and after that a glass of local red Bouzy wine, very rare now, in the rue Gambetta.

Yet though it was a moment for rejoicing, both of us felt shy. Despite the backslapping, the free drinks, it was almost a sense of nervousness. After years on the run, I had become instinctively furtive, almost afraid to announce, even to a barman, who I really was.

I was frightened of something else—ironically, the future—and what peace might bring. The war had provided a kind of hiatus in which all our family questions had remained unanswered, like dusty letters accumulating through the mailbox when the house is empty. One day soon I would arrive home—and have to sort out the pile of unanswered questions.

Certainly the changes that had washed across France had affected my father and mother. My brother, Guy, was a different person, as was my sister, Anna, rescued from a brothel. Nor could I forget Olivia, who, with Anna, had been tortured by the Gestapo such a long time ago. But most of all I thought of Sonia. Beautiful Sonia, an Italian, an "enemy," but still the woman I had always loved, always would. The wonderful youth we had enjoyed together had been sliced away from us in Douzy, where Sonia had been almost a member of the family before she married, where without warning unseen hands drew closed the curtains of time.

Of course I had to report eventually, and late that evening, with the city of Reims erupting in song and dance, and the champagne spilling over every café pavement, I stopped the first military policeman I saw. He looked me up and down—my blue blouse, my uncut, dirty-blond hair, my scruffy face fringed with beard. Then leaning out of his Jeep, he asked me, chewing gum, "What's the trouble, buddy?"

I swallowed hard. There was no need now for subterfuge, but when I said, "Corporal, I'm Major Astell of the U.S. Army," I felt the sudden grip of panic that comes to the hunted, terrified the corporal would disbelieve me.

Hastily I added, "I've been told to report to Colonel Nolan of Com Z. I'm from Department QJ." Com Z might mean nothing more than a gigantic communications network, but the magic letters *QJ* signified much more—a magical formula commanding instant respect. Still, I felt an odd quiver of apprehension. I had never tried out the secret letters—after all, you were supposed to use them only once in your life, and now I was half afraid that they wouldn't work, that after one look at my filthy clothes, my gaunt, dirty face, someone would snarl, "Beat it!"

"Okay, sir. Jump in," said the MP.

Colonel Nolan was very agreeable if a little fussy. He had sandy hair and large horn-rimmed glasses. An armchair soldier, but none the worse for that, he was intrigued by the secret nature of my work, by my unkempt appearance. But he immediately asked an orderly to bring me my first cup of good American coffee for months, made me welcome in a building in the northern suburbs which had been commandeered in his name, and promised me some clean civilian clothes. He also had a tendency to feeble jokes.

"I won't ask you about your work, major," he smiled, "except to say that if you want to take a bath, we've got unlimited hot water right here—though I expect you've been in plenty of hot water yourself lately."

I laughed politely.

"I've been told," he added, "to give you any help I can. I guess you know that General Patton has established his headquarters in Châlons-sur-Marne—about twenty miles southeast of Reims. We've established our Div headquarters—the 90th—here at Reims."

I nodded. "What I would really appreciate is a little personal help."

"Anything I can do for you, major."

"Well, it sounds crazy, but I used to live near here. Only a few miles from Reims. I've learned that my grandmother was allowed to keep a couple of rooms but then the Germans kicked her out. I'll soon find out where she is, but I'd like to see the house again if you could provide transport."

"Why sure! But you mean you actually used to *live* here. An American family?"

I nodded again. "What's left of them."

"Anything I can do, major," he repeated. "I don't know what you've been up to"—again he looked at me with hope—"but I've been told by Div headquarters to give you top priority. Though you look kinda young for—"

"Early thirties," I grinned, "but I feel sixty. I'll wear better when I've taken you up on that bath. And colonel—do my orders say that after I'm debriefed I can have a furlough? I haven't had leave in months."

"For Chrissake! You're due for a long, long leave—and you can go where you want. Paris? Back home stateside? You name it."

"Switzerland—to see my girl."

"*Switzerland!* Hold up, major. I'm willing to do everything I can—but hell, I don't know whether I'm *permitted* to send army property into a foreign country. And then there's the problem of gas. There's none left. Even Patton's run out of fuel. Getting a gas ration for you will be like—"

"Don't worry, colonel. I've got all the gas I need—and my own car. I hid it before the Germans took over. I'll tell you about it after that bath."

In the end Colonel Nolan offered to drive me himself to our home. Like all Com Z officers he had a big car, a driver, and an armed GI ("in case we need assistance," he explained).

"That's too much trouble, colonel, sir," I murmured.

"Feel free," he said. "It's in a town or a village or what?"

"Well—actually"—I hadn't thought about explanations really—"it's by itself. Rather isolated."

Most of Colonel Nolan's Com Z sector in the 90th Division was centered north of Reims where the N-44 highway straggled through the undistinguished suburb of La Neuvillette, a drab series of apartments and shops in busy streets, though soon we reached the busier, wider avenues of the sprawling city center.

As we edged our way through streets jammed with excited French men and women trying to shake hands with the colonel, some offered flowers, others offered kisses each time the traffic slowed down. In the streets the girls threw their arms round the GIs and kissed them as though their love would never die. They were not in love with any one man, I thought, but with life itself. How could anyone *not* fall in love with liberty and freedom?

Nolan was enjoying himself. He waved paternally, local leader of an army of liberation. He loved the cheers, they loved the handwaves, so everyone was happy. And I too began to catch the frenzy of excitement, though not in the way Nolan did. For though I was an American officer, we were at this moment driving through one of the most historic cities in France, the ancient citadel of Reims, where French kings had been crowned throughout the ages, where in the 1914 war only eighty houses and buildings had escaped damage; and I was an integral part of this city. Here was the first school I attended as a kid, the first football games I had played, a whole life spent away from America.

The heart that beat with patriotic fervor was a hundred and fifty percent American. I was willing to die for my country—yet I had reservations. I was ready to *die* for America, yes, but I would rather not live in it. I would also hate to *die* for France—yet I would always be content to live in it.

As I looked out of the window of the car, the wildly enthusiastic crowds actually stopped the traffic at the place Aristide Briand, where the boulevard Lundy runs into the boulevard de la Paix and the nearby champagne houses. Looking at the people, the surroundings, pangs of youthful memories tugged at me. Behind the *place* was a great open square where on market days—in the heart of a bustling cathedral city—the busy peasants set up their stalls, selling everything from vests to vegetables.

"And behind that," confided Nolan, "is the best restaurant in town, the Brasserie Boulingrin. Best french fries in France."

I had eaten half a life's worth of *pommes frites* at the Boulingrin, its bustling waiters darting between small square tables with their red-and-white-checked paper tablecloths. How many times as a youngster had Monsieur Leleu, founder of the brasserie, slipped us extra french fries after Papa had said, "Enough, children!"

"I agree with you about the fries, I know the place well," I smiled. "Ever thought why it's called Boulingrin—odd name, isn't it?"

Colonel Nolan shook his head.

"Years back an old lady gave the ground where the market now stands to the city of Reims, as a place where the locals could play *boule,* the French version of bowling. And *boulingrin* is a perfectly proper word—it means a bowling green. And that's where the first Monsieur Leleu founded his brasserie."

"I'll be damned," said the colonel.

"Now the *marché* has taken over." I was looking at the peasants bringing in their produce from the villages that studded the surrounding countryside. It was safer now to use the roads. The vegetable and fruit stalls were not always filled, but they still displayed an assortment of spotlessly clean endives, celeriac, bundles of *mâche,* a score of other vegetables and herbs. Each unwrapped bundle was examined thoroughly. We could see thrifty, knowledgeable housewives handle tomatoes and peaches carefully, testing one after the other, discarding the unwanted against a noisy background of drama—as though the fate of a French wife's stew depended finally on the one single bunch of onions she had chosen above all the others to flavor her dish.

"All this handling of food—it looks darned unhygienic to me," Nolan said, looking at the mounds of vegetables with distaste.

I almost laughed. "The French don't *like* their vegetables wrapped, colonel. They like to pick and choose, handle everything. They like the smell of fresh earth on a bunch of radishes."

After we had passed the *marché,* I showed the driver the way. We crossed the place Royale—an exquisite miniature version of the place Vendôme in Paris—and then passed the cathedral, with its laughing angel to the left of the main entrance. After that it was easy. We bore right until we reached the broad avenue d'Epernay, the main road leading straight as a ruler to Champagne's second most important city, Epernay, south of the Marne.

We didn't have far to go. Soon the open road on either side was flanked by never-ending rows of vineyards that spread like a carpet across the great plain of Reims, fashioned by a beneficent nature to produce a heaven-sent storehouse of riches. Yet the same nature, by a devilish quirk, was able to switch off heaven and switch on hell at will, for this huge flat plain had also from time immemorial provided Europe's greatest natural arena of battle, surrounded by the enemies of a dozen countries anxious to despoil it.

Seven or eight miles farther along the straight road, near the edge of the modest mountain of Reims, we turned left at a signpost marked TO DOUZY, RILLY, MAILLY. All were famous Champagne names.

"Rilly? That strikes a bell," said Nolan. "That's where the Krauts blew the tunnel sky-high. I heard the Germans were hoarding explosives and blew themselves up by mistake."

The rumor factory of OSS—the Office of Strategic Services—was certainly working efficiently. That was exactly the story which had been deliberately—but inaccurately—started.

"Douzy?" said Colonel Nolan. "Funny sort of name, isn't it?"

Perhaps he was wondering what kind of a house he would find when we arrived. "Ordinary" French houses don't conform to the spit and polish of most American homes. The French regard repainting a house as a criminal waste of money, while flower beds are an unnecessary decoration that robs the peasants of a few extra vines.

"It *is* an odd name, Douzy. I believe there's another village called Douzy somewhere," I said as I guided the driver off the road from Mailly, showing him where to turn. "But we acquired the name by honest-to-God French logic."

"How come?"

"It was christened Douzy by two families who founded it after leaving two other neighboring villages," I explained as our car bumped along. "The villages are still there. One is called Dizy and the other, a few miles away, is called Bouzy."

This was a simple and true explanation, but Nolan was much more impressed when we turned off the pale-yellow, chalky, two-mile private road and he read the weather-worn wooden signpost with its flat statement: VERS LE CHATEAU.

"A château?" he exclaimed.

"Yes, colonel. Our home. Hope you like it. Over there! You can just see the roof through the trees."

"A *château!*"

And that was how, after years of war and waiting, I finally came home to Douzy. As I looked around, driving slowly from the main road, my heart started thumping wildly. I had the curious feeling that I had been catapulted back in time and struggling inside was a small boy looking with wonder at what I was doing.

The ground sloped away in a dell, where in winter I had sledded down a thousand times as a child, every fold of the long, dipping, tree-studded grass as familiar to me as my own hands. I saw it in memory as carefully tended, but even now the weeds, the thistles, the knee-high grass couldn't rob me of its beauty. I felt a surge of elation, memories stumbling through my brain as we drove past the silhouettes of old barns, derelict buildings, signposts of history along the pathways of my youth, my innocence, my family, my loves, my home.

Through a gap in the trees I saw the distant hills, and beyond them the tree line, where the vines gave way, leaving the higher ground to be ruled by the trees. In the center stood the black outline of the village church, not in the village of Douzy itself, but outside the cluster of white houses, alone, defiant, in the midst of the vineyards.

As we stopped the car outside the courtyard of the château, I led the colonel through the white stone archway. For all my life the gravel had been free of even the puniest weed, but though it was choked with grass, with more thistles, it still looked beautiful.

The house was deserted. I could see the disapproving brown, closed shutters. But the very fact that it had been occupied by the Germans was an affront. It assaulted my senses, and I had a sudden desire to kick the door open, if only to let in the fresh air.

"It's unlocked," cried Nolan, twisting the knob.

"Saves the cost of a new door," I said. "Please—after you."

Inside the large entrance hall with its tiled floor, Colonel Nolan put down his field cap on the ormolu table with its gilded legs which had stood up against the wall—always with a bowl of flowers on it—since before my father was born. From there, double doors led to the main reception room.

"It's magnificent," the colonel breathed with awe. It *wasn't* magnificent—but the colonel stroked a polished table and muttered, "Beautiful, beautiful. It was used as a German officer's mess? Thank God nothing was broken."

In fact most of us hated this formal room, and I felt I had to apologize for it, if only to show that we were Americans.

"I'm afraid it's rather pompous," I explained. "Grandma only liked stuffy French furniture. Come into the next room, colonel—you'll find it more comfortable, and I'll get us all a drink."

But as we moved into what had been our usual, warmer living room, Colonel Nolan exploded with rage. The room was a shambles. Champagne bottles, glasses, plates, many broken, looked as though they had been hurled round the room in an orgy. The striped French wallpaper was stained; remnants of food littered the Aubusson carpet; lumps of chicken and German sausages were stuck between the cushions of the deep easy chairs. The room reeked of a bar parlor which a careless landlord hadn't bothered to clean up.

"Bloody Krauts!" snorted the colonel. "Sergeant!" he shouted to his driver, "get someone on the RT to send in a detail to clear up the place. You've got a map reference?"

Without thinking he picked up an empty champagne bottle from a table, scrutinized the label with a puzzled frown, pickup a second, a third, and observed me, reading out a bottle label.

"Astell champagne," he read out. "Same name, eh?"

With a sigh I admitted, "Well, yes, sort of a family business. My grandfather founded that mark."

"Your *grandfather!*"

I said nothing.

"Good God! You make champagne!" He examined a bottle again. "What does this mean?" He pointed to a second label, *"Reserviert fur Angehörige der Deutschen Wehrmacht."*

My German was good enough to know what *that* meant. "Reserved for the Wehrmacht," I translated.

"No longer!" cried Colonel Nolan. "Not now, by God." Then, as though still unable to grasp the truth, he asked, "You mean to tell me you lived here for three generations?" He invested the final words with a special awe. "As it's your home, maybe you could take me on a tour."

"Sure."

I led him through the ground floor. It was a tour for me too, a tour of memories, though each door I opened seemed to produce more evidence of the filth left behind by the invaders. In the library, once Papa's pride and joy, all the books had been stolen. In the conservatory most of the plants were dead, some thrown on the ground. It was the same everywhere. In the kitchen I arrived just in time to hear mice scurrying away. The laundry room was six inches deep in water from some broken pipes.

"It's disgusting," cried the colonel. "Those bastards will pay for this!"

Pay for what? How could anyone pay for a torn-up past?

Trying to cheer me up, the colonel said, "At least I hope you managed to hide your best champagne. Is that kept in back?"

"No." I shook my head. "There's a back entrance some distance away—through the Home Farm, which I showed you, and then there's a main entrance to the champagne cellars about half a mile down the road to Rilly."

"I remember about Rilly—the tunnel being blown up—and now I'm remembering the name Douzy. Wasn't there something about a huge underground cave?"

"You mean the Douzy and Rilly pyramids?" I knew of course that they were in their way quite famous.

I tried to explain briefly the extraordinary phenomenon of the Douzy Pyramid, cut deep into the hillside by the Romans nearly two thousand years ago when they were excavating for chalk, which they prized highly as a building material, especially for inside walls.

"I don't get it." He was puzzled. "Why underground—and how?"

"The Romans wanted the chalk, but they couldn't use open-cast mining because chalk can easily be damaged by frost or rain. So they used to dig a shaft into a convenient hillside, which they could cover at night, then haul the first blocks of chalk from it. As they dug deeper, they excavated outward and deeper from the original shaft—always underground—until eventually the Douzy Pyramid was a hundred and twenty feet deep with a base fifty feet wide in each direction. Centuries later, when champagne was invented, someone discovered it was the perfect place to store it."

"Can we go and see it?" he asked.

"I don't think so. That's the tragedy. When the Germans blew up the Rilly tunnel"—I hesitated, for I didn't want to let him know that I was the one who had blown it up—"it blew in both the Douzy and Rilly pyramids which were astride the railway line."

"Too bad," he commented. "Sounds fabulous. Let's take a look-see upstairs."

Standing on the main landing, he suddenly asked me, "How's about your mother and father? They okay?"

"My mother is in America," I said. "I'm afraid my father is dead." I spoke rather shortly, I didn't want to have to elaborate.

"I'm sorry about that. Tell me—is the rest of your family
safe?"

"I hope so. But my sister married a German—"

"Ah! That's bad." He was almost treating me avuncu-
larly as if I were his protégé. "But don't give up hope."

"And I have a younger brother. He had a rough time. He
had a Jewish girl friend." I paused, memories stirring.
"It's a long story." I didn't want to go into details.

At the top of the staircase I showed the colonel my father's room, which overlooked the stark outline of the
lonely church framed in endless vineyards.

The bedrooms were arranged on either side of the broad,
spacious corridor, which was filthy. Some of the pictures
had been broken, so had a table. The corridor was wider
than the word suggests, the walls decorated with old
French silk, a little faded now, but warmer and more
friendly for all that. For a moment I almost forgot the damage the Germans had done and the other Americans, for I
was not just walking past a row of doors, I was rummaging
in the cupboards of my life. I hardly realized that I said,
"This was my old room."

"You'll be wanting to move in after your debriefing,"
said the colonel.

"I won't use it," I said without thinking. "I prefer this
one." I reached the far end of the corridor and pushed open
the door.

The room meant nothing to him, of course, he hardly noticed it, but this was Sonia's old room, the room she used
every time she came to stay at the château de Douzy, first
as a schoolgirl on vacation when her diplomat father and
mother were posted far away, later as a growing girl. Darling, wonderful, black-haired, impetuous Sonia with those
startling cornflower-blue eyes, how many times, how
many hundreds of times, had I made love to her in this
room after the house had gone to sleep, tiptoeing to the
warmth of her bed, her arms, her kisses.

"Sonia's room," as it was always called, had even been
decorated according to Sonia's whim, with matching wallpaper and curtains, even the ceiling papered with the

same design of red poppies, so that when only one small lamp glowed dimly, it was like making love in a bed of flowers.

That room had been an echo of our secret lives. All gone, all empty. Revisiting the years of youth, I felt a sudden shiver, as though muffling myself against melancholy, a sense of loss for happy times which had slipped away in carefree days.

I was thinking of the day in 1931 when we first became lovers, when she was only seventeen, long before any of us contemplated an end to the happy days of peace, for that was when it all began, and those were the times I liked to remember, those enchanted days of Douzy.

Part One

1931–1937

1

As that particular summer's evening drew to a close—I was nineteen at the time— the white building glowed almost pink, and the west wall—the lower half covered with American pillar roses—was warm to the touch.

It was a long wall, and in the center my grandfather had built a conservatory to catch the afternoon and evening sun, a large glass room adorned with flowering plants and white summer furniture. It looked down over the dell, the far end hedged by giant rhododendrons giving a blaze of color in spring, grassed banks falling away from the other side of the drive, so that as children, when we sledded down in winter snows, we could also skate on the small lake beyond. By the flowering shrubs a wicker gate led to a rough orchard, and beyond that the vineyards stretched in tight, symmetrical rows.

In the pink evening, walking back up the winding path of the dell, past the shadows of day's end already shrouding the flower beds, the last of the sun shone on the stone and set fire to the window panes of the conservatory.

Here the Astells had lived since 1873 when Richard Astell, the twenty-two-year-old son of a San Francisco real estate millionaire, set off from Nob Hill to acquire a little "culture" through the Grand Tour of Europe and fell in love with Jacqueline de Villebrun, an only daughter whose father owned vineyards both north and south of the Marne, and whose grapes were eagerly bought by the great champagne houses.

17

The château was discreetly hidden. Even from below, from the main road linking Epernay and Reims, you could never catch more than an occasional glimpse of slate roofs glinting like blue-gray steel, for the house lay couched in a wooded park. The curving drive wound from the main road for more than two miles past vineyards, then tree-studded lawns so sloping they could be trimmed only with the scythe, past the kitchen garden—my French grandmother had a fetish for fresh vegetables—and then the long, rectangular flower bed, almost hidden from the graveled drive—ablaze with every kind of bloom from snapdragons to roses—because this bed was used only for cutting blooms to fill vases in every room.

It was not a pretentious building, not grandiose in the manner of most French châteaux. It had no fountains gurgling, no neatly trimmed box hedges cut in intricate patterns to comprise formal gardens. But all the same, the three-story building—white stone with a steep gray-slated roof and slender ornate chimneys—was not only impressive, it was beautiful, perhaps because the shape and the way it nestled between trees had been cunningly devised to make Douzy château look smaller, less ostentatious. It gave the impression of being a long, low country house, somehow disguising its third floor.

From the top floor, dormer windows peeped out like square eyes in the sharply sloping roof, and here the domestic staff lived: Jean, the butler, who had worn a clean white jacket for each meal for twenty years or more; Aubergine, a nickname for the chief parlor maid; Yvette, the cook; and sundry others, all related to the vignerons working for my father, and who came and went as they grew up, became pregnant, and hastily married. At least in retrospect, that is what seemed to happen all the time.

The first floor contained what house agents call "the principal bedrooms," and there were seven grouped on either side of a broad landing, reached from the ground floor by a wide and handsome staircase. For as long as I could remember, the decor of the landing had never changed from the dark-red silk walls—faded, but no one seemed to notice—mostly covered with scores of old sepia photographs which had, through the early years, recorded the changing history of Douzy champagne.

No one ever thought of changing the framed photographs, or adding to them, perhaps because Grandma regarded the landing as her own photograph "album," and also because she hated change.

How she had shown her shocked disapproval when my parents installed a bathroom in their bedroom, the grandest bedroom in the house, with lovely views beyond the Douzy church. A *private* bathroom connected directly to their bedroom! A bathroom that would be used by only two people! The thrifty men of Champagne sniffed as audibly as Grandma when years ago that bathroom was installed, long before the passing years had allowed modern plumbing to make the bedroom floor of Douzy a warm and comfortable oasis for tired men and women and children.

The ground floor was different—a mixture of Grandma's stiffness and Mama's warmth, largely determined by the layout of the building. The large hall could never be used for any other purpose for it was bordered by the courtyard, which you reached after driving past the cutting flower bed and turning left behind some yew trees, where an arch of white stone in the wall led to the graveled courtyard.

On the right were the old stables, to the left double front doors led to the hall and an even larger—and very formal—reception room, a *salon* the French called it, and it still bore the stamp of Grandma's formidable character, for she regarded all the furniture other than French period pieces as vulgar. So out of deference (and fear?) the salon remained as it was in her day. It didn't really matter, for it was used only rarely, when the Astells entertained "officially." Behind the salon lay warmer rooms, a sitting room of low, comfortable armchairs, the walls covered with paintings by artist friends of my father.

Within a few years of my grandfather's marriage to Jacqueline de Villebrun, her parents died, and then my grandfather, some years before he died, took a momentous step. Against all the advice of his neighbors and friends, he decided to bottle his own champagne instead of selling the grapes to the big producers. Jacqueline had inherited nearly thirty acres of vineyards—about twelve of them on the mountain of Reims covered by the famous Pinot Noir red grapes. The rest provided the white Chardonnay grapes, which grew south of the Marne near Epernay.

The decision caused a furor. It was an unheard of step, for the production of champagne—in which several wines of different years are blended—is risky and costly, and most people who were lucky enough to *own* vineyards did much better for themselves by selling instead of making. But since champagne—like port and cognac—is a blended wine, the name of the producer, not the vigneron content to sell his grapes to a big firm, decorates each label.

However, that, it seems, was just what my grandfather wanted—to see his name on the label of every bottle of champagne produced from his own vineyards.

My father did something else. Since two-thirds of his vineyards were planted with Chardonnay white grapes, he decided to bottle *blanc de blancs,* produced entirely from white grapes. Other firms had produced small quantities of *blanc de blancs,* which is a lighter champagne than that produced by the traditional blending with red grapes (which have to be pressed more quickly than white ones to prevent the skin staining the juice). But though my grandfather knew that the blend of red and white gave more body, he always believed that *blanc de blancs* was more subtle, was a more delicate champagne, "the perfect drink," he always said, "at midday."

He designed a special bottle not unlike a Dom Pérignon in shape—though with a longer, more slender neck—and so founded Astell champagne; not a big-quantity-selling brand—he rarely produced more than fifty thousand bottles a year—but both his blended champagne and his *blanc de blancs* were an instantaneous success, a champagne of superb quality in high demand wherever it could be bought.

Since the Astells were never short of money—even after

my grandfather died—my father was in the enviable position of never having to compromise. If the vintage was not up to standard, then we drank Astell *blanc* still wine in place of champagne. Astells produced only the best—or none at all—and so it became as much a hallmark of quality as a French watch by Cartier or a pair of British shoes by Lobb. There just couldn't be anything better.

I was nineteen, and hoping to be a writer, on that eventful day in 1931. I worked three days a week in Paris, learning my trade under the watchful eye of Papa's brother, my uncle Oregon, who was the owner and editor of a weekly newspaper, the *Paris American*. My brother, Guy, and his twin sister, Anna, were two years younger, and so was Sonia, whose father, Signor Riccardi, was Italian ambassador to Paraguay. But then Sonia, who even went to the same school in Switzerland as Anna, was like a sister to us, a daughter to our parents. It had always been like this, so that even now, in the early summer, Sonia customarily joined the family for the half-term break.

During the afternoon I had caught sight of Anna and Sonia vaguely helping Mama in the garden. Whenever I saw Mama with any gardening implement, even a pair of shears, I hid, or pretended to be deeply immersed in some book. I hated gardening, the more so as there was no need for it. We had plenty of helpers from the vineyards.

But Mama always felt she had green fingers—though her notion of gardening never included onerous chores like weeding or cutting the edge of the lawn; that was a gardener's job. She just enjoyed nipping off dead flowers in the herbaceous border or clipping off overblown roses. She also liked company, and so Sonia or Anna would listen to her chatter.

Mama was adorable. Still under forty, she was as American as apple pie, whereas my father, even though he was half American, was as French as *tarte aux pommes*. And as both our parents knew, these two culinary masterpieces, cooked with more or less the same ingredients, are separated by a common factor—the Atlantic.

That evening, just as I was about to join Mama and Papa in the living room, I paused outside the doorway to admire her—almost surreptitiously. A mother of three teenage children—two of them strapping sons—she had kept her figure as trim as a Chanel model's. Her legs were straight and slim, her ankles as good as her wrists, her blond hair untinted. She was simply, as someone put it at an embassy party in Paris, "a darned good looker." I agreed. I was proud to escort Mama anyplace, and I was always suffused with sudden pride when I saw guests eyeing her. She liked it too. I could tell.

Still unaware of my presence outside the room, Mama picked up a magazine, laughing to herself, enjoying a kind of private joke.

"Can I share it?" Papa asked.

"Share what?"

"The joke that's making you chuckle."

"It's nothing really, it's Sonia!"

"But what?"

"Sonia was nipping off dead heads, squatting down. She was wearing a short white skirt, and as I looked at her across the flower bed I could see—*well,* I could see *everything,* but I didn't realize it at first and without thinking asked her, 'Why on earth do you wear black panties with a white skirt?' And do you know what she replied? 'Oh Auntie, I never wear panties in hot weather! That's *me* you're looking at.' "

As Mama added, "Apart from anything else, it's most unhygienic," I hardly heard her. My mind was racing, twisting, turning, painting an erotic picture of a beautiful girl squatting on that May afternoon in the garden, and as I imagined Sonia, I writhed with desire.

Even before we became lovers, I had, in the half-formed way of the young, dreamed of Sonia without any clothes on. I had wondered if I could peep at her; I had even had messy and ecstatic dreams about her. But still, it never entered my teenage head—not even in my dreams—that I could ever make love to her. She was like a member of the family. It would be almost like doing it with Anna! Though

Sonia *was* different, for she had inherited from her mother
—who was half Italian, half Russian—a wild streak as well
as a kind of wild beauty.

Mama was still smiling as she added, "No one's ever
going to tame *that* one! When she knows what she wants
nothing will stop her getting it."

At that moment Sonia came up behind me, unaware
that Mama had been talking to Papa about her. Her black
hair above the bright blue eyes had been mussed by the
wind, and she was laughing with pure happiness. As I
looked at her, compared her with the cool beauty of Mama,
I remembered what Uncle Oregon had once said, "Your
mama is like a carefully tended plant. Always cool and
beautiful."

And this one, I thought, looking at the daredevil twinkle
in Sonia's eyes, mentally undressing her, is like a wild
flower. No one's ever going to put *her* in a vase.

"Anyone seen Anna?" Sonia rushed unconcernedly into
the room while I stood transfixed, thinking of what Mama
had told Papa, stimulated by such a compound of desire,
imagination, frustration, it seemed impossible that she
could fail to notice the physical change in me. My thoughts
spurred by a dozen words, I was almost bursting out of my
gray flannel trousers, my mind focusing on a picture of a
dark-haired girl helping out in the garden. I swore under
my breath that I would discover for myself whether or not
Sonia wore panties—without ever giving a thought to the
long, tortuous, agonizing, ecstatic, and at times unhappy
trail along which that vow would lead me.

The chance came two days later—chance being engineered by me. I woke with excitement to a perfect morning, throwing open the windows at exactly the right
moment, as the sun rose over the rim of the wooded hills,
then slid effortlessly into another dreamy Douzy day. Only
later a storm threatened. It was sultry for May, but I said
to Sonia, "Let's go and pinch some raspberries."

The kitchen garden, with its netted soft-fruit section, lay
beyond the orchard and the Home Farm, and—as I well
know—the orchard itself was a secret garden which none

could overlook. It was a wild orchard—apple and pear trees, plums, a gnarled crabapple, a couple of twisted old cherry trees, all growing in a sea of untended knee-high grass, studded with poppies like a painting by Bonnard. If you traveled a thousand miles across France, you couldn't find a more secluded place.

For a moment, standing at the top of the dell, shading her eyes against the hot sun, she pointed to the gentle scene beyond.

"It's so beautiful," she said. "I feel I never want to leave."

It was. Beyond the long rectangle of the farm buildings, which you could see from this point, the vineyards stretched like rows of orderly soldiers, each acre of land busy with workers. May was turning into June. The first spraying against pests and diseases had almost been completed, though I could see a couple of figures in blue, their metal canisters strapped to their backs, glinting like brass in the sun. They wielded long hose pipes with nozzles, searching out the vital spraying areas.

In the next vineyard placid, sure-footed horses, tossing their heads against early flies, unerringly trod the yard-wide pathways between the rows of vines, drawing the old-fashioned machine behind them for the first hoeing of the vineyard year. The horses rarely ruined the vines, which were never permitted to grow unhindered, so that the fat, round bellies of the horses moved above them. With their legs invisible they sometimes looked as though they were swimming in green water.

"It's like a painting," said Sonia.

"You're right." I repeated her earlier words, "I too never want to leave." For even though I knew that one day I would be a writer instead of following in Papa's business, the vineyards were a way of life to us all, had been since the day we first started to walk. Sonia too. She had known, even as a toddler, how the young vines had to be coddled, as prone to sickness as we were. I had myself learned to use the hoe, to keep the soil loose, never compact. Even when I was ten I had started to learn how the foliage of the vines

had to be reduced each year to give the sun more chance to
help the grapes on their way—and take care not to remove
the wrong branches and leaves, which could cause the pol-
len to fall to the ground instead of blossoming.

And, too, Douzy was "a family"—one that included all
the children of the vignerons. Each one of us was involved.
After all, when you own thirty acres, with up to four thousand vines on each acre, there's a lot of work to be done.
Wires running the length of the lanes of vines, supported
by metal posts three feet high, had to be repaired. Each
row had to be inspected regularly. So did the vines themselves, "Champagne's children" my grandma called them,
the shoots about a yard apart with a life span of around
thirty years, and bearing fruit four years after planting.

"Let's go to the farm and get a sandwich," I suggested.
The Home Farm kitchen had always been a haven, for
there was no other room like it; it was the headquarters of
a multiple organization, not only the horses, the cows, the
pigs and hens, the churns where we made Douzy butter,
even Douzy cheese. That was only one end of the farm, for
the other end of the farm was like another building, filled
with workshops above ground connected with wine making.

"Any chance of a *casse-croûte?*" Sonia knew she could always beg a sandwich from Madame Robert, wife of the
farmer, a typical farmer's wife with five children and,
like so many farmers in Champagne, half an acre of vineyards, her badge of independence. She stretched above the
huge old table—always used to feed the vignerons each
harvest—and sorted out strings of garlic and onions and a
dozen *saucissons.*

She cut off two thick, slightly moist slices, walked over
to the fireplace, which never seemed to die out, and took
down from a hook one of a dozen black hams curing in the
smoke of its own fire. Slicing a *baguette* longways, she
smeared it with homemade butter, slapped the lot together.

"Madame Robert, you're an angel," I said, and then, the
earlier stirrings forgotten for the moment, we sat down on

the roadside behind the farm, munching away until, without warning, Sonia asked, almost too casually, "What about those raspberries?"

Instantly the image which Mama had painted returned. I threw away the rest of the oversized sandwich as she cried, "Race you to the orchard!"

We dashed off into the dell. I realize now that she knew as well as I did that the orchard, and the chasing, represented the first sensation of an undefined love—not yet to be taken completely—because each time the chase ended we tumbled in the long grass, and just for a moment—with no words spoken—we were locked like wrestlers, and though it hardly entered my head that I could kiss or fondle her, those stirrings were so real, so much of a temptation, that we both experienced a delicious tingle of anticipation. Even then I knew that Sonia wanted to be touched, however briefly. But what she didn't know this time was that I was thinking of Mama's conversation—and that when I caught her (as I always did) I was determined to tip her up.

She was off like a streak. I chased her. We fooled around, dodging round trees, laughing, losing breath, touched by secret excitement, before I grabbed her and we fell together, hidden in the grass.

"Got you!" I cried, and in one swift movement I grabbed her ankles and held her legs up. Giggling, she held her skirt between her thighs, screaming but still laughing.

"Stop it, you wretch! Stop it!" she shouted.

I didn't—until suddenly she panted, "I give up!" As though some invisible force had pulled her arms away from her skirt, she let go and—all in a matter of seconds—the white skirt fell away from her legs and I knew what Mama had meant when she talked about black panties.

She laughed and kicked out. I loosened my grip, rolled away, and instantly, the beautiful triangular black vision became a forbidden mystery, hidden by one thin piece of cloth more impossible to tear away than the bars of a prison.

Sonia wasn't angry, but as I started to reach for her—I

think this was the first time I wanted to kiss her secretly—the angry clouds spilled out the first huge drops of rain. They were enormous, the herald of a cloudburst.

"Run for it!" I shouted, and grabbed her hand as we raced, panting up the dell, reaching the shelter of the conservatory at the very moment a jagged fork of lightning split the sky. Within two seconds the thunder clapped in a gigantic explosion—the storm was directly overhead—and then a curtain of rain blotted out the end of the dell.

"Just in time," I gasped. "You all right?"

"I love thunderstorms," she nodded. "I'm going to stay here and watch."

Papa's two black Labradors, which had been chasing us too, slid through the door and lay down panting, pink tongues lolling.

Still breathing hard, I stood facing the back wall with its climbing geraniums. Then Sonia did a strange thing. Almost ostentatiously ignoring the summer chairs, she picked up a flowered cushion and threw it against the back wall. She was directly opposite me. She sat down on the ground facing me, her straight back against the wall, her legs—the skirt above the knee—drawn up until they were almost touching her chin. It was the natural way to sit on the floor, but it was not natural for her legs to be slightly parted.

All this was done without a word, but in a significant silence, broken only by the thunder after each vicious, jagged fork of lightning and the hiss of heavy rain and the noise as it hit the glass roof.

I stood looking at her—everything—and she, pretending to be unaware of the way she was sitting, looked back at me, silent blue eyes unwavering, lips slightly apart.

Had she spoken I might have thought her pose accidental. But she didn't speak. Not a word. She just looked at me steadily.

Two days later Sonia and Anna returned to their Swiss finishing school, and I did not see Sonia again until the end of term—July—when I drove down from Douzy to Switzerland to pick the girls up and drive them home.

I had been given my first car, and I wanted to drive my supercharged T3 MG on a long run, and what fun it would be—or so I argued—for me to drive down to the school and give the girls a treat. Far more exciting for them than taking the stuffy old train from Lausanne to Paris, and *then* having to be met and driven by Gaston, our driver.

Permission to drive to Switzerland faced one stumbling block: my grandma, known to everyone in Champagne as La Châtelaine. My mother might be understanding—at least she hid her apprehension when I drove too fast—but Grandma was a firm believer that no cars were safe unless driven by a chauffeur.

A formidable French lady approaching her seventies, she inspected most of "her" vineyards daily—by bicycle. La Châtelaine cycling with determination through sun or rain was a sight often pointed out proudly to visiting tourists. She symbolized the toughness of a *Champernoise,* for she was a genuine eccentric. Morning or evening, rain or shine, she was always adorned with ostentatious diamonds or other jewelry. And though sometimes in bad weather she would cycle in a pair of corduroys, she always wore her jewels. Everything she did was energetic, perhaps because she used so much of her body in the vineyards, fingers especially, for she could bend down, *feeling* whether something should be done to a particular root of the vine. Her fingers were almost alive with decision; when she wore gloves she never had to work her fingers into them, they slid in with the ease of a second skin.

Once a week Grandma was driven to Reims, the leading center of Champagne. She always made straight for Boulingrin's, not only because she enjoyed the food there, but because the restaurant was like a club where she could be sure to meet friendly champagne producers. Lunch was only one part of her day, the best part was spent in the hour she gossiped with friends.

In the home she exuded what my brother, Guy, called "crinoline sounds." She rustled as she moved from room to

room, she wore long, starchy dresses that seemed to have
been left over from another age, and though she sat comfortably on the horrid French chairs in the salon, she always perched uneasily on the edge of Mama's American
chairs, as though they were made of glass.

"Apart from anything else," snorted Grandma, "this
dangerous car doesn't seem to have a *top*. It can't be safe."

"But Grandma," I implored her, "the top, as you call it,
has nothing to do with the car's safety."

"In case of accidents, *non?* If there's no top, what's to
stop the girls falling out?"

My father said nothing; I think he was terrified of his
mother. Even though he was recognized by now as one of
the foremost experts in the champagne industry, he found
it hard to stand up to her. He was very tall and thin,
though not skinny, very handsome in a lean way, yet
somehow—and sadly—slightly remote. Perhaps he spent so
much time in the cellars and the vineyards that he just
didn't have enough time for us.

"Perhaps we should wait—these small cars—" my father
began doubtfully.

"But, Papa, this is the finest car in the world. It's an
MG!" As though that resolved any doubts.

Finally, as so often happened, the day was saved by my
father's younger brother, Oregon Astell, so nicknamed because years previously he had worked as a newspaperman
in Portland and the name had stuck. He had long since returned to Paris to found his modest weekly paper called
the *Paris American.* He would never make a fortune, but
he loved the work.

Uncle Oregon was two years younger than my father,
and because Grandma insisted on regarding him as beneath saving—*"un journaliste!"* she once said witheringly—he was the only one who cheerfully told her not to be so
silly.

"Don't be such an old fogy!" Oregon said bluntly.
"You'll be driving with a red flag in front next."

My American mother had said nothing. She just smiled
tolerantly, giving my father time to maneuver a few hesi-

tant protests, safe in the knowledge that if Uncle Oregon was present—and he was a regular visitor to Douzy most weekends—he would overwhelm Grandma. That is just what happened now.

"Of course Larry should be allowed to make the trip," said Oregon. "He's old enough to be a soldier—he's old enough to die for his country."

"Exactly!" shot back Grandma, "and old enough to die in a car crash! You are a fine one to give advice, I must say. If anything happens," she crossed herself, "don't blame me for encouraging such stupidity."

Everyone finally agreed. I set off in high spirits, spending the night at the Hôtel Richemond in Geneva, where I tried in rather desultory fashion to pick up a girl, failing through lack of enthusiasm, even though the MG, with its strap across the hood, was a great lure when on the prowl.

The next morning, after a large helping of toast and black cherry jam, I drove along the beautiful road bordering Lake Leman until I reached the small town of Rolle, halfway along the lake. This was the headquarters of St. Agnes, where Anna and Sonia were both boarders. I reached there by half past nine, giving us plenty of time to drive back home to Douzy, and I saw Sonia the moment she stood at the top of the wide staircase—the stairs and banisters a vague picture of shiny, varnished, pale brown wood.

Almost demurely, she walked toward the large tiled entrance hall where countless moms and dads usually waited at the end of each term for their equally demure daughters. Only now they had all returned home, for St. Agnes had broken up the previous evening, and that morning I was the only person waiting.

With a sudden constriction, a dry-throat feeling of excitement, I watched as Sonia reached the bottom step and, with a hint of a giggle, gave a mannequin-style turn so that her pleated skirt twirled like a kilt.

I can't remember Sonia ever looking more beautiful. Her blue wide-apart-eyes set in an oval face were framed in shining black hair, straight, almost down to her shoulders, with a fringe over her forehead. But it was the contrast between the black glossy hair, thick and glorious, the white teeth showing in a smile, and her two-piece linen dress that made me blurt out, "You look stunning! Would you say it's coral—the color?" I asked.

"Like it? I call it cherry pink."

"You look like a painting," I said, and indeed she did. No artist could ever have chosen two more beautiful and contrasting colors.

"To say nothing of that shiny hair," I said.

"That's my secret," she smiled. "I always rinse it with rainwater."

Standing there smiling, looking a perfect product of a Swiss finishing school, very "correct," well brought up, beautiful, but not flashily dressed—as behooved young ladies at St. Agnes—I almost blurted out, "And underneath that beautiful pink skirt—are you wearing panties?"

"And now let me look at you." She pretended to study me critically. "Hmmm! I see a tall, handsome, loose-limbed young man with rather long blonde hair and trusting brown eyes," she laughed, "and what looks like a very expensive English sports jacket and a pair of very posh suede shoes."

And as I walked forward to greet her, she added, still laughing, "I love the way you walk—as though you want to dance. Oh, Larry! It's great to see you again."

"Term's over," I laughed to cover the feeling inside me, and as I kissed her on both cheeks, asked, "All set? The car's outside. Anna ready?"

For a moment she looked me full in the face, large blue eyes unblinking, then she took a deep breath and said simply, "Anna's fine, don't panic, but she's not coming with us. We'll have to drive to Douzy alone, just the two of us."

2

LOOKING AT SONIA, standing there radiant and calm, I was for a moment seized with hidden fears, imagining the worst. Not that Anna had been suddenly struck dead, but—oh, anything, that she'd run off with someone, bolted, been expelled even. But then, watching the slow, almost ironic touch of Sonia's smile, I realized with blinding excitement that this was Sonia's doing. She had engineered this sudden vanishing act by Anna. Still . . .

"Not coming?" I cried. "What on earth do you mean? What's happening?"

"Don't panic! We phoned your mother last night. Take me to Hoffner's for a coffee before we set off and I'll explain."

Hoffner's, in the lazy main street of Rolle, was a pastry shop and café patronized during term time by the rich and boisterous boys being educated at Le Rosay, the most expensive school in the world—or so it was said; consequently Hoffner's was out of bounds to the girls of St. Agnes.

"But term's over now, so there's nothing to stop us going," said Sonia as we sat in a corner. I ordered coffee and assorted cakes. The waitress brought a clean tablecloth with the startling injunction, uttered in the singsong Vaudois accent, *"Un moment, m'sieur, je vais vous napper!"*

"But what's *happened?*" I asked when the waitress had gone. "Why? Is Anna in trouble—expelled or something?"

"Nothing's the matter. Anna phoned your mother yesterday that she's twisted her back slightly and felt she couldn't stand the jogging in your silly old car." Her smile showed she wasn't being rude about my treasured MG. "After all, it doesn't have much in the way of backseats. We did phone—but of course, you'd already left."

"Jeez! If you'd phoned earlier it would have saved me the trip."

"Very gallant, I must say!"

"Sorry. I didn't mean that. But if Anna has hurt her back, shouldn't you be with her on the train? It all seems very sudden, this last-minute attack. What happened?"

The girl arrived with two large *cappuccinos,* the tops of the broad cups foaming with hot milk forced out under pressure, the foam sprinkled with splashes of tiny chocolate chips.

Sitting there, overlooking the sunny main street with its baskets of flowers hanging from every lamp post, I knew even before she started to speak that Sonia and Anna had planned this. They must have done—and for only one reason: Sonia wanted to drive back alone with me. And that meant—well, after that curious incident in May when the storm broke, it could mean only one thing. My first thought of excitement and desire was followed by a second one, What a girl—and what a nerve! How very Russian to plan an adventure like this!

She could not have known what I was thinking, how I was imagining where I would take her, when we could stop, what we would do—if I dared to do anything! She looked at me with those big blue eyes and started finally to speak.

"Darling, beautiful Larry," she said. "No, *don't* interrupt—you *are* beautiful—in a manly way, even though you are the world's biggest nitwit! We didn't telephone Douzy earlier because I didn't *want* to stop you coming to fetch me." I felt the growing excitement increase. "And your precious sister is perfectly all right, probably stuffing herself with Toblerone in the train. She might give a realistic twinge or two when she gets to Douzy—but there's nothing the matter with her back. She's as fit as I am."

I decided to ask only one question. "But surely Mama said you should go with Anna—and leave a message for me at the school?"

"She *was* starting to say something about that, but then we got cut off—well, don't be cross Larry, I put the receiver down on the hook."

"You *what?* The nerve of it!"

"I asked Anna to go by train. I even bought the ticket for her. And," blue eyes looking steadily into mine, beautiful lips slightly open, "darling Larry, you *must* know—you *must* realize—that I've always dreamed of being alone with you."

"Me too." I was so stunned I felt my legs didn't belong to me as the increasing urge of physical excitement hit me with the force of an expanding iron rod, so that I could only repeat, "Me too!"

As she rested one pale hand on the back of my brown hand on the table, squeezing it gently, I realized, with blinding excitement, that at this very moment, sipping coffee, the car round the corner, I faced a turning point in my life. Before the day was out I was going to make love to her. Everything about her—from her face and her body, the way she looked, the way she walked, the touch of her hands—radiated the deep-seated physical passion of an Italian, but too, the equally deep-rooted but longer-lasting mental passion of a Russian.

"I hope you don't think I'm—" she hesitated, "well, setting the pace, but—" she looked down at the table, "I felt that—well, you're so *nice,* Larry. I know you feel kind of responsible—you've been told that, so you'd never make the first move and—I know it sounds silly when you're only seventeen, but your mama was only seventeen when she got married—and I'm so *pazza* about you, Larry."

"Pazza?"

"It means crazy about you, but *nice* crazy, Italian crazy."

"Russian crazy is more like it."

"Just *pazza,* darling. I just want—well, to be alone with you for one day. I've been praying for a beautiful day.

Maybe we can stop on the way and buy a picnic lunch—a *baguette,* some pâté or ham or something, and a bottle of vino—and eat it in a field."

"Come on," I said thickly. "It's a long drive."

I paid the bill, leaving all the loose Swiss change as a tip, and we walked unsteadily to the MG, which I had parked in the small square by the lakeside. Across the blue water rose the hills of France. The car was shaded by a row of plane trees, bark peeling, great tufts of summer leaves jutting out from branches pruned back into knobby stumps the previous autumn.

Then, with neither of us seeming to do anything about it, she was in my arms and I was kissing her, at first just our lips closing on each other, soft and gentle, pressed against each other, and then her mouth opened slightly, and mine too, just a little at first, touching almost as though by accident, tips of each other's tongues barely touching, just brushing each other until, almost with a groan, both our mouths opened together, and we stood there locked to each other.

Very tenderly, all the teasing, all her mischievous sense vanished, she stroked my cheek, and there were the beginnings of two large tears as she whispered, "That was my first kiss, Larry. It was like sipping each other's love. You'll never be able to leave me now."

We drove out of Switzerland via Vallorbe, leaving the trim Swiss villages and neat, clean streets at the foot of the long, twisting climb over the Juras, the road lined with thick, dark, sinister belts of fir trees, reminding me of Gustave Doré's illustrations for *Don Quixote.* The bends of the closed-in forest finally reached the town of Pontarlier, the main street filled as usual with heavy trucks and carts loaded with timber.

Suddenly, driving with one hand, the other resting lightly on her knee, I said, "I need a drink—a beer. I've got the most terrible thirst."

"I wonder why?" she asked innocently.

"Excitement."

"And love?" she asked.

"Forever."

Ornate stone gates marked the entrance to the bustling main street, giving the impression of a town fortified with ramparts. And this was true, I thought, as we stopped at a street that actually was called the rue des Remparts. It gave the broad main street, backed by woods and mountains, the flavor of a frontier town. The first café we entered even had a swinging door, and I almost expected to hear shooting during a poker game or to be greeted by one of those saloon girls who are always called Belle. It *was*, I suppose, the last town before France became Switzerland, and it had the busy, unfinished air of a place where only physical labor could earn a decent living. There must have been pale, black-suited clerks somewhere in Pontarlier, but all the brain was hidden by brawn.

The man behind the bar pulled down the porcelain handle, filled a large glass of *bière à la pression*, half of which I gulped almost before Sonia had time to sip her *café filtre*.

"That's better." I pressed the palm of my hand on the metal filter section of her coffee to try to force a few drops through the cup below, and when she had sipped half of it we set off in the MG with a roar, Pontarlier looking like a one-horse western township, with me whirling her away across my saddle, saving her from the clutches of the villain.

The country changed soon into a more open landscape as we drove toward Dole, and my mind was racing at the prospect she had made so clear, unless she had second thoughts! Perhaps when it came to the point *she* would say no. Fun, but only necking. Scared, suddenly realizing what a momentous step it would be for her to take. Especially as it was her first time. Must be. Or supposing she *did*—and I got her into trouble. The daughter of an ambassador! There'd be hell to pay. Yet that kiss at Rolle—that surely was a kiss of promise? I suddenly felt reckless. Suddenly I didn't give a damn, as we sped along, top down, wind in our hair.

"There!" I cried suddenly, pointing to a glade where the

sunlight dappled through the trees on a rough cart track
leading to open fields behind. "In there!"

For half a second she panicked—and so did I, though mine
was a different fear: that we would be lying there and some
angry French peasant with a shotgun or a big dog would
come charging across the fields and kick us off his property.

"Don't be scared," I said as we reached the end of the
belt of trees and I switched off the ignition. The car was
hidden from the road, and ahead of us was a huge field of
corn ready for the harvest, acres of waist-high gold in the
hot sun, the gold picked out with a sprinkling of red poppies. No one could have invented a more perfect day, the
blue sky spotted with cotton-wool clouds wandering aim-
lessly above, their shadows racing along the surrounding
cornfields in echoing formation.

"Are you scared?" I asked her.

"A bit. I've never done this before."

"Never?"

"Never," she looked around nervously. "So long as no
one sees us. I'm scared of that—and everything."

"Want to drive on?"

She hesitated, said, "It seems so easy when you just talk
about it."

I picked up the rug from the back of the car.

"Don't worry," I reassured her, "even if anyone sees the
car, we'll be hidden in this corn."

We walked hand in hand to the edge of the corn, then I
somehow managed to hold her away from me, holding her
shoulders, looking at her full in the face, and said, "You
know I'd never try to force you—but I *do* want to. Are *you*
sure?"

For a moment her lip trembled. I realized she might be
going to say no. I had a frantic fear that she *was* going to
say, "Perhaps we should go back to the car."

"Don't say it!" I cried. "Don't say it. Trust me! I'll always love you, Sonia, always!"

It wasn't very good the first time, it was all over before
she had a chance. It had to be. I mumbled, "Sorry, darling,

I couldn't wait—" She stroked my face, and there were tears as she whispered, "I could *feel* you when you—you know—" a little shyly at the use of the word, "when you came inside me. At school all the girls said it would hurt, but it didn't."

For perhaps half an hour we waited, lying in each other's arms, and during that time she became excited with the satisfaction of a conspirator.

"Are you all right, darling? Not worried? Shocked?" I asked.

"A bit. But I know I was the one who set it up—though I wasn't sure how far I would dare to go." She hesitated. "I've always loved you, Larry. Do you think it was bad of me that day I let you look at me in the orchard? I'm so happy I don't feel guilty—well, not very."

She sat up, pink linen skirt for the moment decorously over her thighs. Stretching out one slender, brown arm, she plucked out some poppies from the golden corn and laid them across my tummy.

"I shall call you Monsieur Coquelicot—Mister Poppy. And that will always be a secret code between us. If *ever* we fight—we never will, of course—and one of us says 'Monsieur Coquelicot,' we have to stop. And if ever one of us feels like we do now, and there are lots of people around—and we can't do anything—I'll ask you, 'How's Monsieur Coquelicot?' and you'll know that I love you."

As we lay there before the second time, I said, "You know that all these books about sex which you buy in the Tauchnitz editions—they're full of stories about girls having orgasms a dime a dozen. It's not true."

"I know. I read Henry Miller—we smuggled it into school, *Tropic of Cancer.*"

"Me too. But I don't want to leave you in the air again—so what I'm trying to say is, darling, before we make love, let me help you while we kiss."

As I touched her, she shuddered and—eyes closed, mouth open—as I slid inside her effortlessly, she gently pushed my hand away and replaced it with her own and I knew then it would be all right for her, and it was.

Lying there afterward, with her blouse on but unbuttoned, while I stroked her beautiful firm breasts, her skirt pulled down, my trousers pulled up, she put her hand inside them and caressed me and said, "That's what I hoped it would be like. That's what I dreamed about in bed at night. But I never thought it would be quite so beautiful. You're not sorry, Larry? Did I please you? Did I make you happy, was I all right?"

"You know you did."

"Tell me you'll always love me, whatever we do to each other, wherever we are—even if we're apart. Uncle Oregon says there'll be a war one day—tell me you'll always love me."

"You know I will."

I lay by her side, hands inside her open blouse.

"I'm still vaguely scared of that farmer with a shotgun," she said, "but I'll never love anyone else."

I felt the prick of tears, all the love bursting out of me, and I was thinking, I feel the same. There will never, never be another woman in my life. And if there *is* a war one day, I'll wait for Sonia forever. "I just adore you," I said.

"You don't think I was brazen for planning to get rid of Anna—and all this."

"I would never have dared to do it. I've dreamed about this before—but I never thought you'd go through with it if I asked."

"I wanted to, so often!"

"Me too. But I was scared to."

"I nearly didn't go through with it," she confessed. "This morning, at Pontarlier, I almost decided to ask you to understand. And then, when I looked at you after we started driving, our hair in the wind, I realized that we were in love, and I didn't feel guilty." She shivered suddenly.

"Cold?"

"No. I was thinking of the future, looking at you. Those big shoulders, and your chest like warm silk," she lay her head on it, "not hairy," she laughed. "I like it better this way."

"So long as nothing else happens—you know what I mean."

"A baby."

"Ever thought of that?"

"I don't care," she said with the recklessness of someone who doesn't really know what she is saying, "if anything happens I'll go to a Swiss doctor. I'd never let *you* know."

"You'd have to find one."

"Three of the girls at St. Agnes have had abortions. It's quite easy, so don't worry."

"I might want to worry."

"Well, it won't happen I'm sure, but if it does, yes, darling Larry, I'd like you to worry. Because the two of us—it is wonderful really—we've been brought up almost like brother and sister. How many holidays have I spent at Douzy? And I always swore I would never make love with anyone else but you—so that it would be perfect. And it *has* been perfect. And even my prayers were answered—the sun has never stopped shining—and, darling Larry, I love you and I'm *pazza* about you."

Impulsively she threw her arms round my neck and kissed me and cried, "Isn't life good to us! I'm starving! Let's forget the picnic idea and have a slap-up lunch."

We lunched at a bistro not far from Arbois, where—to the amusement of the patron—she took up a chicken leg in her fingers, pulled off a piece of meat with her teeth, then offered it to me. "Yes, yes," she urged me, "it's like our kisses. This chicken has been in my mouth and now it goes in yours. Then you give me a piece of yours."

It was not until we were eating our wild strawberries, however, before I had a wild idea. Why couldn't we pretend the car had broken down, then we could spend the night together?

"Dare you promise me something?" I asked her.

"If I can." She scooped up a spoonful of the tiny wild strawberries, ate half, and gave me the rest.

"Promise? I can be *pazza* too!"

"Pazzo for you, darling," she laughed. "You're masculine, that I do know. *Pazza* for me, *pazzo* for you. Dare I promise?"

"You dared everything this morning."

"Well—you know that if I can, I will."

"It's very simple," I said a trifle too airily. "I want to wake up tomorrow morning in a large double bed and have breakfast with you."

"You're right—you're more crazy than I am."

"I don't see why it should be so difficult. If my car broke down—we'd be stuck, wouldn't we?"

"Your car break down! Your precious MG! You always told me it would *never* break down. Oh, Larry! I'd love to, I would. But I'd never sleep a wink!"

"There's nothing to worry about really—and it *could* break down. Millions of cars all over the world are breaking down at this very moment!"

"But your mama? What about her? She'd have a fit. She'd suspect the worst."

"She'll probably never know. And anyway, if she did suspect, she couldn't prove anything."

It took a great deal of persuasion, but before lunch had ended she agreed. I admit I was nervous. I had never done this sort of thing before, but we made a detour on the N-1, passing beyond Dijon toward Avallon, where I knew a wonderful old inn—a glorified pub really—in the Vallée du Cousin, a wild narrow cleft of land hidden a few miles beyond the main road. The family had spent a night once at the Moulin Blanc, which backed onto a dribbling trout stream. "I only hope they don't recognize and remember me," I said as we approached the old courtyard.

"So long as I don't have to appear until everything's fixed," she made me promise. I jumped out of the car in front of the low, white building. I didn't dare to admit that as I sauntered toward the entrance I was as terrified as she was.

I walked into the pretty reception room, smiled at the reception clerk, and then all my nervous fears evaporated, simply because no one seemed even remotely interested once I handed over my American passport and completed the police *fiche.* Even I knew that in France, country of discretion, no one ever asks for "madame's passport."

"Nothing to it," I whispered loftily as the porter came to the car and took our luggage up the stairs.

"Violà!" The porter opened the door onto a romantic bedroom with a huge four-poster in the center, the curtains round the bedposts matching the same blue-and-white-flowered wallpaper.

When I had tipped him and the door was closed, we both jumped on the bed at the same time, almost whooping with excitement. It wasn't only love—or a teenage crush. It was the *excitement* of our impertinence, so that we were almost giggling at the thought of how we had fooled our parents.

"God! Grandma'd flay me alive if she found out," I said.

"We've got a secret they'll *never* discover. Even if they find out about us later, they'll never know about the Moulin Blanc."

But above all it was the gentle intimacy of doing something together for the first time in our lives that touched us magically. We had our *truite aux amandes* on a small table on the end of the river. The only light came from candles. And when dinner was over, and we went to bed, it was knowing that the perfect day in the sun would end with a night which could never be interrupted until it was time for breakfast.

We made love all night long, but there were gentle times of sleep in between, and sometimes I woke first and by a trick of light—the moon shining through a crack in the curtains—I could see her sleeping face as she lay there, in the position I would come to know so well, lying in the crook of my right shoulder, the sheets half pulled off her bare breasts, her lips in a faint smile as though she was in the midst of a wonderful dream.

In the middle of the night she suddenly sat up, naked, and switched on the small light on the right-hand side of the bed.

"What on earth's the matter?" I asked, half asleep. "You all right?"

"Yes. But Larry, I just had to know at this moment—
now—do you *really* love me? Was this day just for fun—or
will you love me forever?"

"Forever, you crazy Russian."

"Russians *do* love people forever. It comes from inside. I
don't want to think it's just making love that counts for
you. Being in love does make you do that all the time—but
it's real love—"

"My sweet, I adore you, but it's four in the morning."

"But you *will* love me forever?"

"I promise."

"It's a solemn vow. We will love each other forever. I'll
swear it. Do you?"

"I swear it." And more awake now, I added laughingly,
"Do you want me to marry you to prove it?"

"Marry! You're only nineteen. You must be crazy! Love
like ours comes from the heart and soul. Marriage? At seventeen? I can't explain what I mean but—the two things
don't seem to have anything to do with each other."

"But they *should,*" I retorted rather priggishly, for to
my juvenile, muddled way of thinking, the two *were* inseparable. It took me many, many years of our loving before I
could really accept what she said.

"But so long as we *love* each other—and you've made a
vow, remember, we'll never be able to leave each other."
And then, typically Russian—and that part of her character seemed predominant—she switched off the light, murmured softly, "Love you," and lay her breasts against my
shoulder and chest and gently fell asleep, waking only
when the old waiter brought the *café complet,* which I
had ordered for 8:00 A.M., and we ate the featherweight
croissant sitting naked in that huge double bed, she insisting that we share each piece of the fresh croissant and
jam.

We reached Douzy in time for lunch. Papa and Mama
and Grandma had not returned from Paris, and there was
no reason why they should ever question the time of our
arrival. If they did, I would of course tell them that my car

had broken down and where we had spent the night—in separate rooms. But why should they ask? The servants probably hadn't the faintest idea where we had come from. We might, for all they knew, have been in Paris with my parents. Anything could happen with crazy Americans. Only Mlle. Lisette, our onetime governess, and now a "fixture," gave me a long, hard look and pursed her lips. But even her sour look could not stop me from singing aloud with pure happiness.

The next morning when I came down for breakfast, ravenously hungry, Sonia was nowhere to be seen. Only my sister was.

"She went for a walk to church," said Anna.

"At this time of the morning!"

"I know. I was as surprised as you—especially," with a sidelong glance in my direction, "when she said she was going to confession."

Long, long before that I knew, even at nineteen, that the night in Avallon, with all its tenderness and beauty and closeness and warmth—and, yes, innocence—would change my life forever.

3

I͟T͟ ͟L͟A͟S͟T͟E͟D͟ ͟A͟L͟M͟O͟S͟T͟ ͟T͟W͟E͟L͟V͟E͟ ͟M͟O͟N͟T͟H͟S, that idyllic period of
love, the love coupled with all the fire and excitement of
youth.

After the summer vacation Sonia and Anna returned to
Switzerland for their last term, and at the start of the new
year, I was not only working full time for the *Paris American* but also beginning to write occasional news stories
for the *Washington Globe,* whose Paris correspondent,
"Tommy" Tomlinson, rented an office in the *PA* building
and called on me for extra help if he was too busy to handle
the news on his own. I was well paid, but more important
to me, I was slowly becoming a cog in a big American newspaper.

During the week I lived at first in the Astell apartment
in Paris, driving down to Douzy most weekends. And then,
early in 1932, Sonia, her schooling finished, got a job as a
translator in Paris. "Instant translators" were just coming
into vogue, and Sonia was ideal; she was completely trilin-
gual in English, French, and Italian. She was not only
stunning to look at, she was highly gifted, and she worked
for an international agency which hired her out to attend
important functions or conferences, so she didn't have to
go to a dreary office from nine to five translating dull documents.

Her father, Signore Riccardi, was still *en poste* as ambassador to Paraguay and was delighted when Sonia decided
to live in France, where the Astells could keep an eye on

her. At first she stayed with an Italian friend of the Riccardi family, but this posed problems. We were still madly in love—though at nearly twenty, far too young even to think about marriage. But finding places to make love presented problems.

Paris in the thirties was made for lovers, yet though we saw each other almost daily, we were both anxious when I took her home to the family apartment in the rue des St. Pères, the beautiful, narrow street on the Left Bank, with its antique shops and small galleries linking the quays on the banks of the Seine with the boulevard St. Germain.

I *did* take her of course, often late at night after eating at some small bistro or dancing, but it was a tricky business, for it *was* a family apartment, in which I had one of the three bedrooms. And though I was the only member of the family who worked *regularly* in Paris, relatives had a habit of turning up without warning. Papa might have a business trip and elect to stay the night. Mama wanted to do some shopping. One evening Grandma arrived, driven in from Douzy by Gaston, the chauffeur, to spend a couple of days seeing old friends. When at midnight I crept in, unsuspicious, with Sonia, only the sound of snoring made me scuttle for the door and take her home, after which I returned to the apartment—alone.

The following morning at breakfast Grandma, a forbidding figure in a long white gown and a kind of loose, linen cap hiding unmade hair, dunked a croissant in her coffee and looked at me reflectively.

After a brisk good morning, she asked, "I hope you slept well, Larry?"

"Thank you. And you, Grandma?"

"No. I did *not* sleep well."

"I'm sorry. Did I wake you?"

"Not *you!* But nothing wakes anyone more quickly than the tapping of high heels on a parquet floor. And," even more dryly, "it's very bad for the parquet."

As I choked on a mouthful of croissant, she added sardonically, "If you *must* entertain ladies in our apartment at all hours of the night, perhaps you could ask them to remove their shoes when they enter the front door." And as I gulped again, she added—and I had to hand it to the old girl for her final remark—"I imagine they would have to take their shoes off eventually anyway."

Fortunately she didn't seem to have any idea who the visitor had been. Still, we had to do something, and after a few weeks, Sonia found the perfect place.

It was a tiny bandbox of an apartment at the corner of the rue des St. Pères and the rue de l'Université. On the entresol, over an antique shop, it was little more than an extra floor squeezed by a rapacious landlord between the ground and the first floor, almost a shelf jutting into the dark, cavernous, and not too clean entrance hall. It had once been a lodge for a concierge, but there was no longer a concierge and so we snapped it up, all of two tiny rooms, a small bathroom and a kitchen no bigger than the bathroom. But it had a charm, with windows from both rooms looking out over the street barely twelve feet above the passersby.

No white paint could ever make the dark living room lighter, but Sonia found some poppy wallpaper identical to that in her room at Douzy and a Spanish painter called Fernandez, who decorated both rooms. Then we furnished it with bargains from the Flea Market. The room was just large enough for a double bed. And this was new—a house present from me, bought at the Trois Quartiers.

I also brought another "present"—this time of a nonlasting nature. I drove down to the flower market on the Île de la Cité near Notre-Dame and filled the MG with a hundred red roses—and one white one.

Then, knowing that Sonia would be out at work, I filled the small bathtub with what looked like a scarlet flower bed, with just the single white rose in the middle.

She hadn't the faintest idea when she arrived home and tugged open the sliding door leading to the tiny bathroom. She shrieked with joy, then a few tears of happiness stained her cheek.

"You are a fool!" I dried her tears on my handkerchief. "My own Monsieur Coquelicot! Who else in the world

would make me a surprise like this? My darling *pazzo,*
nothing on God's earth will ever stop me loving you."

Soon I more or less moved in. There wasn't enough room
for my clothes as well as Sonia's, but that didn't prevent
me sleeping there and dashing out each morning to the
boulangerie in the rue Jacob for freshly baked croissants.

At first I was worried lest Sonia might have a baby. If
only I had realized what a simple solution to our future
problems such a quickly forgotten "scandal" would have
been! But as she said, after calling at Geneva on her way
back from a trip to Italy, "The Swiss know how to fix
everything. Now I have a diaphragm."

Sometimes I went late to the office so that we could go to
the *marché* at the top of the rue de Seine, the narrow street
lined not only with shops selling every kind of food, but in
front of them, stall after stall, crowded together, barrows
piled high with fruit and vegetables, so spotless it looked
as though each apple or leek had been individually polished, each radish personally scrubbed. There was great
bargaining in the *marché*—especially among the fat,
cheerful, blowsy women, loud-voiced, many·still in their
cloth slippers, for they had just come down the rickety
stairs from their nearby apartments. In their overalls,
hair done up in curlers, they examined each piece of mer-
chandise with expertise before opening their small leather
purses.

Sometimes we dined at Marcel's, farther along the rue
Jacob, opposite the place Fürstenberg, where Delacroix
had had an atelier in a tiny square with clusters of gas
globes on tall, straight lamp posts, which looked like a set
from a period movie.

Marcel's was one of the cheapest, smallest restaurants
in the *quartier,* and though we could have easily afforded
to visit more expensive ones, we preferred Marcel's once or
twice a week because I think we were eager to be accepted
as people who were a part of St. Germain des Prés. I was
perhaps envious of the struggling writers and painters
who had lived there—men like Hemingway, Joyce, and
other undiscovered literary giants who had gathered at

the feet of Gertrude Stein or borrowed books from Sylvia Beach at her bookstore, Shakespeare and Company, in the rue de l'Odéon.

In those Paris days Sylvia provided a central haven for anyone—rich or poor—who enjoyed books, for she was a warm, generous woman with a happy smile below her brown eyes and wavy brown hair, and she loved gossip, so that when she knew I worked not only for the *PA* but for the *Globe,* she was a source of information.

Occasionally Sylvia came to have a quiet dinner with us at Marcel's, for she hated what she called "touristy places" and certainly Marcel's never attracted a tourist. Its zinc bar, with hard-boiled eggs on the counter, and saucers piled up in front of you to keep a tally on the number of drinks served, was tiny. In summer you could sit out on the pavement, in winter inside a glass extension, steamy with heat and the smell of Gauloises.

But the shabbiness of Marcel's was like a welcoming cloak, for it had none of the frostiness of formality. Most of the regulars were lonely men, clerks perhaps, professors or schoolteachers. They nodded to us gravely, not with familiarity but out of politeness, and we never noticed the off-white walls, the stains on the tablecloths, the one shambling waiter, for he was our friend, *their* friend. When elderly regulars arrived he knew without asking which newspaper, rolled up on its wooden rod, he should take off the wall rack for them. He rarely offered a menu to the regulars like us. We would take the dish of the day because we knew it had been cooked by Marcel himself, good home cooking, with no frills, and always marked with chalk on a large slate standing near the cash till where "Madame Marcel" held sway.

Sometimes, after a good dinner with Sylvia Beach, as on this evening, she walked up with us to the Deux Magots, another haven, where for the price of a drink or coffee people sat for hours on the terrace watching the crowd saunter along the boulevard St. Germain. At times I caught her regarding us almost quizzically.

"Are you two ever going to get married?" she asked with a smile.

Sonia shook her head.

"Why not?"

I started to speak, but in her dark, husky voice Sonia said first, "We're too happy to spoil it."

"How Russian!" Sylvia laughed.

That was the way our lives passed by. Unless Sonia went to Florence when her parents were on leave, or if they came to visit her in Paris, we were inseparable, and in those days, when we would dance until the dawn, go to her apartment to make love, and still be ready to face a day's work, there was no city in the world as wonderful as Paris.

Paris was one part of our lives, but then, as though switching off a film, we shared our other kind of life at weekends: the magic of Douzy. To me Paris represented fun and work in a wonderful city, but Douzy was home, a serene beauty, a wonderful family, the gentle seasons of the vineyards illustrating the rolling countryside of Champagne.

And this was a special weekend—the biggest fête day in France and also my twentieth birthday. For I was born on July 14, the *Quatorze Juillet,* France's equivalent of the Fourth of July. It always meant a double celebration in the Douzy household, for we always celebrated birthdays with a few glasses of *blanc de blancs* in the cool white splendor of the Douzy Pyramid, one of the showplaces of Champagne.

Luckily none of us knew that within a few hours Sonia and I would be discovered—and that she would be packed off away from me, from Paris, from our beloved Douzy.

4

"THERE'S ONE THING about a cocktail party in the pyramid," my father said to Willi Frankel, a German engineer and a friend of Anna's who had spent several weekends at Douzy. "It can't last very long. No, it just *can't.*"

Willi looked mystified until I explained that Douzy Pyramid was not only a remarkable natural phenomenon, it was also a "working" cellar over a hundred feet below ground in which we could store up to a quarter of a million bottles from various years.

"Perfect for keeping champagne," I said, "but the temperature always hovers around eleven centigrade. Don't worry! We keep a supply of old Sherlock Holmes-type cloaks for anyone who feels chilly."

Willi, Guy, and I led the way. Papa had gone ahead. Anna, Sonia, and a girl called Olivia Jacobsen, who had been invited by Guy for her first visit to Douzy, followed. Grandma had promised to come, but was visiting a vineyard some distance away.

It was a beautiful morning as we walked along in the warm July sunshine, picking the occasional wild flower, or blowing the tops off the fluffy "She loves me, she loves me not" dandelion puffballs. Everyone was happy. Anna was obviously intrigued with Willi, tall and blond with very correct manners, from Düsseldorf. Guy had become friendly with Olivia at first because she was helping him with his art studies, but I also felt that, though she was several years older than any of us, her creamy complexion,

composed face, quiet and serene, attracted Guy as much as
her painting.

Halfway along the half-mile walk to the pyramid, we
passed the Home Farm, with its large rectangular buildings, the outer wall of weathered brick enclosing barns,
the manure of the farms and horses, the cow sheds, the
dairy where we churned butter, even Douzy *fromage.*

"It looks enormous," said Willi, walking along the
never-ending wall that bordered the lane. I explained that
only half was a farm proper. The far end housed the buildings of the *cellier.*

"Underground? Is this where we are going down?"

"No, no. Underground are the *caves*—the French word
for the cellars, if you like. The *celliers* are not cellars,
they're the name given to the champagne workrooms
above ground—the press which can handle four tons of
grapes at one pressing, the bottling plant, mixing rooms
where sugar and sometimes an older vintage of champagne are mixed with the new vintage to pep it up. That's
where Papa is a real expert—remember champagne's a
blended wine, and he's the best in the blending business."

"Life at your Douzy is very good, is not?" said Willi. "So
why you prefer to live in Paris, hard work as a newspaperman, *nein?*"

"Not easy to explain. I *love* this place, Willi—it's my
home—and yet, I don't know why, half of me is always
yearning to get out of it."

I waved a greeting to an old vigneron called Pagniez,
who, like so many people, had spent his life working with
the Astell family—*with* us, my father always insisted, not
for us. And usually as a family. One of Pagniez's sons
worked in the vineyards with his father. I could see him a
few yards away. Pagniez's daughter had worked in the
château since she left school—a school paid for with pleasure by Papa, who called her, as everyone did, Aubergine,
a nickname derived from some baby-talk mispronuncia-
tion.

I found Willi's question hard to answer. All I knew was
that I found it boring having to listen to "champagne

talk"—my father's friends discussing the influence of supracretaceous chalk soil on Chardonnay grapes—to say nothing of production units, presses, blending, *dégorgement,* and a hundred other technicalities. What I *really* wanted was to see my own name on my first novel (if I ever got around to writing it) or else my by-line on page one of a famous American newspaper.

It would come, I knew it would, I had a complete faith that I would one day succeed. I was lucky in one thing: Papa was understanding, he never tried to force me to follow "in father's footsteps." His was a French life really, more than an American one. He was immersed in a totally French business. He almost always spoke French. He was very quiet, he tended to shirk any man-to-man talks as though they embarrassed him, but on the other hand, he was tolerant enough to understand that I wanted to make a life of my own. He was gentle, considerate—unless he was so occupied that he hardly noticed our presence. When he was with friends, "on parade," as his brother, Oregon, called it, he was good company. But he was the epitome of a man married to his job. At forty-eight he was a handsome man, very tall, and had a trick of raising and lowering his voice to accent certain words, as though to give them a special significance that others missed. When he was explaining something, I would hear Papa say in his special voice, "Oh *really!* I *must* say."

"I think I understand," said Willi, who, after studying at the Sorbonne had worked for a year in a British engineering works, spoke passable English. "I lived with my parents in a village for many years, and now I get excited living in Düsseldorf. Of course," his next words didn't sound exactly complimentary, "I work as an engineer, is different, much more important."

"Jesus!" I laughed. "I don't spend all my time in bed waiting for inspiration you know. I *do* work."

"Of course. But *you* do not mind the big change." And then a little slyly he added, "You think is different for a woman—someone like, well, Anna—to make a home away from Douzy?"

"Anna? You mean the idea of Anna living in Düsseldorf?"

Willi blushed slightly. "Maybe one day, who knows?"

"She *is* only eighteen."

"I know," said Willi hurriedly. "If we are still fond of each other, of course I wait." He almost clicked his heels.

"Papa wouldn't like it." I kicked some loose pebbles to the edge of the path. "He's not enthusiastic about the Germans. And what about this Hitler man? Now he has made some sort of alliance with Hugenberg in Harzburg."

"How you know this?" he looked astonished.

"I *am* a journalist," I laughed.

"You can forget Hitler. He was only a corporal."

"Well, I wouldn't ask Papa for permission to marry yet," I laughed—but I meant it. "Not until you've got rid of Hitler, anyway."

Shortly after midday we all reached the Douzy Pyramid. I knew Willi would be astonished when he saw it for the first time, though so far he did not seem impressed. The sloping country lane led to large double doors set into the hillside. An old-fashioned sign at the end of the drive announced ASTELL & CIE, NEGOTIANTS DE CHAMPAGNE. That was all, an almost supercilious sign, as though the product needed no further introduction.

Inside the outer office I could see Willi doubtfully eyeing the bits of furniture, a few charts on the white walls, some sample bottles in an old-fashioned rack. I smiled inwardly. It *looked* ordinary, but I had never met anyone who could resist the sense of shock when they first saw the pyramid.

"This way." My father led Willi to the far end of the office, where a flight of stone steps dropped still farther downward. They were very broad, a hundred and five of them, but as easy to use as those leading from a dress circle to a theater foyer.

"Here we are!" My father threw open a second set of doors at the foot of the steps. There was a faint odor of sourness, of damp. And it was chilly. "After you." He held open one of the doors politely. "This is your first visit."

We stepped onto a white, chalk-stone terrace cut into the

wall and illuminated by dim lights. Two butlers in ceremonial white ties and tails, each with his silver tasting
dish on a ribbon round his neck, were preparing tulip
glasses for the drinks.

"It's a kind of uniform for ceremonial occasions," I whispered.

Willi gaped in astonishment.

"O Gott!" he cried. "Is not possible, Larry!"

In front of the observation platform we looked upward
toward the apex, a tiny patch of light far above, then downward another fifty feet or so to the huge rectangular base
below. Everything was blinding white.

"Is incredible," cried Willi. "What engineering! How did
anyone build this miracle? Nothing like it in all the world."

My father, who loved the role of guide, pointed to the
apex.

"This pyramid started when the Romans dug that hole."
He pointed upward. "As soon as they'd excavated a
vertical shaft, rather like a well, they dug downward, outward, all underground. Look carefully!" He flashed a
flashlight onto the nearest wall. "You can see the marks
made by men digging out the shaft. Those marks were
made by the Romans."

The balcony on which we were sipping champagne was
ringed with railings to form a semicircular observation
platform. On the floor area below, a dozen dark and tiny
figures scurried round like ants caught in a field of snow.

"Is like a giant crevasse at the South Pole," said Willi.

As the butler gravely poured out more champagne, my
father pointed out the steps built into the sides of the wall,
together with other platforms at various heights, and the
dark holes of tunnels.

"Gives us extra storage space," he explained. "We store
our best vintages here and in the adjoining tunnels. We
use a long chain and pulley on wheels to haul up the bottles six at a time in special baskets. And in the large tunnel," he pointed it out, "there's an ancient truck on rails
that leads to the railway at Rilly."

"This pyramid—is the only one?"

"Good Lord, no," I shook my head. "There's another one on the other side of the Rilly railroad, and in Reims itself there are forty pyramids, with connecting tunnels."

"But all this engineering under the ground—I think is very difficult," said Willi.

"They had no choice if they wanted chalk for building," said my father. "Chalk that's exposed immediately to rain or frost cracks or breaks. The Romans *had* to quarry under the ground and cover the whole thing at night with a slab of stone no larger than a table."

It was the vignerons who discovered that chalk cellars provided the perfect place to store champagne, which matures in bottles, unlike most wines.

After the birthday toasts, my father signaled to the butlers that we were ready to go, explaining, "There are more than a hundred miles of underground tunnels in the area, like a subterranean city, some broad like avenues, others branching off, some like small city squares; trucks on rails, ventilation shafts—yes, we have everything."

"Will they ever build more tunnels?"

"Not in my lifetime, if ever," my father shook his head. "Apart from anything else, remember that the champagne market is as flat as vinegar. The international market has gone. The Russian trade vanished with the Revolution. The American market vanished with Prohibition, while France and Britain are still wallowing in the wake of the 1929 recession."

This was our home in Champagne, once the bed of an old inland sea which over thousands of years had deposited its thick, chalky sediment and become a vast plain of dry and undulating chalk, with only a thin layer of alluvial soil over it. Here stood the mountain of Reims looking down on the valley of the Marne; hardly a mountain really, for the highest point of the horseshoe-shaped range of hills was barely six hundred feet above the plains. But different enough for the former to produce "the wine of the mountain" while the vineyards nearer the Marne were always known as "the wine of the river."

And in answer to a question by Willi, I replied, "No. I'm not going to waste our time taking you to Reims. It's the dreariest, most provincial town in France, filled with priests from the cathedral and colleges."

To my surprise Willi suddenly announced, when we had returned to the house, "I have bought you a present. Is too difficult to wrap up." Everyone gave each other gifts at birthdays, but I hardly expected one from Willi. However, he presented me with a thick malacca walking stick.

"That's great," I thanked him.

"And useful."

"Sure, I like walking."

"No. Look. Let me hold it." With an almost theatrical flourish he tugged hard at what looked like an ordinary walking stick. It came apart in his hands, revealing a beautiful sword stick, which he could slide back into the malacca cane, using it as a sheath.

"That's terrific." I examined it with new interest.

"In case Hitler attacks you," said Willi solemnly—before bursting into laughter.

That evening we held a warm, cozy supper with a few local friends, mostly Americans, after which we drank still more Astell birthday toasts in "le living room."

This was Mama's favorite room—long, with a high ceiling in beautiful proportion—and better still, she had furnished it without regard to Grandma's tight-lipped disapproval of any "foreign" furniture. Grandma Jacqueline might have "the right" to keep her family heirlooms in the salon; but enough was enough, and behind the stiff, unyielding French furniture, Mama, with her American flair for friendly rooms, had her way. Two long, deep sofas, colored in oatmeal, each big enough to seat four people, filled one corner. In front of them was an extraordinary glass-topped coffee table, three yards long, more than a yard wide, with a top made of plate glass an inch thick. Four men could not lift it off the crossed stainless-steel legs that supported it. It had been designed years ago by the firm which supplied Papa's champagne bottles. A dozen people could sit round the table for drinks.

In winter a log fire always flickered on the walls. One wall was covered with paintings, many signed personally by Vlaminck and Dufy, and (my own favorite) a large picture of some sunflowers, dated 1909 and painted by Goncharova, the frail Russian lady who lived in the rue de Seine near our Paris apartment. The other wall was lined with bookshelves—something very much against the French tradition, for many people preferred to house their books in a formal library. No doubt this was because newly published French books had only paper covers, so most families had their books specially bound and that seemed to change them, to clothe the books with a sense of formality, whereas many of our books came from New York or London and had cheerful, bright dust jackets that gave an added warmth to the room. They stretched along the entire forty-foot length of one wall.

The far end of the room offered a tantalizing glimpse of the outside world, for it was here that the french windows opened onto the conservatory, always filled with plants, ranging from bowls of daffodils and tulips and azaleas in spring to tubs of fuchsias through summer, and barrels of Michaelmas daisies and chrysanthemums in the autumn. Gardeners carried flowers in bloom from hidden greenhouses so that with the changing seasons, the conservatory, overlooking the dell, seemed to be magically endowed with the property of an everlasting summer. And behind them, clinging to the wall, were the scarlet blossoms of climbing geraniums, thrusting up between the rows of wires, and which seemed to bloom even as another winter approached.

Talking to Sonia for a moment I suddenly thought, She's right—Douzy is a benediction. If only life—and love—if only all of this could go on forever.

Someone else apparently thought the same.

"That's a very beautiful young lady," said a voice in my ear. "I think you should introduce me. I just came to Douzy for a predinner drink on my way home, but looking at this vision I'm tempted to invite myself to dinner."

It was Monsieur Maurice Pol Roger—not only the head of the famous champagne firm, but the mayor of Epernay since the end of the war.

Sonia murmured something polite.

"A picture, sir! Yes, a beautiful picture. A photo *sans besoin* to *retoucher.*"

It was a pretty compliment. *"Mais, hélas,"* said the mayor. "I have to go. Keeping two jobs going is hard work."

"He keeps *three* jobs going," I whispered as soon as Papa took the mayor to the front door. "He's our local eccentric. He goes to the office at eight o'clock every morning and leaves at half past nine, only an hour and a half later."

"A hard day's work," Sonia laughed.

"It is. Know what he does? He changes in his car, then spends the entire day shooting or fishing. He's already bagged over five hundred wild boars in the woods up on the mountains, and then—believe it or not—sharp at half past five each evening he returns to the office to sign his letters."

"Larry, darling," Mama interrupted my thoughts. "Could you be an angel and fill my glass for me."

Mama looked wonderful. But there were moments when she sat sadly staring into space.

Guy, Anna, and Olivia were talking together with my father, and Jean-Pierre Malherbe, who lived near Reims and automatically came to any party, stood looking at my sister with worshiping eyes. He was openly envious of Willi, who at the Sorbonne had passed every engineering examination that came his way without any apparent effort.

When Anna nearly knocked over my glass, I looked in Willi's direction and said to her, "Don't become too involved with a German. He might become another Hitler."

"You're a fine one to talk!" You could never get the better of Anna. "You and your Sonia. She might become another Mussolini. Yes, she's over there, looking at you."

I stood watching her. In fact I was imagining Sonia naked in bed with me—until I caught Mama's eye. Seeing her quizzical look, I wondered if Mama knew that I had started my birthday by making love to Sonia before breakfast and that soon, when the party was over and the house was darkened, I would creep out of my room to hers and spend the night with her. "Parents know nothing," Anna had once declared decisively, but I wasn't so sure now, at this moment, when Mama looked first at me and then directly at Sonia.

Sonia was sitting in a deep armchair near the french windows, talking now to Jean-Pierre, who was learning the skills of champagne production with one of our neighboring firms; with him were two elderly ladies.

I walked across to them. Sonia had suffered long enough at the hands of Jean-Pierre, an orphan whose American father and mother had been killed in a car crash, but who had lived in France all their lives, so that the only American thing about Jean-Pierre was his passport. He had been brought up by the two delightful American maiden ladies sitting next to Sonia, known all over Champagne as the Misses B and B—Miss Brewer and Miss Barron. Miss Brewer was a distant relative of Jean-Pierre's and had taken him into her care. Miss Barron had originally been engaged as a companion to Miss Brewer, but for many years there had been no boss, no servant. They were now friends who clung to each other with a desperate fear of loneliness. They had a tiny apartment in Paris and a cottage not far from Douzy.

"It's a fine party, Larry," Jean-Pierre stood up politely. "Have you seen Anna?"

"She's with her new boyfriend." Sonia sometimes had a mischievous streak. "You've seen him—Willi something."

Jean-Pierre blushed and immediately Sonia touched his hand, as though asking forgiveness.

"Don't worry," she smiled. "He's a German. A silly engineer or something dull. Doesn't sparkle like a true son of champagne—like you and Larry."

I saw Miss Brewer say something to Jean-Pierre, but he

didn't hear her. On purpose perhaps? The Misses B and B were gentle, kind, nondescript, gray-haired, plump, talkative—and also came to all our parties. Perhaps Jean-Pierre was stifled by their gentle kindness, but even if he tried to escape he failed, for as he crossed the room he was trapped by Grandma, who loved to talk to "a real Frenchman," as she put it acidly, "instead of listening to all those American accents."

The fact that none of the Astells had the faintest trace of a foreign accent when speaking French—rather the reverse in fact when we spoke English—had never convinced Grandma that we ruined the French language every time we opened our mouths.

"I want a breath of fresh air," cried Sonia. "Isn't the café in Douzy village open?"

"It is," I said. "Let's pop in for a final nightcap. Maybe we could get some beer as a change from champagne. Night, night everyone." This to the older ones, with a big kiss to Mama and a fervent "Thank you" for my birthday present.

Looking at me fondly, Mama whispered, "Don't forget to kiss your grandma good night—and thank her for the shaving set."

"Good night, Grandma Jacqueline," I cried. "Tomorrow you'll see me with a polished new face—thanks to your new shaving set."

Grandma's eyes rarely softened, but she stood up, all creases and hidden noises from her stiff dress, and offered two cheeks to be kissed. I obliged, and as the others prepared to leave, Willi bowed stiffly and said formally, *"Bon soir, madame, et merci beaucoup."*

It was a polite gesture, for after all it wasn't Grandma's party. But she was unbending, giving poor Willi only a frigid inclination of the head.

"I don't think she likes me," said Willi.

"Well, you're not your grandma's boyfriend," Anna said cheerfully, "so I wouldn't let it worry you. Grandma

Jacqueline won't be satisfied until the last German in the world has been buried."

My father was just behind, and as I walked out of the salon into the hall, grabbing my gloves from the ormolu table, I asked him, "As it's my birthday, Papa, can I borrow the Hisp?"

He nodded almost absently, adding, "But don't smash it up. We've all had a few drinks tonight. Yes, *indeed.*"

"Promise. And thanks for everything."

I had my precious MG, but Papa's family car was much grander, a long, gleaming Hispano-Suiza, driven usually by Gaston, the family chauffeur, another of old Pagniez's sons. The Hisp, as we nicknamed it, was like a battleship. The 1931 model, it had a nine-liter V-12 engine and would hum along at more than a hundred miles an hour.

We all ran out into the warm summer's night, and I shouted to Guy, "You want to drive my MG? Take Olivia with you and follow me."

Sonia jumped in next to me, Jean-Pierre and Anna sat in the back with Willi.

There was no shortcut by which you could drive from the château to Douzy village, though you could walk there across country in fifteen minutes. But with a car you had to drive almost down to Rilly, near the main Reims-Epernay road, then double back up a chalky, narrow strip of road, shining pale gold in the moonlight. Not that the detour mattered. July was a benevolent month, it was warm, it was only a couple of miles, and the Hisp purred along like a silky cat. It was a joy to drive her, though I kept the speed down—apart from the Hisp, I didn't want Guy going too fast and smashing up my MG.

It was not only exhilarating, it was beautiful as we made first for the church with its ugly grayish square tower and squat apology for a spire. At night the church looked abandoned, forbidden, dirty, as if it needed a wash, for the walls had been erected four hundred years ago by mixing big white stones with plaster, giving it a speckled look. But the graveyard with its horizontal family memorial slabs—ornate and often one on top of the other in French peasant fashion—was neat and tidy, and so was the gray stone plinth bearing the names of local fathers and sons who had died in the Great War.

Silhouetted against the vineyards, the church was an anachronism, nearly a mile from its village, but as we drove on toward Douzy, it wasn't difficult to see the reason why. The village of Douzy might just as well have been built on a switchback.

Anna yelled from the back seat, "Let's stop at the *mairie* and see if anyone's getting married."

The *mairie* was an unpretentious house in the steep curving rue Clémenceau, for the village didn't merit a "mayor's parlor." The mayor worked in the vineyards and had a plot of land, and this was his home—despite a front door decorated with special pronouncements: the new, revised postal times, a discreet notice that the mayor had some potatoes for sale (by the sack only).

Anna struck a match to peer at the only wedding notice. "It's Anne-Marie Drouet," she shrieked. "She's the girl who works in the *épicerie.* I *thought* she was in the family way when I saw her last week."

"Who's the unlucky man?" someone asked.

"Dunno. One of a dozen, I imagine."

A few yards down the steep hill stood the Café des Sports, faint lights glowing behind steamy windows, with a sign in bold, black lettering, the *C* and *S* emphasized in red. Opposite, Madame Roisin's *épicerie,* where the unfortunate Anne-Marie worked, was closed and so naturally were Douzy's other two shops—the bakery and the butcher. The owners were probably at the Café des Sports celebrating.

Douzy was an integral part of our lives, perhaps because it had grown naturally in the hilly vineyards surrounding it and so was different from many of the neighboring villages, which often consisted of one long street, straggling and deserted. Douzy clustered rather than straggled, so that our tires sqealed as we twisted and turned through the village streets leading to what the *Guide Bleu* called "the surprise view" at the corner of Douzy's public-washing trough, shaded by a steep roof and surrounded with peeling plane trees. In front of us spread miles of vineyards like black lines of regimental soldiers, black now at night through a trick of the moonlight, which robbed us of the green lines of daylight.

Back up the hill, we all trooped into the Café des Sports and ordered cold Slavia beer, while Roland, the patron, who knew everyone and everything in the village, said slyly, "You're twenty today, I hear. *Bonne fête!*" And casting an eye at Sonia sitting at the stained, wooden table—even the way she drank her beer was exciting—he added, "Soon time to settle down and get married, eh?"

Sonia caught the look, and in her dark, throaty voice she just said, "I'm not ready to get married yet, Monsieur Roland, but, all the same, I'm not going to let Larry marry anyone else."

The party over, I undressed hurriedly in my bedroom, taking a last look at a pair of cuff links which I placed on the dressing table. They were beautiful—and Sonia's expensive birthday present to me. I waited a few minutes. The last guests had long since departed, Papa and Mama were in bed.

Gently—the movement born of long experience—I half-opened my bedroom door, looking for telltale bands of light below open doors. Darkness! I tiptoed the length of the corridor, gently pushed open the last door on the right, and slid into her room.

Sonia was already in bed—well no, it was a warm summer's night, and she was on the bed, lying on her back, hands clasped under the back of her head, legs together, still naked, her black hair tumbling over the white pillow. Only one small bed light lit up the poppy pattern on the walls, the ceiling, the drapes, turning the small room into a basket of red flowers.

"This is our real present—to each other, *mio adorato,*" she whispered as I snuggled naked against her.

I have no idea how my father found out. He must have

been suddenly suspicious, because I set my alarm at five thirty each morning, giving me plenty of time to sneak back to my room before the house awakened.

He couldn't have heard the alarm. I had bought it especially because it gave out a discreet buzz instead of the usual bell.

At five thirty it rang and I turned it off, nestled in Sonia's arms for the best part of half an hour, as I usually did, loving her gently and quietly so that no one would hear any creaking beds.

By six o'clock I carefully pushed open the door, which opened into the corridor, peered out to make sure no one was about, then prepared to turn left.

As I gently eased the door shut, my father, who had been quietly standing on my right, hidden by the open door, tapped my shoulder without a word.

I spun round with a cry. I heard a gasp from Sonia. My father, in his dressing gown, looked at me with a kind of cold scorn and then without uttering a single word pointed to my room. The gesture was an order—and one that could not be disobeyed, especially by the twenty-year-old son of the house.

Not until after breakfast did he ask me, quietly, even politely, to go to his study, after an embarrassing breakfast shared by a silent family, who could sense that something was wrong.

My father asked the usual questions. How could I be so stupid? How long had this been going on? Was I sure she was not pregnant? "I don't blame you entirely, she's terrific, but I hope you agree you've been stupid—and worse," he said. Finally, he came to the point.

"Sonia will leave this morning." The tone of his flat statement horrified me.

"But she works in Paris! She's got a job."

"I am not interested in her job," said my father sternly. "She will resign from it and leave."

"But you can't force a girl who's independent to give up her job," I shouted angrily.

"I can—and I will. I'm giving you two damn fools a

chance. If you want to save Sonia's"—he hesitated over the word—"honor, you do it my way. If she goes quietly," he permitted himself a wintry smile at the allusion to police procedure, "then we will all keep this despicable skeleton in our own cupboard. And that means that Sonia's mother and father need never know how you've seduced their daughter."

"And the alternative?"

"If you insist on behaving stupidly, I shall cable Signore Riccardi that you have seduced his daughter and broken up a family friendship that has lasted for years. Then *he* would order Sonia to return."

"That's blackmail? *That's* despicable—to use your own word."

"But I've only got Sonia's welfare in mind. And perhaps you'll remember that your mother is Sonia's godmother. Responsible for a girl's welfare. You're a selfish idiot, thinking of yourself all the time."

"She still might not go." I felt a sudden stubborn streak. "She might insist on staying."

"She's a minor. As a newspaperman, you should be a little more intelligent in sizing up people. With his diplomatic powers, Signore Riccardi could have her *permis de séjour* canceled within twenty-four hours. Don't be so naive."

"But I love Sonia. We love each other."

Until that moment my father had kept himself under control—as he always did. But the word *love* sparked off a sudden outburst of fury.

"What in hell's name do you know about love!" he cried. "Is it your idea of love that you cheat a woman like Sonia's mother just because you want to get her daughter into bed? And in my house. God preserve me from modern youth!"

"I don't care what you think—or what you say—we've got nothing to be ashamed of." And with a sudden rush of anger, I cried, "I want to see her. Right away. I suppose she knows?"

"You see her? In no circumstances. Yes, your mother

has spoken to Sonia. And she agrees with me—you will *not* see her. Not alone. *You* may not be ashamed, but understand this. You've behaved like the worst kind of bastard. The daughter of one of our oldest friends. You may not be ashamed of youself, but I'm ashamed of *you,* yes, I am."

"I still want to see her," I muttered.

"Just remember one thing. Italian men don't like their daughters to be—well, soiled. I'm talking about a prospective husband for Sonia. By sending her away I'm protecting her, protecting her family name. If anyone in Florence ever found out, it'd cause a scandal."

"They won't find out. You've no right to stop me. And you can't." Now I began to get really mad, borrowing the temper from my father. "And if you're so worried about what people think, we'll get married."

"At your age?"

"Why not? Mama was younger than Sonia when she—"

"That's different, yes, *different.* You're both too young. You've no career—not yet—"

"Well," with a touch of sarcasm, "you'll be relieved to know that Sonia doesn't want to get married."

"More sense than you have."

"But I *am* going to see her alone and say good-bye."

"You're not."

"I am. What are you going to do about it? Try and stop me by force? If you try, I'm off. I'll leave home. And then you can thank yourself for breaking Mama's heart—for that's what'd happen if I left. And I will if I have to. I can be as stubborn as you."

"Where will you go?"

"Anywhere. I don't give a damn."

"And live on?"

"I won't ask you for money, if that's worrying you."

He hesitated. For the first time my anger began to simmer down for I knew I had won the small battle. Better—or was it worse?—I realized that my father wasn't really angry. I was the angry son, he was the hurt father. Suddenly, I was aware that, with his strict code of principles, he was ashamed of me. *Ashamed* of what I had done. Of the possible disgrace. Was that it? What a stupid, old-fashioned way for father and son to start a fight. Over a woman, like so many fights in life. He was ashamed, as though I had broken a law, as though I had raped Sonia, seduced her.

"All right," he said heavily. "Arrange the good-byes with your mother." Then he left the room without another word. With supreme irony he would probably never believe that it was Sonia who in the first instance had seduced me.

I was still seething, so angry that before I did anything else—before I even tried to see Sonia—I felt a desperate urge to get out of the house into the fresh air, go for a walk, give myself a chance to cool off. Almost running across the courtyard I rushed through the arch and nearly fell into the arms of Anna and Willi, locked in a torrid embrace behind the yew trees.

"Sorry!" I shouted and prepared to walk down the hill.

"Wait!" cried Anna, gesturing to Willi to leave us alone. "I'll see you in a minute or two," she said to him. And to me she asked, "What happened?"

"Caught in the very act." I kicked some loose gravel savagely. "Father was actually waiting for me when I walked out of Sonia's room at six this morning. Jesus! Was that one helluva row."

"What's going to happen to you—and Sonia? She told me she's leaving. Oh, Larry! Poor you, poor Sonia."

"It was too good to last."

"Willi and I will probably be next," Anna prophesied gloomily.

"What on earth for?"

"Papa hates the Germans. He's been indoctrinated by Grandma."

"Silly old cow. Yes, I mean it. But you'll be all right. Get rid of Hitler—he's bound to go—and then—"

"Couldn't you bear to wait for Sonia? I mean, let it all blow over."

"That's the idea, I suppose. But its so damned stupid—having to wait."

Suddenly, Sonia appeared, walking through the arch quietly, almost sedately, all the fun gone from those laughing blue eyes. She looked at me a little awkwardly and said, "Your mother said you'd probably be here."

"I'll dash off and find Willi," said Anna.

"Darling Sonia," I cried. "Let's walk down the dell. Though I suppose," I added bitterly, "I'm only allowed to see you if we keep in sight."

"That's true." She was very serious but close to tears. "I did make a sort of vague promise to your mother. She's been very sweet."

"What's sweet about separating us?"

"Don't let's part like this, darling. It won't be forever."

"But why not get married? Run for it, bolt this very minute in the MG and get married at the American embassy?"

"You know it's impossible." We were walking slowly down toward the bottom of the dell, following the pale ochre path, the green lawns falling away to the bank of the rhododendrons and the orchard beyond.

She kicked at some loose stones before repeating, "You know it's impossible. It's not only *your* parents—it's mine. I'm only eighteen. There'd be a terrific row if Daddy became involved in a scandal—through me. Especially as Daddy is returning to Europe. If he found out what's happened to his only daughter, he'd have a fit."

"But we can't just accept this." I must have sounded desperate, for she linked her arm in mine so that, unseen by anyone looking at us from the house, she was able to take my hands, lock her fingers through mine.

"We have to—for the time being. It's the only chance—for me to behave—and then we'll try and fix something. I don't know what."

"We don't even know what'll *happen*. We don't even have any say in anything. Your father could be posted anywhere—Australia, *anywhere!* And if he took you with him, we'd never meet again."

"We will," she continued to hold my hand, squeezing herself close to me as we walked along. "I was thinking," she laughed, but not with any happiness, "here we are holding hands and this is the first time I can remember not feeling excited when you touch me. I feel as though I've been pushed into a cold shower."

"Me too."

"But I do believe that if we wait, we'll be together again. And in the meantime, here's a little present for you. Don't open it until I've gone. The car's coming to fetch me in less than an hour."

As soon as I returned to the house I had a talk with Mama. "But we *love* each other," I pleaded. "You of all people must understand, Mama. You were younger than Sonia when you married Papa. I love her." I added, lapsing into French, *"Je l'ai dans la peau.* What I don't understand is—why can't we just get married?"

Mama was sitting next to me on one of the large oatmeal-colored sofas by the big glass coffee table, and suddenly she leaned across and held my hand.

"Believe me, I do understand," she said. "But I'm her godmother, I gave my word to God, in church, that I would look after her. And now, I've failed. Perhaps that's the problem—the way she's been brought up as your sister—it makes me feel that the way you've behaved isn't very"—she was searching for a word that wouldn't hurt—"very clean."

"It was the only way," I said miserably.

"You could have waited, darling."

"We *love* each other!" As though that excused everything. Then I added, "Would you like Sonia to marry me?"

"Later, yes. But now, no. You want to be a newspaperman, a writer. Even Uncle Oregon says it's hard work. You shouldn't be tied up at twenty, really, darling. You can wait. If Sonia goes to Florence, you can write to each other, and then, when you've got rid of all this sneaking business, you'll see her for what she is a—a future wife, a wonderful girl. Then perhaps you can get engaged."

"But if she goes to live in Italy, she'll probably run off with someone else."

"If she did, then she wouldn't be worth waiting for, would she?"

"But if we get married now?"

"At twenty, darling?" she asked. "What you've done, Larry—all that deceit in our own house—is not very nice, though I try to understand," she sighed. "I'm not angry with you. But your father is right. And I think you owe it to Sonia's mother not to hurt her. If she found out, it would break her heart. Later if you want to get engaged, the past will be forgotten, you'll have made a clean new start."

Alone in my room, still hearing the crunch of tires on the gravel as she left in the Hisp, I opened Sonia's present, the one she had said didn't cost anything. It was a flat parcel, and as I tore open the flimsy white tissue paper, it turned out to be a Moroccan-bound Italian diary, the sort with one whole page for every day.

And in it she had throughout the weeks filled every page for the first six months of 1932, ending on the previous day, my birthday; each page covered with her thoughts for me, the wonderful things we had done together, every happy day and night we had spent together, warmed by each other's love.

5

I WOULD HAVE BEEN AN ABNORMAL twenty-year-old had I not for months displayed all the classic symptoms of a broken heart. I lost weight, I went for long walks alone, outwardly calm but secretly railing at the cruelty of life and parents and my own stupidity at being caught, the greatest crime of all.

Two days after Sonia left on that bleak day in 1932, and I had rushed out of the courtyard to the privacy of my bedroom, I prepared to return to Paris, to work on the *PA*. I had to. I also made a big decision not to live in the rue des St. Pères during the week. For I had guarded one secret the family *didn't* share—the existence of the tiny apartment in the rue de l'Université. Luckily I had signed the lease in my own name.

So, for what it was worth, I got a touch of revenge. The days at Douzy had passed in stony silence—not aggressive, more silence because no one could find the right words to say to each other. But on the evening before I was due to leave, Mama asked if we would all be having breakfast the following morning.

Breakfast at Douzy was a ritual, held in the large dining room, with its shining silver lining the back of the long sideboard. On it stood chafing dishes warming not only bacon and scrambled eggs, but from time to time American hotcakes with maple syrup and even a mass of soggy—and delicious—corned beef hash with poached eggs.

Punctuality was never insisted on at breakfast. It really *was* a movable feast—until half past ten when the table was cleared. Otherwise people trooped in, some still rubbing their eyes, and took helpings of whatever was left, and filled their own cups of American-style coffee—Papa's only real addiction to an American habit; he could not stand the bitter chicory-flavored liquid that passed for coffee in France.

We were all grouped round the polished table, and Aubergine was handing some croissants or home-baked bread to Guy when I looked at my watch.

"Time to be off," I said.

"Drive carefully." Mama never changed her Monday morning plea.

"I promise," I smiled—though I felt miserable. I could see that *she* felt for me. Then I dropped my bombshell, enjoying briefly the casual words.

"And by the way," I said, "I shan't be staying at the rue des St. Pères anymore."

"What on earth do you mean?" asked Papa sharply.

"I need a change." Adding almost defensively, "I'm old enough to hold down a job. I'd rather be on my own."

"But, darling, *where?*" asked Mama gently. "You can't just rush out and—" she looked hopelessly at my father.

"Yes, where?"

"You don't have to be scared, Mama. I've arranged to sublease an apartment from a friend, that's all. Just for a few months, it's handy for the office and the rent is peanuts."

"But *where?*" insisted my father.

"On the Left Bank. I'll let you have all the details when I've got the place in order, I just don't want anybody to see it until then."

At first there was a steady stream of letters, but Sonia was not a good correspondent, while I was always worried about pouring out my heart in case letters were opened by her parents, who had returned to Italy. On the other hand, Sonia could have written to *me* without any danger of discovery, especially after I gave her details of "a new apartment I've just moved into"—with the address of *her* place. She knew what *that* meant, and she did write then, a sad letter "thinking of distant places and the lost lands of love."

But the pity was that whereas I, by now exercising an almost daily facility in writing, could have poured out page after page of passionate letters, I had to mask all my true thoughts as a matter of precaution. Sonia, on the other hand, faced no such restrictions; she could have poured out her heart to me, yet found herself incapable of translating the passion of the spoken word into the written language.

Both of us were frustrated, and in the thirties telephoning was virtually impossible. I tried from time to time, but France was cursed by a special brand of witches—usually female—who seemed to enjoy a fiendish glee every time they connected anyone to a wrong number after hours of delay. The Italian service was just as bad.

Still, though I missed Sonia, I loved her old apartment with its walls of red poppies. Despite the original fear that nostalgia would make me wallow in self-pity, exactly the reverse happened. It reminded me of Sonia every day, I felt I was sharing it, but not sadly. I would have despaired much more had I stayed in the rue des St. Pères, knowing that someone else was living in our old apartment.

As I became more and more involved in my work as a newspaperman, the stream of letters began to dwindle. Apart from anything else, I had discovered that the newspaper world, which I had regarded as comparatively undemanding when writing only for the weekly *Paris American,* had become a tough, exciting, fascinating taskmaster by the time I moved more and more into daily newspaper work.

"It's like having a new girl friend," said Oregon after I had done a major piece for the *Globe.* "You just don't have time to go looking around for other girls."

In a way it was true. Of course I still loved Sonia but—busier than ever—I didn't miss her on any particular day, that *very* day. Much more, I missed the memory of *all* the days of happiness we had shared. If that sounds silly—even pretentious—it is because I can't really explain my feelings as the months slid by.

And I discovered something else: the year of intense physical lovemaking before we parted, the physical expression of my love for Sonia, had been true, not just the randiness of a young bull. With Sonia's presence I had needed to make love all the time. Without her presence I didn't—apart, that is, from the occasional therapeutic night out with a pretty passing flirt.

But most important, the longer we were parted, the more exciting my work became. Each morning was a new adventure, a morning to which I awakened rarely knowing what it would have to follow.

If the weather was fine, I walked to the office, making first for the river, with the tiny tugs straining as they hauled a line of barges along the Seine, or watching the first portable bookshops open under the huge elms or peeling plane trees, the first persevering fishermen reserving their places for the day. I crossed the Tuileries, walked up the avenue de l'Opéra, then bore right toward the Bourse until finally I reached the narrow, congested rue du Sentier.

The offices of the *Paris American* and the *Washington Globe* were at the top end, facing the boulevard Poissonnière. The narrow three-story building looked as though it had been squashed between a textile warehouse and Madame Yvette's bistro, where she served unlimited red wine, Pernod, or *fine à l'eau* on credit to the small staff of four or five journalists and the handful of printers.

Each morning when I stepped into the narrow hall, its walls a "post office" yellow, the air smelling of printer's ink, Charles, the porter, emerged from his concierge's cage to greet me. Short, with rheumy eyes, he pulled open the latticed door of the ancient elevator, where visitors were greeted with an uncompromising sign hanging on its surrounding metal cage: ON NO ACCOUNT MUST THIS ELEVATOR BE USED FOR DOWNWARD JOURNEYS.

The elevator shuddered to a stop on the second floor, where the editorial staff worked, the squeaking machinery begging for oil as I tugged the latticed door open. The circulation department (consisting of one man) and the advertising department (more important, two men) were on the first floor.

Because Tommy Tomlinson, the Paris correspondent of the *Globe,* had rented rooms on the floor above me, he was giving me more and more work on a free-lance basis, simply because if he wanted a rush job, he just came down one flight of stairs to see me.

I found myself *suggesting* more and more exclusive stories for the *Globe,* partly because the Astells *did* know many people in Paris so that often I stumbled on fascinating tidbits of news before anyone else. Papa was a close friend of Bill Bullitt, the American ambassador. A member of the Travelers' Club in the Champs-Elysées, he knew many politicians. And he often passed on to me casual information which might lead to a story.

Oregon helped even more. He was not only an experienced newspaperman who had deliberately opted out of the international scene to run the *Paris American,* he had become a living legend in Paris. He was, or had been, close friends with everyone from James Joyce to Hemingway, from Henry Miller to Gertrude Stein. They all loved Oregon, not only because he was wise but because, with his private income from his share of the champagne estate, he was always willing to stake writers during difficult times.

Unlike my father, who was tall and rather elegant in an aloof way, his younger brother, Oregon, was effusive, chubby, with a round face, alert eyes darting behind spectacles, eyes always alight with ideas. He talked with the same exuberance that made his eyes and his articles twinkle—enthusiastic, always in such a rush to pour out his thoughts that often he had no time to finish his sentence. He chain-smoked Gauloises, lighting one with the stub of the last. A trail of ash decorated his jacket lapels—it always did.

Since the day someone had dubbed him "Oregon" years ago, no one remembered his given name of Ronald, except it was on his passport and *carte d'identité.* He had long since discarded the name, like an old jacket which once fitted but which now sat oddly on his shoulders.

Often I drove Oregon to Douzy, for I still spent the weekends there whenever I could. After the first anger I had never really harbored a grudge against my parents when Sonia was sent back to Italy; and anyway, if I missed Sonia, I also missed the gentle life of Douzy, its calm and peace, the warm hillsides clad in vineyards. At first the homesickness had been all for Sonia on those walks along paths we had known since we were children. But now, by the middle of the thirties, years had passed, and the homesickness was more for Douzy.

People came and went. Willi had become a regular visitor, for by now he was highly placed in Staffens, his engineering firm in Düsseldorf, and he traveled regularly to Paris. Anna adored him—much to Grandma's disapproval, for she hated all Germans; even my father was worried as, with the thirties galloping away, the Fascists, then the Nazis, seemed to become more and more powerful and evil.

"It's not a question of whether or not there'll be a war next week," said Oregon, one afternoon at Douzy. "There won't be. But there *will* be a war before the end of the thirties. Impossible to stop it. Hitler's Nazis are winning everywhere. Mussolini is taking over any country he likes. The Spanish people are torn by civil war. There's no hope—not for Europe, anyway."

"I see the French have agreed to extend the Maginot Line," said my father.

"Useless!" shouted Oregon.

Willi had joined us, and I'm not quite sure why, but Oregon suddenly asked him, "No offense, Willi, but do you ever feel you'd like to get out of Germany?"

"Leave my country!" Even his precise German accent betrayed his horror at such a step. "You mean because of Hitler? Just wait till big business gets frightened. They'll soon kick him out. And as for the German high command! *They're* not going to take orders from a corporal!"

"I hope you're right," said Oregon, "but I think he's here to stay, and if the West doesn't do something to stop him—one day we'll have to pay the check."

"Nein, nein!" cried Willi.

Olivia, who came almost every weekend to see Guy, said in a matter-of-fact voice, "The Jews will come in for more beastly treatment, you watch. I'm Jewish and when I listen to that sort of evil—" The words trailed off and her large brown eyes were sad.

* * *

Oddly enough it was Willi Frankel who gave me my first big break on the *Globe*. The *Globe* had already printed dozens of my stories, but nothing could compare with this.

In July 1934 Willi had visited Paris on business, followed by the weekend at Douzy. And it was during a walk in the vineyards, beyond the orchard and the lake, that he told me the most extraordinary story.

We had read a brief account that Ernst Roehm, one of Hitler's oldest friends and head of the Brownshirts, had been executed. But that was all we knew. The details had been hushed up in Berlin.

"I heard a rumor that scores had been killed," I said.

"Scores!" Willi looked at me with disbelief. "Not scores, but hundreds, *thousands* even. Hitler himself is ordering the execution of thousands. Such a bloodbath it has been!"

"Then why are you a party member?" I couldn't help asking Willi, as from the top of a rise we looked down on a magic carpet of blossom during the brief week of the flowering.

"This is a foolish question. You know that no one can get a big job in Germany unless he joins the party. It is like being a member of a trades union in America. You are a member but it means nothing."

"I'm sorry, I didn't mean it. But—know any more details?"

"Ja, ja. One of the chief engineers at Staffens escapes by a hundred meters. Roehm is on vacation with friends at the Hotel Hanslbauer at Bad Wiessee near Munich for a jolly night or two." I barely stifled a smile at Willi's description of such a grim night.

"Roehm is a homosexual, you know," Willi continued. "Most of his friends are. The men sleep together in the hotel. They don't like girls."

"I'd heard rumors. You're sure?"

"Ja. The Staffens engineer staying at Wiessee, he is very pretty, and several times the Brownshirts ask if he would like to meet Roehm."

Slowly, as we walked, Willi filled in the background to the story. Roehm had started the Brownshirts—the *Sturmabteilung,* or SA for short—and it had grown to four million strong, making Roehm more and more powerful, especially behind the scenes. Now, according to Willi, Hitler believed that Roehm had grown so strong that Hitler was worried. At the same time Hitler badly needed the backing of Germany's armed forces, which despised the onetime corporal.

"That is true," said Willi. "So it seems Hitler decides to get rid of Roehm."

"But how, Willi? Hitler only came to real power early last year. You can't just overthrow an army of four million men like that."

"Remember the German navy and army hate the rabble of the SA," Willi explained. "So Hitler does a deal with them. Early in April, and this has never been told, Hitler left for a secret meeting on the pocket battleship *Deutschland*. They sail from Kiel. Admiral Raeder, the head of the navy, is there. So is General von Blomberg."

"What happened then?"

"Hitler makes a secret pact. The German navy and army will agree that Hitler succeeds Hindenburg as head of the state if Hitler agrees to suppress the SA. And kill Roehm."

According to Willi's informant, Hitler and Himmler stage-managed a nonexistent plot in which Roehm was supposed to be planning to kill Hitler. In fact Roehm and his cronies were at Wiessee, "having fun and games," as Willi put it. To me the fascination of this inside story for the *Globe* was that though the bare details of Roehm's execution had been printed, lack of detail would whet the appetite for more. But how safe was Willi's source?

"As safe as—what is it you say?—as safe as my house," Willi explained. "My friend from Staffens is at Wiessee when Roehm is there—but he is lucky, his hotel is at the far end of the village. Finally Hitler drives to Wiessee—to confront Roehm. My friend sees him arrive. Hitler goes into the hotel himself. Roehm is arrested and taken to the Stadelheim prison in Munich."

"It's sensational," I exclaimed.

"Very much," said Willi. "This will become the—you might call it the turning point for Hitler."

"But why didn't Hitler just order Roehm's execution?"

"Because he is an old chum of Hitler's—once they share

a cell in jail—Hitler offers him a courtesy." With a wry smile, Willi explained, "He leaves Roehm a loaded gun in an empty room. Is a classic gesture, but Roehm refuses to be classic and ignores the gesture of honor. So he is executed by Himmler's SS."

According to Willi, thousands were shot in Munich, while in Berlin Göring supervised the deaths of hundreds more.

"I am telling you, Larry," said Willi seriously, "that this is very exact. Staffens is working on secret tank construction, there are many people close to Hitler. Even they are horrified. For twenty-four hours all Germany echoes to machine guns. The executioners, they must work in squads of eight, but only for an hour at a time."

"But none of these details have been printed."

"It couldn't be printed," he shook his head. "No Germans will dare to. And no American journalist in Berlin could get a cable through the censor."

"Can I print it?"

Willi made only one stipulation. "You must let me spend three days back home in Düsseldorf before you tell America. I would not like it to be associated with you here. And I am afraid of this man Himmler. He used to be a chicken farmer—did you know this?—but he has spies everywhere."

I promised, of course. But five days later I had my very first lead story in the *Globe*—right across page one, said the herogram—the name given to congratulatory cables from the *Globe*'s foreign editor.

Even Papa was impressed when the clip from Washington arrived by sea mail: WHY HITLER EXECUTED ROEHM, THE FIRST FULL DETAILED STORY and underneath; From Larry Astell, Exclusive.

It was the first of many more scoops I landed during the next two or three years, when I often seemed to be working seven days a week—ninety percent of the time for the *Globe*. The odd thing was that I had never met anyone on the Washington newspaper except Tommy Tomlinson—until the day early in 1937 when he phoned me in the *PA* office from his room above.

"Hi!" he greeted me. "How's about keeping a day free for lunch?" Though this big, burly man had been correspondent in Paris for many years, he still couldn't speak more than a few words of fractured French.

"Could do," I grinned. "You paying?"

"Nope."

"Then I'll have to think about it."

"Please yourself. Only—I think I ought to tell you, Henry Vance, the owner of the *Globe*, is arriving on the *Berengaria* and he asked to lunch with me—and he wants to meet you too."

I whistled.

"The big time." Tommy had a sardonic attitude toward newspaper owners.

"What gives?" I asked.

Tommy shrugged his shoulders. "Far be it from me to unravel the insane workings of a newspaper baron's mind."

"But seriously?"

Tommy harbored no jealousy because I wrote as a free lance for the *Globe*. He was a tough old stager, quite content, now that he was in his early fifties, to stay in Paris until retirement age. "He's obviously heard about your stories—or maybe," he said with a wry smile, "he actually reads his own paper. Most proprietors only look at the ads—the cash flow. You should get *your* old man to invite my boss and his wife down to Douzy for lunch and dazzle him."

I did just that. My father invited the Vances and Tommy for the weekend, sending the Hisp to Paris to drive them to Douzy. And even Mr. Vance was entranced when he made the usual "first time" visit to drink a vintage Astell in the Douzy Pyramid.

"Never seen anything like it in the goddamned world," he said, peering up and down at the extraordinary white *cave*. "What a place to hide secrets. Yes, sir, thank you, I *will* have another glass of champagne."

Mrs. Vance was equally impressed, especially at the way the servants looked after the guests—a tradition at Douzy.

"No one has ever looked after *me* like this before," she said after being cosseted by Aubergine. "I just tell you,

Henry Vance, you'd better start improving the standard of
housekeeping back home, or I'll be pinching Aubergine,
though why she's called by that name I wouldn't know."

We had to explain. And Mrs. Vance, when she left, gave
Aubergine the biggest tip she had ever seen.

Tommy's remarks about making friends with the boss
were absolutely correct. From that day, I was more than
just a cipher to old man Vance, even in faraway Washington. I was a name; he could put a face to it; he had been to
our home with its strange white pyramid.

That afternoon, after the Vances had left for Paris,
Mama squeezed my arm and said to me, "Be an angel,
Larry, and help me in the gardens. It's a lovely day, and
anyway, we never get a chance to talk." And when we
were snipping off the crimped, dead pansies round the border, she added, "I'm so pleased about your success with
Mr. Vance, darling. I think he likes you. You *are* clever."

"Thanks largely to you," I laughed.

"Not entirely. Your father says you're the sort of man
who'll always recognize a chance and seize it. It's wonderful."

There wasn't really much to do in the garden. But I had
the feeling that Mama wanted to talk. Over the years,
dealing often with strangers from whom I was trying to extract information, I had developed a kind of instinct which
told me when the time was ripe for imminent exchange of
confidences. Sure enough I was right.

"Do you ever miss Sonia after all these years?" Mama
asked me almost shyly.

"Not really—well, that's not true. It's a long time now—
three or four years—but of course I think of her often."

"Any other girls in view?"

I shook my head.

"Nope," I said firmly. "Nary a one. A good newspaperman must be a loner. Uncle Oregon told me that."

"But you must have girl friends?" Was Mama probing?
Or was this just normal parental interest?

"A few. Not very exciting though. I like being alone during the week, then coming to Douzy on Fridays—unless the *Globe* asks me to do a Sunday stint."

Mama sounded a little guarded, watchful, when she asked almost casually, "Have you heard from Sonia *lately?*"

"Not for ages. Why? Any particular reason?"

"Only," Mama hesitated, "that I heard from Sonia's mother the other day."

"I didn't know you even wrote to each other."

"Not often. But it seems there's a vague chance— nothing more—that the Riccardis may be coming *en poste* to Paris."

"You mean it—really! And . . . ?" I left the question unfinished as I picked up some dead flowers.

"I don't know, dear. I know nothing really."

"But why Paris?" I blurted out. "That's wonderful."

"Why *not* Paris?" asked Mama with a laugh. She explained the details of the letter she had received. Apparently Riccardi had, in the normal course of diplomatic duties, done a stint at the Italian foreign office after leaving Paraguay and now, according to Sonia's mother, was senior enough to be given a fair number of choices when the time came for him to take up a new post.

"And he's expecting to be offered Paris," she said.

"And Sonia?" I insisted.

"I don't know," Mama laughed again. "Really! Why don't you phone her and find out. I suppose she would come to Paris—if this appointment goes through. Do you still love her? It's been a long time since—but you say there's no one else."

No, there wasn't. The thought—even the mere possibility that Sonia might return to Paris after all these years—made me realize how much I had missed her. How long was it now since I had seen her? Four years—no, more? Perhaps she or I or both of us would be different when next we met. Maybe the years apart would have robbed us of the innocence we had both at first enjoyed. I certainly didn't feel the white-hot surge which had always seized us in the past even when we brushed against each other. But you couldn't expect that sort of feeling to thrive on an absence of years. And during the years when I had moved ahead as a newspaperman, I had become more preoccupied with living rather than loving. There was hardly time to *think* of love, let alone make it.

Of course if I saw her again, God knows what my reaction would be. I didn't think I could ever resist her—not only because of *my* feelings, but because she always made it so clear that she couldn't resist me. On the other hand, Riccardi might never come to Paris. And Sonia might be busy in Italy, or she might not want to reopen the past after all these years. She had hardly bubbled over with passionate letters in the intervening years.

"I'll believe it when I see her," I laughed. "In the meantime, I'm a loner."

"You're right—it's probably only a rumor. All the same, Larry, I don't like to think of you so much alone in Paris. It doesn't seem natural."

"Mama, I'm surrounded by friends—well, acquaintances. They're not so intense as"—I could afford to smile now at the painful, beautiful memories—"as Sonia was. Of course sometimes I'm lonely, but it doesn't worry me."

As I shoveled up the dead flowers into a barrow, I had the sudden feeling that I wasn't the only one at Douzy who at times was lonely, and I felt a twinge of guilt at the casual way in which we accepted Mama, the dodges we got up to to evade "garden duty," forgetting that Mama didn't *need* to do any gardening, it had become to her a therapy more than a passion, something to *do,* something to keep her hands busy, her thoughts occupied, when she was bored.

"Yes, I am lonely sometimes," she confessed, asking me for the pruning shears. "The trouble is—men change. At first when we were married, even if your father enjoyed his work, it was only *part* of his life. But now he's become *too* successful." With a laugh she added, "All he *had* to do was watch people fill bottles of champagne and let nature do the rest. But now—my dear, he's the head of this and that, the vice-president of this, he works on the *Comité* and the *Appellation contrôlée.* He's hardly time to say good morning to me. Yes, I am lonely at times," she added thoughtfully, "but thank God for Guy."

"Let's hope he doesn't choose his girl friend, Olivia, instead of Douzy."

"He won't!" she said almost ferociously.

"Mama! She's very pleasant. I admire Olivia. She's no Sonia, but she has a certain serenity. And she *is* a good painter."

"I didn't mean it," Mama straightened her back. "I was only thinking it's not my idea of fun living alone in this big house when you all leave home. You've gone already. And what's going to happen between Anna and that German boy? And after that," suddenly she was sad, "I'll be all alone except for Grandma and Mlle. Lisette. They're hardly scintillating companions. Soon there'll only be Guy left."

"Don't you think," I asked suddenly, "that it's a bit of a bore having Mlle. Lisette around—I mean, an ex-nanny living in the house? After all, how many years is it since she *was* a nanny?"

Mama shrugged her shoulders. "She's all right," Mama said, curiously defensive. "And there's plenty of room."

"She's such a prune, it's bad for you to have her around. You need younger company. I think she should go."

"No," said Mama with sudden firmness. "Let's forget the subject."

"You're the boss," I said cheerfully. "But at least why don't you come to Paris more often? Even live there? Or visit America for a few months. How about that? Doesn't it tempt you?"

"Sometimes. At least shopping in Paris would make a change," she said half humorously, "from gardening."

"Next time you come to Paris we'll go out for dinner. We'll find a boy friend for you."

"Maybe," she said thoughtfully.

A few evenings later I mentioned to the family over dinner that I had been invited to meet Otto Abetz, the German minister in Paris with special responsibilities. Grandma's immediate sniff of disapproval was distinctly audible.

"He should be shot!"

"But, Grandma," said Guy, "you can't shoot everyone."

"The Germans are the natural enemies of France." She made statements like this with an air of finality that brooked of no argument—and in fact we had long since found it easier to accept Grandma's dictums than to start discussions which we could never win. To her the French were God's chosen people, the Germans were the Devil's disciples.

"But," wailed a pretending Anna, "you can't want to shoot Willi—*please.*"

"You watch your step, young lady," warned Grandma darkly, but without specifying any reasons.

My father helped himself to some more pink *gigot*—like most Frenchmen he preferred his lamb underdone—and some *mange-tout.* "I always thought," he murmured, "that in these dangerous times, with a lunatic like Hitler in command, we should all be trying to *avoid* war. *Really!* It seems to me that Mr. Abetz is at least *trying* to help—to promote understanding."

"I still prefer dead Germans." Grandma cut her slice of meat as savagely as the poor lamb's throat, then folded her hands across her lap, always a sign that the last word had been said.

"There, there, boys and girls, that's enough killing for one night," said Mama tolerantly.

"We don't want to run out of coffins," whispered Oregon.

Otto Abetz, it transpired, was paying one of his regular visits to Paris in his role of "ambassador-at-large." Many French people were deeply suspicious of his motives. He was apparently very close to Hitler. The French anti-Fascist clique firmly believed that Abetz and his followers were building up a pro-Nazi fifth column strong enough to betray France in the event of war. Others, like my father, felt Abetz was striving to improve Franço-German relations. He *seemed* to be a Francophile with an impeccable pedigree. He had a charming French wife called Suzanne. He spoke the language perfectly. He was at home with French history and literature, he could keep his end up with any French intellectuals.

"He likes people to think," said Oregon, drawing on his

after-dinner cigar, "that he's the one German above all others who's determined to prevent war with a country he loves. Personally, I think it's a load of crap."

"Well, the Europeans are behaving very strangely," said my father.

"They sure are," Oregon said, touching the plate with the end of his cigar so the ash would drop off gently, "and not only with German-inspired riots in places like the Sudetenland, and Halifax in Britain, crawling to appease Hitler. The Italians have joined the German-Japanese Anti-Comintern Pact—bloody strange bedfellows I must say. And Franco is winning all along the line."

"They should all be put behind bars," said Grandma. "And Abetz first—tomorrow. Better that than you, Larry, kowtowing to a German."

"I still think it might be interesting to meet him."

"Sure. But watch it. He'll be charming. My bet is that before the end of the party, you'll be invited to a free junket in Germany."

"After the piece I wrote about Roehm? He must have seen it?"

"He'll have forgotten all about it. Anyway, he's big enough to take that sort of criticism in his stride."

I met Abetz the following week in his house in the rue de Rennes. His French wife was at the door of the salon to greet guests and couldn't have been more charming. Almost instinctively, I took in every detail of the room, the tall french windows, the pale green walls, the gold leaf that touched the moldings of doors and ceilings—and of course an assortment of Louis XV furniture, without which no political home was complete. It was a pretty room, particularly as a whisper of sunlight shafted through it.

Abetz obviously knew who I was, for he came forward to greet me. I was surprised to find a handsome man, tall with big shoulders, and a face that looked paler than it actually was because of his reddish-blond hair. He had a big smile. It was his eyes, though, that fascinated me. They were blue, yet they didn't go with the smile. The smile and the eyes seemed to belong to two different people. The smile was wide and generous, the blue eyes above the smile like two chips of ice frozen with a bluish tinge.

"It is a pleasure to meet you, Mr. Astell." He couldn't have been more charming. "I have admired your work very much."

The more I listened to him, the more intrigued I became. He seemed to make a great show of being an understanding friend of France, he exuded cordiality. He also made a great number of intelligent observations and yet, I couldn't tell why, I found him shifty.

There were about twenty people at the party, and we made small talk until another guest arrived with something of a flourish, as though the late timing had been carefully engineered for effect. It was the Countess de Portes, mistress of Paul Reynaud, the up-and-coming French politician. She was not with her escort as Abetz stepped forward and kissed her hand while she cooed, "So nice to see you again, dear Otto."

I had met Hélène de Portes before but only briefly in a crowd, and I had never studied her carefully. I found it hard to like her. She wasn't particularly good-looking. She had a somewhat angular face, a large mouth, and I noticed that her complexion was sallow. Still, she was dressed in the height of fashion, her dark curly hair swept upward in the style of the day.

She had been Reynaud's mistress for nearly ten years, and behind her back her enemies called her *la porte à côté*. It was a double-edged nickname, for she *was* the side door through which anyone who wanted to see Reynaud had to pass; but *à côté* was also a snobbish term, so that to her detractors, she was "a little *à côté*," "a little ordinary."

"Perhaps, *chère madame*," Abetz had joined us, "you can help me to persuade Monsieur Astell to visit us in Germany. We have already invited several prominent writers, but not yet an American. All we ask of our visitors is that they write the truth and not propaganda lies."

"You should go," said Madame de Portes.

"May I introduce you to the writer Jean Luchaire," said Abetz. "He has already visited us in Germany."

I knew Luchaire well by reputation. He had been
Suzanne Abetz's boss before she married the German. Luchaire was blindly pro-Nazi.

"And his delightful daughter, Corinne," murmured
Abetz. And Luchaire's daughter *was* delightful. Only seventeen, Corinne Luchaire had shot to stardom in a French
film called *Prison Without Bars*.

"I congratulate you on your performance," I said, adding sincerely, "and—well, you *are* beautiful."

Luchaire was accompanied by Paul Ferdonnet of the
Agence Prima, another pro-German writer, and I knew
that Abetz had arranged for several self-appointed intellectuals who were sympathetic to fascism to have their
unpublished books published in Germany—with Abetz
footing the bill, and paying staggering advance royalties
out of all proportion to possible sales. In short, bribery.

We had almost reached the end of the party, the guests
were beginning to drift away, when Abetz, seeing me in a
corner talking to his wife, Suzanne, came up and said, with
the studied air of someone skillfully planting a casual remark, "By the way, I hear that an old friend of your family
is coming to live in Paris."

I was on my guard, I could sense his interest by the way
he watched my face.

"Oh yes?" I hadn't the faintest idea of the bombshell—
the double bombshell—about to be dropped on me.

"I mean Signore Riccardi. He's just been appointed to
Paris."

"Riccardi!" I echoed. "How did you know he was a friend
of the family?"

Abetz shrugged his shoulders as though explanation
was superfluous. "I can't remember offhand who told me.
The countess, perhaps?" And with that charming smile of
his, he said, "Did you mention it, Suzanne? No? Does it
matter? The main thing is that old friends will be reunited. That *can't* be bad in these difficult days."

I was puzzled. It was part of my job as a newspaperman
to keep track of all the important changes at the Quai
d'Orsay and on the Paris diplomatic list, and I would

surely have known if Riccardi was about to replace the present ambassador.

"Oh, no," said Abetz. "He's going to be an ambassador-at-large, so to speak. You may say that Signore Riccardi will have very much the same job I have. In fact we will be working together—for peace and understanding, to encourage happy relations between our countries."

I was still puzzled, suspicious. How could Abetz have possibly known that the Riccardis and the Astells were old family friends?

Then, even more casually, Abetz dropped his second bombshell.

"I hear that Signore Riccardi's daughter is positively beautiful," he said. "I'm looking forward very much to meeting her."

"She is," I said, in my enthusiasm dropping my guard. "A real stunner."

"I'm only sorry," murmured Abetz as he said good-bye, "that her fiancé, who works in the foreign office, won't be able to join her in Paris."

6

I COULDN'T BELIEVE IT! Sonia engaged! *And without telling me!* That angered me most. At first, filled with the indignation of a spurned lover, I was furious—forgetting that over the years I had hardly encouraged her to keep her love.

I slammed the MG into third and, taking the back way to the office, avoiding the *Grands Boulevards,* I roared up the rue du Quatre-Septembre toward the rue du Sentier.

And there in the office, of course, was a letter from her. One glance at the postmark told me it had been delayed, as letters in Europe often were these days. I was in no hurry to open it, but for a few moments studied the Italian stamp, deciphering the smudged date, the blue envelope with its strong upward-sloping handwriting.

What excuse could there possibly be in the unopened letter lying on my desk, taunting me? Sadness? Apology? Reproach?

After a few moments, anger diminished, I realized that she couldn't know how Abetz had deliberately told me in advance about her fiancé. Sitting at the old wooden desk where I had passed so many hours of my life, I was thinking of that sun-drenched day when I had driven her from Rolle and we had stopped the old MG in the cornfield and everything had happened, and the days which had followed and which could never be forgotten. I suppose that had been the happiest year of my life. It had been very near to heaven in those carefree days when, in spirit if not in fact, we always seemed to be walking hand in hand, laughing, through some enchanted garden. "Everywhere" was our garden in those days, it made no difference whether we were walking along the Left Bank or helping with the *vendange* at Douzy, or typing in my office. I think it was her feminine instinct—that and her Russian blood—which enslaved me in those happy months.

Sighing, I slit open the blue envelope with one edge of the pair of long scissors without which no newspaperman's desk is properly furnished. I started to read.

"Darling Monsieur Coquelicot," she began, "I want you to be the first to know two things—that I am engaged to be married, and that I still hope you realize that I will always love you more than anyone else in the world."

I straightened up, almost with a jerk, for this was no ordinary letter to a jilted lover.

"It looks awful, so stark, written like that," she continued. "But what I am trying to say, darling Larry, is that the love we have known for each other can never be replaced by any other man, and yet if I have not written to you for a long time, there have been many reasons. Daddy has been in trouble—not yet resolved—and I have been able to help him, but in a way which has made it impossible for me to do what I really wanted to—run away to your arms and marry you, my love. One day I will explain.

"Italy is not America and the diplomatic service is not like producing champagne. I remember your papa once telling me that if he didn't approve of the harvest in any particular year, he just wouldn't bottle any champagne. But you can't make decisions like that when you are a diplomat—or, alas, a diplomat's daughter. You have to carry on, and play a part if needed."

I turned over to the back of the first sheet and read on. "Francesco, my fiancé, is a career diplomat who has had his problems too. We don't live in ordinary times now. Il Duce is in charge. Our problems are not terrible, but the life of a diplomat is not easy and I think I have been of help. What I am trying to tell you is that in Italy—and certainly in the diplomatic service!—it is sometimes more important for married couples to be good friends than passionate lovers like we have been. So when/if we meet, you must understand that sometimes life is not easy for a dutiful daughter."

There was a great deal more in the three blue pages, but I was wondering, what did she mean by having to play a part? And that it was more important to be good friends than passionate lovers? It sounded like a recipe for a miserable marriage—not that she was married yet, only engaged. But was she whispering discreetly that love, as she had so often said to me, had nothing to do with marriage?

Mama received a letter from Signora Riccardi a few days later, and when I arrived at Douzy for the weekend and she told me, I professed only a mild interest. Mama and Papa exchanged noticeable glances of relief.

"Sonia's fiancé has a title," said Mama. "He is the Count de Feo—Francesco de Feo. But it seems they won't be having an early marriage. The Italian diplomatic corps likes a man to get settled before he saddles himself with a wife. Very sensible."

Sensible! Who the hell wanted to be sensible with a hot-blooded girl like Sonia? What a terrible waste of a beautiful woman! I thought. But of course she must have changed. Now she must be twenty-three. Perhaps *she* was "sensible" now.

Then, a few weeks later, Signora Riccardi wrote to Mama again, this time giving the date when Riccardi would be arriving in Paris, where they would live in a "diplomatic" house in the rue de Longchamp. Her husband would be ambassador-without-portfolio. And I knew that the appointment would cover many secrets. This had to be an important promotion, for it came after a previous promotion. Riccardi's stint at the Italian foreign office had been a direct reward for remarkable diplomatic help given by Riccardi—some said undercover help—in persuading the countries of Bolivia and Paraguay to end their bitter war in 1936. He was obviously a formidable man.

Sonia was engaged, of course, so that except innocently we would never see each other alone. But I couldn't pre-

vent a tingle of anticipation at the prospect of meeting her.
A few girls had shared my bed since those happy days in
the rue de l'Université, but not one had stirred me, loved
me, as Sonia had done. The day after Mama had read the
second letter, she cornered me in the living room.

"I imagine we'll be seeing quite a lot of the Riccardis,"
she began tentatively. "After all, they're old friends—and
you're bound to be thrown in contact with Sonia. But,
Larry," she hesitated slightly, "I trust you to—well, remember I *am* Sonia's godmother. It sounds so old fashioned! But be *good,* darling, if you know what I mean. It
would be very unfair to everyone."

"I will," I promised her, and I meant it.

Besides, I had other things on my mind, no time to moon
over a schoolboy crush which had ended six years ago. I
was now a professional newspaperman. I could say that.
I had graduated. I was working so hard for the *Globe* that
I had little or no time for the dear old *Paris American,* even
though I still worked in its building. I wasn't a staff member of the *Globe,* but that was because I preferred it that
way. As a stringer—paid by the day or by the quality of a
story—I was earning as much as a staffer simply because
France and Europe dominated the news and Tommy Tomlinson couldn't cope single-handed. Yet the arrangement
suited the *Globe* because as a nonstaffer it wouldn't be sad-
dled with long-term responsibilities if I vanished when
war came. By now in 1937 we all talked about *when,* not *if.*
I was equally satisfied with the arrangement because
though I was paid well I retained my freedom. Naturally I
consulted Tommy about everything, but as a stringer I
didn't have to send Washington a cable every time I took a
day off.

"Once you're on the staff, they like to keep track," said
Tommy. "You've got to send them a signal even if you
fart."

I was free. I worked hard. I was well paid. But the *Globe*
didn't own me.

Yet apart from my work, and long before Sonia reap-

peared, all was not well, though I find it difficult, looking
back, to pinpoint the moment when I realized how the
calm and ordered life of the Astells was slowly beginning
to show signs of strain. Nothing dramatic happened. No
one ran away from home, Papa wasn't surprised in bed
with another woman, we didn't lose our money. The *Paris
American* actually put on circulation.

Perhaps it was an echo of the discontent, the masked
fear that chilled all Europe each time the posturing Hitler
tightened his grip on a dictator's world, each time the an-
tics of Mussolini posed new threats. No one was *really*
afraid—not day after day after day—but occasional stabs of
fear came and went, like a tooth abscess that flares, quiets,
then flares again.

I saw what was happening in the family mostly in episodic flashes when I returned to Douzy for weekends, or
when members of the family visited our Paris apartment
during the week. Perhaps I didn't realize what was happening at first because I was so busy with the *Globe*.

Then Sonia returned to Paris—and despite all the promises, I was soon caught up in a web of deceit, smiling lies,
broken promises, furtive meetings. Did that somehow help
to sour the life of Douzy? Did the families suspect, did the
ripples of what happened secretly turn into larger, eddy-
ing circles that touched others?

Because, of course, when Sonia finally arrived in Paris
and drove with her father and mother to spend their first
weekend with us at Douzy, we were lost. Don't ask why, I
make no excuses. I was determined to keep my promise to
Mama, and it never entered my head that an old lost love
would be rekindled the moment our hands touched. It was
electric, needing no words, the effect of just shaking hands,
the feeling of desire, as though we had never parted.

She seemed hardly to have changed; the same perfect
complexion on that heart-shaped face, the same wide, open
blue eyes, as though she was always surprised at the joy of
living, the eyes as bright as ever. I drew in a deep breath.
Her tailored suit—even I knew that women liked their
suits to be tailored by men—was in gray *Prince de Galles*

checks, a jacket and skirt that showed off her figure and long, straight legs, in their silk stockings. And when she took off her jacket I could see that she was as slim as ever, breasts pointing upward under her silk blouse, just the right size, round and firm and pointing gently, not aggressively.

The most extraordinary thing of all was that she knew it too, she wanted me, without any word spoken, as desperately as I wanted her. And there was another extraordinary thing. It wasn't lust. I wasn't panting physically with desire. I can't explain it, I was above that feeling. I just wanted to wrap her in my arms, smother her with kisses, and slide into her body.

I tried to think—what to do? I was bemused. At first I could only stand there, holding a book. I was on the verge of panic, if I didn't control myself I would shout aloud, "I need you! Now! *Now!*"

I remember that Anna had told me she was going into Reims to meet someone for ten minutes. She would drive over about five o'clock, return in half an hour. It was my chance: almost deliberately ignoring Sonia, who was talking to Tommy Tomlinson, who had come for the weekend, I chattered first to Signora Riccardi for a few moments, glanced at my watch—half past four—and buttonholed Anna, showing her the new book I had been handling, pretending to search for the illustration.

"Listen quickly," I muttered as I turned the pages, "don't ask any damn fool questions, but for God's sake, Anna, get Sonia to drive with you to Reims. But drop her at the far end of the orchard. I'll leave first with Tommy, pretend I'm going for a walk. Sonia and Tommy can swap places, change back when you return home. I must see her alone. I *must.*"

I saw the quick glitter of conspiracy shine in her eyes. She had always known about Sonia and me since that first drive from Rolle in Switzerland. And now Anna had her own conspiracies with Willi.

"Okay," she whispered. "You go now. Take Tommy

with you, and he can come to Reims with me for half an hour."

It was as simple as that.

"How's about a walk through the vineyards?" I said to Tommy.

"Me? I'm no walker," he began, fortunately out of earshot.

"Come on," I muttered savagely, and said to the others, "Tommy and I have a problem to solve—our next assignment. We'll discuss it over a walk. Bye girls, see you soon!"

The far corner of the orchard backed onto the road leading through the vineyards, at the spot where village boys sneaked in to pinch apples each autumn. As we walked down the dell I explained to a mystified Tommy what was expected of him.

"For a bureau chief, you're very understanding," I said.

"Anything to encourage romance," he chuckled. "Make a good story, wouldn't it?"

Five minutes after we had crossed the orchard, Anna's Citroën appeared round the narrow road, at times almost as yellow as a lemon. From this spot, the route led to the main Reims road.

My heart was banging against my ribs as though a hammer were striking them. The car always went slowly round the tricky bends of the drive, and when it stopped Sonia jumped out of the car without a word.

"Hop in, Tommy," cried Anna. And as she started to move forward slowly, she added, "Be ready to swap places in half an hour." Then the back of the Citroën disappeared round the next bend.

Without a word we scrambled across the bank, stumbling through tall stalks of frothy hedge parsley and poppies, and into the orchard. Then, and only then, we almost fell to the ground, hidden in the long grass, and kissed each other as though the world would end when we stopped.

Still without a word, lying on her back, she pulled up her skirt and there, after six years, was Sonia as I remembered her, the long, slim legs, the flat stomach creamy white against the black. It sounds incredible, but I had no time to think of her, I pulled down my trousers with one hand, stroking her with the other, feeling her damp with desire, and then, after barely one move inside her, it was over before I knew what happened.

Only then did she speak. Lying there next to me, stroking my hair, my face, she kissed me again and again and whispered, "Don't worry, darling. I came before you—the second I saw you looking at me." Kissing me again, she added almost wistfully, "Almost at this very spot, where I first let you look at me. Remember?"

I nodded.

"And here you are," twisting my blond hair, "the same Monsieur Coquelicot. Remember him?" She lay back smiling, shining black hair spread out in the long green grass. "Do you forgive me?"

"Of course," I said.

While we still lay back in each other's arms, she whispered, "Got a hanky—one you don't need again?"

I gave her the one from my breast pocket. She tucked it between her legs, keeping it in place with her panties. "Lucky I was wearing panties today."

Watching her, filled with the electric clarity that always follows true lovemaking, I suddenly thought, I shouldn't be watching her—I shouldn't have done anything. Aloud, I said, "I am taking away another man's fiancée. I can't help having a feeling—well, you know—"

"Don't feel that way, my love," she whispered. "Remember the first time, Mr. Coquelicot? It's me that should feel guilty. Do *you* forgive *me?*"

"Of course—if there's anything to forgive. Here—let me clean you up." I was worried lest our parents would notice anything.

"It takes a lot to ruin a Caraceni of Rome," she laughed. "Brush my back, will you, darling?" With a kiss and a light laugh that showed she didn't care, she said, "He's the only tailor in Italy who really specializes in Prince of Wales suits. Costs a fortune, fifteen hundred lire."

"There! That's better." I dusted a little dirt from her shirt.

"Thank you. And I'm so glad. I missed you so much. I find it difficult to write letters—"

"I know," I laughed too. It was extraordinary how, in the space of a few minutes, it was easy to joke, the tension eased after the urgent physical need.

"I know." Echoing my words, she smiled back. "You used the right words—a physical need—because the second we touched each other in the living room, it was as though I could hardly stand up."

"That's just how I felt. If I'd left the room, I wouldn't have been able to wait, even for you, even for this."

We didn't make love any more that day. In a curious way there was no need to. We had fallen in love—against all the promises to behave. We had released the desire, and so, knowing that we did love each other, as we had done six years ago, the act of making love again wasn't, for the moment anyway, necessary. Satisfaction was taking over from urgency, anxiety from desire. The moment of meeting had been the moment of falling in love again, indeed that touch had been the moment of making love.

So it all started again. Only this time it was different from the earlier deception. It was better and worse. Then I had only kept a secret from my parents. Now I was involved in the betrayal of the man Sonia had promised to marry; though he was still in Rome, it would have appalled my father and mother, if discovered. To say nothing of Sonia's parents.

Yet there was no way in which we could stop meeting during the months that followed. We tried. I wasn't an absolute fool, I knew I was behaving badly, and so was Sonia for that matter. Often I felt ashamed of what I was doing. Then at other times I caught myself thinking that it wasn't all my fault. Sonia was no quiet, unassuming fiancée. With her Russian blood, she had a temper that flared, she was impetuous, strong-willed, and though she might consider the wishes of her father, and thus never discuss the possibility of breaking her engagement—not at this stage—she was determined that we should not miss one moment of our love if it could be kept secret.

In an almost bizarre way, Sonia even advanced what she considered to be a perfectly rational attitude to our behavior—one that made it clear (to her) that we had no need to be ashamed of what we were doing.

"After all," she said, "it's not as though one of us picked the other up and started an affair. We fell in love six years ago. The others stopped us. We're only," she searched for the words, "resuming where we left off."

"It's not the kind of philosophical argument that would stand up in a debate!"

"I'm happy about it. It satisfies my conscience. After all, if we'd never been discovered, we might eventually have got married."

"How extraordinary you should say that." I was thinking back to a conversation at Douzy. "Mama actually told me once that she was sorry we'd been discovered. What a pity, my darling Sonia. It would have saved me so much trouble."

"It's too late now." Her voice was suddenly abrupt. She seemed to hate discussing a more permanent relationship. But this time I stood firm.

"Look, we love each other," as though that solved every problem, which, to my uncomplicated way of thinking, it did. "Breaking an engagement isn't the end of the world."

"But it would be—for me."

"But why? Is it your father? Or Francesco? After all, darling, it *is* a bit odd, come to think of it, you become engaged to a man you obviously don't love—and as soon as we meet we fall into each other's arms!"

"One day I'll explain. I haven't committed murder if that's what you're afraid of. But I need help and you can't help me. Kiss me—and don't look so worried, one day I'll tell you everything. But not now. Don't spoil everything."

"But I want to know," I said stubbornly. We were lunching at the Brasserie Lipp in the boulevard St. Germain. "I have a *right* to know."

The moment I used the word *right* I knew I shouldn't have.

Almost scornfully she looked at me—like a different woman. Her wide-apart blue eyes seemed to narrow, and she went almost white with anger. "What *right* do you have?" she said furiously. "How dare you lecture me about *right?* Isn't it enough that I give myself to you—"

"And take from me!" I said angrily.

"Oh!" Her anger turned to sarcasm. "Now you're doing me a favor each time we make love."

"I didn't mean that."

"Then don't say it, you pompous idiot," she flared up. "Why the bloody hell can't you accept things as they are?"

At that moment the old waiter came in with our dish of *choucroute* and laid the tray on the table.

"You can throw that damn stuff away," she said to him, and without another word stormed out.

I tried to follow, to make peace—everything had blown up in a matter of seconds—but in my rush I upset the tray. The *choucroute* tipped over—much of it on my trousers, but some on the trousers of the waiter. The prim lady behind the cash register screamed faintly, then beckoned to the headwaiter, demanding payment before I left. "He's drunk, he's a disgrace to a respectable place," I heard her cry.

By the time I had paid, Sonia had vanished.

I too was boiling over with anger. That was the end of that! It served me right for getting mixed up with a woman about to marry another man. And what a bitch! No woman had ever walked out on me before in a restaurant.

On an impulse I walked across to the Deux Magots, bought a *jeton* from the waiter for the pay phone, and dialed Tomlinson's number. Only the day before he had asked me if I would like a quiet trip to Fontainebleau to write an undated piece for the Sunday supplement on "the new Barbizon School" of painters—the inheritors of those who had worked mostly in the forest of Fontainebleau, the people like Rousseau, Millet, and Daubigny.

"Okay if I go today?" I asked him.

"You sound mad at someone. But sure."

I spent three utterly miserable days at the Hôtel Fleuri et Forêt at Barbizon, surrounded by the forest of Fontainebleau. The weather was warm and sunny, but I felt cold and miserable; the food at the hotel was superb, but I felt starved—for love. I drove round the area, searching out promising painters, making notes, yet all the time beset by a nagging thought, Perhaps I should phone her? I wanted to. And I swear it wasn't nastiness that stopped me. I didn't want to be nasty to *her*. It was a feeling I entertained that even if I was miserable without her, I must have a few days in which to breathe, to consider the future, the slippery slope down which I was sliding helplessly to what could only be a sticky end.

I didn't give in. I didn't phone and I never expected her to, for she also had a stubborn set to her jaw. Three days later I drove straight to the office, parked my car outside the rue du Sentier, and as I walked through the doors, Charles, the doorman, his watery eyes blinking as he opened the doors of the rickety elevator, said, "Pardon, monsieur, there's a lady to see you."

"Now? It's only ten o'clock."

"She's been here, sir," he coughed discreetly, "since last night."

She was asleep on my leather sofa in front of my desk. By her side was a half-filled cup of cold coffee and the crumbs of a croissant. Charles must have brought her breakfast and she had fallen asleep again. But it wasn't that which first stunned me. The office was filled from floor to ceiling with poppies—hundreds and hundreds and hundreds of them. There must have been twenty to thirty vases standing on the desk, the floor, even the windowsill.

I leaned forward and kissed her gently on the eyelids and her cheeks, and I could taste the salt.

Without rising, just emerging from sleep, she just put her arms round me and, still with a trace of tears, murmured, "Oh, my darling Monsieur Coquelicot, never do that to me again, never, never. Promise? I'm sorry! I love you, I behaved abominably, you're the only real thing in all my miserable life. All the rest is like acting out a horrible play."

And when she had said that and made up her face and I'd opened a bottle of champagne from the office fridge—even though it was still only just after ten in the morning—she explained, though only in part, why she had agreed to the engagement.

"I didn't want to involve you and I still don't want to," she said. "But Daddy begged me to accept Francesco's proposal. He said his entire future—his very life—depended on the engagement." But beyond that Sonia would not satisfy my curiosity.

So the quarrel was forgotten, and the secret months that followed were as wonderful as if we had never quarreled or for that matter had never been parted.

True there were differences as the months slipped by. For one thing I still couldn't say that I enjoyed the thought of Sonia being engaged to another man, even though he was living far away in Rome—and she didn't seem to love him. Yet there was a different reason why I was uneasy—her father's vaguely sinister work in France, something that seemed to forestall any discussion of our future.

I still thought it perfectly simple for Sonia to break off the engagement and marry me. But she was afraid to. She *wanted* to marry me, of that I am sure, but as she said time and again after that quarrel, she could do nothing that would upset the diplomatic relations between her father, Count Ciano—now foreign minister—and what was happening in France.

"And Francesco *does* come into those relations," she sighed. "Not with me—but with Ciano—and even Mussolini. I only pray, darling, that we can sort it out. You know I want to marry you one day. But be patient."

There was nothing I could do—but carry on, work hard, and make love in secret.

First, I found a place where we could meet. I did once take Sonia back to the rue de l'Université, but it was more for old times' sake than as a refuge of safety, and both of us were nervous of being discovered, for both Papa and Mama had recently visited the apartment.

"We've got to find another place," I said, and we did. I was an old friend of a tall American photographer called Alex Rhys, who often worked for the *Paris American.* He was a bachelor in his fifties and lived in the rue du Cherche-Midi, across from the boulevard St. Germain. And when he suddenly announced that he was leaving for Asia on a year's assignment for a major American magazine, I grabbed the chance.

It wasn't the rue de l'Université, though it was even smaller than that beautiful poppy-bedecked apartment. And it was on the fifth floor—without an elevator. But Alex had turned the one-room atelier into a charming apartment, every wall decorated with huge blowups of his photos. It had a shower and a bidet. The kitchen consisted of a glassed-in corner with a couple of burners and a fridge—enough for a bachelor, and enough for us. There were a couple of deep, comfortable armchairs, a table that would seat four at a pinch, and in one corner a wide divan surrounded by bookshelves.

It was perfect, and within a month we had a second "home," a beautiful and secret place of our own. There we could meet whenever we could snatch the time, and there both of us could live in a world of make-believe limited only by the hours when Sonia had to go clattering down the rickety wooden steps.

7

OVER THE NEXT FEW MONTHS I began to wonder more and more about the "duties" of Sonia's father. What exactly was the sinister role being played by Riccardi? It must be very serious—and secret—for Sonia was insisting that it would be impossible for her to break off an engagement to a man she didn't love.

I might be unduly sensitive to Riccardi's behavior, even his power to influence Sonia's fears, yet I had an instinctive feeling that he had not been appointed to Paris merely to initial new trade deals or discuss the plight of migrant Italian workers. His work smacked of intrigue, especially as he and Otto Abetz met regularly. I knew that Abetz was trying to undermine French resolve in these critical years. It seemed incredible, but was Riccardi working with him?

"Daddy was supposed to retire even before he was posted here," said Sonia. "But when Mussolini appointed Count Ciano foreign minister, Daddy became one of Ciano's right-hand men. Mummy's delighted," Sonia added with a laugh. "The job rates a chauffeur and servants."

Ciano was Mussolini's son-in-law, and I knew that when you marry the boss's daughter you often end up thinking and acting like the boss. In Oregon's words, "It's the only sensible way to protect your investment." And Mussolini, engaged in enlarging the Italian empire in Africa, was not my favorite character. He had poisoned the wells in North Africa, in effect murdering thousands of civilians. He had proclaimed King Vittorio Emanuele Emperor of Ethiopia.

He had already demanded—and *got*—part of France's East African possessions. He was finding it all so easy—easy enough to start demanding the "return" to Italy of Nice, Corsica, Tunis. All over Italy the three words had become a battle cry.

"I shouldn't say this, but I have the feeling," Sonia rarely sounded uneasy, "that Mussolini is up to no good in France. It's the hints my father drops."

"Such as?"

"He told me to be careful because a number of Italians here are—well, spies, I suppose, though he didn't use that word. But they're reporting back to Rome on all Italians in France who are against Mussolini's regime."

"I'm not surprised."

"He was vague. Just said that sometimes countries don't see eye to eye. And that it could happen with our two countries. And I don't like Otto Abetz. Father sees him all the time. He doesn't want me to be in the middle of any trouble."

This particular conversation took place in bed—as usual in the early afternoon or at lunchtime, safely hidden in the one-room studio on the fifth floor of the rue du Cherche-Midi.

"Sometimes I feel that we've never been separated," Sonia said, "as though this terrible interval has just been an awful dream."

"It wasn't," I said sadly. "You *are* engaged to be married. And not to me. Why don't you—?"

She put a finger to my lips and, remembering that first day when we lunched together on the way back from Switzerland, said, "Here, let's share our food."

"But I love you—more than ever," I said. "It can't be wrong to marry the man you love. Can it? *Can it?*"

"We've been through all that, darling, don't spoil it. It *can* be bad. Daddy's walking a tightrope. And if he makes one false move—like breaking off my engagement to one of Ciano's most promising helpers—well, it's been made clear to me—" she sighed.

"Even so. If I spoke to your father? I could even turn you into an American citizen."

From Sonia I had built up from casual remarks a picture of her life with Francesco in Italy as an engaged couple. The Count de Feo had great taste, a large estate, excellent manners. He was at his best chatting to any pretty woman sitting on his right or left at a grand dinner party—"Rather different from this room." I looked ruefully round Rhys's flat.

"You know how much more I prefer this one," she replied.

I took some consolation from the fact that though Sonia must have been the most beautiful guest at any dinner, Francesco seemed relatively immune. I couldn't understand how he could resist her physically. "How can any man keep his hands off a girl like you?" I asked, not exactly jealous, but hoping she would say that he had never been to bed with her.

"He hasn't," she said. "It suits me perfectly. He doesn't like that sort of thing—not much. I love no one else but you."

But, I asked her, weren't there others, even if her fiancé was prepared to wait? Again I asked, how could a sexually stimulated girl like Sonia resist other men? Didn't she herself feel the urges of sex?

"You'd be surprised how it stops when you don't love someone," was all she said.

"But your fiancé—how can *he* wait until you're married? Nobody does these days."

"He does." I began to understand in bits of conversation over the happy weeks that Francesco wasn't what the Americans and British then called a nancy boy, but that even if he didn't like men, he had never loved women. "He loves to be surrounded by them," she laughed once, "but not on *top* of them." He was, in a word, neutral.

"I think the term is narcissist," she said gravely.

"Then why the hell did he ask you to marry him?" I asked almost savagely.

"Darling Larry," she kissed me, "don't talk anymore,

please. We have an hour before I must go. Make love to me in our special way. What did you call it once?" She laughed. "The nonchalant way! What descriptive powers!"

Lunchtime was the safest time to meet, and we usually ate thickly buttered *baguettes* packed with pink, slightly moist ham. We were already in bed, munching and occasionally sipping cold beer, while Sonia snuggled closer to me as we indulged ourselves in "nonchalance." It was exciting—and typically Russian. Outwardly we were like a married couple, tucked into bed, talking about the problems of life—the office, my latest scoop, on this particular evening the problems of Sonia's father. But that was only superficial. The object of the game—which Sonia had invented of course—was to see how long we could discuss mundane topics while our hands were busy with each other underneath the bedclothes, sending delicious shivers of anticipation through our loins. And yet even by the time she could not stop moving slightly when I touched her, and my excitement matched hers, we still pretended—even discussing the weather—until finally neither of us could wait another second, and without a word I sank myself inside her, not on top, but both of us lying fully stretched side by side so that not only our lips were locked, but so were our feet, even our toes. This way, smothered with kisses, I did not have to do a thing as she, nearing her climax, moved faster and faster while I gritted my teeth with the effort of waiting for her final shudder of satisfaction.

For a few minutes afterward, I lay back, my breath coming faster with the effort of making no effort. I reached across her to the bed for a cigarette. Part of the "game" consisted of pretending afterward—until we got dressed —that nothing had happened, of carrying on the conversation where we had left off, as though it had been interrupted only because the phone had rung. Only this hadn't been a phone, and we each needed a few moments of relaxation, and during that time, almost like the schoolgirl I had first known, she lay back clutching my right hand in hers. I inhaled my first puff and blew out a long stream of bluish smoke.

"As I was saying, there's one way out of your problem. All we have to do is get married," I continued, "then you'll be an American. And whatever happens in Europe—even if there is a war—you'll be a neutral American. America will *never* get into a war in Europe, not after the Great War."

She borrowed my cigarette, inhaled, and said, "Larry, darling, you're so *practical.* I love you, you know I do, but you know I can't."

"But a broken engagement? That would soon be forgotten!"

"It wouldn't—not by Ciano," she said.

"But if our love is so beautiful—why not get married—and to hell with everyone! Unite our families as well as ourselves."

"You make it sound like a business merger! One day I'll tell you." There was no irony in her voice as she jumped out of bed, beautiful when naked.

"I'm off to Douzy tomorrow," I said. "It's Friday."

"We'll meet next week?"

I nodded.

"And darling Larry—never forget that I love you more than any man, and I always will. But don't worry—one day, who knows?"

One day? I had to wait many many days before I learned why she and Francesco became engaged. Even then I never dreamed it would be Francesco, of all people, who would be the one to tell me.

Despite the late, watery sunshine, the autumn weekend had a sour note to it. The first thing I noticed when I arrived was that Guy and Anna weren't on speaking terms—and making it very obvious. Mlle. Lisette, our ex-nanny, walked around the house wearing a permanent sniff of disapproval. Mama was tight-lipped. Olivia, who had arrived at Douzy on the Thursday, looked embarrassed and almost anxious to leave. Only Papa seemed unperturbed. Normally Anna and Guy were as close as twins usually are, though their characters differed. But usually Anna took Guy's odd moods in her stride, never let minor differences erupt into issues.

Mlle. Lisette also usually kept herself to herself. It was a long time since she had bathed us all and looked after us, and now she had grown into a middle-aged spinster who had gradually taken on the duties of a factotum, a kind of superior housekeeper who was regarded almost—but not quite—as a member of the family. The line of distinction had been subtly drawn. Mlle. Lisette lunched but never dined with us. She didn't meddle in anyone's affairs, though she signified disapproval by the way she walked. To me she typified the frustrated middle-aged virgin.

"What the hell's up?" I cornered Anna. "Anyone'd think the Eiffel Tower had fallen across our vineyards."

At first she shook her head. "Nothing." She had Mama's habit of clamping her mouth closed with an air of finality.

"Come on, Anna, don't give me that crap." I held her lightly by the shoulders. "Not me!"

For a moment she hesitated, then she searched for her tiny white handkerchief and blew her nose—hard. I realized she was on the verge of tears.

"Trouble between you and Willi?" I knew he hadn't been to France for some time. I wondered for a moment if he had ditched her.

She shook her head. "Willi's wonderful," adding bitterly, "when I get a chance to see him! He asked if he could come to Douzy this weekend, but Mama said it was unsuitable." She drew another deep breath. "Unsuitable! It's the last damn straw. Mama has allowed Olivia to come and live with us—yes, *live* at Douzy—all to make her precious Guy happy. She told Olivia yesterday."

So *that* was behind the pursed lips. It seemed odd. I liked Olivia—she was quiet, a good painter. She had none of the artsy-craftsy mannerisms so popular in phony art circles. Even so, a visit was one thing, but hell! *living* at Douzy was a very different matter.

"Did she ask to stay—or I suppose Guy asked?" I was still puzzled.

Anna sat down on a sofa. "I'm so damn mad my hand is shaking. Light a cigarette for me, will you, Larry. You're the only one I can talk to."

I was horrified at the bitterness when she began to tell me the story. I already knew that Guy had several times hinted at leaving home to study art in Paris. He had cited me as an example, arguing that since I was following a chosen career, why shouldn't he? What was the difference between writing and painting? It sounded fair enough. To me he had said, "Paris is the only place to study art."

I had asked him then, half in fun, "Would you be so keen to work in Paris if Olivia lived in Marseilles?"

Guy never did have a sense of humor. "That's a damn stupid remark," he had said, and walked off in a huff.

I shouldn't have said that, I knew it. Poor Guy suffered from the curse of being a younger brother. And though I couldn't really see him as a young Picasso, I had the feeling that one day he would change. Mama had a streak of toughness in her. So had I. So had Anna. And I don't doubt that one day that toughness would break out in Guy.

Anna perhaps didn't see it that way. "Of course, it's Olivia," she almost snorted. "They've been lovers for ages. I've got eyes in my head. And so has Mama."

"Well, Anna," I said mildly, "you can't blame Guy for that. You're not going to stand there and tell me that you and Willi haven't popped into bed together."

"That's nothing to do with it. Of course we have—but *when,* dammit? Ten minutes in the orchard is about our limit. For Guy sex is laid on. For me it's a crime!"

"You're a girl. Like it or not, it *is* different."

"Okay, I'm a girl. So I try to be discreet and not upset Mama. But *Olivia!* She's not only come every damn weekend for the last year—even for Christmas—but now she's going to come and *live* here. Yet Willi can't come for dinner without special permission."

* * *

I heard only later, from Anna, how the crisis had arisen. Anna was staggered when Guy first broke the news that he was planning to leave Douzy; for though I was in Paris, the family, according to Anna, was sitting down for dinner when Guy said, "I've got something to tell you," and drew a deep breath.

Everyone looked up.

"Mama," he announced in a flat voice, "I've decided to go and study art in Paris. I hope you don't mind, but I *have* to go. I need help in my studies."

"I *say,*" said Papa. "I might be able to get Raoul Dufy to find you a teacher. What about *that?*" He looked pleased at solving the problem.

Mama took a very different view.

"Oh, no!" she wailed—as she had wailed every time Guy hinted at leaving.

"You'd want to stay in the apartment, I suppose?" asked Papa.

Guy shook his head. "No, Papa. Larry's got his own apartment. I want to be on my own too. To work—and to learn."

"You *can't* go. Please, Guy," Mama begged. "You're my youngest boy—the last one—all I've got now. Just wait a bit longer, darling, just a few months."

"I've *got* to go," said Guy desperately. "I'm losing my grip. You're very kind letting Olivia come to teach me at weekends, but I can't succeed alone."

Turning to Guy, Mama added tearfully, "Of course you have to leave home one day, darling—but not yet. *Please.* Just a little longer."

All this I learned from Anna, who at this point said, "It was awful! I felt like throwing up. Larry, you can't imagine what the scene was like." She hesitated, at a loss for a metaphor. "I know I shouldn't say this about Mama, and you know I love her, but it was the way she *begged*—like an elderly girl friend begging a young lover not to leave her. It was awful, Larry, awful."

"Poor Mama," I said. "It must be hell for her. She must love Guy very much. The youngest, I suppose—"

"Don't give me that garbage," said Anna angrily. "I happen to share that doubtful honor."

"So what happened?"

"Can't you guess!" It was a statement more than a question. "Mama knew perfectly well what she was going to do. Yesterday at lunch she told Papa that Guy *should* be encouraged to pursue his art studies and then turning to Guy suggested that Olivia should come to live at Douzy. *Live!* I ask you! And what's more, she could have the room next to Guy's. And that, as we all know, used to be a guest dressing room, with a communicating door. It's nauseating, Larry, it's perverted."

"What did Papa say?"

"You know Papa. 'Oh *really.*' " She mimicked his rising accent perfectly. "He's sweet, he accepts anything. Thought it rather a good idea."

"Well, it's kept Guy at home—for a bit," I said.

"I've nothing against Olivia," Anna's voice was a bit too harsh for truth, "but Mama's actually encouraging Guy to sleep with a girl who's several years older than he is. And just in order to keep Guy at home."

"I must say—it's a bit hard to take—but mother love—"

"Oh shit, Larry," said Anna inelegantly. "It's unhealthy, especially as there's more to it than that."

"What on earth do you mean?"

"Why do you think Mama's hanging onto Guy? It's not just because he's the last son at home. She's jealous because *she* hasn't got a man."

"Honestly, Anna!"

"It's true. Mama *needs* a man."

"You can't just talk like that about your mother—"

"Honestly!" She mimicked *me* this time. "What's *dishonest* about saying so? Olivia needs a man. I need a man. What's so different about Mama—who's young and pretty and healthy?"

"But Papa?"

"Come off it, Larry. We all adore Papa—but as far as

that sort of thing is concerned, I'll bet he's as useless as a bottle of flat champagne."

"Shut up!" I said.

"Sorry, Larry. But about the other thing—Guy and Olivia," for the first time she laughed, "you should have seen Mlle. Lisette's looks when she heard."

"How *did* she hear?"

"No idea. But talk about virginal disapproval! If Mlle. Lisette's looks could have killed, Olivia would have been dead and buried before she had a chance to unpack."

Anna was calmer now, but after she had started another cigarette, she added, "I know that really it's no concern of mine. But what *does* make me mad is that when Willi rang up yesterday afternoon and told me he was coming to Paris unexpectedly on business, Mama said it was too late to make the arrangements for him to come to Douzy. It makes me sick. Anyway, I'm off tomorrow."

"Off?"

"Sure. I'm off to Paris. In theory to spend the weekend with a girl friend. But in reality—well, Willi's booked a suite at the Crillon and I'm going to spend the time in bed with him."

I liked Willi—very much. He was decent, honest, good-looking in a Germanic way, and he was obviously brilliant, already well launched on a highly successful career at Staffens. All the same he *was* a German—a typical German in many ways. He walked in a determined, forceful way, so that sometimes I found myself thinking there was a hidden goose step in every stride. I wasn't being racist; just realistic. After all, racism and realism were often connected. One day—who could tell what might happen? The Germans were behaving like tyrants. The swastika now was Germany's official flag, Hitler now wielded supreme power. Conscription had been introduced. I knew that Germany was quietly building an air force, training its pilots of tomorrow secretly on gliders. Only a few days before Anna and I had our talk, Hitler had outlawed all Jews in Germany.

"That's your Willi's Germany," I said. "I wonder how

Olivia will react when she has to shake hands with Willi the next time he comes to Douzy."

"That's politics," sniffed Anna. "Willi's not that sort of man."

"Well, the Germans are on the warpath. I'm very fond of Willi, darling sister. But don't get too involved. One day Europe and America might even have to fight the Germans again."

"Warmonger! What nonsense!" She was happier now, excited at the prospect of her secret weekend in Paris. "Live for today!"

Anna set off for Paris on the Saturday morning. She had her own car by now—a Citroën—and after I saw her off at the front door I grabbed my malacca cane—"Willi's present," we always called it—because I had promised to meet Papa by the lake and go for a walk with him. I was just about to leave when I heard a voice ask gently, "Larry—can you spare me a moment?"

It was Olivia, and at first I was irritated; she might be a good painter, she might be Guy's girl friend, she might be very pleasant, but she *wasn't* an Astell, and as a family we had always abhorred discussing family affairs with "outsiders." On the other hand, no one could be irritated with Olivia for long, because her large, brown, pleading eyes disarmed all antagonism.

She was also very good-looking, with a long, intelligent face, the creamy white complexion accentuated by her hair drawn tightly at the back in what these days would be called a ponytail, showing off the back of her long, graceful neck.

"I feel terrible about Anna," she said with a directness I liked, "but I didn't *ask* to come here. When your mother told me, I was surprised as—well, as I suppose *you* were."

"I *was* a bit surprised." I thought she might like an equally direct reply. "It was the adjoining bedrooms."

"I suggested to your mother that perhaps I could live in one of the vineyard cottages, but she refused."

"Did she now?" That did surprise me.

"It surprised me too, but I admire her for what she said."

"What *did* she say?"

"That if Guy and I were in love with each other, she didn't want any furtive business. Sneaking in and out of each other's bedrooms. Those were her words. Then she added something I thought rather curious. She said there'd been enough of that in the house."

"She said *that!*" For a moment a surge of anger toward Guy bit into me. Goddammit, all those years ago I had had to leave the warm arms of Sonia in order to keep a secret—or so we thought—and now Mama was actually *helping* Guy to do what had been forbidden in my day, with —for Guy—only a communicating door to lend a spurious air of respectability to the proceedings. Did Mama know that Sonia and I had become lovers again, I wondered? Serve her right if she did! The stab of anger passed. It wasn't Guy's fault, more his good luck. And anyway, thank God, I was out of the house now, only a visitor at weekends. I loved Douzy, every stone of it, every square inch of our land, but in Paris I was free.

Olivia had spoken the words without any malice and obviously hadn't the faintest idea what I was thinking about, for she said, "So now I feel I ought to leave."

"I wouldn't do that." I chose my words carefully. "I understand. Let's see how things work out."

"Thank you, Larry. And you know," she said a little diffidently, "I *can* help Guy. He does need me."

"For art—or for—?" I left the sentence unfinished.

"One helps the other," she said gravely, and without a trace of annoyance. "Some people—van Gogh was one—produce their finest work when they're miserable. They thrive on unhappiness. Others—like Monet—need to be surrounded by happiness. That's how Guy feels."

"And you?"

"I haven't discovered yet."

As she went back into the house I walked through the archway toward the dell, thinking of what Olivia had said—and without any thought of an extraordinary incident about to take place.

I was making my way to the lake, as it was always called, even though it covered only about two acres, with a man-made island in the middle just large enough for the wrought-iron pergola which rose from its grassy slopes. The lake was ornamental really, part of the view, for even though it lay behind the orchard at the foot of the dell, its blue-gray sheen could be seen from the house, standing as it did on high ground.

My father had gone ahead to have a few words with Jacques Pagniez, the old vigneron who acted as general help; one of his duties was to clean up the lake from time to time, using a small rowboat from which he raked the dead leaves or algae.

At the bottom of the dell, with its long grassy slope, I was about to open the wicker gate leading to the orchard, which I would have to cross, when I heard voices. I stopped to listen, the action instinctive because in the autumn we were plagued by village kids pinching apples. It was easy for them to walk through the vineyards and, when they were certain no one was watching, wriggle through the high grass. I wanted to catch the youngsters red-handed, though I wasn't contemplating drastic action. I knew most villagers by sight, and the threat of telling their fathers— many of whom worked for us during the *vendange*—would scare them off for a month or two.

I crept behind one of the huge rhododendrons that served as a ten-foot hedge between the dell and the orchard. I could see no one, hear no more voices, and wondered if I had been mistaken—until I stiffened suddenly.

On the other side of the bush, only a few feet from where I was trying to hold my breath, a woman's urgent, angry voice cried, *"C'est dégoûtant!"* Then she continued in French, bitterly angry, "You're all the same! No thought for other people. To bring that woman to live in the house!" She repeated her first phrase, "It's disgusting! What you do in another house, or anywhere, is none of my

business, but here—where," the voice became a low hiss
and I missed the words, until I heard, "is living."

I knew that voice, typical of so many nannies the world
over. It belonged to Mlle. Lisette. For a moment I thought
she was angry with one of the manservants—until the man
replied.

"For Chrissake, Lisette!" said my brother, Guy, equally
urgently. "You're not my nanny anymore! You can't go
around telling me what to do with my life!"

"Lisette! Not *Mlle.* Lisette!" I had never, never heard
anyone in Douzy use that name. Guy called her that. What
the hell was going on? By now, eavesdropping or not, I was
damned curious, especially after Anna's disclosures. What
on earth had "that woman" to do with Mlle. Lisette, who
in fact lived at Douzy only as an act of charity.

I heard no more.

"Damn!" I muttered as the voices faded and I heard feet
walk through the long grass. What the hell had she
meant—*"in another house"*?

I could hardly tell Papa what I had heard—especially as
there might be an innocent enough explanation—but no, I
thought, as I crossed the orchard, wading through the
thick grass where I had upended Sonia such a long time
ago; no, there could be nothing innocent about what I had
heard.

When you are deep in thought following an experience
that leaves you puzzled, it is a shock to be cheerfully hailed
by someone who hasn't the faintest notion of what happened to you only moments ago. The fact that it *had* happened so quickly made me feel that the other person must
have known too.

"Ici, Larry," my father waved as I reached the gravel
path that ran round the lake. "Been waiting for you. Look
how Jacques has tidied up the lake."

The old vigneron gave me a *"Bonjour, m'sieu."*

"Really," said my father. "Clean as a new pin. Splendid
work, Jacques, I *must* say." And to me, "Can you stand a
walk to the other side of Rilly? Take us about an hour. A

bit chilly, but we'll stop at the local bistro—they've just opened their 1933 *Crémant*—should be good and dry. Yes, *very* good, I *must* say."

He set off, long frame striding out, ashplant swinging forward and then jabbing the ground with each step.

"Wonderful day for a walk," he said exuberantly. And indeed it was. The pale sun shining on the vines and the creamy yellow pathways gave everything a muted, gentle air. The acres of stripped vines rolling away from us always looked so *tidy*. They exuded an atmosphere of sobriety, of thrift—very different from the exhilarating end product. We walked past a group of farmhouses built of stone, solid, plain, the rough plastered walls an austere gray, the narrow streets or farmyards flanked by high stone walls concealing private lives, with glimpses through heavy gates or an open courtyard with a trough, a pump perhaps, a few dying hollyhocks straggling near lines where lettuces and peas had grown, and at the back, like a fence—as though the owner had planted something with an eye to the distant future—a row of spindly poplars, their bases and roots covered with straw as cozy—and as efficient—as a coverlet protecting a child against cold nights. At that moment a skein of geese flew overhead like a formation of aerobatic aircraft.

"It *is* wonderful," I agreed. "Like an aquatint."

Papa's walks were rather special. He was, in his own words, "a one-way walker." Whenever he went for a walk, he never walked back, a habit which, looked at from his point of view, was eminently sensible. He would choose a target—one of the innumerable bistros, small hotels, even cafés, which dotted every village. He knew just how long it would take him to walk there. He then added half an hour for time to sample the local wine, at which time Gaston would arrive with the Hisp and drive us home in time for lunch.

"May sound silly," he confided to me once, "but in fact if you look at it sensibly—yes, *sensibly*—it's a *good* idea. Walking never seems quite so attractive after a couple of drinks."

We all felt guilty if we didn't occasionally walk with him, but he inevitably started long discussions on the champagne market, and the trouble was that none of us had any common ground for conversation with Papa, while he regarded a walk as a wonderful chance for talking about the vineyards through which he walked.

He stopped to examine them for diseases, fungus, red fly. He passed the time of day with every neighbor and discussed prospects—either for frost, bloom, the *vendange,* according to the season.

As soon as we passed Douzy church and branched right along the track leading upward to Rilly, he spotted one row of vines.

"Look at this!" He stopped and plucked off a leaf from a vine. "Not one ours, thank God. Not *ours. Very* bad management."

The leaf was dented in the middle, as though someone had pressed its center. The shoot of the vine had been flattened too.

"And that means court-noué." I knew exactly what my father meant—a disease that normally attacked Chardonnay vines; no one has ever really discovered what caused it. Some said it was due to a small fungus that flourished in the roots, others believed it was caused by poisoned soil.

"Thank God, it's not infectious," said my father. "Half these vines will have to be uprooted. Who do they belong to?"

I had no idea and we walked on.

I don't know how the conversation started, but I suddenly found myself pleading the cause of Anna. It started innocently enough when I said, "I'm sorry Mama wouldn't let Willi come for the weekend."

"It's not a question of *not letting.* Really! Oregon is here for the weekend. Olivia is here."

"I didn't mean it that way. But after all, if Guy can have his girl friend here, it's a bit hard on Anna to leave Willi out. Instead, Anna's so upset she's gone to Paris to spend the weekend with a friend."

"To Paris?" Startled, he jabbed his ashplant hard into the ground.

"Well, she's a grown-up woman," I said. "She doesn't have to account for everything she does. Any more than," with a sly dig, "Guy has to account for his taste in girl friends."

"Anna—well, it's different." He jabbed his stick into the ground again.

"Because she's a girl?"

"Good Lord, no." He looked positively astonished at my simpleminded attitude. "No, *no*. Because Willi's a *German.*" And with a touch of asperity he added, "And don't take me for a fool, Larry. If she's gone to Paris for the weekend, I don't imagine she'll be spending her time at the Louvre."

"Sorry," I laughed.

"It's Anna's future I'm thinking of, yes, her *future,*" said Papa. "This fellow Hitler—to say nothing of Mussolini— neither of them can carry on forever making an economic mess of their country. When they go too far down the slippery slope there's only one way out—blame neighboring countries, and if necessary fight them."

"Hitler doesn't *seem* to be making warlike noises," I said.

"He's too smart," said my father. "I had dinner with Madame de Portes and Paul Reynaud the other day. He's smart. He told me that Hitler doesn't *make* plans—he waits for other countries to make mistakes, then takes advantage of them. And he watches while the morale of our countries crumbles. Look at France! No resolve, no"—he searched for the word—"no old-fashioned guts. Why don't the police do something about these anti-Jewish riots in Paris—the French Fascists, Cagoulards."

"They're crackpots," I said.

"I'm not so sure," my father disagreed. Then changing the subject he asked, "Do you think Anna is getting *really* serious about Willi?"

There was no point in hiding the obvious.

"Yes, I do," I replied. "I think he'll be knocking on your

study door one day, clicking his heels, giving you a stiff German bow, and asking for permission to marry your daughter."

"Oh! I *say,* not *really!*" Papa looked alarmed. "I thought Germans only behaved like that in films."

We had passed Rilly by now, ordered our drinks, and he sat there, all six feet three of him, slim, a handsome face, a man without an enemy in the world, but constantly surprised by the most elementary facts of life. *"Really!"* he said again, with his rising accent, "I wouldn't know *what* to say."

"In this day and age, I don't suppose it would make any difference." I tried to sound philosophical. "If Anna wants to marry Willi, she will. I think Willi would be worried if you said no, for he feels he should ask you formally. But when the time comes it'll not only be formally, it'll be a formality."

My father called the waiter for another glass of the Crémant. "Really, *very* passable." He held the glass by the stem to the light. "Don't misunderstand me," he said, "I *like* Willi. A very intelligent young man. But just supposing—"

"You mean a war?"

"Exactly."

Gaston arrived with the Hisp, and as he drew up the car Papa called out, "There's a drink waiting for you, Gaston."

"Merci, m'sieu." Gaston pushed open the door of the bistro. They all knew him in every village, for Gaston was not only their friend and neighbor, he was always offered a drink during Papa's walks. After all, Gaston was more than just a chauffeur, he was an old friend—certainly of mine, for I was a Walter Mitty racing driver and he was great at tuning the engine of my MG. Gaston was a handsome man, a worthy son of Jacques, the vigneron, and so it was only natural that we had played together in the fields and the woods as kids. Everyone, including Gaston himself, had automatically elected to work with the family.

And after he discovered a natural bent for tinkering with newfangled cars, everyone was delighted when he became the family driver, none more so than Jacques, who regarded Gaston's new job as a step up in the world. And life had also been made easier by a gesture of my grandfather's, before he died: he had rewarded several old members of the estate with their own small plots of vineyards. They might not be extensive, but even so, everyone working in Douzy had a slice of independence, a few vines he could call his own, enough for each family to bottle its own wine or sell the grapes to the cooperative.

As Gaston returned to the Hisp, Papa asked him, as one villager to another, "What do you think of this year's red, Gaston?"

"Not as good as Douzy, *m'sieu,*" said Gaston frankly.

"You're right," agreed my father. "Would you mind stopping for a few minutes at the *celliers.* I just want to see how the fermentation is going."

We drew up at the entrance to the Home Farm, where the buildings at one end housed the machinery needed to produce champagne before it was taken to the *caves* below. The fermenting shed was at the far end, and it was like stepping into an oven; from the time of the harvest in late September, the wine juice had been kept in forty-four-gallon casks at a temperature of around sixty-five degrees.

"How's it going?" my father asked one of its *cellériers.*

"We'll be able to let the fires die down in another two weeks. Then we'll open the windows and let in the cold air." This sudden change in temperature was vital, because the cold caused a precipitation which threw off the impurities, allowing clear wine to be drawn off.

At this stage, around the end of the year, the casks would then contain only *vin nature,* but my father would be able to start judging, even from this rough wine, how to make it perfect by blending wine from our different vineyards to ensure that we maintained our special characteristics.

Sunday evening Mama had invited several people to dine at the château, including the Misses Brewer and Barron.

"My spies tell me we're having *pintade* for dinner," Oregon said as he offered them champagne.

"I always feel so sorry for the poor guinea fowl"—Miss Brewer had been listening, nodding—"being shot like that. It seems so cruel."

"There, there, dear," Miss Barron consoled her. "They probably suffer less than if they lived to be old and then died because they were too weak to find food."

Did birds really become too old to find food, I thought idly as the other guests arrived? Perhaps the Misses B and B were right. The two old ladies fascinated me, for they, too, were birdlike in appearance. What would happen to *them* if they had to search for their food? What would happen to them if, say, a war came and their safety, even their modest incomes, were endangered?

Looking at the two frail old ladies—Miss Brewer nodding her head as she always did, Miss Barron eagerly agreeing with everything anyone said, a legacy of her days as a "companion"—I had a sudden wild vision of German troops overrunning our beautiful countryside, shelling the women's pretty little cottage, forcing their staid and uneventful lives to erupt into violence and chaos. They would die of shock, poor dears, though perhaps—like the *pintades*—they would suffer less than by growing old and feeble. They would never be able to cope.

Happily they were like Grandma Jacqueline, convinced that war was out of the question. I heard La Châtelaine say, "I met Monsieur Chautemps. He told me there would never be another war and I believe him." Miss Brewer nodded approvingly, as I wondered what she would say if I told her what I thought: that Camille Chautemps was a weak, vacillating political leader who might easily lead France into war. Of course I said nothing, and luckily the silence was interrupted by two sounds.

Just as we were passing into the dining room, Jean, in his white jacket, came to me and murmured, "It's Mr. Tomlinson on the phone, sir, in Paris."

"Excuse me, Mama." I went into the study where there was an extension.

"Hi!" cried Tommy. "Hope I haven't disturbed that family dinner, but I've only got a couple of minutes. Gotta go to Rome tonight. Train leaves at ten o'clock. Just received the goddamn cable from Washington. I've got my interview with Musso, and I've got to report to Ciano tomorrow lunch. It's all been planned at high level in Washington, but they only got the okay today. Can you pinch-hit for me for a week? Usual dough."

"Sure," I replied. "Need me tonight?"

"No—so long as you're on the end of a phone. I've told Washington where you are and that you'll be in Paris tomorrow."

That was that. No problem, especially as it was already the middle of the night in Washington.

But after dinner the phone rang again. This time it was Willi Frankel on the other end of the line. Thinking of Anna I felt a momentary apprehension, but Willi's voice reassured me.

"Sorry to intrude on you so late"—Willi was always very polite—"but it is a big story I have for you. Yes, it is about Hitler and de Gaulle; *Ach!* It will be a scoop, *nein?*"

"Can I meet you Monday for lunch?"

"No, this is my problem. Before lunch I am to leave. Must be back in Düsseldorf. Any chance we have breakfast together?" I could hear the wry chuckle in his voice. "Isn't that what Americans always do? The working breakfast?"

"You're sure it's worth it?" I asked.

"Is important, I assure you," he said solemnly. *"Very* important."

"Okay. I'll be there, eight thirty for fresh orange juice and all the trimmings. Okay?"

After all, I was in charge of the bureau while Tommy was away in Italy. What a way to start the week if I could land another "Willi" exclusive.

8

WILLI WAS STAYING AT THE CRILLON as he always did, and in a suite. He enjoyed the trappings of luxury that went with a good job.

I had been nervous that I might meet Anna when I parked my car on the Concorde at eight thirty on the Monday morning. It was one thing for him to spend the weekend with my sister, but I didn't want to see visible evidence of it in the form of a bright and cheery couple sharing breakfast. I needn't have worried. Willi was far too circumspect. Anna had already left.

Still, Willi did ask me as he helped me to coffee, "It is at the—the departure—Anna and me—well, we should get married. What would your father say to my—what is it?—my *troth?*"

With a sigh I answered, "He wouldn't like it, Willi. Nothing personal. He admires you very much But she *is* his only daughter, and he's afraid—of the future."

"If there comes war, you mean?"

I nodded.

"If there comes a war"—Willi's tone suddenly became bitter, almost savage—"it will be the fault of France and Britain."

"Hey!" I protested. "You don't have to shove Hitler's propaganda crap down my throat, Willi—not at breakfast. Don't spoil a good croissant."

"Who is saying about Hitler? Europe it is who is *making* Hitler. The French, they fight themselves, they are scared of their own extremist politicians, they do not like to think about Germany. France, she is very weak, so she gives Hitler more courage—you understand? I hate Hitler. But French politicians are very pathetic. They are more scared of communism than Hitler."

"You're exaggerating." The waiter brought us more coffee. But all the same I was wondering if Willi *was* exaggerating. He had a new authority since he started climbing the ladder at the Staffens Engineering Corporation—high enough to warrant not only a suite at the Crillon each time he came to France, but also back home, so he said, a driver to take him to work. Success had given him a new stature, even a slight touch of German imperiousness. And he seemed to know what he was talking about. Suddenly he said, "Sorry for becoming angry. *Entschuldigung!* Excuse me! Is only because I am frightened. But to business—about one man in France I *do* admire though. You ever hear of a French officer called de Gaulle?"

I nodded. "I've met him once or twice. Prickly sort of chap, though he was polite enough to me." I gave a short laugh. "Perhaps because he was so surprised to find that *any* American could speak French. I met him with Reynaud."

"He writes a very good book," said Willi. "You are reading it?"

I shook my head. "About tank warfare, wasn't it? You say it's good, but I read that it was an almighty flop. The military reviewers tore it to shreds."

"I understand why. He calls the army leaders a lot of *dummkopfs*. Is no way to help his military career!"

"I don't even remember what the book's called."

"A good title—*Towards a Professional Army.*"

I wondered idly why Willi should be so interested in de Gaulle, or for that matter in military strategy, and with a touch of sarcasm said, "Don't tell me that Hitler is thinking of challenging the French army!"

"God forbid. Hitler is not being so foolish as to take on the finest army in the world." He gave a sardonic grin.

"But I will tell you what *is* fascinating. Hitler gets hold of de Gaulle's book and he is going crazy about it."

"I didn't know he could read!"

"He has ordered Otto Abetz in Paris to buy up all the copies he can get hold of—for his general staff. They are being ordered to read it and send the Führer written reports."

"Are you sure?" Willi had been right. It *was* a good story.

"Absolutely. My boss at Staffens is sent a copy, he is told to write a report. I see the letter myself."

"I still don't get the idea."

"I can understand. Our Führer believes he is a military leader in the Clausewitz tradition. And ever since Germany occupied the Rhineland, he is dreaming of a new concept of war—self-supporting armored divisions—using tanks as independent attacking units, not just to help the infantry. But all the top men—Keitel, Rundstedt, and Guderian—are politely turning him down. They say to each other Hitler was only a corporal. But now all his theories are appearing in print—and by Germany's enemy."

"So he's pinching de Gaulle's ideas?"

"Not exactly. They both have the same ideas but—please, never say this to anyone or it will be bad for me—the Führer is—well, not known for great thinking. He shouts a lot. But de Gaulle, he is a professional, and what he has done is give Hitler the practical explanation of how his dreams can come true."

"It still has to be worked out."

"It can be. After all, we make tanks, Larry—the men in our works are crazy about the book. It's not for any *aggression*—Hitler he says many times that he has no territorial ambitions—but he wants a strong Germany for world respect." He looked at me almost defiantly. "This is not unreasonable, is it? You admit, I hope, Germany has been very badly treated since the Treaty of Versailles."

It *was* a hell of a good story for the *Globe*, though I realized I must make sure Willi wouldn't be involved. The last time he had given me a big story—about the Roehm

massacre—he had asked me to wait a few days before filing.

"Maybe you do the same again," he asked me, and of
course I agreed.

"I don't want you to be tortured," I said half jokingly.

Willi laughed out loud—a real German belly laugh.

"Honestly! Americans have amusing ideas about Germans. We are not eating babies for breakfast! The Gestapo? They are everywhere, but they are not *torturing*
people. We are Germans—civilized people. Do not please
confuse the Gestapo with Mussolini's bully boys, who force
people in their jails to drink castor oil by the pint as a punishment."

I didn't need to clear the story with Colonel de Gaulle,
because he hadn't given me the information, but I took
care to describe de Gaulle as one of France's most exciting
military brains, and to say that he had been attacked by
the old fogies of the French high command because they
were jealous of him.

It worked. First I got a herogram from the *Globe* foreign
editor saying, "Your exclusive leads page one," and when
the paper arrived, there it was under the headline HITLER
STEALS BRILLIANT FRENCH OFFICER'S IDEAS. And the strapline
above looked good too: Exclusive from Larry Astell in
Paris.

I later sent a clipping to de Daulle, who wrote a pleasant
thank you letter, and the next time I met him at a reception, he shook my hand, bending over my modest height.

"Well, sir," I said diplomatically, "even if Hitler copies
every idea in your book, the Germans will never be a
match for the French army."

I will always remember de Gaulle's reply, given in measured tones. "The French soldier will fight to the last drop
of his blood. Rest assured of that. But if German tanks—
my tanks with German swastikas painted on them—turn
the Maginot Line in the north and then sweep south, no
one will be able to stop them."

* * *

Willi had mentioned Otto Abetz, and the next time I met
Sonia in the rue du Cherche-Midi, she also mentioned him.

"Odd how that man's name keeps cropping up," I said.

"I had lunch with him yesterday and dinner on Saturday."

"Otto Abetz! You had two meals with him! Tommy Tomlinson calls him Hitler's hatchet man in France."

"Horrible." She screwed up her nose. "He was lunching
with Daddy and asked me along—deliberately, I think.
Twice in a weekend."

"What do you mean, deliberately?"

"He gave me the shivers. He meets Daddy all the time.
It's spooky. We had lunch at Maxim's, and he told me that
he thought Mummy and I would be wise to leave France
and return home to Florence."

"But you've only been here a few months! Did he give
any reason?"

"I wonder if Daddy put him up to it. His reasons were ridiculous. He said France wasn't safe. He said something
about the Cagoulards. That they're going to increase their
bombing campaign. Do you think Monsieur Abetz is behind them?"

"Abetz and—your father?"

"Oh, no!" She looked genuinely horrified. "Daddy's a
diplomat. He'd never get mixed up in anything like that."

That was probably true, but in addition to the Cagoulard
evidence of Fascist activity there was the sinister—and
unsolved—murder of two Italians in Paris. Both were violently anti-Fascist writers. Carlo Rossello was shot dead.
His brother Nello was stabbed to death in a wood near
Bagnoles-de-l'Orne. The crime had not only remained a
mystery, but all news of it had vanished from the front
pages of the newspapers. It smacked of a typical French
cover-up.

"It's a bit sinister, all coming together," I said.

"You don't think it was a political business, do you?"
asked Sonia.

"I'm sure it was."

Sonia was free that evening, and we decided to risk detection and have dinner at Marcel's. Instead of walking directly along the rue de Seine, we strolled along the *quais* toward the Institut before doubling back. It had been raining that afternoon, and it had given the *quais* a smell of freshness. The rain had washed not only the streets, but the walls of the buildings and the trunks of the trees, so that the bare yellow patches of the plane trees shone golden in the lamp-lit evening and everything smelled good and clean.

Yet as we sat down at Marcel's and looked at the blackboard to study the *plat du jour—daube de boeuf,* which we knew would have been *mijoté* on the stove for hours—I could sense that Sonia was unhappy.

"It's not your father who's worrying you?" I asked.

She sprinkled a little salt on her chunk of fresh *baguette.* "No, not Daddy, but love—for you—and then, too, the fact that Abetz, a German, could warn me to leave—almost as though a German is giving orders to my father. That's what frightens me—the sense that my father is working with him, even for him, in such a mysterious way."

"There's such an easy way out of everything," I said again. "Break your engagement! Marry me!" I reached out and took her hand, which was lying on the white tablecloth. "Just marry me. After all, we love each other. It's only a question of going to the American consul. You do love me?"

She was silent for some time, toying with her meal.

"I never realized until we met again how much I loved you. I *want* to marry you—but I'm afraid. It may sound overdramatic, but I'm sure Abetz has some"—she searched for the right word—"some *hold* over Daddy. Or perhaps it's Ciano. As you know, he's Mussolini's foreign minister, and he certainly has the Duce's ear."

"But it makes no difference, surely, if we break an engagement?"

"It does, I'm afraid. I daren't break it off, though I want to. But I *have* done one thing. I've suggested to my fiancé that we should wait a bit longer—I'm playing for time."

"That's something." I tried to be cheerful. At least, I thought, it's a step in the right direction.

The next day in the office I cornered Oregon. "I've got a question for you," I said.

"What gives?" Oregon, plump and cheerful, eyes twinkling, bustled into my office.

"What's the latest news on Otto Abetz?"

"Just that he's still a die-hard Fascist of the worst kind who poses as a friend of France. What's the story?"

I explained what Sonia had told me—that Abetz might in some sinister way be using her father.

"Sounds feasible." Oregon lit another Gauloises and wiped the ash from his jacket. "He's dangerous—got friends in high places, including Reynaud. Though Abetz isn't exactly Reynaud's friend, more his girl friend's—the Countess de Portes."

"I know. I met the countess with Abetz. She's not my cup of tea."

"I don't suppose Herr Abetz is bothered with her charms," said Oregon dryly. "It's her influence he's after."

I found it difficult to imagine the rather dumpy Countess de Portes as a "woman of influence." Of course several French ministers had semiofficial mistresses who seemed to run their political lives, but Reynaud hadn't struck me as a ladies' man, so perhaps he had to be content with what he could get. It never entered my head that it was the other way round, that it was she who had got him.

"Don't underestimate her, m'lad," Oregon chuckled. "Reynaud's intelligent and forceful, while she's consumed with ambition. That's a formidable combination. I wouldn't be surprised if she doesn't make Reynaud prime minister one of these days. Then she'll be the power behind the throne. And if the political situation gets worse, it's always in the cards that Madame de Portes could hold the fate of France in her hands."

"God forbid!" I said. "She and Abetz!"

* * *

About a week later, Sonia and I dined "officially" at Maxim's, with Willi, who had unexpectedly returned to Paris and phoned Mama, asking if Anna and Sonia could make a foursome. It was all very respectable. Maxim's was off my beat—unless the *Globe* was paying, or Papa was in Paris, for it was his favorite restaurant. But it gave us a chance to dance.

Anna was staying in the rue de Longchamp with Sonia, so I teased Willi while the girls were in the powder room. "No hanky-panky this trip?"

"Nein. Is time for truth, Larry. Anna and I want to marry. We need your help. Advice perhaps, but quickly." In his excitement he lapsed into German, *"Ich fahre Morgen ab."*

"Leaving tomorrow?"

As we prepared to take the corner banquette on the left—Papa's usual table, given to us automatically by Albert, the imperious headwaiter with his fleshy, hanging jowls wobbling like liver about his tie—Willi whispered, "Anywhere will do."

"Anywhere will *not* do," I explained. "The top people in Paris always sit on the left as you come in. The right is reserved for tourists and riff-raff."

A quivering Albert led us to Papa's table, facing the band. I had to admit that all the gilt and faded red plush did give one a feeling of opulence.

"Let's all have martinis, for a change," cried Willi.

"No champagne, Monsieur Astell?" Even Albert looked astounded when I shook my head. "It's Mr. Frankel's party," I said, "so we'd better do as he says."

Willi superintended the ordering. I think he rather fancied himself as a gourmet, and he discussed the menu with authority, though I already knew I would settle for a *sole Albert.* It was the best sole served outside Waltons in London, where we always ate on our rare visits to England.

Finally the ordering was over, and then Willi said abruptly, "Anna and I want to get married."

"It's definite?" I looked at Anna.

"Definite." Her eyes were sparkling with happiness and I thought (nothing to do with the subject under discussion) what a couple of corkers we had dining with us! I had already noticed a few pairs of tired middle-aged male eyes stray covetously in our direction. For Anna in her own way was every bit as attractive as Sonia—especially when she was happy. She had the same mischievous glint in her eyes, the same outgoing personality; only when she was in a bad mood or unhappy did her mouth become a straight line—rather like Grandma's.

How different she was now, here in Maxim's, with the band playing "le fox trot." Willi is good for her, I thought. She's a woman, she's in love, she's been having an affair with Willi for a long time, and it's crazy to keep them apart just because our parents think of her as someone who might be affected by international politics.

"Why don't you just *get* married?" asked Sonia.

Willi was really shocked. "That is the last resort. Such a course of action is most improper. My parents would not like it, and I could never do such a thing behind Mr. Astell's back."

"Then you'll have to go to Douzy and stand up to him."

"I still can't see—why don't you just go off and get married?" said Sonia.

"You're a fine one to talk," I said.

Looking back now, it might seem foolish of Willi to have been so nervous. Why shouldn't he and Anna just elope? But it wasn't as simple as that. The Astells were a warm, united, happy family, despite our problems. And in those days sons and daughters didn't *want* to upset their parents. They might hurt them if driven to take desperate measures, but not until every possible means of conciliation or persuasion had failed. We all wanted the best of all worlds. Anna wanted to marry Willi—and I sensed that, come what may, she would—but I am sure she would have been horrified if she had been told she could never return to Douzy, even for vacations. Life without Douzy was unthinkable. As a wife in a strange country, with no friends, living amid a regime of which we heard awful rumors, she needed the *thought* that Douzy would always be there as a refuge.

We didn't solve anything that evening—I don't think that was really the purpose of dining at Maxim's.

"What we really want is moral support," Anna summed it up.

"When are you coming to Paris next?" I asked Willi.

"In three weeks."

"Right. I'll start softening up the parents. I don't see how Mama can object to anything in view of the way she's behaved over Guy."

"It's rather different." Anna seemed doubtful. "I'll have to go and live in Germany."

"It's next door," I said cheerfully.

The next day, quite by chance, I again met Otto Abetz. The *Globe* had been so intrigued by my story of the way Hitler was studying de Gaulle's book that they asked me for a follow-up story. In the first article I had mentioned that Reynaud was a great admirer of de Gaulle's, and so Washington asked me to get a quote from Reynaud.

I telephoned Reynaud's secretary, explaining what I wanted. I pointed out that I had already met Reynaud socially, and no doubt the name Astell meant something, for twenty-four hours later I got a reply. Reynaud was holding a small cocktail party at his bachelor apartment—as distinct from his main house, where Madame Reynaud presided. Of course many politicians, harassed by long nights of discussion at the Assemblée, kept small one-room flats near the Parliament building, Reynaud included. His apartment was in the place du Palais-Bourbon, very close to his work, but it could scarcely be called a "bachelor" apartment since he had installed Madame de Portes in it.

Reynaud had charm and a strong personality. Like many short men he was vain, with a tendency to aggression, as though to make up for his lack of inches. He was well aware of the power of the press, especially American newspapers, which was no doubt why I had been invited.

There were only a couple of dozen guests, including Madame de Portes—and Abetz. Reynaud immediately said that he had read my piece on de Gaulle and had understood my request for some comments on it. "And so, *mon cher,* I have already dictated some material for you." He fished in his pocket for a neatly typed foolscap sheet. "Efficient, *eh bien?* Now instead of talking business, we can enjoy ourselves. *Voilà!* I will introduce you."

Madame de Portes could not have been more charming. "I too have seen your article on the colonel. Paul showed it to me." She whispered almost as a conspirator. "The colonel is a very intelligent man, but a bit hard to get on with, eh?" She laughed. "You are as good a writer as your champagne is famous. Here we have Moët. I hope you are not insulted."

"It makes a pleasant change from home, madame," I said, and she thought that very funny. Madame de Portes brought me up to Abetz, saying, "You know each other of course, Herr Minister."

I studied again the square shoulders, the cold blue eyes, and the reddish-blond hair. He seemed relaxed and cheerful.

"Of course, it is a pleasure," he said, shaking hands with me.

I was about to make polite noises when Madame de Portes gushed, "Herr Abetz is, as you know, one of France's greatest friends. He is the man who stamps out all the silly rumors about quarrels between our two countries."

"A lot of nonsense is talked about Germany," Abetz explained. "It is my task to see that truth prevails. That is all."

"Rather like a friend of mine from Italy," I said, "Signor Riccardi."

For a moment—a split second—his mouth tightened. Then affably he said, "Of course—I remember—we talked about Signor Riccardi the last time we met."

"Yes. He's an old friend of the family. And so is his daughter. She was brought up with my family when her father was serving in South America."

"A delightful girl."

He lit a cigarette carefully, eyeing me. "Very interesting, Monsieur Astell. I wish you well." He gave me his half bow and strolled off to talk to other guests. I left soon afterward—with an uneasy feeling gnawing inside me that I had behaved like a fool in front of this smooth and rather frightening man.

9

WE WERE MOVING toward the winter of 1937 by now, and I
was even more thankful that I still lived alone in the rue
de l'Université—to say nothing of our secret hideout on the
other side of the boulevard St. Germain. Paris was filled
with people doing early Christmas shopping. Grandma
visited the apartment regularly, so did Papa on business
trips, so did Mama, who telephoned me without warning
one day and said she was arriving to do some shopping.

"What about that lunch you promised me?" she laughed,
sounding gay and happy.

"Wonderful. But dinner, not lunch. Remember your
promise?"

"Darling, I'm in such a rush. Papa had to go to Bordeaux. He'll be back tomorrow night. And I've promised to
dine this evening with the Sardis." She mentioned a couple of old fogies I hardly knew.

"But Mama!" I protested. "This is *Paris!* And the Sardis
are exactly the kind of people we want to *avoid* in Paris."

"Lunch, Larry, please. You'll just take me out like a
young man escorting a lady."

"You *sound* terrific," I said. "It's going to be quite a
lunch. Where shall we go?"

"What about the Pré Catelan? We can lunch indoors and
look at the *Bois.*"

"Right. I'll pick you up at one."

"I'll collect you," she said. "As Papa went by train to
Bordeaux, I kept Gaston—he's got some relations in Par-

is—and then he can collect your father at the station when he returns to Paris, pick me up, and we'll both drive home."

"Suits me," I said, and I must say, we had one of the happiest lunches I can remember. She seemed a different person. She was dressed in a beautiful Chanel suit, which showed off her blond hair perfectly. And the surrounding frame of green from the trees and the last of the flowers in their formal beds showed her off too.

"You look as though you've started a new life," I said. "Just watch that old man in the corner eyeing you! I'm sure he thinks you're my mistress."

"Really, Larry!" But I could see she was pleased, as the sommelier filled her glass with Montrachet.

"It's very expensive," she examined it, "but never mind."

"It beats me how you do it," I said, "how you look so young," and she did look young, really beautiful, but more than that, she exuded a kind of suppressed sexuality, a kind of hidden excitement that I had never seen in her before.

"Come on, Mama," I offered her some more *quenelles de brochet.* "Tell all. You been up to something?"

She almost giggled and shook her head. "I just feel great, that's all."

Even her departure had a touch of Astell style. This was still the era of great automobiles in France, the Delages and Delahayes, but nothing could equal the gleaming black and silver of the Hisp when Gaston drew up in front of the gravel drive with its meticulously trimmed beds.

"Hy'a, Gaston," I greeted him.

"Bonjour, monsieur." Gaston still had that rare knack of being able to translate a boyhood friendship into the different relationship of adults. There was nothing snobbish—or servile—in our friendship. Gaston was the first to crawl with me under the bonnet of the MG when it needed tuning, and the first to shout, "Pass me the number three wrench, Larry." But with the true instinct he never used my name in front of others.

Mama had arranged to give me a lift to the office at the

corner of the rue du Sentier and the boulevard Poissonnière, and it was the only time she mentioned Sonia. But
what she *did* say left me dumbfounded.

"Do you miss her—do you still love her?"

"You shouldn't ask questions." I avoided a direct answer with a laugh. .

"Do you? I want you to be happy, Larry. And Sonia—you
remember what I once said—what a pity that you were
ever found out. Have you ever thought of—well, getting
her to break off her engagement?"

"Yes," I said flatly. "I do love her, Mama. I always will."

"Do you see her—I mean—?"

"How dare you!" I laughed again to cover the direct
question.

"Well—I wouldn't blame you. Try again with her," said
Mama. "Try, she's a wonderful girl. I blame myself a lot
for—well, everything. And I want you to be happy. I want
us *all* to be happy."

It was strange how the smiling happiness of that lunch
communicated itself to me. I had been very touched by Mama's declaration, by her *obvious* happiness. But what I
didn't realize, until the next time we met, was that Sonia
had changed too.

We could still never meet regularly, of course. I had to
wait for her to telephone me, and sometimes we met in the
afternoon, sometimes in the evening.

"But this time, if you're free?" she began.

"I'm always free for you."

"Well, darling—surprise! What about all night?"

"Explain before I burst a blood vessel!"

"Daddy and Mummy have left to open a new trade center for Italian goods in Lille. They've already *gone!*"
She could hardly contain her triumph. "So if monsieur
pleases!"

"Monsieur does please—see you in the Cherche-Midi in
an hour. And darling Sonia, let's dine again at Marcel's—to hell with the risk. If anybody ever does see us, we

can always say you phoned me because you couldn't find anyone else."

"A likely story!"

I could sense the difference in her the moment she kissed me, throwing her arms about me before we set off for Marcel's. She was quiet in the warmth and coziness of the restaurant. She sat there after dinner, her coffee in front of her, just sat there silently, eyes dreaming, looking at nothing, never noticing the admiring eyes of the other diners, never realizing her beauty. Then as I watched her, she put forward a hand, touched mine, and her eyes belonged to me again.

After our *café filtre,* walking back to the rue du Cherche-Midi, she was even quieter. Winter was creeping toward us, it was a chilly night, so that, as she held me tightly and we walked arm in arm, I thought that maybe she was keeping her mouth closed against the bitter night air.

Once in our tiny apartment I poured out a *marc de champagne,* the golden liquid made from discarded grapes, and offered her a glass. She shook her head. I switched on the cheap portable radio and looked at her. At times—and this was one—I would again catch her watching me quizzically, intently, with a faint ironic smile, as though summing me up.

"Why don't you turn off the radio, darling," she said in her sleepy, dark voice, straight from the throat. As she spoke she slid out of the armchair, and the next moment she was half kneeling, half sitting on the floor, in front of me.

For a few moments she said nothing, just leaned her head against my chest while I ran my fingers slowly through her silky black hair. Then she looked up. "Have I been wrong all these years?"

"To love me? No."

"No, not love. Wrong to think that this"—she waved to take in the room—"is better than marriage?"

"You know what my thoughts are on the matter," I said lightly.

"I think I *was* wrong." Her voice had a slight catch to it.

I didn't say a word. I didn't dare. I just held her very close, stroked her hair, and waited for her to speak again.

"Do you still want to marry a crazy girl like me?" she finally looked up.

"More than anything in the world. I've always loved you. I've always wanted you. But, darling Sonia, what about de Feo—the engagement? And your father?"

"I'm proposing to you, aren't I?" She laughed a little unsteadily.

"I can't believe it!" I held her away from me, looked at her from arm's length. How long was it since first we had fallen in love? How many happy, carefree years? That was the word—*carefree*. It was the carefree nature of our life and love that we had cherished, guarded so preciously.

"I'd almost given up hope," I cried. "Six years since that wonderful day when I brought you back from school. Come closer and let your fiancé—nice word, that, I like it!—let your fiancé kiss you."

Later, I started to think about the future, thoughts racing through my head. What *about* this fellow de Feo? What *about* the so-called protocol of upsetting a diplomatic marriage, which would probably infuriate Count Ciano? What about the hold Riccardi had over Sonia or her fiancé? I was so excited, so happy, so tender with the excitement, that I found myself saying, "Nothing matters really but us—all the other problems can be solved. But you'll have to tell your mama and papa," adding with a laugh, "you can't have two fiancés at the same time."

"Leave it to me," she whispered. "There'll be a hell of a row—but I can only say the truth. I can't live without you. I've known it all the time. I've tried to be a good dutiful daughter, but I can't—not anymore. Even though, it's going to hurt many people."

"We could get married secretly?"

"We'll see, beloved. But just for tonight, let's forget all the problems and spend the night loving each other."

I suddenly felt a wild desire to dash out into the street, maybe grab the MG and race around the block.

"I think I'll go and wake up Cartiers," I cried, swinging her in my arms. "Do you think they'd sell me a ring at this time of night?"

She kissed me, holding me tight.

"I'm overwhelmed!" I said.

"I meant you to be."

"Well," I laughed, "you don't face any in-law problems. You're already a member of the family. Papa adores you, he'll be delighted. In fact I'm going to phone him. What time is it?"

"Don't do that darling, let's sleep on it. I was thinking it would probably be easier to get married quietly."

"You really think so?"

"The thing is," she said, "that by marrying quietly, no one could do anything about it. People couldn't try to change our minds. And I *am* worried about Daddy. And that horrible man Abetz—and poor Francesco de Feo. If we got married secretly, nobody could do *anything* about it. Don't you agree?"

That *was* a point in favor of a secret wedding. I had always dreamed in the past of Sonia and me getting married from the château and the village church in Douzy, surrounded not only by our Champagne friends—hers as much as mine—but surrounded too by the vineyards and the villagers. I suppose the thought had first come to me when the Riccardis were thousands of miles away.

"Okay. Why not?" I agreed. "I'll go to see the American consul first thing in the morning. Getting married is and should be our affair."

Almost as an afterthought, I said, "There's one point. As a good Catholic you'll have to have a church service later."

"You're a Catholic too."

"But not a good one. No honestly, I'm thinking of our parents. Our mothers will be terribly upset if we don't have a church service."

"We will. As soon as you like we'll have a benediction in church—but let's get the consulate over first."

"Suits me. I just want to get married. I want to be your husband, not your lover."

"Or both?"

"I hope so, darling. It's forever, and the first thing I'm going to do tomorrow is go out and buy you an engagement ring."

"Oh, no. Not yet darling."

"Yes, I am. No discussion."

"But Larry—this is still a secret, remember. And you're so crazy—" She was thinking back. "Remember the day you bought me a hundred roses?"

"And you almost cried."

"I did. It wasn't the money you spent on them—not even the fact that the flowers would have to die in a few days—it was *you.* You think of things. But a ring? Not yet."

"I insist. What time is your father returning from Lille?"

"Tomorrow afternoon."

"Super. I'll be back before lunch. We'll have a sandwich here."

"You shouldn't."

"Please! You can pretend it's a junk ring, costume jewelry or whatever they call it. But let *me* buy it for you. And you can wear it on your other hand. A *secret* engagement."

"Oh dear, you're already a bad influence. What can I say? Have you ever met a woman who doesn't love jewelry? But please, I'm coming with you to see you don't get swindled."

"You're doing nothing of the sort. I know just what you want—and what I want."

Finally she agreed. I went to Arnaud's, a small, beautiful jewelers in the faubourg St. Honoré, which Mama had patronized for years. I had been there often enough to be recognized by Monsieur Arnaud. Sonia would certainly approve, for I knew from the original gift box that this was where she had bought my birthday cuff links.

And at this moment in my life I came across perfection. There is no other word for it. Even I—with my total inexperience—recognized that I was looking at a ring more beautiful than I had ever seen. It was a huge, pure, sky-blue star sapphire, its beauty caged in a brilliant circle of diamonds.

"Your mother admired this when she was shopping here the other day," said Monsieur Arnaud, "but she said it was too expensive. *Tout de même,* I thought you would like me to show it to you—it's one of the sad facts of life that beautiful things cost so much," he sighed. "Sky blue."

"Is it very expensive?" I knew I had a sizable sum of money left to me by my grandpa when he died, and I'd never touched a cent of it.

Politely—was he a shade condescending?—he mentioned a figure. Astronomical! Then he prepared to put the ring back into the safety of his counter case.

"Hey!" I cried. "Is there any law stops me looking at it a little longer?"

"I'm sorry, sir." Unobtrusively Monsieur Arnaud eyed his watch—Cartier, I noticed. He obviously felt he was wasting his time.

"Okay!" I said to his astonishment. "Wrap it up." Then as he gaped I added, "Just one condition."

I saw his eyes darting covetously, followed by doubt. Was I going to ask for long-term credit? Easy terms? It was a path strewn with hazards for any jeweler. You might start confidently buying something you couldn't afford, but when the crunch came, fathers and mothers had a habit of returning jewelry which their sons shouldn't have bought in the first place.

"No sweat," I said. "I'll give you a check right away. The ring's perfect."

"The condition, sir?" He seemed as puzzled as he was delighted.

"I want a certificate of insurance—for half what the ring's worth. Just in case the lady concerned needs to insure it. I don't want to embarrass her."

He obviously thought I was dotty. So did I! I went whooping into the MG as though executing a war dance, and this time when I reached the apartment just before lunch, there were no tears. I patted a place for Sonia on my knees, then I let her open the velvet case.

She first gasped with sheer astonishment, then wonder, and then gave a deeply drawn breath. And finally, when she had looked at it, she followed with a shriek of joy.

"You *are* mad," she cried. "You *are* crazy. I always knew you were, but *this!* Larry, my *pazzo* Larry, you shouldn't." But with a laugh, "I'm a woman—so it's too late to take it back. It's *mine*. The most beautiful ring in the world. And it's mine forever—like my idiot American fiancé who I will always love. I will keep this ring all my life—then one day, a long, long time ahead, it will belong to our daughter."

Getting married—or rather making plans to get married—didn't seem to involve any serious problems. I rang up Jim Parks, one of the American vice-consuls with whom I played an occasional game of tennis at the Racing Club, and arranged to meet him that same day for a prelunch drink at Harry's Bar.

I was almost on my way out of the office, deciding to walk across the Opéra to the rue Daunou, when a rewrite man on the *Paris American* came in and asked, "Got any more bumf for the 'Comes and Goes'?"

This was our nickname for "Arrivals and Departures." As we were a local newspaper, we printed a list of important Americans leaving or visiting Paris, and sometimes we didn't have enough material to fill the *PA* column because Oregon resolutely refused to dilute it by putting in trash.

I picked up a folder filled with leftovers for "Comes and Goes" and was about to say, "Take a couple from here if you need them," when my eye hit on a list of names. It is one of the odd factors of journalism that a practiced newspaperman can look at a page even in a directory and pick out unerringly one significant name. Almost without *looking* I read in a list of departures, dated some time back, "Mr. and Mrs. Henri Sardi."

Odd I thought, trying to work out the date of my lunch with Mama. Well! Mama didn't dine with the stuffy old Sardis after all—for the very good reason that they weren't in Paris.

My first thought was that when I reached Douzy I would get Mama aside and tease her gently. But then I thought back to that happy lunch. Was the look in her eyes one of anticipation for the evening to come? Or had she in fact merely made a mistake in the date? No, that was impossible because the date had been arranged in a rush, with my father away. Conveniently away? It must be—well, I thought, I am not, repeat not, going to mention the Sardis to my darling mama. I don't know what the hell's happening, but she is my mama, and she deserves to be happy, and I'm not going to spoil it by putting my nose in some business that doesn't concern me.

At the Racing Club, Jim Parks gave me the necessary forms to sign, asked for the requisite photographs and birth certificates. That was about all.

"I'll process everything in about a week or ten days," Parks assured me. "Then I'll phone you, make a date, and one of the counsuls will marry you. After that it might take a while for Mrs. Astell's citizenship papers to come through, but if your pa has a quiet word with the ambassador, I'm sure Mr. Bullitt will speak to Washington and there'll be no sweat."

Sonia Astell!

10

THAT WAS THURSDAY.

Before I left for Douzy the following evening Sonia told me, "I know we must keep things secret, but you can tell Anna. We've been so close—she even fixed us up with our first date that time in Switzerland. I think you owe it to her."

But I never had the chance to tell Anna. I drove down on the Friday evening. It was winter now, and it had turned bitterly cold. The roads were treacherous, and on some flat brown land, black skeletons of trees showed up against leaden skies.

Near La Ferté-sous-Jouarre I stopped for a swig of brandy from my flask. People were skating on a small pond that came almost to the edge of the main road, men and women with woolen caps, brightly colored, long scarves twisted round their necks and flying behind like pennants. One couple holding hands swirled to a stop by the grassy bank of the road, which was stiff and white with rime. The man shouted, "What time is it?" I told him it was nearly half past four. Then, waving to the skaters, I put my foot down hard and reached Douzy in fifty minutes, just as the sun was shrinking, burning away the last fiery particles behind the trees. And just in time to land right in the midst of the biggest family row I can remember.

As I closed the front doors to shut out the biting cold, I heard raised voices screaming at each other in the living room behind the formal salon. Suddenly one voice—Anna's for sure—screeched above the others.

"Goddamn hypocrites! That's what's wrong with this lousy family."

"Anna, darling, it's for your own good." That was Mama's voice.

Throwing my thick coat and long scarf on the ormolu hall table, I strode into the living room, taking in the entire group at a glance—Mama, Anna, Guy, Olivia. Everyone seemed to be talking at once. All looked up at the sound of the door opening. Anna was crying—but with anger, I thought. Mama was crying—but with sorrow, perhaps. Olivia—what the hell is *she* doing here in a family row, I thought savagely?—had a stony, slightly aloof look. Guy was trying to touch Anna, to console his twin sister, but she turned on him shouting, "Take your paws off me."

"What the hell's the matter?" I asked.

"Oh, Larry!" Anna wailed as she almost fell on to my shoulder.

"Here." I pulled out my handkerchief and dabbed her eyes. "Well?" I asked the others. "What's the row about? And where's Papa?"

"Papa's gone out for a reception and dinner at the Syndicat de Champagne," said Guy.

"You're the only man around the house—you tell me what's the trouble."

"Better ask Mama."

"Okay. Mama, darling?"

Before my mother had a chance to speak Anna burst out, "They've found out about Willi and me spending the weekend together at the Crillon."

"Oh *that!*" I tried to simulate a nonchalant approach. "Is that all?"

"All!" cried Mama. "The only daughter of the Astell family—in bed with—"

"Go on, Mama," said Anna, her voice dangerously quiet, "go on—say it—"

Mama hesitated, finally said, "A man."

"That wasn't what you were going to say was it? You were going to say 'a German.' "

"What the hell difference does it make?" I cried in exasperation. "You can't make a row over the fact that a grown-up girl has been to bed with someone." I was thinking, What about you, Mama? "Come on, Anna, dry your eyes. Anybody'd think you'd murdered someone."

Mama made no reply, but at least I gave everyone a breathing space.

"It isn't as though Anna is—well, *wild*, Mama," I said. "She's in love with Willi."

Olivia hadn't said a word, and she shouldn't have spoken now, but she did.

"I think I should go to my room," she said very quietly to Guy. All she meant, of course, was that this was a family row, in which she had been caught by chance, and she was in fact withdrawing from a painful scene with tact and consideration. The pity is that she just didn't disappear without a word, for the enraged Anna seized upon those two words *my room.*

"Your room!" she shouted. "Who the hell said it's *your* room?"

"Shut up," cried Guy. "It *is* her room. You mind your own goddamned business."

Guy, I thought, is beginning to grow up. Perhaps it was Olivia who had made him tougher, taken him away from my "elder brother shadow," given him a personality of his own. He *had* guts—and anger—*and* determination. His persistence in learning to paint was only a manifestation—one day to be forgotten, I was sure—of an inner toughness.

Anna was not so reasonable, for almost with a sneer, she asked, "Is it? Well, I'd like to know how many hours of darkness she spends on her side of the communicating door."

"Anna!" cried Mama sharply, the original cause of the row forgotten for the moment. "Don't speak like that of Olivia."

"I'll say what I like to whom I like," shouted Anna. "That's what's so goddamn wicked about this house—yes, wicked. The goddamn hypocrisy. I'm a grown-up woman, I go off for a weekend of"—she looked at Mama almost with a sneer—"fornication, I think that's the word. And you

treat me like a kid. Yet all the time you tell me I'm wicked,
you, Mama, are letting my twin brother go to bed with—"

"That's the damn end," shouted Guy, and for a moment
I thought he was going to hit Anna. Everything seemed to
happen in one jumbled moment. I rushed over to try to
quiet—protect?—Anna. Mama looked furious—yet strangely impotent.

Olivia said quietly, and I must say with great dignity, "I
didn't ask to come to Douzy. It wasn't my idea, and I'm
sorry if I've embarrassed you. I'll pack my bags and leave
as soon as I can."

"Over my dead body," cried Guy. Again I thought he
was going to slap Anna's face, but he thought better of it
and said, "If Olivia goes, I go. And for good."

At that moment I tried to cool an explosive situation by
asking Anna with an assumed innocence, "How was this
terrible crime of yours discovered?"

"Mlle. Lisette saw us going into the Crillon when she
was visiting Paris," said Anna. "Then she promptly came
back to Douzy and told Mama. *Quelle vache!*"

It was not the first time our ex-nanny had told tales out
of school—long after we had left school, so to speak, at least
long after she had ceased to be our nanny. She didn't discover our innermost secrets perhaps, but she had a habit of
telling Mama quietly that she didn't think we ought to go
to a certain bistro, or that when Anna had said she was too
busy to garden, she had found her reading a sexy novel. It
had been one thing to behave like that when we were under her charge, but what right did she have to interfere
with our adult lives?

"Anna's right," I said to Mama, still trying to divert attention from the main row, "Mlle. Lisette *is* a trouble-
maker. I don't know why the hell we keep her."

What I *didn't* know was that, typically, Mlle. Lisette
had been quietly listening to our shouting from the salon
next door. When events didn't concern her directly she presumably stood there in the salon, drinking everything in.
But suddenly *her* name was brought into the argument.
She stormed into the living room. I had a sudden vision of a

furious woman, wispy gray hair flat against her head, glasses with steel rims.

"Would you really like to know why I am still here?" she shouted.

"No thanks," I said quietly. "Why don't you just go to your room, Mlle. Lisette."

"Because I prefer to stay. Because I have every right to stay." She spat out the words with fury, wielding a verbal dagger.

Olivia started to leave the room. Then Guy made to follow.

"Not you!" screamed Mlle. Lisette. "You stay. I know all about what happens in your room at night!"

"Everybody knows it," I said airily.

"You should talk," she turned on me. "You're as bad as the rest of them. You think you can say anything you like. Do you *really* think I didn't know how you used to stand and watch me through the crack of the open door when I was getting undressed?"

I felt myself going cold. It was true. Mlle. Lisette had been younger, prettier, when I was fourteen and discovered that she had the habit of leaving her door ajar when undressing at night. By peeping through the crack I could see everything, so I used to sneak up regularly to watch, confident she couldn't see me. I had thought it a great adventure in those days.

"That's enough," I said thickly to the ex-nanny.

"No it isn't! You're as bad as the rest. You thought I couldn't see you, but I could. I saw you all right, doing a dirty thing as you watched me. I used to stand there undressing until you'd finished."

"Get out!" I shouted. "Get out, you bitch."

What I had done—and long since all but forgotten—was not very serious, even though in those days all boys were solemnly warned that if they played with themselves too frequently they would end up in an asylum. Still, it was not the kind of thing I wanted Mama to hear.

I saw Mama put a hand across her eyes as though to blot out some unpleasant picture, and I had a sudden premonition. Mlle. Lisette's revelation about me was only a beginning. I sensed a fear in Mama, a real fear. It could have nothing to do with me.

"Are you all right, Mama?" I asked. "Why don't you go upstairs and rest before dinner?"

Before Mama could get up out of the chair, Mlle. Lisette started her ravings again.

"Come on, Guy," I cried, "kick that bitch out of here. Get her out before—"

But Guy stood silent. I looked at him. He was deathly white.

"Guy!" I cried more sharply, my mind flashing back to the incident near the orchard. This was not "Mlle. Lisette." This was Lisette.

"Guy," I said, "what's the trouble?"

"She'll tell you. She's been threatening to spill the beans for years. Go on you bitch—tell."

"I will," sneered Mlle. Lisette. "Pigs, all of you. Do you really know why your kind and supercilious mother keeps me on here—on full salary? Ask Guy!"

For a moment I thought Guy was going to keel over. I looked at his face—pasty, dirty, gray. Then I looked at Mama. Her face was creased with agony. I determined to kick the bloody woman out of the room, to use force. As I moved toward her, she shouted, "Ask Guy! Ask your precious Guy!"

"Ask *what?*" shouted Anna as I struggled with the woman.

"Ask Guy," Mlle. Lisette shouted back at us. "Ask Guy who's the father of my child."

The bombshell was followed by an agonizing silence, in which nobody seemed to have the courage to look at anyone else. Even the row over Anna was wiped off the slate— for a few moments, anyway.

As Guy stepped forward, Mlle. Lisette, beside herself with fury, tried to grab Mama, shouting, "Everyone was happy before that Jewish bitch came into the house."

Guy tried to hit her. I somehow stopped him, almost pushed her out of the room as she shouted, "Pigs! *Salauds!*"

Turning to Olivia, I said, "I'm sorry you were dragged into this mess."

She smiled. She had behaved with dignity, and now she turned to Mama, who was crying softly, and said, "Please, Mrs. Astell, don't worry. It was a long time ago. I'm going to leave now."

"No don't," Mama implored. "Please stay."

I stole a look at Mama, suddenly realizing *one* reason why she didn't want Guy to go. Was Lisette blackmailing her? How poor Mama had changed from that happy day of smiles at the Pré Catelan! I caught myself thinking, It's bad enough about Guy, but what the hell, who cares? It's Mama who counts, Mama who suffers, Mama who helps. And thank God Mlle. Lisette had only been blackmailing Guy and hadn't been snooping around Mama's private life. And thank God Mlle. Lisette had only spotted Anna at the Crillon—and not Mama, dining with some unknown admirer at some secret rendezvous. That *would* have played hell with the weekend.

"It could be worse, so don't worry, Mama." I kissed her, but she looked agonized, almost as though she had painted on a new face suitable for a different occasion—or was it a new mask?

Of course you can't just ignore the sudden revelation that your brother has had an illegitimate child with the local nanny. A hundred questions danced before my thoughts. Where was it? Did Guy see it? Was it a boy or a girl? Yet, though I was flabbergasted at the news—Guy a father!—I had a curious sensation that Mama wasn't taking in the seriousness of the situation. Perhaps she had lived with the secret for longer than I realized. I had no idea when this wretched woman had gone to bed with Guy. Perhaps time, the situation itself, had dulled the effect for Mama.

But there was something else. Not for the first time during the quarrel, I wondered, was Mama more concerned about *her* secret life than about Guy's and Anna's? She wasn't behaving as I would have expected in a traumatic row like this. Mama, after all, was self-possessed and quite capable of controlling a situation, especially in her own

house. She might be lonely—she might be unhappy—but
still, she could with one sharp command have brought the
rest of the family to silence, even that cow Mlle. Lisette.

Maybe, only maybe, her mind was on other things, another man? And among all the family I was the only one to
realize that Mama faced problems of her own. Did she
guess that I knew? I couldn't tell, but I do know that, as we
stood there, my heart went out to her, and fearful, fanciful
impossibilities flashed through my mind in a second. She
was about to run away and join her lover—forever! That
was why she hadn't controlled the family quarrel. Who
gave a damn about Guy? No, she wasn't running away, she
had been discovered, she was being blackmailed and suicide was the only way out. *That* would make Anna's problem unimportant. Crazy thoughts!

"Larry—you're the elder son! Won't *you* help me—me
and Willi?" cried Anna, breaking in on my thoughts.

"Leave this to me," I patted her shoulder. "This Guy
business"—I nodded toward Guy, who was sunk in gloom
in a chair—"must have been a hell of a shock. But," I
turned to Mama, "let's deal with Anna. She's going to
marry Willi. There's nothing you can do to stop it, Mama.
And after all that's happened today, I think you should
give Anna your blessing. I don't know where they'll be
married, but if it's in Germany, then I'm going there to
give Anna away. She's had a raw deal—the toughest of any
of us—and I for one am going to try to make up for it. I
think you should, too, Mama."

"You know I love you, Mama," said Anna. "I don't want
to hurt you. But I *do* love Willi—terribly."

"I understand—I try to—we all like Willi—we only want
you to be happy."

I felt like saying that our parents had chosen an odd way
to prove their love for Anna, but instead I persisted, "So
it's agreed?"

Mama nodded, and after a long pause, she said, "Of
course, Anna. You can telephone Willi and tell him you
both have our blessing."

* * *

Not until after dinner did I drag the whole Mlle. Lisette story out of Mama. Apart from curiosity at opening a cupboard containing such a fascinating skeleton, I was intrigued by one fact. If Mlle. Lisette had had a baby, where was it?

"We had it adopted," Mama told me when we were alone and she was more composed. "It seems such a long time ago."

Guy was only seventeen when it happened, while I was nineteen. Mama either didn't know or refused to discuss the details. However, the Astell children had long since ceased to need a nanny—so why had Mlle. Lisette been kept on?

"You can only see one side of her," Mama explained. "You don't realize the way she brought you all up. She made you what you are today, darling."

"For what it's worth," I couldn't help saying, "I'm not sure she did a good job."

"It's human nature, I suppose," Mama sighed.

"But what's that got to do with keeping Mlle. Lisette on after we'd gone away to school?"

"It's simple. She liked being with you all, especially Guy. So she not only became part of the family, but nannies are getting harder to find, and I thought that one day—well, you'd all be getting married and she'd be able to look after my grandchildren. She's a queer stick, but I liked her—until Guy and she—" she shuddered.

"Didn't you fire her even then?"

"I wanted to."

"But she did *stay,* Mama."

"She went away to have the baby—four months before, so you and Anna wouldn't notice. The child was adopted. None of us—including Guy—ever saw it."

"But then—she came back? After what happened with Guy. For God's sake, Mama, why?"

"She sort of—drifted back."

"Deliberately?"

"I suppose so. Guy didn't seem to mind."

"And since then? Look at me, Mama. You didn't *ask* her back, did you?"

Mama shook her head.

"She forced her way back. That's true, isn't it?" I asked. "And since then she's been blackmailing you. Isn't that the truth? Come on, Mama," I began to feel exasperated. "I'm not a child. I'm twenty-six. Tell me everything."

"Blackmail is such a nasty word—but," rather pathetically, "I only paid her wages, Larry. Nothing more. And she's been useful around the house."

"And her keep—no wonder she can't stand the sight of Olivia. Well, anyway, we've damn well kicked her out this time." A sudden thought struck me.

"Does Papa know? Know everything?"

"Oh, yes. I couldn't keep a secret from him."

Are you sure? I wondered, looking at Mama. I was sorely tempted to tell Mama that Sonia and I were planning to marry in less than two weeks, for she badly needed news to cheer her up. And though I disliked the way Olivia had come into the family, it was only now I realized that Mama hoped Olivia might drive out Mlle. Lisette. And, though much delayed, the ploy had finally succeeded. Mlle. Lisette had gone.

"Your troubles will soon be over!" I fetched her a *marc*. She enjoyed one—but only one—small glass after dinner. "The main thing is—don't panic. Let poor Anna marry her Willi in style. And don't worry so much, Mama. Anything could happen. There probably won't be a war. Anna could leave Willi if there is one. She'll keep her American passport. It's such a crazy world there's no point in getting excited about anything—because it may never happen. Promise me not to worry."

"You're very persuasive."

"I'm not. I'm just practical. Since Anna's determined to marry Willi, let's give her a good send-off. I'm going upstairs to tell Anna to phone Willi again and tell him they're going to be married at Douzy. The first marriage here since yours, Mama! We'll have a white wedding as soon as we can fix it."

"I suppose you're right. In fact Papa has already said that he knows it was bound to happen sooner or later."

And that, I thought—and hoped—was the end of a painful day and night. I stole off to bed as soon as I could after dinner—partly because I didn't particularly want to have to listen to Mama and Papa, or have to intercede.

In the middle of the night, almost as though I was waking from a nightmare, I sat up suddenly. One sound dominated the blackness—the mournful tolling of a bell, driving all thoughts of the family quarrel away. It was the Douzy bell—and everyone knew what that meant in winter.

I heard my father's voice shout, "Up everyone! There's not a moment to lose. Quick now!"

A stranger staying in the house might have thought it was a fire alarm, but it was nothing of the kind. The single sound of the bell told all of us who lived in the area that disaster was threatening the world of champagne.

I knew that from every house in every neighboring village, men and women would be scrambling out of beds, as I was, grabbing the warmest clothes they could fling on hurriedly, swilling faces to wake up, and then going into the cold night air in a race against time to save the vineyards from their greatest winter hazard—frost.

This was worse than fire, it was a malevolent nature's cruelest, craftiest enemy, for it struck simultaneously over an area. And so far no one had discovered a speedy way to outwit it, even though, when the temperature started to fall, "sentries" were designated to make regular checks on the nighttime temperature.

Now it had fallen below zero.

I had felt the cold when driving from Paris, especially when I stopped near the skaters for a swig of brandy, but it was surprising how much milder it usually was in Champagne, especially in the protected folds of the vineyards planted on the sloping west-facing hilly areas. The vineyards are also planted between four hundred and five hundred fifty feet above sea level, sheltering them to a certain extent from frosts, while the forest above them gives a soft moisture to the ground below, which stabilizes temperatures.

My father was running down the stairs, still crying, "Every second counts!" For there was only one way to beat a sudden frost in those days—by employing an army of

willing helpers bearing lighted torches, always kept in the
outhouses of the Home Farm. As I ran down the lane, with
Olivia and Anna just behind, I thought I was leading the
way—until a wobbling figure flashed past the slight downward slope. It was La Châtelaine cycling into the fray.

At the farm we picked up our torches—kerosene-soaked
rags tied to sticks—and made for the nearest vineyards.
Old Pagniez and his daughter, Aubergine, joined us.

"Plenty of time," grunted the vigneron. "We'll have the
smudge pots going full blast within the hour."

Suddenly I saw another fleeing figure—right next to me.

"Oh, no, you don't," I grabbed Mlle. Lisette's arm
roughly and spun her round. "We can do nicely without
any help from you!"

"Every helper counts."

"Get off our ground. I'd rather lose everything. Clear
out, you bitch!"

Running on, I didn't see her again as I made for the first
smudge pots, man's only invention against frost. They
consisted of small, rusted kerosene stoves, about two feet
high, always left out in winter, containing fuel at the bottom with a chimney sprouting above. Hardly noticeable,
half hidden in the vineyards, they stood at ten-yard inter-
vals along every fifth or sixth row.

It was bitterly cold—it was now three in the morning—
as the first men and women arrived, torches flickering,
spreading out from the edge of a vineyard, slowly advancing, because every single kerosene can had to be touched
with the torch to ignite it. And there were hundreds of
them—yet this was the only way, in those days, to provide
warmth. I often wondered what it would be like to fly in
the dark over the vineyards and see below thousands of
twinkling, slowly moving lights advancing in formation.

As we darted between the plants, more smudge pots
belching black smoke, we started coughing and spluttering, for it was not the kerosene in the pots that warmed
the vines against the frost, it was the dirty smoke—made
worse by those who fueled the fire with old tires—that was
effective. It settled like a blanket, loitering in every nook

and cranny against the iron-hard soil, covering the vines with the warmth of the smoke, moving like an old quilt where it was most needed.

At 5:00 A.M. all helpers who weren't ready for bed trudged into the salon of Douzy château. It was a tradition, the equivalent of the British tot of rum after a naval battle. Only a few sneaked off home before gulping one—or two or three—glasses of *marc de champagne,* fiery enough to melt an icicle.

Papa hadn't yet arrived. "He's clearing up in the farm," said Mama, whose face was sooty, her hair bedraggled. She was laughing—just as Grandma Jacqueline dismounted and demanded her tot. She was wearing her "emergency kit," consisting of a pair of old corduroy trousers tucked into fur boots, a long black cape with a fur collar, a woolen skiing hat, and thick mittens.

"Bravo!" she toasted us. To the vignerons, this was high praise indeed, and there was a cheer as she downed her first glass of *marc* in one gulp as though it were water, then calmly asked for a second glass of liquid fiery enough to make a stranger splutter.

At least the night of crisis had one beneficial effect. It took Papa's mind off family affairs. At breakfast he was so full of the magnificent way the people had responded that he forgot the earlier problems.

"I'm very proud of everyone, *really,*" he helped himself to bacon and eggs. "Such loyalty! *Really.*"

Only later did he remember Mlle. Lisette, though Mama must have told him earlier of the terrible row. He made only one reference to our ex-nanny. It was a curious trait of Papa's, who had behaved in exactly the same way when he discovered me leaving Sonia's bedroom. He seemed to make up his mind, make a decision, announce it—and then, incredibly, forget it, or brush it from his mind as though it didn't exist.

"No doubt she egged Guy on, considering the difference in their ages," he said with his rising voice, "yes, *probably.* But I can't allow a woman who has been wronged by our

family to be thrown out and *forgotten*. Not after all the
years she's spent here. *Really*, we've passed the days of
throwing—er—immoral women out in the snow. Yes, the
snow."

"But she can't stay here, Papa?"

"Of course not. But we still have a few cottages in our
Mont de Champagne vineyards, and it happens that one of
them is empty. Madame Delamonde moved after her husband, who worked in the south vineyard, died a month ago.
She's gone to live with her son. I will let Mlle. Lisette live
there rent-free and arrange for the Crédit Lyonnais to send
her a modest monthly allowance. Yes, I think so, yes."

"And Anna?"

"She will marry her Willi," adding with a touch of wry
humor, "We don't want any more unexpected children in
the Astell family."

At that moment Anna came down for breakfast.

"Darling Papa!" she cried. "I've spoken to Willi. He's so
excited. Thank you for understanding."

"Not actually *understanding*," said Papa without any
malice, "so much as accepting. Your mother and I want
you to be happy, yes, *happy*. We may have had reservations, but never mind. It's your choice and we shall do
everything we can to help."

How wonderful, I thought, that the two kids—Anna as
well as Sonia—should both be overcoming the problems of
their love lives at the same time.

Later that morning, I told Anna, swearing her to secrecy.

"What a pity we can't have a double wedding," she said.
"I'm so happy for you, darling brother. Happy for everyone."

Well at least, I thought, we've had enough drama for one
quiet weekend at Douzy.

Or so I thought.

11

ON THE SUNDAY AFTERNOON while we were having tea, the phone rang. It was Paris. Sonia.

I had left her on the Friday, laughing and happy. Now on the phone she cried without preamble, "Oh, Larry. It's Daddy! He's been expelled from Paris. Tonight. And I'm afraid for us."

"What happened?"

"Come to Paris!" It was a cry of distress. "Every second counts. The Quai d'Orsay has declared him persona non grata."

"What on earth for?"

"I don't know, *I don't know,*" she cried, impatient with frustration. "Just come, *please!* Mummy's still in the house packing up, but Daddy's taken a suite at the Ritz. Just come, for God's sake."

"I'm on my way, darling. When does your father leave?"

"Midnight—in theory. But the Rome express leaves at ten. That just gives us time to tell him about us—because he said something I didn't understand—about me."

"Don't worry, darling." Without bothering to put on my coat I dashed round to the old stables on the far side of the courtyard and brought the car round to the front door, where I left her idling to warm up. When I went inside for my coat Aubergine helped me into it and found me an extra scarf, for it was very cold by now, with a threat of snow in the leaden sky.

I had little time to explain to Mama what had happened

to Sonia's father—and I deliberately didn't tell her about our wedding plans. Then I was off, twisting downhill past the dell toward the main road—and Paris.

I reached the place Vendôme at about seven and made my way straight to the Riccardis' apartment on the third floor.

Signore Riccardi opened the door of his suite the second I pressed the bell, almost as though he had been standing there to greet me before I saw Sonia. She gave me a wan smile. Riccardi looked more creased with worry than anger, but I could tell immediately that Sonia had told him about us.

"I'm sorry about the bad news," I tried to commiserate, without having the faintest idea how much worse the news would be in a couple of minutes. "It seems a bad time to talk about Sonia and—"

"A very bad time," he said bitterly. "To break up a future husband's life without so much as a warning—"

"It was my fault, Daddy, I couldn't go on with it."

"This is no time for argument. I understand about people in love, I understand you two. But you play your cards badly. And you have no hope now."

I didn't like the tone of *that*—though I didn't know why.

"May I say, sir, our families are old friends—"

"Don't be such a *cretino,*" he shouted suddenly. "We're not playing *giro tóndo!*" I remember the Italian version of ring around the roses. "You two couldn't marry now if you wanted to."

"But I'm an American," I blurted out.

"You can be Lord God Almighty," he said, "but what you don't know is that Sonia has been expelled too."

My mouth dropped open.

"Is this true?"

She nodded miserably.

"Tonight?"

"They've given me three days to leave," Sonia whispered in a small, frightened voice. "I can't believe it."

"Three days! But that's eternity! I'm sure I can fix—"

"You can't!" said Riccardi harshly. "Apart from my daughter's sacred promise to another man, you wouldn't have the time anyway."

"I would," I cried. "Please understand, Signore Riccardi. We love each other—not only Sonia and me—but the families—"

As patiently as his Italian nature would permit, Riccardi explained that he understood everything I said. He had often thought in the past that Sonia and I would make a happy couple. But times had changed. Her fiancé was an important member of Foreign Minister Ciano's team. To start a scandal at this delicate moment—with her father kicked out of France—would be disastrous.

"There's something more you haven't told me," I said. "You can't stop us."

"Diplomacy isn't just a question of giving orders anymore," he said bitterly. "Why do you think I have been declared persona non grata? Intrigue—and not by the French. They are after Sonia too. I do not think you could marry if you tried." Adding with a wintry smile, "Not even with your American influence."

"But if we can?"

"I want to marry him so badly, Daddy. What does Mummy say?"

"I don't know. I don't know anything," he wiped his forehead. "She's still at the house packing personal things ready to be sent on. I don't know."

"If I can?" I begged him.

He turned to Sonia, and stroked her blue-black hair.

"Carissima," he said, "I would like you to be happy. And I like Larry, I do. But you do not understand everything." He was wavering.

I knew in my heart that I could pull the right strings. But then Riccardi asked me, "If there is no time to get married before Sonia is sent away, what then?"

"Then she'll go, and I'll wait a bit and say nothing—for the moment anyway—if that helps you," I promised. "I'm sure we can get married, but if there's a hitch I'll agree—if

Sonia does—not to break her engagement to the other man until the timing is better."

"I don't want that!" cried Sonia.

"We'll be married, don't worry," I promised her. "In a couple of days."

"If not? It may sound silly to an American," speaking softly, Riccardi almost ignored Sonia, "but to an Italian, honor is very important. Especially in the service. And I have problems. If Sonia stays *here* as your wife, it will be *her* honor that is dirtied. If she remains engaged and then breaks it off after a few months, honor will be satisfied all round."

I didn't really like the sound of it—mainly because I was convinced Riccardi was lying—that he was using a pretty feeble excuse about "honor" to cover up a far more sinister reason why he hoped the engagement would continue. I *knew* Riccardi was in trouble, and perhaps needed Sonia, even de Feo. But what had he done? There were no clues, though the drawn face of Riccardi and the silence of Sonia told me it was serious. Yet I could not challenge Riccardi, call him a liar in front of Sonia.

"What do you think, Sonia?" She nodded—reluctantly.

"It is generous of you," said Riccardi. "I don't like what is happening, but we are in much deeper waters than you think, and there are people who will stop at nothing. Now I must prepare to leave. This suite will be kept on for Sonia until she goes."

Inside me, I was exulting. For I had made a deal which I was convinced would enable us to get married. And Riccardi had *promised* that if we got married before Sonia had to leave, he would accept the situation—not that there was anything he could *do* about it while Sonia was in Paris and he was in Rome. So the promise not to rock the boat if she went to Italy would not apply.

"I do not have much time," Riccardi looked at his watch. "So perhaps I will say *au revoir* to you as I am expecting guests before the car picks me up at half past eight to go to the Gare de Lyon."

"Daddy, I'm so angry with the French for this."

"Don't worry, *carissima*. Diplomacy is no longer for gentlemen."

He put his arm on Sonia's shoulder. They were standing
by the window of the oak-paneled sitting room overlooking
the private Ritz gardens, and he looked tired, though still
handsome—I could see where Sonia inherited her dark
beauty. But I could also see a middle-aged man's dreams of
his daughter making a good marriage to a titled diplomat
crumbling about him. "Yes, *mia cara*," he said sadly, "all
will suffer now, and we cannot fight them. They are stupid,
these people, so stupid they never listen to discussions.
One man gets his orders—from whom? you may ask—and
then everything goes on a belt of assembly and nothing
can stop it."

"But why?" asked Sonia desperately. "They can't do
this without giving both of us a reason."

"They can. They do. I do not know why. The French at
the d'Orsay are very polite. However they insist they have
orders to cancel your residence permit." He gesticulated as
only Italians can. "I argue with them, I tell them it is
against all the code of diplomacy. They are very, very
sorry, they say, but these are orders. Whose orders? I ask.
They will not tell me. They don't even know why they do
this, they cannot tell us."

I had never seen Sonia so destroyed. Her face seemed to
have fallen in with pain.

"It's monstrous," I muttered. "It's bloody infamous.
They *can't* do this. Just because a pack of bloody Frogs—"

"Please," said Riccardi coldly, "try to control your language. I know you must be very upset."

"I'm not a diplomat," I suddenly shouted. "I know it's
not your fault—but Christ! The damn French can't do this
to us!"

After I had said good-bye, I took the elevator to the
ground floor and walked past one of the gilt and plush
chairs opposite the concierge's desk—at the exact moment
when Otto Abetz came marching through the front door.
He had two men with him—bodyguards, I guessed.

He looked as he always did—tall, shoulders squared up

as though for a fight, blue eyes seeing all, pale face contrasting with reddish-blond hair. And always carrying
with him, like a cloak, a sinister aura.

"Ah so!" he held out a hand which I unwillingly took. I
hated myself for lacking the moral fiber to refuse it.
"When are you going to take up my offer of a trip to see our
beautiful new Germany? The offer still holds, you know.
We need good writers to see for themselves the wonderful
things our Führer is doing."

Abetz knew I would never go. He knew damn well I was
violently anti-Fascist. So he wasn't *inviting* me. He was
goading me, and the thought made me mad as hell.

This man, I was convinced, knew why Riccardi and
Sonia were being kicked out of France. He might even
have engineered it to protect himself.

I saw it this way: obviously Riccardi's visits to Paris had
held sinister motives; he might even have been involved in
plans to liquidate the two Itallian anti-Fascists murdered
during the summer. If so, Riccardi would certainly have
consulted Abetz as senior partner.

Above all, however, Abetz had to protect his own front as
a lover of all things French, his role as confidant of Madame de Portes, his influence with the right-wing die-hard
French politicians, for this was his cover while he organized a fifth column in France. But what if Sonia's father
had blundered somewhere, been indiscreet? If Abetz
thought this had happened, he wouldn't hesitate to get
Riccardi and his family out of the way before the French
began to ask awkward questions, which might even impli-
cate Abetz. This was speculation, I knew, but Abetz, I was
sure, had used his influence among pro-Fascists at the
Quai d'Orsay to declare the Riccardis undesirable aliens.

Abetz had one terrifying, snakelike trait in his character, one confirmed by many other newspapermen. It was
an uncanny ability to read your mind. He could see the
rage boiling inside me, and with his sharp intuition he immediately knew the cause of it. It must have been so, for
standing there, slightly supercilious, he suddenly said the
most extraordinary thing.

"So please come and see our Germany"—his voice was as smooth as silk—"and I promise you, Monsieur Astell, an unending supply of our most beautiful *Fräuleins*. We keep them handy," his voice held a trace of a sneer, "as a sort of therapy in case any of our guests are suffering from broken hearts."

For once in my life I thought of the right answer before the other man had a chance to leave.

"I don't like making deals with men who fuck up my love life," I retorted, unable to control my fury. "But I will make a deal with you. I'll come to Germany with *you*—the day the French come to their senses and kick shits like you back home where you belong." Then I added one last homemade "German" word which I had once invented as a joke to tease Willi. It had a very effective sound.

"Gefundenshite!" I said and pushed my way through the swinging doors into the clean, cold air of the place Vendôme.

I was round at the U.S. consulate almost before it opened, dancing with impatience until the girl led me to Jim Parks's door.

"Christ! You look mad," he greeted me.

"Mad! I've never been so livid in all my life. Know what these sodding Frogs have done?"

As coherently as I could, I outlined the events of the previous evening. "They can't *do* this sort of thing to innocent civilians," I cried.

"It's life in *la belle France*," Parks sighed. "Might as well remember it."

"I don't give a shit," I cried. "We've got three days. That gives us time to get married, doesn't it?"

Parks, his jacket on its hanger, Arrow-type white shirt newly starched, fingered one of his embassy-issue yellow pencils with the standard rubber at the end, and said softly, "I hate to say this, Larry, but no dice. You're out of luck."

"But I'm *American*. Don't I have any rights?"

"In France, fuck all. And as for an Italian—she may be beautiful, Larry, but when the French are looking for an

Italian, consider yourself lucky they haven't picked her up in the *panier à salade* and taken her to the local jail."

"It's not *possible* that people can stand by and ruin other people's lives. I love that girl, Jim. My *father* will vouch for her."

"I wish I could help, Larry," Parks shook his head, and he really meant what he said. "But the only way you might have been able to pull rank was if you'd got the lady pregnant. And you've left it a bit late for that."

After a few more moments of futile argument I stormed out of the white embassy building, jumped into my MG, and missed almost every pedestrian unlucky enough to be on the avenue Gabriel.

"I'll find *some* way," I swore as I grated the gears into second.

But I didn't. I *couldn't*. When it became obvious that there was no way of delaying the cancellation of her *permis de séjour*—not even after I had been to the prefecture—I had one last thought: I would take her to America the following day, and we'd get married there. But she didn't have a visa. And that would take time. Finally I suggested that I would travel with her to Italy, and we could get married there. But she shook her head. I had promised.

"Well, what about forgetting my promise and breaking off your engagement?" I suggested.

Sadly she looked at me. "You heard what Daddy said. He's tied to Ciano's apron strings."

She held out her beautiful hand, displayed the sapphire on the third finger. "There's where it stays," she promised me. "It's our engagement ring—but it's an unofficial engagement, just for the time being. I don't want to tie you down. To tie *anyone* down. Though Monsieur Coquelicot is mine forever, whatever happens."

And that, after a lot more discussion, was how we left it. But when finally I realized that I must, for the moment anyway, accept what had happened, I resolved on one thing. I would never spoil the time we had spent together by a bitter leave-taking. We would part as friends—can

lovers ever really be friends? Sonia had once asked me—
until I came to marry her.

I had Sonia's address near Florence, of course, so I decided on impulse before she left to write to her so that a
message would await her when she arrived in Italy.

At the nearest souvenir shop on the rue de Rivoli arcade
near the statue of Joan of Arc, I asked the girl, "Do you sell
postcards?"

"Mais oui, Monsieur."

"Give me fifty please," I said with a deliberate nonchalance. "As many different as you can, please."

At the office I posted every one to Sonia.

I didn't go to the *PA* on the last day, for I was haunted by
a feeling that we would never see each other again, certainly never as lovers. No doubt the Riccardis and the Astells—the young as well as the old—would meet again as
old friends in years to come. But, I told Sonia, it could
never be the same for us.

"It will, darling, it will," she promised as we sat down at
Marcel's for our final dinner in the bistro we loved so
much. Two or three of the elderly, solitary regulars bowed
politely to us as they always did. I wondered what their reaction would have been had they known she had been
thrown out of France.

I couldn't even begin to eat the *boeuf bourguigon,* which
came to our small table piping hot, its sauce redolent of
good wine. And matters were made worse when Marcel
himself, in chef's hat and blue-and-white-checked apron,
looked horrified. *Nobody* refused Marcel's cooking (even
though occasionally it was below standard) if only because
most people who dined at his restaurant were so hungry
and so poor they would eat anything.

"I'm just not hungry," I apologized.

"Can I change it, monsieur?"

I shook my head. For a moment I had a wild impulse to
blurt out, "She's going!" But I resisted the temptation.
There was nothing anyone could do about anything.

"I think he should have a cognac," said Sonia gently to Marcel.

"On the house, please," Marcel bustled over to the tiny zinc bar.

Sonia took my hand. "You should eat a bit, darling, just a mouthful."

"Plenty of time for that tomorrow," I wallowed in self-pity. Yet it wasn't only self-pity that robbed me of my appetite, it was the fact that my misery was combined with a sense of foreboding which I could not dismiss from my mind. I loved Sonia, there would never be another, but I was, I hoped, man enough to know that life would go on after she had left, even though for a time it would be empty and I would be as miserable as hell.

Her leaving—and the sinister overtones that caused her departure—seemed symptomatic of the hatred, the beastliness, the downward trend of all life in Europe. It wasn't only our lives that were being torn apart, through no fault of our own. Europe itself was crumbling as 1938 approached.

"Let's go home, darling," said Sonia when I had downed my cognac. "Let's go to bed in each other's arms."

We walked back down the rue de Seine, past the tiny apartment where Goncharova—who had painted my favorite sunflower picture—lived, then along the quai Malaquais until we crossed the boulevard to the rue du Cherche-Midi.

Then we went to bed, but not to make love. I tried. Did I want to prove my love? I didn't know, but I couldn't. I lay there in her arms, wanting to, I tried again and again, waiting for the dawn, but I couldn't make love.

On the last day I took her to the Gare de Lyon and saw her comfortably installed in her reserved first-class wagon-lit. After I had kissed her for the last time, she leaned out of the window and said, "We'll meet again, my beloved Larry. I promise you."

I wondered, as I drove back to Douzy, whether we ever would. When the car slid effortlessly round the bends toward the house I felt that each rhythmic turn of the train's wheels rattling toward Italy was taking her farther from me, that she would never again set foot in the enchanted garden of Douzy which we both loved.

Reaching the courtyard, I had a sudden urge to turn round and race away. I resisted it, but I felt for the moment that I never wanted to see Douzy again. What had to us been a magic garden was, without Sonia, just another estate with its workaday chores.

I prayed we *would* meet again. Yet, somehow or other, I already had a premonition that the next time we *did* meet, she would be married. And not to me.

Part Two

1938-1939

12

Anna was married at Douzy in the spring of 1938 "to her German," as Grandma Jacqueline said, with a withering look which meant, Well, I did my best to stop them!

Despite parental doubts, however, it was a beautiful white wedding. The couple were young and handsome and obviously very much in love, and if anyone had doubts about the wisdom of marrying into a German family in these troubled times—"What the hell," as Oregon said, "just think of Krug, Mumm, Heidsieck, and Bollinger—half the families in Champagne are descended from the Germans."

Papa had decided on one thing: to give the guests the choice of wearing the traditional formal cutaway jacket with striped trousers or a dark, sober suit.

"That or a blue lounge suit, I think, *yes,*" he said in his up-and-down voice. "*Really,* as this is a village wedding, a dark suit will be—well, quite *practical,* yes?"

"Blue suits! You mark my words," Grandma snorted, "this is the sort of thing that's turning France into a Communist country. Blue suits do *not* go with champagne."

Oregon, the only one who dared to tease his mother (and still called her Grandma Jacqueline), said brightly, "Let's serve beer instead."

"It'd be more suitable," muttered my grandmother, adding when she was sure Willi wasn't in the room, "it's the only thing the Germans drink anyway. They *swill* it down—by the bucket."

175

"I do seem to remember wines like Niersteiner," my father mentioned timidly.

Grandma glared at him. "No one in France drinks *German* wine," and searching for a suitable simile, sniffed, "it's like serving mint sauce with a *gigot*. All right for foreigners."

Most guests would wear cutaway morning suits—if only to do justice to what promised to be Anna's stunning wedding dress, for almost as soon as the date had been fixed, Mama said firmly, "It may only be a village wedding, but Anna is our only daughter, and she's going to wear the most beautiful dress in the world. Mainbocher promised me personally."

This was the couturier who had designed the wedding dress for the Duchess of Windsor—a forty-eight-year-old designer from Chicago. Originally called Main Rousseau Boucher, he had edited French *Vogue* in the twenties before telescoping his name and then setting up shop in the avenue George V.

"Main," as Mama called him, was a personal friend who took enormous trouble with clients he liked. He had arrived at Douzy with a selection of sketches and, when one had been chosen, sent a fitter to Douzy half a dozen times to make sure everything was perfect.

On the day Anna looked exquisite. I had an impression of white lace that looked almost like a crinoline, hundreds of seed pearls, and Grandma's "heirloom lace" worked into the train.

"And no nonsense about etiquette," Mainbocher had insisted. "I know a train is only supposed to be three yards for a church wedding or six yards for a cathedral, but *you're* going to have a six-yard train."

More than a hundred guests arrived from Paris. All the leaders of the champagne houses had been invited. Fifteen of Willi's friends came from Germany, including a charming couple called the Mollers and Willi's mother and father, who were quiet, very pleasant, but couldn't speak a word of English or French. A marquee—which could be reached only through the house—had been erected as an extension to the conservatory—deliberately, for though Papa hated class distinctions, he knew that lines had to be drawn when the wedding guests included Bullitt, the American ambassador, and Paul Reynaud, who had each accepted.

"We couldn't—er—throw them in at the deep end with the vignerons," Papa admitted. "Both would be embarrassed." He was right, for the villagers—friends to us, but unknown to guests from outside the area—arrived early, hungry, thirsty, and clutching all the sticky children in the village.

They made their way from every direction—up the dell, along the drive, through the orchard, past the cutting bed. Just behind the big yew trees and the courtyard arch, long trestle tables and three hundred folding chairs had been arranged. Everyone reaching the top of the dell was greeted by an unlimited supply of Astell nonvintage, with soda pop for the kids. You could sit down where you liked; in front were mounds of food ranging from every kind of home-cured *charcuterie* or pâté to canapés of smoked salmon. Nearby two huge pans hung over the embers of a large fire. One contained *boeuf bourguignon,* the other a *cassoulet,* in which even the geese had been fattened on the farm before going into the stew pot.

From time to time we left the marquee to visit the village celebrations at the top of the dell. The biggest cheer of all, however, was reserved for Reynaud when he made a brief appearance before the vignerons. After all, he was minister of justice; he apologized for the absence of his wife (and not, of course, mentioning his mistress) and then, a true son of France, insisted on toasting the bride and groom "with all of those here who I know are her most trusted friends."

A dozen arms held out champagne bottles from the tables. No one could find a clean glass, but that didn't worry Reynaud. He picked up the nearest cup, grabbed a bottle, poured in a little champagne, swilled it round to clean it, then refilled it and drank the toast.

The vignerons loved it—but soon the amount of cham-

pagne began to tell. I saw several sly boys and girls grab
piles of smoked salmon canapés, stuffing them into their
pockets or handbags. One little girl put some up the elastic
of her knickers.

The young unmarried men and women began to disappear, making for the dark hidden corridors of the yew
trees, from where I could hear sudden giggles, rustling of
hands in clothes, squeals of those who preferred necking
—or anything else—to pâté and champagne.

The younger children played under the trestle tables, or
rolled down the side of the dell littering it with paper, dirty
plates, glasses, half-eaten *baguettes*.

"It's filthy," I said to Mama as we looked out of the
striped tent toward the dell. "I'm not going out there
again."

"They'll be all right tomorrow, they'll clean up. You see,
Larry, if one or two *do* get drunk, it's not because the
champagne's free. It's because they *are* Papa's family.
This is a great day for *them* as well as for Anna. I only
wish—" she stopped short. I knew that just in time she
stopped uttering the word *Sonia*.

"How do you think I feel?" I said bitterly. "The only girl
I've ever really loved all my life—and Anna's best friend—
yet she's not even here. But perhaps it's as well she
couldn't come to the wedding," I muttered savagely, not
saying it aloud, for despite all the past, despite the uncer-
tain future, I had—even to the last second—hoped wildly,
impossibly, that she might by a miracle arrive at Douzy for
this day and that I would suddenly see her, cool and beautiful, sipping champagne in the marquee.

"I know, Larry darling," Mama twiddled the stem of her
flute glass and smiled to someone, "I only wish I could say
something. But, after all, she's living in Cairo now, it's a
long way away."

"Oh! Don't get maudlin," I said irritably. "What's the
point of saying anything?"

Sonia had never been a prolific letter writer, but she had
dropped me a brief note—short and sweet, yes, very, very

sweet—to say that her father was being posted as ambassador-without-portfolio to "handle affairs" along the North
African coast. They would live in Cairo—it was an obvious
trouble spot. Italy was demanding more and more territory in North Africa. The French, on the other hand, were
relying on their huge North African empire to provide
them with the cannon fodder for the next war. They didn't
put it quite so crudely, but that was what they meant.

When I told Oregon of Riccardi's move to Cairo, where
he would have his headquarters, his first response was
"Ciano must think very highly of Sonia's father. She going
with him?"

I nodded.

"North Africa could be a vital war theater—if war
comes, that is," said Oregon. "Riccardi is probably laying
the ground, just as he did in Paris."

"Maybe," I agreed. "And Sonia tells me he's got a new
assistant."

Oregon cocked an inquiring eyebrow.

"Yes, her dashing young fiancé, the Count de Feo. It
seems he's gone to Cairo to be trained by Riccardi for a
more important job."

"Espionage?" asked Oregon, not speaking sardonically
as he so often did, but seriously.

"The Italians seem to specialize in it," I sighed.

Cairo! Half a world away from my modest beat as a
newspaper correspondent, virtually confined to writing
stores about events in Paris.

Oh, Sonia darling, I said to myself. Drop everything!
Come back! If you still love me, if you are still barred from
entering France, return to Italy, and I'll take the next
train to Rome and we'll get married by the American consul in Rome. And then? I'll give up my job if you like, settle
for a life in Douzy. Anything you want providing we can be
together. Remember, above all else, what Douzy repre-
sents to me, to you, to us. Douzy is more than just a place to
live, a business, a name, a trademark, a beautiful château.
Douzy is the living symbol of a way of life that may one day

vanish. If the world goes mad, and Douzy's way of life has to go, let's at least live it for the time still left.

That's what I thought, that's what I *dreamed.* But that seemed to be the limit of what I could do, for feelings of depression were not confined only to thoughts of Sonia. As spring turned warmer, all Europe that summer of 1938 was suffering from a kind of malaise as it was forced to face up to a question it had for so long tried to shirk: would Hitler fight?

Early that year, Hitler had assumed supreme power over all Germany. He had simply engulfed poor Austria. Against him in France Léon Blum had been no match and had been replaced by Édouard Daladier as prime minister. In Vaucluse, where he had been born, the son of a local baker, Daladier was nicknamed the Bull of the South, but though he had a tough exterior, he was a hollow man inside. I was horrified at his appearance when I first met him. He looked dirty. A cigarette always hung out of the corner of his mouth. He stank of absinthe. He looked more sly than clever.

And because I knew Reynaud, I was fascinated by one other aspect of Daladier's character. Despite his dark-skinned complexion, his crude manners, despite the lock of greasy hair always hanging over his forehead (dreams of Napoleon, perhaps?), Daladier, who was a widower, had managed to entice a titled lady into his bed as his acknowledged mistress. She was the Marquise de Crussol, and the Countess de Portes was her arch rival.

"The world's not big enough for both these women. One of them will have to go," Oregon prophesied—a truth for which he didn't have to wait long.

Daladier was symptomatic of most French leaders—no guts. We all had feelings that none of them was strong enough to stand up to Hitler. And this indifference permeated through the entire European structure.

"It's hard for us, yes, it really *is,"* said Papa one day, "to realize that France is very *tired.* Yes, *exhausted.* You can't lose a million and a half men as France did in the Great War without having a feeling of 'never again.'"

"De Gaulle told me when I interviewed him recently," I said to Papa, "that France doesn't have enough tanks and planes to fight a war anyway. The French aero industry is on strike. Tank production has been hit too. He says half the Renault work force is Communist. Arms production has declined every year—1936, 1937, and now 1938."

"That's all part of the 'never again' malaise," explained Papa. "France doesn't *want* to fight. And really, I don't blame her. Especially on the pay they get. A few cents a day—it's appalling. Napoleon used to talk about an army marching on its stomach. They'd march better with full pockets."

"And the fifth column doesn't help," said Guy. Everyone nowadays was talking about the fifth column, the term which originated in the Spanish civil war when General Mola boasted that he had four columns outside Madrid—and a fifth one inside the Spanish capital.

"Led by Abetz?" I said.

"He should be shot," interrupted Grandma, pausing at the door on her way to bed.

"But by whom?" asked Oregon slyly.

"Well, it won't be the army," said my father.

The feeling of disquiet in those summer months was worse in Douzy than in Paris, because of the gap left once Anna had gone to live in Düsseldorf, the gap and the fear.

"It gives you an awful empty feeling without her around," sighed Mama. "I never realized how much you can miss someone you've always taken for granted." With a worried look she added, "I do hope she'll be all right. Things seem to be so gloomy in Germany—this talk about guns before butter. Do you think she's getting enough to eat?"

I could sense Mama's apprehension in the sudden, quiet evening moments at Douzy, the times when she looked at nothing, said nothing. I could almost hear her asking herself, Will Anna be safe? Can she ever be happy, an American living in a beastly country like Germany? She had just been reading a report on the way children were being taught to inform against their parents and report them to Nazi bully boys.

"You mustn't brood on it," I begged Mama on one of her down days. "You feel that way about Anna, but I feel that way about Sonia, living under Mussolini, who's forcing pints of castor oil down the throats of men and women who say anything nasty about Fascists."

"You know what I think," said Papa, turning later that evening to Mama. "You should go for a week to Germany, and—"

"Hear, hear!" I interrupted. "It's an easy journey, and Anna wrote that her apartment is ready. Go on, Mama, phone Anna *now.*"

Well, Mama didn't phone *that* day—but I could see immediately that she was excited. And two days later in Paris I telephoned Anna from the office.

"Mama's thrilled at the idea of visiting you," I explained to Anna. "But why don't *you* phone *her*—without having phoned me, if you get my meaning?"

"And you can come another time," said Anna. "Split it up so I've got two visits! I miss you, Larry—and—well—"

"I will." I cut her short before she started asking about Sonia. "Now phone Mama right away."

Originally Mama had planned to take the train to Düsseldorf, but somehow she gave us all an impression of worry, presumably because there had been several minor strikes on the French railways. She puzzled me; Mama was not the kind of woman to be nervous, yet a few days later she said to Papa, "Wouldn't it be awful if there was another strike and I was stuck in Germany."

"But they're not serious, Mama," I protested. "They're only one-day token stoppages—and there probably won't be any more anyway."

"I don't like the idea of the train," she said. "Only—" the rest of the sentence trailed off.

I'm not quite sure how Mama's alternative suggestion was broached, though I do know that it came from Papa. But did he make his suggestion out of the blue? Or did

Mama skillfully lead up to "his" idea, plant the seeds in him? Or was the whole thing just an accident?

She did say, I remember, "We'll go to see Anna another time. But" she said to Papa, "it would be a good idea if I went the week you have to go to Switzerland on business."

"Hardly business," he said. "More of a bore. It's the annual conference of the Comité International des Vins in Bern the week after next. Yes, really, a bore, I *must* say, but I'm the champagne chairman this season and I *must* go."

"Of course you must," agreed Mama. "But—" I realize now that Mama knew perfectly well what *she* wanted, but was determined to let the suggestion come from Papa. And it did. As she said, "But—I was wondering—" Papa said, "Wait! I have an idea. Why not go by car?"

"By car?"

"Well, my dear, I'll be away for a week—going by train of course, the Swiss never go on strike! Why not take Guy with you—I'm sure he'd like to see Anna. Olivia's in Paris and he's simply moping about—especially after that scene with Mlle. Lisette. And you, Larry?" he said, with a look in my direction. "You'll be working, I suppose? Such a pity."

"Yes, I will," I nodded. "But don't worry. I'm already planning a trip to Germany later for the *Globe.* I don't know how, but I'll make it soon."

"Well, that's fixed then." Papa seemed really proud at solving a "difficult" problem which had never been considered before simply because his thoughts were so concerned with champagne that he never thought of it—until somehow, skillfully, Mama jogged his brain in the right direction.

"And of course," said Papa as an afterthought, "you must go in the Hisp. No Citroën for you. Gaston can drive you and Guy. After all, it's only a hundred and fifty miles."

"You are clever!" Mama rarely displayed such open excitement. But then, it was her first trip to see Anna since the wedding.

That evening everything was arranged. Papa would be

leaving on the Sunday to catch the train to Bern, so I would drive him to Paris the same day, and then collect him at the station on his return. No point in driving first to Paris in the Hisp and then collecting Mama, as Reims was well on the way to Germany.

We telephoned Anna and started making final plans. The Frankels had only one spare bedroom, but Willi arranged for Guy to sleep at the Borse Hotel, just round the corner in a quiet street near the Kreugstrasse. In Paris we started filling in forms for the cumbersome bundles of paper required for an international trip by car—the *triptyque,* the *carnet,* an international license for Gaston, another one for Guy. Mama didn't bother. She *could* drive—she held both American and French licenses—but she hated driving in traffic.

The visit started off without a hitch—well, almost. I telephoned both Mama and Guy in Düsseldorf to check. According to Guy, Mama found Düsseldorf pleasant—but with reservations. She thought the whole Ruhr area was pretty horrible, said Guy, "and the noise was awful. You know I can sleep, even if a hurricane hits Tampa, but the streetcars and buses start hooting at six o'clock. After the first night, I swapped places with Mama."

"How come?"

"Easy. I'm sleeping in the spare room, and I let Mama sleep in the Borse Hotel. It's near the apartment and the street's quiet. So it suited everyone."

"Guy is an angel," said Mama on the phone the next day. "I must tell you, Larry, it's a pretty horrible city. But the hotel is clean, and I come round every morning for breakfast before Willi goes to work. And Anna is wonderful."

"It's a success?"

"It's more. It's a joy to see her again—and, if I'm really honest, the change for both Guy and me won't do either of us any harm."

She certainly sounded happy.

13

Two THINGS HAPPENED the next morning. The first concerned Sonia and me only; the second had worldwide repercussions.

A letter from Sonia was waiting for me at the office. And, though her few letters had always been tender and loving, this one held a note of despair.

"It's not a question of not loving you," she wrote. "You know I will always love you whatever happens, but there seems no hope now of planning to break off my engagement. It's always wait and see, wait and see." She underlined the words savagely, I could visualize her anger when she wrote them down. "I sometimes wonder if I dare run away, but if I did it would hurt and disgrace so many people. I'm so depressed because I can see no road leading from the present to the future. I am trapped here in Cairo by events which I can't control."

What did the word *disgrace* signify?

There was much more in the same vein, and I, too, was afraid. Worse still, anger and frustration were burning me up. It all seemed so damned pointless. She had only to *insist!* As she said—run away! I would do the rest. If she gave me the word, I would gallop in on the equivalent of my white charger and take her away forever. And yet I knew in my heart that this was no solution, any more than it would have been easy for Anna to run off and marry Willi.

Sometimes I found myself wishing—oh, how I wished!—

that I could find another girl who could wipe out forever the memories that haunted me. But I knew I never would.

The second event was very different, and tragic. That same morning a poor, half-demented, seventeen-year-old German or Polish Jew shot the third counselor at the German embassy in the rue de Lille in Paris, just round the corner from our apartment, and when the man died two days later all hell broke loose in Germany.

It was a tangled story. The youngster, called Herschel Grynsban, was living secretly in Paris with an uncle. Suddenly his German-Jewish parents of Polish extraction were among twelve thousand people deported from Germany to Poland. The trainload of refugees reached the frontier. The heartless Poles refused to accept it. The train set off on the return trip to Germany. It was not allowed in. For days the luckless men and women were shunted from one country to another. Four women on the train died for lack of attention. Herschel's father somehow got a letter to his son, and in a blind fury the boy walked into the German embassy and shot the diplomat, a man called Ernst Vom Rath, fatally wounding him.

It was the signal for an anti-Jewish pogrom surpassing in ferocity thus far anything ever witnessed, even in Germany. All Jewish newspapers were ordered to cease publication, cultural associations were dissolved. No Jews were allowed to attend university, all Jewish children were expelled from schools. Then bands of young Nazis, acting simultaneously all over Germany, set fire to synagogues, smashed Jewish shops, stoned Jews in the streets, forced many to crawl in public on their hands and knees. Men, women, and children were dragged from their beds, men taken to concentration camps.

Much of this fearful persecution took place near the area where Anna lived, for the Ruhr was ablaze with hate and vengeance. Papa was frantic. But we were helpless. As the pogrom gathered momentum all telephone communication with Germany was cut. We even thought of driving to Germany to rescue Mama and Guy—not to mention Anna, but the frontiers were sealed. Finally I asked Washington to try to contact Düsseldorf through the *Globe* bureau in Germany, while Papa begged Bill Bullitt to phone our embassy in Berlin. We did get a message through. No one had been harmed, the Frankel house had not been touched—and Mama would leave as soon as she could.

But that was days ahead, for the pogrom increased. On the radio Dr. Goebbels, the Nazi chief of propaganda, screamed, "The justified and understandable indignation of the German people at the cowardly Jewish assassination has been vented in a wide degree."

In all, fifty thousand Jews were killed or wounded or lost their homes and the right to work. Inevitably the outraged Jewish communities outside Germany reacted violently—while all the time Mama was virtually trapped in Düsseldorf. As the pent-up hatred spilled across Europe we got a message from Bullitt. The U.S. embassy in Berlin had secured permits for Mama and Guy to leave Germany. They had left that morning.

Almost at the same time, during the afternoon, Mama's voice came through loud and clear to my office.

"We managed to get to Copenhagen," she said. "Oh, darling, it's been so terrible—and my heart breaks for Anna. I'll tell you everything when I see you."

"Why Copenhagen?"

"It's the only border that was open—across Schleswig-Holstein—I hope that's how you pronounce it. We're staying at a hotel called the d'Angleterre, it's very beautiful and peaceful. We'll set off tomorrow for home. I've so much to tell you."

As I was saying good-bye Tomlinson rushed in crying, "All hell has broken out on the Right Bank. Thousands of Jewish rioters. Let's go."

Already on the previous day rioters in Brussels had gathered in the Grand Place, forcing their way into the beautiful fifteenth-century Town Hall, apparently searching for Germans supposed to be hiding there. A protest meeting in Trafalgar Square had been so jammed with Londoners that traffic was suspended round Nelson's column for four hours. Now, according to Tomlinson, a rampaging mob of thousands had assembled at the Châlet, with the idea of marching to the French Chambre des Députés and handing in a written protest.

At first it was quiet and controlled, but by the time I raced along the Opéra and reached the area, the mob had got out of hand. A few angry youths, a few officious policemen, started a minor scuffle. It spread with the speed of a brush fire. As the *flics* started swinging their murderous blue capes—the hems lined with lead—the first heads were cracked open. Within minutes infuriated men and women were tearing down railings, paving stones, upturning cars and setting them on fire. The police brought in more reinforcements.

Clanging bells announced the arrival of the first ambulances, but they took away only injured policemen, leaving the Jewish protesters lying on the pavement, ignoring frantic appeals to the police for first aid.

It was then that I saw Olivia Jacobsen. The forward section had reached the quai du Louvre on its way to the Concorde, where the Jews planned to cross the bridge. But police arriving from the other end of the Right Bank started laying into them, even though there was no fighting.

I had parked my car on the opposite bank, near the Pont de Carrousel—not far from the family apartment in the rue des St. Pères. By the time I saw Olivia police were chasing ahead, leaving the wounded to fend for themselves. Between twenty and thirty stunned and bleeding men and women lay stretched on the broad sidewalks bordering the Tuileries.

I had no time to think of the others. I picked up Olivia. She had what looked like a gash on her left forehead—the slanting, narrow split in the flesh that so often comes from a swipe with a policeman's loaded cape—but as I picked her up she actually smiled and said, "Are you one of us?"

"You're too heavy," I joked back. "Here! See if you can make it to the car, then I'll take you home."

She was able to walk, dragging her feet, the strap of one

shoe wrenched off, which made walking difficult, stockings torn, blood on her white blouse. But I felt that she looked worse than she felt, despite the cut.

When I got her upstairs I gave her a stiff *marc* —we never kept brandy in the house—and then went to the kitchen and returned with a basin of hot water and a cloth.

"This'll help." I cradled her head on my shoulder and carefully dabbed the bloodied part of her face. Luckily the bleeding disguised my first impression that the cut was along the forehead. Her forehead was scratched, but not as deeply as the left cheek.

"I'm going to phone for Dr. Malherbe," I decided. "It's not a serious cut, but you might need a couple of stitches to make sure there's no scar on that beautiful face of yours."

"I'll be all right," she said. "Sorry for all the bother I've caused you." Then she almost laughed, "Do you think I could have another *marc?*"

"And get plastered?"

"I won't, I promise you."

Waiting for the doctor, I poured out another large measure, and took one for myself.

"But, Olivia," I said, "you *are* a bit rash, dashing in like that. You could have been killed."

"Somebody had to do something."

"I understand. What's happened to those men and women in Germany is terrible. But you're not *there,* Olivia. A protest in France against the bully boys of Germany is like —swatting a fly."

"It might stop people doing the same thing here," she sounded bitter.

"They'll never behave like that in France. You know that. But I'm frightened for you—you're so fierce about it!"

"It has to be done."

"But was it worth it?"

"My God—of course it was."

"But that poor boy who shot the German—how many deaths has *he* caused?" I asked.

"It's terrible, I know, but it's a kind of war."

"I didn't even know you were in Paris," I said.

"I came specially. I had to help."

"But all the same, Olivia, you can't win the war in a day. You must be more—well, patient, even tolerant."

"Tolerant?" she asked sadly. *"Tolerant* —isn't that just another word for indifference?"

The bell rang. Dr. Malherbe arrived and after a brief examination said firmly that he would give Olivia a local anesthetic and put in two stitches. He finished quickly, packed his bag, and said, "She'll be all right after a good night's rest."

"You'd better stay the night here," I said after the doctor had gone. "Does it hurt?"

She smiled—she had a very warm smile. "Not a bit. But what would your mother say?"

"I think she would understand," I smiled back.

"And," she hesitated, "Sonia, if she knew?"

"Ah, Sonia! She *would* be furious. She does get a bit jealous. Or did."

"You really love her! I've always known it from the way you treated her when we were all at Douzy. I remember the first time I saw you."

"You do?"

She nodded. "Your sports shirt was open at the neck, as though the collar couldn't hold in your vitality, and your tie was knotted loosely, like a multicolored silk necklace. I thought," eyes downcast, "you were very beautiful. And in love with Sonia."

"It's in the past tense now. She's engaged to an Italian diplomat with a title. My bet is she'll marry him, and we'll probably never see each other again. If there's another war, we'd be enemies. Not like you and Guy."

"My art teacher!" she murmured slyly. "If you like to put it that way."

"What other way is there?" I hesitated.

"It's difficult to explain," she lay back on the bed. "I have a kind of warmth for Guy, but you know, Larry, he doesn't own me. And he's away—and you're away too—and Sonia doesn't seem to own you either."

"I love her—even though I had the real brush-off in her last letter to me. I'm sure now we'll never get married."

"Well then," she said gently. "You and I are old friends blooded in battle. And I read somewhere that violence makes people passionate. And you can't take a vow of chastity just because—"

"I never did take one."

"And," she hesitated and smiled again, "my cheek doesn't hurt anymore."

"We shouldn't, Olivia—and yet I do want to."

"Do then," she whispered.

"I don't want to hurt Guy."

"He'll never know. I promise you," adding almost gravely, "just this once. To cement a friendship. Nothing more."

After that there was no question of saying no. Apart from the fact that I was on the rebound from Sonia, there *is* a curious link that binds close friends who are the lovers of others. Where did I read that most married men have an urge to make love to their wife's sister? And, though I had never thought of really loving anyone but Sonia, I wasn't a monk wallowing in self-imposed continence. If I didn't do it as often as most other men I knew, it was because I couldn't be bothered. But this was different. It was an excitement adorned with the quality of friendship. That and the fact that Mama had telephoned after leaving Copenhagen that she had reached Brussels—which meant that she and Guy would be incommunicado until morning. I know I should have harbored feelings of guilt about Guy, but I didn't. And it wasn't as though I had made the first move.

Quite apart from the beauty of Olivia, it was so long since I had made love to a girl—any girl—that I had almost forgotten the feeling of aching pleasure that comes when you are inside the warm, soft, yielding flesh of a woman. For a few moments I lay beside her in my own old bed, the one I used before I moved out. My chest was squeezed against her warm full breasts as if they were cushions, and our pubic hairs scratched each other as she gently and expertly fondled me between my legs. The whole of her body

was the same creamy white as her beautiful face, and
when I started to speak she kissed me quietly.

"No need for words," she whispered. "It's as though
we're two other people."

"You mean it doesn't count," I smiled as I looked at her
body.

"It will count—in your memory," she replied gravely,
and stopped stroking me between the legs, fumbling until
she found and gripped me.

"Do nothing," she almost ordered me, but quietly, then
rolled on top of me, then she gave a secret smile and said,
"This is our way of making love."

I didn't see how it could be that different, but she was exciting, and there was about this strange encounter an ele-
ment of risk, of excitement, of once-and-for-all.

With her left arm holding herself away from me, she
used her right hand to guide me, gently, just touching the
entrance to her with the top of me until I was afraid it
would all be over before I started. Then, still on top of me,
half sitting, she pushed herself until I was inside her.

"I can't wait," it was my turn to groan. "I *can't*, Olivia,
I'm sorry but—"

"You won't come," she kissed me. "Not yet. Can you feel
anything?"

Suddenly as she kissed me again I felt the inside of her
grip me, squeezing me inside her with such force that I
could hardly move. Suddenly the grip relaxed. I was
gasping—with the sheer pleasure of it, the excitement, it
was a feeling I had never experienced.

As I lay there underneath her it came again. I was being
gripped tightly, as though the velvet gloves of her soft inside had suddenly been replaced with the equivalent of an
iron fist. She was so tight round me, I almost cried out with
pleasure or pain. Then she relaxed, then used her muscles
again. And again —and again. Starting me, stopping me,
prolonging the sweet agony until finally, her lips wet with
overkissing, she cried one word, "Ready?"

I gasped out, "Yes, yes."

Almost frantically, she cried, "Quick, quick!"

* * *

Later, as we lay in bed, each decorously wearing a dressing gown, each with a large Scotch and Perrier, I knew that she shared with me the peculiar, if never to be repeated, calm that is almost a sense of relief. It can come only to people who have made love yet who do not really own each other, but rather are long-standing friends like we were, enjoying themselves.

Raising my glass, I toasted her and said, "Olivia, you are fabulous, truly."

"I made you happy?"

"Christ! I've never known anything like it in my life. You're a witch—a sorceress. How do you do it? It's as though you've an extra hand inside of you." I laughed again, and said, "You're out of this world as a lover. How, please?"

She hesitated, but smiling, and I knew she wasn't withholding any secrets. Perhaps, I thought, we just fit. Yet as I watched her, waiting for her to talk to me, I knew it was more than that.

"I know I've got a beautiful white skin," she began tentatively, "because everyone tells me so, but you might be surprised to know that though my father is Jewish and French, my Jewish mother—she's dead now—was half Egyptian. A small half by the look of me," she smiled. "I was born in Alexandria."

"You can be a Hottentot for all I care."

"But I'm explaining," she laughed, and I felt a sudden quiver of pleasure as her dressing gown fell off one shoulder uncovering one creamy, full breast.

"I'm sorry," she saw where I was looking.

"No, don't please—leave it like that. You were explaining." I poured two more Scotches.

"You'll make me drunk," she laughed, and said, "Egyptian Jewish girls are very special. And they have always had the reputation of making wonderful wives. They're," a little more shyly now, "supposed to be very beautiful as well."

"They are—but—"

"Beauty is not enough," she said modestly. "Our mothers always told us that though women were treated as chattels by Egyptian men, a woman could always triumph over a man if she could keep him faithful. So we were taught."

"But how? You can't be born like this."

"We practiced," she said demurely. "From the moment we started to menstruate."

I couldn't believe it—or understand it. All I knew at that moment, looking again at that bared breast, was that she had somehow *gripped* me secretly and at will. I had never known a pleasure even remotely like this—a physical pleasure, not a love pleasure, but a pleasure to be enjoyed time and again, one that made me want to scream with the excitement of making it last forever while at the same time wanting to reach a climax.

"It sounds awful, putting it like this," she explained, "but girls are taught muscle control in order to please our husbands. Now you're making me feel embarrassed."

"Go on—please."

"Give me another drink," she held out her glass. "Then I won't be so embarrassed!"

She took a sip, then lay down, opened her dressing gown, and stroked me. I began to feel stirrings again, and as I touched her between the legs she too showed signs of excitement.

"We shouldn't," she whispered, "but this promise of only once does mean that 'once' can last all night," she had a wry sense of humor and shivered as I touched her again.

"Tell me first, the secret," I said. I wasn't ready yet, only fascinated.

"Put your finger in—go on, inside me," she whispered.

I did—and immediately felt it gripped by her.

She laughed. "It's an old method, practiced by our mothers and their mothers forever. I can't remember who told me—but everyone knew that girls were taught to control their muscles—inside. I used to be told how to sit with my legs as wide apart as I could, and exercise. It was hard at first, but in the end my muscles there were so strong I could control them. And now you know my secret."

And then we made love again. Afterward, she whispered, "Don't be angry with me."

"Angry!" I echoed. "How could I be?"

"And you don't have to feel," she was searching for words, "any sense of—obligation, that's the word."

"I won't, I promise you—so long as you believe that I'm not a very good liar, and I don't want to lie to you, but I do want you to feel—forever—that what happened was a very natural coming together of two people who like each other. Do you understand what I'm trying to say?"

"Perfectly." And almost sleepily, she said, "I hope I pleased you, Larry."

"You know you did. More than I can ever tell you."

"That is *my* reward. Because you pleased me too. I know you'll always be in love with Sonia, but this doesn't count. I said that and I mean it. We're not in love with each other—I'm not even in love with Guy—but I think making love with an old friend you like is the most wonderful experience on earth. And I've just had that. I just wanted," shyly again, "to please you because you are a wonderful person, Larry. And in doing so, I pleased myself as well."

The next morning I drove her to the station. As she jumped into the MG, I examined the strip of plaster on her left cheek.

"Doesn't hurt too much?"

"I'd forgotten all about it," she smiled, but even in the smile there was a special intimacy.

I would have driven her to Douzy, but I didn't dare to leave the office untended.

"I *do* work for a living," I smiled. "You know I'm not the sort who'd spend the night with you and then put you on the nearest bus to get home by yourself. But—"

"That night never happened," she said gravely.

"But something did," I said "and I think I ought to tell you. We *have* changed Olivia. No, it's not love, I'm not going to make an idiot of myself, I just want you to know that from now on I shall always think of you not just as Olivia, but as a member of the Douzy family."

"Thank you for that," she said simply, "and I promise you I'll always behave."

"I know you will."

"But," with the faintest touch of a smile, "it *was* fun, wasn't it?"

"It was wonderful," I replied.

14

THAT WAS WEDNESDAY MORNING. The next afternoon Mama and Guy arrived back at Douzy. On Friday evening I drove home from Paris, arriving too late for dinner.

"What about Anna?" It was the first question I asked after Jean poured me a coffee.

"She's fine," said Guy. "A bit shaken—"

"She's *not* fine!" burst out Mama. "Nothing *happened* to any of us in Düsseldorf, but it was terrible and Anna was in an awful state."

"But if nothing happened?"

"It was the *knowledge* that terrible things *were* happening around us. That non-Jewish people," with a look of apology to Olivia, "were unharmed, untouched. But even with the censorship, people like Willi *knew* of the terrible things taking place—literally round the corner. We all knew. One friend of Willi's who worked with him at Staffens just vanished. Someone went round and found his apartment smashed up."

"Were you hurt? Molested?"

"Not like Olivia here," said Guy.

"You're all right now?" I asked her, carefully casual. "Sorry I didn't ask before."

"Fine," she smiled back, one stranger to another. "I should be thanking you for rescuing me and taking me to the train."

I think all of us were anxious not to *talk* about Anna— though that didn't mean we loved her the less, didn't

197

worry about her, wouldn't have been glad had she come back to Douzy. But casual conversations released the tensions. That was probably why Mama said, "Olivia must have been terrified. Knocked about like that."

"You might have driven her back to Douzy instead of dumping her at the station," Guy said jokingly.

"You try working for a living, sonny," I grinned, "and you'll find there isn't always time to drive a girl seventy miles home."

"Okay," said Guy with mock resignation, "I know I'm just a poor artist. They never work."

"You're very conscientious," Olivia defended him—and I felt the faintest twinge of jealousy.

"It's time you got a *real* job." Grandma didn't realize that Guy was being sarcastic, she really believed that artists didn't work, just dashed off the occasional picture when inspired.

"When are you taking the stitches out?" I asked Olivia.

"Day after tomorrow." We both spoke with studied normalcy, as though that eventful Tuesday evening never *had* really taken place, that it was just a dream.

During the morning I took the MG to the small working garage behind the stables, for one of the mufflers on the exhaust pipe wasn't working properly and I needed help. "It smells of burning," I said to Gaston.

"I'll look underneath."

"Sure you're not too exhausted after the trip?" I asked him.

"Take more than that to tire me," he grinned and disappeared under the car, finally shouting, "You need a complete new exhaust unit. The old one's cracked, burned through. I'll phone Paris to have one delivered to your office, then I'll fit it on your next visit home."

Gaston had a knack of sliding out from under a car, and when he stood up, wiping his hands on a bit of rag, I said, "Thanks. Hope you weren't too bored in Germany."

"Not a bit," he grinned, showing beautiful teeth. "It was a change. I prefer our wine but—"

"I'm told the German girls are hot stuff!"

"Not for me. Too dumpy."

"Anyway, thanks." I walked back into the house, saying to Mama, "I don't know how we'd manage without Gaston."

"Why do you say that?" asked Mama.

I shrugged my shoulders. "Nothing special—except that he's not only a good mechanic, he's so—well, even-tempered." Then changing the subject, I asked, "What about Anna? We must do something about her."

"She loves Willi—that's the real—well, I don't like to use the word *problem* about two people who are crazy about each other, but you know what I mean," sighed Mama.

"Then there's nothing to be done, *nothing,*" said Papa.

"And what does Willi think?"

"He says it's all madness. He was very upset, especially about that friend of his in the business, but he does believe it'll all pass over."

"Did you ever suggest—yes, *suggest,* but *delicately,* my dear—that Anna might—well—a vacation in Douzy. Perhaps stay here for—"

"I did, carefully," Mama said to Papa. "Anna was very angry—she said I was trying to break up their marriage. I said it wasn't true—and Willi said Anna was exaggerating. Willi is convinced that all this Hitler business will blow over."

"Perhaps it will," I said, lying.

"The trouble is"—Mama was trying to explain her attitude—"that the *feeling* is so awful. We knew that not far away the Fascists were behaving like beasts, but we never *saw* anything. And when we got lost on the way to a museum, a policeman with a car actually told us to follow him and led us all the way."

"All in the cause of art," I laughed to Guy.

"I wasn't there. Probably the policeman took a fancy to Mama driving behind Gaston in their flashy car."

"You missing out on art!" I *was* surprised.

"Oh, no, I wasn't," said Guy. "Anna took me to a staggering modern-life class. There's no way you can get in without special permission—she fixed it. Mama wanted to go to the famous Museum of the Ages. It's Düsseldorf's greatest reason for existence."

Later that evening when Mama and I chanced to be alone, I said teasingly, "In fact, darling Mama, you seem to thrive on terrifying experiences. I know you must have been very worried about Anna—"

"I am."

"But, well, you look as though the change—however brutal —has done you good."

"I think it did. It took me out of myself."

"You look so young—and—the word is *vibrant.*"

"It did me good to see Anna. But vibrant? That sounds a wonderful thing to say." She kissed me gently. "Mmmm. Vibrant. Yes, I like that."

"It's wonderful what mother love can do," I murmured. "Would you look so happy if you were seeing me after a few weeks away?"

She *did* look attractive. There was a sparkle to her eyes, she seemed to walk with a spring in her step.

"I haven't seen you looking so exciting for years," I said. "It's a good thing you had Guy as a chaperon. We don't want another German in the family." I was thinking of another day, another time, when she had also looked beautiful and happy beyond the normal.

"Of course," I cried, "I remember now. You remind me of that day when we had lunch together at the Pré Catelan. You remember, I told you then, I'd never seen you look so beautiful, as though you were in love all over again."

"Silly boy," she kissed me on the cheek again. But not before I saw that those beautiful soft cheeks of hers were tinted with the faintest of blushes.

So the summer dragged on, a strange mixture of forced gaiety disguising the apprehension.

"It's funny how much happier I feel about Germany now that I've actually seen Anna's apartment," said Mama one evening. "I can picture her whenever I want to. I'm not half as worried as I was."

"You've no need to be, really," said my father. "I was lunching with Bill Bullitt yesterday, and he's convinced that Hitler is bluffing."

"There's no need to bluff if you're holding a straight flush," Oregon still enjoyed the occasional game of poker.

"You mean he isn't bluffing?" asked Miss Barron, who had come in for drinks.

"Half and half, I *think* so, yes," said Papa. "All these threats about Czechoslovakia. It's a bluff in a way because he senses that France doesn't really want to get into a war. He trades on that—yes, *trades* on it."

"I won't listen to a son of mine saying the French don't want to fight," said Grandma angrily. "They're the finest army in the world. We should thrash the Germans now—declare war immediately."

"They'd need help," ventured Jean-Pierre, who had also come in for drinks. "Would England fight?"

"There's not going to be a war," said Mama.

"No, Britain wouldn't fight, not at this time," said Oregon.

"We don't need Britain," Grandma snorted with finality, as though that problem had been solved, adding with a toss of her head, "we're better off without them"

Rashly I ventured, "I'm not so sure about that," but as Grandma started to bristle I caught sight of Mama, the trace of a sardonic smile lighting her face as she gave a tiny shake of her head. No use getting involved in an argument. I smiled my agreement back to Mama, though I was too late, for Grandma continued firmly, "You should read more history, my boy—learn from it, learn the lessons of France's greatest leaders. Have you read the new biography on Napoleon?" And without waiting for an answer, she continued, almost with relish, "No! I thought not. Very silly of you. It's called *If Napoleon Lived Now!* That would put the Germans in their place."

I dearly wanted to blurt out that Napoleon hadn't shown how to put the Russians in their place, so why should his ghost succeed against the German army of today? But I didn't like to disagree so angrily, even though most reviews had panned the book.

Even so, I *was* worried about Hitler. I wasn't worried by actual threats—not any more than the average healthy young American could be worried. It was the unreal atmosphere in Paris that summer which left me vaguely disturbed, as if the city were determined to dance the night away until the dawn, knowing it would be bad.

There had never been a summer like it! There were an astonishing three million foreigners in Paris, many living there, others visiting. They included fourteen thousand Americans living in Paris, plus all the visitors, bringing with them bulging wallets and insatiable appetites for a good time. To the dismay of French purists, pretty girls on the boulevards, using their own new slang, some said they had had a "spiffy" evening—especially if their escort looked "snazzy." Love letters from America started reaching France with the letters CYK on the envelope! "Consider Yourself Kissed."

The brooding image of Germany was so evident that I found myself using slang words borrowed directly from Hitler. On the dance floor a man complained, "Hey there! I can't move. Give us a bit more lebensraum." When I went shopping at the *marché* in the rue du Seine, one American who lived in the neighborhood warned me, "Don't like the flavor of those *saucisson* over there. They're a bit ersatz."

The packed hotels, the rowdy night clubs in turn attracted top entertainers. Maurice Chevalier returned from Hollywood to sing at the Casino de Paris. The Negro boxer Panama Al Brown won a fight in Paris and promptly doubled his fee by tap-dancing at the Cirque Medrano, the most famous circus in Europe. As if to provide an extra dollop of ice cream for the big spenders, the king and queen arrived in Paris from London in mid-July. The Hotel Crillon was decked out in cloth of gold. The fountains at the Rond-Point des Champs-Elysées managed to color the water, giving the impression that the most beautiful fountains in Europe were spraying gold dust. The visit caused the biggest traffic jam ever known in the capital, which went wild with excitement. "The French love royalty," said Oregon dryly. "They must be darned mad they cut off all those royal heads and did away with the system."

It *was* exciting—but it *was* make-believe. Until in September the warning bell in the office announced a flash on the Associated Press teleprinter.

The French government had devalued the franc. And that—to politicians, let alone men like Oregon and Tomlinson—meant a political rather than a financial crisis, the one brought on by the other.

True, the Americans thought it great news. Until September 193€, you got twenty-nine francs for your dollar. With devaluation you got thirty-seven. The British now got one hundred seventy-eight to the pound sterling instead of one hundred forty-seven. It couldn't be bad—for those on holiday.

For the world outside, though, the fall in the franc—which had decreased by over fifty percent in two years—was the signal everyone had been waiting for: that the mounting tension between Germany and Czechoslovakia had reached bursting point —one in which the French government was deeply involved. Within days France and Germany were poised on the abyss of war.

"But how does France come into this?" asked Miss Brewer, who had come with Miss Barron for a quiet supper at Douzy.

"It's simple really," explained Oregon. "Czechoslovakia is France's most powerful continental neighbor. The two countries have a mutual defense pact, binding each one to fight if she's attacked. Now that Hitler is threatening to take over the Sudeten Czechs—and that will eventually mean the entire country—President Benes of Czechoslovakia is demanding that France stand by its treaty obligations."

"And the other countries?" asked Mama.

"They're not in it," said Oregon. "Britain, for example, doesn't have any defense treaty with the Czechs."

That evening Tommy Tomlinson phoned that he had

been ordered to Germany for a few days. Would I pinch-
hit? I arrived on the Monday morning just as he was
shoving some carbon paper into his typewriter case.

"I'll bet Daladier's scared," he grinned, "to say nothing
of that arch creep Georges Connet. He might be foreign
minister, but he's the biggest appeaser in the business.
And that's saying something." To me he added, "Mind the
shop. I hear tell that Daladier's going to London to beg,
steal, or borrow some help, even if it's only words."

"I don't see Britain offering to fight a war for France,"
said Oregon. "But France might try to get help of another
sort. After all, Churchill said the other day that if France
and Germany went to war, England would be drawn in."

Fortunately for Mama's tattered nerves, telephoning to
Germany had become normal again, comparatively easy;
unlike France and Italy, Germany was efficient, the operators rang the numbers you asked for. And Anna didn't
seem in the slightest degree worried.

"It's all talk, Mama," she said. "The Germans don't
want a war, and we're not going to have one. It's tub
thumping, that's all. Did I tell you we're just buying a new
Mercedes? An office car, but I'll be able to drive it."

But the shouting didn't die down. Instead the momentum of tension and fear increased, sweeping across all
France. Daladier did fly to London, and as a result Chamberlain agreed to fly to Germany to try as an "honest bro-
ker" to persuade Hitler to moderate his demands. He spent
several hours with Hitler at Berchtesgaden, the Führer's
mountain retreat, but when the awkward, shambling figure of Chamberlain returned to Heston, then London's airport, it was clear that his mission had failed.

That was the moment when panic set in. Overnight the
face of France seemed to change, as though the cheerful
mask of those summer months had been ripped off by a
mugger. It was not so much the nauseating sight of the
rich fleeing Paris in their expensive cars, but the immediate preparations for a war that everyone knew France
could never win. It was as though Hitler had told the
French via the British government that Germany would

not hesitate to fight, knowing that the French *couldn't* fight, whereupon the French—who also knew that Hitler was more powerful—decided to bluff the Germans by preparing to fight.

Overnight practically every fit man in the country under sixty was mobilized—two and a half million of them.

Overnight there wasn't a mechanic, a plumber, a carpenter to be found in Paris and other big cities. Yet there was no immediate threat of war. It was serious, yes, but the Germans were still talking. Chamberlain decided to make another attempt to save Europe, flying off within the week to see Hitler and try again, leaving a Paris shrouded in hooded street lamps, with piles of sand at every corner as the only defense against incendiary bombs.

The panic spread even to the Americans, for Jim Parks phoned me at Douzy to tell me that the State Department was planning to evacuate all fourteen thousand American residents in Paris.

"And if you take my tip," he said, "you'll get your folks away before the rush starts."

"He's right," said my father when I told him. And turning to Mama, he said with more firmness than he usually displayed, "My dear, you must go—really, very quickly. For once, I am determined, really *determined.*"

"You can be as determined as you like," retorted Mama cheerfully. "I'm not going anywhere—not while Anna is in Germany."

"But you must—"

"I won't." It was one of the few times I saw her eyes glint with anger at my father. "And anyway, even if there is a war, it won't be our problem."

All the same, it sounded ominous. I was horrified the following day when I saw Jim Parks. "You may be a hero," he grinned, "but the State Department doesn't rate your chances of survival in France very high. We've just anchored two American cruisers off Brest."

"Two *cruisers!*"

"Sure. They're there to take off the U.S. citizens who're anxious to leave."

The American embassy, where I had gone to see Parks for a story, looked like the headquarters of a besieged city. Stocks of food, gasoline, with fleets of vehicles, had all been prepared so Americans could reach Brest.

"And then?"

"All U.S. nationals will be given temporary refuge in camps being prepared on the island of Madeira."

"Always wanted to visit there," I laughed.

"Now's your chance," said Jim laconically.

Everyone had forgotten Chamberlain, who had returned from his second—and apparently abortive—visit to Germany. Many Frenchmen were anti-British anyway and derided him, for Chamberlain could hardly be described as *sympathique*. If not downright ugly, he didn't inspire confidence—any more for that matter than Daladier did. The British fleet—the world's greatest—was mobilized "as a precautionary measure" on September 27, and another wave of fear gripped France, with everyone desperately trying to clutch at any straws.

The straws, however, were just out of reach—until two days later when, with an electric suddenness, with a kind of excitement that really did hit you with the force of an electric shock, Daladier announced that he was flying to Munich to meet Hitler. The conference had been arranged by the forgotten Chamberlain, who would also fly to Germany. Mussolini was arriving by train.

"Well, that's that," said Oregon to Mama. "You can relax. Europe's okay—for the time being anyway. The big powers would never risk a full-blooded conference unless they'd fixed everything in advance. It's got the sweet smell of success."

I didn't realize Oregon was being sarcastic until he added bitterly, "And the sour stink of a sellout. That's the end of the Czechs—they haven't been invited. They're being sold down the river."

Oregon was right. When the conference ended Chamberlain waved his piece of paper and cried, "It is peace for our time." Europe went mad with relief. I was at Le Bourget airport for Daladier's arrival. The long, low terminal

building, the apron behind, the parking spaces, even the
main highway were jammed solid with rejoicing people.
Men wept with joy—or relief. Strangers rushed up and
kissed each other as though they had just won a war, instead of, well, avoiding one. All sense of shame evaporated.
"France has been saved," someone next to me cried. Later
in the Deux Magots, it was drinks all around on the house.
Within hours President Roosevelt's photo—and a translation of his two messages of encouragement—were printed
in tens of thousands, to be pasted on every shop window,
every wall.

"I don't care," cried Mama when she hugged me as I returned to Douzy at the weekend. "I know I should feel
ashamed and sorry for the Czechs, I know I *should*. But I
don't feel any shame, darling. I only feel a sense of relief.
And, when I think of those awful days in Düsseldorf, and
poor Anna, I can't feel anything but gratitude to that Mr.
Chamberlain for what he has achieved."

Europe thought as Mama did. I showed her a copy of *Paris-Soir.* "They've opened a special fund," I told her before
Papa arrived back from the pyramid.

"For what?" she asked.

"You guess. To help elderly cripples? Or cancer victims?
Go on, you guess."

"I never was any good at riddles."

"It's a fund," I spoke slowly, "being raised by grateful
readers of *Paris-Soir* to buy Neville Chamberlain a retirement villa with a trout stream somewhere in France."

"I would like to send a subscription to the paper"—
Mama was almost in tears—"to say thank you—from Anna
and me."

A week later I received the first letter for weeks from
Sonia, and before I tore it open, even while I was looking at
the illustration of the pyramids on the Egyptian stamp, I
knew the news would be bad.

It was. She had married, and her husband, the Count de
Feo, had been posted to Paris as ambassador-without-
portfolio.

15

I WAS DETERMINED on one thing: it was over between Sonia and me. She was married and in a way I was thankful; it would save me from complications. I had been uncomfortable enough, lying and deceiving, as the lover of a woman engaged to be married to another. And though I knew that many married women had boy friends, the deceit wasn't for me.

The feeling I had for Sonia was still confused. At bottom, everything was passion. A passion that overruled instincts which reason dictated should be kept in check; nothing to do really with marriage. She was not only Russian-wild but jejune on the subject of marriage. I don't think she was ever really anxious to get married to me.

When I told Oregon—before anyone else, as Sonia's letters were always sent to the office—he had a theory of his own.

"Sonia's problem is very simple," he explained. "She's never really grown up. She's got a childhood fixation, perhaps because her parents meant so little to her. She missed out on a childhood with them. So she's making up for it now."

"Sounds a bit steep—a bit Freudian."

"It's true," he insisted. "She's not really marrying this de Feo—at least she thinks she isn't, she's playing with her dolls. And all this nonsense you've told me about in the past—the blind obedience to her parents! I'm not denigrating Sonia—I adore her as much as you—but she regards

them in the same way as a teenager. They're a symbol of
authority—they have to be obeyed without question."

Was that true? I wondered. She told me once that her
ideal marriage would be to the kind of husband who wasn't
too demanding. What an awful recipe for happiness, I remember thinking. Had Sonia tried to relive the past, the
happy days at Douzy when Monsieur Coquelicot slid under
her blankets at night? Did she still feel like that? After all,
I was thinking as I reread her letter, sometimes first love
can be best love. But this one had lasted long enough.

And, of course, people change. Does a girl change just because she becomes a wife? How, I wondered, had Sonia
changed? After all, *I* had changed, I could view her marriage with some impartiality. Distance, a change of circumstances on her part, an increasing absorption with
work on mine.

All the same, I couldn't help feeling sad at the finality of
it all. Sonia had written that "my husband and I"—and
that did give me a nasty jolt, seeing it above her dashing,
upward slanting signature—"expect to reach Paris around
April."

She would, she wrote, be allotted the same home her parents had occupied in Paris, one which I had visited several
times. It was in the rue de Longchamp, almost at the corner by the river, a long, low house with a beautiful garden
completely ringed by trees, which effectively screened it
from neighbors, making it a perfect setting for garden
lunches or cocktail parties. And since the house was owned
and staffed by the Italian embassy, the food and drink
were as good as any in Paris.

I couldn't help a wry smile, and I told Oregon, in the *PA*
office, where the new Contessa de Feo was going to live.

"Hope the food's as good," I said.

"Under the same management, it should be. But you
keep away," he grunted.

"But if I get invited—in the cause of duty?"

Oregon hesitated, looked at me, his gray hair like a
curly wig round his bald pate, his lapels covered as usual

with a trail of ash, a man who had steered me steadfastly on the road to journalism.

"I hope not," he said, deliberately pausing to light one Gauloise with the butt of the first. "No, no! Don't get mad. She's a great girl—and when I think of what you two have been up to for all these years, I'm jealous as hell of my wasted youth! Lucky dog! But you're no longer a carefree youth, you're moving forward, you're on the way to big things. And she's bad news for you."

"I can take care of myself," I said shortly, not sure whether to be annoyed.

"That's just the problem. Where Sonia's concerned, you can't—and even worse, *she* can't. You attract each other like iron filings in front of a magnet."

"Well, this time it'll be different."

"Hope so. Care to bet?"

"Ten bucks?"

"Make it fifty." And more seriously, Oregon added, "Watch it, Larry. And remember, you'll be a neutral when—not if, anymore—when the war comes. And being American you'll have a head start as a neutral newspaperman in Europe, specially on the *Globe*. Don't spoil it. You're going right to the top of the heap."

Mama gave me a similar comment when at the weekend she learned that Sonia and her husband were coming to Paris to live. It wasn't really a warning so much as a sigh of relief.

"I know you used to love her, Larry, probably you still carry a torch for her." She was arranging a mass of roses in her favorite blue and white Chinese bowl. "So I'm glad for *your* sake that Sonia's married. So much more final."

I almost laughed. "It *is* final," I promised her, "though not for that reason, but because I want it that way. Being married has nothing to do with still being in love has it? Lots of married women have boy friends. Why shouldn't Sonia?"

"You've been reading too many romantic novels!"

"I've not! What I say is true!"

"You *are* a romantic. Books or no books. Pass me the pruning shears, please."

"So are you," I handed them to her. "And sometimes, Mama, I wonder about you. I've seen a sparkle in *your* eyes that makes me think twice."

"At my age! Don't make me laugh. You ought to be ashamed of yourself." But all the same I could see that the notion pleased her.

"For telling the truth?" I asked.

"For making up romantic nonsense."

"Well," I grew suddenly serious, "tell me, Mama—you and I, we've never had any secrets—dare I ask you?"

"No, you daren't," she was suddenly sharp tongued.

"Sorry," I apologized.

"That's all right." Suddenly she put down the vase and left the room abruptly. But, I wondered, were her eyes shining —or was that the beginning of a tear as she walked quickly from the room?

The early part of 1939, before Sonia's arrival, followed the same political pattern of the previous months: euphoria born of relief, all shame ignored, hidden like dirt brushed guiltily under the carpet.

There was even a new vacation idea to rival the normal skiing or winter-sunshine holidays of winter. A French travel agent was advertising a regular five-day all-included *Voyage de la Paix*—from Paris to Germany, with stopovers at Munich, Nuremberg, Bad Godesberg, and Berchtesgaden. It was organized by the Compagnie Française de Tourisme, and it was a sellout.

"Nice choice of words," said Oregon dryly when I told him.

But long before that, of course, the Germans had marched into the Sudetenland in a deal that spared the rest of Europe—but not poor Czechosolovakia—the agony of war.

I had no news from Sonia, and though we all wrote to her and her husband—polite letters of congratulation—I deliberately made no inquiries about the proposed date of her

arrival. Apart from anything else, I was kept busier then
ever before. There were political stories to be covered when
Tommy was busy or away, as when he accompanied Daladier on a flag-waving visit to Algeria, Tunis, and Corsica—a
ploy to offset Mussolini's demands. When he returned he
asked me if I would like to visit the tattered remnants of
five hundred Americans who had volunteered to fight in
the Spanish civil war and who had suffered terribly during
the closing stages.

The civil war was all but over, a towering defeat for
those who had fought against Franco for freedom. Hundreds of thousands of refugees had fled across the frontier
and were living in hastily erected camps near Perpignan.
Conditions were appalling. Guarded by Senegalese, they
were virtually without food. The lucky ones had a single
blanket and slept on the ground. The vanquished who had
fought against tyranny were dying every day, even as the
foreign powers duly recognized the Franco regime.

My brief was to search out the remnants of the Fifteenth
International Brigade and write a story of the survivors.
There weren't many left to interview. Out of about five
hundred under the command of their American leader, Robert Hale Merriman, four hundred were either killed or
missing. The picture of those bedraggled yet heroic men
haunted me, and one night when I dreamed of the faces I
had seen, I somehow mixed them up with Anna's.

Mama had been to Düsseldorf, for a second trip to see
Anna, soon after the turn of the year. There had been no
violence, no anti-Jewish pogroms on this occasion, but
even so, when Mama returned home, she was very depressed. She had invited Willi and Anna to come to France
for a holiday, but apparently everyone in Germany now
faced difficulties in getting exit permits.

"I just have the awful feeling," Mama told us, "that
they're prisoners—a jail without bars. After all, you *should*
be free to go abroad if you want, but when the German government won't let you *leave* the country without signing
dozens of forms, it's the same thing as prison."

"But why, I really don't see the *reason,*" said Papa.

"The Germans say it's because they won't allow anyone any foreign exchange. The deutschemark is in a terrible state."

"But that's nonsense," said my father. "If we pay for their holiday, really, it's no drain on the wretched Germans."

I tried to cheer up Anna on long-distance, speaking regularly to her on the office phone. During the spring I had an increasingly vague, disturbed feeling that she wasn't really happy—nothing to do with not loving Willi, more the misery of living in a country doomed to dictatorship. The threat stood out to anyone who cared to see—and to poor Anna, with memories of Douzy, it must have been hard to bear. We had discussed a possible holiday for her—could she come to Douzy for a month?

I only hoped she would be allowed to, for Hitler was tightening his grip. The original sellout at Munich had—by arrangement with the big powers—given autonomy to the Sudetens, but in March Hitler flouted his earlier promises made at Munich and marched straight into Czechoslovakia.

The French president and Mme. Lebrun were on a state visit to London at the time. The glittering scenes, with Mme. Lebrun dressed magnificently by Worth, the Paris couturier, and the queen in her tiara, were shown on newsreels in the French cinema—together with film of the German entry into Prague.

Probably the irony passed unnoticed, for to many French men and women Czechoslovakia was an unknown country, a hybrid one, and if anyone had ever heard of the Czechs, it was as an exporter of cheap gloves, boots, and Czech glass. As for fighting for this unknown country—to the average Frenchman the idea seemed senseless.

All the same, Daladier was immediately granted wider powers in the Assembly to speed rearmament—and the man who had to find the necessary cash was Paul Reynaud, who had been raised from his post in Justice to become minister of finance—a big step up the ladder.

"Not that *anything* makes any sense anymore," Papa sighed. "No *really!* Whatever happens, everyone is going to lose, yes, *lose.*"

"Especially here!" Oregon had come, as he often did, for the weekend, and I was spending the morning with them in the white and mysterious Douzy Pyramid, which was still, even after all these years, invested for me with an eeriness when I looked up to the tiny hole far above and imagined how, centuries ago, the Romans had started digging for chalk.

Spring was a critical time for Papa, for last year's 1938 champagne crop had been allowed to reach the high point of the first fermentation—the first of the two fermentations that would eventually make the champagne sparkle and pure. For at this time—spring—it was not a sparkling but a still wine. It still had to be blended. Papa, with his flair for blending different wines, was quite at home with all the paraphernalia needed to mix different champagne wines from different localities. Even the grapes grown half a mile from the next vineyard had a different taste, and the skill of producing the best champagne in the world lay in mixing all the different wines together—through tasting and selection—to get a balance that suited Papa. He was the final arbiter.

"Taste this," said Papa, "and tell me what you think."

Papa knew that my knowledge of champagne was negligible, but he liked to feel that this was a family concern, even though I was writing and Guy was painting.

"Actually it *does* taste good," I tasted a sip from another vineyard. "We don't need to use any old wines from previous years, do we?"

Papa shook his head, delighted. If a crop from any particular year, like this one from 1938, hadn't been quite up to standard, Papa would have mixed in champagne from previous years, all stored deep down in the cellars; but once you added years to a new batch, the champagne couldn't legally be classed as "vintage."

"But this one *will* be vintage—hopefully," said a beaming Papa. "We can mix enough of the thirty-eight crop without adding any other years—and that will make a good wine."

It wasn't champagne yet, of course. Papa had to add a small quantity of cane sugar and fermenting agents, then put it in bottles, resting in cool, deep cellars while the fermenting agents reacted slowly on the sugar, causing the head. And even then, after months, the bottles had to be skillfully opened to get rid of the deposit—and closed before the bubbles escaped.

"But that's a helluva way off," sighed Oregon, "and I wonder if there'll be anyone to drink it by then—or to come down to this pyramid. It's sad—a sort of a second home to the Astells."

"I wonder," Papa washed his hands under the running cold tap. "We've just started to get over the Russian Revolution and Prohibition and—and now? Just when the British market was starting to pick up too. It really is very discouraging."

"Well, there's not going to be any champagne in England if war comes," I said.

"You're sure right," said Oregon. "Seems a long time since that fat old womanizer Henry the Eighth used to keep a special envoy at Ay, barely ten miles from Douzy— yes, all year round, just to buy wines for him. Even though they didn't sparkle in those days."

The de Feos arrived in spring to take up their post in Paris, and almost before they had settled in at the rue de Longchamp, Sonia telephoned Mama. Mama, not me, which I found irritating and significant—as though she, like me, were not about to reopen pleasurably self-inflicted wounds.

I could also tell from Mama's replies, the excitement in her voice, what was happening.

"How wonderful for you, Sonia. Yes, I'm sure we'd love to come. Your *first* party as a diplomat's wife." Pause. "Sonia darling, we didn't send a present, it was all so sudden." Pause. "It's just a party to meet your husband and his friends? Oh yes, of course, your friends too." Pause.

"Two weeks, on Thursday? Of course. If there is anything else, we'll cancel." Laughs. "And your husband—it's terrible of me not to remember his name." Pause. "Of course, Francesco, so beautiful. Yes, Larry is doing very well—of course he'll want to come." Pause. "No, Sonia, I can't say I'm really happy about poor Anna. I went to see her just after Christmas. But the world's in such a state, who knows *what's* going to happen." Pause. "Yes, they adore each other, but sometimes I get depressed about her future." Pause. "Yes, I've noted the date, all very informal, but as soon as you can, you and your husband must come to Douzy for the weekend."

"That was Sonia." Mama finally put down the phone.

"I rather gathered that," I replied shortly, to mark my disapproval—no, irritation is the better word—that she hadn't even asked to say hello to me. After all she was *my* girl, not Mama's. Or, I suppose, had been.

Mama looked at me a little oddly. She always could detect any nuances in my voice. However, she decided to say nothing, except to add, a little too brightly, "Sonia's giving an informal party for her friends—and Francesco's. We're all invited. I sometimes can't believe she's married, a *contessa*, the wife of an ambassador. And still only twenty-five."

"At least she's not a mother yet," I replied.

"You'll come, won't you?"

"I might," I said airily. "Depends on my engagements." I knew I would, of course, if only out of curiosity.

I had forgotten how beautiful the garden looked behind the rue de Longchamp. It didn't depend on masses of blooms arranged in symmetrical flower beds cut up into crescents or circles. It had always been more of a wild garden, with a mass of green trees forming a semicircular backdrop. Instead of beds the flowers had been arranged in ochre pots, Italian style—hundreds of them, some grouped round the trees, others clustered round the steps leading from the terrace, which I had last visited to meet Sonia's parents when they lived there. It seemed odd that though

Riccardi had never owned this embassy house, his wife had
been the mistress there, and now Sonia was the mistress of
the same house.

There was no protocol on this occasion, but there was a
casual, cheerful "line" so that as the guests arrived—some
known to Sonia, others only to her husband—people
queued up near the doors to the main salon to shake hands
or touch cheeks with perfunctory kisses, and offer their
congratulations, before passing on to diplomatic flunkies
bearing salvers laden with drinks.

We entered as a group. Until she saw us she wore a
slightly fixed smile of welcome, the sort duplicated in a
thousand embassies the world over. But then Mama and
Papa came just ahead of us, and Sonia's face broke into the
old, warm, all-embracing smile and her entire face seemed
to change.

"Mama! I can call you that?" She laughed and kissed
Mama and Papa. "It's wonderful to see you," and with a
whispered aside, "as soon as I've met the last of Francesco's friends, I'll come and look for you. I can't get used,
really, to this formality."

Then to her husband, "Francesco, this is Mummy's
great friend, Mrs. Astell, my godmother, and her husband.
They almost brought me up."

He seemed a very pleasant man—tall, brown hair, good
face, chiseled with a straight Italian nose—and he immediately grasped Mama's hand and said, "I feel I've known
you all my life. I've heard so much about all your family."

"And this is Larry, and this is Guy Astell." She looked
at us both, kissed us on the cheeks, and suddenly I found
my heart pounding.

She looked more beautiful than I could ever remember
her. Absence lending an added enchantment? No, it wasn't
that. Her blue-black hair was done in a different way,
more formal, not the sort of hair she used to shake out
when she wanted to kiss me suddenly and it was falling
over her eyes. The hairdo of a woman rather than a girl.
That was it, she looked more grown-up. Lips painted a different color, nail polish to match. Now, married to another,

Sonia had reached the ultimate moment of peerless beauty. The schoolgirl who had fallen in love with Monsieur Coquelicot had been replaced by a person who exceeded the promise of the past.

She looked at me, magically silent—yes, even though she was talking, making introductions, small talk, she was still magically silent within herself. I knew she was occupied with thoughts of us, as though telling me in secret, "Life has thrust us apart, but I was yours before anyone else possessed me, and I gave you everything I had to make you happy."

For a moment I wondered if her husband could hear my thumping heart. I shook hands and Francesco muttered some polite greeting; and I wondered, too, whether Sonia's father had ever said anything to him about us. But of course no one was even remotely noticing my heartbeats, and as for Sonia's husband, he had the true trained diplomat's face. Not by the slightest gesture, hesitation, or sudden emotion did he deviate from the automatic gestures of a warm greeting to old family friends of his wife's. You have to be trained to look like that, I thought. A diplomat's disguise—it covers any emotion, from jealousy to boredom.

As at most parties, Papa and Mama knew a fair sprinkling of the other guests, and so did I for that matter, but as soon as she could Sonia came across to us and hugged Mama again.

"Tell me first," she said, "how's Anna? You must miss her dreadfully."

It seemed hard to realize that this self-possessed Sonia, who had been Anna's lifelong friend, had years ago engineered Anna's phony illness so that I could drive Sonia alone from Rolle. And passed that truly eventful night which had started all our loving. And now, Sonia was married, and so was Anna, living in different countries, knowing hardly anything about each other's lives.

"I'm worried about her," sighed Mama, and after Papa had made some noncommittal remark and Guy had met an old friend who was also studying art, Sonia said, "And you,

Larry? I heard from someone that you're now the top man
on the *Globe.*"

"Hardly! That must be Oregon talking—he always
thinks in the future."

"But work goes well? Still," the slightest hesitation,
"still happy?"

I would have given the world to think up a brilliant retort off the cuff. But I could only say, "Sure. And you?"

"As well as can be expected."

A gushing middle-aged lady rushed up to her and kissed
Sonia on both cheeks profusely, and wouldn't stop talking,
and as others moved around her, I realized how beautifully
dressed she was. She had always been well dressed, but I
used to say in those days that she looked like a rich
playgirl slumming on the Left Bank. She had dressed then
with the simplicty of youth. Now she had an added sheen
of beauty. She wore a pale blue silk crepe outfit, almost severe in its line, looking at first like a dress, but which was
in fact a two-piece affair, with tiny self-buttons at her
waist and wrists.

Mama, I realized suddenly, was watching me with an
amused smile. "That dress is a marvel," she whispered to
me. "It'd make even a fat woman slim. But then it's a
Mainbocher."

"How can you tell, Mama?"

"To be frank, I'm surprised. I thought that as the wife of
an Italian diplomat Sonia might *have* to wear clothes made
in Italy. But it's made by 'Main' all right. I can tell his
work anywhere. His flair sticks out, as though he's sewn
his trademark all over the outside of the dress."

The garden was soon crowded, and I was busy being civil
to people I had never met before. It was so strange seeing
Sonia again, so different yet the same, name different, status changed, an ex-schoolgirl now a diplomat's wife, married to an apparently agreeable husband.

Mama looked relieved that I had accepted the situation
so cheerfully. I never quite knew what Mama felt—what
son does?—but I had the feeling that the romantic streak
in her imagined me starting a fight with Sonia's husband.

Of course it was nonsense. Papa was much more down to earth. Probably he had long since forgotten our youthful indiscretion and presumed that I felt the same way. Only Oregon, with that conspiratorial twinkle behind the fringe of white hair, knew how I felt—or might feel.

It was strange for me though, because, despite the promises I had made to myself, the words of banality which she offered seemed strangely unreal—"Have another drink," "Do try this caviar," "I'd like you to meet Mr. and Mrs. Johnson," "Yes, the trees are beautiful at this time of the year."

I seemed to be aware of other drinks, other food, other people, other trees, other times, whatever she said to me. She didn't *do* anything. She laughed and joked and spoke the jargon of the day. She smiled politely to everyone —what she had once described to me as "putting on my standard party smile." She introduced me to other guests, but though the movements of her eyes, her hands even, the way she spoke, smiled even, were totally normal, there was an almost imperceptible secret movement to every action. I knew that very first evening of the party that she was thinking as I thought: that though Europe might be poised on the brink of war, we faced an equally dangerous future—we were again poised on the brink of love.

When later, back home, I tossed and turned through a night when sleep eluded me, I tried to recall in my mind the series of secret signals she had emitted, yet which no other person in the garden could see, extrasensory signals, like the unheard noises of some birds who can communicate with each other by sounds humans can't ever hear. We were like that.

I was thinking of the past, too, all gone, remembering for no reason half-forgotten moments which had made up our joint lives—the night I hurt my hand, the giggles and laughter when she tried to tie my bow for my dinner jacket. We had been going to someone else's diplomatic party that evening. Or the way we passed the later evenings, circumspectly, after she had become engaged to de Feo, planned excursions to our favorite hidden restaurant.

Lying there unable to sleep, the latest Steinbeck un-
read, I turned over the imaginary pages of another book,
my own life story, some of which I had reread many times,
and yet, as I lay there, I was hesitating, almost afraid to
turn the page over and start a new chapter.

Of course the thought that we could meet as "friends"
and cheerfully relegate all the memories of our past to
semi-oblivion was doomed from the start. I fought against
it, I even quarreled in an attempt to prevent a return to the
past. I really tried. I know Sonia did too, but she had more
of a volatile temperament than I had. She was apt to become "Russian" at a moment's notice, as she did the time
when we met during the Harvard Glee Club ball some
weeks later.

Bill Bullitt had organized the ball in Paris to honor the
visit of the Harvard Glee Club, and he had spared no ex-
pense. "Everyone," was invited, including the Astell family en masse. There were two bands playing in turn in the
main embassy ballroom, and in the immaculate gardens
behind the avenue Gabriel, two huge marquees had been
erected, one as an intimate nightclub with Django Rein-
hardt, then the rage of Paris, the other as an outdoor-
indoor running buffet, where all the guests could help
themselves whenever they felt hungry, with the promise
that at 5:00 A.M. eggs and bacon would be served.

I can't say that as a rule I enjoyed this sort of shindig,
but Mama did, and I danced the latest hit, "Begin the Be-
guine," with her and several other friends of the family,
and it was almost by accident that I partnered Sonia. I
hadn't gone out of my way to ignore her, we had just been
at opposite ends of the room or even in different rooms until we met face to face.

"Come and dance," I asked her, perhaps because she
looked more breathtakingly beautiful than I had even realized. She was dressed in pink, and even I could see that
the chiffon skirt contained yards and yards of material,
giving it a fairylike fullness. Her shoulders were bare ex-

cept for two straps holding up the pink top encrusted in diamanté.

"You look ravishing," I muttered.

I remember that I had some old-fashioned notion about "married women"; oddly enough, the prospect of going to bed with someone *else's* pretty wife just for the fun of it didn't really worry me—and there was plenty of temptation in the shape of bored wives during that last-fling summer of 1939. Immoral it might have been, but that sort of adventure was to me unimportant compared with deliberately reopening an affair with Sonia, recently married and closer in the past with me than she had ever been with her husband.

That was different. That, I felt in some silly way, was being dishonorable. I would never make any advances to her. Nor was Sonia guilty of tempting me. For weeks we had met at parties, even a weekend or two at Douzy with her husband. Everything was very correct, though when we touched by chance, brushed against each other getting into a car, or whatever the circumstances, I could sometimes feel her hand tremble, and I could tell by the way in which she touched the corners of her dry lips with the tip of her tongue that she was finding it difficult to control her emotions.

We danced round the room to the soft, lilting music of another new hit in Paris, "South of the Border," and then suddenly she held me slightly in front of her, away from me so that she could look at me straight in the eyes. Her face was almost desperate.

"I wish to God I'd never come back to Paris," she said almost savagely. "It's asking too much, here together like this—"

"Come and have a bit of cold chicken." My voice was just as urgent as hers. "I know, Sonia, I know, darling—but come into the marquee. Only—never say you're sorry we've met again. Never say that."

"Why not? What the hell good is it standing in front of each other like this? It's worse than being apart."

We walked across the lawn and into the striped supper

tent. Violins from Monseigneur, the Russian nightclub off the Champs-Elysées, had been engaged for the night, and they were playing a Russian folk song.

"Not that," said Sonia again angrily.

It was a haunting, sad little Russian tune called "Kalitka"—"The Gate" in English, she had told me once—and the corny violins throbbed with love and temptation—and sadness.

"They *would* play damn Russian music," she went on. "It makes me want to cry. Get me something to eat, will you."

"What?" I began.

"Anything! Hell, I'm not going to *eat* anything. I only want to get my bearings."

I walked over to the table along one side of the tent. It held a vast selection of cold meats. I put a little pressed duck, some foie gras, and some Waldorf salad on her plate; then the same for me. A butler brought some glasses and a bottle of champagne, which he stood on a small table by our side.

"It's not even Astell," she said nastily.

"Don't be cross, darling," I said. "We'll work something out. But you know—you *are* a married lady now. And we agreed—"

"I don't give a damn what anyone agreed, married or not. We've always loved each other, it's hypocrisy for you to sit here looking like a stuffed dummy."

"Thanks!" I said.

"Well, dammit," she cried, almost stamping her foot, "if politicians can break agreements between countries, so can ordinary people like us. I hoped—yes I really did—that this would all be over when we got married. I hoped I'd never come back to Paris. But we're here. And I can't *help* myself. I *can't*, Larry."

Only a few guests had started to eat, so for a few moments we talked without interruption.

"You talk like that," I said. "But what about Francesco? He's no fool. What about him?"

"Never mind him."

"But you must—we must. Dammit, for all I know he's just outside the tent waiting for you. You're *married* to him now."

"Marriage is one thing—and love—let's meet alone, soon!"

"That was fine when we were both much younger—but no longer. And after all"—I was beginning to get annoyed myself —"you say it doesn't matter, but I *did* ask you to marry me. I even asked your father's permission. But hell, *you* jilted me. And in my book that's a damn good reason not to get entangled again—however much I love you."

The violins were raking out the ashes of another sentimental love song, sweeping the haunting music past us like a warm wind. "You've forgotten—I *wanted* marriage. Remember?" I asked.

Perhaps I shouldn't have added that last question, "Remember?" It made her furious.

"Are you saying no to me? Are you?"

I shook my head miserably. "No—but can't you see that I'll always love you, Sonia—always. And it's that which makes me hesitate. Love."

"Are you—" Her voice was suddenly very quiet with anger. "Are you saying no to me?"

"Let's see what happens, darling. Please! In good time, you know I will always love you—but, now?"

"I'm bloody well offering you myself—my body, my soul if I've got one," she almost hissed. "And you—you stuck up sanctimonious prig—yes, that's what you are. A prig. Perhaps this will cool you off."

I didn't have time to deny the charge, or agree with it, for I realized she was right. I was a fool—and a prig. But at that moment she whispered savagely, "I don't want to make a scene so I won't throw the glass of champagne in your face. Instead—" And without another word she leaned across me, by the side of the small circular table, and poured the entire glass of bubbling liquid down the front of my trousers. With that, nobody noticing, she walked out of the marquee, head high, while I made my way to the wash-

room to explain a perfectly normal occurrence—that someone had bumped into me.

The glee club ball didn't end until 6:00 A.M. on the Saturday morning, and I think she must have left early for I
didn't see her again. I stayed on in spite of everything and
didn't reach the office in the rue du Sentier until midday. I
always had a weekly Friday conference with Oregon before he put the paper to bed.

"You look a bit—well, ragged," he said. "And mad."

What I liked about Oregon was that he could read my
face like a book. "Girl trouble?" he beamed knowingly,
looking even pinker in the face than usual, almost cherubic—except that cherubs don't chain-smoke.

"Don't worry"—he lit up another Gauloises—"where
women are concerned, the motto is—masterly inaction. Always let *them* come round after a tiff. Never be the first to
give in."

"This one won't," I muttered.

"Then I wonder why she asked for you on the phone
about ten minutes ago?" he said dryly.

Ten minutes later Sonia phoned again. "Oh darling
Monsieur Coquelicot." It was years since she had used that
word, a password that was supposed to heal all quarrels.
"No, no, darling Larry, I'm a beast, I hate myself, but you
promised that whenever I needed help and called you that
you'd come to me. I need help now, Larry. I do. I've only got
a moment. I'm phoning from a pay phone."

"Outside—not in your home?"

"No. All our phones in the house go through a central bit
of machinery—oh, I don't know what you call it, a switchboard —but the Fascisti have their own men in the rue de
Longchamp. Two live in my house. I just want to talk to
you—to try to explain one or two things—and oh, Larry, to
tell you how much I love you. Can we have lunch in our old
restaurant—on Monday perhaps, Marcel's in the rue Jacob?"

She must have sensed my hesitation because she added,
"I'll never ask you another favor, Larry. But *please* —if
you want to make me happy, if you really love me."

"All right," I said. "Anything you ever want—you know
that."

"I won't be able to phone back. And I don't think it
would be very sensible for you to phone me at home."

I agreed. "One o'clock on Monday at Marcel's," adding,
"and don't worry, darling Sonia."

On the Sunday morning I went for a long walk with
Papa through the vineyards to the other side of Rilly, past
the neat little train station, and at the far end the yawning
hole where the single-track line disappeared into the
mouth of the tunnel.

The vineyards were looking at their most beautiful in
July. They always did because of an added bonus. The
flowering in the vineyards usually coincided with the flowering of the summer lilies that decorated hundreds of
small gardens.

Papa examined some of the tiny vineyard flowers and
said in his sing-song accent, "Well, I only hope we'll all be
here for the *vendange,* yes, the *harvest.*"

By tradition the grapes were always picked a hundred
days after the flowers, which lasted about a week, had
died. There were exceptions of course, sudden hailstorms
or other acts of God or the Devil, but we had stuck to that
timetable in Champagne for longer than any of us could remember, and it usually seemed to work.

Rilly produced a very good still red wine—not as good as
ours, we liked to believe, but still very drinkable, and after
all, even though it wasn't sparkling and came in ordinary
looking bottles, it *was* still champagne.

"Yes, *very* drinkable." Papa looked at his watch to time
Gaston's arrival, allowing him time for a drink. "Yes, *very!*
I left the ball at the embassy early on Friday night—well,
really, Saturday morning. What time did you leave?"

"Six A.M.," I grinned.

"Disgusting. How you young people can do it. Did—er—
Sonia stay that long?"

A sudden sixth sense flashed out "Warning, Warning,
Warning!" As though a red light had signaled "Take

Care!" that this was not an innocent remark but a loaded question of Papa's.

"No idea," I was cheerfully able to tell the truth. "I saw her in the supper tent about midnight, then I didn't run across her again."

"I see."

"Why? Anything the matter?"

"No. No. But I have a feeling, Larry—nothing to do with your past, er, escapades, yes, I think *that's* the word—that we shouldn't see too much of the de Feos."

"Why on earth not?" My mouth must have fallen open with astonishment.

"Well, it's not serious, but still—" he hesitated.

"But it *must* be serious—our oldest friends on a blacklist."

"I say—*really*. That's a most unfortunate word to use. No, I don't like *that* word."

"I didn't mean to use it. But what are you saying?"

"It's extraordinary, and probably it means nothing. But two things happened during the ball. Colonel Malcom, one of the military attachés at the embassy, told me that de Feo is very closely linked with Abetz, who is running an espionage network from de Feo's house."

"I can't believe it," I cried, but all the same, my mind racing, I was thinking of Sonia's warning, that her telephone was being monitored.

"I'm sure it's all exaggeration," said Papa, "but you know the Italians are becoming more bellicose in their demands against France. And, there's something else. Reynaud told me that your old friend Abetz is being told to go."

"Abetz!" I whistled with surprise. "Leaving for where?"

"Kicked out, yes, *kicked,"* said Papa. "Apparently the French have finally agreed to expel him from France for his pro-Nazi activities. I can't say I'm sorry."

"That's the best news of the day," I drained my glass as I saw the Hisp coming round the corner from Rilly's main street.

"I thought you'd like it. But our embassy believes that

any—er—abnormal tasks that used to be performed by
Abetz will be taken over by de Feo."

"But what tasks?"

"Well, someone will have to keep a secret radio transmitter open from France to Germany, and I'm told that it's
going to be located in the rue de Longchamp."

"And you think Sonia—?"

"Of course not," he retorted sharply, and with an irony
he failed to perceive, "Sonia's one of *us.*"

"Was," I said.

"Better that way," he agreed. "Just for the sake of peace
and quiet. I don't mean that we can't meet as a family
whenever we want to. Of course we can—but—well, ahem!
Don't start getting caught in any—well, I hate to use the
word, but—any compromising situations. Remember you
are a newspaperman as well as an Astell."

As Gaston drove us back to Douzy I didn't think it was
quite the right moment to tell Papa that I was lunching secretly with Sonia the following day.

That Sunday evening at dinner, when we had just
started the consommé, Jean leaned over my shoulder and
whispered, "Pardon, m'sieu, there's a trunk call for you."

Mama was used to my telephone interruptions by now.
"He's a newspaperman," she would explain with a certain
pride. "He lives on the end of a phone."

I hadn't the slightest idea who could be phoning me, especially as I knew that Tommy Tomlinson was in Paris. A
disemboweled French voice said faintly, "Please wait to
receive a call from Lausanne."

Switzerland? Who on earth could be phoning me from
Lausanne?

"Who is it?" I asked.

*"C'est la gare à Lausanne, m'sieu. Attendez un instant,
s'il vous plaît."*

Impatiently I waited, racking my brains. It suddenly occurred to me that it might be Willi, perhaps on business
and taking the opportunity to telephone freely from Switzerland—something that we had long since realized was

impossible during the guarded telephone calls between Düsseldorf and Paris.

But it wasn't Willi.

"Larry! Can you hear me? It's me!"

"Me?"

"Anna, you ass."

"In Lausanne?" I heard her laugh. She must have caught, even over the distance, the sense of improbability in my voice.

"Where's Willi? What on earth are you doing in Lausanne?"

"Willi's in Germany. Listen, Larry—I've only got a few minutes."

"Fire away, I've got a pencil ready. What's the phone number of your hotel?" By now I always had a pencil, and I always asked for a phone number before anything else.

"I'm not at a hotel!"—I *thought* I heard a catch in her voice—"I'm calling from the station. I'm catching the night sleeper to Paris just before ten oclock. I'll be in the Gare de Lyon soon after noon tomorrow. Do you think you could meet me in Paris? Your darling sister—before—well, the others."

"Of course. Anything wrong? You and Willi?"

"You *are* an ass. It's not Willi. He's the most wonderful husband in the world. But Germany—I'll tell you all about it."

"Sounds great. *A bientôt!*"

"*A demain.*"

I went back to the dining room in a state of suppressed excitement.

"What is it?" asked Mama, suddenly worried. "You look as though you've seen a ghost."

"I have—in a way," I hesitated. The news seemed too momentous to blurt out quickly. Then I drew a deep breath.

"Anna's coming back," I said.

16

WE SEEMED TO STAY UP HALF THE NIGHT talking about Anna's arrival, though I was careful to point out that Anna hadn't said she was returning to *live* in Douzy.

But the business of going to Switzerland, telephoning from the station, was intriguing. Anna would normally use a hotel phone even if she wasn't staying in the place. But a public telephone in a railway station! It was quite out of character and, too, the direct railway trip from Düsseldorf to Paris was much quicker.

The electric effect of the news was spiced by the unknown dangers of the future, for this *was* the summer of 1939—early July—this *was* a time split by tension. Even the warmth of that last summer of peace could never dispel the chill winds of fear.

"I must admit," said Mama, "that I hope in my heart Anna will stay a while. I'm sure she doesn't get enough to eat—you've all read about that guns and butter business?"

"They don't say guns before frankfurters," said Oregon. "The Germans won't starve. Not Aryans." Then, with a look at Olivia, "Sorry, m'dear."

"Well, I'd like her to stay," said Mama, "for a long time if she wants to."

"If she stays more than a few weeks," said Oregon dryly, "she won't see Willi for years. Once the war breaks out, she'll be stranded—here."

"Better here than there," said Papa.

"Poor Anna," said Olivia. "She must be very torn and worried."

"Are you sure she will be better off in France than in Germany?" I asked. "You're the one, Papa, who's always saying the Champagne area will be right in the path of a German advance."

"If they ever reach that far," said my father almost stonily. "They haven't declared war, you know, and as for invading France—don't you think you're jumping the gun a bit?"

"Perhaps there *won't* be a war," I said, thinking of my morning conversation with Papa. "After all, we keep on getting nasty shocks and then—it all passes."

"Anna should never have married that German Willi," said La Châtelaine. "He may be better than the usual run, *mais tout de même, il est un Boche!"*

The first thing I had to do on reaching Paris was to let Sonia know I couldn't keep our lunch date. Yet I didn't dare to phone her. The only alternative was to drive round to Marcel's and leave her a note, telling her that I had been called on urgent business and that I would meet her in Marcel's several days later. I did so, though I could *not* tell Sonia that Anna was arriving, that this was the reason I couldn't meet her. I had been very shocked by Papa's remarks. And while I knew that Sonia would never have any direct dealings with the Germans—let alone an espionage network—I had felt for years that Riccardi had never been the innocent diplomat he pretended to be.

I caught sight of Anna as the conductor offered her a helping hand negotiating the steep steps of the brown and red wagon-lit. She saw me at the same instant, and for a moment I thought she was going to burst into tears—of relief. The porter in his belted blue blouse pointed out her two suitcases.

"This all you've got?" I asked.

Despite the relief, the hug of welcome, Anna looked tired, drawn.

"I didn't dare bring any more luggage"—she *was* on the point of tears, and her tone was bitter—"I only got an exit permit for a week."

As she moved toward the platform entrance, ready to offer her tickets, clutching her travel documents, I noticed that she was holding her American passport.

"You can still use it?" I asked.

"I did it deliberately," she replied. Again the bitterness. "You've got to learn how to keep ahead of the law in Germany. It's the only way to survive."

"As bad as that?"

I didn't like to ask too many questions, not too soon anyway, especially when I suggested to Anna, "Would you like to phone Willi from the apartment before I drive you to Douzy?"

"Phone Willi! From Paris! When I'm supposed to be in Switzerland." She shook her head vigorously. "My exit permit is made out for Switzerland only, and I can't afford to have any other immigration stamps on it. That's why I switched passports in Lausanne and used my old American passport. Perhaps later you could phone Willi? Discreetly. Don't mention my name, or anything like that."

Anna and I set off for Douzy as soon as the porter had put the bags in the back of the car. I knew that Mama wanted to see her before anyone else. But the trip, less than two hours, gave both of us the chance to fill in some of the background to her life. Sometimes it is easier for brother and sister to exchange confidences than for parents and offspring, however close they may be.

It was clear that Anna was deeply torn by three emotions —love, hate, fear. Love for Willi, hate for the Germans, fear of the future.

"Willi and I both share the fear," she confessed, "and that's really why I'm here. To have a breather. I hate Germany, it's so darned scary. And poor Willi tries to understand and be kind to me. But of course he's a German, so he can't see things my way."

"In what way?"

"Two instances that are really extraordinary. The first

is so ridiculous. Some damn official came one afternoon, produced a card of authority—you know how the Germans like authority—and said he was from the Ministry of Child Welfare."

"But we haven't any children," she told the official.

"That's the problem, Frau Frankel," said the man severely. "Why not? It's—"

"I told him that was our affair." But, according to Anna, it was *their* affair. "Germany is supposed to be surrounded by enemies and all that crap," she said, "and needs to produce more children."

I couldn't help laughing. "What did you do?"

"I tried the sob stuff. Couldn't have any children and so on. I'll tell you one thing, Larry, nothing would ever force me to have a baby at this time."

"And the other problem?"

"More serious. It may sound melodramatic, but we're locked up in Germany now. No way to leave without official permission. I didn't *want* to go to Switzerland. I applied for an exit visa to visit France. Perfectly good reason —to see my family."

"And what happened?"

"They turned down my application flat. Damn it, Larry, I'm an American—well, sort of."

"Did they give a reason?"

"I gathered from Willi, who was furious, that some German bigwig is on the point of being expelled from France— there's already been a preliminary story about it in the newspapers—and so this is a kind of reprisal. No one is allowed to visit France."

After some hesitation I asked her, "Do you ever wonder if you'll stay in France?"

"Willi wants me to," she answered frankly. "Even if it means being parted—for the time being. He's scared. But I love Willi, and we're so happy, despite the problems. And he can't go. He couldn't get a job anywhere abroad. And so we're trapped—because even if he wants me to go, I couldn't leave him. But at least, darling brother, I'm here breathing the good clear air of Champagne for a few days."

"What fun we had," I sighed, "that night the four of us danced at Maxim's."

"What a long time ago it seems," she sighed too.

I told her the latest news about Sonia—omitting what Papa had said, but explaining that Sonia had specifically asked me not to phone her at her home. It would be different if Anna phoned later in the day, I suggested, with the perfectly innocent news that she had suddenly arrived in France.

She promised to do that, and by then it was time to sweep up the winding drive past the dell, through the arch to the courtyard, and as Mama came out and gathered Anna into her arms, I could see that both of them were crying gently.

Even a couple of days of good clean Douzy air did wonders for Anna. The color returned to her cheeks, but more important, she lost the tenseness I had noticed when we met. She was home—not at "her" home really, I suppose, but still the home where she had been brought up.

"It'll always be home, always," she said. "I can't imagine life without Douzy. That's what tears me in two in Germany. I love Willi—but I love Douzy."

We had set off for a long walk through the vineyards, and from the heart, she said, "We all seem to have made such a mess of our lives. Fancy *you* not being married to Sonia. It's unthinkable for you to marry anyone else."

"I know."

No one could spend any time in the warm countryside of Douzy without that warmth trickling through to the souls of the people who were part of it, and Anna was no exception.

That morning, as I looked across the dell, opening the windows of the conservatory to invite the sweet smell of summer inside, I was thinking of the day of the thunderstorm when Sonia and I had raced from the orchard to escape the rain.

It was a day just like this, I thought and looked down. By the far end of the drive a lane led to the Home Farm, lined

with knotted hedges polished by the daily rubbing of the
cows on their way to grateful milking. Wild flowers lined
either side of the ochre lane—multi-colored willow herbs
tall as hollyhocks, the thick green stalks of hedge parsley
jutting out into spikes of creamy white blossom—and
beyond the orchard and the lake the countryside spread
out, the vineyards green and brown in rows, and beyond
that the ripening corn, a glittering gold, while near the top
of the rise beyond Douzy church was a carpet of more vivid
yellow, a huge field of mustard, "Champagne's other
crop," as Papa called it. Now that the flowering had ended,
workers in the vineyards were trimming the ends of the
vine stalks to make spraying easier and to give the sun
more chance to ripen the grapes.

"It's the best time of the year"—Anna walked along
with pure pleasure—"as though the whole world has been
getting ready for me to come home."

Slowly, almost hesitatingly as though embarrassed by
sharing secrets, Anna began to unwind. And in doing so,
she told the family in Douzy some horrific stories.

"In Germany, love isn't enough," she groped for words.
"I find it hard to explain. I know that in France everyone is
scared there'll be a *war*. But that's a *natural* fear. In Germany people are not only scared of *war*—but they're frightened of *life."*

It was nothing one could lay a finger on, she told us,
there was nothing tangible, but always there was a feeling
of hidden terror. People were afraid to speak to each other,
even to laugh openly. It sounded crazy, she told me one
evening, but people even disappeared—and with no trace,
no warning, no clues.

Their neighbors the Mollers, who lived in the same
apartment complex, were such good friends of Willi's that
they had even come to Douzy for the wedding.

"You remember, you liked them," Anna said to Mama.
"And they were such fun. He worked in an architect's office, so in a way the two men had a kind of link, architects
and engineers." One day Mrs. Moller told Anna she'd be

giving them some hard-to-get food she was getting from relations in the country—butter, pork products, all sorts of things from the farm.

Anna didn't have the cash ready when Mrs. Moller delivered the parcel, and Willi had insisted that he would accept the food only on the understanding that it would be a "business transaction." Two days later Anna went up one flight to pay the bill and, she thought, have a coffee. But in those two days the Mollers had vanished. "They'd gone," cried Anna to Mama. "They'd just vanished."

Another family had been allocated to the apartment, even taking over the furniture.

"But I must find out where they've gone," Anna cried to the new neighbors. When she tried to get into the front door—half expecting to be invited in by the new arrival, a woman she had never seen—the stranger just stood there. But from the doorway Anna could see that one of the Mollers' own paintings was still hanging in the hall. And on a table she saw some old silver-framed family photographs that belonged to their friends. Pointing to them, she said to the new arrival, "So the Mollers are coming back? I see their photographs are still there." Anna really thought they *were* going to return. But the new tenant, delighted to be allotted this apartment, said vaguely that arrangements were being made by the authorities to "forward" all personal effects.

"It's the authorities this, the authorities that!" Anna exclaimed to me. "It drives me mad. That—and the danger of asking too many questions. It's awful in Germany. The moment you ask a simple question, people begin to regard you with suspicion."

Anna never did find out what happened to the Mollers—until Willi finally learned that Moller was part Jewish and had been transferred to a different town.

"And I can guess what the word *transferred* means," Olivia interrupted.

Anna nodded. Jews were being stripped of every penny, then kicked out of Germany, often to Shanghai, where no passports or visas were required when landing at the International Settlement.

"Once they reach Shanghai, those who have some connections can sometimes get visas for America or Britain. But for every lucky one there are a thousand—ten thousand—who have nowhere to go. It's terrible. You know, Olivia, when I first arrived here at the beginning of the week and I met you again, I felt a real sense of shame—of being German, of the way the Germans have treated the Jews."

"You're not a German!" Olivia said gently. "You never will be."

I was concerned about one thing.

"What's going to happen if you don't return to Germany soon? You say you've only got an exit permit for a week—but the time's already up."

Almost defensively, Anna said, "They can't *force* me to go back to Germany right away if I want to pay a visit to my family."

"But you switched passports."

"Then when I return to Germany I'll switch passports again. I'll travel to Switzerland on my American passport and go from there to Düsseldorf on my German passport, and just say I was taken ill."

Almost without thinking I asked her, "Where was your new American passport issued? In Germany?"

"What new passport?"

"Aren't you Mrs. Frankel now?"

"Oh, I see. I didn't bother to get a new one. This hasn't expired. I just hung on to my old passport—the one I had before I married. It doesn't seem to have stopped me traveling—so far."

"All the same," I said, "I think you ought to get your marital status changed. You may find it very useful one day to have dual nationality. But if someone spots a technical error—like forgetting you're a married woman—well—"

"I'll get it done right away."

"Don't leave it too long," I warned her. "Jim Parks will

fix it for you while you wait. It's only a question of writing your new name on the inside and stamping it."

"I promise," she said, but knowing Anna, I doubted if she would remember.

Thank God I arrived first at Marcel's for my postponed "reunion" lunch with Sonia. And that I had come by car—in my latest MG, changed a year ago from the T model for a brand-new snazzy model WA, in racing green, with wire wheels, four windows, and running boards joining up to the rear fender. Altogether more luxurious.

Because Marcel's was closed. The standard sign read FERMETURE ANNUELLE. A smaller sign announced that the restaurant would reopen on Monday, August 21.

Everyone—the butcher, the candlestick maker, to say nothing of restaurants and shops—closed each August. But it was not yet August, only the middle of July, and I had noticed that more and more places were closing down earlier. Oregon had had his own explanation. "One hell of a lot of people are wondering when they'll get their next vacation," he said.

Sonia arrived within five minutes. She was dressed in a blue linen two-piece suit, with a topaz clip on one breast and a scarf casually knotted round her throat.

"Blue always did suit you." I kissed her on the cheek, a sisterly kiss, smelling her faint perfume. "And so does Arpège," I remembered—how could I ever forget it? "But look," I cried, "Marcel's closed."

"Oh, no." Her sudden exclamation of dismay, the way she put her hand to her mouth, was so genuine I felt a sudden urge to touch her on the arm. Years apart tend to make people forget the habits of others. Sonia had always felt a special bond toward people, who had dealt with the two of us as lovers. She had a gift for sharing love, communicating it to others who could see how happy we were.

"That's terrible," she said. "Where shall we go?"

"Let's drive into the country," I suggested. "I know a lovely place at Marly."

"You haven't been there with—"

"No girl, if that's what you mean."

"I was so looking forward to meeting Marcel again. Oh! You've got a new car. How super. And it's bigger."

"Yes, it's got a bit more room—and two point six liters of motor. It'll get us out to Marly before you know what's hit us. You're not afraid to be seen with me?"

"Maybe it would be better if you put the top up."

Marly was only a dozen miles from Paris, a onetime royal hunting lodge surrounded by beautiful forests. A new road had been built bypassing Versailles, so there would be no problem.

"And the restaurant is pretty expensive," I grinned, "which means that it'll keep any tourists away. They'll be having their picnics. It's called the Auberge du Roi. Of course Charles the Fifth stayed there."

We drove at high speed along the flat straight road bisecting the beautiful forest, the thick green belts of trees on either side, with here and there sandy tracks or bridle paths, indicated by small green signposts.

Suddenly she said, almost breathlessly, "Stop the car. Just for a second!"

I slammed on the brakes, slid off the road to the grass verge near the corner of a riding path, and she said a little unsteadily, "I know this is going to be a respectable lunch, but, darling Larry, just one kiss before we reach the *auberge.*"

She leaned across, again the wisp of Arpège, and as I leaned across the low steering wheel toward her, she said in that husky voice of hers that always betrayed excitement, "If you knew how long I've waited for this kiss, Larry. Oh, Monsieur Coquelicot, how I love you! And how I have missed you."

I pushed one hand along her neck, underneath her thick blue-black hair; she kissed me, slowly at first, never to be rushed, until finally, when my breath had gone, I cried from the heart, all thoughts of behaving properly forgotten, "Why did I let you go? Why, oh, why? What a bloody fool I was!"

"No," she said sadly. "I let *you* go. I'm the fool though I had no choice."

We kissed again, and I could feel myself stirring, and I knew she felt the same, for she said, "It can't be wrong to be in love. Not us. But where can we go?"

"Nowhere," I said. "You know that, darling—and perhaps it's for the best. This is just about the most public forest outside Paris. There's a peeping tom behind every tree."

"But I must—I *must!*"

"I'll find a place after lunch," I promised her, not knowing how—or even if I should. "Take it easy."

"Take it easy! You Americans! You must be mad. Can *you* take it easy? Let me feel you." Almost savagely she undid my trouser buttons and pushed a hand inside my underpants. "Oh, darling, I want you—now. And you say take it easy!" She moved gently. "We've got to do something. I don't give a damn if some tourists do see us. We must. Christ! We're as good as married—or we were. I don't care what you do—but I can't go to lunch like this—come on, darling, do it, do it, and don't bother about anyone else."

"I can't. Not in this damn car."

"Then let's do it to each other," she urged me. "Now, before lunch. Kiss each other in the car—and touch each other or ourselves, nobody'll be able to see. Wait, I've got some paper hankies for you in my *baise-en-ville.*" She used the slang word for a large bag which girls sometimes carry when they know—or hope—to spend a night away from home, slang because *baiser* means to make love.

"Here"—she pushed the handkerchiefs inside my underpants—"now nobody can see us, we can kiss and love each other." She pulled up the blue linen skirt, leaving herself bare, black and white, for there was nothing underneath.

It *was* all over in a few seconds. And when the kissing stopped, she said, "That's better, isn't it, my love?"

She started to straighten her skirt, pull it down, then dabbed a little eau de cologne between the inside of her thighs—a typical Italian and French habit—and dipped

into her capacious bag and took out a mirror and wiped
away the lipstick and, catching sight of me through the
mirror, looked at me almost mischievously and asked,
"Now a glass of champagne will taste really perfect, *non?*"

We drove on—quite sedately, except that I was holding
her hand most of the way.

"I suppose if our parents knew what we'd just done,
they'd be disgusted," she wondered. "But how sensible we
are. We know everything there is to know about each
other. And by a very simple process, we've," she almost
giggled, "calmed ourselves down."

"Mama would have a fit if she knew!" I laughed.

"Do you realize"—she still left her hand gently in
mine—"that this is the first time I've seen you laugh since
I came back to Paris. Isn't it wonderful, playing with yourself and each other? And," again mischievously, "it's not
only relaxed me, it's given me a huge appetite."

The Auberge du Roi was suitably rustic, a reflection of
the famous royal forest. A spattering of genuine antiques
decorated the reception area. And behind the half-empty
dining room lay a peaceful garden framed by an English-
style herbaceous border with a lawn in the middle as green
and smooth as a pool table. A large bill discreetly pushed
into a willing palm ensured that we had a quiet table in
the corner of the open-air veranda. And a bottle of champagne, which *did* taste good.

The menu looked enticing. "And I'm just as ravenous as
you are," I laughed again. "Just looking at you gives me
an appetite. God, Sonia, you're so—so wonderful, and I love
you so much. I was determined to behave now you're married. But I couldn't."

Drinking our champagne, we sat, at times holding
hands, silent in our thoughts, looking over the garden with
its bowers of roses and the bright green lawns.

"It's at times like this," she sighed, "that I wish we'd
taken photographs of all our wonderful times together—
pictures so that in the years to come, if things don't turn

out well for us, we could for ever and ever turn to them and relive our memories."

"But I can remember everything. It's all there," I touched my head. "*Everything*. The beer in Pontarlier on that first day—you dressed in pink. The cornfield, the gentle times we've had whenever other people would leave us alone. No, I don't need to be reminded by any fading photographs."

We finished a whole bottle of champagne, leaning across the table, holding hands, the small vase of home-grown flowers pushed to the side until finally we heard a discreet cough and the waiter asked if we were ready to choose.

Before I could ask Sonia what she wanted she turned to the old head waiter, gave him her most radiant smile, and said, "Would you choose for us, please? We are very much in love—and—"

"I understand perfectly," he was as gravely concerned as only the French can be when confronted with romance.

"Except *ris de veau*," I said as an afterthought. I had never been able to stomach sweetbreads.

In the end he brought us some *feuilleté de langoustines* wrapped in puff pastry so light and flaky it almost dissolved as we ate it. And after that some breast of duck cooked in olives, and to top it off—"You're still hungry?" I asked her, and she smiled to the waiter—an ice cream, over which the waiter poured a liberal portion of *framboise*, the lethal white distilled liqueur made from raspberries.

I had forgotten my cigarettes, and as I walked back across the lawn from the car, I saw that she was watching me intently.

"What are you looking at?" I asked.

"The way you walk. I love the way you walk—as though you want to dance. You'll always walk like that, darling—not gangling, but an easy walk. *You* know. As though you haven't a care in the world—except me."

"You always."

"*Carissimo*. I love the way you talk, walk, and—"

"Not now! Don't excite me again. It's not fair!"

It was over the second cup of coffee that I told her about

Anna being in Douzy, and all about Anna's worries about Willi and living in Germany. "How terrible for her, Larry! But naturally I'll be *discrète*. And I do hope not much time passes before I see her."

And then Sonia had some news for me. "I'm hoping to acquire—I think that's the right word—a small house in Switzerland."

"What on earth for?" I was astonished. "And what do you mean—acquire?"

"From Daddy. I know it sounds crazy, but if there's a war, the Swiss at least might stay neutral—and it'd be a good investment."

"Sounds wonderful. I still don't quite see why, though."

"It'll be *mine,* don't you understand. And you will be able to come and see me there—a bolt hole. I haven't got it yet, but with luck—"

"I didn't think the Italians could export money."

She looked embarrassed, just for a moment. "Daddy's got a bit tucked away in Switzerland," she admitted. "I haven't got the house yet, but if I do—oh, Larry darling, just to have a place where we can go—a place of our own. I'm so much in love."

"Me too," I said huskily. "But you've forgotten. You *do* have a husband. I feel guilty, even here with you."

She hesitated, trying perhaps to arrange her thoughts.

"Don't feel guilty," she said finally and very gently. "I'm not betraying anyone."

"Your husband?"

"Least of all him. He's very understanding, very considerate—you see, everything was arranged, it had to be—and he knows about our past. All he asks is discretion."

I didn't really understand. Her husband didn't seem to be a queer—"He's not," she laughed. "But don't *try* to understand," adding gravely, "after a wonderful day like this, just learn to accept."

And so it all started again.

17

MIDWAY THROUGH THE SUMMER, when the previous year's feeling of relief at the Munich sellout had begun to evaporate, it suddenly dawned on France and Britain that Poland was now wide open to invasion, that the only hope of averting a European war with the madman in Germany was for Hitler's archenemy, Russia, to form a defense pact with France and Britain. None of the three powers were very strong, yet such a pact would surely mean that, in the event of war, Hitler would face enemies on both fronts. And even he could not be as mad, as suicidal, as to invite such a prospect.

By July the talks were proceeding slowly after a dismally ineffectual opening in June. Incredible Western bungling had virtually prevented any hope of success. Even the Poles—the only people to be threatened directly— flatly refused to allow Russian troops on their territory in the event of war.

"With the Germans we risk losing our liberty," said Field Marshal Smigly-Rydz, the Polish commander, "but with the Russians we lose our soul."

The British led the Anglo-French delegation, with France very much the junior partner, and a British admiral was in charge.

"You'd have thought that since they're going to talk to the commies," said Tommy Tomlinson, "they'd have the brains to play down the English lah-di-dah lord stuff. But Jesus, they must be off their nut in Whitehall. Let me tell you the name of this guy—and imagine what the Russians are going to think. No—" as an afterthought, "I haven't got enough breath to tell you his name. Here, read it yourself."

And there, incredibly, was a copy of the London *News Chronicle,* announcing, "The British delegation is headed by Admiral Sir Reginald Aylmer Ranfurly Plunkett-Ernle-Erle-Drax."

"Can you beat it?" Tommy read it again. "The Russians will die laughing."

Before they started, the delegation ran into more trouble. To avoid crossing Germany by train the navy had chartered the *City of Exeter,* with the idea of meeting the Russians in Leningrad in four days. But only after boarding the *Exeter* at Tilbury, near the port of London, did the admiral discover that she'd made only thirteen knots, so she couldn't possibly arrive in time.

"And I've heard a rumor from our Washington office," said Tomlinson, "that Ribbentrop has sent a team of his yes-men to Moscow to talk to the Soviet high-ups."

Yet against all this background of mounting despair, Paris in the summer of 1939 seemed gilded by splendid receptions, dances, night-long festivities. The prospect of war was an ever-present ghost at every party, but even so people refused to acknowledge the reality behind the fears. Each new crisis was like a splinter of glass that scratched, might even draw a drop of blood, but was not savage enough to wound badly.

The madness in the air was a last-gasp attempt to enjoy ourselves while we could, a collective national need for illusion, by a patient with an incurable disease who knows that death will come at any moment.

Even the 1939 parade for the *Quatorze Juillet* on the Champs-Elysées, though splendid in its panoply, seemed out of place, echoes of past grandeur. The foreign legionnaires, the Zouaves, the polished glinting breastplates of the cuirassiers, even a platoon of British guardsmen in scarlet tunics and bearskins, seemed an empty gesture on this, my twenty-seventh birthday.

My duties for the *Globe* kept me from Douzy that birthday, for the first time in many years. But my photographer friend Alex Rhys had set off on another long trip, and I had been able to move from the rue de l'Université flat back to his fifth-floor bandbox of an apartment in the rue du Cherche-Midi. And just because it *was* my birthday, Sonia had somehow planned to spend most of the day with me at "home." Though cooking was hardly part of the daily duties of a diplomat's wife, Sonia, like many Italians, was a born cook and she produced an enormous dish of *spaghetti carbonara.* "*Al dente,*" she said, "and with real belly pork in it, not bacon, the way they do it in restaurants."

I was sitting in the most comfortable chair, leaning back, legs outstretched, watching her.

"Cooking over a hot stove like any housewife," I murmured.

"Just because I'm a diplomat's wife doesn't mean I can't cook," she retorted. "Especially *spaghetti carbonara.*"

But it wasn't cooking that intrigued me on this occasion. It was the way she had dressed—"for comfort," as she put it. "I hope you don't mind, but I decided to leave a nightie and dressing gown and one or two bits and pieces—just in case we can spend more time together."

"These your cooking clothes?" I laughed, for she was wearing a beautiful white crêpe de Chine nightdress with a thin dressing gown over it.

"Mummy would have a fit if she knew," she laughed. "These clothes are part of my trousseau. All my lingerie came from Nataline Serni in Florence."

"So long as they didn't come from—" I had a sudden stab of jealousy at the thought of him seeing her in that nightie.

"No, my beloved," she came over and kissed me after biting off an end of spaghetti to check. "He didn't buy them. I bought them—and I vowed, even then, that I would never wear them except for you. It was a present from me to you—bought by me, for the day when I knew we would meet again."

With assumed nonchalance, I said, "Very interesting! Lunch ready? I'm famished."

"Horrible beast! I spend all my days cooking for you and—"

"Come and kiss me—"

"And then?"

"You choose. Lunch first or after."

"And I've got another surprise for you," said Sonia on the way home. "I had lunch the other day with the Polish ambassador—I think he's got a crush on me. You've read about his ball in the embassy? Well, I've got invitations for the whole Astell family. You *must* get Anna to go, it will be good for her. It's going to be the greatest ball of the season. It's so sad to think," she said, "that this might be the last such ball for quite a while."

"How did you fix it?"

"I asked him. He's met your family, and of course he admires both your Papa and Grandma for having stuck to their dual nationality—French as well as American. It's so easy to become American and forget the rest of the world."

"Does Francesco know?"

She shook her head, but the very mention of Francesco's name jarred the beautiful sleepiness of the afternoon. I had been wondering about him, and what his specific duties were, because Abetz had by now been kicked out of France and replaced by another roving German diplomat, a large fat lump of a man called Albrecht, who looked as prone to paranoia as his predecessor.

Albrecht was a frequent visitor to the Italian embassy. I knew this from the *Globe*'s agency contacts, men whose job it was to "cover" the routine comings and goings of people at embassies, consulates, the Quai d'Orsay, and so on. They obviously didn't report everything they saw or heard about, but somehow over the months, patterns began to form which a trained political observer like Tommy could fit into some sort of picture.

It was these snippets of news that made Tomlinson say, without realizing its significance to me, "In the days when

Abetz was top dog, first Riccardi, then de Feo used to go and see him. They were ordered to go, I'd guess. But now it's changed. Albrecht goes to see de Feo. I wonder if Abetz blotted his copybook while de Feo is close to Ciano."

Maybe, I thought, but close for—what? I had tried carefully over the years to pry clues from Sonia about her husband's secret work—and secret it was, I didn't doubt that. I had even told her once of a story in the Paris rumor factory that de Feo had got his appointment only because Count Ciano had been to bed with Sonia. But we both laughed at that.

Yet Sonia had always evaded any tactful questions with a sigh. Now I hinted again.

"Does your Francesco, and your father, have some secret—well, it sounds so melodramatic—but some kind of hold on you, darling? I don't mean anything wrong, but—"

"I know, my darling Larry, how puzzled you must be," she said, "we all have to protect our parents—and ourselves—from time to time. But don't worry. I've done nothing wrong. And now we are living for today—don't let's force open any cupboards that might contain skeletons."

There had never been a ball like the one at the Polish embassy. The Astells went *en famille;* but despite my best efforts, Anna said she would prefer to stay at home, she was in a sad mood, wondering about Willi, from whom we had heard no word. But she did one very sweet thing. She gave her invitation to Olivia, and I was delighted—for Olivia's sake. She didn't go out much. Papa was in tails, I was in black tie, the girls looked wonderful, and the atmosphere of exhilaration—and a kind of gossamer make-believe—was so beautiful that at first sight even the most jaded guests gasped with phrases like *"C'est merveilleux."*

It *was* wonderful. In the beautiful gardens the trunks of all the trees had been covered to a height of ten feet with garlands of fresh flowers. All the trees and lawns had hidden lights so that the mood changed with lights that never produced a glare, but color changes so gentle they ran into each other, like differently tinted clouds or sea. And it was

more beautiful than ever because the scenes of unreality
lent it a wistful note, a frenzied anxiety not to miss anything while it lasted. Julius Lukasiewicz, the ambassador,
had spared no effort to make it a night no one would ever
forget—especially by those who wondered if there would
ever be another night like this. "Luka," as he was known
to his friends, knew perfectly well that the Russo-British
deal had foundered and what that meant to Poland. I felt
that he had decided the end was near and he was determined to go out with a bang.

He had invited all the most beautiful women in Paris,
and at three in the morning, under a warm sky, he made
his final defiant gesture. He led his entire embassy staff,
all of them barefoot—the ladies in crinolines—in a polo-
naise across the cropped embassy lawns, which were bordered with white marble statues. The effect was pure
magic, for they and the beautiful girls were illuminated by
large red Bengal lights; the pots of fire lit the lawns, the
dancers, the white statues with a macabre, moving red
glow. Sonia was dancing with Francesco; I was dancing
with Olivia, and suddenly as she looked at me smiling
—Olivia was such a beautiful girl, I thought, remembering
that one night together—her face was bathed in a soft reddish glow shining through her hair, and I shivered suddenly. The girl, and those near her, looked like corpses
dripping with blood.

The moment passed, the music changed into a fox-trot,
difficult to manipulate on grass, but when I suggested sitting down Olivia begged me to continue, not possessively.

"I adore dancing," she pleaded, "and Guy—well, he's not
much for it. So give me one dance more please, even
though I have the strangest feeling, as though we're dancing ourselves into the war."

"You look positively dazzling," I tried to turn away any
morbid thoughts. And she did look dazzling. Mama, who
knew all the couturiers in Paris, had asked Edward
Molyneux to lend Olivia a ball gown, a model dress. It was
often done by good clients like Mama, who might ask a big
house to lend a dress to a daughter for an important dance.

It cost the dress house nothing, and providing the girl was pretty, it was a good free advertisement. Olivia was wearing a long white dress that spread out from her waist almost like a crinoline—not really as full as that, but that was the only way I can describe it. "Classical Molyneux," said Mama.

"I suppose I ought to be grateful that Anna's not here," said Olivia. "I do hope you can help her to stay in France."

"Germany *is* her home—well, her husband's."

"I know. But if there's a war?" she said.

"What about here? And anyway, she'll decide. Anna knows what she wants."

Mama came along, and though I wouldn't have minded dancing again with Olivia, I thought it more polite to dance with Mama—especially as I had already danced three times with Sonia. I was intrigued by Olivia, by the skill with which she wordlessly had made it quite clear that what had happened on that one night in the apartment was never to be repeated. She had never said anything—and I, being more in love with Sonia than ever by now, had never of course made any approaches. But Olivia did have extraordinary gifts.

"She's a helluva good girl," I said to Mama. "It seems a long time since we had that awful row."

"I know. And now, with Anna away, she's become a kind of second daughter to me. Strange how it all works out."

After another dance, I looked at my watch. Half past four. "I'm pooped," I told Mama. "It's okay for you people who dance the night away, but I'm a working man. If the Hisp is ready—and if poor Gaston isn't fast asleep—I think we ought to go."

Mama nodded, and we started to collect the Astell brood.

As I waited in the hall for Guy to pick up Mama's wrap, a sixth sense made me turn round. I *knew* that someone was talking about me. And I moved so quickly that I actually caught Sonia's husband pointing me out—quite definitely. And the other man was the fat Herr Albrecht, who had taken the place of Abetz. We had met previously, but now I saw the German nod to de Feo—almost as though he was obeying orders, being told by the Italian diplomat what to do. As soon as they saw me, they both waved to me.

We had all tended to shy away from the question of Anna's future plans—deliberately. All that any of us at Douzy could do was try to persuade her to stay, but, understandably, too much persuasion irritated her, sometimes causing her to erupt in the kind of anger that makes people shout, "Why don't you mind your own business?" or "Leave me alone, will you!"

She had to be handled carefully, poor Anna, her lovely young face now creased with worry bordering on bleak despair. She *had* to work out her future herself, while we could only hope she would stay. And she had stayed—so far. Her original permission to stay a week in Switzerland had long since expired. If she remained long enough, she might be too afraid to return. Wouldn't that be the best solution?

The chance scene at the Polish embassy ball, when Sonia's husband and Albrecht had obviously been talking about me, had an intriguing sequel a few days later in early August, when Albrecht called me at the *Paris American* office.

Our meetings had usually been brief, often at the International Press Club functions, though unlike Abetz, who had only toyed with writing as a dilettante, Albrecht was a professional journalist, though not a very likable character.

He tended to call all foreign correspondents by their Christian names, impervious to snubs by those who disliked him. Perhaps I was also prejudiced because his clothes seemed to hang on him, giving him a dirty, shifty look. His jackets had the telltale slanting pockets of the Germans, and no doubt they were expensive. If he looked a mess, it was not the fault of his clothes, but of the shapeless mass of blubber struggling to burst out of them. On the other hand, he had been recruited by Germany's propaganda chief, Dr. Goebbels, and liked to be regarded as a "fellow newspaperman."

"How are you, Larry?" he began. "Good. Listen. We've had an inquiry from a German national whose wife is missing. Inquiries have asked if you can help."

"Me?" I knew perfectly well what he was leading up to.

"Yes," he explained. "She's a Frau Frankel. It seems she's your sister. Is that right? I'm terribly sorry. Had no idea. But apparently her husband is worried."

I said nothing, hoping he found the silence disconcerting.

"I'm sorry, Larry. Can you hear me?"

"Sure."

"Well, then—?"

"But," I said mildly, "you didn't ask me any questions. You just made a statement. That's fine. Thanks for letting me know."

"But your sister—we got a message—she went to Lausanne for a vacation."

Again I said nothing.

"You are hearing me?" he sounded exasperated, as I hoped he would. Poor Albrecht was so used to making flat statements as a means of grilling people that he had lost the art of trying to frame polite questions.

"But she's left Switzerland," he added.

"It's a free country and she's over twenty-one," I said cheerfully. "What do you want me to do?"

"Her husband is worried. He asked me to make some inquiries."

That, I was convinced, was a lie. I had been trying for days to contact Willi. And high-ranking diplomats didn't waste their time making personal calls to newspaper colleagues just because someone had overstayed an exit permit.

"What do you think, Larry?" He finally asked a direct question. I answered with the first thought that came into my head.

"Do you think she's run off with another man?"

"Why you say that?" he asked.

"But you're sure she isn't in Lausanne? How can you tell? It can't be a problem for Germans—in Switzerland, surely?"

"We have discovered that she left suddenly. She gave no forwarding address. Perhaps she had come to see you?"

"If she's run off with another man? Hardly likely. Would *you* go to see your family if you bolted with a new girl friend?"

"She might come to your château," said Albrecht finally. "You will let me know?"

"With her husband?"

"No. He is in Düsseldorf."

"I've been trying to telephone him. I can't seem to get through. Could you help?"

"Perhaps his wife," he persisted.

"From Lausanne?"

"She is *not* in Lausanne," said Albrecht heavily, "and I think you know this without me informing you." And with an attempt—equally heavy—at sarcasm, he added, "Thanks for all your help."

The more I thought about Albrecht's heavy-handed hints, the more I was convinced that de Feo was vaguely involved. I didn't flatter Anna by thinking that de Feo was moving heaven and earth to get one single German-American girl back to the Fatherland; but the Nazis and Fascists *were* dedicated zealots, and it was quite possible that Albrecht, knowing that de Feo's wife was Anna's lifelong friend, had mentioned her "disappearance" at some routine joint meeting. And how astonished Albrecht must have been if de Feo announced that he had dined with Anna Frankel only the previous week—for Francesco and Sonia had been recent guests at Douzy.

That would have explained the talk between the two diplomats at the Polish ball. And the sequel. And it couldn't have come at a worse time, for finally Anna was beginning to crack. On the Saturday—that would be August 19—she admitted to me that she had told Willi to phone me at the *PA* from an office outside his building for news, but no news had come through. She was sure Willi's phone was tapped.

Suddenly she burst into tears and cried, "I'm going back to Germany. Something terrible's happened to Willi. I've got to go."

"You can't," I told her. "You're in trouble yourself for overstaying your visit out of Germany. Knowing the Nazis, they could chuck you into jail."

"I've got to go," she muttered. "I can't leave him without a word—oh! I hate the Germans. I hate them!"

"You're not going," I said. "Not yet."

"You can't stop me!"

"I can."

"How?" she asked.

"Because I'll go first and see what's happened," I said, not suddenly, but after some thought. "I can go on a trip as a newspaperman. No problem. I'll check out that Willi's okay, what he wants to do, then report back in a couple of days."

She kissed me impulsively, "You're an angel. You will? Right away?"

"Couple of days," I said. "Don't worry, Anna. I'll only be able to stay in Germany for a night or so, but I'll find out what's happened."

I set off by train on Monday the twenty-first and even I could feel the claustrophobia that gripped me as we passed the frontier and the guards examined our passports, with a couple of stony-faced men in Gestapo uniform watching in silence, unblinking, never missing a trick, spies not only on the innocents on the train, but on the German officials checking the innocents' passports. It passed through my mind as the train restarted inside Germany that the frontier epitomized all that was terrifying in Germany. I patted my malacca sword stick with a sense of security—and irony that Willi should have given it to me. Not that I would ever use it—or need it—I thought.

I found a cab easily. No problem with the address, a prosperous-looking apartment block, Willi's name on a list by the front door, though when I rang the bell in the apartment, I half expected no reply. After all, every attempt to contact Willi had failed. Maybe he *was* having a secret affair with some local floozy—that *would* be ironic after my jocular suggestion to Albrecht that Willi's wife had a lover. But no, Willi was highly intelligent. No man in his right senses would vanish without a word if he had a girl friend. He would cover his tracks.

Then I heard movements inside the apartment—a vague shuffling from inside the room, behind the front door. A voice, which didn't sound like Willi's, mumbled something in German. I could just make with in my limited German, *"Wie heissen Sie?"*

It *was* Willi! But a Willi who sounded disoriented.

"It's Larry!" I shouted. "Open the door. It's Larry!"

"Thank God," Willi's voice behind the door suddenly broke into a grateful sob. I waited impatiently to the sounds of bolts being drawn back—and then, with mounting horror, I managed to catch in my arms the broken, sagging figure grabbing a hall stand in a vain attempt to stand upright.

"Jesus Christ, Willi! What the hell's happened?"

"Es ist ein Unfall passiert," I could hardly recognize the bloody torn mess, as he repeated in English, "an accident."

His face was one blotch of purple and red bruises. Both eyes were blackened, barely visible. His lips were puffed or split, I couldn't tell which. The blood on his face was matted where the skin had split—obviously as a result of someone's fists.

"Come on, for Chrissake," I cried urgently. "Let me help you."

I tried to take an arm. He gave an almost animal yelp of pain. "Nothing fatal," he gasped, "but in the ribs there is much pain."

Somehow I got Willi to the sofa in the living room. I had brought with me a bottle of Scotch, and I poured a huge dose into his throat until he spluttered with the fire—and no doubt the stinging effect against his cuts.

I took off his jacket carefully. His arms were all right;

but his body was black and blue—and green and the dirty yellow of bruises changing color after their first contact with flesh.

Willi's wounds were horrific—yet I didn't need a practiced eye to realize that he had been beaten up scientifically. Maximum pain but no broken bones. Lips split but no teeth knocked out. Puffy eyes almost closed, but no danger of losing his sight. Someone—and I could imagine who it was—had arranged for Willi to be taught a lesson—yet not a fatal one.

"When did this happen?" I asked harshly.

"Tuesday night," he replied weakly.

"Tuesday! That was two days ago. Haven't you done anything? Seen a doctor?"

He shook his head. "Too weak to leave the apartment. I sleep. No one comes in. I cannot eat. My phone is not working and, anyway, better not to involve friends."

"But you could have died."

He managed a feeble smile. "Not likely, They could do this so easily, but they do not want to. Is good to see you, Larry, so good. And what news of my *liebchen?*"

"She's fine. She sends you a big kiss."

He managed a twisted grin. "No kissing for a few days."

"Before anything else," I said, "you must get some medicine. And food. No, shut up, Willi"—I stopped his interruption—"I'm going to put you to bed, then go out and find some cotton wool and bandages and iodine or whatever you need."

He tried to stop me, but I managed to get the rest of his clothes off and put him between the sheets, though in truth he was almost faint with pain.

I managed to find a pharmacist who understood English, and he gave me all the necessary supplies—as though beating up was a common occurrence. He showed me the salve to use for split lips, the iodine for cuts, the other medicines for bruises. On the way back I found some milk, a couple of loaves of dark bread, and a pair of fat, long sausages. Willi would not be able to eat much until his mouth was better, but I could boil some milk for him to sip.

Almost the first thing he asked me when I returned and put the food on the kitchen table was "And how is Douzy? Still as beautiful?"

I almost choked on the words. Douzy! So far away from this mad country! Perhaps at this very moment, Anna was wondering whether Willi and I had met yet. Perhaps she was having her predinner drink, talking to Mama, perhaps getting moral support from Papa. But never—O God!—never imagining such a horror as this; poor Willi broken and beaten. The contrast between Douzy and this apartment, reeking of blood and vomit, was almost more than I could bear.

"At least Anna is safe," he managed a wan smile.

"She's fine," I reassured him. "We were worried about not hearing from you, so I came along to see for myself. Thank God I did."

"I will be fine. And please, Larry, don't tell Anna about this. I will be better soon. Don't worry her. What you see"—it hurt him to smile, but he still made an effort—"what you see is fairly normal around the streets of Germany these days."

"But why, Willi—*why?*"

"I'm not sure. They ask where is my wife." He tried to sit up in a straighter position.

"Never mind the explanations now," I said, "the most important thing is—where can I get you a doctor?"

"No doctor. Better not. Maybe if you can get me into hot bath, I soak in it."

It did help, though only after a long struggle to get him into the big iron tub. His entire body was covered with bruises. I let him soak for a long time, topping up the water each time it began to cool. Finally I found a bathrobe and half carried him back to the bedroom and poured some more Scotch into him before discovering what had happened.

Three Brownshirt thugs in uniform had suddenly rung the bell—and Willi remembers that for the first exciting moment of its sound, he even thought that by a miracle

Anna had arrived unexpectedly. Instead the three men marched in and closed the door behind them.

"One look and I knew why they were coming to see me," Willi remembered. "They didn't speak, they gave no reason, and for me there is no escape."

"This is beyond all reason—they damn well nearly murdered you."

"Before I can argue, even ask why, they start to beat me up. Very methodical." He winced with pain as he tried another smile. "One man stick plaster over my mouth to stop screams, then they take the turns. Two men hold me from behind, while third man hit me. I can do nothing, not even move face. And they kick too. When one man is tired hitting me, another takes his turn. This way they go on hitting me for long, long time."

"Poor bugger," I breathed softly. "You think it might be because of Anna?"

Willi was not sure. The punishment seemed to be too drastic for a husband whose wife had done nothing more terrible than overstay a holiday abroad. And it couldn't be anything to do with his work at Staffens. Willi was sure of that. He had recently been promoted, he was working on new and important contracts. He was, he said, a party member in good standing. He had broken no rules, revealed no secrets. Yet suddenly his telephone had been disconnected, all attempts to call Douzy had been frustrated. He could surmise only that it was a warning—that Germans with foreign wives should keep them at home.

I suddenly found myself saying, "I won't tell Anna the details, Willi, not if you don't want me to—but I hope you love her enough to stop her coming back to Germany for the time being. *You've* been warned. But what about her? I don't imagine they respect women any more than men?"

He shook his head. "She must never come back," he agreed, "not till this madness is over." He hesitated, then added, "I must write and tell her this, make her promise. Would you mind taking a short letter from me to Anna?"

"Of course not," I replied.

Willi hesitated.

"I think you have to hide it," he said. "I want to beg Anna not to return to Germany. Is not enough if I ask you to tell her. I have to put it down in words. You understand?"

"Of course. Don't worry," I said—but *I* was worrying.

When Willi finally handed me the letter it covered two closely written pages.

"No envelope?" I asked.

He shook his head. "It must be carefully hidden."

"But, Willi," I cried, "surely they won't search my *papers?* I mean—I'm not German, I'm not Jewish, they've no reason—"

"They have. I know what happens when men like me get beaten up. They wait to see who your friends are—maybe they are hoping Anna is to return. Your presence here is probably reported—perhaps by the pharmacist where you buy the drugs. And someone will follow you to the station when you leave."

"If what you say is true—it's terrifying."

"It is terrifying, I tell you," said Willi. "Here! Flatten each page into a square and then put one inside each sock. Please!"

Though I took off my shoes and socks and put the pages against the soles of my feet, I had the feeling that everyone could "see" them. I tried to forget my anxiety by preparing some food—Scotch was not enough sustenance for Willi. Rummaging in the kitchen, I broke up a couple of slices of bread, carefully taking off the crusts, then boiled some milk, dunked the bread in it until it was almost mushy, and produced that good old standby of nursery food—bread and milk. Willi managed to get some of it down, and afterward he felt better.

"You know what they sometimes call bread and milk in America?" I joked. "Graveyard stew!"

"The only thing that makes me happy is Anna—that she is safe," he said. "I didn't tell you until now, but as well as the beating, one of the men demands my party card and tears it up, and hands me official document that I am expelled from the party. Why? I ask. They never tell.

There can be no reason—jealousy, something I do not know about? I have been a good worker, I have helped very much. Now," said Willi, "this means I lose my job at Staffens. Is very secret work, only party members can work in armaments division. For me there is only one thing—join the army."

I hesitated. I was horrified at what had happened—at what I had seen, a generalized picture suddenly brought into the fine focus of a bleeding, torn mouth, black eyes, bruised ribs. This was Germany, I thought bitterly, the master race.

"The senseless brutes."

"Yes," sighed Willi, "this is the master race that Hitler promises will rule the world for a thousand years."

"But I have to return to Paris. What are we going to do? Are you sure you don't want Anna to come back to Germany?"

"*Nein, nein!*" He tried to shout. "It is over, life here in Germany. War comes very soon."

"Sounds tough on you," I said, "but, Willi, I agree. Anna may be married to a German, but she's still an American— and that means neutral. Looking at it from her point of view—and yours if you really love her—why should she suffer in a war that's no real concern of yours? But what are we going to do with *you?*"

"What can anyone do?"

"Can you get out? Leave?"

"Not possible, Larry. Germany is sealed tight. And even if I could go, where?"

"Do you mean to say there's nowhere you could go to?"

He shook his head. "You do not realize what happens in Germany. I have no passport anymore. How can I even get past a railway station? And if I escape, who will help a German? We are hated by everyone in Europe."

Sealed tight. I had never before thought that people other than criminals could be denied the right to a passport, freedom to travel.

"I work all my life, very hard," said Willi bitterly. "I pass my exams, I am top-class engineer—but maybe someone does not like the fact I have a foreign wife, or that my friend Moller's great-grandfather was half Jewish."

I was thinking, trying to solve a puzzle which no one could solve. "And there's no chance," I hesitated again, "Of—well, fixing you with a new passport? Or of escaping —is there no way out across a frontier?"

"Is impossible."

"But if we knew in advance—if I could start the ball rolling—I'm sure that since you're the husband of an American citizen, Papa could pull some diplomatic strings."

"I tell you, Larry, war will come soon. I am lost in this kind of new Germany. The only way I will be able to find food to eat will be to join the Wehrmacht."

"But Anna?"

"She will stay with you. Is my great joy. That and the goodness you show in coming to see me."

I hated the idea of leaving Willi and hated even more the prospect of telling Anna what had really happened. But I had to be back in Paris by the twenty-third.

"Just tell her the half-truth," Willi begged me. "That I lose my job, but not that I look such a mess. And one thing more, I would like a promise."

"If I can," I agreed.

The war, he said, would be brutal and protracted. And France could never win against the might of Germany. "This you must believe. We know from secret information that France will never be able to withstand Germany." As for Britain, well, Willi felt that she would probably compromise. Hitler, however, would never dare to involve the might of America. "So maybe I fight in France, who can tell. But maybe the Astells of Douzy remain neutral, *nein?* What I ask is—please do remember that when I join the army, I am like millions of Germans—I don't *want* to fight. But I have no choice. It is that or a camp. So please do remember this if we ever meet again. Remember I am not a free man—never until Hitler is dead and Germany is beaten."

* * *

I left Willi in time to catch the early morning train to Paris-Nord on August twenty-third. On the way back to the Düsseldorf station in the Bahnhofstrasse, I decided that Willi was right. There was no point in telling Anna how badly Willi had been beaten up. Especially as he felt reasonably certain there would be no repetition.

Even in the comparative peace of the first-class compartment, the air of tension was suffocating. I sat down in a corner seat which bore my name on a ticket, and put my briefcase and overnight bag on the rack above. A large fat woman sitting opposite opened a packet of sandwiches, looked at me suspiciously, and carefully held them so that I couldn't see what she was eating.

I stood up to take down the briefcase and get out the latest Eric Ambler, *The Mask of Dimitrios*, which had just been published in London. As I returned my briefcase to the rack the fat woman, still eating, looked down at my shoes. So did the other two people in the compartment—an insipid middle-aged couple. As though they had all heard Willi's letter crackling in my shoes because of my sudden movement, three pairs of eyes were suddenly fascinated by my shoes. The sweat broke out again on my forehead. Any of these people could be a Nazi agent.

At the frontier with France we all had to get out, queue, have our passports stamped, check with the customs. I had been warned that any Jews would be stopped and searched physically in an effort to prevent them smuggling out valuables.

An officer in gray uniform, backed by a couple of armed soldiers standing nearby, looked hard at me, wrote down my name, then let me pass through to the customs, but only after he had whispered something to a nearby clerk.

In the next room where the customs search took place, I saw the clerk whisper to the officer, who asked me quite politely to open my bag. He must have known who I was—or at least that I was known to Willi—for he examined every single thing. He opened the screw top of my toothpaste, examined my toilet bag, felt inside the spare pair of shoes. After the bag, he searched every corner of my briefcase.

Even then the search was not over. As I prepared to return to the train a second officer stopped me and asked if I would turn out my pockets. They took out everything—from my *carte d' identité* to my fountain pen. But not until they actually started to frisk me did the sweat beads start again.

"Please to go!" he said, and I saw him shake his head to someone. Thankfully I flopped down in my carriage seat. I felt as though I had been subjected to a third degree. But I *had* got Willi's message past the customs!

Two minutes later we moved across the frontier. As though a voice were crying "Freedom" a Frenchman pulled open the sliding door of the compartment and cried cheerfully, *"Passeports, s'il vous plaît!"* and *"Avez vous rien à déclarer?"*

Hearing me reply in French, the fat woman leaned across and offered me a sandwich, saying, "I was frightened to talk to you, I thought you were German."

"I thought *you* were German."

"Main non! I come from Dieppe."

Even so, I had to admit that as the train steamed away from Germany, I did wonder if I would ever see Willi again. It was a hope that diminished to zero by the time I arrived in Paris—just in time to read the sensational news that stupefied Paris and was now being announced in the biggest and blackest headlines ever seen in France.

While most of the country was on vacation, those two archenemies Russia and Germany had brought off a coup that stunned the world. The headline in the evening papers told the story: RUSSIANS AND NAZIS SIGN NON-AGGRESSION PACT.

At first I couldn't believe it. German Foreign Minister von Ribbentrop had, it appeared, turned out to be a master diplomat. At one stroke of the pen, or rather two strokes, he and Stalin had removed the direst threat facing Germany—the nightmare of a war on two fronts, the danger

which all Europe had hoped would prevent Hitler from his
final act of folly.

Now there would be no danger of a second front, for Germany and Russia were "friends."

"And that," declared Oregon, when I reached the rue du
Sentier, "means certain war. It's a matter of days now, not
weeks or months."

18

THE MOMENTOUS NEWS of the pact between Russia and Germany sent waves of apprehension which seemed almost visible in half-empty Paris—as though we had all caught a glimpse of the four grim horsemen of the Apocalpyse riding by, licking their lips. So profound was the sense of shock that at first it seemed impossible that millions of people hadn't yet heard the news, didn't yet realize its significance—that the two ill-assorted bedfellows were preparing to carve up Poland between them, and that Europe was doomed.

Why should they know? France was on vacation. In Douzy on that warm August Wednesday afternoon, with the sunshine rippling beyond the vineyards and over the yellow mustard fields, Papa was at the *cellier* and Mama never turned on the radio until Papa came back to the house. And so they still presumed that I would be returning late that Wednesday, as I had promised to tell Anna about Willi.

Of course I couldn't go—not immediately.

"On this date—the day the world has decided there's going to be a war!" exclaimed Tommy Tomlinson.

"Larry, I've had a cable from Washington," he continued. "You're working full time on retainer as of now. I don't need you weekends, I'll mind the store Saturdays and Sundays. But even now, Paris, like every other capital, is demanding reaction stories. I can deal with most of

them, but you might ring up your chums in the army and
politics—and Madame de Portes if you like."

I couldn't say no to his offer. I would still be free most
weekends; I was virtually on the staff and that meant
more responsibility, more involvement. And Vance, through
Tommy, had already suggested I might like to become a
Globe staffer. In a way that would be great, but on the
other hand, once a staffer, bang would go my independence. As a staffer there would be no way I could disobey
an order—even if the paper sent me as bureau chief to any
place from Singapore to Santiago. My way was best.

I immediately telephoned Anna.

"Willi all right?" Her voice was harsh with worry.

"Of course. Super," I lied.

"Why didn't he phone?"

"Phones don't work as well in Germany as they used to
do. It's guns before phones now, not only butter." I tried to
keep my tone light, but with the first words she detected
the half-truth in my voice.

"Something's wrong, isn't there?"

"Look, Anna. There are problems," I admitted. "But I
can't talk on the phone." I explained the news that had
broken. "This affects all of us—the whole damned world,
including Willi as well as you."

"Okay. What are you doing this evening?" Her voice
sounded determined, edgy, bossy almost.

"Nothing. I'm on standby duty. Just in case—"

"Larry, bless you for phoning, but I can't wait till the
weekend for news of my—" she hesitated, "my husband.
I'm driving into Paris right now. I'll spend the night at the
apartment in the rue des St. Pères. If I have to, I'll come to
the office. Otherwise, can you spare time for a *casse-croûte*
at home? I don't feel like going out to dinner. I'll cook for
you."

"Okay," I agreed, "seven o'clock."

It seemed vaguely peculiar, the prospect of having a
meal in the old apartment. In the past so much had happened in those beautiful, spacious rooms, the gray-paneled

dining room, the tiny study with its sedate bookshelves, the bedroom Guy and I shared as kids when Papa and Mama took us to see the Cirque Medrano or the Eiffel Tower; all the beauty of youth, and often with Anna and Sonia there too. In those days it had been a real home; a second one, true, but we always *felt* at home there as we scampered through its rooms. For long now, though, it had been relegated in my mind. The heart had gone out of the place, the excitement of youth had long been wiped off its walls. Now my Paris home consisted of my beloved Coquelicot rooms in the rue de l'Université. Going to the family apartment was like going visiting. Indeed I felt like a stranger as I parked my car round the corner in the rue de Lille and passed through the courtyard before climbing the handsome, wide circular staircase to the second floor. Anna had already arrived. She was sipping a Scotch and Perrier.

"And here's one ready for you," she knew that I enjoyed an occasional whiskey. As she poured out the Perrier in silence, I looked at her, wondering what form the next few moments would take—and how much I could withhold. For she looked so miserable, I was afraid to tell all.

When she saw me watching her, she touched up her hair slightly, patting it into place.

"I'm afraid I look an awful sight," she said.

It was not for a brother to admit this to a sister—even though it broke my heart to see her like this, so different from the beautiful bride on that spring day at Douzy, barely a few months ago. How she had changed! How was it possible that in a few weeks lines of worry or anxiety, or just plain fear, had furrowed her face, not only the forehead, the eyes, but two deeply etched creases leading from the corners of her nose to her mouth. And the hair of which she had always been so proud, but which she now nervously patted again and again—all the sheen or gloss gone. It looked dull and mousy, what Oregon once described as "old maid's hair."

"I've got to begin with one bit of bad news," I said heavily. "Willi's lost his job."

Anna didn't seem surprised. "I somehow expected it," she said flatly.

I explained as best I could that Willi had been expelled from the party after some Nazi official visited him at the Frankel apartment.

"Did he say who?" She was asking questions almost like a robot.

I hesitated.

"Come on—I'm not afraid," she said harshly.

"Brownshirts."

Suddenly she burst into uncontrolled sobs. "Oh, no, my poor Willi," she cried, and turned her tear-stained face to mine, "I knew them. Scum! Did they—hurt him?"

"No, no," I lied again. "According to Willi they roughed him up a bit when he was slow answering questions. But"—and I was on safer ground now because it was true— "though there was nothing for us to celebrate now he's lost his job, we did manage to drink a bottle of Scotch between us."

She tried to compose herself, but every now and then she was racked with sobs.

"But Willi must have said *something*—"

"I think he was afraid his apartment was wired." I told her everything—everything except the naked savagery of Willi's beating—until she had quieted down.

"Sorry about this"—she searched in a blue bag for a wisp of handkerchief and dabbed her eyes—"but poor Willi, it's so terrible for him—such a brilliant engineer—one of the best in Germany. What will he do now? What *can* he do?" Her voice trailed off.

Again I hesitated. But I had to tell her.

"He's talking about joining the German army," I said finally.

"The army! Those bloody clodhoppers!" she said savagely, and I was glad, for it was better to see her angry than weeping. "What a waste, what a stupid waste of a fine engineer."

"I know, Anna," I didn't really know what to say, but

added, "I think Willi felt that a few months of nonentity might be a good idea. I don't know what he's done—"

"Nothing!" she cried. "That's what's so damnable." She asked a hundred questions, wanting to know everything about him. Had Willi lost weight? Who was doing the cooking for him? And making his bed—"our bed," she started to cry again, then said, "It's the tank he was working on at Staffens that caused all the trouble."

I didn't understand.

"It's highly secret," she explained. "Supposed to be the finest tank in the world when it's ready. And several times people came to question us—very politely. But in the end I realized that the friendly meetings were always directed at me. About my family. All of us at Douzy, and America, Everything. I'm the one who got Willi into trouble, I'm sure of it."

"I think you're exaggerating." It was all I could say.

"I know it. Willi was engaged in highly secret work— and he was married to an American. That bloody beast Hitler is paranoid about American spies."

"Willi gave me a letter for you." I handed the pages to her.

"Did he? Thank you, Larry. I thought everyone was searched. I'm surprised you dared to carry it."

"Willi warned me," I said. "Thank God he did. The Gestapo on the train had obviously been tipped off. I think I was trailed from Willi's flat to the station. They searched my overnight bag with a fine-tooth comb. Even checked the contents of my pockets."

"Where did you hide the letter?"

"One page in each of my socks."

"Bless you, Larry, You've been wonderful."

I hadn't read the letter, but I knew what was in it.

"And Willi told me to stress above everything else," I said, "That you mustn't return to Germany. He's a marked man, Anna—and technically, I suppose, you're a German citizen and you're marked too."

"I wonder they didn't kill him. Thank God he's safe." She was reading the letter but it was so painful that she started crying again, and I took out my larger pocket hand-kerchief. "Here, Anna," I handed it to her, "This is bet-ter."

And later, after another Scotch, thinking that sorrows shared are sorrows halved, I said, "If there *is* a war—and there's bound to be one soon—Italy will surely be dragged in as a partner of the Rome-Berlin Axis. And that means Sonia will be an enemy too."

"I suppose so," she stopped crying, perhaps grateful for a change in conversation. "And you'll miss her. Do you see her often?"

"Whenever I can. I've never told you, Anna, but—well, we became lovers again soon after she married Fran-cesco."

"I wondered. And her husband?"

"He doesn't seem to care. And we're both very discreet."

Anna sighed. "Poor you. Poor us! I suppose if life had worked out differently, it would have been better if I'd never married Willi and you had married Sonia."

"Sonia wouldn't have me," I said bitterly.

"She loved you. Still does, I can tell," Anna insisted. "I often wondered *why* she didn't marry you. I always felt there was some reason—"

"You feel that too?" I asked.

"Yes, I do. I remember Sonia telling me one day that you were the only man in the world for her—but there were problems. Those were her words—problems."

"One day we may find out," I said. "My own belief is that somewhere along the line Riccardi, who I have never really trusted, blotted his copybook—and the price of his future somehow involved Sonia not marrying me."

"We'll never know. It is bloody, isn't it? *You* don't know why Sonia was afraid of some trouble—and I don't know why Willi's in trouble." She thought for a while, then added, "You know, Larry, this apartment makes me de-pressed. I'm not going to feel *much* better, but I don't feel like cooking—not even a *croque-monsieur.*"

"Let's go round the corner," I suggested. "Better for both of us. I'll take you to Lipp's."

So we walked along the rue des St. Pères, crossed the boulevard St. Germain, and found a bench-type table in the famous Brasserie Lipp.

"*Choucroute garnie* for two," I ordered, "and two large glasses of ice-cold Slavia."

"By the way," said Anna during dinner, "I forgot to tell you, but while you were in Germany Sonia invited herself to Douzy again for the weekend."

I must have looked very pleased.

"Yes," it was the first time I saw her laugh that evening. "Her husband's been called to the foreign office in Rome. So she rang up Mama. You mean to say she didn't tell you?"

"She can't," I explained. "It's awful, but the telephones in her house are tapped. She daren't phone me except from a phone booth, and I can never phone her."

"Still," she said, "you'll see her soon."

Anna drove back to Douzy early on the Thursday morning, and almost before I had reached the rue du Sentier, Sonia was on the phone.

"From a phone booth—so early?" I asked.

"Francesco has already left for Rome," she sounded breathless. "Every foreign ministry in Europe is in a panic. I'm sorry for *them*," with her throaty laugh, "but it's wonderful for us. You've heard about the weekend? And our staff of spies are now so overworked, I think the Italian Fascisti have vanished."

"For God's sake, be careful—for your sake."

"I'm not risking the phone—but I think the bloodhounds have been called off—so any chance of lunch?"

"Can we go someplace where I can kiss you?"

"That will be the most important part of lunch." She still spoke in that special voice of hers, almost as a signal, warning me she couldn't wait long before we met.

"Think it's safe to go to Marcel's?"

"Is it open—in August?"

"Sure," I replied. "You remember it was closed the last

time in mid-July. And there was a notice, reopening on August twenty-first."

"Then Marcel's it is," I could almost feel the warmth pouring across the telephone line, flooding through her at the prospect. "It'll always be my favorite restaurant."

Though times of crisis usually meant extra work for the *Globe,* lunch was fairly safe, simply due to the time difference: the editors in Washington were barely eating their bacon and hotcakes as we ate lunch. But I did manage to sandwich in a reaction story before I made my way to the rue Jacob. I went to see Reynaud to get it.

Reynaud had agreed to see me for ten minutes—in his apartment behind the Chambre des Députés. And among his remarks about "grave danger for Europe" and the usual political guff, there was one significant passage—though it didn't come from Reynaud but from Madame de Portes, who entered Reynaud's private sitting room without warning and said briskly, *"Bonjour, cher Larry.* These are stirring times! But exciting!" She caught sight of herself in an Empire-style gilt looking glass and automatically touched her *bouffant* hair.

"But one thing, *cher* Larry," she exclaimed. "That man Daladier will have to go if it comes to war. He's not the kind of leader we need to rally France in times like this."

"Then who do you think will succeed him?" It wasn't exactly an innocent question on my part.

"Who do *you* think?" she asked almost archly, and her question was answer enough, so that when I wrote my story, I started, "Informed sources close to the Quai D'Orsay believe that Monsieur Daladier may have to resign, and though no one has yet suggested a successor, many favor Monsieur Reynaud."

That, I knew, would please many people—especially one—and make it difficult for Reynaud to refuse later requests for interviews.

I arrived at Marcel's at ten to one, and five minutes later, while I was waiting at the bar, Sonia opened the narrow door with its frosted glass panes and stood for a moment framed in it, almost like a model posing, dressed in a plain white and brown dress with a narrow belt, a suede bag over her shoulder, a tiny straw hat like one of Maurice Chevalier's. She looked incredibly—well, saucy. She was wearing the sheerest stockings that money could buy and on her narrow feet, a pair of brown suede moccasins.

As I kissed her—no need for shyness at Marcel's, everyone knew we were lovers even though we didn't go there often—she looked up, came toward me, and asked, "Do you approve?"

"I run out of words trying to describe you—and out of breath. And that hat! Every time I see you, you look more desirable!" I held her out at arm's length, studied her almost clinically, she looked so beautiful, then ordered a glass of champagne for her; though it wasn't very good, it was the only alternative to those awful sickly French aperitifs like Kina Roc.

"Even three days away seems like an age," she said huskily. "I'm so glad to see you."

"Me too."

"Was it awful in Germany?"

I nodded. Anxious to change the conversation, I said, "I love those shoes—they're new, aren't they?"

"You notice things!" Like any woman she was delighted.

"I just thought that moccasins show off your legs."

"Made for me, that's why. By a man called Gucci who has opened a shop in the Via della Vignia-Nuova."

"Never heard of him," I said rather impolitely.

"Remember your twenty-first birthday party?" she asked as we sat down at our usual table. "Such wonderful days—and nights."

Nothing had changed—not there, not in Marcel's. Only we had changed. As the wife of a diplomat, Sonia was busy, much in demand, though always finding ways for us to meet. But I, too, had changed. Now I spent most of my time working on the *Globe* with stints helping out on the *Paris American.* I was earning good money, simply because there was so much news in Europe to be covered that Tommy Tomlinson couldn't cope unaided.

"It must be months since we were last here," said Sonia. "Hold my hand, darling. Across the table. Don't be shy."

I wasn't shy, but she always pretended I was.

"You know, Larry, I don't think I've ever loved you so much. Perhaps it's because I'm afraid—no, that's not an insult. It's the truth. Francesco says it's only a question of days now. But, darling, we'll always have a place to meet."

"Sorry, darling—I don't get it."

"My house in Switzerland."

I had long since forgotten the "cottage" she had planned to buy in Switzerland.

"You mean you've got it?"

She nodded, the fear of war replaced by the excitement of a new toy. "One we can share, neutral America, neutral Switzerland. Darling, it's for you and me. No one else will ever be allowed in."

"Where is it?"

"You'll never guess. It's at Rolle, just behind the lake. Not far from our old school. Remember St. Agnes? I don't know what's going to happen to Francesco and me, but if there's a war—well, I'm trying to think of the future. Switzerland will *always* be neutral—and as a diplomat's wife I hope I'll always be able to move around a bit."

"And Francesco?"

"Papa's given *me* the cottage—it's *mine*. It's nothing to do with anyone else."

"Has it got a name, in case I have to come and search for you?" I laughed.

"You remember the coffee shop? Well, almost opposite, by the fountain, a small lane leads off the main street. It's up there, first house after you pass under the railway bridge. It's got an odd name, Three Circles Farm."

"I wish we could escape now," I said, suddenly thinking how awful it would be—on our best behavior for the coming weekend at Douzy.

"Why couldn't we?"

"Now, now," I laughed. "None of your mad ideas. Keep the Russian in you at bay!"

"I love you, I love you, and we'll spend the weekend alone."

"On Sunday Papa has called a family council of war—to discuss the future."

"Well, Saturday—and Friday—with Douzy as a perfect alibi."

"We couldn't. I wouldn't put it past your Italian bloodhounds to phone Douzy and speak to Mama—deliberately to check on you."

She thought for a moment. Then, looking at me, straight with those blue, blue eyes, she said, "Why not tell your Mama what we're planning?"

"But where would we go?"

"What about that place in the village near la Ferté-sous-Juarre. It's tucked away. It's halfway to Douzy. We could drive there on the Friday, and on Sunday just drive on and join the family for dinner. And your council of war."

I wondered. Anyway, as I thought to myself, what the hell, I'm twenty-seven, I'm free, and if I can't tell my own mama my innermost secrets, whom could I tell?

"You're right," I admitted. What made it easier to agree was the fact that Mama was spending the Thursday evening in Paris to attend some formal dinner. Gaston was driving her in, and surely there would be time for me to pop round to the apartment for a drink and sound her out before dinner. All the same, I was a little nervous. It was one thing for Mama to *know* about my affair with a married woman, but something else to *condone* it.

That Thursday, sitting in the big salon in the rue des St. Pères, drinking my second Scotch, I summoned up my courage and said, "Mama darling, I want to talk to you. You can tell Papa later—if you want to. It's up to you."

"You mean about you and Sonia?"

"You *did* know?"

"I guessed. I'm not as old and decrepit as you seem to think."

"But that wasn't what I wanted to talk to you about."

"Oh!" she seemed surprised. "I thought—"

"Now that Sonia's officially invited for the weekend—we wondered—well, her presence there with you could provide us with a super alibi. Could we sneak off for a couple of nights? It's so sad, always having—"

"To go home?" she asked, and held out my arm. "I know how sad it must be for you. Mornings are so beautiful, waking up, and—" she hesitated.

"Would you mind if I didn't stay at Douzy? On the Friday and Saturday anyway. Just so that we can be alone."

Surprising me, she stroked my cheek, and said so gently, "Poor Larry, my love child. You are doomed to love, that's the fate of the love child. And we took Sonia away from you. I'll never be able to forgive myself for stopping you when you were young. I shouldn't say yes—I shouldn't. But," almost mischievously, "there's a world of difference between a snatched afternoon and an entire night."

"Mama!"

"I understand—it's the least I can do, Larry. But come back Sunday afternoon—for the party at the pyramid. And I'll make apologies for you."

"Mama, you are wonderful."

"Where will you go?" she asked, suddenly conspiratorial, "you two illegal lovebirds?"

I wrote down the name and number of the hotel.

"Have we time for another drink, Mama? To celebrate?"

"I'd love to, but I haven't time. I must dress for dinner."

"Who with?"

"The committee of the American Hospital," she laughed. "So dreary. I'd much rather be with you."

I had arranged to pick up Sonia soon after lunch, but before that I had to spend a morning at the office helping Tommy Tomlinson, and also Oregon, with the last lines of information for the *Paris American*. It was an uneasy morning, imbued with a sense of urgency, suppressed panic.

There could be no question of Chamberlain and Daladier

trying to placate Hitler this time. Action was outstripping words, tomorrow's history being enacted as we gaped at the awful news, and I was horrified at the way in which we could only stand and watch preparations for the disintegration of the only world we knew.

Daladier, it appeared, was in a panic—almost more afraid of the French Communists than of Germany. He banned *l'Humanité,* the official organ of the French Communist party, and ordered the arrest of all its Communist staff. Then he took an unprecedented step. He ordered the arrest of all Communist members of Parliament, though this was a direct violation of their parliamentary immunity. Known Communists in the armed forces also were thrown into jail.

On the Friday morning—the day I was planning to leave with Sonia—Oregon and I went for a quick stroll along the Grand Boulevards to judge the temper of the crowds. The string of boulevards, with their separate names joining one into the other, and called collectively "Grand" were already pasted with mobilization posters on every spare inch of wall.

"But Christ!" I pointed out the frightening headline AP-PEL IMMEDIAT to Oregon. "This is Friday—it's only a couple of days since the Russians and Germans got together."

"Daladier's right. There's no time to lose," said Oregon grimly. "Look at that!" A convoy of trucks emerged from the corner of the boulevard Haussmann into the boulevard des Italiens. They were packed with rows of helmeted troops, each man grasping a rifle by the barrel, the butt on the floorboards between his legs. "They're on the way to the Maginot Line."

Tommy Tomlinson had asked me if I could collect local-interest material for a piece that he would be writing later in the day. We often helped each other by pooling information.

"I'm going to take a quick look at the Gare de l'Est." I left Oregon and drove to the station—which I knew led to the Maginot Line area. The *gare* was jammed with the stark evidence of war, with troops everywhere. Some wore the khaki uniforms which had officially replaced the French blue uniforms in 1935. But many still wore the famous *bleu horizon*, not only out of pride, but because, as reservists, they had never been issued with replacements. Every man carried his manganese steel helmet with its unusual shape—still identical to the 1915 issue, stamped in one piece with an identifying badge.

Most of the men came from the infantry—it was easy to spot them with their blue uniforms, or in khaki with the blue piping on their kepi, or peaked cap—whereas other branches such as the artillery or infantry displayed different colored piping. Here and there tank crewmen strutted past with their special pride in being part of the elite "new army" which de Gaulle had envisaged. They had their own uniform, including their three-quarter-length leather coats and blue berets, and carried special helmets with neck guards and padded feather fronts.

There seemed to be hundreds of women crowding the station, some in tears, some kissing with the passion of a last farewell, sergeants shouting, officers swaggering in their neatly cut uniforms, and, above all, the long black columns of trains splaying out from each entrance to each platform, that and the steam above. It was a shambles of mixed patriotism and tears.

For every man there seemed to be two women, or perhaps it was an optical illusion, though there *were* two types of women: the younger ones—the sweethearts rather than the wives—locked in embraces, yet not crying, proud of their men, caught up in the infectious fervor of martial music calling the brave to arms, each girl convinced that her heroic man would return; it was the older women who had the drawn faces, the lines etched in by memories of another war, weeping quietly when saying farewell to sons who had never known their fathers.

On the way back to the office I passed the Louvre. It was already closed, the trucks drawn outside, the first crates taking away a national heritage to some secret destination. From the office I phoned the American embassy for the latest news. Jim Parks told me that even the American

Hospital at Neuilly-sur-Seine was packing up, ready to be evacuated "lock, stock, and syringe," as he put it, to Etretat in Normandy.

The first early editions of the evening papers carried whole-page ads warning the people of Paris to leave the capital unless they were needed on essential work. ENEMY BOMBS MAY BE REDOUBTABLE cried one headline.

"But there's no war yet!" I said to Tommy as I typed out a few helping paragraphs. The ads, which were duplicated on posters on nearby walls, even across from the windows of the rue du Sentier office, urged people not to hoard food and staple necessities. But by the time I set off to pick up Sonia, the first queues—for everything from sugar to gasoline—were forming. A sign AVIS A LA POPULATION gave instructions on how to shield car lights after dark and how to make improvised curtains for the home. The age of the blackout had arrived.

I had planned to meet Sonia in my MG outside the rue du Cherche-Midi. She was always afraid of being seen, and as she jumped in and I kissed her gently, the sudden noise of a roll of drums startled her. An old-time village town crier—for St. Germain-des-Près was a village in the heart of Paris—was beating a roll. A small crowd gathered as he announced in stentorian tones that under pain of severe punishment all members of the reserve must report to their units.

The decrees had already been promulgated, but the sight of this old man, crying to the "villagers" as his forefathers had cried to our forefathers before their past wars, before their past unnecessary deaths, made me shiver. It was a ghoulish illustration of the futility that gripped us all.

19

THE CHEVAL BLANC, in a tiny village a few miles east of La
Ferté-sous-Juarre, was the perfect place for a quiet weekend.

I had stopped there several times for drinks on the way
back to Reims and Douzy, and had fallen in love with its
charm. A small hotel with eight rooms which had achieved
gastronomic renown out of all proportion to its village location. Originally it had opened as a small bistro with a few
simple rooms to accommodate visiting farmers or trade
visitors—the sort of men who couldn't afford the better
hotels. But then Monsieur and Madame Roland, who
owned it, began producing culinary delights far better
than anything offered either in Reims or Epernay. Their
food was superb. People started driving from Paris for
weekends, even though six of the rooms only boasted a
cabinet de toilette. And above all it was discreet. It had
become not only a haunt for gourmets, but also a hotel
where gentlemen could safely bring the wives of other
gentlemen.

It stood in its own ground—a courtyard lined with pots
and tubs of annuals, of the type known to seed merchants
as hardy because they had to flower all summer through.
There were tubs of orange calendula edged with lobelia,
and the inevitable pots of petunias that grew, died, and
regrew.

"It's so beautiful, isn't it?" Sonia squeezed my hand. Behind the restaurant was a large pond on which some

ducks—no doubt kept for a specific purpose—quacked, almost the only sound to interrupt the magical silence.

The trees were colored a dozen different shades of green.
It all looked so peaceful that the impending beastliness of
war seemed a million miles away. The Cheval Blanc cast a
spell that made the short weekend as gentle and sweet as
any I can remember. Perhaps it was also because we both
knew there wouldn't be many more weekends together—
that the same disruption in the lives of Anna and Willi
would soon disrupt ours, make artificial enemies of each
other. It was a weekend beautiful yet tinged with sadness.

We went for long walks. The countryside was different
here. The fields of corn and barley were more sweeping, so
that with each passing cloud a shadow rolled across the
golden sea like a black wave. No one seemed to notice us,
as if (though this was fanciful nonsense) all the world
knew we were lovers on the verge of parting, and so
tactfully left us alone. In truth the entire area seemed
empty, as so many small villages are empty in France.
This one didn't boast one single shop, not even a *tabac.*
And the quiet village streets led across the fields, which
were different from those near Douzy. These were lazy
fields, inviting, the fat black and white cows as much in
place as the buttercups and other wild flowers that dotted
the green grass.

Hungry after our long walk on the Friday evening, we
ate a huge dinner, in which almost everything was home-
grown, homemade, and home-cooked, from the *terrine de
lapin,* the finest Charantais melons to start with, and the
dish of succulent yellow *girolles,* the mushrooms which
were sautéed, stalks and all, with a whiff of garlic so subtle
it was as though Sonia had chewed a clove and breathed
over the dish. Or for Sonia, as a vegetable, a dish of *hari-
cots noirs,* the delicious skinny string beans that start out
with blemishes of blackish spots which mysteriously vanish and turn green after cooking.

This weekend we made love in a peaceful, serene way,
perhaps because of the war clouds rolling across our horizon, darkening the blue August skies; perhaps also be-

cause for two mornings—the Saturday and the Sunday
—we were untroubled when we woke; no anxiety, no need
to dress quickly, no need to part hurriedly with backward
glances. Instead we ordered our feathery croissants and
coffee when we felt like it, not when we had to, before or
after making love. Even the act of lovemaking was different here; it had a quality of gentle repose.

"It's like being married," Sonia kissed me.

We arrived at Douzy during the late afternoon of Sunday to find the family assembled for a champagne party
that was about to start in the pyramid.

"I'm glad you both arrived in time," my father eyed me
warily. I was wary too, I wasn't sure whether or not he
knew how I had spent the last two days.

"Why the party?" I asked.

"A sort of temporary farewell, yes, I think that describes
it perfectly," explained Papa, while I continued to look
mystified.

"It's a mobilization party," explained Guy laconically,
"for those in the vineyard who've been ordered to report to
the military authorities."

A sudden rush of nausea hit me. It had been one thing
earlier that week to watch the frenzied, excited crowds at
the Gare de l'Est on their way to the front—watching them
as a reporter, as impersonally as if I were watching a news-
reel.

But this! The men at Douzy were actually on the point of
leaving for an unknown life. For where? For how long? For
life or for death? Poor devils! It seemed only a few weeks
since I watched the last remnants of the Spanish war
victims—victims only because they had been on the losing
side; several hundred idealistic young men who had volunteered to fight for a free Spain, many of them butchered by
Germans with guns or planes. And now, all over again.

Oregon, who was spending the weekend at Douzy, must
have seen my sudden silent anger, for he squeezed my arm
gently. "I know what you're mad at"—he seemed to read

my thoughts—"that a bunch of stupid political leaders are responsible for this, while we—"

"You're dead right," I replied. "Nobody wants a war."

"I agree with you—but only partly," he lit another cigarette in preparation for the short trip to the pyramid. "There *is* one thing you can't really ignore. It's too *easy* to say that nobody wants a war, so therefore it must be the fault of the world leaders. But aren't we—the ordinary people—to blame too? It's not only the leaders who are tyrants—the masses can be tyrants as well."

We walked down to the pyramid—all except Grandma, who had been making her rounds of the vineyards and whom we eventually saw approaching from a different direction, a stalwart old lady riding on her bicycle from one of the outlying vineyards where she had discovered some foliage which had not been trimmed well enough to let in the last weeks of the sun.

"Good afternoon, Grandma," I said politely as she dismounted.

"And where have *you* been, young man?" she asked, though fortunately—perhaps with advancing age—she never bothered to wait for an answer. "The number-five field," she said to one of the vignerons who was making for the pyramid, "needs more trimming."

He smiled assent. He knew that even if *"les salles Boches"* arrived at Douzy, La Châtelaine would make her rounds and give her orders—and expect them to be obeyed without question.

We trickled into the pyramid, more or less lining up at the tables draped with white cloths, at the back of the observation platform, scanning the faces of those I knew would be going, feeling a twinge of guilt, even though it wasn't my war—I wouldn't even be allowed to enlist had I wanted to. Which I didn't. If—that eternal if—it did come to war, I hoped that I would then be able to report it for the *Globe*.

Some of those who had received their mobilization orders were somber, some excited; looking at the white pyramid high above and all around us, I whispered to Sonia, almost shivering, "It looks like a bloody shroud."

One of Jacques Pagniez's family—a cousin of Aubergine's—came to shake hands. "I'm leaving on Wednesday," he volunteered the information. "Ordered to the Maginot Line."

"So he'll be safe, monsieur," said Aubergine, with the touch of pride that signified an appointment to a "safe" location.

"Yes, monsieur," he said, "I'm one of the lucky ones. One of the officers told me I'll probably never see a German. Do you know that some of our guns can fire twenty kilometers? Fancy shooting someone you've never seen!"

"Less uncomfortable for the soul," said Oregon.

"Sir?" The young man looked startled at the mystic word *soul*. Somehow the word didn't go with killing, and neither he nor Aubergine had the faintest idea what Oregon had meant.

The usual couple of formal "butlers" were serving champagne. Dressed in white tie and tails—a uniform to them—and wearing their badge of office, a silver tasting cup suspended round their neck by a multicolored ribbon, they dispensed champagne at every reception; they had never actually been vignerons—or full-time butlers—for when no one was giving a party both men worked in the accounting department. Serving as butlers was a spare-time job which they performed with dignity and, by now, a professional touch.

"I'm afraid I'm leaving, sir," said one of them, the middle-aged Pasteur. "Called up with the reserves."

"But who's going to—" I asked.

"We're not irreplaceable," he smiled. "Actually, monsieur, I'm really looking forward to it. I don't get on very well with madam, my wife I mean—and—" he shrugged his shoulders.

"I'll have to help you out," I smiled. "But I won't be as good as you are."

"Very kind of you to say so, sir."

Papa turned to kiss Sonia on the cheek. "We shall miss

these boys. But I'm *very* glad to see you, my dear. And how's"—he stumbled over the forgotten name—"your husband. Really! I've never got used to you as someone's wife."

"Francesco's in Rome," explained Sonia. "Very busy, as you can imagine."

"Yes, yes, of course. This must be a very busy time for him, very troublous, yes, that's the word, *troublous.*"

Anna was standing up by the rails, looking down into the white pit below, talking to Guy. Even though one was a man, the other a woman, at times the twins, when seen in a certain light or at a certain angle, were astonishingly alike—even though Guy looked quite masculine and Anna had a feminine face.

As Sonia walked over to talk to them, and I shifted away from Aubergine, who had been introducing me to yet another relative, Mama came up to me and said, "I think Anna feels much better, if that's the right word, but you know what I'm trying to say—now that the future is—well, resolved, I suppose you might say."

"Or inevitable would perhaps be a better word," said Oregon.

"Whatever. But she's not torn by having to make decisions. She may be miserable, parted from Willi. But there's nothing she can do about it now."

"One thing does worry me," I said, talking directly to Papa. "If the Germans do start a war, won't Anna be in trouble? A German national, I mean—sort of an enemy alien in France?

"She's American!" my father almost spluttered.

"Is she? She might be an American in America. But what would she be if the Germans occupied France and she was still here?"

"A disgusting thing to say!" La Châtelaine had overheard my remark. "I would kill myself before I let the Germans take my home." She gave an indignant rustle of her old-fashioned, rather long skirt. "It's wicked even to *suggest* such a thing as occupation."

"I'm sorry, Grandma."

"I should think so. Occupied! By the *Boche!* Unthinkable!"

"Of course," I agreed quickly. "But I was thinking about Anna." And then as Grandma, with a fine toss of her head, spoke to someone else, I elaborated to Papa, "It's true that Anna has dual nationality, but even so, you know how suspicious the French can get. It's not only the Germans—what about those French who whisper that she's married to a German, that her name is Frau Frankel, that she has a German passport? If war comes, she would be an enemy alien, even if Germany didn't occupy France. She could be interned."

"In prison!" cried Mama. "Never. Not Anna."

"You know what red tape is like in France," I said.

Grandma was back, and snorted, "The *Boche* will never beat the French. If this war comes, it'll teach the Germans a lesson they'll never forget."

"It won't be our problem, thank God," said Oregon.

"Of course it will," Grandma said angrily to Oregon. "France is your country too, and don't you forget it, my boy." The words *my boy* made me realize how odd it was to listen to Grandma giving her son a dressing down. "Never forget that even if America stays out of the war—and frankly it's none of our business, the French don't need them—we owe everything, our lives, our fortunes, to France. That's why both my sons have dual nationality. And that I am French. *Vive la France.*"

"Vive la France!" cried the others, hearing her raise her voice, without having the faintest idea what she was talking about.

"Meanwhile, what about Anna?" I asked.

"We'll talk about it after dinner," Papa suggested. "Larry's right, of course. She should get out of France." And to Mama, he added, "And so should you too, my dear."

"We've been through all that," said Mama with a touch of asperity.

I was about to agree with Papa when—perhaps fortunately, as it broke the tension—Gaston came along. He was politely talking to Olivia, almost earnestly.

He approached my father and asked, "I wonder, monsieur, if it would be all right to give Mademoiselle Olivia her final driving lesson tomorrow?"

"Driving lesson!" I looked at Gaston. "What on earth do you mean? She's the best driver in Douzy," adding with a laugh, "after you and me."

"I know, monsieur, but," Gaston hesitated. "Monsieur agreed that mademoiselle should spend a little time driving the Hisp. It *is* large for a lady driver, sir?"

"Ah yes, of course," Papa agreed.

"But why?" I suppose I should have realized.

"Because on Wednesday afternoon," said Mama quickly, "we won't have a driver. Gaston's been mobilized."

"Oh no!" I couldn't believe it. Gaston and I had the bond that only two people who have grown up together *and* loved cars can share. The same age as me, a man of impeccable manners, a quiet charm, the son of an old friend of the family who had spent his life working for us, and who had produced Gaston, who in turn worked for us and had become the perfect chauffeur as well as a friend to me. He was good-looking, didn't smoke, drank only wine, and was completely honest. He was like another member of the family.

"But, Gaston," I suggested, "couldn't you qualify for a reserved occupation or whatever it's called?" I turned to Papa. "Surely we could help?"

Gaston looked embarrassed.

"I don't want that," he said. "I'm only worried about letting you down."

"And so," explained Papa, "we've got a new driver. Yes, a chauffeuse. Yes, chauffeuse, that's the word. What do you think of *that?*"

"And that's why I'm getting a few last minute tips," Olivia laughed. "I call the Hisp the monster. I only hope I don't smash it up."

"Her, please, not it." I laughed too, but couldn't help asking, with a trace of sarcasm, "Then what's going to happen to Guy's painting lessons?"

"Did I hear someone call my name?" Guy crossed the

platform. "Art? Oh, that!" he said cheerfully. "On the advice of my mentor and art master, I've decided to give up painting until the war's over. I'm going to work full time for Papa in the vineyards or the *cellier*. Only until the war's over, mind you."

"Hardly worth bothering about. If those Germans have the guts to fight, the war will be over in a couple of months," said La Châtelaine fiercely—the look of fierceness accentuated by her eccentric clothes, the long tweed skirt (rather unsuitable for summer) and the thick leather belt with a huge buckle, and her hair in a bun.

I'm sure that Oregon loved his mother, but even so he couldn't stop the whisper, "All she needs is a pair of cycling clips and she'd be a man!"

Turning to Gaston, I said, "It's going to be tough without you, but let's hope Grandma is right—and that it'll all be over before it starts. Any idea where you'll be posted?"

"I hope to go to North Africa in the transport corps or tanks. Thought I might as well get a free bit of travel on the government."

"No luck?"

He shook his head. "I've still got my application in," he said, "but now I've been told to report on Wednesday to Arras. I imagine my application has been pigeonholed."

"I think you're better off here," said Mama. "At least you'll be able to come and see us when you're on leave, and Madame Robert will be able to get you some extra food from the Home Farm. And, you'll be with your family. Africa? It sounds horrible. And," hesitating, "if my husband can help—"

"I'm very grateful, madame." I could see that Gaston really meant it, was touched. "And I'll continue with Mademoiselle Olivia's final lesson?"

"Of course," said my father as Gaston walked away. "Salt of the earth that lad, yes, the *salt.* Trust him with my life."

The Misses B and B, together with Jean-Pierre, came for a quiet dinner that evening, and Miss Brewer in particular

was a perfect foil for Grandma, nodding approval each
time Grandma made a new and outrageous statement.

This was also a farewell dinner for Jean-Pierre, who had
gained a commission as a second lieutenant and was being
posted to the Maginot Line.

"On Thursday," he said in answer to Papa's question.

"We shall miss Jean-Pierre very much," sighed Miss
Brewer. "The cottage will be very empty."

"Don't you think you should close it up and move to your
small apartment in Paris?" asked Mama. "If there is going
to be any fighting, it's sure to be around the Champagne
area, whereas the Germans will never reach Paris."

"We did think about it," Miss Brewer nodded more urgently than ever.

"But you see," explained Miss Barron, "it would suit us
best to remain here. The cottage will be so much nearer for
Jean-Pierre when he gets leave."

To me it seemed incredible that though this nationwide
mobilization was urgent *and for real,* it was still invested
with the unreal quality of a war-games exercise. Nobody
seemed aware that when the battle burst upon Europe,
leave wouldn't matter a damn—you could be shifted from
one theater to another without telling anyone, to say nothing of the fact that thousands and thousands would be
killed or maimed. People like the Misses B and B—and
others—seemed totally unaware of the disruption and
bloodshed which war would inflict. Miss Barron had actually consulted the railway guide for information about
trains between the front line and Reims. To her the front
line was static, Jean-Pierre was safe, nothing would interfere with his routine leave or weekend passes. Did they
really think war was still a game between "gentlemen"
who abided by a set of rules?

Of course, like everyone, I didn't think they *would* be
killed, but when I said this to Oregon, he answered, "No
one would ever go to war again if they didn't feel certain it
was the other guy who's going to get killed."

"I'm quite looking forward to it," said Jean-Pierre,

"though I'm worried about what'll happen during the *vendange.*"

"We'll be short-handed too," said Guy, "so we'll have to help each other."

In fact the *vendange,* or harvest, though not due until the end of September, might well cause problems, for the speed with which the grapes were picked depended on employing casual labor from mining families in Lorraine who had over the years become regular visitors—and experts in harvesting.

"But as most are miners," explained Papa, "the government is certainly not going to let them have their annual vacations to pick grapes."

After dinner Papa carefully broached the subject of Anna's departure. We were sitting in a corner of the conservatory having coffee.

"I don't really want to go anywhere," confessed Anna miserably. "If I can't stay with Willi, I want to stay at Douzy."

"Very understandable," agreed Papa. "Yes, *very.* Nothing matters, of course, if there *isn't* a war. But technically I suppose you are a German. And quite apart from red tape, people are getting, well, suspicious of their neighbors."

"Suspicious of someone like me!" Anna almost laughed. "But everyone round here knows me. *Everyone!*"

More gently than usual, Oregon explained, "It's the fifth column, Anna. It's become a sort of cult. Everyone is looking at everyone else—looking for traitors, Nazi sympathizers."

"It sounds awful," said Anna. "I don't *want* to go, but even if I did, where *could* I go?"

"America?" I asked.

"God forbid. At heart I'm a European, Larry, and you know it."

"England?"

"They wouldn't let you in with a German passport, or stay with an American one," said Oregon.

"Then I'll stay here," decided Anna.

It was at this moment that Sonia drifted toward the conservatory, listening to the end of the conversation.

"I've got an idea," she hesitated. "What about my house in Rolle?"

"What's this about a house in Switzerland?" Both Papa and Mama looked mystified.

"Of course, I haven't told you." Sonia explained how she had come by the house. "It's not very comfortable yet," she admitted, "but Anna could stay there." With a laugh at the happiness of the past, she said, "At least it's got more comfortable beds than those we slept on at St. Agnes."

I could see that Anna was tempted.

"It seems a *very* good idea," said Papa. "Just until this nonsense blows over."

"I could come down with you to take a look-see and help put the place in order," said Sonia. "We could have such fun! It's probably in a terrible mess—but the Swiss are good at things. They'll fix it up in a week." And squeezing Anna's hand impulsively, she implored, "Come on, Anna! Just for the time being. Just the two of us."

I realized for the first time that Anna was frightened. Not deeply. Perhaps apprehensive would be a better word. But to her, Switzerland represented a haven, while the prospect of living in America was unsatisfactory because it was too far from Willi—not to mention Douzy. Switzerland was different. It was small and cozy and next door to everything.

"Want a lift down?" I asked.

"Thanks—another time." Even Anna was laughing again, and with a hidden meaning that only the three of us could understand, she said darkly, "We know what happens when you take girls out in your seduction cars."

Before the end of the evening it was decided. There was no suggestion that Anna would stay in Switzerland for a long time. But even she had to agree that the name Frankel on a German passport could be embarrassing.

"You two girls fix up the details between you," I said, "And I'll see you safely on the train."

It was shortly after this that Mama came into the conversation, astonishing us with a rare outburst of anger.

The girls had gone off on their own—it always added to the warmth of my love for Sonia to see how close she and Anna had always been, still were. Shades of the days when we were all conspirators. And here they were married to different people, living different lives, but we were still like a trio who loved each other. Papa was explaining that Sonia had suggested taking Anna to Switzerland.

"A temporary refuge, yes, the word is *refuge,*" he said, rather pleased with his choice of words.

But this remark led to another. "Of course I would have been happier, my dear, if Anna had gone to America—with you." He turned to Mama. "After all, you haven't seen your mother for years, and she's an old lady," adding mildly, "I see mine every day."

"Too often," grunted Oregon. "No offense, but mothers should be seen and not heard. Why do you think I started the *Paris American?* So that I wouldn't be bullied in Douzy seven days a week."

"Well, I'm not going anywhere," Mama's voice was firm.

"I know how you feel about staying here," said Papa. "But it won't be much fun here, even for a neutral."

This casual remark, directed originally at Anna more than at Mama, almost led to a row. I couldn't believe the intensity of Mama's feelings.

"We've been through all this before," she said crossly, "and once and for all, I'm not going to leave France." As I looked up, surprised at the vehemence in her tone, she added, "I don't know why you insist on carrying on about it."

"The war could last a long time," said my father dryly.

"Or a very short time," snorted Grandma as she entered the room. "The *Boche* will never get past the Maginot Line."

"There is *one* thing Anna would do well to consider." Oregon was hastily changing the subject. "She's going to find a German passport an—encumbrance. I don't know what she can do with it," he hesitated, "but if she can—well, conveniently forget she ever had it—" he left the suggestion in midair.

"You mean just use her American one?" I asked.

"Sure," Oregon added. "You told me the other day her American passport is still valid. Great. Only even though she does have dual nationality, she'll have to be careful."

"About what?" asked Papa.

"About getting caught," said Oregon, "with the German one. By accident, I mean. Germans aren't exactly popular around Europe, and more and more travelers are being searched at the frontiers."

I had had to work in Paris all that last week in August—and "all that week" included trying to make head and tail of the abortive moves by Daladier and Chamberlain, both trying desperately to pacify the Germans.

"Daladier can't do a thing," said Tommy Tomlinson in the office. "He's too weak."

First thing on Monday morning, I booked tickets for two sleepers to Switzerland for the Wednesday—that would be August 30. I had a hell of a job getting reservations, everything was booked up, but with a little help from embassy friends, I succeeded. The storm clouds were darkening every day. The feeling of edginess in Paris was claustrophobic, yet I found, too, a ring of patriotism, as though everyone were echoing the cry of Grandma, "The *Boche* will never stand a chance!"

On the Wednesday afternoon I took the girls to the Gare de Lyon. Everyone seemed to be making for the southbound trains—or were the traffic jams by the Hôtel de Ville always so jammed with traffic?

It was evening and spattering with rain, as it so often was when the trains for the south departed. The rain added to the sense of foreboding. In normal times trains are exciting to watch, to board—but not now. The packed platforms were thronged with wet people, looking more bedraggled than ever in the blue wartime lighting, making the unending rows of platforms seem even longer under the huge arcs of the glass roof. People struggled at the narrow entrance gates, and at first a fussy ticket collector tried to stop me until Sonia explained her diplomatic status. We fought our way toward the train reserved for passengers to the south, hardly able to hear ourselves as the old-fashioned engine whistled away its steam.

It was deeply depressing. And yet I was delighted at our joint success in persuading Anna to leave, for what would in effect be the start of a new life. For I could see no return to the past.

The station was crowded, not so much with troops now—they would be making more for the Gare du Nord or the Gare de l'Est. The people bumping into us now were mostly civilians in the process of running away. Like Anna, I suddenly thought.

Travelers going only to southern France—Lyon and the surrounding area—were able to board the train immediately upon producing tickets, but passengers making for Switzerland, for which there were three special coaches at the rear of the train, had to go through immigration and a vague customs check. I knew that the customs operated stations specifically to deal with occasional passengers about whom they had been tipped off, men or women carrying gold or perhaps drugs. In the same way passengers, especially those with foreign passports, were subjected only to a cursory examination. The police and immigration were more interested in looking for criminals.

I could see Anna and Sonia through the window of the immigration room off the station platform. The moment the officer looked at Sonia's diplomatic passport, he saluted smartly and even gave her a small bow. A moment later Anna presented her American passport, and I saw the officer, apparently perplexed, motion to Sonia, asking whether they were friends and traveling together. Then I saw him consult a thick black loose-leaf reference book. I guessed it consisted of a list of names, and I saw, but could not hear, the beginnings of an argument. Barging through the door, I tapped Sonia on the shoulder.

"What gives?" I asked.

Anna had gone white."It's the passport!"

The French official was not only polite, he was plainly apologetic.

"Can I help, officer?" I asked. "This is my sister."

"It is unfortunate"—he displayed Anna's passport—"and I can assure m'sieu that this is only a technicality. But the name of madame—and the passport."

"Oh, no," I groaned. "Oh, Anna—you didn't get your passport stamped with your new name."

Anna was in tears. "There never seemed to be any time—I—"

Sonia was whispering to the immigration officer, "trying to pull rank," as she told me later. But there was no rank to be pulled. I saw the officer apologize profusely. Something about the man's manner, polite but acting under specific orders about a specific person, crystallized into a sudden suspicion that this was not an accidental problem at the station. Someone had warned the immigration authorities to watch out for a "Miss Astell." How otherwise could he have known that there was anything wrong with what appeared to be a perfectly valid American passport? How could he know enough to ask if Astell was her real name?

"I don't understand, officer." My voice had an undercurrent of anger. "Why should you pick on my sister? She has a dual nationality. How did you even *know* she had a married name?"

"Monsieur, please, I beg you, this has nothing to do with me. I am only presented daily with a list of names. As you know, even if it is innocent, it is strictly illegal to travel under a name that is not correct."

I *knew* what had happened—knew inside my guts, even if I could never prove it. I said to both girls, "It's that sod Albrecht. He knew you were in Paris, Anna, he's tipped off the neo-Fascists in the Quai D'Orsay." Adding, "My God, Anna! How could you be so bloody stupid as to forget your passport problem."

As I led the girls back to the car I was thinking, God! how powerful the Germans are—and the fifth column. And how thoroughly ruthless, how deep-seated the determination to beat the hell out of anyone who stood in their way. No wonder that poor innocent men like Willi—anyone who crossed their path—were watched, and beaten up or exterminated.

I hoped—though I had my doubts—that the "technicality," as the immigration officer called it, could be resolved quickly. And it had already occurred to me that if the Germans behind the French were able to stop an American leaving Paris for Switzerland, they might be equally capable of stopping a Frau Frankel.

So it proved. It would take at least a week for the U.S. embassy to process the documents. New photos would be required. They needed her marriage certificate, which meant getting a duplicate from Douzy. The formalities were endless.

"We'll start the ball rolling," I said. "I only hope we will get the new passport through in time."

I had to leave the girls after dropping them at the rue des St. Pères. Sonia refused to travel to Rolle alone. Anna decided to stay at the apartment until Friday evening when I could drive her back to Douzy for the usual weekend break. But before that—and right away—I had one phone call to make as soon as the ancient elevator creaked and groaned to the second floor of the rue du Sentier.

It was to Herr Albrecht.

Whatever he might have wondered, his first remarks on the phone exuded his spurious air of camaraderie, that of the fellow journalist delighted to talk with a colleague.

"Cut out the hearts and flowers crap," I almost shouted. "I know damn well you brought pressure to bear to get my sister stopped at the station."

"That is outrageous, Larry."

"You and Abetz. What a pair of shits."

I could feel, even on the phone, his anger matching mine.

"I would remind you, Herr Astell"—the "Larry" had

gone for the moment—"that your sister insisted she was in Switzerland, *nein?*"

"Well, how do you know she isn't?"

"She shouldn't dine with an Italian diplomat, my friend. Women who are on the run should be more circumspect. After all, Italy is a member of the Rome-Berlin Axis."

I felt sick. I had known that was the obvious link, but had thrust it out of my mind. Could it really be true that de Feo—the husband of Anna's oldest friend—had betrayed her?

At least Sonia could have nothing to do with it. So she must never know. If, that is, my guess was right. I prayed it wasn't, and said to Albrecht, "Are you there, Herr Albrecht?"

"Ja, ja."

"Then listen. Keep right out of my way. I warn you. I don't give a shit if you're Hitler himself—but the next time I set eyes on you, I'm going to beat the hell out of you, in the same way you beat up my brother-in-law. I'll start by crushing your balls together. Okay, fatso? Now just you remember—keep out of my sight."

I felt better—a bit better anyway—when I slammed down the phone.

After checking with Tommy Tomlinson, I left on the Friday for Douzy. I knew there was no hope of seeing Sonia that weekend, and I had the feeling in my bones that the bubble of our lives was about to burst at any moment. So I set off in the MG, arriving in the late afternoon.

The first person I saw was Gaston, polishing the Hisp.

"What on earth are you doing here? I thought you'd gone with the others, the day before yesterday."

"I got some good news," he seemed excited. "They're drafting me to North Africa after all."

"I knew you wanted to go. When?"

"On Sunday. Catching the train to Paris to report, then to Algiers."

"Well—*bonne chance,* Gaston. Algiers can't be that bad, though I don't suppose you'll ever see a German."

The second person I saw was Papa, taking an early evening stroll in the courtyard.

"Just ten minutes for a breath of air before dinner," he explained.

"Mama around?"

Papa shook his head. "She's having a rest. She told Aubergine to wake her in time for a bath before dinner."

"Nothing wrong?" Papa seemed tense.

"You obviously haven't heard the news."

"Nothing—not since I left Paris."

He sighed. "It upset your mother. Germany has invaded Poland."

"Oh my God!" I cried. Until the very last moment, despite the overwhelming news of sinister German troop movements, I had clung to the hope that it wouldn't—that it couldn't—happen. "So this is it," I said dully. "There's no way that France and Britain can keep out of the war now."

"None," said Papa.

"And Anna. How's she?" I picked up "Willi's" malacca cane and found myself strolling out of the courtyard, in front of the yew trees toward the path at the top of the dell. In the early evening sun the lake in the distance shimmered like a burnished tray catching the light.

"I'm very worried," confessed Papa. "Yes, really. This business at the station was *very* unpleasant. That sort of thing has never happened to the Astell family before."

"The station business was deliberate," I told Papa. "A plant—set up by the Germans using French Fascists in the government."

"But what's going to happen to her?" My father looked anguished, nervously prodding his ashplant into the grass verge of the path. "War is certain, yes. And then—do you realize Anna could even be interned."

"She *is* American."

Papa shook his head gloomily. "She's not—not technically. She is American—but only in America."

"If she holds an American passport?"

"I don't like it, Larry, I don't like it at all. If the worst

comes to the worst, and we can't get her out of France, we
may have to hide her."

"You must be joking!" I could hardly believe my father's
words, as though he was panicking.

"I am not joking," he said crossly. "I am not. Please realize that Anna is a German. And whatever Grandma may
say about the French, we all know—you and I—that they
could cut through Champagne like a knife through butter.
Yes, *butter.*"

"But we're neutral."

"We may be neutral, but so is the lightning that strikes
a neutral man dead in the middle of a field."

"And Mama won't go to America? Definitely, not even
now?"

"Absolutely not," he sighed, jabbing again into the
grass. "Really, women can be very difficult. They don't understand that if they love a man in wartime all the husband wants is peace of mind."

But astonishingly Mama confounded the family later
that evening by calling us into the living room and announcing—without any arguments—that suddenly, inex-
plicably, she had changed her mind.

"Perhaps it's because my mother is getting old, and who
knows if I'll ever see her again," she said in explanation—or was it only part explanation? It sounded a little
too pat for me. But then it occurred to me that perhaps she
was doing it to try to get Anna away too.

"Is Anna coming with you?" I asked.

"That was my hope—still is," said Mama, but Anna
shook her head—firmly, as though she didn't want to discuss the matter. "I wish," began Mama, "but I can understand about Willi." And changing the subject abruptly,
she said, "When do I have to leave?"

"Tomorrow, I'm afraid, it's the last chance," said Papa,
half happy for her, half sad.

Papa, it seemed, had made all the practical arrangements long before. He had agreed with Bill Bullitt that she
should leave on Saturday with a seat reserved on one of
the many aircraft now flying between Paris and London.

From there the embassy would look after her, meet her, transfer her to the boat train to Liverpool.

"I've never been on a plane," Mama confessed. "I'm a bit nervous."

"No need to be," said Papa cheerfully. "People are flying all over the world these days. Why, there hasn't been a single crash since Pan Am started its first commercial flights between Europe and New York in May! I'd have sent you on one if you'd left earlier, but they've been suspended for the moment. However, it's okay between Paris and London."

"And then there are those awful submarines."

Patiently Papa explained, "My dear. We're not at war, you know. We may never be. And you know, *really*, Germans won't use their submarines when ships are going about their—what's the phrase?—their lawful occasions on the high seas. *Yes.*" He seemed pleased to have discovered the exact description. *"Lawful occasions."*

He paused for a moment, then added, "And anyway there's no fear of being sunk even if Germany does start a war. No, certainly not. She's not only a fine ship, but she's carrying a couple of hundred children, nearly three hundred American citizens, and around five hundred Canadians. Even the Germans wouldn't dare to sink a neutral passenger ship carrying over three hundred *Americans.*"

"When exactly does she sail?" asked Mama.

"Sunday evening—that's September the third," said Papa.

"The *Athenia.*"

20

AT 5:00 P.M. ON SUNDAY, September 3, France declared war on Germany. We sat waiting, ears glued to the radio at Douzy, though we all knew the actual declaration to be a formality, for Chamberlain had announced the grim news six hours earlier on the BBC, at eleven o'clock on that warm Sunday morning, and his sonorous voice in London had been followed almost immediately by the dismal wail of air-raid sirens as a signal for the people of Europe— friend and foe alike—to start the life of troglodytes.

It had been a false alarm as it happened, but now that war was a reality our first agonizing thoughts were of Mama. Somehow I had always felt—or I suppose *hoped*— that in the end we would somehow settle for another "Munich," that people couldn't be so mad as to go to war, that even if Mama did sail off to America she would be back once the hullabaloo had died down.

During the official announcement on the French radio, we were gathered in the living room—Anna, Guy, and Olivia, and of course Oregon. Jean had already prepared a silver tray with flute champagne glasses and a magnum of the prized '21.

"Shall I serve it, sir?" he asked when Papa switched off the radio and rang for him.

"Please," said Papa, "and a glass for you too, Jean."

The butler carefully eased open the cork of the large bottle, taking care to avert a bad-mannered pop.

When our glasses were full, Papa said simply, "To

Mama!" Adding hastily, with a quick look at Anna, "To absent friends, all of them. Yes, *all.* And to victory. Yes, a *speedy* victory." As we drank our champagne Papa looked at his watch and said, "She should be sailing just about now. *Bon voyage!*"

Yet it was worry rather than fear that we felt. Though we had heard a great deal about German submarines, even seen some photos of their ugly black silhouettes with the letter *U* and a number painted on each conning tower, their presence was impersonal, it had nothing to do with us, they represented no danger to neutral passengers, to women and children.

There were others, too, who were worried that day. What about poor Anna? I stole a glance at her, almost afraid to let her catch me watching her surreptitiously. She was sitting in one of the deep oatmeal-colored sofas near the big glass coffee table, twiddling the stem of her champagne glass, her thoughts miles away, eyes glazed with misery. Poor Anna! She not only had Mama to worry about, but one extra person, Willi; an enemy now, an enemy of the France that Willi enjoyed so much.

And what of Olivia?

"Santé!" I toasted her. "It's strange to think that here we are, in this beautiful home of ours, and you're the only French person among us."

"Don't say that to Grandma," Oregon chuckled. "She may have an American passport—but that's the only American thing about her."

"The *Athenia* is a good ship," my father, miles away, was thinking aloud rather than talking, masking his worry.

"No point in upsetting yourself," said Guy, trying to cheer him up. "You'll only work yourself up into a state. Just put your mind forward a few days. In a week or so Mama will be hitting the high spots in New York."

"I know you're right," Papa admitted. "Stupid of me, especially when I *am* so glad she took my advice."

"But you can't help thoughts, can you?" asked Olivia gently. "If only people could control their thoughts! Think only of happy things."

"If only we could!" said Anna. "If only Willi—"

Sensing the tautness in Anna's nerves, Oregon, trying to change the subject, asked, "Where's Grandma?"

"Upstairs," said Papa. "She wants to stay in her room until dinner."

"No doubt reveling in dreams of glory—how the French are going to thrash the Germans," Oregon was chuckling.

"You mustn't tease her," my father reproved his brother gently.

"I won't," Oregon promised. "But sometimes I think a bit of humor, even if it *is* forced, is the only way to keep sane. What about my problems?"

"What about them?" asked Guy.

"Never occurred to you, did it, that behind my cheerful exterior, I, too, could be in the dumps?" Striking an attitude of mock despair, Oregon lit another Gauloises, looking around for an ashtray in which to put the stub of the one he had just finished. Then, peering through his glasses, cherubic in appearance, he added, "I'll be out of a job soon. I'm going to have to close the *Paris American.*"

"But you can't!" It was Olivia, always sensitive to the unhappiness of others. "You can't!"

"You can't," echoed Anna.

"I can't," mimicked Oregon. "But tell me—who's going to read it when the last Americans have gone? Oh, yes, they'll go—the day after the first air raid on Paris. And who's going to advertise in it?"

I said nothing, I just felt sick at the thought of Oregon sitting there, not even noticing that the trail of ash from his cigarette was falling on Mama's precious, thick, white pile carpet, still trying to crack a joke, to take life as it came. The *PA* had been his baby—and in a way I was suffering too, for I had been journalistically weaned on it, learned my trade, helping to fill its columns; and if it came to that, learning everything I had to learn through Oregon's selfless help.

Deliberately changing the subject Oregon turned to Olivia, "And you? You're quite happy to carry on with your new work—Champagne's first lady chauffeur!"

"If I'm good enough to keep the job," she laughed. "I've

no desire to go back to the big city, apart from driving the Hisp into Paris when I'm needed. But I love it here, especially since you've all been so kind"—I could sense that she was speaking under a certain strain—"I never had a real family of my own until," shyly, "now. And I love the country. And I *hate*," with a sudden rush of vehemence, "big cities like Paris."

"You've never really got over that pogrom business, have you?" I asked.

She shook her head. "I don't wake up at night with nightmares about it, if that's what you mean. After all, Guy and Anna and your mother had a far worse time than I did. They saw it in all its beastliness. I only saw the fringes. But it's not a question of being afraid *today*. It's the future that frightens me. If—well, you know, there is a powerful clique of right-wing Frenchmen who are as violently anti-Jewish as any Nazis. So you see, I feel safer here."

"I don't think we've got anything to celebrate"—I tried to be cheerful—"but I'm inviting anyone who wants to come to Boulingrin's." It had been months since we had dined at the brasserie in Reims.

"I'm just in the mood for a steak and *pomme frites*," cried Guy. "Especially if you pay. Remember! I'm no longer a struggling artist. Now I'm a struggling vigneron. The pay is even worse."

In the end the four of us went. I think Papa and his brother, Oregon, were relieved to dine quietly at home with Grandma. For with Mama on the high seas, Papa was bound to be more miserable than we were—not because we were heartless, but because youth isn't as pessimistic as middle age. We were all certain that a cable from Mama in New York would arrive within days.

The Boulingrin was crowded, and Monsieur Leleu had great difficulty in finding us a table.

"How are you all?" To him we were friends first, customers second. "Just have a drink at the bar, and I'll put you at the head of the queue for the next free table."

A man drinking near us put his glass down on the zinc

bar and slapped Guy on the back, crying, "To victory! You see—it'll all be over in three months!"

He was half right, but he insisted on opening a bottle of champagne—which none of us really wanted, anyway. Fortunately Leleu rushed up, a sheaf of red and white paper tablecloths in his hand, and whisked us away from the man, who promptly offered the champagne to someone else.

"What a sad day!" cried Leleu. "But never mind, my old friends. There's no rationing of good red meat—not yet."

Everyone was so busy eating and talking that it seemed almost embarrassing. This was a terrible day in the history of the world! Surely in British or German restaurants people would be eating quickly, imbued with a kind of decorum. But here! Crash! Bang! Wallop! as the American comics said. There were no inhibitions here. We ordered our steaks, one *bleu,* one *bien cuit,* two *à point.*

"Here's to your mother," said Olivia suddenly, gravely. And we all drank a toast to Mama in the first of four bottles of *vin ordinaire,* which we knocked back between us before saying good-bye to Leleu, who doubtfully regarded my slightly raffish appearance and then the equally raffish MG.

"Don't worry," I laughed, "I can drive this damn thing blindfold." I roared into first gear with a noise that could have wakened the dead and soon rolled gratefully into bed.

At 2:30 A.M. I was sunk into a sleep so deep and concentrated that I didn't even hear the stutter of the special phone in my room, which usually jerked me into instant wakefulness like a fire alarm would.

For this phone *was* a kind of fire alarm. The normal phones at Douzy were used at normal times—day and evening—but some months previously Tomlinson had arranged for a special phone, with its own number, to be installed in my bedroom to save the rest of the family being awakened if I was called in an emergency. It didn't happen often at weekends, but even so, I could never ignore the fact that as far as the *Globe* was concerned, it was only eight o'clock in the evening when it was one in the morning in France.

I knew it had to be Tommy on the other end of the old-fashioned phone.

"It's two in the morning," he whispered instinctively. "Sorry to wake you."

"Two o'clock! You crazy?" I heard the noise of the office teleprinter. "What the hell are you doing at the office?"

"Emergency. Called me out of bed from Washington via the embassy. I'm in my sodden pajamas with a raincoat on top. It's bad news."

Suddenly I shivered, a premonition of disaster slapping me in the gut as though I had actually been physically punched and was about to be sick.

"Bad news?" I repeated. I could smell it—seeping through the phone wires from Paris.

" 'Fraid so," he said heavily. "For you."

"Well, tell me, for Christ's sake," I almost shouted. "I'm not a kid."

"Easy boy, easy. There's no suggestion that anyone we know is dead or anything like that but," again the hesitation, the agony of having to impart bad news over the phone, "brace up, Larry, you've got to know."

"It's Mama?"

"I hope not."

"Then *what?*"

"The *Athenia* has gone down. Sunk by a German U-boat. The first casualty of the war. I had to tell you."

"Of course." I seemed to be discussing other people, almost as though I were writing an objective, unfeeling story about people caught in death, but people who didn't matter to me. A story.

"Go on," I said after a pause. "Any news of Mama?"

"No, no," he cried. "The flashes are just coming through. There's every chance most people will be saved. She was torpedoed late yesterday evening, but all I know is that"—he hesitated again over that dreaded word of war—"casualties are light. So your mother hopefully will be okay."

"And other people's mothers?"

"Don't carry on, Larry. There are lots of survivors, so keep your fingers crossed."

"Mama?" I asked again.

"No news of individuals. And no news is good news. Sounds corny but it's true."

"Poor Mama." I suddenly felt the tears trying to push their way past my eyeballs. O God! What about the others? I would have to wake them up. For a few seconds, the prospect almost drove away thoughts of Mama herself.

"The *Athenia*—was she badly holed?"

"She's sinking. Those German pigs just opened fire without warning. They didn't give a shit about the kids on board, let alone the women. No warning—the damn captain just let her have a torpedo amidships."

"God Almighty!" I was thinking of Mama, I could picture the body floating in the sea, and then said, thinking aloud, "How the hell can I tell Papa? And Anna?"

"Don't do anything now," Tommy advised. "I had to warn you about it, otherwise you'd have heard it on the radio first thing in the morning. But there's every chance that—hang on! I'm just getting a new flash on the AP wire."

In the background I could hear the stuttering wire machine, imagine the long snake of white paper tape trailing to the floor when the machine was unattended, the words spewing out letter by letter, as though some unseen hand were typing.

"Sounds much better. You there, Larry? A large yacht, the *Southern Cross,* arrived on the scene almost immediately. Two British destroyers, the *Electra* and *Escort,* were right by. And a couple of Norwegian and Swedish vessels seem to have been around too. Here! Listen to this. Quote—several hundred survivors already picked up. Unquote."

"Thank God for that. When did it happen, Tommy? Where?"

"Soon after dark, I guess, and a couple of hundred miles west of Ireland, place called the Rockall Bank, but it means nothing to me. Go to bed now, Larry, but wake up early, before anyone else listens to the radio. Give you a chance to break it gently. If I get any lists of survivors—if your mother"—again the awkward hesitation—"I'll wake you."

"Thanks, Tommy," I said. "But I won't get much sleep tonight."

It was a long black night, and the morning that followed, after Papa had broken the news to everyone, was even blacker, despite the watery September sun. Everyone seemed to talk in whispers—or suddenly, loudly as though unable to control their voices. There was nothing any of us could do except listen to the radio.

Everyone was on edge, though the family was perhaps better equipped to hide fears or prepare for grief than the others. Jean served breakfast as though this would be the last meal ever to be prepared in the house. Aubergine sniffed so persistently that Papa, who rarely raised his voice, shouted in exasperation, "For God's sake, stop that sniveling!"

The French radio, which we listened to in the living room, was spouting the nonsense which it always feels compelled to utter in times of crisis—declarations of the infallibility of French arms, the deterrent of the Maginot Line, the proud tradition of neighboring Belgium, the German lack of aircraft. One announcer even proclaimed, "The entire population of France is prepared to play its part, and *now,* for our latest information points to an imminent attack on Germany in order to neutralize the German air force before it has a chance to bomb our homeland."

What incredible balls! I thought. We *knew* this wasn't true, and at one time, when Papa was out of the room, Oregon sighed, "The trouble with the French is that they despise everything that isn't French, so they can never bring themselves to believe the Germans are more efficient than they are."

In normal times we would have switched off this drivel, but no one dared to in case there was news of the *Athenia.* This, so far, was the only action of the war, and news bulletins about the U-boat attack constituted the only firm news amid a welter of theories, surmise, promises for the

future. As a newspaperman I could hear the creaking hand
of the censor in every official handout.

The sinking of the *Athenia* was not a "French" story; the
passengers were not French, neither was the vessel, but
it attracted attention because of morbid discussions on
whether the deaths would be an "advantage" in persuading neutral America to take stern reprisals against the
Germans after the sinking of a neutral vessel, even perhaps help to draw America into the war. It gave us, the
family waiting for news, an increased sense of the macabre
as we listened to "experts" discuss whether the loss of a
few lives—perhaps Mama's—might not in the long run
prove a cheap price to pay for extra American help.

"Not a hope," declared Oregon. "Someone will have to
sink a few U.S. battleships before the Americans fight in
Europe—or anywhere for that matter."

We didn't expect the French radio to announce any casualty list. I don't suppose the radio newsroom even knew
that the passenger list included one American wife whose
home was in France. On the other hand, Tommy was keeping in touch through the wire services and had alerted the
Globe in Washington. Papa had spoken to Bill Bullitt, so
we had all avenues of news covered.

During the late afternoon Sonia managed to get through,
but she asked for Anna, not me, as we were both convinced
her phone was tapped. There was nothing she could do—
except hope. And then halfway through a dinner for which
nobody had any appetite, we heard that Mama was safe. It
was about eight thirty when the phone rang, and as Papa
was nearest the dining-room door, he jumped out of his
seat and almost ran into the next room. We sat on the
edges of our seats for what seemed an eternity until Papa
gave an almost wild shriek, to make sure we could hear,
"She's safe! She's all right!"

We had to sit in the dining room a few more minutes
waiting for details, but when Papa returned, his ashen
face was touched by the first spot of color I had seen during
all that desperate day. Bill Bullitt had managed to get
through from Paris. Mama, he told us, had been picked up

by an American vessel, the *City of Flint*. Out of fourteen hundred passengers and crew, one hundred and twelve had been lost, including twenty-eight Americans.

After official confirmation we had to wait several days, for only then were passengers who had taken ten days to reach Canada able to send cables. Mama's read, "All love but miss you terribly." She had obviously been restricted to a short message. Five days later a second cable arrived from New York, "Settled down none the worse for Atlantic ducking, letter on way. Will miss you at the *vendange.*" I liked her reference to the *vendange!* But we still had to wait for our first letter.

I had almost forgotten this important autumn festival at which Mama always helped—until Papa phoned me at the office a few days later.

"We're in trouble, yes, I think you could say trouble," he began. "We seem to be at peace with the world in Douzy, despite the war, but we can't get the usual labor for the *vendange.*"

By tradition the annual harvest in the vineyards took place a hundred days after the flowering—and we always relied on casual labor to help out.

"Guy is really working like the devil," I could sense a rare chuckle on the phone. "Really, Larry, if he had painted as hard as he works now, he'd have filled the walls of the Louvre. Yes, the *Louvre!* Are you coming to help out—for a few days at least?"

"It might be difficult. We're having a hell of a time. But I'll try, for a long weekend at least. Have you got the government's okay?"

"They agreed yesterday," he replied. Even in wartime government officials made regular tests throughout Champagne to ensure that the harvest contained a satisfactory quantity of sugar and the necessary acid content. Only after an affirmative nod would the strict controllers of the Champagne region allow the harvest to proceed.

"If I get a call from the *Globe*—"

"Of course," replied Papa, "I'll understand. But, any-

way, it'll be good to see you—and the family. And we need
every man we can borrow now that many of the regulars
have let us down."

These were the men, women, and children who com-
prised the "task force," as Grandma used to call them, almost always recruited from coal miners in the Lorraine
who brought their families with them to help out with the
different aspects of harvesting. It was also a kind of family
holiday.

"I suppose a lot of them are either mobilized or reserved
as coal miners. But what about the women and children?"
I asked.

"That's the trouble. They want to come, but transport is
difficult."

"Don't worry," I promised Papa, "I'll be there if it's hu-
manly possible, and I'm sure Oregon will be there. And
since every spare body will be needed, have you ever
thought of asking Sonia?"

"Would she come?" I could see that Papa was wondering
what her husband would say.

"No harm in asking—providing the request comes from
you, preferably to Francesco."

"You'd like it?"

"You know I would. That's why I suggested it."

In fact Francesco agreed immediately that Sonia could
stay at Douzy for a week and help out. I imagine he was so
inundated with work that he was almost relieved, especially as this was an official invitation to work at a vital
seasonal job Sonia had tackled many times in the past.
Francesco even offered to come down to Douzy for a day
and help, if he could spare the time.

So I had taken one major hurdle in my stride. Now I
faced the next—how to get some time off. And that proved
easy after I received an intriguing proposition from the
Globe.

Back in Paris I warned Oregon that he would be expected to help out for the *vendange.*

"Already!" he cried. "The weeks fly by so quickly, I
seem to spend all my time reading the Sunday papers."

Time did flit past—yet the war was less than three weeks old. Mama had barely had time to arrive safely in New York. No letters yet. And, most astonishing of all, hardly a shot had been fired in anger by either side.

I was talking to Oregon when Tomlinson phoned down to my office on the floor below and asked if I could spare him a couple of minutes. Something in his tone suggested an unusual request. There was a tinge of suppressed excitement in his voice.

"Larry, I've got news for you," he started without preamble.

"Good or bad?"

"Depends on which way you look at it. Want the bad news first?" I could tell from his banter that he wasn't really serious.

Leaning back on his swivel armchair, feet up on his old-fashioned French desk, he said with mock sorrow, "I've had a telex from Washington. Sorry about this—but they don't have any more use for you as a stringer. It seems they're about to appoint a staff man."

It might have been said half humorously, but still, his casual drawl gave me an immediate reaction. I felt as though I had been pushed under an ice-cold shower. "Don't say that sort of thing. For a moment I thought you meant it."

"I do. It's for real."

"What the hell?"

"Temper, temper!" he grinned and explained the good news. The *Globe* wanted to employ me as a full-time bureau chief for France. They were offering me three times the amount I had been earning as a free lance or stringer, who is usually paid for material used or requested, or, alternatively, by the day when sent out on an assignment. I had been happy with the arrangement, but I was beginning to realize that if I wanted to reach the top in journalism, I should join the staff of a prestigious paper. And the *Globe* was the voice of Washington. To be appointed bureau chief in Paris, a senior member of the staff, was a big step up.

"And as far as money's concerned, you'll soon be matching me," said Tommy. "Not that champagne producers
need any money."

"But what about you?"

"Don't worry. I've got a new job."

He had indeed. Middle-aged but ever youthful, Tommy
Tomlinson had been secretly nursing an ambition which
only Hitler could fulfill. He had long wanted to be a war
correspondent and had been furious when the *Globe*
turned down his request to cover the civil war in Spain.
When he threatened to resign they had compromised by
promising Tommy that he *could* be a war correspondent if
there was a war in Europe—Vance being confident no war
would interrupt Tomlinson's last years as one of the best
Paris correspondents in the business.

"Vance sent me a humdinger of a cable when I reminded
him of our arrangement," Tommy chuckled. "Practically
said I'd fixed it with Hitler. I cabled back that I was being
measured for my uniform."

Now of course they couldn't find anyone but me to handle the political news. According to Tommy, Vance had
had an eye on me as a possible successor in Paris since our
first meeting, but excited though I was, two things worried
me, and I said so right away. It was one thing for me to
write a "set piece"—a situationer as it was called in the
trade—in which I had all the time in the world to research,
then write about, something I hoped I knew about; it
would be very different dashing off cables under pressure
day after day as bureau chief.

"Not to worry," said Tommy. "I shouldn't be saying this,
or you'll be asking for a raise, but you write like a dream,
Larry. You're going to do the *Globe* proud, and I'll bask in
reflected glory. And you won't be troubled by day-to-day
chores. Routine filing is going to be too expensive, and all
the routine business will be taken care of by the agencies.
And your second gripe?"

"I don't want to leave France." I knew it sounded impertinent for a beginner to start making terms after being offered a great chance, but I was operating from strength,

not cussedness, because there was no way I *would* leave Douzy.

"No sweat," Tommy agreed cheerfully, "I knew you'd make that stipulation and told Vance as much. He agreed. He'll give you a contract for the duration, France only, and as a special-feature writer."

"Meaning exactly what?"

Tommy explained. Reporting a war was going to be very different from reporting in peacetime. What the *Globe* wanted were stories that no rival newspapers carried— stories in which the contacts I had cultivated so assiduously over the years would tip me off with fresh angles.

"If you can deliver one big French political story a month," said Tommy, "you'll have earned your pay. Now sign here." Like a conjuror he produced a letter signed by Vance to be countersigned by me. "That will constitute a legal agreement." He handed it over to me.

"What's the date?" he asked as I read it through.

Thinking suddenly of Papa's urgent request for help with the *vendange*—and that Sonia would be there—I said, "Can we make it two weeks from now? Give me a bit of leave before I start."

He nodded. As I signed I said, "You took a lot for granted."

"I told your Uncle Oregon yesterday"—Tommy grinned an admission—"and he told me he'd kick your ass to kingdom come if you turned the offer down!"

Later that week I had new profile photos taken for my press card and *carte d'identité* and for credit-filing facilities. I had thought the old photos would serve, but the idiotic bureaucrats of the French civil service, puffed up by war, decreed otherwise: all "official" photos not only had to be in profile but had to show the right ear clearly.

I soon received a couple of very agreeable cables. Tommy must have told Vance why I wanted leave, for he cabled, "Welcome to the world of the *Globe*. And I hope I may have a raincheck and visit you for the next peaceful *vendange.*" The *Globe*'s editor, Schill Scotter, whom I had never met,

cabled more laconically, "Welcome aboard stop any ideas
proexclusives postvacation query."

At the same time, I was introduced to the world of the
censors and Ministry of Information, a group of half-baked
citizens who were already convinced they were the nation's guardians of truth, for even if there was no war to report, that did not prevent the Ministry of Information from
rapidly building up an enormous sluggish empire centered
round the Hôtel Continental in the rue de Castiglione. It
was hardly the proper image for the pulsating heart of a
grim operational war room. The wallpaper was pink and
flowery. The uncomfortable gilt furniture was bogus Louis
XV. The chief press officer dealing with the American and
British reporters worked in an office so ridiculously large
it could have been a banquet hall.

Not even the remotest criticism was allowed to sneak
past the censor. Every day Colonel Thomas, the Ministry
of Information spokesman, held a conference for newspapermen. He was tall, thin, with closely cropped hair and a
mustache. On the bridge of his long thin nose he had old-
fashioned pince-nez. He looked like a cartoon from a by-
gone age and was a hopeless anachronism.

The weather was perfect as the time of the *vendange* approached. Yet it was extraordinary, that month of inaction
by nations who in theory were willing to fight but who in
fact were unwilling to commit themselves to large-scale
losses. It was, as one newspaper put it, "the war that never
was." Everyone had been preparing for a terrifying on-
slaught. The British cabinet had secretly estimated that
the maimed and wounded in devastating air attacks would
total a million casualties. Yet the French newspapers had
to struggle to find stories of military fervor. The first British troops had arrived in France, at least giving the Paris
press a few pictures of lads in kilts and girls draped over
tanks.

Odd things, though, started to happen. While we were
preparing for the *vendange,* while the nucleus of our temporary work force began to arrive, who should telephone

from the Misses B and B's cottage but Jean-Pierre. The war was less than three weeks old, he was an officer in one of the biggest forts in the Maginot Line, yet he was at home when I arrived to spend a Sunday at Douzy.

"How come you're back on leave so soon?" I went round to see him.

"No place to sleep," he laughed rather shamefacedly. "I mean it. Sounds crazy but we're overmanned all along the Line. I had to sleep on the floor, so they sent me home for a week. Still," proudly, "I've already been in action."

I looked surprised.

"Yes. I think our team was one of the first to fire the big guns. Though between you and me, the whole thing was a bit of an anticlimax."

Jean-Pierre had been sent to the Hochwald Est fortress and, when he saw that I was interested, said, "You won't breathe a word to anyone will you? The press, I mean?"

I shook my head.

"Well, you know, three days after war was declared, we opened fire with a seventy-five-millimeter gun. It jammed. Most of the shells were old and defective. We tried the bigger gun—the one thirty-five—but two out of every three shells failed to explode. One of our guns at Hochwald Est fired shells over two thousand yards with one barrel, but less than nine hundred yards with the other. But the worst thing of all is the overmanning. It's crazy—even I can see that. Half the *poilus* should be sent back—to work in industry. At least I'll be here for the *vendange.*"

"And we've got air cover here," I said. "You didn't know? The British fighters have arrived to protect us."

In fact a hundred and sixty Fairey Battle planes of the RAF had arrived in the airfields of Champagne; and airfields in those days really meant fields, for there were no runways for the Battles, whose main duties were to protect French reconnaissance planes.

These first few weeks of war—as they affected me both in Paris and Douzy—left everyone bewildered by the almost uncanny lack of action, as though someone had forgotten to wind up several million toy soldiers. Nothing happened.

War and violence were supposed to be synonymous, but
there was no violence. In Paris the cafés were crowded
each evening, and several times I could not find a table at
the Deux Magots, even though I was a favored old customer. The cinemas played to packed houses—especially
Ninotchka, Goodbye Mr. Chips, and *The Wizard of Oz.*
Long queues formed to *book* for *Gone With the Wind,* which
wasn't due to open until mid-December. Such was the faith
of the average Parisian!

But though threatened German attacks had never materialized—giving French newspapers the opportunity to
jeer at German cowardice—I found the atmosphere chilling with apprehension; the more so as no one in Paris
made any adjustments to normal life which we all felt
should be made in the name of war. There was no point in
hoarding for there was enough of everything. Only the
blackout was, in the words of one commentator, "a ridiculous bore." One newspaper headlined the front page satiri-
cally LET THERE BE LIGHT! In a curious way the lack of heroic
action made one feel almost ashamed. The only "war"
which we, as newspapermen, could discover was in the gilt
halls of the Hôtel Continental, where the censor waged
an unremitting fight against all foreign correspondents.
Their most positive action was to provide each of us with a
gas mask, to be slung around the neck in a cardboard box,
and a tin helmet.

For the rest of it we soon became part and parcel of what
was quickly labeled *la drôle de guerre,* in England, "the
phony war." I see it now in memory, those first weeks, in
flashbacks of war oddities: the newspaper kiosks near the
Métro stations all barred, and the day's papers, magazines, books, dumped unceremoniously on the sidewalks.
The anger of thousands of crossword enthusiasts when
their puzzles were suddenly banned from print in case the
clues contained fifth-column codes. The blackout with the
street lamps painted blue or violet giving an uncanny
glow.

Unlike the famous Café Flore, which had closed down,
the Deux Magots still opened its doors, though outside the

terrace, with its small circular tables squeezed as close to each other as loving couples, men were filling sandbags from a pile by the roadside while one solitary North African hawker did a good trade selling peanuts. When Oregon and I ordered our first drink we could no longer—as we always had done—pile up the traditional saucers as a guide to our total bill. Now we had to pay cash with each separate order. Too many customers, it seemed, had conveniently bolted when the sirens emptied the streets.

From the inside of the terrace we looked up at the gray barrage balloons and—for the moment unthinking—I said to Oregon, "This is the end of our world."

"It isn't," he growled. "This is not the end of anything, it's the beginning of everything."

We strolled after lunch on that sunny afternoon through the Luxembourg gardens, I don't really know why. The first golden leaves were drifting down. A group of soldiers was digging trenches, but they had the air of men who didn't know why they were expending such energy, almost as though they suspected the work had been ordered only to keep them occupied. The lake in the gardens had been drained, and we both had to hold our noses as we walked quickly past the noisome stench. Not far away three of four young women were arguing as they walked along, and I saw one soldier wave, another shout a garbled invitation, a third cry, "They look as though they could do with a wash!"

It was a mild exaggeration, but it was a sign of the times: it was not "done" to be too chic anymore. The French girls were already adopting a new "fashion"—not to use makeup or extravagant hairstyles while there was a war on. Only there wasn't a war, not a real one. And anyway I couldn't see the link between war and their defiant gesture, almost as though they were trying to prove something.

All this, of course, was far from the peace and serenity of Douzy, where, while Tommy remained in Paris, I went to help out with the *vendange*—and wait patiently for Mama's first letter.

21

ON THE DAY I DROVE BACK to Douzy for the *vendange* the first letter from Mama arrived. It had been opened by the French—there was no censorship in America of course—but nothing seemed to have been deleted.

It was long, a little incoherent, and some of the earlier parts had been written on the *City of Flint* so it had become a kind of diary. Mama was not a very good descriptive writer, and it was hard to visualize what had happened. However, she was able to reassure us on several points which had worried us, for I had had visions of her struggling for hours in the water; in fact Mama had managed to clamber directly into one of the lifeboats, "thanks to the wonderful crew members."

There had been twenty-six lifeboats, Mama was told, and as the vessel took fifteen hours to sink, most people got away. "Most were killed near the number five hold, where the torpedo hit the *Athenia*. Someone gave me his life belt and then ran off before I could stop him. I was wearing a long evening dress when it happened. Do you know, I was still wearing it when the *City of Flint* reached Halifax, in Nova Scotia, on September 13," she wrote.

Describing the orderly scenes as she was lowered to the lifeboat, Mama added, "I even had time to grab my leather attaché case containing my passport and other papers and money, and I hung on to it like grim death, but then when I was being transferred from the lifeboat to the *Flint*, I dropped it, and there was no time to retrieve it."

I had also worried about the conditions on the *Flint*, but the Americans had apparently provided for possible Atlantic dangers, and though Mama had to share a small four-berth cabin with no toilet facilities, "they were very nice people who didn't snore too much, and we became great friends."

Sonia had been driven down to Douzy by an Italian embassy chauffeur, who had requested permission to remain at the château, offering to help in the harvest, while "in the service of Madame l'Ambassadrice." I had been warned about this via Papa, and in its way it was quite normal for a rich wife to ask for a room for her driver. The man—whom I regarded as a spy—would not sleep in the house, but in one of the farmer's rooms. I was beginning to feel sure that de Feo knew we were lovers. But I also had the curious feeling that he wouldn't be unduly concerned providing we were *seen* to be behaving correctly.

Studiously I kept out of the way when Sonia's car crunched across the gravel courtyard and Aubergine emerged to help with the luggage and Anna arrived and the two girls hugged each other. From an upstairs window, I heard Anna cry, "Oh! It's wonderful to see you. Just like the old days—the *happy* days."

It was like that all the time of the *vendange.* Even though we missed Mama, and often thought of her with longing, the knowledge that she was safe had stifled all our worries about "the war that never was." And each evening, as we all sat down for supper and I touched Sonia's feet or leg under the table, it was as though the intervening years had been a bad dream: even Oregon had overcome his initial depression at the closing of the *Paris American.*

There was something about the *vendange* that made you forget the miseries of the world. After all, the end of September, the vital ten days or so, represented the climax of a year's work and worry, so the harvest time always was a festive affair—not only for us, but evident in the holiday atmosphere of the pickers, who not only earned good

money, but enjoyed magnificent food served each evening
on the long oak table in the kitchen of the Home Farm.
Nothing seemed to have changed, not even the smell of
freshly baked bread, not even the ceiling festooned with
hanging food—the hams, the salamis, the sausages.

There were some problems this year, mainly due to a
shortage of casual labor, though many of the regulars did
turn up with their families, ready for a working holiday
that would last until they all celebrated the end of the harvest with the *cochelet*, a traditional feast, washed down
with unlimited champagne, with a local band engaged for
dancing in one of the barns.

The day before work officially started we all went for a
walk—the three girls, Guy, and me—and it always gave
me a peculiar feeling of continuity to come across "old
friends" whose faces were familiar, even though we saw
them only once a year.

Basically the activities would be divided into two sections—one, outside in the vineyards, where La Châtelaine
ruled: the other, inside, where my father handled the problems of the pressing once the grapes had been gathered in.
The division of labor worked without a hitch, but then as
Oregon once explained to me slyly, "Your father and his
mother can't really have a row—because they never meet
until it's time for dinner."

"We're about a dozen people short," said Grandma that
evening. "The wretched government doesn't seem to realize this is an emergency. Ridiculous! Not giving enough
men permission to help the champagne industry."

"Coal is important," said Sonia meekly.

"What for?" snorted Grandma. "We don't kill anyone,
there's no fighting, they just let officers run around in big
cars. Stop their silly war for a week, and we could have our
harvest."

We were having supper on the Friday evening after our
arrival; the food was similar to a dinner, but tradition dictated that supper—not dinner—was served at Douzy on the
Friday before the harvest began.

At seven the next morning we all trooped out, meeting near the barns in which the helpers had spent the night after supping on the big kitchen table. Grandma had been there for an hour. Every migrant helper who knew her reputation held her in awe. To them, she had, as a widow, inherited the vineyards and (without the help of a husband!) turned vines into liquid gold. Despite her eccentricity—especially in clothes—she was never reduced to a figure of fun. Not the indomitable, irreplaceable figure of La Châtelaine.

"I'm going to make a tour of the southern vineyards," she announced to one of the vignerons. "Keep these people on their toes." A farmhand puffed out cold morning air as he pumped up her bicycle. She was dressed in a green overcoat, rather long, of the shade favored by Austrians. It had large officerlike lapels with a double row of buttons, which I felt should be brass, instead of leather. A muffler had been thrown round her neck, for the early morning had a keen September nip to the air. On her head, hiding knotted hair worn in a bun, she sported a green felt Alpine-style hat—the same color as her coat—with three of four brightly colored feathers stuck in the band.

"She looks quite jaunty," said Guy.

Four types of workers were involved in the harvest. First on the scene came the gatherers, who worked in *hordons* as they were called. Using pruning shears they cut the bunches of grapes and stripped the leaves, putting them into small baskets.

From boyhood I had always been fascinated by the fact that men could work on the coal face in Lorraine for eleven months of the year yet were careful enough, gentle enough, at Douzy to handle fragile crops that could be ruined by careless bruising.

By 10:00 A.M. I was at the south vineyard overseeing the *carriers* at work. They were loaders really, and their job was to empty the small baskets of grapes into wicker trays, where the nearby pickers examined each bunch almost grape by grape. This was the *épluchage,* and it was vital to discard any grapes not up to standard. I saw a watchful

Grandma, who had just arrived on her bicycle, pounce like a hawk on one picker sorting out bits of stalk and overripe or green grapes—but not throwing them away.

"Merde! Idiot!" Grandma cried. She was merciless during the *épluchage*.

"She knows," I whispered to Olivia who had been watching, "that it's absolutely vital to keep only the top-quality grapes if you want top-quality champagne."

As the pickers filled their trays, the *"clean"* grapes were placed carefully in one-hundred-fifty-pound baskets called *mannequins*, then stacked with great care into carts, which took them to Papa's domain, the pressing room. Champagne, as he never forgot to tell us when we were young, was a blended wine, and the blender was the man who could make or mar the quality.

The shallow presses were designed so the fast-running juices would not have time to become stained red by the colored skins of the Pinot Noir grapes. And each press held exactly four tons of grapes, from which Papa expected to extract thirteen casks of juice, each cask containing forty-four gallons; the ten first casks usually produced the *cuvée*—the best wine. In any event the strict laws governing production imposed a limit of juice to each four tons of grapes. Once the quota of thirteen standard-sized casks had been filled, the remainder was sold off as still wine, either locally, or to mix into *vin ordinaire*. In no way could it ever be called champagne.

As Papa ended the third day's pressing he said with a satisfied aside to me, "A very good harvest so far, yes, *good*. Of course selling it might be a different matter, with all our markets closed. But we can always keep it." And to one of the hands, he said, "Well done, Georges. Take it to the boiling sheds after labeling."

Each forty-four-gallon barrel was labeled to show not only the year but which vineyard it had come from—very important when it came to blending—and would be stored for several weeks in fermenting sheds for the "boiling," as the first frothy fermentation was called. There the casks would remain for as long as necessary in a temperature—

for once in their lives—well above that of the cellars of Douzy. When they were finally opened for a second fermentation, the contents of the casks would have no sparkle, of course, but at least the grape juice had become a still wine, ready for the long journey that would transform it into bubbling champagne.

Some of the casuals noticed differences at this *vendange.* For the first time that anyone could remember, two tall, white flagpoles had been erected. Atop one flew the flag of France; on the other the Stars and Stripes fluttered. In half a dozen places large wooden notice boards, stuck on stout poles, had been erected. They all read UNITED STATES PROPERTY.

One stood at the entrance to the drive, where it branched from the road to Rilly, east of the main Reims-Epernay road. Others boldly proclaimed America's neutrality on the main gates to the Home Farm, on several of the vineyards bordering local roads.

The most intriguing work, however, yielded no clues to the curious men and women who had arrived from Lorraine, for all questions about the "construction work" going on behind high wooden barricades were met with blank stares or vague shrugs.

In fact the construction work appeared to be an extension to the *cellier* at the far end of the Home Farm, near the building which housed the great press and the boiling room, and it was apparently taking place inside the farmyard, near the point where the steps led down to the cellar tunnels, lined with thousands of bottles, and which continued all the way to the Douzy Pyramid.

"It's just a precaution," my father had explained mysteriously. "Yes, I think that would *describe* it, but really, there's no need to advertise what we're doing. It's a private building, really."

Behind the tall wooden screens Papa was constructing a sloping roadway about twenty-five-feet long, running parallel to the cellar steps, and which, if you continued to dig, would lead into the old cellars themselves. However, the

sloping roadway came to an abrupt end—blocked with
newly laid bricks, the plaster still fresh.

"They're going to be dirtied, whitewashed, and then
you'll never be able to realize that it's a new wall," said my
father. "And behind that wall, completely bricked up, but
with air vents, there are ten thousand bottles of the thirty-
three vintage. Yes, I think you could say the finest vintage
of the *decade.*"

"Papa! You cunning fox!" I cried. "That's genius. At
least if this war ever gets going we'll have something to
celebrate peace with."

"Absolutely. And a vintage that will shoot sky-high in
price if champagne production suffers."

"But why the path?" I asked.

"You realize that originally, behind this hoarding, was
the old wall of the warehouse. That will be replaced, and
then nobody will ever know that the wall was knocked
down and rebuilt."

"But still," I said, "what's the point of a road leading nowhere?"

"The Hisp," said Papa simply. "I love the Hisp. I'm not
going to risk losing that if the war ever reaches Champagne. Look!"

He had also built fireproof gasoline storage tanks I had
never seen before, housing thousands of gallons. They
would be bricked up; a smaller store of gas would be hidden in another cellar so that if I needed any, I could find it
without knocking down the walls. He would, he explained,
leave the hoardings up until the last minute if danger
threatened. Then he would drive the Hisp into its wartime
cave, jack up the wheels, and disconnect the battery. After
that he would rebuild the wall, "a few coats of dirty white-
wash on the bricks, and *really* nobody will be able to discover our secret."

It was one thing to hide a car and a stock of champagne.
It was a very different matter to hide something much
more precious.

"What's going to happen to Anna?" I asked. "Officially

she's now a German citizen. The French have already announced that all German nationals in France are to be interned."

"Not Anna," said Papa. "If the Germans ever come that *would* pose a problem. But for the present, I've been to see the *préfet de police* and we have come to an understanding —yes, that's the word—to leave matters as they are for the time being. Yes, as they are," he added in his up-and-down voice.

I didn't doubt that some consideration had been shown to the *préfet,* but to be on the safe side—in case the Germans ever did reach Champagne—my father had turned the old stables facing the main entrance on the other side of the courtyard into a self-contained little apartment, stocked with the kind of provisions and articles, like candles, which many people had already stored in their air-raid shelters. And in a business like ours, in which loyal workers included odd-job men who could turn their hands to anything, it had been easy to erect a stepladder at the back, down which anyone could climb and vanish into the woods behind.

"I only hope nobody talks—gives any of this away," I said.

"You mean *spies?*" My father, who had a charming streak of innocence, was horrified. "What a terrible, yes, terrible, thing to suggest! Why on earth should *anyone* do a thing like that? They're our friends, Larry. *Really!* Our friends."

"I'm sure you're right, Papa," I reassured him. But all the same, I had my doubts. In this strange world of fifth columnists, anti-Jewish French Fascists, men and women who believed the future of Europe lay in a strong Germany—why should *everyone* be a friend?

The week of the *vendange,* with Sonia so relaxed and happy, had been like a honeymoon. The need for brawn as a change from using brains, the outdoor exercise, the fun of everyone racing against time to gather in the grapes, the warmth of our love, the tenderness which sometimes springs from fear of the future had all combined to make it a memorable week of—strange to use this word, but it was true—peace in the midst of war.

Douzy was like an elixir of life. If you took it in regular doses, no harm could befall you. And Douzy was an elixir of love too.

Now Sonia had to return to Paris, for a couple of days, before leaving to see her parents in Florence and then going to Rolle to visit her new house. She would be away for two weeks—and though she telephoned me once from a phone booth, I was unable to meet her before she left.

Two weeks—it seemed an age. I felt the loneliness so acutely that, back in Paris, I went off by myself to the Apollo cinema near the boulevard des Italiens to watch the latest American hit movie called *Stagecoach.* It took me out of myself for a couple of hours.

Luckily I had a lot of work ahead of me, for as the new Paris bureau chief, my first task was to land a major political article for the *Globe.* I faced an immediate problem of another kind, however. When Tomlinson had run the office, he had employed me as a stringer. Now I was chief of the bureau and *I* needed a stringer.

The head office agreed immediately to my request—and I already knew the man I wanted. He stood head and shoulders above everyone else and, as it happened, he had lost his job. He was, of course, the one and only Oregon. He knew more about France, politics, and journalism than I would ever know. What's more, the *Globe* was still operating from the offices in the rue du Sentier—paying rent to Oregon who owned it—so he even knew his way around "the shop." It would be an ideal wartime job for Oregon now that the *Paris American* had ceased publication. The arrangement I planned was not without a touch of irony—the onetime pupil offering a job as assistant to the master who had taught him everything. But I entertained no worries that Oregon might suffer from hurt pride or wounded dignity. He was a pro—and proud of it.

When I tentatively suggested the idea to him, he positively twinkled behind his glasses.

"I've always said"—he lit another Gauloises—"that I'll die the day I don't work for a newspaper. My boy! you've saved my life."

I had been turning over an idea in my head since I met Jean-Pierre and found him on leave so soon after the outbreak of war. Barely a couple of weeks! And the reason was ludicrous—that he had nowhere to sleep, an officer of the French army in one of the key forts of the Maginot Line. After talking things over with Oregon and then meeting some high-ranking followers of de Gaulle, who favored a streamlined army, I could visualize the headline in Washington before I wrote a word—FRENCH ARMY IS TOO BIG.

After a few days of research and interviews, I came up with an astounding set of facts and figures, proving that the French mobilization machine was ponderous, bogged down with bureaucracy, overambitious. One man in eight was now mobilized in France, compared with one man in forty-eight in Britain. The French had called up so many men that industry was being crippled. Thousands of conscripts were already undergoing the laborious process of being demobilized. There was a tug-of-war between the army, which liked to control large bodies of men even if there was no fighting, and the needs of industry. Then I discovered, after thinking about Jean-Pierre's faulty guns in the line, that a huge proportion of French artillery was still in storage. By the third week in September, when mobilization was complete, the French had in theory fifty-seven divisions—yet only seven were available for the western front.

"It's dynamite," cried Oregon. "Now let me dig out some facts about the effect on civilian morale. The fact that all the men have vanished, but there's no war, no work." There was a bitterness among the civilians as well as among men at the front, a sense of anticlimax. The Germans hadn't rained destruction from the skies. Accidents in the blackout were more lethal than among the troops. There were restrictions on gasoline—though anyone who knew the right friend could get as much as he liked.

"That's a fine piece." Oregon read the finished draft

through carefully, and that was high praise indeed. "But you'll never get it past the censor."

I had wondered.

"Not a hope in hell," said Oregon. "Your only hope is to file from Bern. No censorship in Switzerland. But even if you can get it there, you can't use your by-line, even on a Swiss dateline."

"Well, then what?"

There was only one way—and I knew it. Forget my by-line, make the ultimate sacrifice on my very first dispatch as a staffer. But it had to be. If my name appeared on that story, the French might even cancel my accreditation.

As Oregon added, "Hell, Schill Scotter, the editor, and Vance will know you did it, and they're the only ones who really count. The rest is just vanity. You'll get a lot of respect from them."

That was what happened. As a stringer—and as an American citizen—Oregon took the train to Bern one day, handed over the cable and some explanatory details to Tixerand, our man in Switzerland, and returned to Paris the next day.

Three days later I received a cable from Scotter. It made no sense—except to me. It read, "Unable contact Tixerand stop if you contact please onpass congratulations to Tixerand on gaining his majority."

Scotter knew that in no way could I phone through to Switzerland. And as for Tixerand's "majority," he was in the mid-fifties. It was Scotter's way of telling me, "Good work, you've grown up now."

22

THOUGH I KNEW that Sonia was spending a few days in Switzerland, there was no way I could sneak off to meet her there. She did telephone the dates when she would be in Rolle, but I now had to realize that I was a member of the *Globe* staff. I couldn't just walk out of the Paris bureau for a couple of days to meet a beautiful girl. That had been the prerogative of the free lance.

It is curious how things work out in life. I didn't go to Switzerland for one simple reason—I couldn't. And on the very day when I would have been with Sonia in Rolle, had I been able to make the trip, I found myself instead dining alone with Sonia's husband.

I could hardly believe it when the Italian embassy phoned.

"I'm the Count de Feo's personal secretary," said the girl. "His Excellency wonders if you would care to have dinner with him quietly on Thursday?" Adding, before I could catch my breath, "His Excellency asks me to apologize for such short notice. He wondered if perhaps Maxim's would be agreeable to you."

I gulped. Thursday! Yes, it *was* the very night I would have been in Rolle. And only two days before Sonia was due to return to Paris. Why the hell did he want to see me? Did he know about us? He was the last man I wanted to meet alone over the dinner table. Though Francesco was, in fact, very agreeable and we had by now met often enough to use Christian names, but no man can feel com-

fortable when dining alone with a husband whose wife is
your lover. I wasn't thinking only of emotions like shame,
embarrassment, guilt, I just didn't like the idea of sitting
alone in a restaurant making polite conversation with a
man of impeccable manners and breeding in such a situation.

I planned to arrive first, as a gesture to de Feo's status of
ambassador, but he was five minutes early. Albert, the
headwaiter, fleshy jowls wobbling over tight collar, ushered me immediately to de Feo's table.

"I didn't order champagne"—de Feo always wore a
slightly amused, almost ironic smile—"because I feel you
must drink so much of it at home. How are you? What'll
you have?"

As I hesitated, he asked, "May I suggest a new drink
I've invented. Albert knows how it's mixed—bitter Cam-
pari, vermouth, gin on what you call the rocks, with a
splash of soda. Do try it. One day I'm going to think of a
name for it."

At that moment the Negro boy who served coffee and
was always dressed in fancy Oriental costume came past
and piped up, *"Bonsoir, Votre Excellence."*

"That's what I'll call my new drink," exclaimed de Feo
delightedly. "A Negro! No—that would upset our African
friends. I know—a compromise—a *Negroni.* Perfect!" He lit
a cigarette from his long holder, and as I sipped the new
drink I found that it had a pleasant bitter taste.

I didn't often have the opportunity to size up Francesco;
I had to admit that he was good-looking. He had what I can
only call an "open" face—something I didn't usually asso-
ciate with diplomats. He had a good head of hair, slightly
wavy—though not marcelled, thank God. He had the
straightest of noses, and he was no doubt generally regarded among the ladies as a dashing Italian Romeo. He
had become highly successful in his chosen profession
while still in his early forties.

I continued to study him as we decided on the menu. His
dark blue Italian-cut suit was exactly right. So was his
bow tie—the *papillon,* as "butterfly ties" were commonly

known in France. The white and blue spotted tie matched a spotted silk handkerchief, and the initials under a coronet on his silk shirt were so discreet you could barely see them. He was, in short, very elegant, from his oval gold and enamel cuff links to the distinctive gold watch with its "D" strap, which also whispered "Cartier."

We both ordered the same dinner—foie gras followed by roast beef—"And some *raifort,* Albert," adding to me, "It's not so much the beef I like here, it's the horseradish sauce."

Spreading the foie gras on a corner of wafer-thin warm toast cut in small triangles, de Feo said, "I'm so pleased your father asked Sonia to Douzy for the *vendange.*

"The change did her good," he continued, adding before I could say anything, "One of the reasons I asked you to dine with me tonight was to talk to you about Sonia. I know that you're," he coughed slightly, "a very privileged friend, and I don't think she's very happy."

I said nothing. This was one of those moments when, faced by a highly intelligent man, I needed to watch every single word—and let most of them be uttered by him.

"But first I have an apology and confession to make," he paused while the sommelier poured out a little Puligny-Montrachet for him to taste.

"Thank you," he nodded to the sommelier, then said to me, "Larry, you have to believe me when I tell you that I had absolutely nothing to do with that terrible business in the railway station about Anna. I am as horrified as you. Apart from anything else, Anna is Sonia's best friend—I was shattered."

"But you did give her away?" I asked.

"I had *nothing* to do with that," he replied firmly. "It was a mischance, and I'd better explain what happened right away."

The *mischance*—his own word—had, as I imagined, happened on the night of the Polish ball; he and Albrecht had been talking together while Guy was fetching Mama's wrap. How vividly I remembered the eerie sensation that I was being watched. What I didn't know until now was that

Albrecht had been merely asking de Feo if he knew me, and Francesco had added innocently, "My wife has known the family for years. And I know Larry Astell's sister. We dined with her last week."

He motioned to the waiter to remove the small blue plates and replace them with warm toast wrapped in a stiff napkin.

"And that was enough," said de Feo. "I had no *idea* your sister was not supposed to be in France. Why should I have? Sonia *had* told me that Anna was married to a German, but even so—why shouldn't she visit France? And I didn't know anything about Abetz running a vendetta against you."

"A vendetta?" I echoed.

"Perhaps the word is a little dramatic. Do you mind if I smoke between courses? It's a deplorable habit." He carefully pushed the end of his cigarette into its long holder and again moved his lips into that special, slow, slightly ironic smile. "But I've known Abetz for years. Once he refused to drink Astell champagne at a party. When I asked why, he said you insulted him in public—before his colleagues. In the Ritz Hotel, I believe. What on earth *did* you say to him?"

"Gefundenshite!" I rolled the word round my tongue. "I made the word up myself and it gave me one hell of a lot of satisfaction."

"And caused you a great many problems," murmured de Feo dryly.

"How do you know about this?"

"I was posted to Germany as a junior in the Italian foreign service and worked with Otto Abetz. I was supposed to be his protégé. It was understood that if or when Otto wanted a key figure planted in Paris for the Italian foreign service, Hitler would ask Mussolini, politely of course," again that faint sardonic smile, "to appoint me. Abetz wanted someone he could trust."

"Does Sonia know all this?" I said.

"I don't suppose she does. We never discuss politics," answered de Feo after a pause. "And that brings us to Sonia, doesn't it?"

What I have to tell now is the final unfolding of the tangled relationships between Riccardi, Sonia, de Feo, and Abetz; how their fates were interlinked, and how, because of them, marriage had always eluded Sonia and myself. Each appeared in the drama, though only from time to time; thus the problems appeared in episodic fashion, lacking continuity.

Now, however, at Maxim's, and later over brandies in the rue de Longchamp, I was able to piece together for the first time words and actions which had hitherto baffled me—especially as any suspicions had always been brushed aside by Sonia.

When it became obvious that de Feo was about to unburden his soul, my first puzzled question was why. Why tell me diplomatic secrets which had for so long been so carefully hidden? It never occurred to me that the reason was simple: Riccardi was dying of cancer and soon there would be no need for any more secrecy. This was why Sonia had gone to Florence. The second basic factor involved both Riccardi and de Feo. Both had skeletons in cupboards which they were anxious to keep locked. And the man who held the key to those cupboards was Otto Abetz.

Riccardi's troubles began in Paraguay, the landlocked country in South America which in 1932 went to war with its neighbor Bolivia; both countries laid claims to the vital Chaco River and the surrounding Chaco Plain, then—wrongly as it happened—believed to contain oil.

The Bolivian army was officered by Germans under General Hans von Kundt. Mussolini sent "technical advisers" to the people of Paraguay, where Riccardi was ambassador in Asunción, the capital. Riccardi became a kind of legend. With Italy's help Paraguay won the war at the end of 1935, and by 1936 their military hero, Colonel Rafael Franco, a close friend of Riccardi, had been elected president in a coup. Immediately he formed a semi-Fascist

regime modeled on Mussolini's Fascists. In it he appro-
priated four million acres of land from the rich, shared
among peasants and soldiers—except for a "present" of
land worth one million dollars, which had quietly been
promised to Riccardi as a reward.

There was one problem: it took years for Riccardi to sell
the land secretly, which explains why he refused to leave
Paraguay for better diplomatic posts. Nor could he easily
siphon the cash to Europe. Mussolini had set up an exchange institution through which all foreign money trans-
actions had to be routed. Riccardi *had* to work through
secret channels. It was the only way. He did finally manage to sell most of the land and transfer the cash to Switzerland.

While all this was happening—as I put de Feo's story
into sequence—Francesco went as a junior diplomat to
Germany. He had been picked to study infiltration and
subversion under Otto Abetz.

Abetz, however, never trusted anyone unless he could
control him, through fear or blackmail. Shortly after his
arrival in Germany, de Feo was compromised. In the
heady days when Hitler dreamed of an Aryan superrace,
with Francesco perhaps the most handsome man in their
group, the cult of comradeship among men was strong. To
be the friend of a man was far better than being the lover
of a woman.

"That didn't mean that we all went to bed together," observed de Feo wryly, "but most of us did have friendships
of the kind British boys at public schools go through. To be
frank, Abetz trapped me one evening after we had all had
a great deal to drink. It was pure schoolboy stuff. Nothing
really sordid like sodomy."

With a real sigh of regret de Feo continued, "I never
wanted to get married. You have no idea how I used to *love*
my bachelor life. It was perfect. I had marvelous servants,
lots of women friends who enjoyed a good dinner and were
delighted not to be bored by amorous advances afterward."

To de Feo, who by now had returned to the foreign ministry in Rome, the Berlin episode had been forgotten. But

then the ministry, guided by Abetz, called Francesco in and accused him of being homosexual. Though he denied the accusation, he was under a cloud. But Abetz had no intention of ruining de Feo's career, he just needed to control him, so at a time when Mussolini was hysterically ordering every suspected homosexual in Italian government circles to be deported to Sardinia to work in the coal mines, Abetz moved to save de Feo, for he needed him. He suggested that Francesco could avoid the coal mines very easily—by getting married.

This was long after Sonia had been sent away from Douzy "in disgrace," and Riccardi, working in the Italian foreign office, was behaving oddly, making sudden trips to Switzerland. Sonia was not stupid. She knew something was wrong.

But Abetz had heard the first whispers of Riccardi's "secret treasure"—for a very good reason. Hitler had been furious at the way his general had been humbled by Italy in Paraguay—and Riccardi was the man responsible. The Germans kept files on Riccardi—and on left-wing leaders in Paraguay. With the end of the Fascist government there, rumors about Riccardi multiplied.

As Hitler was deeply suspicious of all Italian motives, Abetz was ordered to have Riccardi watched. What better way to do this than through his onetime protégé de Feo? And since Francesco was in trouble, what better way to *use* him than by forcing him to marry Riccardi's eligible daughter?

Riccardi was panic-stricken when he discovered from a German diplomat that Abetz knew that "something intriguing had happened in Paraguay," and that a daughter married to de Feo would make Abetz ignore the conversation. No doubt the story was even more tortuous than the manner in which I have tried briefly to untangle it. But Riccardi *was* sitting on a million dollars—and liable to exposure. Sonia met de Feo, by arrangement. Francesco was presentable, with a title, and when he proposed, Riccardi warned Sonia that if she refused, he would commit suicide.

Soon Riccardi was posted to Paris. Sonia, by now en-

gaged, returned to Paris, relieved that she had not yet
been forced into a quick marriage to de Feo. Once again
the influence of Abetz prevailed. He was engaged in many
devious plots while posing as an ardent friend of France,
and he needed someone like Riccardi to do the undercover
work for him in Paris, while Abetz posed as the Francophile.

In Paris, though, there was an unexpected development.
Whispers of the "Riccardi affair" had not only reached
German intelligence but also left-wing governments in
South America trying to stage a coup in Paraguay. Left-
wing anti-Fascist underground movements were beginning to work together, sharing information. Among the
first to learn of the rumor were two Italian brothers, Carlo
and Nello Rossello, who had fled from Italy, and were
plotting in Paris against Fascists. Finally, one of the
brothers confronted Riccardi and threatened to denounce
him unless he handed over the gold.

Riccardi realized that the two brothers must be elimi-
nated, and arranged all the details through professional
thugs. There is little doubt Abetz knew what was happening. From Riccardi's point of view it was a perfect murder.
Mussolini even cabled him congratulations on the way in
which the troublemakers had been liquidated.

Riccardi's stock actually soared—but not for long. Abetz
never trusted *anyone*—especially someone who had instigated murder. He wanted to be sure that Riccardi was out
of the way. So when Abetz felt the time was ripe, he
dropped hints to the French government about the murders. And Riccardi was kicked out of France. And of course
Sonia had to leave too.

Now came the final silky twist in Abetz's devious plot.
After Abetz was declared persona non grata in France, he
asked Count Ciano to appoint de Feo roving ambassador in
Paris so that Francesco could keep an eye on Albrecht,
Abetz's replacement, for him. Moreover, Abetz insisted
that de Feo and Sonia now marry. If Francesco ever suffered an attack of conscience, his own wife would be involved in the crimes of her father. If Sonia refused to go

through with the marriage, Abetz would leak the whole Riccardi story.

Our brandy glasses had long been empty, and finally I said simply, "What now?"

"What indeed?" de Feo lit another cigarette from his long holder. "I am very fond of you, Larry. I would have been very happy if you two could have married. But," he shrugged his shoulders, "Abetz is still a powerful man—even stronger now, from a distance in Germany."

"But you love Sonia surely—in a way," I hesitated. "No one can *help* loving Sonia."

"Of course I do. Sonia is wonderful, but believe me, when it was suggested that I marry her, I was appalled."

"It certainly took you a long time to get round to it."

"Exactly. I know what you are thinking and the answer is a resounding no. I am not—those vulgar words—a pansy, a queer, a pouff. But Sonia is my wife—and I have a name and family that is honored in Italy, and I don't want it to be sullied."

It was his turn to hesitate, searching for the right words. "I know perfectly well that you love Sonia—and even worse, the poor dear loves you. I am very touched by it—this love of yours that seems to last forever. I wish I knew your secret."

He led me to the front door and opened it. "But we must all take care. For if I'm watching Abetz's successor, you can be sure that he is watching us."

"I will," I promised.

We walked together to my parked car at the bottom of the rue de Longchamp. "I shouldn't be saying this, but make the most of this ridiculous *drôle de guerre*. Soon it will end—and when it does, when the Germans are ready, they will become the masters of all Europe."

Part Three

1940–1941

23

AT HALF PAST SIX on the morning of Friday, May 10, I was fast asleep at Douzy when the insistent ringing of the downstairs telephone stabbed into my dreams. Had the noise come from my private bedroom telephone, I would have been instantly alert, for only Oregon (and the *Globe* in Washington) had the number, but this was downstairs. And my father, who valued his sleep, had long since disconnected the phone in his bedroom because it irritated him.

I switched on the landing light, cursing the prospect of answering a wrong number; but no, I thought, that wasn't likely; no one would insist on phoning for such a long time unless he was sure.

All the same, I almost barked into the receiver in the hall, "Yes? Who is it?" as though saying wordlessly, "And what the hell do you mean by phoning me at this time of night?"

Almost apologetically, the voice, which I recognized, astonished me. "It's Francesco."

I was suddenly wide awake, nerve ends tingling—with fear that something had happened to Sonia.

"Yes!" was all I could say.

But it had nothing to do with Sonia.

"I shouldn't be telling you this"—de Feo's voice sounded urgent—"but it won't be a secret for long, and I thought you might be grateful if you could make an early start to Paris."

"Francesco! You're talking in riddles. What's this all about? Nothing wrong with—your wife?" I hesitated over the last two words.

"Nothing—but the balloon's gone up!"

"How come?"

Speaking very deliberately, like a political spokesman reading the text of an official communiqué, Francesco said, "At first light this morning, a hundred and thirty-five German divisions invaded Holland, Belgium, and Luxembourg. They're making straight for France, and the front extends from the North Sea to the Swiss frontier. My friend, *Dio ti protegga!*"

As I started to mutter a thanks for the warning, he added, "I have to go. I'm speaking on my private line. *Arrivederci.*"

Without another word he hung up. As I stood there in my pajamas, I suddenly shivered, thinking, Yes, we would all need God's protection now. And then another thought —it was damned decent of Francesco to call. He would realize that news of the German invasion could have already reached Washington from Berlin or neutral countries, and as it was now just before midnight yesterday in the *Globe* office, there was nothing I could do in France. Even so, the sooner I reached Paris the better.

For this day, I knew, was the moment of destiny for France—and I was afraid. I was haunted by a few words which Hitler had said to his chiefs of staff the previous October and which I had read somewhere: "I place a low value on the French army's will to fight. Every army is a mirror of its people."

I only prayed that Hitler was wrong, but he had an uncanny instinct for hitting on the truth.

Rushing upstairs I grabbed my dressing gown, then made my way to the kitchen to get some coffee. At first I thought no one else was up, but when I was heating the water Gaston poked his head round the kitchen door.

"Hello," I cried. "Heard the news?"

Of course he knew nothing. Seeing him there, and with an oblique reference to Jean-Pierre's unexpected leave, I laughed, "I thought you were in North Africa. Don't tell me you've got nowhere to sleep either."

"Embarkation leave. Off tomorrow night." And after a moment's hesitation he added, "You're up early—not going to Paris by any chance? Could I beg a lift?"

"Sure. I'm leaving as soon as I get dressed. Have some coffee first."

We sat across the kitchen table, the open door leading to the early sun at the rear of the house. Gaston explained that he had relatives in Paris and wanted to say good-bye to them. "I'll get a lift back to Douzy or Reims somehow."

I remembered that once before when Mama was being driven from Douzy to Paris, Gaston had stayed with friends there. "Sorry I can't guarantee a ride back," I said, "but God knows when I'll see Douzy again. Still—you never know," thinking that maybe Oregon might want to go to Douzy while I remained in the office. "Phone through to the office before you go back—just in case."

Already, on the journey to Paris, there was an air of expectant secrecy, pompous bustle. At half a dozen important junctions officious military police demanded to see our papers.

"The news seems to have got around," I whispered to Gaston. I dropped him at the Châtelet—what a long time ago it seemed since Olivia had been hurt during the riots there. "This okay?" I asked.

"Fine, thanks. The Métro from here takes me straight through to Levallois-Perret, where my aunt lives."

Paris was beginning to awaken by the time I sandwiched my MG between two trucks loading cloth in the narrow rue du Sentier. Upstairs the tape machine rattled along in jerks, but there didn't seem to be any hard news beyond the original terse flash. We had reached the stage of reaction and background stories.

Oregon bustled in around nine o'clock, the prospect of action pumping his adrenaline like a tonic. His eyes twinkled with excitement, his voice had an undercurrent of exuberance that comes only to men and women—politicians, war leaders, and, yes, newspapermen—when they are des-

tined to play a role in momentous events. And though it
was true that journalists were only onlookers, we *were*
privy to many secrets which readers of our newspapers
were rarely permitted to see. Like Oregon I, too, felt a
surge of excitement, even the macabre thought which I
couldn't control, They might bomb Paris today!

In fact at first there was nothing to report at all, though
everyone knew the real war had started. When I passed
Madame Yvette's bistro, next door to the office, I heard an
announcement on the radio that there was *"rien à sig-
naler."*

I could do nothing about the day-to-day reporting of the
war—the agencies were faster and better equipped than I
was; however I could interpret, prophesy, and seek exclusive interviews, while Tommy Tomlinson lived with the officers and men in the Maginot Line, sending eyewitness
dispatches.

The news on the whole was electrifying. But one thing
never entered my head—that the German attack couldn't
eventually be contained. The combined Allied forces—
French, British, Dutch, Belgian—were numerically superior to the Germans. We could muster one hundred and
fifty-six divisions—twenty-one more than Germany. We
had four thousand tanks—mostly French—and though
cumbersome, they should be more than a match for the
Germans, who had fewer than three thousand. Only in the
air could Germany boast of superiority.

Even so, when I switched on the French radio, another
solemn voice was crying, "The nations of Europe are
united as never before, and we are ready to repel the in-
vader and defend humanity against the hordes of Hitler."

I switched it off, irritated by this drivel, but then
switched it on again. It might be a good idea to listen in
case there was a communiqué. Funnily enough I was more
worried by Mama's reaction to American newspapers than
I was by real fear. The Americans would splash the news,
distort it, probably be drawing maps showing how they
hoped to break through Champagne—and we could do
nothing to tell her that most of it was nonsense.

Among the papers on my desk was a message to ring Jim
Parks at the U.S. embassy.

"No, it's nothing to do with war—well, not directly."
And I could imagine his grin as he added, "We leave that
to you blood-sucking leeches."

"Thanks a lot. So what?"

"An extraordinary thing has happened. Lots of unsorted
cargo, parcels, even some luggage were rescued from the
sea when the *Athenia* went down. Don't forget she took fifteen hours to sink. Among the bits and pieces was an attaché case with your mum's name on it. Not in mint
condition; the clasps, locks are all rusted and so on. But it's
got her passport and documents in it. Will you accept it on
behalf of your father—he's next of kin, I guess?"

"Fantastic," I cried. "I'll call round as soon as I can.
Keep it for me till then."

As it happened I was summoned later in the day to the
Hôtel Continental by Colonel Thomas for a Ministry of Information briefing. I learned nothing—absolutely nothing
—so after the meeting broke up, I walked round from the
gilt rooms in the rue de Castiglione across the Concorde to
the embassy. I was fascinated at the stroke of chance by
which Mama's writing case had been saved, not least because it was well remembered. We three children had
bought it at Hermès years previously for a joint Christmas
present to Mama, and as I showed my pass and ran up the
stairs to Parks's office, I could imagine the case bobbing in
the water, remembering from Mama's letter how it had
fallen into the sea just as she was being transferred from
one vessel to another after the sinking. I could see in my
mind's eye the anguish at that moment as it slipped from
her grasp, as she tried in vain to clutch it, only to see it
bobbing away. Probably it contained all her papers—not
only her passport, address book, but even jewelry perhaps.
According to Parks it had been sent first to Britain, and
then when the embassy in London discovered that it belonged to someone living in France, it had been forwarded
to the embassy here.

As I signed for it, Jim said, a trifle too casually I

thought, "It's not locked, of course. The clasps broke as soon as anyone touched 'em. But you'd better just open it for a look-see before you hand it over to your father. Never know, it might contain something that doesn't belong to you."

What an odd remark! Back at my desk, I undid the string. The back of the writing case was almost coming apart, the clasps were rusted and useless, the beautiful leather with its distinctive Hermès stitching was covered with circles of green mildew.

Almost without thinking I opened the case—and caught my breath—as though someone had thrown a bucket of cold water full in my face. I looked at the soggy mess on top. What I saw *couldn't* be true! It was a picture of an attractive, smiling woman embracing a handsome, young man, an obvious keepsake photo. And my mother had never looked more beautiful.

At that moment a knock sounded, and as I hastily closed the top of the old writing case Gaston popped his head round the door. I must have looked irritated—or maybe so stunned I hadn't yet recovered.

"Sorry," he said, "but I was almost next door and I thought I ought to tell you I've got a lift back tonight. Thanks for your help."

"Okay," I said almost absently. *"Bonne chance,* Gaston!"

As he closed the door behind him I opened again the writing case, almost savoring the moment of anticipation. There was my mother, and even through the once-wet photo, I could see the pure happiness shining out of her eyes and the adoration—yes, that is what it looked like— the real adoration for the younger man in the secret photo. And I knew the younger man too—in fact I almost ran to the door of my office to call him back.

Gaston of all people! *Gaston.* My age, Papa's driver.

I couldn't believe it. I closed the top of the case hurriedly as though someone had caught me peeping through the keyhole at a couple of lovers. A thousand thoughts flashed through my mind: the time when Papa was saying in his

up-and-down voice, "Salt of the earth, Gaston. Trust him
with my life." Life, yes. Wife? That was a different matter.
How *could* she? I opened the case, looked again at the large
photo. Of course he was handsome—even dashing, he had
good manners, but in *bed* with my mother. Where? How?
How had they done it?

I remembered the time Mama had lunched with me in
Paris, refusing dinner because she had an engagement
with some old fogy—and I had later discovered that the old
fogy hadn't even been in Paris at the time. And then there
was Germany. Of course! Mama had even managed skillfully to arrange to sleep in a hotel instead of with Willi and
Anna. How excited she must have been when they couldn't
get away, then the night in Copenhagen, another in
Brussels.

My God, I thought. How long has this been going on? I
had another sudden desire to rush down the circular stairs
shouting "Gaston! Come back!" I resisted the impulse. I
would have been too late anyway. If Mama had still been
at Douzy, I might have done something—though I hadn't
the faintest idea *what.* It wasn't *my* life, it wasn't *my* wife.
Nothing to do with me. And I couldn't suddenly feel a
surge of hate for Gaston because whatever had happened,
Mama must have been the one who instigated the affair.
Still, I could hardly look at him with the same eyes the
next time we met. Thank God he was off to Africa. And
then I realized that *this* was the reason why Mama had refused at first to leave France, and had suddenly changed
her mind. She had refused to leave Douzy hoping that Gaston would remain in a reserved occupation, but perhaps
Gaston had been torn by different loyalties; and once he
decided to volunteer for service in North Africa, once he
was booked to leave, Mama knew that she had lost him
and decided to bolt.

Oddly enough, on this first afternoon, I didn't give much
thought to poor Papa. After all he didn't *know;* and indeed
he hardly ever noticed anything. And I would take good
care that he never would know.

A brief search showed that there was nothing else in the

case that Papa shouldn't see. And I suddenly felt a wave of sadness for poor, darling Mama, trying to pick an autumn crocus, thinking of the casual remarks she had made to me. "Yes, it is a bit dull here in Douzy. . . ." I was sure—hopeful?—that Gaston and Mama didn't really love each other, that it was the physical attraction which a beautiful, middle-aged woman who sees life slipping by feels for a handsome, young man, by a woman who asks for one more chance to remember her youth. "Bless you, Mama," I whispered to myself.

Before I could change my mind I decided to tear the photo to shreds—praying that Gaston hadn't left one of his own to look at in North Africa. Well, we wouldn't meet—any of us—for months, perhaps even years, perhaps never. I felt almost guilty tearing the photo up, but I couldn't post it to America. Yet how she must have clung to it! How many times, I wondered, had she thought about destroying such damning evidence. She must on occasion have been terrified that it would be discovered by accident—an accident just like this. What torture it must have been for Mama, wondering, in love, or a kind of love, clutching to one photograph as the only tangible memory of those stolen nights in Düsseldorf, Paris, or wherever. With real regret I tore the photo into hundreds of pieces, sprinkled the bits of paper with lighter fuel, and then burned everything to the last morsel of ash.

Within a couple of days the first details of the German assault began to filter through, though all mention was rigorously suppressed in the press. It seemed that at daybreak on May 10 every available German aircraft took off. The Luftwaffe's targets included Belgian and Dutch airfields, French airfields at Calais, Dunkirk, Metz, Bron, and Châteauroux, and Valdahon camp. From the North Sea to the Rhone Valley the sky was filled with a heavy drone. At the same time the Germans dropped almost the whole of their airborne strength over Holland.

At half past five that morning the bulk of the Wehrmacht attacked along the western front. The one hundred

and thirty-five divisions included ten armored and eighty
crack divisions, moving against Holland, Belgium, and
France.

Now the world as we had known it was really crumbling
about us. Soon there were government changes. Reynaud,
who had succeeded Daladier as premier, called in Marshal
Pétain, the hero of Verdun, as vice-premier. General Maxime
Weygand, who was seventy-three, replaced Gamelin as
commander-in-chief. At Douzy hordes of refugees from the
Low Countries and Denmark poured across their frontiers
into France, impelled by fear or an instinctive urge for security; long caravans of men and beasts, the Vikings with
their blond hair and ruddy cheeks standing out against
their dark-haired neighbors. Sometimes when I saw them
approaching from afar on some distant hillside, they
looked for all the world like a covered wagon train awaiting attack by hostile Indians.

I was not often in Douzy during the early days, but according to Papa, he managed to keep most of the nomads
away from the precious vineyards. Some were aggressive,
some were violent, "as though we owed them a living,"
said Papa, "yes, a *living.*" They raided crops, became bel-
ligerent if we dared to protest.

"So what did you do?" I asked Papa.

"I sent for Grandma," he gave a wry smile. "The first
time she threatened them they thought she was a joke. But
only once. I must say, only *once.* She laid about the largest
man with her walking stick. In the end he bolted. Remarkable, *quite* remarkable, the way she followed it up with a
tongue lashing." At the memory of the moment Papa
chuckled, almost with relish, "Yes, that's the perfect
word—*tongue lashing.*" He rolled it round his own tongue,
as though physically enjoying the words.

"And then?"

"There must have been fifty in that group. Grandma
chased some cows that were too near the vineyard, ordered
the farmers to graze them in the orchard, and shouted to
the refugees, 'Follow me!' They didn't dare to refuse and
followed her to the Home Farm, where they were all given

bread with ham or *saucisse* and as much wine or milk as they could drink."

"And they behaved?"

Papa nodded. "The word went round. Those who behaved, as they moved on, told the others they could depend on one free meal a day if they respected the house rules. Yes, the *rules.*"

This conversation took place a few days after the German invasion, on the first occasion when I was able to get to Douzy for a few hours to see how the family was faring. Five million men, women, and children were on the march across Europe, all fleeing the spectre of German brutality, running anywhere, although they must have known in their hearts there was no real hope; the carpet of humanity was being trodden underfoot by the Germans with the indifference of men squashing ants.

"There's an old proverb," said Oregon when we were discussing the refugees, "which goes, 'What's the use of running when you're not on the right road?' It's a German saying, by the way. Ironic, isn't it?"

The only information we could glean about these momentous events came through the Ministry of Information, and though any news of retreat was firmly withheld, I was able to fill in some of the broad outlines of the picture. Three Panzer corps were in the van of the German attack which had been launched that Friday morning. The Germans swarmed through the Ardennes in southern Belgium and Luxembourg, obviously making for the river Meuse. Already by the end of the first day's fighting, it was clear that the Belgians were retreating and there was no way the brave Dutch could hope to hold out. Though valiant, the Hollanders had only a quarter of a million men and less than a hundred and fifty planes. They were doomed from the moment German airborne forces seized key airfields and bridges.

In fact, thinking back to those first days of the real war, the most extraordinary thing is that when the big push did come, even when almost immediately the Germans started

pouring toward the Meuse, there was no sense of real
panic. Sure, France would receive a few hard knocks before the Krauts were beaten off, most people thought, but
the issue could never be in real doubt because Europe was
not only more powerful but fortified with an even stronger
weapon—right—on their side.

Of course the rich—as usual—took their precautions. A
well-known American hostess in Paris, Mrs. Laura Corrigan, promptly closed her Paris house and moved into the
Ritz Hotel—it was said that she occupied the entire first
floor. But even so, that indicated a *lack* of panic. The
Corrigans of this world could have just as easily flown off
to Mexico or Rio, but all they wanted was to stay in Paris
and be cosseted.

I could hardly get away from the office for several days,
but on the Sunday—it happened to be Whit Sunday—Sonia
telephoned me from the rue de Longchamp. Francesco had
been ordered to Italy for a two-day conference with Ciano.
We agreed to meet at the terrace of Fouquet's on the
Champs-Elysées, so that if by chance she were followed,
our encounter would have all the appearance of a chance
meeting.

Sipping a beer, I waited in the sunshine, glancing
through *Le Monde* until she arrived. The Duke of Windsor
had entertained King Zog of Albania at a charity gala in
Paris. The Académie Française, busy composing its new
dictionary, couldn't agree whether the wing of a chicken
was a limb or a muscle.

She arrived along the avenue, gave a well-simulated
smile of surprise and a wave as she greeted me, and I gravely invited her for a coffee, after which we strolled down toward the Rond-Point. From some unseen window or café a
gramophone or radio churned out the latest haunting hit
tune, "J'attendrai." Near the Palais de Glace gardeners
were carefully planting early flowers.

"It's a perfect summer's day," Sonia almost sighed with
happiness, the long hard winter—the worst in the history
of France—forgotten with the buds of the chestnuts opening out all along the Champs-Elysées. It seemed impossi-

ble, feeling the sun on our faces as we strolled along, that during the winter the Thames in London had frozen over and that Paris had been a city of burst pipes—with hardly a plumber in sight.

"Let's lunch at the Ritz," I said suddenly, probably thinking of the unknown Mrs. Corrigan. "It's a change and the food's good."

"Anything you like, darling, even though—well," with a low happy laugh, "when you leave your beloved Left Bank for the Ritz it's rather like lunching in a foreign country."

I just felt that the easy elegance of the Ritz matched the mood of the May sunshine and the phrase on everyone's lips *"Chantons quand même!"* Why shouldn't we sing just because the damn Germans wanted to stop us.

Georges, the barman in the small bar off the rue Cambon, always joked when I arrived, "Sorry, m'sieu, but we've run out of Astell."

"Don't worry," I replied airily. "I'll forgive you this once. Anyway I have a sudden desire for a cocktail—a side-car." It was years since I had tasted an old-fashioned cocktail—and I couldn't even remember the ingredients though I think it contained Cointreau and brandy. I just felt the need for a sharp, tangy flavor.

"Sorry, sir," Georges looked at a sign over the bar. "It's a dry day." I had forgotten that on three days a week no hard liquor was served anywhere in France—excepting at home. But of course wine didn't count as liquor, so we settled for champagne after all. Georges also whispered a warning as I tasted the champagne. "Only two courses allowed and there is no *pâtisserie* today. All cake shops close three days a week."

"So we have to settle for a two-course lunch," I cried in mock despair as I steered Sonia to a corner table in the quiet paneled dining room—it was too early yet to lunch in the garden.

"Not to worry," I added, "we'll start with a *risòtto con scampi* followed by *poulet de Bresse.*" I knew that at the Ritz they served the finest roast chicken in France.

Suddenly, halfway through lunch, without knowing

why, I asked, "I wonder what poor Willi is having for lunch today?"

"A tenth of what we are eating—if that," said Sonia. "It makes me feel embarrassed to think of it."

"I was thinking how ridiculous it is that suddenly Willi, a good friend, can so easily become an enemy."

"Of the French, not of us."

"You know what I mean. You might be the next enemy. Francesco more or less said it was bound to happen in the end."

"Not yet," she laid a hand on mine.

"No, not yet," I echoed. "But one day for certain. What's going to happen to us then?"

"There'll be a way. There has to be." She was suddenly silent, doubting perhaps, afraid, as the waiter poured out the black coffee and asked, "Anything else, Monsieur Astell?"

I shook my head.

"I suppose," Sonia was thinking aloud, "that the real answer for me would be to live mostly in Switzerland. It's neutral. Francesco says all nations at war need one or two neutrals for convenience. And as you're a neutral American too—well, we could meet there."

"And Francesco?"

"He'll have to understand—and I think he does. He told me about your talk," she hesitated. "You see, everything's changing. Poor Daddy is now in the hospital. The end is very near. A priest is waiting to administer the last rites if necessary. I know I should be sad and weeping, but I can't really feel that way. He's in terrible pain in Florence, he cries to Mummy that he wants to die, and—does this sound brutal?—I want him to die. And when that does happen, then the threat that hangs over him will die too—and I won't be needed again, not by anyone. Except you. Do I sound very—what's the American word?—tough?"

"Of course not. I understand. And for you as well as me, it's"—I was searching for the right phrases—"it's important that you say this and explain it to me. It's a terrible thing, talking about imminent death and suffering, but—" the words trailed off.

"What's so awful is that I can't see Daddy. I daren't go to Italy in case there's a war and the French wouldn't let me return. And if I have to choose I want to remain with you, the living, until the very last moment of our lives together. You don't think me heartless? And there's another thing —I'm really afraid of what most French people regard as the impossible—a German victory. Do you think—?"

"I daren't *say* so," with a smile that broke the tension. "If Grandma heard me, she'd flay me alive."

Sonia smiled too, nodding as the waiter offered more coffee. "Probably she's right, I'm getting into a panic for nothing. France *is* very strong?" She posed the last remark as a question, her voice betraying doubt, hoping for assurance.

"Not as strong as she pretends," I had to admit.

"That's the real reason I don't want to leave you, it's *because* anything terrible could happen and I won't be away from you until we are dragged apart by events bigger than we are. If the war goes on with no result, why shouldn't I stay—at least until Italy declares war, if she ever does."

"It's selfish, but that's all I want too. Every hour together with you is a bonus."

We parted after lunch by different exits, for I knew by now that Francesco's main concern about us was the need for discretion. I walked back through the Ritz shopping arcade and out into the rue Cambon, turning right along the Grands Boulevards. Despite the war, despite the sandbags at "strategic corners," despite the despondent groups whose rags and tatters and wide-eyed curiosity proclaimed them to be refugees, I felt the spring of love in my step as I strode toward the office. It had been a gentle, beautiful lunch filled with love. We had to stay together, we *had* to. I caught myself quietly humming "J'attendrai," for despite the refugees, this seemed at a first glance like any other Sunday, with the crowds reveling in the sunshine, even turning their faces upward toward it as though to warm themselves after the cruelty of winter. Reality returned

when I reached the office and opened the elevator at the
second floor to hear the jangling telephone.

It was Papa. I had been trying in vain since Friday to get
through to Douzy, always to be told by the invisible vinegary spinsters who manned the French switchboards that
the number was engaged. Papa had succeeded where I had
failed—it was easier with local knowledge to pull a few
strings, or telephone wires.

"It's bad news," Papa said without preamble. "We don't
really know anything here at Douzy—except that the Germans are advancing everywhere. It's pretty awful, yes,
awful. I went to Reims for a bite of dinner at Boulingrin
last night, and it made my stomach turn—yes, really
turn—to hear the army types swilling champagne and
talking about their impregnable Maginot Line." And then
he came to the point. "Any chance of you getting to Douzy—just for a night?" I could sense that my father needed
me if only for moral support. "We must decide what to do
about Anna. I don't like her staying here."

"I'll try," I promised him. "I think I could get back for
one night. How's everyone—Guy and Olivia?"

"I'm worried about her too, of course," Papa's voice rose
up the scales. "There was a nasty anti-Jewish demonstra-
tion near Reims the other day. But it's Anna who really
worries me. She's German, Larry. She should go to Switzerland as soon as possible."

"Could she?"

"Really! Why not? Not by train, but is it too late to go by
car?"

Papa seemed to ignore the fact that the Germans had at
one point advanced almost to the borders of Switzerland.

"I'll try and get back home for a few hours sometime this
week," I promised him. "I want to see you too of course. Oregon can mind the shop."

Papa was just explaining that he could provide me with
a tank of gas when the sirens sounded.

"It's a raid," I shouted to him. "I'll have to ring off, but
I'll be seeing you soon."

The insistent wail of the air-raid warning was, I thought,

the most depressing of all sounds made by war. Gunfire
was bad, and I had never heard the whistle of falling
bombs or the terrible sound of the Stuka dive bombers, but
the sirens had a depressing sound all their own; it was the
noise of a world summoned to live underground, to revert
to the life of the caveman. I could see through the windows
the *flics* forcing people into makeshift shelters even
though there was no sound of gunfire or planes overhead. I
knew we should be grateful for their solicitude, but during
the only time I had been caught in the street during a raid
an officious policeman had insisted on bundling me down
the steps into the nearest Métro station. It was jammed.
The smell of sweating bodies, old women on the verge of
panic, the claustrophobia, the feeling that if a bomb did
fall and block up the entrance we would be trapped were
awful.

This time I was in the haven of the office, and I stayed
there, listening to the concert of sounds, shouts, slamming
doors, wardens' whistles.

There was no bombing and the flash of the all-clear came
up on the tape machine in the office almost as the sirens
announced that the nonexistent raid had ended.

The other news, however, was bad. By the Sunday, after
little more than two days of fighting, the Germans had
crossed the Albert Canal at Maastricht. A squadron of
British Battle planes based at the RAF fields near Champagne had volunteered to fly suicide missions to attack
bridges over the canal. All had been shot down. The only
light relief came when a British correspondent arrived in
Paris from London, bringing with him the Sunday newspapers. The main headline on the *Sunday Chronicle* read DE-
SPAIR IN BERLIN!

It was obvious that official communiqués were distorted,
but finally the foreign press corps cornered Colonel Thomas and literally demanded that they must be given regular off-the-record briefings, if only to combat German
propaganda. It was not just a question of getting news, we
all argued, but of being kept in the picture so that we

didn't make fools of ourselves and thus unwittingly distort the truth through ignorance.

Colonel Thomas finally agreed and adjusted his pince-nez on his aquiline nose, and gave us a depressing but at least fairly accurate account. Not only had the Albert Canal been breached, but advance guards of the three Panzer corps had penetrated to the east bank of the river Meuse along an eighty-mile front between Dinant and Sedan. Within a few hours—May 12 to 13—General Guderian's Panzers established bridgeheads close by a sleepy old provincial town which meant much more to Hitler—and to France—than just another strong point to be stormed or defended.

Sitting astride the river, Sedan—as any of us who had studied European history knew—was one of those key points in war and peace whose fate had changed the destiny of Europe. Here in the nineteenth century it had been the scene of France's greatest humiliation when Napoleon surrendered unconditionally with a hundred thousand men to Field Marshal Moltke of Prussia. Now Sedan was to be the scene of defeat again.

During the night German columns lining the Meuse positioned themselves for attack by seven armored divisions supported by three air fleets. At Sedan the Meuse is a swift, narrow stream running between steep banks. The river line was an ideal barrier and the French were convinced they could hold it. They had reckoned without the superior air power of the Germans. For hour after hour, from early morning on May 13, Stukas low-level bombers screamed over the Meuse, giving the defenders no rest. The covering guns were pounded into silence. The Germans crossed the river in boats and inflatable dinghies, setting up pontoon bridges and then establishing beachheads on the west bank. Within hours the advance guard of the German troops took Sedan without a fight, and as the news of the German victory rattled its letters along the office tape machine, neither Oregon nor I needed to add the one significant factor which both of us knew: that Sedan was less than sixty miles from Reims—and Douzy.

"You'd better go and see your father," said Oregon quietly. "Only come back to Paris soon—all hell will be let loose before long."

I drove down late on the Friday. With Whit Sunday behind us the weather had turned even warmer. The sun seemed to shine every day, and on the first evening Anna and I went for a long walk, up past the bleak outline of Douzy church, through the twisting streets of the village, stopping for a beer with Monsieur Roland, the *patron,* at the Café des Sports.

Even after only a short absence Douzy never failed to tug at the strings of nostalgia. When I walked down past the dell to the orchard, or up to the village, I felt as though I could never bear to leave the place and sometimes would curse myself—muttering aloud—for choosing to live in a city.

"What *are* you muttering about?" Anna laughed. I hadn't realized I was talking aloud.

"I was thinking that there just can't be another place in the world as beautiful as Douzy," I sighed. "Listen!" We could both hear the growl of gunfire like a distant thunderstorm. "And to think we're going to lose it all."

"Nonsense!" Anna spoke quite sharply. "Don't ever say that. It's defeatist—and oh!" with a catch in her voice, almost the kind of break that signals waiting tears, she added, "if we don't look on the bright side—if we don't *hope*—what the hell is there to live for?" She hesitated, and then added, "I love Douzy more than life."

We had finished our drink, and Anna was walking by the side of the lane, framed to the waist in feathery cow parsley. "If someone tried to take it away from us, I think I'd kill them," she said.

"I feel that way too. And so in a way does Sonia. Never forget that. It's the only *true* home she's ever had. But Anna—don't you think you ought to get out of France? What if the Germans—"

She shook her head vigorously. "Never! I still love Willi —I think of him more than you'll ever know—but I'm not going to be kicked out of Douzy by Nazis. And anyway I'm not going to leave Olivia. At least I do have a kind of American passport, but what chance is a Jewish girl like Olivia going to have if the Germans take France?"

"Not much," I admitted.

"Nothing can happen to me," she said.

"Don't tempt fate by saying things like that."

"I said so and I mean it—I'll kill the first German who lifts a finger against me," she said. "I will, I swear it, Larry. I loathe the lot of them."

"Not all. There must be millions of decent Germans like —well, like Willi."

"Willi's only a German by accident," she almost shouted. "To me he's not German or American or French. He's my *husband!* My husband! Do you ever think of Sonia as an Italian?"

"I don't suppose I do—except perhaps when I worry about the future."

"Well then," she looked at her watch and suddenly changed the subject. "Let's start for home, shall we?"

After dinner Papa also brought up the subject of "the girls," as he called them.

"I must say we should do something," he declared rather helplessly. "Yes, I do, *really.* The Germans are less than fifty miles from Reims. You're cutting it rather fine, you and Olivia, yes, *fine* is the word."

Apparently all attempts by Papa and Guy to organize some way of spiriting the girls to the south of France or Switzerland had been thwarted by one stumbling block: female intransigence.

"If it's dangerous to use the train, couldn't we smuggle the girls across the frontier into Switzerland?" asked Guy.

"First, it's not so easy for an amateur to cross frontiers illegally," said Anna. "And second, we don't *want* to go."

"Quite impossible, I agree." Papa must have nursed some half-forgotten memories of an old war film, for he added, "Girls scrambling over all that barbed wire. Out of the question, yes, there must be a better way."

"But what?" asked Guy.

"Please, Papa," Anna was beginning to lose her patience. "Don't worry. I'm a grown-up girl now—I'm married —and I can look after myself."

I knew what she meant. But did Anna have the slightest idea of what the future might hold for her if the Germans overran the area? The trouble was that after the months of inactivity, not a soul realized how subhuman the Nazis could be if anyone got in their way. I hated to think what they would do if they got their hands on Olivia in some anti-Jewish purge. "Some of the stories of German savagery are unspeakable," I said half aloud to Papa.

"I've heard about them," but had he heard the real evil details, I wondered, as he added, "but still, I *must* say, this *is* American property. They'll have to respect it. They can't just—"

"Papa! Face up to the truth," I cried, exasperated. "And you've got to realize this, too, Guy. They can do *anything*. With the Germans, might really *is* right. Have you thought about the embassy? Couldn't the embassy help Anna? What about Bullitt?"

"Really, Larry!" Now Papa sounded annoyed. "Do you think I'm a child? Of *course* I've been in to see Bill Bullitt. I think he could fix it. But there's one problem."

Patiently Papa and Guy explained that Anna had become so close to Olivia that they had decided to stick together.

"They say they face the same problems," said Guy. "I don't really know how to explain it. Both losers, I guess. One without a husband, the other without a family, Jewish, on the run if the Germans arrive."

"I can understand," I said. "They're both damn good girls, and each one is determined not to let the other down."

"Really, it *does* complicate things." Papa sounded frustrated, defeated by circumstances.

I felt a sudden pang of pity for Papa. We were all so busy with our own lives we forgot the quiet way in which he had carried on after Mama left for America.

"You must miss Mama," I tried to console him. "Have you heard from her?"

"No letters," he shook his head. "And as far as I can see not much hope of getting any for the time being. But I've had fairly regular short messages through the embassy. Mama's living in New York—and she's taken a flat at the corner of Fifty-sixth and Lexington. A *very* convenient place for St. Patrick's."

At that moment I heard the peal of the old-fashioned brass pull bell outside the front entrance.

"Really, a bit late for callers, yes, it *is,*" Papa frowned and looked at his watch. He always considered it bad manners for anyone to arrive without warning after dinner, and as Aubergine came in to announce the visitors, he said almost testily, "Do we know them?"

There was no need for an answer. The Misses B and B burst into the living room.

Miss Barron's face was drained of all color. Miss Brewer's was streaked with tear stains.

"Jean-Pierre's dead," said Miss Brewer dully. "He's been killed in action."

24

DAILY THE NEWS GREW HEAVIER, though, as if deluding themselves—or being deluded by others?—only those in high places realized it. Even men returning from battle seemed under the impression that *their* experiences were those of an unfortunate unlucky episode. *We* knew—the foreign press corps particularly, for many of them came and went from one country to another and between them could piece together a more coherent picture of unmitigated disaster. To me it was as though the heart was being torn out of France. And I could sense something equally tragic—the sense of futility among men fighting under leaders with 1914–1918 mentalities against a revolutionary war machine so fearsome that nobody believed it was possible.

One of Jean-Pierre's friends whom I had met when both were on leave had promised to call me when he reached Paris, where he lived, and tell me how Jean-Pierre had died. He had stayed with the Misses B and B the time when Jean-Pierre had been sent home because the Maginot Line was too crowded.

"That was the trouble," he was a young man of twenty-two called Boisseau. "As they had no room we were all sent up to the front line on the river Meuse. It was murder."

We had met for a drink near the office, where he told me the horrific story. Jean-Pierre and Boisseau and their unit had been sent up the line to bolster the morale of raw re-

cruits. Many had been training for only six weeks. The two
thousand or so men had only eight hundred rifles between
them. Only two hundred were modern mousqueton French
rifles, the rest were obsolete, some rifles dating back to
1891. "I had a long thin Remington weighing twenty
pounds, with a lock so worn the cartridges kept falling
out," said Boisseau. "Others had rifles too rusty to load."

When the unit set off for the front line they had no knap-
sacks and had to wrap their belongings in waxed cloth.
They were issued with rations of eleven biscuits each, one
tin of sardines and one of pressed meat. "The cans were
coated with blue paint, and when I scraped the paint off
mine, I found I could read the date when the meat had been
canned. It was 1917."

Everyone could tell a similar story—but since none of
them ever passed the censor, it was easy for the government to build up a false picture among civilians. By hiding
bad news they gave the impression that though the French
were suffering some setbacks, nothing was out of control
and soon the tide would turn. But we *knew.* The French
government knew. It could pinpoint every disastrous defeat as the Germans thrust westward and to the Channel
ports, where more than a quarter of a million British
troops had miraculously escaped after being trapped by
the Germans at Dunkirk.

"Everyone knows how badly the war's going," I said bitterly to Sonia during one of our quiet lunches, "everyone
but the French. The Germans are taking France as easily
as picking our grapes."

We still met whenever possible at Marcel's, but even
there it was hard sometimes to throw off gloom. The sense
of adventure which had made life so exciting had been
drained out of both of us. Once or twice, when sitting at the
square table, I caught her looking sad.

"A centime for your thoughts," I smiled.

She smiled back. She looked so beautiful on that warm
June day, no hat, black hair silky, lips slightly apart.

"I'm not *afraid* of war. It's only the dreariness of it all
that terrifies me. We hardly ever laugh these days, it's as

though we're already too old to enjoy life. A girl too old at twenty-five! Isn't it a terrible confession—not to have a sense of fun anymore? That's what sometimes makes me depressed."

She hesitated, still thinking, then asked, "What do *you* think about?"

"I don't know." The old waiter brought a small dish of *charcuterie* and some radishes, and we counted ourselves favored clients. "I just feel an awful weight of sadness, partly for a country that's going up in smoke around us, but—sounds selfish"—I tried a grin—"but especially for us." I was thinking, as though in the past tense, how we had shared such a beautiful, laughing love together, not just the physical side but the tenderness.

As if reading my thoughts, Sonia sighed, "I wish we were in Douzy now, this very minute."

"The war can't go on forever," I protested. "And then Douzy will still be there—to welcome us back."

"But will it be the same? Will *we* be the same? You can't just brush away years apart and expect to remain unchanged."

It was during this lunch at Marcel's that we finally agreed it would be stupid to ignore the fact that Italy soon *would* be an "enemy." And that we would have to be parted.

"But where would you go?" I asked.

"The house in Rolle is ready," she replied. "I've got an official resident's permit. So it's my home—in theory. Our ambassador in Bern fixed it for me with the Swiss. But I should go there before Italy becomes involved, otherwise all of us at the embassy will leave together in a sealed train for Rome. It's the normal practice. And if that happens I might get trapped in Italy."

It made sense, I said, as long as Francesco accepted the situation.

"He will. He understands."

"You'll have to go soon?"

"No, no, no!" she cried. "Not until the very last second of the very last day."

"I don't think it'll be long," I sighed. "The Italians are making threatening noises. And you know there are rumors that the French government is going to evacuate Paris. If that happens, Mussolini will *have* to declare war—to be sure he gets a share of the spoils."

"I wonder how long it will be?" she sighed.

My conviction that the government would leave Paris soon was reinforced after I met Jim Parks for a drink at the Tante Claire bistro not far from the embassy. Even Jim's image of the cool efficient young diplomat was getting a little frayed—at the edges, as I noticed from the soiled cuffs of his shirt sleeves.

"Yeah, I know," he said bitterly as he saw me notice them. "Now I can't even get my goddamn laundry done."

"Things must be bad," I laughed.

"We're all set to run for it—contingency plans ready and tested."

"For?"

"There's no secret about this. We reckon the government will have to make for Tours and set up some sort of government there and then we will have to go with them."

"And a temporary embassy?"

"We've already taken over the Château de Candé in the Loire Valley, the place where the Windsors got married. It's been lent to us by its American owner. We've already got a skeleton staff there, and we've prepared it down to the last bottle of vino."

"Of course the government might not have to go," I suggested.

"Nothing's certain in a crazy situation like this—with an enemy that sits on its ass doing sweet eff-all for nine months, then bang! hits you in the crotch when you're not looking. But I don't see the French holding out for long. Take my tip, get some authority—a special pass or something to go south—just in case."

He was right, and I decided to ignore all official requests for a pass. I would be bogged down in paperwork for the duration: Reynaud I could not approach, however considerate he was. For with a country fighting for its life, I would never get within a mile of him. Madame de Portes, though, was different. It was worth a try. She was always accessible.

In fact she couldn't have been more helpful—though the scene when I met her was bizarre, even shocking, in the midst of a war.

Her secretary was arranging an appointment for 6:00 P.M. the following day when she must have grabbed the phone, for in that special voice of hers she interrupted, "Come to the Ministry of Defense, *cher* Larry. Paul is up to his eyes in work and he's also got a cold, so I'm helping out."

She was indeed.

I drove to the Ministry of Defense in the rue St. Dominique. Reynaud preferred to work there—where Napoleon had once had his offices—instead of at the Hôtel Matignon, the official residence of the premier of France.

I arrived just before six. "You're expected on the first floor, monsieur," said the secretary.

As I reached the waiting room the male secretary seemed embarrassed. So did the only other man waiting for an appointment—a man I knew, Pierre Lazareff, editor of *Paris-Soir*. He was gazing in astonishment through the open door leading to Reynaud's office—not at Reynaud, he wasn't there, but at Madame de Portes, who was energetically presiding over a noisy conference of elderly statesmen.

"C'est impossible!" Lazareff nodded to me, for I, too, could see that Reynaud wasn't in the room. How *could* you hold a war council—or whatever was going on—without the prime minister being there? And at the very moment when the government might have been discussing with anguish whether or not it should flee from Paris.

The countess caught sight of me, came out in a rush, crying, "Please don't be impatient. We'll be finished soon." Then she moved over to a third opening, and while Lazareff and I sat almost aghast, I heard her say through the

door, "Are you all right, Paul? Just relax! We're working."

She bustled back to the conference room. Ten minutes
later a group of dispirited cabinet ministers trooped out.
Lazareff was waiting to see one minister. As they went
downstairs together Hélène de Portes cried, "Come in,
cher Larry. It's good to see someone so young and healthy
after talking to all these old fogies!"

"I hope the prime minister isn't too ill," I said.

"No, no. Just a bad cold. But he has a great responsibility, you know, and I must make sure that he conserves all
his energy. That is why I help if I can. Now tell me, Larry,
what can I do for you?"

I explained—tactfully adding that I didn't for a moment
suggest that the government would *need* to leave Paris, but
that as the correspondent of an important Washington newspaper, I must be prepared for all possible contingencies.

"You shall have your request while you wait," she said
cheerfully.

I must say that—in direct contradiction to most French
government offices—Madame de Portes did get things
done. She worked like a dynamo.

"Sit down, Larry," she bounded into the outer office. I
heard her dictate a letter of accreditation. When the secretary brought it in, she read it, made Reynaud sign it in the
adjoining room. Then the secretary stamped it with the official seal, and almost with a flourish she smiled, *"Voilà!*
These may be bad times, but even the Germans couldn't
match that for efficiency."

Back in the rue du Sentier I told Oregon what had happened.

"It's a madhouse," he cried. "With that damn woman
wielding all the power. What *really* frightens me is that if
things go badly for France, she'll make Reynaud sign the
instrument of surrender as quickly as she signed your bit
of paper."

During the first week in June the phone in the rue du
Sentier stuttered one lunchtime, went dead when I picked

it off the hook, then the bell shrilled again, and a voice croaking with exhaustion, but still with an unseen grin in it, cried, "It's Tommy. Any chance of pinching a bath at Douzy? I'm at Reims, taking a couple of days off. Haven't washed for days."

"Tommy! Wonderful to hear from you. Go there right away. Papa must be around but I can't phone, it's too hard to get through. I'm just filing a story, but I'll drive to Douzy when I've got my stuff through the censors. See you later this evening."

I was so excited at the prospect of seeing Tommy Tomlinson again that I almost forgot to go to the Hôtel Continental for the afternoon briefing. I was on the point of leaving when the phone rang again. It was Sonia.

"Francesco's just left for Rome," she sounded breathless. "He says it's a question of days now. Ciano has sent for him. But, Larry—it means that we're free for a couple of days," adding with unconscious irony, "Isn't it wonderful! I'll go straight to the rue du Cherche-Midi and wait for you."

"No, no!" I cried. "I was just going to risk phoning you. Tomlinson's on his way to Douzy. He's driving over from Reims. I've got to go to the Ministry of Information for a briefing. Come to Douzy for a couple of nights, darling. I plan to leave as soon as I can get away. Can you get one of your embassy drivers to take you to the office? Wait for me and we'll drive off together." I felt suddenly exhilarated.

I was kept at the Ministry of Information for nearly an hour for the afternoon briefing. Colonel Thomas was dressed in a beautifully cut uniform, specially tailored, severely masculine, the cloth pale khaki, the texture of tweed, with bound edges. He was being cross-examined (in effect) by another American correspondent who had just returned from the front line—part of France which Thomas had obviously never had the time to visit. He was forced to admit that "for the moment, only temporarily you understand, monsieur," the Germans had air superiority around the Meuse area. Yes, he agreed, civilian population masses were clogging the roads in many areas, "But that, monsieur, is a situation that will soon cease and the requisite measures are in hand."

"What measures?" asked H. R. Knickerbocker, one of America's most respected correspondents.

"That, monsieur, I am not permitted to divulge," said Colonel Thomas, picking up his briefcase and bowing as he strode across the splendid room with its gilt ceiling and ballroom chairs.

We reached Douzy just before dinner, and it was extraordinary—especially when I thought back to our sad lunch at Marcel's—it was truly remarkable how the moment the car crunched on the gravel the air of depression lifted.

The doors burst open before Aubergine could reach us, and out rushed Anna, Olivia, and Guy, together with a shambling figure balancing a champagne glass in one hand and a huge cigar in the other.

"You old so-and-so!" I cried. "That's my suit you're wearing, Tommy. And my silk shirt!"

"Everything is borrowed"—Tommy gave a lordly wave of his cigar—"even the cigar, one of Oregon's, I'll never be able to return *that*. My new friend, Aubergine, is washing my clothes, pressing my uniform, and I feel like the king of the castle."

From the very moment I hugged him, then kissed the girls—and they in turn rushed to embrace Sonia, who had appeared with me out of the blue—the few hours were like a birthday party. Everybody was suddenly on fire with happiness. We even started off with a joke after our first welcoming drink.

With mock gravity Anna announced, "We're rather short of space now that Tommy's arrived unexpectedly, but you won't mind sharing a room, will you, Larry?"

"Share a room—with Tommy! Never! He snores."

"How do you know?"

"Not with Tommy," said Anna sweetly. "I thought Tommy deserves a long night's rest on his own. But if you and Sonia could be persuaded—"

We dissolved into laughter just as Papa, who had been working late, arrived home.

"You sound happy, *very* happy, yes, it sounds just like the old days," he beamed, and as he kissed Sonia he examined her more closely.

"You look more beautiful every time I see you," he said as though it was a mystery and unexpected. "Yes, more beautiful, very attractive."

We didn't *do* anything to make that brief spell of "freedom" any happier than countless others. It just happened that way, perhaps aided by the presence of Tommy. An unexpected friend can often help to ease family tensions. Perhaps also it was because those hours were in a sense stolen, as though we were all on leave. Only Mama and Willi were missing to complete the atmosphere of a family party.

At one stage, when Sonia and I sat together on the large sofa, my feet on the corner of the huge plate-glass table, and the others talked or joked, I teased her, "Another centime for your thoughts."

"I was just thinking of the magic which this house holds for me. Douzy is our real home, isn't it, where we first fell in love. Sometimes I imagine I'm married to you, not Francesco, and settled down here. It's so peaceful. So stable. It's the only home we've ever really had. If only we could stop the clock and stay here forever."

Later, as was inevitable, there were moments when the conversation grew more serious. Apart from anything else I wanted to hear all Tommy's latest news. He was with the 35th Division in the French army, where for three weeks as a war correspondent he had been with soldiers holding a sector fourteen miles south of Sedan.

"After the big breakthrough?" I asked.

He nodded, explaining that after the Germans had crossed the river they had driven north and west, leaving German infantry to widen the gap and turn the Maginot Line. North and west the Germans were advancing up to fifty miles a day, bypassing strong points.

"You've never seen such a shambles," said Tommy.

"The men in our sector were in some cases literally starving. The field kitchens were often ten miles behind the lines, and the food was delivered once every twenty-four hours—each midnight. Stone cold. Sometimes the trucks couldn't get through, and then there wouldn't be anything to eat—not a biscuit—for forty-eight hours."

"Where does this leave us?" I asked. "I mean Reims, Douzy, the family?"

"Not a hope. No use kidding ourselves. Reims will fall within a few days. Nothing can stop the rot; only the goddamn censor would never allow us to tell the truth."

"Papa doesn't think so," I said doubtfully.

"No offense meant," Tommy hesitated, "but there's a world of difference between your father and Oregon, his brother. Oregon *loves* the French. Your father *admires* them. That's a helluva difference. And so you see your father can't realize that for a century—since Napoleon and then the Great War bled France white—France has been a second-class power flattering herself she was a great one. It's a pity, it's led her into masquerading as an empire that's no match for the Germans."

"Does it really matter if or when France gives in?" I asked Tommy. "I'm not being cynical, but does it really matter? The British will have to sue for peace, won't they? After all, the French hate the British; they like the Germans more than they like the French. And anyway the British don't have a chance."

"What about the Channel?" asked Tommy.

"Do you think the sea counts anymore when the other side has a mastery of the air?"

Perhaps the fact that Douzy was doomed—if only for the time being, we hoped—helped to sustain our feeling of exhilaration and to shrug off the doubts. It gave us an added impetus to enjoy those few hours to the fullest.

I had to leave with Sonia immediately after lunch, before Tommy, who had "borrowed" an old Panhard and planned to rejoin his unit a couple of days later, "if I can find it," he added dryly.

The last lunch was subdued. It was as though the effort

to be cheerful (even though it had been spontaneous) had sapped all our reserves of emotion. In a matter of days Douzy would, even if neutral, be surrounded by German uniforms. This was surely the last time my family, Sonia, and I would meet in this beautiful home as one happy family, and the parting might be for a long, long time. Sonia would have to leave for Switzerland. Anna would become a fugitive in hiding. Olivia would live in fear if she ever dared to show her face. Already the process of disintegration in our family had begun now that Mama was in New York and Willi had vanished, swallowed up in the gigantic German military maw. Meanwhile I would probably leave for the south with the French government. Who knows if I would ever be able to get north again to see Papa and Grandma? I even had to give up my MG—leaving it to be used at Douzy while I drove back to Paris after lunch in the less conspicuous Citroën, which I thought would be more suitable for the journey to Tours.

On the Saturday—that must have been the eighth of June—Sonia phoned me again when I was back in Paris. Her husband was not returning from Rolle to Paris after all because the declaration of war was imminent. That was the word she used.

"He told me not to worry," she said. "All embassy personnel would be given three days to pack up after the declaration, and of course the French would be given the same courtesies in Rome."

"How will you go—I mean travel?"

"The officials here tell me we'll all be collected from the embassy in buses under French guard three days after the war is declared and we'll be put in a special sealed diplomatic train. That's all I know."

"But, darling—war might come any day. And I might have to go south too—any day. The government's wavering. I may have to leave for Bordeaux or Tours at a moment's notice. Everything points to a sudden evacuation by the government. Time is running out. We must meet now—in case it's good-bye—until I can get to Switzerland." Then she dropped her bombshell.

"I'm going with you!"

"Hey! Wait a minute!" I started.

"No, I won't wait. You listen, darling." As calmly as she could—and she was never very calm—she outlined her plans. Italy would declare war within forty-eight hours, she was sure. She would be ordered to go first to Italy. "But I want to go with you."

"I know that, but it's impossible," I cried. "Apart from the fact that I don't know where I'm going to make for, if there is a war—and you are with me—you could be lynched if anyone found out you were Italian."

"They won't. Don't be silly. Everyone at the embassy is getting a special pass with a time limit for the three days. Don't be so afraid."

But I was afraid. Of course the prospect of traveling with her was wonderful. But there were fifth columnists everywhere, and if we traveled on crowded roads, where tempers could burst into angry confrontations, God knows what could happen.

"I'll take that chance," she declared. "I'll have three days of grace—of official protection, guaranteed by the French—"

"Sonia, please! The French can't even control their own troops, let alone civilians."

"It's the only way. If we go south, then you can take me to Bordeaux. I'll get across the frontier into Spain, then go from one neutral country to another, Switzerland."

"It's not on. Too dangerous."

"Don't you understand *anything,* Larry," even at this moment of tension I almost smiled, imagining the way she was stamping her foot at the other end of the telephone as she often did when irritated by my imagined obtuseness.

"I'm throwing myself at you," she cried. "I want to marry you when we can. I'm leaving home to settle down with you. I don't know how or when, but this is our only chance. I'll tell Francesco. He'll eventually be able to get an annulment or whatever they do. But you are my man now, Larry. And despite this stupid damn war," she almost choked with anger, "I'm coming with you."

"Okay," I said huskily. "You're mad—crazy—but I love you, friend or foe, French or Italian or American. It makes no difference."

"We'll do it, darling," she cried, "we will—and this time it's forever."

I never hesitated now that the decision was made.

"Let's leave at dawn the day after tomorrow," I said. "I'm going to a press conference at the Hôtel Matignon this evening—the premier's official office, so it must be an uppercrust briefing. There's only one thing I must do—the only proviso I've got to make."

"No conditions, we don't need any."

"This one. If Madame de Portes is around—and she will be—I'd like to get an extra pass made out for you personally and get it stamped with Reynaud's official seal. She'll do it, I know."

At least Sonia could hardly disagree with that useful information. "It might not be necessary, but it's a good idea if you can pull it off." Then she added, "I'll see you this evening at the rue du Cherche-Midi."

"No, let's meet at the rue des St. Pères. I've got some gasoline and food stashed away in the family flat. I couldn't face carrying the gasoline up five flights so I left it in our place. I'll pick you up at the rue du Longchamp after the press conference."

That was how it worked out. Madame de Portes was there, and because I went to the Hôtel Matignon half an hour before the conference started, she even invited me into her sitting room for a drink and arranged a special pass without any problems.

We decided to leave at dawn or even earlier on the Tuesday, June 11, and spent the last Monday pretending to be carefree lovers without an unhappy thought in the world, almost as though we were on a honeymoon.

For in the hot sun of this Monday, Paris had the appearance of a stage set. The pavement cafés on the boulevards were as crowded as ever, a kaleidoscope of gaily flowered dresses, of men fighting for places at the minuscule tables, ordering a *vin rouge* or a *bière de pression;* yet the roads were so empty they gave the city a nostalgic turn-of-the-century character like an old sepia postcard unearthed from a dusty drawer. I almost expected to hear the clatter of a pony and trap. An occasional taxi driver sped along the Champs-Elyées with the verve of a racing driver who has no competition. An occasional ancient car—many of the rich had already left—rumbled up the avenue, always in the direction of the Etoile, to join the queue leaving the gates of the city for unknown destinations.

Even now, as we strolled along our favorite streets, the people of Paris seemed unable to believe that the worst could ever happen. I knew how their thoughts were running—that France possessed not only the Maginot Line but the finest army the world had ever known, the army that last time had stood for more than four years against German might, the army of glory that Lavisse once described as "one of the most perfect instruments of war history has ever seen." It was more than an army, it was the heart of the nation; it epitomized the very greatness of France. France might have changed; its politicians might be venal, but now more than ever people believed in the words of Anatole France that the French army "is all that is left of our glorious past. It consoles for the present and gives us hope for the future."

The heat shimmered and danced along the beautiful broad avenues, and although many shops were shuttered we saw few traces of war. Near the new Pont des Arts two formal gardens had just been planted on the embankment. In the symmetrical courtyards of the Louvre men—brown and sweating though stripped to the waist—uprooted the early spring flowers and filled the bed with geraniums from loaded trucks.

As we walked down the rue des St. Pères to the Left Bank the bookstalls were open, and down by the *quai*—the dome of les Invalides shining in the sun—a man in uniform calmly set up his easel and started painting. Below him a barge loaded with refugees sailed up the Seine. Not one in ten thousand realized that the Germans were on the point of taking Reims and had crossed the river Aisne and were attacking south of Soissons, while a Panzer division was moving on Rouen.

That last Sunday was beautiful—a tender make-believe day which gave us, as though handing out a farewell gift, a final picture to remember of the Paris we loved, unsullied by the dinginess of war.

"By the way," I said as we prepared for bed. "Got a visa to enter Spain?"

"Of course. And you?"

"Sure. The worst part of a foreign correspondent's job is keeping your visas up to date."

We were both tired, but happily so. The last thing I did before switching off the lights was to turn on the radio for five minutes.

Italy had declared war.

25

THE SHRILL OF THE ALARM tore into the bedroom at 5:00 A.M. We had been fast asleep in each other's arms, and for a few seconds, as I leaned over to shut out the insistent ring, I hadn't the faintest idea where I was. Then with a sick feeling, reality flooded in as I realized that our last hours together were running out for the third time in our lives. Soon the war between France and Italy would separate us, like people who, when clinging together, are torn apart by a great wave that finally engulfs them.

We had two priorities: to get Sonia across the frontier into Spain and at the same time do my job, find out what was happening among French politicians in Tours—if or when they arrived there—and file a story to Washington. This I hoped to do by sending a cable through Drexel Biddle, who was looking after the embassy task force in the absence of Bullitt, who had elected, against the advice of Cordell Hull, secretary of state, to stay in Paris. Biddle's headquarters in the Touraine was at the Château de Candé.

We set off in the Citroën at 6:00 A.M. after drinking some coffee and eating a couple of yesterday's croissants. I had managed to find some American tinned ham and loaves of bread to make sandwiches. We put them in a separate carrier bag with two bottles of Vichy water and one of brandy. We each had an overnight bag with a few spare clothes, and in the trunk I had locked a case of champagne—or what looked like champagne. I only hoped no one would try to drink it.

"For this," I explained to Sonia, "is vintage Astell gasoline. I filled up a dozen magnums in case of emergency. Now let's go, darling. There's going to be a hell of a rush on the roads, though I'm not worried. We've made an early start. We should make Tours easily by tonight."

How glib it sounded, how easy! Tours in a day! A mere hundred and fifty miles, even less. The trouble was that none of us had the remotest idea of the shocks in store for us. Around Douzy we had watched the long streams of refugees, but they had seemed to move along, however slowly. Why should this be so different?

The first few yards set the tone for that awful day. Not the traffic—not at first—but the atmosphere. Even in the early morning, as I drove across the Seine and up the Champs-Elysées, the city had a haunted, desperate air, so different at first light from yesterday's sunshine. It wasn't only the emptiness, the closed shops, the metal grills, the drawn shutters, the naked newspaper kiosks on the pavements, the lack of movement. There was something more sinister, an air of dreaded expectancy.

Everyone "knew" the French cabinet was pulling out of Paris, and this in itself was a signal for defeat. Everyone "knew" the American ambassador had decided to remain in Paris to hand the capital over to Germany in some sort of neutral capacity. And that was a sign the French were being abandoned by the Americans. And so everyone "knew" that it was only a question of time before the swastika would fly over the public buildings of an occupied city.

Only it hadn't happened *yet.* So we all watched, as though the patient was suffering from a terminal illness. It would have been almost easier to bear if death had mercifully ended the protracted suffering and put the patient —and his relations—out of their misery.

"At least the roads are quiet," Sonia tucked herself into the right-hand seat of the Citroën. "So there shouldn't be too many problems."

It looked as though she was right. Halfway along the Champs-Elysées, at the Rond-Point, an old flower seller was quietly preparing her stand of brightly colored blooms

as though this were a perfectly normal day. The few cars
were mostly old, I noticed, probably dragged out of ancient
garages at the last minute by people who had only just decided to abandon homes or offices and bolt.

We had decided to drive through the Bois, leave Paris by
the Porte de St. Cloud, and make our way to Versailles,
then Chartres, and on to Tours. At first all seemed to go
well, but it was an illusion. The roads were only empty at
first because the exodus from Paris had started long before
we had even woken up. Before we reached Versailles we
had to slow down, though at first I assumed we had just
been caught in a local traffic jam.

"We'll be through this in no time," I patted Sonia's leg.
"Though we may find a few more bad spots like this."

What we didn't know around seven o'clock that morning
was that the traffic jam consisted of one solid block of vehicles stretching virtually without a break on any main road
from Versailles to Chartres, more than fifty miles ahead.
Nor did we have the faintest idea (until many years later)
that we were living through one of the greatest mass
flights of human misery in the history of Europe, with in
all seven million people on the march across the face of
France. They moved forward instinctively, as relentlessly
as a colony of ants, some spurred by blind terror of the unknown, others impelled by a dogged determination to
escape—struggling to reach a ghostly terminal that didn't
exist.

I don't know the exact moment when instinct warned me
that I had made a fearful error. I had chosen what I
thought was the one main road and that was bad. I had to
get onto the secondary roads.

"I've bloody well erred!" I said as the traffic ground to a
stop. An assorted collection of vehicles filled every inch
of road ahead: everything from an expensive chauffeur-
driven Delage with white-walled tires, in which a middle-
aged woman sat in the back ignoring everyone around her,
to a wizened old couple beside the car—old and panting,
but insisting that they push their creaking overloaded

handcart festooned with pots and pans that regularly clanked as they swung against the car.

Every few minutes the procession started, then stopped; as the old couple drew abreast of the Delage, the chauffeur became more and more enraged each time their pots and pans scraped against the immaculate maroon paint job.

At one point he got out of his front seat and started to berate them. The old man doffed his blue beret to the lady in the car, who didn't seem to notice him. Then, with an expressive use of the hands, the old man made it as plain as if he had told her, *"Eh bien!* What can I do? It's all these people who keep pushing me."

Every time the jumble of vehicles stopped the same thing happened, with the old man and his wife finding it impossible to steer the ancient handcart in such restricted space.

"I wonder if I can find a better way across country," I said to Sonia. "It might pay me, even if it's longer."

The next time we stopped I jumped out and stood on the running board to see if there were any side roads or lanes I could take. Or even, I thought, I might turn round. I looked back.

"What is it?" asked Sonia.

"Come and see! We shan't be moving for a few moments." She stood on the running board, stretching on her toes for a better view. Now it was no longer just the road *ahead* that worried me. One look *behind* told me I would never be able to turn. Thousands of vehicles boxed us in —cars, horses and carts, a hearse, bicycles, and an old-fashioned three-wheeled tricycle with one wheel punctured. Every now and again a car wheezed to a stop, perhaps overheated or out of gas, blocking the road. Those behind unceremoniously pushed the vehicle to the side of the road, the ditch, or a village courtyard. I had the curious, ugly feeling that each time a car stalled everyone else experienced a moment of grim enjoyment. Each one that fell by the wayside diminished the number ahead.

In the open country linking the quiet villages many tried to bypass the traffic by driving across the fields. They

vanished in the distance ahead, sometimes cheering at
their victory. But sooner or later we caught up with them.
Sometimes a field would end in a wall, a wood, even a
ditch, and then there was nothing to do but for those who
had taken a shortcut to try and rejoin the main road. They
never did. With an almost ruthless fury those who had
taken hours to cover their stretch of road blocked every attempt to let the clever ones back in the mainstream. With
vehicles nudging each other nose to tail, this, too, gave
those on the main roads a savage pleasure.

"We're trapped," I said to Sonia. "We couldn't turn
round if we wanted to. We can only go ahead."

Long columns of men, women, children, and vehicles
grunted under a hot sun. In front of us an elderly woman
stumbled, too late for the helping hand offered by a father,
brother, or son. Someone behind pushed. The small group
of walkers threatened to be engulfed, separated, to fall behind the others. I could see the old lady's arms, the wrists
like knotted rope; then she started retching, the filth of the
raddled old body pouring out of her mouth. Who would
have thought that an empty shell of an old woman could
vomit such a quantity of liquid?

Did anybody care in this torrent of frightened human
beings? Yes, miraculously, love came in the form of the
husband or son or whoever he was. Gently he wiped the
vomit from the old lady's face with the only piece of cloth
at hand in the emergency: the tail of his shirt, which he
somehow ripped away.

The old lady mumbled, but no real words came out. I
glimpsed for a moment a look of terror in the sunken eyes
and I knew what it was—the fear of being abandoned as
those behind were forcing the press of people to move on.
The father or son put a reassuring arm around her. All she
wanted was to live! To suffer, to starve, to bring up a half-
famished family with love and care, anything so long as
she could live for another day, another hour, another minute.

There was hate too, hate and greed disguised with a
smile.

"Look," I pointed to some peasants leaning over the five-barred gate of their field. To the bedraggled, tormented people, they cried out, almost cheerfully, as though offering sweets for sale:

"Come on, ladies and gentlemen! Out with your money! Ten sous a glass of water, two francs to fill your bottle."

On the notice board outside one Hôtel de Ville, where the jam seemed never to end, I saw dozens of pitiful signs, advertisements for people trying to mend broken hearts: Madame Lefarge, c/o Hôtel de Ville, asks for news of her daughters Marie-Louise and Hélène, 6 and 5 years old, lost near here on June 9.

By noon we had covered perhaps twenty miles. The sun baked everyone, tempers frayed with heat as much as with the delay. The interminable changing of gears started to give me a cramp in my right ankle as the muscles knotted up. I stopped for a moment to walk on it, to alleviate the cramp. A cacophony of Klaxons signaled their fury. More and more overheated cars began to stall. All were bundled onto the side of the road or a field, despite the screams of outrage from those who hoped (probably rightly) that the cars would start again after they had been cooled for an hour or two. With the heat and the stoppages, both of us were soon too tired even to talk.

Soon after midday, when we were well beyond Versailles, nothing moved for an hour. Nothing. It seemed as though all the vehicles in France had been welded into one solid mass.

"What the hell's happened?" I groaned, for always, everyone was afraid to leave a car in case the road suddenly cleared. "You can walk ahead a bit," I suggested to Sonia. "Stretch your legs and tell us what happened."

She returned a few minutes later.

"You'll never believe this," she mopped her forehead. "But it's not a car that's causing the jam. It's a garbage man in his cart."

"A garbage man!"

Others crowded around, besieged Sonia for news.

"What happened ahead?"

"Why can't we go on?"

"The garbage man," Sonia explained, "has driven his cart from Versailles. It's filled with files and documents. But now it's stuck in a narrow street."

Because it was hidden from our view, we never did discover how the trash cart was moved, nor did we ever pass it. Soon there was another holdup when a tour bus stalled and was finally pushed off the road by a nearby tractor.

The coach was painted brightly PARIS DE NUIT! It had been used for highly popular tourist trips, in which tourists paid a fixed sum for a tour of nightclubs, with a glass of indifferent champagne at each stop, often ending at a *boîte* where girls were available. The coach bore the legend "We promise you the most beautiful girls in Paris."

It was abandoned at the exact moment when I read the slogan ". . . the most beautiful girls in Paris." It was also the precise moment when the occupants of the saucy coach descended—a couple of dozen decorous, fluttering nuns, all in stiff white coifs. They tumbled down the steps before deciding how to continue on their journey.

Not far from us—and the old couple pushing their handcart—the more healthy pushed their way through. A very old lady in a wheelbarrow was being carried by a young, stalwart curé, sweating in his long black soutane. He passed several cars and other vehicles by the simple expedient of keeping to the narrow edge of the road. The nuns fluttered round him and offered to help, but I heard him cry cheerfully, "I'm only pushing my passenger to her sister in the next village."

I looked at the curé and the old lady. She seemed very frail. Should I offer them a lift? More than once I had wondered whether I should make room for pedestrians, but several factors had prevented me. Above all others, I had not yet seen one instance of a *lonely* old man or woman, even a couple. Everyone had a handcart or a baby carriage, and often seemed to move in families. There was another reason. Pedestrians made better time than we did. They could take shortcuts across the fields. All but the invalids could easily outstrip our car by walking.

"I do feel bad sometimes," I confessed to Sonia, "but I couldn't pack a large group in."

And there was one more reason—selfish, but important. The crowd often turned ugly, and it was easy to forget that I was on an assignment for the *Globe.* However slow the progress, I had to reach Tours and file a story. I wasn't part of the exodus really, I was making my way to a specific place to do a job, and I didn't dare to let in strangers who might force me—even with violence—to change my route. I had already seen some nasty fights. Several toughs had tried to open the rear doors of the Citroën, which I kept locked.

The curé, however, was different. When I heard him say that he was going only to the next village, I shouted, "Why not jump in, Father—with your passenger?"

"That's very kind of you," he seemed grateful. "I'm fine myself, but my passenger is very, very old. Jolting around in a wheelbarrow can't be good for her."

She looked very frail. Sonia got out of the front seat to help her get into the back. Then she sat down beside her and asked the curé, "Why don't you sit in front, Father."

"Thank you, my child. Perhaps you would be kind enough to hold this altar vase. My friend attaches great importance to it."

"Of course," Sonia looked at it casually. It was not particularly attractive, decorated with a frieze of religious figures.

"It was the only object I had time to take from the church," explained the curé. "This lady presented it to us many years ago, and we use it on the altar for flowers during the harvest festival or weddings. You understand—it's of no value really, but very precious to her."

"I'll take care of it," she promised him.

As we drove on a dozen men started fighting each other like savages—and all for the possession of the wheelbarrow which the curé had used.

"How can we expect to win a war when people behave

like this," I asked the curé, "when half the people in
France are greedy or corrupt? How can we *trust* the people
of France?" As I spoke one of the men lurched against the
Citroën and started cursing, then peered inside and crossed
himself. Another had already smashed up the wheelbarrow and hit the nearest man across the head with the barrow shaft.

The curé was young, with ruddy cheeks, and despite his
bulky clothes, there was the hint of a powerful country
body beneath.

"You can trust them at first," he replied cheerfully, "because men at heart are simple creatures. At first they're
easily dazzled. But then the shine rubs off, doubts replace
trust. You are not French, are you? Your command of our
language is to be complimented." He spoke in the slightly
old-fashioned way of someone who had spent years in a
seminary.

"American," I smiled. "A newspaperman."

"Ah! So you probably know about politicians. You sound
as though you don't like them."

"They make me angry."

"Anger is a futile emotion," he said gently. "The man
who is angry loses more energy than his victim. So if you
are angry, you lose out."

"But I can't help it—not when I meet politicians who
are—"

"Wayward?" he suggested the word. "Does it really
matter so long as men respect each other? All of us have to
make the best of a bad job—which is what life is really all
about."

"It's sometimes easier," I said, "living in a village, in
the country."

"Yes, I am surrounded by peasants. I prefer them to city
people." Passing through the edge of a hamlet, he added,
"Look how the locals stand watching you."

The farmers and their women, often leaning against
their gates, silently studied the file of refugees as though
watching a parade.

"When a war comes," explained the curé, "the only

thing that matters to a peasant is its effect on his own personal life. War or peace are only extensions of storms or sun. Mobilization or occupation are unimportant only when compared to sowing and harvesting."

We dropped the curé at the next village—but it was not until we had driven through the straggling street that I realized the old lady had left the vase behind.

I peered ahead and around. Sonia opened the door as we idled along, standing on the running board to see behind in case the curé called to us. There was no hope of stopping.

"I feel terrible," I said. "We promised. But it *was* such a scramble when they got out."

"Don't worry," said Sonia. "We'll keep it in trust. One day we'll find him and return the altar vase."

"Let's hope so."

The curé had brought a breath of fresh air into our tiny, boxlike world. But did he really believe what he said about peasants, or were men of religion so isolated from reality that sometimes they were deluded?

"I don't think he even realizes the French are losing the war," I said to Sonia, "that what's happening is"—I searched for the word I wanted—"cataclysmic."

It was—to me anyway. This was not just a pitiful queue of craven men and women scrambling to an illusory safety. In the sweat and the stench and fighting, we were witness to the death of a nation, the last rites of France, of all Europe barring the master race. Each step forward on that hot and dusty roadway was in reality a step backward, another step on the road to defeat, another step on the road to victory for tyranny.

How wonderful the warm air might have been, with the sun shining, the fields of corn ripening! But the sun that baked us was also an illusion; the road of the exodus sloped downward as man descended into the gloom of a night which would never see the sun.

"I'm sick of the French," I said, "not because a better army is beating them, chewing the so-called invincible French army into mincemeat. No, it goes deeper than that."

What sickened me most was the all-pervading smell of corruption. The way people had been betrayed. This was the root cause of defeat, this far more than cowardice or ignorance. These people around us were running away because they were realists, aware that corrupt leaders were responsible for their plight.

There was a stop while a car ahead was pushed off the road. I took the opportunity to give Sonia a swig of water from the warm bottle of Vichy, and then found a towel and wiped her face. Both of us were drenched in sweat, much of it brought on by anger and impotence.

Most political leaders in France were rotten to the core, I thought. And everyone except country parsons knew it. Was it fair to blame some small-town clerk and his church-going family or some working man from a factory for the mess we were in, for not taking his cue in corruption from a political leader? After all, the French prided themselves on their logic. What could they say, how could they react at the spectacle of a middle-aged "happily married" premier like Reynaud dyeing his hair in order to impress a mistress with whom he was infatuated? Who could blame the logical French for realizing that if the going got rough, French leaders like Pierre Laval would sell out the French people to save their own skins.

In a way the ribbon of road ahead of us was like a river, the water dirty, yet composed of human beings. Tears, sweat, heat, the stink of selfishness and greed; the ever-present torment of fear surrounded us; the river of people and vehicles moved relentlessly forward like a tidal bore, slow but inexorable.

A commotion in a straggling hamlet halted the traffic yet again, this time barely a few paces ahead of us. A girl in her early twenties—long brown hair, a checked skirt, a pink blouse—screamed without warning and threw herself onto the ground, threw herself deliberately. She did not fall. She bent almost double, gave a bewildered look before she was seized by an epileptic fit, arching her body, writhing in contortions, the pretty mouth slipping into a slack, dribbling face as she twisted her body like a savage performing an indecent war dance. Two burly men pulled her screaming to the side of the road, and the river of traffic poured on as though the sluice gates had been reopened.

It was like that all day, a combination of all the worst elements in nature: heat and sweat, hunger and thirst, weariness and fear, cowardice and hysteria. Man was rapidly being reduced to the level of an animal. Men and women, cooped for hours in small square boxes that moved only in inches, suddenly reached a moment—women in particular—when they had no choice but to squat next to the nearest man or woman to relieve themselves. For men it presented no real problem.

"You're lucky," sighed Sonia. "You're built in such a way that you can use the waterworks standing up."

You *could*, standing against the side of your car. But the women had to rearrange clothes, pull up skirts, pull down panties, nervously realizing that men could see everything, were almost brushing against them.

"I've been holding myself for hours," confessed Sonia. "I can't wait much longer."

"You'll just have to sit down next to the others; or squat, I suppose, is the right word."

"I *couldn't,*" she said. "I wish I could. I know that if I tried I'd jam up. All those men looking at me." And then she added almost desperately, "Haven't you got something I could use?"

A broken-down car ahead had caused yet another jam, and I was able to lean over the seat.

"Only this." I picked up the porcelain vase with the wide neck. "We can't use that. It's the curé's altar vase."

"Give it to me." Suddenly Sonia at the the sight of it gasped with the effort of controlling herself. "Come on, for God's sake. I can't hold it another second. *Give it to me!*"

As always in summer, she never wore pants. With her skirt hiding her knees she perched on the edge of the front seat, held the neck tight to the join of her legs. When she had finished she edged the door of the car open a few inches and poured out the contents.

"I'll wash it when I get the chance," she promised. "I'm sure the curé would understand."

"Don't worry," I said. "He *would* understand. Feel better?"

"A new girl. You know, this is the sort of problem you never see when the heroine faces a long and terrible journey in a romantic adventure movie."

Yes, it was like that all day. Everywhere the once-beautiful countryside was littered with the signature of refugees—broken bottles, filthy paper, young people defecating, old people vomiting, torn umbrellas, punctured tires, suitcases that had fallen off and burst open, straw mattresses split in two. Everything seemed to conspire to make the journey more frustrating.

Suddenly the dreary scene was enlivened by a breath of different fresh air. Out of the blue, on a country road leading to la Malmaison, we came across a truck drawn up by the side of the road. Grouped around it were some British Tommies in their ill-fitting uniforms. Most were singing lustily, two were shaving, dipping their brushes in their tin drinking mugs. When I shouted a greeting in English they crowded round our almost-stationary Citroën.

"Blimey!" cried one. "You English?"

"American."

"Next best thing!"

"Got any fags, guvnor?"

"Know where the fucking 'ell we are? Begging your pardon, miss."

"Don't let them offer you a cuppa tea," another laughed. "We've been shaving in it."

It almost restored our sense of humor—the wolf whistles, the gratuitous advice.

"Keep the door of your car locked or someone'll nick your girl."

"You need any help driving, lady?"

"Clean your car for a tenner if you come back to Blighty with us."

With a wave we nudged forward, pushed there by the

cars behind, klaxoning like mad; barely half an hour later
we passed another bunch of soldiers. They were leaning
out of the windows of a train siding that now ran parallel
to our road.

But there were no songs, no jokes this time. These were
poilus. These were glum, silent human beings being
shipped like cattle, ordered to some battlefield God knows
where, probably by some idiots who would decide any moment that the war was in vain—apart from killing.

And there was something else.

"These poor devils are fighting in their own country,"
said Sonia. "Those British boys we saw—they looked as
though they were *enjoying* the war. To them it was a kind
of adventure in a foreign land. But these French boys in
the train—this is *their* own country they're fighting over.
There's no spirit of adventure there."

"It's not only the soldiers," I ground in the gear too low,
as some kids ran across our path, "I never realized my different feelings about the refugees until now." When we
were at Douzy we had been surrounded by an endless
stream of refugees escaping from Holland, Belgium, eastern France. Now, though, we were not *watching* the exodus of a nation. We were part of it, Sonia and I. Every
stumbling figure, every face torn with fatigue had become
a part of the patchwork of our lives.

Nowhere was the feeling of being part of the scene more
evident than when we could see some distance ahead or behind. At the top of a small rise leading to Rambouillet, I
looked back at the long, slow-moving procession, traveling
along the white ribbon of road framed in poplars black
against the sunlight, and on either side fields of corn. It reminded me of an old painting which La Châtelaine had always insisted on keeping in the salon—the flight of the
Israelites, a long line of tired, broken people. It was a scene
straight from one of those old-fashioned Bible illustrations. Only the trees behind me, the poplars, straight and
dark, seemed suddenly to look like prison bars from which
there would never be any escape for the innocents fleeing
the enemy.

* * *

It took us nearly two hours to drive through Epernon, then finally I managed to leave the main road for one I knew would eventually bypass Chartres.

"It goes through Maintenon"—I traced the route on Sonia's map—"and better still, not far from Chartres, but in a tiny hamlet, there's a small gas station used mainly for tractors. I had a puncture there once. I know we've got spare gas, but we might as well top up if we've got the chance, and anyway, with all this low gear work, we'll need oil and water. She must be heating up like hell."

Sonia put the question I hadn't dared to face.

"We'll never make Tours tonight?" She flattened the map on her knees and traced the route.

" 'Fraid not. We'll be lucky if we get past Chartres. I'm going to try and make for a village called Blandy. It's near Châteaudun."

"Not on the map," Sonia was trying to find it.

"It's just a small village. But it's got a superb *maison de santé*, not really a clinic, but a plush kind of health farm for very rich people who want to relax and unwind. It's called the Bellevue, and it's run like a five-star hotel —with prices to match."

"If we can get in?"

"We might be able to stay there for the night. I know the owner, I helped him with a piece in the *Paris American*. So he owes me one. Then we'll press on to Tours tomorrow."

Once we left the N-10 main road, the route was much less congested and we were making better speed when suddenly I heard the roar of engines, followed by a whine that turned into a terrifying screech chilling the blood. Planes were diving out of a cloudless sky.

"Heads down!" I screamed, jamming on the brakes.

Only then, as the screech grew louder, did I realize that we were not the target. Out of the side window I saw four fighter planes attack the main road in the distance—the very road we had left. I couldn't see the target even when I opened the door, but I could see the planes and, even worse, hear them.

"There they are!" I pointed to the sky, instinctively clutching Sonia.

We could see the planes go into their dive. I knew where the main road was by the distant line of poplars on the horizon, marking the road along which we had expected to drive, perhaps the very spot where we might have been trapped. The planes wheeled like gulls, then in perfect formation roared into their dive. Until the very last moment they looked as though they would hit the ground and burst into flames.

"If only they would!" cried Sonia.

As I heard the distant rattle of machine-gun fire the four planes flattened out, then puffs of smoke covered the row of poplars. Out of the smoke, like genies out of a bottle, the planes zoomed up against the blue sky, sullied now with slowly enlarging clouds of gray, drifting smoke. Then the planes vanished high into the sky.

I hadn't realized that Sonia was crying softly.

"How can people do this?" she asked, leaning her head on my shoulder.

"I know, my precious, but this *is* what war's about."

"But these are peaceful people," she watched the smoke shrouding the main road. "What have these planes got to do with *them?*"

"Come back into the car," I led her in gently and closed the door.

"And just thank the Lord," I said as I sat beside her, "that we took this country lane. Otherwise—"

"Don't say anything," she wiped away the tears. "I'm a baby, but I just suddenly thought of one thing—it could have been us. I only pray that if anything does happen, both of us will be together at the same second." She searched for my hand, squeezed it very tight. "So that we'll never know."

"Stop being so morbid!" But the same thought had flashed through my mind, "O God! If it has to happen, let us die together."

* * *

I remembered the small gas station, just a single hand-operated pump used mainly by locals filling up their tractors. It didn't have any forecourt or fancy buildings which, I felt, would make it less known. And it was right at the end of the hamlet. I found the place behind a narrow street, deserted except for the occasional horse and cart returning from the fields at the end of the day's work. And there was the pump with a solitary car just leaving, and a man standing by the pump.

"Just what we need," I said cheerfully, thinking that in a few minutes we should have passed Chartres. As I edged into the right position near the pump, I saw the man lock it up and pocket the key.

"No gas left?" I groaned.

"Doesn't look like it, does it?" He was surly.

"Not just a few liters? And I need oil and water."

"We're closed!" shouted the man.

I swore softly and prepared to drive off. Then I caught sight of the automatic gauge with its figures on the side of the pump. Suddenly I realized that the pump *wasn't* dry.

"Hey!" I cried. "You've got some gas."

Though I knew I had spare gas in the back of the car, I had, as always when working on a story, one thought—that nothing, certainly not some bad-tempered sonofabitch, must stop me taking every precaution to get to Tours, to save Sonia, and file my story. Every liter counted.

Without turning the man snarled, "What if I have? I've been pulling that handle all day long. I'm tired. If you want some gas, come back tomorrow."

"But, m'sieu—" I tried politeness.

The *garagiste* didn't speak English of course, but again he snarled, and this time his words were the equivalent of "Fuck off!"

"Et ta soeur!" I shouted the most perjorative insult I could think of and bounded out of the car.

"Come back," shouted Sonia. "Forget the bastard."

"Just a minute," I said.

"Come back!"

It was too late. I wasn't so angry about the lie he had told me, it was the pent-up frustration. I didn't give a damn *how* tired he was. Everyone in France was tired, an entire nation was tired. I offered to pull the handle of the pump myself, but he pretended not to hear, and instead said softly, "What did you say about my family?"

He wasn't a big man, but he had the knotted, tight arms and shoulders of someone whose livelihood depended on his physical strength.

"What did you say?" he repeated menacingly.

"I need oil and gas. I offered to do the work. I've got the money."

"Fuck off!" he repeated.

"You shit," I said in French. "It's shits like you who are losing the war."

He picked up a heavy-duty jack.

"You'd better get out of here quick, sonny," he said, "before I bash your damn brains in."

"I *won't* budge," I cried desperately. "It's your duty. Here," I fumbled for some money.

"I said get off my property," his voice was soft, more menacing than when he shouted. "I don't like little shits who insult my family."

He moved nearer. I was frightened, praying desperately for some car to come along, to break the tension, to interrupt. Damn! All day we had been hemmed in by cars, now there wasn't one in sight. The pump was at the end of nowhere. I saw his knuckles show white as he gripped the jack.

There was no turning back. I was out of the Citroën and that was that. I couldn't climb back in again and quietly drive off. I should have tried, I suppose. The old adage about discretion. But I *couldn't.* And anyway, I knew he wouldn't let me, I sensed that. All the same, I realized that in a straight fight I would never stand a chance.

Sonia shouted desperately from inside the car, "Please, darling—come back, forget this man."

"Yeah—why don't you, sonny," the man jeered.

The stubborn streak increased—determination born out

of fear? Masculine pride in front of "my" woman? I shouted
back to Sonia, "Stay in the car."

In the seconds that seemed an hour I looked round for a
weapon. The place was as empty as a padded cell. I might
have grabbed the handle of the pump, attached to its rubber hose, but it was locked. The only object was an old watering can, half filled. A sudden thought sent a fresh
shiver of fear through me. Even if I dodged his raised arm,
he could *throw* the jack at me. Even a glancing blow could
break an arm or crack a skull. Again I looked round, ready
now to shout for help if I had to.

At that moment I saw a second tube, longer, thinner, unlocked. It was near the main pump, but separate and with
a much longer hose.

It was the pump used to force air into flat tires under
pressure. It took me half a second to remember how Gaston
and I used to play a game with the tire pump we always
kept at Douzy, which showed me how the force of compressed air could knock down quite large targets as easily
as if a water hose had been used. Air was as tough as water
under pressure. Only you couldn't see it.

With my left hand I grabbed the watering can, hoping
the man wouldn't realize the significance of the small nozzle in my right hand. I knew now what to do—my only
chance, ignoring one last wail of despair from Sonia.

It couldn't have been more than a minute since we first
traded insults, but now I shouted, "I'm going to smash the
lock on your pump."

Holding the half-filled watering can, I swung it at the
lock. I knew I could never actually break it, but I would
take his mind off the nozzle in my right hand by giving a
good imitation. I smashed the can at the pump again and
again. He roared with anger, like a bull, arm upraised.

"Leave that alone," he shouted. "You bastard, you'll
pay for this."

In his anger I don't think the man realized that, as I kept
on bashing the pump, splashing water all over with each
new effort, I still gripped the thin rubber tube in my right
hand.

He charged toward me. I had to wait until the very last second, almost to the moment when he prepared to hit me with the jack. That was the toughest moment—waiting, controlling myself as he actually raised his arm for a blow that could split my skull, so close I could smell the garlic on his breath. He almost knocked the watering can, and then I pointed the nozzle—not twelve inches from his face. The jet of air came out of the nozzle with the force of a fire hose. It would never kill him, but for one second, two perhaps, I hit him full in the open eyes with the blast, knocking him off balance. He screwed up his eyes, grunted "Bastard." I needed only those two seconds. I grabbed the jack and hit him with it—straight across the nose.

I heard the crack as the bone broke. Then the blood poured out of nose and mouth as he keeled over, spitting broken teeth out of split lips. He wasn't unconscious—but he wasn't going to attack me because, apart from screams of pain, he was for a moment blinded with blood.

"Let's get out of here," I gasped to Sonia and tore open the door.

I pressed the starter. Thank God it roared into life at the first touch of the button. I jammed in the gear—still shaking, though everything had happened in a couple of minutes. Then through the rear mirror I saw the man stumble to his feet.

"Quick, darling!" Sonia begged me.

"I'm off," I inched the car toward the empty village lane that would lead me to the south.

Two seconds more and we would have been clear. But I didn't have those two seconds. Sonia, in the right-hand seat, was nearest the pumps, even as we started to draw away. I heard the bellow of spluttering rage, the voice incoherent. With the instinctive reflex of a violent man, the *garagiste* picked up the jack and hurled it at me, at us, at the car.

It hit the right-hand corner of the windshield, next to Sonia. And though we had safety glass, even in those days, it splintered. And Sonia was sitting in front. She must have seen the man hurl the jack, for I remember she instinctively ducked and shielded her face with her arm as I braked.

The bonded glass broke the force of impact and the jack fell to the ground outside. Jagged edges of glass tore through her silk blouse, ripping the right sleeve from shoulder to wrist in shreds. Without a second's delay—as though someone had thrown a tin of red paint at her— Sonia's right arm and shoulder were stained with blood.

She screamed. I held out an arm around her and, steering with the left arm, reversed toward the man. If Sonia hadn't screamed again, I think I would have run over him. She couldn't possibly wipe away all that blood. Yet I could sense that the wounds were only superficial. Because it was safety glass the smashed window had fallen inward. It hadn't sprayed.

"It isn't worth it," she whispered. "Please—I beg you —let's go and find a doctor."

I raced around the corner, out of sight, stopped, tore off my jacket, then my shirt, ripped it into bits, and tried to tie up her arm and wrists. The cuts weren't deep, though the forearm where she had held up her arm was bleeding badly. There were no deep gashes, but I realized that she must get the wounds cleaned in case they contained particles of glass dust.

The glass seemed everywhere—on her knees, the floorboards, in the pocket on the dash. Every time I tried to wrap some cloth around her wounds I scratched myself with unseen glass.

"We'll be there soon," I said with more assurance than I dared to hope for.

Just as I was turning off the back road to regain the road which I knew should lead me to Chartres, I saw an old weather-beaten wooden signpost: CHÂTEAUDUN, ROUTE INFÉRIEURE.

It might be inferior—it looked little more than a cart track—but it might be empty, off the beaten track, and the springs of the Citroën were tough enough to withstand any shock treatment.

"We'll try it," I said. She looked pale and I suddenly remembered the bottle of brandy. I had forgotten all about it until this moment.

"Here," I held it up, "Take a swig, darling—from the bottle." She did and almost immediately a touch of color brushed her cheeks. I could see that below the elbow blood had already started soaking through the makeshift bandage.

"It's all my fault," I said. "If I hadn't been such a damn fool—"

"You're what we call *un tipo robusto!*" She tried to smile.

"Can you lie back a bit?" Seats in those days didn't recline, but I folded up my jacket to make a pillow, and she lay back gratefully and closed her eyes.

Half an hour later the *route inférieure* suddenly blossomed into a proper, if narrow, road, and before long we reached Blandy and I saw the white building of the Bellevue in the distance.

"We're there," I said and she opened her eyes. "I'm not asleep," she smiled. "I'm fine. I'm only scared about these bits of glass."

"We'll have you in bed in a few minutes," I promised her.

The Bellevue was on the edge of the place des Epars, the sprawling heart of the village with its marketplace, patch of green, rows of shops, and the inevitable roofed washing trough of the local "laundry."

Because the Bellevue was a kind of hotel, hundreds of other people had made their way there, and the *place* was a jumble of cars, trucks, crowds, people sitting on piles of luggage round the edge of the square. Somehow I managed to double-park the Citroën alongside the entrance.

"Hang on while I get the owner." I didn't dare to imagine what would happen if he wasn't there. I remembered his name—luckily it was familiar, Monsieur Lelong, the same as that of the couturier. I had once lunched with Lelong when he visited Paris and I was trying to arrange for someone to keep us informed in the *Paris American* about Americans visiting the area.

"Hang on," I said to Sonia again.

There was a moment of farce as I strode up to the ornate reception desk.

"No beggars or tramps here," spluttered an irate clerk in striped trousers. "Get out before I call the police."

"My wife's been badly hurt—"

"No place for tramps. Get out."

I had forgotten that I was bare to the waist. No wonder they thought I was a tramp. "The name is Astell," I said, knowing that everyone in the "hotel" business would recognize that name.

"Get me Monsieur Lelong."

At that moment Lelong walked out of a salon leading to the main foyer.

"Hi!" I cried. "Remember me? Larry Astell."

"I didn't recognize you, monsieur, in those—er—sporting clothes. *Comment ça va?*" And more seriously, "This is a sad time to be meeting."

"Sadder than you think. A bloody maniac has attacked my—fiancée. She's bleeding. Can you help?" I explained briefly what had happened.

"Every regular room is occupied," he apologized. "The clinic is a shambles. But some of the *femmes de chambres* have bolted—and if you wish—at least the beds are good."

"You're too kind, *cher ami.* But first a doctor."

"Don't worry. We have several resident doctors."

Lelong snapped his fingers as though the milling crowds overflowing the foyer didn't exist. A hall porter materialized.

"I'll look after the lady," I told him. "Here's the keys. You take the car into the garage and bring in the luggage in the backseat—but leave the trunk locked. Monsieur Lelong will tell you which room to go to."

So we arrived at Blandy. It had taken us over twelve hours to drive there from Paris—a distance of around seventy miles as the crow flies.

Sonia was nearly done in. She must have lost more blood than I realized. I helped her into the foyer while Lelong prepared to take her upstairs when he had found the doctor. People on either side moved back in order to give her more space—or perhaps, I thought, since they were French, to make sure bloodstains didn't ruin their clothes.

Once in the foyer I stood appalled. The Bellevue looked more like a transit camp than the elegant *maison de santé* I had known in the past. Everywhere was a mess; ornate chairs were piled against the pink papered walls in a pathetic attempt to save their gilt value, mattresses were torn and bursting on the litter of the beautiful carpet. Every square inch of occupied territory was jealously guarded. I had managed to find a chair only because Lelong had brought it from the office. Anyone else searching for a place to rest was met with hostile stares. Luggage was piled in one corner, an uneven craggy leather hill. A vague smell permeated the room, a compound of tobacco, dead cigarette ends ground into the carpet or overflowing from ashtrays, and unwashed bodies, men and women past caring. It was the smell of war.

"What an awful mess," I said to Sonia.

She was obviously in pain, but even she was horrified at the spectacle of a beautiful "hotel" in chaos.

"We're *really* in the war here," she smiled weakly. "War is much more dangerous behind the front line than in it."

She's right, I thought. Here in this beautiful lounge we were in the heart of war. War was no longer a set piece, the soldiers in scarlet dominated by unseen generals, in the days when war was a kind of chess game played by opposing military forces. Now it was *our* war. It was right here.

"Oh, Larry," her voice was close to tears as we waited for the doctor. "Oh, Larry, darling, what I wouldn't give to wake up next to you in our coquelicot room at Douzy. If we could only turn the clock back."

The room under the eaves of Bellevue was more comfortable than I had expected. Though small, ours had been used by two maids so there were twin beds, and even a *cabinet de toilette*.

"But *hélas, madame,*" Lelong apologized, "there is no hot water."

The doctor was professional and reassuring. He asked me to leave while he attended to Sonia, and by the time I had returned she looked a different person—still pale, still drawn, but the doctor had covered most of the wounds with tape, though the forearm was bandaged where he had put in three stitches.

"Medically, you didn't really need the stitches," he explained, "but it's a question of *esthétique.* This will prevent you from having a scar on your arm for the rest of your life."

When he was on the point of leaving I said, almost without thinking, "We're off tomorrow to Tours."

He looked at me in blank astonishment.

"You must be mad!" he exclaimed. *"Absolument fou!* You are proposing to take this lady, who is suffering from shock, to Tours—on roads jammed with traffic. Anything could happen. She needs her bed, someone to make her rest for at least twenty-four hours."

"I thought if we had a good night's sleep—"

"My good sir, you are very young and, if I may say so, very foolish. The aftereffects of shock can be very bad. If she leaves the Bellevue tomorrow, I accept no responsibility."

At the door he returned to Sonia and said, "I will come to visit you tomorrow. And hopefully you'll be able to travel the following day—if your husband insists."

Outside our small room, while Sonia was washing, I explained to Lelong how urgent it was for me to reach Tours and contact the American embassy. I did not, however, mention our plan to drive later to Bordeaux and then send Sonia across the frontier into Spain. Nor did I mention that she was Italian. Because of this Lelong made the obvious suggestion.

"Why don't you travel to Tours through the night. It'll be much quicker. I'll make sure Madame is well looked after, properly fed, then you can drive back to Blandy tomorrow evening, sleep for a few hours, and return to Tours or wherever you go on the Thursday. Coming back to Blandy to collect Madame shouldn't cause any problems. It's less than seventy miles from Tours. Traveling from Tours *toward* Blandy should be easy."

It made sense. I was certain in my own mind that the French cabinet would eventually make for Bordeaux, and if I drove there with her after her day of rest, I could easily drive on to the frontier later. The problem of filing urgently would have gone. Of course I felt torn on one point. I didn't want to leave Sonia, even for one night. But I *had* to contact the French cabinet at Tours. I should have been there already. And I was sure that cables from the *Globe* would be awaiting me at the Château de Candé, Drexel Biddle's American headquarters, which I would be using as a place to receive messages. And then, once I had got Sonia across the border, I could return to Bordeaux and await events, probably ahead of the competition. The *Globe* would, I hoped, put it down to my astute foresight. It was not for me to enlighten them that I was there partly because of Sonia.

I was worried about Sonia's reaction, I knew that she would be concerned about my job.

"I do hate being parted," she admitted after I had helped her to drink a bowl of soup. "But the doctor has given me one pill which I've already taken and another one for tomorrow morning."

Lelong swore that she would be looked after night and day, and I believed him. It was just after 9:00 P.M. now, and he said, "You must have a good meal. We have a small private dining room for the executives. Come. I will give you a steak."

Long before I tiptoed out of the room Sonia was dozing. I ate my steak and fries, and the Bellevue garage gassed up the Citroën and even replaced the smashed window from the spare Citroën parts which even the smallest hamlet always stocked.

Before leaving I said to Lelong, "See you during tomorrow night. I'll just run upstairs and say good-bye to Sonia."

Half-asleep she held my hand—hers was damp and feverish. She whispered, "I know you have to go—but I hate the idea." I sat on the edge of the bed and stroked her hair. "I've got a sort of premonition," she mumbled, fiddling with the cuff links she had given me so long ago.

"Sssh, it's time you went to sleep, darling, and rested. And don't worry, I'll always be with you."

"But if anything does go wrong?"

"It won't—ever. We're going to be married somehow. Remember? Even after we've got you across the border, whatever happens to us, always remember—we love each other."

She was already asleep when I kissed her gently on the lips. It was the sleep of a drugged patient, and I knew how badly she needed it.

"I'll be back tomorrow," I whispered, though she couldn't hear me and didn't stir when I gently kissed her again.

It had to last us many months, that gentle kiss in the maid's room at the Bellevue.

26

I REACHED TOURS around dawn—to find the city in a state of utter shock—disoriented, disorganized. On the verge of panic, every motorist moved toward the center of this lazy old cathedral town, abusing each other as they fought for their right to put a few more inches between themselves and the Germans.

Above all I needed a shower and a change of underclothes and shirt, which I had carried in my overnight bag. I managed to get a room at the Métropole in the rue Jean-Jaures, where the Astells had stayed from time to time, and where I had a nodding acquaintance with the manager, the tall, elderly handsome Monsieur Roland Audermard, possessor of a magnificent pair of mustaches which we had once photographed for the *Paris American*. He was also a fervent admirer of Astell champagne.

The hotel was packed, and even in the sedate reception area there was a great deal of squabbling among the indignant mistresses of government officials who felt that their status—or at least that of each political lover—required better accommodation.

"But the real problem," confided Monsieur Audermard, "is that when the government requisitions rooms from me, I am given a voucher in payment, a kind of promissory note. But I ask you, will it ever be honored? I have to carry on paying the staff, but will I ever see my money?"

"Never," I said firmly, producing a large wad of French

francs and American dollar bills. "If you can spare me a room—I only want it for a few hours."

I planned to tour the government offices, see Reynaud, file my story, snatch a couple of hours' sleep in the evening, then drive back to Blandy by dawn the next day. There, all being well, I would pick up Sonia and return to Tours, then drive farther south, even as far as the frontier if possible. Haunted by the memories of the exodus, however, I had as a precaution paid in advance for the second night at Tours.

Once I had showered the sleep from my eyes—only cold water, but that helped—then shaved and put on a clean shirt, I made my way to the newly installed Ministry of Information, which was housed in a couple of buildings in the rue Gambetta, through streets crowded not only with cars and trucks, but with the city's pretty blue streetcars, which would have been better left in the garage.

A colleague in the hotel told me the rue Gambetta led off a small square distinguished by a memorial to the dead of the Great War.

"You'll spot it easily," he said. "It consists of a statue of a nude lady wearing a helmet. She's sandwiched between a *pissotière* and a café. It's got food—some good coffee too," he added as an afterthought.

The café was obviously a favorite haunt of newspapermen, no doubt because it was so close to the Ministry of Information. A. J. Liebling, the American writer, was there. He had spent the previous night trying to sleep in his car. Drue Tartière, who worked for the French Radio Mondiale, was luckier—she had borrowed a bed in the local brothel; while one junior British diplomat and his wife, who had arrived late, started the first night of their honeymoon bedding down on a bench in the nearby park. His name was Donald Maclean.

The ministry was a sorry comedown after the splendor of the Hôtel Continental in Paris, with its rose-covered wallpaper and Louis XV furniture. One of the requisitioned buildings had been the Bourse de Travail, the other a dingy post office. Here the ministry had established a corps of censors.

Every newspaper dispatch had to be passed by censor. For though I hoped to file through the embassy, they would never permit me to use their facilities unless I, too, had my copy stamped by the authorities. The press office was at the top of a flight of winding steps—a few dirty rooms furnished with ancient school desks, the kind with chairs and desks in one piece. A British correspondent was listening to the German radio. The man was announcing in a throaty accent, and for a moment I imagined it was the voice of Willi speaking. Of course it wasn't, but where was he, I wondered?

"The French government," said the German voice, "is now in Tours, the provisional—the *very* provisional—capital of France." The tone was a sneer so pronounced that one French correspondent almost knocked the Englishman down as he switched off the portable radio.

"Hey, you!" shouted the Englishman. "Leave my sodding radio alone. I'm making notes for filing."

"You're a traitor, listening to that," screamed the Frenchman.

"Nine out of ten Frogs are traitors, bud," said an American as the Englishman switched back to the German broadcast.

I bolted—just as one man punched the other and they started scrambling on the floor.

I had my own personal story to consider. I hoped to get an exclusive interview with either Reynaud or de Gaulle or, if the worst came, with Madame de Portes. I wasn't in Tours to cover "routine" agency news. I wanted to cash in on my contacts among the politicians.

The greatest problem of all, however, was *finding* the government officials. The ministries had been dispersed to châteaux throughout Touraine—as a precaution against air attack, I was told; and at the same time local newspapers had been forbidden to publish the addresses of government departments in case fifth columnists tipped off the Luftwaffe. In fact, the government, its cabinet leaders, the army were totally cut off from the people of France and, even worse, from all reality.

I drove first to the Château de Candé—an American-owned fairy-tale pile of glamorous turrets and battle-ments, already famous as the place where the Duke of Windsor and Mrs. Simpson had married.

Now it had become the provisional embassy headquar-ters headed by Drexel Biddle. After crawling along dusty roads it was as though I had stumbled on to an oasis. The owner had installed a large pool—which, alas, I didn't have time to use—a badminton court, a golf course, archery butts, even artificial brooks to encourage ducks to breed.

More important, the generous owner of the Château de Candé had made his millions as an industrial efficiency ex-pert; consequently, everything worked. A telephone had been installed in every one of its twenty rooms. It boasted its own internal switchboard. And when my car crunched to a stop on the graveled driveway I was even greeted by a real English butler in striped trousers, left behind, I heard later from the owner, in case Biddle needed personal atten-tion.

"Whom would you wish to see, sir?" he asked gravely.

"Mr. Matthews if he's available." Freeman Matthews, known to everyone as Doc Matthews, was a counselor, al-ways willing to help. He was a mine of information.

"Certainly, sir." The butler ushered me inside with the urbanity of one greeting guests arriving for a weekend house party. "And who may I say is calling, sir?"

"Mr. Astell of Reims." I knew that any butler worth his salt would know *that* name. He did. "Of course, sir, and if there's anything I can do to make your stay more comfort-able, my name is James."

He *was* able to help, for though Doc Matthews had driven off with Drexel Biddle to some other château, the inestimable James—I almost called him Jeeves—produced a list of personnel staying at the château to see if I could spot a friendly name.

"This one is fine," I exclaimed as my finger stopped on the name of Jim Parks.

What's more, Jim had some cold American beer, and it was he who first outlined to me that state of panic already gripping the bewildered French government.

The British ambassador, Sir Ronald Campbell, was installed several miles away at the Château de Cléré. The French foreign minister was at Langeais, the finance minister at Chinon. Reynaud himself was installed with Madame de Portes at the Château de Chissay, above the river Cher, midway between Tours and Amboise.

"It's madness," exploded Jim Parks. "You'll never believe it, Larry, but when Reynaud arrived here he found three hundred coded telegrams waiting for him—and the fucking French refused to decode them because they said they were too tired."

"I'm going to try and see Reynaud," I said, "but I'm worried about censorship. Even if I quote Reynaud's own words, the censors are liable to cut 'em out. They're a law to themselves. Especially if you come across one who doesn't like the prime minister. I've got written permission to use the embassy line to Washington for cabling, but only if they're passed by censor. Any way I can get round it?"

Parks thought carefully. "We don't expect the boss or Doc Matthews back until late," he was weighing his words, "but I guess that if you could get Reynaud to approve and sign every page—every one, mind you—and you got the cable to me before the others return, I'd just *have* to make the decision—and let it through. After all, if he *is* premier, so he must be chief censor. Trouble is, Larry, you'll never get to see Reynaud."

"I know him—" I began.

"Sure. I know you've got an in with lots of top brass. But how're you going to *make* contact? Set it up—make the date?"

"I'll phone Madame de Portes."

"You'll never get through. Reynaud's got a hundred rooms in his château, but only one antiquated, hand-operated telephone. It's linked to the nearest village, where the goddamned lady in charge closes for two hours every lunchtime and switches off at six sharp each night."

"Then there's only one thing to do," I tried to disguise my misgivings with a laugh, "and that's pop down the road to Reynaud's place and invite myself in for a drink."

It was now 9:00 A.M. Candé must have been ten miles from Chissay—and Candé lay twenty-five miles east of Tours on the road to Orléans. But I still had a good road map (hidden, all maps were now forbidden as a precaution against fifth columnists).

"I'll be back before six with my cable signed by Reynaud," I promised cheerfully—though doubtfully.

Jim Parks looked worried—even more worried than I did. But at first I didn't realize why. At the last moment he hesitated, almost as I was on the point of leaving.

"I shouldn't say this"—he mumbled something like "Thank God this place isn't bugged," then blurted out— "Reynaud isn't at Chissay. Won't be there until late this afternoon."

"Well, thanks," I said sarcastically. "You might have told me earlier."

"I couldn't. I shouldn't even now. It's restricted."

"But I'm on your side! Remember me? I'm supposed to be your buddy—and the voice of 'Washington in print.' What gives? Why the hell are you holding out on me?"

"I know, I know," he said. "But there are certain things I'm not supposed to talk about. Christ! You must know that, Larry."

"Not with a guy who once tried his best to help me to get married," I joked.

"For your eyes and ears only?" he asked. "Promise?"

"On the flag if you say so. But what's cooking, for Chrissake. And where *is* Reynaud?"

He took a deep breath, hesitated, then finally said, "Reynaud is with Winston Churchill."

"*Jesus!* So Reynaud has flown to England?"

"No. Other way round. Churchill's here. Not far away; flew in yesterday."

"In France! God Almighty! What a story!"

"You'll get me fired," sighed Parks, "shouting like that."

"Where is he then?"

"Place called Briare. It's the new French military headquarters. General Maxime Weygand, the C-in-C, met Churchill there last night."

"Never mind Weygand. But *Churchill in France!*"

"He landed yesterday, in a foul temper I'm told. The car to meet him never turned up. It was a worn-out old Citroën and broke down on the way. Churchill was furious—left standing on the tarmac fuming until they could find another vehicle."

"Where's—what's the name of this place?"

"Briare. About thirty miles southeast of Orléans. Just follow the river until you smell an expensive cigar. But seriously, you've got a head start, because Candé is twenty or so miles along the Main Tours-Orléans road."

"Do you know who's going?"

"I don't know Churchill's gang, but I gather de Gaulle's there. And Pétain. And of course Weygand. Churchill's flying back to England this afternoon, but maybe you'll be able to pick over a few bones if you step on the gas and catch your chum Reynaud."

I had no problem finding the headquarters of seventy-two-year-old General Weygand, the commander-in-chief, at his headquarters in the Château du Muguet—translated literally as Lily of the Valley Château. It lay at the end of a narrow winding road past the village of Ouzouer, about eight miles from Briare itself, where there was a small airfield.

But there I was stopped. Two French soldiers stood guard in front of a pair of handsome wrought-iron gates flanked by large stone pillars decorated on top with masses of petunias planted in two urn-shaped stone bowls. The soldiers had fixed bayonets.

"Restricted area," the first growled, moving threateningly toward me. "The grounds are private."

It was hopeless even to think of asking for permission to

pass those gates and eavesdrop on what could possibly be
the most momentous war council in the history of France.
And indeed, as I opened the door of my car, the sentry said
something and waved me away from the gates with his rifle.

"Restricted area," he shouted again.

"I'm a friend of the prime minister's," I said. "Here!" I
produced Reynaud's letter of authority, and he did allow
me to step forward and examine it while the other sentry
covered me with his rifle.

"Doesn't count," he said. "This a war zone. Under military authority. General Weygand is the boss here," adding
with a laugh, "Reynaud's got no power here—nor his girl
friend."

I would never have a chance of entering a restricted military zone—I realized that immediately. But I also knew
that so long as I remained in this country lane, minding
my own business (and obviously not making a fool of myself by taking photographs), no one could really force me to
leave. If on the other hand, I behaved stupidly, threatened
anyone, even the dumbest *poilu* wouldn't hesitate to shoot
and ask questions after. My job was to play for time in the
hope of picking up a few crumbs when the feast was over.
In the meantime it was a waiting game.

I was half asleep in the front seat of the car. And I was
hungry. But two hours of patience later I awoke as though
shot. The sound of a hand-operated siren tore into the still
air. Obviously it was a signal to the sentries at the front
gate. I had long since turned the car around on orders from
the sentry and parked it on the grass verge well away from
the gates. I jumped out—taking care to keep well away
from the gates as the sentries spruced themselves up a bit.

In the distance I could see groups of men walking or
waiting, gesticulating, strolling along the broad flag-
stoned terrace of the château with its classic facade behind, and its large french windows open to the warm day.
Some seemed to be shaking hands, bidding each other farewell. I made out—vaguely but unmistakably—the tall fig-

ure of de Gaulle towering head and shoulders above the others.

I heard the spurting roar of motorcycle engines being kicked into life. Three cars came slowly round the back of the château, which was hidden from me. Doors opened, bulky figures clambered in through the low French automobile doors. The motorcyclists opened the throttles of their noisy machines, the group which remained behind waved good-bye from the top of the terrace, the convoy slowly started to move across the long drive through open parkland dotted with drowsy cows, hidden only once for a couple of moments as it passed behind a clump of chestnuts.

Then the sentry was opening the gates. The four police motorcyclists roared past, helmets hiding faces. They hardly noticed me; their job was to make sure the VIPs faced no traffic obstructions. Three Citroëns followed, slowly as they approached a ridge in the park drive just before the gates. As they passed the gates and accelerated I caught a glimpse through the nearest back window of a large man puffing away at a cigar. The car disappeared.

"Well," said one of the sentries sardonically, "now that you've interviewed your Monsieur Churchill, I suppose you've got enough material for your story."

Actually I got the "material," as the sentry put it, by luck less than half an hour later. Perseverence too, though I say it myself. I had spent hours "wasting" time on a summer's afternoon with droning bees and the sweet smell of the countryside making it difficult to stay awake. But some instinct told me I must hang on, because I knew that Reynaud would have to leave for Chissay before long as he had a cabinet meeting, and I did have his signed letter of accreditation. When he left, perhaps I could follow him, flashing passes, anything, to become part of his convoy until I could speak to him. For after all, he knew me, trusted me, respected my father, needed help from the Americans. Everything was going in my favor—except contact. I hoped when Reynaud passed through the gates I could stand near him, and he might recognize me—and give me a chance to ask if I could follow him to Chissay—officially.

It happened almost that way—but then luck stepped in, when two motorcycle policemen swept from the front door toward the main gates, followed by only one car. It *had* to be Reynaud's.

The gates were drawn open. The soldiers presented arms—sloppily, I noticed. I stood by the car respectfully until, as I moved forward, the police officers waved me away with a shout. One just bumped me, throwing me off balance to the ground, forcing the car behind to jerk to a halt.

I jumped up, waved politely to Reynaud as he looked out to see if anyone had been hurt. Reynaud was seated in the backseat by the righthand window, and he looked squashed and uncomfortable. He also looked astonished to see me there. I was even more astonished—at his cramped position. For five men and the driver were crammed into a car meant to hold four.

"What on earth are you doing here?" cried Reynaud through the open window.

I was so staggered by the mass of people inside that, almost without thinking, I cried, "Excuse me, prime minister, can I drive any of you—help in any way?"

De Gaulle gave me a faintly ironic smile. He always seemed to find it hard to break into a real smile.

"What on earth are you doing here?" repeated Reynaud.

"I've been trying to get an interview with Marshal Pétain."

"Waste of time!" snapped de Gaulle.

"Well, sir, I've got a car, and it's at your disposal."

Their second car, it transpired, had also broken down, and they were planning to drive to the airfield at Briare to pick up one of the extra cars used by Churchill's party.

"But now," mused Reynaud, "we could save time if—"

I thought it better to say nothing—hoping, heart in mouth, as they looked at each other, that I could drive them to Briare. At least it would give me a chance to ask for an interview later.

But then Reynaud made a suggestion that sent me into a newspaperman's seventh heaven.

"Let's bypass Briare," he suggested to de Gaulle as I stood quietly by the open window. "If we have to collect one of Churchill's cars at the airfield—and if by bad luck he's delayed—we'd *have* to remain with him, as a matter of courtesy. But since he's not expecting us to go to the airfield, we could possibly save hours of valuable time if we could ask Astell to drive one of the cars to Chissay."

"I have to go to the American embassy in the end," I said politely, "but if it suits you I could take you to Chissay first, prime minister."

To de Gaulle, Reynaud said, "You'll have to go there, won't you—for the meeting?"

He nodded.

"How did you know that Mr. Churchill was coming to France?" he asked.

"I didn't," I lied. "My whole idea was to ask for an interview with Marshal Pétain."

"Done!" cried Reynaud. "You will be enrolled—temporarily of course—as the only American chauffeur in the French civil service. You might get the Légion d'honneur for this." To de Gaulle, he said, "You sit in the back with me, *mon général.* Astell will drive the two of us." To the others he cried, "You take the other car with the regular driver."

Once inside the car, the policemen kicked their starters, the motorcycles roared, and we set off in style, sirens wailing on the two motorbikes clearing the traffic ahead, gesticulating, shouting, waving. Reynaud sat in the left-hand seat directly behind me. De Gaulle sat on the right, in a sideways position to allow him more room for his legs. I was astonished at the way in which even the most obdurate people ahead of us scattered when the police forced vehicles to the sidewalks. After the day of the exodus, it resembled a royal procession—which in a way I suppose it was. And though probably no one knew the identity of the tall, gloomy man with the big nose, the little cock-sparrow

Reynaud was recognized instantly every time we slowed down.

He might be losing the war, but everyone liked him, felt that he had guts, hardly realized yet that the war was being lost by others, more traitorous. As the Citroën edged slowly past a crowd the men and women shouted, *"Bonne chance!"* or *"Bravo Reynaud!"* and often, *"Merde aux Boches!"*

At first the conversation between the two men was conducted in whispers, as though Reynaud and de Gaulle were discussing state secrets, or reviewing the vital meeting with Churchill. But during a lull, when Reynaud asked me where we were, and after hands pushed through his open window had tried to shake his hand, Reynaud spoke to me. In the rearview mirror I could see that his eyes, below his slightly dyed hair, were lit with a trace of amusement rare in these harrowing times. Sardonic perhaps?

"Tell me, Larry," he asked me not unkindly, "what do you propose to write about?"

My first problem was not writing, but bypassing the censor. With sudden inspiration I replied, forgetting all my earlier ideas, that I had come in the hope of seeing him for one reason only—to help France if I could.

"I know you must be overwhelmed with work, sir," I said, "but the *Globe* would be honored if we could publish even a brief—" I just prevented myself from using the word *appeal* and went on, "a message of encouragement to the people of the United States, who admire the wonderful stand you are making."

"Are words enough?" Reynaud asked bitterly.

"We need guns and tanks and planes more than words," said de Gaulle.

"I know, sir. But words *do* help. Roosevelt *wants* to do everything short of war to help France. A message might help. And, sir, it could provoke the president into giving France a message of—of hope, sir. Hope that might persuade the French to send away their great navy, the planes that remain."

"It sounds very fine in theory," said Reynaud, "but it is too late now to have any effect."

"But, sir," I begged him. "It's *never* too late. Not to hope. And anyway, sir"—it was very difficult trying to look disarming when Reynaud could see only the back of my head—"it costs nothing to try. And if we could do this, sir, I'd arrange for the message to be made available coast to coast on the news agency networks."

I knew the *Globe* would regard this as an astute move, a "national interest" gesture, which would in no way nullify our exclusive, for the *Globe* was our local paper anyway, serving the nation's capital. It made no difference to our sales if we gave the story to anyone from the *Milwaukee Journal* or the *Los Angeles Times*.

De Gaulle was whispering. I kept silent, holding my breath. We were driving through a small town called Sully, halfway between Briare and Orléans, a traffic cop's nightmare, for six roads met at the heart of the square. It took ten minutes for the police to force a passage, and inevitably Reynaud became more and more irritated and the thread of our conversation snapped.

Somehow I had to bring him back to my suggestion, for apart from the value to the *Globe* of a major scoop, I realized that if Reynaud *did* agree to back a nationwide appeal to Roosevelt, he would *have* to override any censorship in the national interest of France.

"The problem is time." At least ten minutes had passed since Reynaud last spoke to me. Now, out of the blue, he suddenly spoke as though I had made the suggestion only seconds before. "But General de Gaulle agrees with me—a dramatic appeal to the United States could be of inestimable value to France."

He was thinking, then he added, "I have a cabinet meeting later this evening, but as soon as we reach Chissay, I will ask you to help the countess to prepare a rough draft, then I'll go through it with you and make any suggestions."

I stole a glance in the rearview mirror at de Gaulle's face. It was expressionless, but I could sense, almost feel,

his irony. There was no love lost between de Gaulle and
Madame de Portes. On the other hand, from my point of
view, it would make writing the dispatch easier and
quicker. No one could say that Madame de Portes was
hidebound or fussy. She was action packed.

"I'll have to add a little background material, sir," I suggested.

"Like how you were the only journalist to see Churchill." Reynaud had a wry sense of humor and knew how
to treat newspapermen—and the poetic license they sometimes needed.

"Well, I did see him," I laughed, adding more seriously,
"But of course, sir, Madame de Portes will show you every
word we write so that you can cross out anything you
wish."

"With a carbon copy for Monsieur Reynaud," added de
Gaulle.

I decided deliberately not to mention the problem of censorship at this stage. I felt that if Madame de Portes became really enthusiastic, she would deal with Reynaud as
I had seen her handle a cabinet meeting in his absence.
She could easily persuade the prime minister to exercise
his right as chief censor. And that was all I wanted to satisfy Jim Parks at the American embassy.

"I'm most grateful, sir," I drove swiftly through the outskirts of Orléans. We were on the last lap now. "And I hope
I can be of real service to you." Then, without thinking I
added, "It may even persuade the defeatists to delay going
on to Bordeaux if necessary."

"Bordeaux!" De Gaulle sat up so suddenly he almost hit
his head against the low roof as he snapped, "Who on earth
said anything about going to Bordeaux?"

"I'm sorry, sir," I stammered, "I thought General Weygand—"

"Bordeaux is the road to defeat," said de Gaulle loftily.
"The prime minister prefers the road to honor. We shall
make our last stand in Brittany."

I almost gasped, as he added, "In Brittany large forma-
tions of troops will be able to hold out until British mer-

chant vessels arrive to transport them to North Africa," he explained, "and Mr. Churchill agrees. We can embark half a million men from a Breton redoubt. I leave for Quimper this evening to make the necessary arrangements."

Quimper, as I knew, meant the port of Brest—and the possibility of evacuating not only a fighting force but masses of equipment to North Africa.

I sped on toward Chissay, wondering how much of this latest startling development I would be allowed to print —if any. On the surface the plan for a Breton redoubt seemed brilliant. At least it would be able to halt the rout. I was equally fascinated by the irony of the choice, of the way various factions were "using" Tours as they plotted for power. Everyone had made for Tours—but for different reasons. Weygand and Pierre Laval, whom I had never trusted, regarded it as a halt on the way to Bordeaux, whereas Reynaud and de Gaulle regarded it as a halt on the way to Brittany.

I would have a great deal to write about when I reached Chissay—if I was given permission: Churchill's visit (though I would never be able to mention Briare by name), and then the Breton redoubt and the emergence of de Gaulle as a more powerful figure in the struggle against those whom I was already beginning to label as defeatists —led by Laval and Marshal Pétain.

Yet all adrenaline flowing at the prospect of writing a major piece was dulled by one other thought. Sonia. For one thing was clear. The plan to establish a Breton redoubt meant the end of all our schemes to spirit darling Sonia away to Spain. It was now the twelfth. By tomorrow at six o'clock (if she did not catch the diplomatic bus in Paris), she would be an enemy alien—subject probably to internment. It wouldn't have mattered had she been making for Spain. It was far from Paris, I had friends in high places in this region, I had always felt certain we could bluff our way through among the horde of refugees. But what could I do with Sonia if I had to go to Brittany—or even remain in Tours? I couldn't hide her for the duration of the war.

* * *

We reached Chissay in half an hour. The fifteenth-century castle, with its three round towers, lay in wooded parkland leading to an abrupt corner which in turn led to a courtyard. It was obviously a tricky curve to negotiate, especially if you met a car coming toward you. I was not surprised therefore that someone was needed to control the traffic.

But what *did* surprise me was the person in charge. It was none other than Madame de Portes, dressed in an outrageous bright red pajama suit. She was busily directing the traffic like an expert.

Only when the police stopped with our car in front of the main entrance did she wave imperiously to someone else to take over her "duties." She didn't seem unduly surprised to see me, greeting me merely with an "Ah, Larry! *Bonjour.*" Before Reynaud started to explain everything de Gaulle gave her an almost perfunctory nod and, contrary to French habit, didn't shake hands.

"He's a cold one," she muttered to me as de Gaulle moved through the door, *"Une grande asperge!"*

I grabbed my typewriter, found some carbon paper in an old study, and composed the majority of Reynaud's speech for him, aided, I must say, by intelligent suggestions from Madame de Portes, who looked over my shoulder all the time.

As it was supposed to be written by Reynaud, I had to employ a few flowery phrases. I didn't want it to be too long because I also wanted to add a general story of the day's events—and some of this might have to be critical, for I couldn't possibly disguise the chaos, the disorder, the gloom, the horrendous defeats on the battlefields, though I *could* take care not to mention the incidents of cowardice, of French troops refusing to fight, the general feeling of betrayal from within. That would have to wait, and I knew that if any of this material reached Washington from agency sources, the *Globe* would be able to work it in alongside my main story. Finally the "Message from France" read:

Friends of France! In this hour of greatest urgency, the fate of our land and our liberty rests in the balance as our valiant armies continue to fight against the forces of tyranny unleashed by Hitler.

France and America have been staunch comrades in arms since we stood shoulder to shoulder against the selfsame enemy in 1914 to 1918, and though I know you cannot join us at this time in the fight against evil, I appeal to you now to give us all the help you can, even though it may be short of war, and declare America to be a nonbelligerent ally.

Such a gesture, though committing no one to armed conflict, would tell the free world that you are with us in spirit, and give hope to ourselves and Britain as the skies darken over Europe.

I on my part promise our friends in America that, with the Germans almost at the gates of Paris, we shall fight in our fair country until if necessary the last soldier has been killed. If we cannot hold Paris, we shall fight in the provinces of France. If we cannot hold the provinces, we shall go to North Africa and fight from there. We shall never give in. *Vive la France! Vive les Etats-Unis!*

Madame de Portes read it quickly.

"Formidable!" she cried. "It is wonderful. I will take it to Paul while you get on with the second part of your article."

"It won't take long, madame," I promised her, for I wanted to minimize the dangers of any high official interrupting Reynaud. If that happened, I might not be able to see him for days. And anyway, I had already written some background material, particularly on Pétain, which had not been submitted to censorship, but which I could now tack on to the general story I tapped out.

I had been worried that Reynaud might cut out references to Churchill in France and also the news about the Breton redoubt, but when finally he sent for me, he immediately agreed with my point that Churchill's visit would be announced in a communiqué. Therefore mine would be an exclusive follow-up color story—far, far better, for every agency would announce the communiqué but the *Globe* would have the only man "present" at the meeting.

Signing each page, Reynaud made no comments until I had almost reached the end and started to read the earlier material I proposed to tack on. Some of it concerned Pétain.

"I can't pass this sort of thing," he said testily. "It's giving aid and comfort to the enemy."

"Anything you say, prime minister." I didn't hesitate, working on the principle that if I could get a quarter of my material past the "censor" I would be more than happy. "What's the passage you don't like, sir?"

"It's where you describe Marshal Pétain."

There was nothing *wrong* with the article, though I knew it might come as a shock to the less informed readers of the *Globe*. It simply stated a fact not often realized in America: that when World War I was about to erupt way back in 1914—yes, World War I—Pétain was *at that time* already fifty-eight and looking for a villa where he could retire. And that was thirty years ago—yet now he was the spiritual leader to whom France looked. Wasn't that a bit old? I asked the readers in my article.

"It doesn't put him in a very good light, stressing his age—and for American readers," protested Reynaud.

"It's true, sir, but it's been published before."

"Yes, I know," Reynaud was no fool, "but by tagging it along at the end of a message from me, it somehow reads as though I approve of what you say."

"Please cross it out," I said urgently. "It's my mistake. You're absolutely right, sir." I was suddenly sweating— one more stupidity and he might tear up the whole story. I breathed a little more easily when Reynaud finally signed the last page.

"Here's something you *can* put in," added Reynaud suddenly. "Much better than that absurd Pétain stuff. General de Gaulle told me we have absolute proof that the Italians have already started sending their Caproni bomb-

ers over southeast France and even as far north as the
Loire Valley. A great many casualties last night. They
didn't waste much time."

I scribbled out the addition on a spare sheet of paper and
asked Reynaud to sign that page too. Then I returned to
Madame de Portes.

"You are a fine journalist!" She herself made sure the
pages were correctly numbered. "Wait here, I will try and
help you a little more."

I stood in the study, idly looking at prints and old photographs on the wall, including an illuminated scroll bearing a French translation from Goethe. The first letter of
each line was enscribed in flowery gold leaf and the text
read:

> Possessions lost, something lost;
> Honor lost, much lost;
> Courage lost, everything lost.

As I read it again, I felt a sudden shiver and had an almost
irresistible urge to tear down the frame and its scroll and
smash it against the table. Then Madame de Portes arrived. Leading me to the door, she indicated the two traffic
cops sitting, legs astride, in front of my Citroën.

"To see you on your way," she cried almost gaily, and to
the policemen, *"En vitesse, s'il vous plaît!* This gentleman
is carrying important dispatches from the premier of
France to the American embassy for transmission to the
president of the United States."

And that was how I returned to Candé to file my copy.
Jim Parks could hardly believe his eyes when, out of the
window, he saw the motorcycle *flics* tear up the drive and,
as I emerged from my car, salute me briskly before roaring
off.

"You sure travel in style," said Jim.

"I told you I had contacts."

"Anything to show for them?"

"Only this—duly signed for immediate dispatch."

"This" was my cable—with the note in Reynaud's own

handwriting: "This letter is my authority for M. Larry Astell to file the attached cable, each page of which has been countersigned by myself." And then following the legal phrase used since time immemorial, he had added, *"Lu et apprové, Paul Reynaud."*

Parks whistled as he read. "Christ! You've hit the jackpot this time. Oh, I almost forgot. There's a cable for you."

It was from the *Globe.* It read: "Paris declared open city stop Tomlinson unable return exwar front stop Return Paris soonest cover entry Germans stop."

Sonia darling, I'll be back in Tours and in your arms soon, I was thinking, but I was also thinking, I'll have to take you back to Paris and try to catch the diplomatic bus by tomorrow evening. I can't disobey an order from the *Globe.* I might have been tempted—but not now, not with you on the run and nobody going to Bordeaux to help you. And, I was thinking too, you are a diplomat, you *are* protected—but only if you obey the rules. And if—no damn it, *when*—the Germans win the war, their Italian allies will be free to travel anywhere in Europe. Even, as an Italian diplomat, to Switzerland, to your bolt-hole in Rolle. I'll be there to see you, don't worry.

27

WHEN I REACHED THE OUTSKIRTS of Blandy, making good time against the main stream of fleeing cars, I had no premonition of the scene that would greet me as I turned the Citroën into the place des Epars and saw the wisps of dying smoke, smelled the sour aftermath of fire—burning wood doused with water. Then I jammed on the brakes as I stepped into a movie scene from an air raid. In the early moments of dawn, the sky was streaked gray and pink. In front of me the imposing facade of the Bellevue provided an ornate smoking background. The village square was filled with men, women, and children lying on the ground, crowded next to each other on pavements, in shop fronts, on snatches of grass, on benches, even on the side of the road, some cuddled up close as protection against the twin chills of fear and night, some covered with newspapers, others with anything they had been able to forage—carpets, tablecloths, the lucky ones with blankets and pillows filched from the Bellevue. I heard cries for help, moans of people in pain. Ambulances, cars, even trucks arrived to carry people away as I watched. Others hobbled to the hospital, if there was such a thing as a hospital in this small village. Mothers searched for children, everyone was coughing or spitting or vomiting because of the smoke.

It was the first I knew of a raid, and I felt the actual stab of pain as fear clutched my heart. Where was Sonia? I had no clue to the events of the last few hours—only the obvious fact that the Bellevue behind the square had received a direct hit. And that I would never be able to drive my car, however slowly, across the mass of people. I started to reverse, remembering the side street leading to the Bellevue courtyard where the porter had first garaged my car.

Suddenly, despite the nip in the air, I began to sweat with fear for Sonia, as a moving figure, a man in a daze, almost walked into my slowly moving Citroën.

"What the hell's happened?" I shouted.

"Air raid. Last night. Got a cigarette?"

I handed him a Gauloises, yelling, "Was it bad?"

"Could have been worse. I hear that fifteen people have been killed. Everyone else had to be evacuated."

"Where are the—the dead?"

"Don't know. Most of us grabbed our bedclothes and spent the rest of the night here in the square. A few people hurt—glass splinters mostly. I heard another bomb killed a lot of people in the suburbs of the nearest town. Could you spare me another cigarette?"

I scarcely heard him, my mind racing with anxiety. *Sonia!* He must have thought I was scared—I was, but not for myself.

"Here, take the pack, I've got some more," I shouted, and started to back the car until I was free of the square, heading for the rear of the clinic.

I *had* to find Sonia—there must be a first-aid post somewhere—but before anything else I had to make sure the car wasn't stolen when I went to search for her on foot. I must put it in the Bellevue courtyard, which acted as a sort of open garage. The double wooden doors were locked. I jumped out, tried to force the lock. It was flimsy, the old doors rickety, but I just didn't have the tools to break the doors open. Finally I inched the car very slowly toward the doors, pushing the fenders against them, and nudging the car inch by inch. The doors began to groan and give—but I had to be careful not to overdo it, not to smash the doors completely, for I had to leave myself a way to close them afterward.

Slowly the doors cracked. Splinters of wood round the old-fashioned hinges broke off, and finally the square iron locks and bolts, screwed into the door, burst open. I jumped out, opened the doors completely. Once I had driven the car through, I closed the doors, then backed my car hard up against them, forming a barricade heavy enough to stop intruders trying to enter the courtyard from the street.

The Bellevue foyer was a shambles of smashed furniture; debris everywhere, smoke, smell, crunching glass, the gilt reception area shrouded not only in dust and plaster but in uncanny silence. The elevators weren't working. The main staircase had been ripped apart, but I knew the back staircase which we had used to go to the maids' room and this hadn't been damaged. I took the stairs two at a time, reaching the bedrooms under the eaves at the rear of the hotel, panting with the effort—and fear. The rear of the building seemed virtually undamaged. Yet as I reached the top of the stairs and turned the knob on the door of her room, a great fear held me back. Where was she? Why had I been such a fool as to leave her alone unprotected even for one night? And yet, I thought desperately, if she was searching for a place that seemed safe, this quiet backwater was perfect to choose.

Finally I burst open the door—half expecting the impossible: Sonia still sleeping off the drug. The room was empty—but as neat as though a chambermaid had cleaned it up. Sonia's overnight bag was there, the room tidy, the bed pulled back, her pair of spare shoes under the edge of the coverlet. Nothing seemed to have been disturbed in the room where I had left her before driving to Tours—leaving her so drugged she probably never even remembered my good-night kiss.

I could only hope and pray that she had left the hotel before the raid had started—perhaps for some simple reason, the need for a breath of air. I could imagine what happened then—panic, as only the French understand the word. But where was she? If she was unhurt, why wasn't she standing in the place des Epars? Why wasn't she by the main gate, waiting for me since I couldn't know where she was?

There had to be a good reason—but what good reason? I must keep calm, I told myself, mind racing with possibili-

ties. She might be in some makeshift hospital, evacuated
perhaps, to the only available place in some nearby village—and then I would never have a chance of finding her.

I refused—by an enormous effort of will—to believe that
Sonia had been killed. And yet, I thought in sudden panic,
though our untouched bedroom indicated that she had left,
it might not have been for that "breath of air." She might
have made her way to the main lounge, now a twisted, tangled pile of wreckage from which none could escape death
or serious injury.

Shuddering, and suddenly cold, I realized there was only
one way I could be sure whether or not Sonia was alive. I
must go the equivalent of the morgue. The village wouldn't
boast such a place, but the police or air-raid wardens must
have designated some building in which the bodies would
await identification and burial.

Angrily I stubbed out a Gauloises. I mustn't think of
such an awful thing. I must think *positively*. I must think
that this is Thursday and that in theory she had to be back
in Paris and on that bus by the evening. She must be alive,
and provided I found her soon, we would still be able to
reach Paris in time.

She might be injured! Outside in the square, unable to
move, I made my way past the front entrance, ignoring the
shouts of the two policemen who wanted to know where I
had come from. Half dazed with shock, I walked into the
"battlefield" of the place des Epars. The "bodies" were beginning to wake up, make more noises as the sun slanted
over the village roofs. I trod as carefully as I could among
whimpering hungry children—the semisleeping figures
stretched out, one or two with bandages on heads, arms, or
legs, though I could see that the most seriously injured
must have already been taken away. Once or twice, coming across a huddled figure, I caught myself thinking,
There she is! but each time even before I spoke I spotted
the telltale evidence that it wasn't Sonia—something as
simple as a shoe peeping out from under a blanket, the
kind of shoes Sonia would never have worn.

Two men came round the corner of the place wheeling a

kind of trolley. On it stood a pail of coffee and some cheap
cups, and people began to form a queue. The children were
the ones I was most sorry for, herded from one place to another as a farmer herds sheep, as bewildered as sheep,
spindly legs moving wherever their parents told them to
go.

I asked one of the men where the casualties had been
taken. The dead had been laid out in the village church,
and I knew I had to go there—and *now.* I had done this sort
of thing before. Every trained newspaperman checks at
the morgue before anywhere else when looking for a missing person. But I had never before done it when searching
for someone I loved.

There was no sign of Sonia in the church. Almost thankfully the fifteen bodies lying in the church were uncovered,
as all the blankets had been needed in the village square.
So I was spared the agony of a long drawn-out examination. The church smelt of death—and the all-pervading
smell of wet, burned wood.

From the church I went round to the local *préfet,* asking
if there were any reports of an accident to "the Countess de
Feo." No one had heard of her. I made my way back to the
Bellevue, in the hope that Monsieur Lelong had turned up
and might have news. He had vanished. I wandered again
through the crowds filling the place des Epars. One group
had grown angry, demanded the right to return to the
Bellevue now that the danger was over. They didn't realize
that the building could easily fall down if somebody inter-
fered with the wreckage. The police were obdurate. Most
sleepers had awakened, people were moving around as I
searched among them—men looking for day-old *baguettes*
to feed their kids. A bar in the corner of the square was
doing a roaring trade in hardboiled eggs. I ate one before
returning to the police station to see if there was any more
news.

Where was she? What was happening? Beginning to feel
more and more desperate, I even asked at several cottages
in case she had been taken ill with shock. But nobody had
heard of her. Fear that she was dead had been replaced by

a kind of anger. Sonia was *there*. I felt it, I *knew* it, yet
there was no way I could find her. She had to come to me,
and if she *couldn't*, there was no way I could meet her. Had
I missed her through bad luck, stupidity? If I had reached
the hotel an hour or two earlier, would I have found her
then? If I had raced round the corners of villages when I almost fell asleep during the drive back to Blandy and had to
slow down would I have been in time to stop her vanishing? If I had skipped a mile and arrived just one hour
earlier—even twenty minutes earlier—or if it had rained,
or if it hadn't rained? The world of vanishing Sonia was a
string of ifs, ifs, ifs.

With a sense of mounting despair I returned again to the
place des Epars. She might have gone back, been looking
for me while I was looking for her. Yet the search seemed
hopeless. Apart from anything else, I didn't know where to
start. The police seemed indifferent, they were busy, they
either couldn't or wouldn't find time to help. I didn't know
a soul in the village except Lelong, not even the name of
the doctor who had treated Sonia.

It was at this precise moment that I did recognize a man
and a woman. I didn't *know* them, I had never spoken to
either of them, yet even the sight of someone I recognized
gave me a surge of encouragement, a feeling of fear diminished when shared, even with a stranger.

The lady was sitting on a pink chair on the pavement in
the square. She was the snooty woman in the maroon
Delage car who had driven near us almost all the way from
Paris. Next to her stood her chauffeur in his matching uniform, though I noticed that he no longer wore his peaked
cap or a tie.

Almost without thinking I rushed up to these "old
friends," and even though the woman didn't seem to recognize me—indeed she ignored me—I blurted out to the
chauffeur, "Do you remember me? We were driving just
behind you from Paris—my fiancée and me. She's vanished. Have you see her? And you, madame? Please forgive
me."

Very politely the chauffeur replied, "I'm very sorry, monsieur. I do remember the lady in your car. Next to the old couple who kept scratching madame's car. But I haven't seen your fiancée since we arrived."

Then the woman spoke. It was extraordinary really, looking back to that strange tableau on the fringe of the large village square—the mass of people, sitting wherever they could snatch an inch of space, the crying children, the strident voices of parents disguising their fear, their hopelessness, their pessimism. The world seemed to have no existence beyond the crowded square that had become a casualty station in a battlefield, with a well-dressed, almost haughty woman ignoring everyone around her.

Then she spoke. She had a beautiful, gentle voice, which was filled with compassion. It made a mockery of her attitude of imperious disdain.

"I recognized your American voice," she said gently. "You are inquiring about your Italian lady friend?"

As I gasped—had she actually met Sonia, confided in her?—the chauffeur interrupted, "May I present Madame la Baronne de Lancourt."

"Never mind, Jules," said the baroness.

"But you've met her! Did she tell you she was Italian?"

"We didn't actually meet," said the woman quietly.

"But *we* never speak Italian! How—"

"I have a certain flair for accents," she answered dryly. "Just as I could tell you were American immediately, even though you speak French perfectly."

"But what's happened to her, madame? *Please?*"

"I cannot tell you much," she smoothed the dress over her pink chair, "I heard her talking to a policeman—just near here the night just after the raid. I heard the policeman ask the lady for her papers."

I waited impatiently, almost angrily, for she seemed determined not to hurry.

"There was a lot of noise, you understand," she continued. "A lot of crying children, some women screaming, and a great many words I couldn't hear. But this I *did* hear— and I can swear to it. I heard the policeman say, 'I'm sorry, madame, but I must ask you to accompany me and prepare to return to Paris.' I understood quite clearly that your friend was being forced to go back to Paris for some reason I couldn't understand.''

"Back to Paris?" I echoed. Knowing more about Sonia's plans than the mysterious baroness, I realized she was without doubt telling the truth. Unless—

"You're sure, madame, it was my fiancée?"

She hesitated. Then, as though sensing that the chauffeur was about to interrupt again, she said, "Please, Jules" and to me, with a touch of hesitation, "I'm sure, even though I didn't actually see the lady."

"Good God! If you didn't *see* her—it could all be a mistake."

"It isn't, I'm afraid. You see I—"

"But, madame," I said angrily, "you *didn't* see."

"It was an unfortunate choice of words, sir," she said gently. "I'm afraid I can't see. I'm blind."

I could feel the rush of blood to my face as I stumbled for words. Now, of course, everything that had happened on that terrible day of the exodus fell into place—the lady's apparent aloofness, the way she sat alone in her car, unconcerned at the misery and suffering around her. What an agony it must have been for *her,* seeking no special preferment. Not once had she complained on that dreadful day.

An instinct warned me that she would not take kindly to a stammered speech of commiseration. Much better to regard her as a normal person, ignore her plight. She would take *that* as a kind of compliment.

"You're right, madame," I said instead. "I can sense you know you are right. I am very grateful."

"Go and search for her," she said softly. "I feel that anyone with such a musical voice as hers must be very beautiful. She had a laugh in her voice even on that dreadful day."

"Perhaps we will all meet after the war," I said. "I hope so." I took her hand. With a perfectly natural gesture she held it out to be kissed in the manner of the French.

"Bonne chance, monsieur, et vive les Etats-Unis!" she said, then added a curious sentence, "Do not worry, monsieur. All of us have a life to get through. So we might as well get through it."

After I had returned to the prefecture, I flashed my press card and drew the officer's attention to the name Astell, which he knew. Then he did remember the name and told me that Sonia had been sent back to Paris for her own good.

"But, officer," I said, "her letter was in perfect order."

"That is true," he admitted, "but surely monsieur will realize that she has been told to present herself at the embassy by this evening."

"I know"—it was hard not to show my exasperation— "but you arrested her when I could have taken her back."

"I didn't arrest her, monsieur, I did it also for madame's safety. I could take no chances. If anyone in this area discovered she was Italian," he shrugged his shoulders, "she would have been torn apart."

"But that's ridiculous."

"No, it isn't, sir, you don't realize that it was an Italian bomber that killed all these people in the square."

Of course the officer was right. And there was no way I could admit that by this evening I had planned to get Sonia, an enemy alien, across the Spanish frontier if possible.

"I understand, officer," I said publicly, though inwardly I was thinking, Is the entire world crazy? All the way *back* to Paris. And when the French give in, all the Italians in the world will be queuing up to take pleasure jaunts back to Paris.

It was mad.

Now I had to reach Paris as quickly as possible, not only in order to file my story when the Germans marched in, but to try to see Sonia at the Italian embassy before the bus left.

I decided to spend a few minutes looking for a little food. I had hardly eaten for twenty-four hours, apart from that one boiled egg. I walked behind the hotel toward the serenity of the church, searching till I found a small shop where I managed to buy three tins of sardines and some pâté that looked none too fresh. Nearby was a bar, though the wrinkled old *patronne* was angry and impolite when I ordered a *bière de pression* and asked her if she could spare me a *baguette* to make a sandwich.

"I've been serving sandwiches half the night," she shrieked as she wiped the froth off the *bière* with her wooden slat. "Why can't you people stay where you belong!"

Everyone was in a foul temper. The solitary old waiter looked exhausted. When one man spilled a coffee he snarled, "Why don't you get out of the way. I'd rather have the Germans here than you riffraff."

Not until I had flourished my considerable supply of *argot*—accompanied by a note—did the old woman grudgingly give me a *baguette*.

I grabbed the hunk of dry bread and bolted for the courtyard of the Bellevue to get my car. The sooner I set off for Paris the better.

I reached Paris at 4:00 P.M., driving against the stream of traffic still pouring out of the capital. It was madness, I kept on repeating to myself. Tonight my beloved Sonia would be forced to leave. Tomorrow her allies the Germans will be masters of Paris and (in theory anyway) she should be able to return whenever she feels like it.

I revved up the Citroën. She was beginning to make a few tired sounds after all the low-gear work, but she still responded as I drove across to the Left Bank and toward the Italian embassy in the rue de Grenelle, quite close to our apartment. One look told me nothing on earth—no press cards, no plea of neutrality, no letter from Reynaud—would get me past the ring of police guards facing the gates of what was now enemy territory. I did try. I cajoled. Everything was in vain.

It suddenly occurred to me—as a forlorn hope—that maybe Sonia had been allowed to drive to her home first.

After all she was supposed to have three days of grace. But at the rue de Longchamp I drew a blank. There was no guard outside the beautiful, low house, but there was no one in either. The shutters had been closed, and when I rattled the doorknob the house sounded hollow and empty, as though all life as we had known it since the day of that first summer party had been whisked away forever.

Halfway up the street I heard the sound of music coming from someone in a small bar. A group was drinking but not boisterous, and one played a guitar. I realized that two or three of them were American. I needed a drink badly—Scotch if it was still available—and I discovered that one of them also knew the words of the most popular song in Paris at the time. It was awful in a way, the contrast between the neutral Americans, to whom war was an adventure, and some nearby sad-eyed Frenchmen waiting for the city to fall. It was a picture of haunting contrasts as one of the Americans strummed for a moment and then they all started singing:

> The last time I saw Paris
> Her heart was warm and gay,
> I heard the laughter in her heart
> In every street café.

I couldn't bear it anymore, I gulped down my Scotch, left more than enough francs on the small round table, and drove back to the embassy to wait.

By evening, as though the news of the impending departure of the Italians had been spread around, a small, anti-Italian group gathered, shouting slogans, and when just after seven o'clock the wrought-iron gates were opened by the police, the crowd surged forward. The first of four buses appeared, armed guards on the step. It made its way slowly to the gates. I shoved and forced my way right to the front—haunted by a sudden fear that the bus might be attacked and that Sonia, as an ambassador's wife, might be given priority in the first bus.

Slowly the bus went past the gates. The small crowd—

there can't have been more than a hundred men and women—shouted obscenities, there was a fusillade of rotten fruit—tomatoes and other things beloved by French crowds. And then, just for a second, as the bus swung right down the rue de Grenelle and headed toward the boulevard Raspail, I saw her.

It was nothing more than a glimpse, but through the unwashed windows of the bus, through the spattered remains of tomato pulp, I saw her, and she saw me too. I didn't dare to make a special sign. I just put my fingers to my lips and smiled. She did too—a sad smile, but still a smile. Then as the bus drew away I felt as if it had taken a part of me with it forever, that we would never again tread the paths of love, and that she was waving a farewell not only to me, but a farewell to France.

28

ON THE LAST NIGHT before the Germans came I couldn't bear the thought of spending the evening alone in my apartment. In my mind's eye I could still see not only the Germans but the green bus with the obscene splash of squashed tomatoes and the face of Sonia behind the dirty windows, like a badly developed photograph.

"I need a couple of stiff drinks," I said to Oregon when I reached the office, "and I don't feel like drinking by myself."

"Don't blame you. I've got some Old Grandad."

"I've not sunk as low at *that!*" I screwed up my face. "I think I've got a bottle of Scotch in my desk drawer."

We drank almost in silence for a while, and then I couldn't even stand the office any longer. I wasn't only wallowing in self-pity because Sonia had gone, I was haunted by imaginary pictures of the awful spectacle that awaited us on the morrow.

"Let's go for a walk," I suggested to Oregon. "How about the embassy? Just to see what's happening?"

It was still light, of course, a balmy June evening of half-empty streets which at first glance disguised the bungling, the wavering, the cowardice, the corruption in high places.

As we turned left out of the rue du Sentier along the Grands Boulevards, I sniffed the very special odor of the Métro when we passed the Richelieu-Drouot station. Without thinking I turned to Oregon and said, "Something's missing."

It wasn't the eerie quietness of the streets and missing strident screeches of taxi tires, it was something else, and at first I couldn't place it. Then I realized—the rumble of the Métro beneath my feet was missing.

"Of course," Oregon echoed my thoughts, "we take it so much for granted. There's something else, the—" he hesitated to use the word— "the *shame* of it. Paris is being given away. Compare that with the heroic stand of the Poles in Warsaw."

"I know." As we walked toward the Madeleine and turned left, I asked Oregon, "What do you think made Ambassador Bullitt stay on in Paris?"

"A sense of occasion," replied Oregon promptly. "The higher you rise in the Pomposity Stakes, the more you need to look for chances to show off your greatness—real or phony," he added hastily.

Even so, it *was* puzzling. Cordell Hull, as secretary of state, was Bullitt's undisputed boss. Hull had insisted that Bullitt should accompany Reynaud to Tours, in other words that the ambassador should follow the legal government—especially at a sensitive time like this. President Roosevelt, who had a special relationship with Bullitt and had often written to him without telling Hull, refused to give Bullitt any actual order, but *advised* him to leave Paris with the government. Bullitt grabbed the loophole and decided to ignore what was only advice.

"For Bullitt it's a perfect moment of destiny," said Oregon. "After all, Bullitt is rich, pampered if you like, he's vain and flamboyant, and he's captivated Roosevelt. Now, toward the end of his career—which has hardly been illustrious—he's been given the chance to preside at one of the greatest moments in the history of Europe—even the world. When the Germans march in they're going to go to see Bill Bullitt, who is the only important foreign diplomat in Paris. And then he's going to hand over the keys of the city, so to speak."

"It's like hiring a butler for the day to hand over the city, in the same way a servant would offer a drink on a silver salver." I had never really liked Bullitt.

"That's all it is," Oregon agreed. "And mind you," he was thinking out his next words, "my guess is that when the history of this little episode comes to be written, Bullitt will go down as the one American above all others who let France down."

We had almost reached the Crillon Hotel when I heard a shout of "Larry!"

It was André Guerin, a French journalist from *Paris-Soir*.

"They tell me the Germans are coming in tomorrow," he said.

"That's what we've been told," I shook hands.

"Britain has ratted on us," said André. "Refused to send in her last fighters to save France. And now America—well, I'm not bitter about America, *mon vieux*. But when I look across there," he waved a hand toward the antiseptic-looking white building of the embassy, the Stars and Stripes, the marine guarding the entrance behind the railings. "It seems incredible to think that when the Germans arrive tomorrow and start stripping Paris bare, all your lot inside the embassy will be getting your normal clothes, Scotch, cigarettes—whatever you want—and all the food you can eat."

There was nothing either of us could say, and anyway André liked us, his words weren't motivated by malice.

As he waved good-bye, I said to Oregon, "It does give me a funny feeling—the thought that the embassy will be just about the only spot in all Paris where war will never physically impinge on us, even if it's surrounded by starving French and overfed Germans."

"It gives *me* a funny feeling too," Oregon admitted. "Those inside that building will be onlookers at everything that takes place in Paris—yet as safe from violence as the Romans were in their ringside seats at the Colosseum."

Oregon left me soon afterward and I strolled up the Champs-Elysées to Fouquet's. Even though almost all the restaurants were closed, Fouquet's offered me quite a reasonable snack, after which I decided to walk home, as though through a city of the dead.

When I crossed the Concorde to head for the Left Bank I looked back at the yawning avenue, in its way the most handsome street in the world, now abandoned by everyone but myself and three stray dogs. Even the four huge flags at each corner of the square hung with a kind of lifeless despair on this last night before other hands would haul down the tricolors and replace them with the banners of the master race.

The first German troops planned to enter Paris before 8:00 A.M., and according to an American embassy official General von Studnitz, the C-in-C of German forces, would arrive at the Hotel Crillon at 9:45 precisely. He had commandeered this building for himself, and arrangements had been made for him to set up his headquarters in the Prince of Wales suite on the first floor and to make a formal call on the American ambassador at ten o'clock the same morning.

Long before that, however, as Oregon and I walked the streets, the endless procession of German vehicles, with their troops looking like fresh, silent, blond robots, pounded through the empty streets of Paris on this, its blackest day. They entered the city north and east of Notre-Dame, their traffic regulated without a hitch by German military police using red disks attached to short handles.

Only a few people watched. Most, I felt sure, were peeping from behind closed shutters, ashamed to be seen watching history in the making. Here and there though, knots of people did stand and look glumly, most of them stupefied by the youth and discipline of the German soldiers, each one looking freshly scrubbed. No one *really* knew what was happening, even how to behave. Paris, by deciding to become an open city, had fallen without a shot being fired in anger. But that was all they did know. Had France lost the war, or had they lost only a battle? Their confusion was increased by the thousands of French policemen in neatly pressed uniforms, lining the streets with

their white batons at the ready. They almost looked as
though they had made a special effort to smarten up for
the occasion—as though royalty were going to visit Paris.

"They look as though they're enjoying it," I instinctively lowered my voice.

"I don't think so." Oregon was watching the smart uniforms of the police. "It's their way of holding up their
heads, as though telling the Germans that though they're
beaten, they're French and proud of it. Poor devils. They
must be suffering."

Perhaps surprisingly, I didn't feel much emotion. Significant occasions, I had already discovered, tend to freeze the
emotions, especially if you are occupied storing up facts
and impressions for an article to be written later in the
day. I was too busy to feel except for the passing thought
that only a few days ago I had been strolling down the
Champs-Elysées in the sun with Sonia, and now she was
God-knows-where, locked up in some bloody train heading
for Italy—and not neutral Switzerland.

And so in a way the day passed by in a series of snapshots. I certainly wasn't going to miss the German commander's visit to Bullitt, and for this ceremony—if that's
the proper word for it—Oregon and I and several other
American correspondents were able to flash our press
cards and stand inside the embassy courtyard. What happened had all the trappings of farce—if it hadn't been so
pitiful.

The Hotel Crillon was, of course, separated from the
American embassy by only one narrow street, the rue
Boissy-d'Anglas. Yet, though von Studnitz could have
walked in three minutes to his nearest neighbor, so to
speak, he was apparently determined to observe strict attention to protocol for the visit to the American ambassador, who would hand over to him the city of Paris on behalf
of the French. He was also determined to extract the last
ounce of drama from this historic moment. From the
American embassy courtyard I could see the German commander climb into a large black Mercedes, flying the
swastika. In this the German commander set off for the

hundred-yard journey, preceded by an escort of motorcyclists, black leather contrasting with gleaming machines. At the front entrance to the Crillon they revved up their motors, then the cavalcade covered the distance in under two minutes, halting with shouted commands in the embassy courtyard.

Von Studnitz stepped out. I caught a glimpse of a short, dapper man wearing a monocle, a small mustache, who reminded me of a démodé cavalry officer. Spurs clinking, his chest a spectrum of medals, his monocle firmly screwed into his right eye, he walked into the embassy—and out again ten minutes later.

I wondered what Bullitt must have been thinking.

"He's too goddamn vain to realize that by staying in Paris instead of following the government it was as though he'd slapped every Frenchman in the face and told them they're finished," said Oregon.

The black day was not entirely devoid of humor. After the ceremony of handing over the city Oregon was talking to a group of correspondents and embassy officials in the avenue Gabriel, outside the embassy gates, when a German lieutenant stopped, saluted politely, and asked, "You're Americans?"

There was a chorus of affirmatives, after which the German asked, "Can you tell us where we can find a decent hotel?"

"You must be joking!" we could not help laughing. "The city's yours, there are hundreds of empty hotels all over Paris. All you have to do is take your pick."

So the miserable day continued. Following hard on the heels of the stormtroopers came experts ready to take over every section of Paris life. Their efficiency was incredible. One group of uniformed engineers drove to the main telephone exchange in the rue du Louvre, while trained announcers and operators, also in uniform, seized the main radio station in the rue de Grenelle. Before midday Radio Paris was broadcasting programs in German and music by Wagner. Before midday four blood-red German flags dominated the Concorde—two over the Ministry of Marine, the other two over the Hotel Crillon. Others floated over the Chamber of Deputies, the Senate, even over the Arc de Triomphe, with the tomb of the unknown warrior and the eternal flame beneath.

I walked toward the Eiffel Tower to see what was happening. The first flag the Germans tried to fly there was too large. It had taken some effort, for the elevator had been sabotaged and the Germans had to walk all the way up—nearly seventeen hundred steps. I could see the flag flapping like a sail and then hear the sudden noise of ripping as the wind tore it. Half an hour later more German soldiers climbed the tower again to replace it with a smaller flag.

All this we took in our stride, eyes on watches to make sure we gave ourselves enough time to meet deadlines.

"This has to be a humdinger of a piece," said Oregon. "For once in the war you won't have to face a censor."

It was true. The Germans planned to open a censor's office the following day, but for twenty-four hours Americans—and a few other neutral correspondents—were being permitted to file anything they wished to write. There were two obvious reasons for this. There was nothing they could say that could irritate the Germans, and there were no military secrets involved. I had arranged to file through the embassy, so I had plenty of time to return to the office and type my piece. Then I made my way back to the embassy to file. I wasn't particularly looking forward to the night that lay ahead—for I knew that as soon as I had handed in my story to the skeleton staff at the embassy, I would have to set off and drive through the night to Tours. Only by leaving around midnight could I hope to beat the jams that would surely build up and choke the roads later in the day.

As I walked out of the embassy doors after filing, I had to stand on the steps for a moment to wait as a low, gleaming Mercedes swept through the double doors of the courtyard and drew to a stop with a flourish. Everything about that moment infuriated me—the soldier in his jackboots clicking his heels as he opened the rear door, the exaggerated

salute, the polished car, and above all the flag, the swastika, on a pennant near the outside fender. Without knowing why, I suddenly thought of poor, shy Jean-Pierre lying
alone—dying before he had even begun to live.

The military driver held out a hand to help the unseen
passenger as he leaned forward from the deep backseat. I
watched—vaguely irritated but still intrigued, wondering
who in the German hierarchy could possibly be visiting
the American embassy so late at night.

Since he was arriving in a chauffeur-driven German
limousine, it never entered my head that the mysterious
visitor wouldn't be a German.

But it wasn't a German.

It was an American. Unsmilingly, the tall, thin man declined the offer of the helping hand, stepped out, peered
through the dim light as he climbed the steps, and then,
seeing me, exclaimed in his special up-and-down voice,
"Well, *really,* Larry! A one-man reception committee? How
did you *know* I was coming to see you?"

I stood there, almost gasping with horror, staring at my
father as though unable to believe what I saw. Then I
looked at the sinister, long black car, the Nazi flag, the
Nazi military chauffeur, and I suddenly realized that it
was Papa—and that he wasn't being facetious, he wasn't
trying to disguise anything, he wasn't even attempting to
apologize or to show some sense of shame. What he *was*
doing seemed to him perfectly natural.

"But Papa!" I exploded. "What the hell are you doing—
being driven around by a German soldier! With a Nazi flag
in a German military car?"

"Eh?" He seemed genuinely surprised. "Oh, that's easily explained. Quite *easy.*"

"I can't see any easy explanation from where I'm standing."

"Really, Larry—why *do* you jump to conclusions?" he
started to climb the embassy steps.

"I can see the conclusions," I cried bitterly.

"I *must* say, Larry," he was suddenly testy, "you are a
very stupid man. There is a perfectly logical reason," and

with a short laugh, "I'm not a—collaborator. I'm a perfectly good American citizen, even if I do have more than a dash of French blood in me." Holding my arm, he guided me up the steps and inside the reception area, where he said more gently, "I have few minutes before I see Bullitt."

For a moment I was so stunned that I almost rushed down the steps without another word. But reason told me there must be some explanation—however misguided. There *had* to be. Whatever Papa might do, he couldn't make a fool of himself like this. And he would never cooperate with the Germans, even though America was neutral and the Germans were not therefore our enemies. Not *technically*—but Papa was half French, he had dual nationality, Grandma was a hundred and fifty percent French! And so anti-German she would, I thought, even shoot her son on the spot if she had seen what I had seen that night.

"Come inside," he said quietly.

My father whispered to the clerk behind the desk, presumably asking him to wait before announcing his arrival to Bullitt. Then he sat down on one of the blue banquettes facing the desk, back to the tall, elegant windows.

"Young people get so excited, yes, *very* excited," he exclaimed. "Anybody'd think—"

"I did think," I said, but more slowly now, more quietly.

"It's so very simple," he sighed as though tired with the effort of having to deal with idiots like me. "When General Guderian occupied Reims, the first thing he did was to appoint a German civilian to control the entire organization of the champagne market. He's called"—even Papa couldn't help but chuckle at the absurdity of the title— "the führer of champagne."

"But what's that got to do with you in a German car?"

"Please, Larry, *really!* The champagne führer, whose name is Herr Gaertner, interviewed the head of several champagne houses to discuss the future. Very bleak, yes, *very,*" he shook his head. "But Gaertner is an expert on wine. He has vineyards just across the border from Alsace, and he's a very sympathetic man. All the same, the Germans have ordained that champagne sales to civilians are to be banned. Production will continue—but most of the output will go to the Germans. This was what I was told," added my father. "I didn't meet Herr Gaertner at the earlier meetings."

"And then?" I was beginning to get more intrigued.

Slowly the story unfolded. It seemed that Herr Gaertner had discussed with all the champagne growers the prospect of electing one man to liaise with all the members of the Bureau de Champagne, the affiliation which since the turn of the century has always protected the interests of champagne.

"Well," said Papa, and I could feel that he was pleased with himself, "all the champagne houses unanimously asked me to become the delegate to deal with the Germans."

"But is that such an honor?" I couldn't quite eliminate the edge of sarcasm in my voice, though Papa didn't notice it.

"Not an *honor,* good gracious, no. But my colleagues feel that even though I am half French, the fact that I am a neutral American might help the—well, the common cause, yes, the *cause*—perhaps getting certain conditions eased."

"What does your Herr Gaertner think of that?"

"In fact," said my father, "he's—well, a gentleman. Intelligent, educated at Harvard, and owns some very large vineyards."

"And the car—why the German car?"

"Really, you *are* cross-examining me! It's no mystery, goodness me, no. I agreed to serve as chairman of the committee, but on one condition—that I went to see Bullitt and placed my problem on record at the embassy. I don't see that there's anything wrong in what I'm doing, but I wanted it clearly understood that I wouldn't take the job if the embassy didn't approve."

As I sat there he added dryly, "Anyway, there was no other way I could drive to see Bullitt, thanks to you, I *must* say."

"Me!"

"Well, you did take my Citroën, and I'm too old to tear around the countryside in the dead of night in an MG. Besides, an official German car makes it much easier to pass through roadblocks."

"I hope you won't regret it," I said. "Treating with the Germans—"

"I'm not treating," he was suddenly angry. "What a stupid thing to say. Yes, *really* stupid!"

"I'm sorry."

"You should be. I've taken this job not to make life easy for the Germans but to make it easy for the *French*. To increase production and to make a profit and to provide jobs for the French. Really, you make me *very* cross, Larry. Now good-bye. I must talk to Bill Bullitt. Will I see you?"

"I'm off to Tours but—"

"I hope to see you in Douzy soon. Meanwhile I will look after the family, my friends—and if I can help them by borrowing the occasional German car for official business with the Germans, I shall not expect you to stop me."

With that he turned to the desk without looking at me again. I had rarely seen him so furious. Or was it something else than anger, I wondered as I walked solemnly across the courtyard to find my car. Was it a simulated anger disguising hidden doubt? Did my father secretly feel a sense of shame at being driven in style by a Nazi chauffeur—and on the very day that a fellow American had handed over this beautiful, tragic capital? Perhaps in a curious way Papa didn't realize the shame of it until he saw me and saw the look of horror on my face when he stepped out of the German car.

29

LONG BEFORE I SET OFF FOR TOURS after the encounter with Papa, the French government, unknown to most people in Paris, had been evacuated again—from Tours to Bordeaux. The idea of a "Breton redoubt" had, I learned later, been abandoned, largely because Madame de Portes and Weygand disliked what she called "a stupid gamble." Anyway she didn't like de Gaulle. So I bypassed Tours, though I did not cross the Gironde and struggle into the great seaport of Bordeaux until the Saturday afternoon—and by then even I could smell the air of defeat in the endless trail of haggard failures. Twice before Bordeaux had been the provisional capital of France—in 1871 when the Germans occupied Paris, and for a brief spell when it was threatened in 1914.

The city was overflowing with refugees. There was hardly a hotel bedroom to spare, but I managed to park my car in the place des Quinconces, which stretched in front of the striped awnings of the Hôtel Splendide terrace. The *place* was not a paved square in the usual sense of the word, but an open space normally reserved for fairs or exhibitions. It was bordered on the far side by the river. The authorities had obviously been preparing for a new fair for there were several abandoned pavilions advertising *Les Vins de France*.

I had already spent one night in the Citroën on the way down and was reconciled to spending another. The American consulate in Bordeaux was in the rue Esprit-des-Lois,

447

where Jim Parks told me it had been elevated to the status of temporary embassy, adding sourly, "I've got to share a twin-bedded room with nine people."

At least Jim was able to put me in the picture. "It's all over bar the shouting," he admitted, "but the boys tell me that de Gaulle is the man to watch. There's a vague rumor going round that if France gives in, he's going to bolt for it—and try to fight on."

Reynaud had set up his headquarters in the Quartier-Général, the headquarters of the Eighth Military Region in the rue Vital-Carles, a short street leading off Bordeaux's main shopping center quaintly named the cours de l'Intendance.

"I'd better go and see if I can contact him," I said.

"Your best bet would be to check with the British," Parks advised. "They've taken over the Hôtel Montré—five minutes away from Reynaud's house, and if anyone *does* bolt for England, you can bet your bottom dollar the British will be around to help."

"I'll go there right away."

"Go to one other place," Jim said suddenly. "The Portuguese embassy. I gather it's just about the only place still issuing visas, and it's hell there—even fighting in the queues. Shouldn't that make a good story, if nothing else?"

I'd already seen that the visa section of the American embassy stretched in a queue half a mile long on the pavements outside. "And it's as bad at the British embassy," said Parks.

Fear born of ignorance had struck terror into the hearts of a population swollen by hundreds of thousands of refugees. Only the brave or the foolish still dared to hope for a miracle. For the rest, nothing could throw off the stupor that blanketed the city. I could see the ugly mood among men and women of many nations who had been funneled by circumstance into this one city, and who could no longer disguise from themselves that they had reached the end of their tether.

Outside the Portuguese consulate, which was near the place des Quinconces, men fought like savages as they

vainly queued for a visa to freedom. Jews, Czechs, Poles,
German, and Austrian refugees—all knowing they were
marked for the concentration camps—tried to storm the
consulate building. The Portuguese officials phoned the
police, who did not even bother to answer the distress call.

Knowing the nature of their fate if the Germans caught
them, these people did not realize that the Portuguese
were issuing transit visas only, and these only to people
whose passports were already franked with a visa for the
country of ultimate destination. And for ninety-nine out of
a hundred there was only one chance of getting this—
unless they happened to know that the Republic of Haiti
was prepared to stamp any passport with a resident's visa
for a hundred and fifty francs.

The Portuguese consulate was near the Splendide, and
as I walked past the crowded terrace of the hotel I could
even hear the welcome sound of ice tinkling in glasses.

During these fateful hours no one had any real news of
the actual fighting. And there was no way of finding out.
Anyway, what did it matter? I tried the British as well as
the Americans. The British were probably better informed
because after all it was their war as well as the war of
France. But *no one* knew. At the embassy, though, I did
meet an old British colleague, Harold King, who worked
for Reuters news agency; he was one of the best-informed
English correspondents in France. He had driven down to
Bordeaux and had a cubbyhole of a room at the Splendide
with a sofa, which he offered me in place of a bed. Better
still it had a bathroom, and after a shower King took me
for dinner in what was recognized as the finest restaurant
in all Bordeaux. It happened to be next to the Hôtel
Montré, the "temporary" British embassy, and they had
booked a large "embassy table" at the Chapon Fin for
every lunch and dinner. The food was impeccably cooked—
everything from lobsters to soufflés. In the far corner of the
room I spotted the swarthy features of Pierre Laval.

But then there were two worlds in Bordeaux during
those last hours before the Germans snapped the hand-
cuffs on France. If refugees without rooms filled the park

benches, shopkeepers filled the shelves of their windows. In the cours de l'Intendance almost every imaginable article was on sale. Provocative dummies flaunted the latest fashions in dresses and hats for women. I replaced my wardrobe with a couple of the latest-style shirts, a pair of slacks, socks, shoes. It was the same even in every food shop. Though penniless thousands were unable to get a square meal, confectioners crammed their windows with mouth-watering displays of chocolate, the perfumiers with scent, the grocers with cheeses, rows of hams, mounds of pâtés, bottles of wine—at a price.

As far as the *Globe* was concerned, I had plenty of color stories, but I gave up trying to compete with spot news. I tried again and again to contact men close to Reynaud, but as the panic spread nobody had the time even to be polite. On the other hand, I didn't have to worry. It was by now becoming increasingly obvious that Pétain and Weygand (with Laval in the background, I was sure) were winning the battle to capitulate against the frenzied efforts of Reynaud and de Gaulle to continue the fight. And Jim Parks told me one other sobering fact: that Reynaud's mistress now believed it would be better to give in and was trying to influence Reynaud. The poor French premier was on the rack—and now his mistress was going to give the screw an extra turn. How long ago it seemed—and yet it was only a matter of hours—since Reynaud and de Gaulle shared a dream to continue the fight in North Africa with the country's great fleet and so keep the symbol of a living France in front of the world.

The dream seemed to have been shattered, but the one thing that never entered my head was the possibility of an alternative dream—one which, though in a different way, could still be the symbol of a living France. It came about late on the Sunday night, when finally Reynaud had resigned and Pétain had succeeded him, and though he had not yet formed a cabinet, it was obvious that he would immediately sue for armistice terms with Germany. To all intents and purposes the French had given up the fight.

I heard the news first from someone in the British-

occupied Hôtel Montré, which I visited every day. I walked
the five minutes across the cours de l'Intendance to Reynaud's office in the hope of seeing him—or perhaps Madame de Portes—to pay my respects to the premier who
had fought so magnificently, if in vain.

Reynaud's house and office in the Quartier-Général had
a small courtyard facing the rue Vital-Carles, and behind
the large front entrance, an imposing hall. There were no
sentries at the door—no longer. It seemed impossible to realize yet that Reynaud held no more rank, but was just a
private citizen of a country that had lost the war. As I
reached the door another man approached. It was Major
General Sir Edward Spears, Churchill's liaison officer
with the French, and a close friend of de Gaulle's. I had
met him at the British embassy, and I nodded to him, and
said, "It's darned dark in here."

It was. The spacious hall, which boasted several stone
pillars, had a wide staircase at the rear. The only lighting
came from one miserable bulb. The entrance hall was
empty except for us. I realized that if I wanted to see Reynaud, I must climb the wide stone stairs. As I stood there
undecided, both of us heard in the eerie semidarkness an
urgent whisper, "General Spears! I must speak to you!"

The man was French—and Spears spoke French as well
as I did. To my astonishment, I saw a tall figure flattened
against one of the columns, shrouded in its shadow.

It was de Gaulle. I couldn't believe it—this haughty, almost disdainful, arrogant leader hiding like a criminal in
an entrance smelling of dust, of the need for someone to
sweep away the mustiness. Urgently he whispered again,
"It's extremely necessary that I talk to you." He caught
sight of me. "Oh! It's only you, Astell." It was not a phrase
expressing arrogance, but more relief.

Spears whispered, "I can't speak now, the British ambassador is going to take me to see Monsieur Reynaud."

"You must," insisted de Gaulle, still whispering and
carrying on, speaking, "I have very good reason to believe
that Weygand is planning to arrest me."

Spears whispered to de Gaulle, warning him to stay just

where he was, virtually hidden. He would, he promised, be back soon. I had at first been astonished to see de Gaulle at all, for I knew that on the previous day he had flown to London to see Churchill.

"I arrived back this afternoon," he explained to me. "In a British plane. Churchill gave orders for it to return to Britain tomorrow morning. And the crew knows that if I want to go to London, they have orders to take me—but they must leave at nine o'clock in the morning."

"If there's anything I can do—" I began, still whispering.

"Perhaps," said de Gaulle gloomily. "Weygand *is* going to try and arrest me. I insist that in some way France must continue the fight. He says that it's treason for anyone to continue fighting after an official armistice. I have great faith in the British—though we don't always see eye to eye. But I'm going to fight on."

"Do you mind if I stay?" I asked. "Or do you want me to leave?"

"Stay if you wish," said de Gaulle. "But no *reportage* until I am safely on British soil."

Of course I promised. But I did need de Gaulle's permission, for Spears was known as a prickly British general who would be quite liable to kick me out of the place without a word. "Perhaps you'd tell General Spears that I'm to be trusted," and hesitating, for I didn't want to sound banal, added, "and your friend."

"I'll do that," he muttered. "Where the devil is Spears?"

A few minutes later the British general returned to the cavernous hall. I heard his footsteps on the empty stone floor. De Gaulle was so well hidden that at first Spears didn't see us, with de Gaulle standing bolt upright, his back to a column so that he couldn't possibly be seen by anyone entering through the front doors.

Moving to the rear wall where we were even more hidden, we held a kind of impromptu conference. The gist of it, in whispered conversation, was that de Gaulle had decided to accept Churchill's offer of a seat on the British plane which was waiting at Mérignac, the military airfield for Bordeaux. But he *had* to make his way in secret early on the following morning, for which he needed a car. He also needed a place to hide for the night.

Spears had his car but didn't advise de Gaulle to take it over. No doubt he thought, as I did, that de Gaulle's presence in an official car would probably be reported back to Pétain or Weygand in a matter of moments.

"As to hiding, well there must be some spare place in the Hôtel Montré," said Spears. "And that is only five minutes away."

"We will take a chance and walk there together," said de Gaulle to me. "Astell can show me the way."

"And I do have my car if you need it tomorrow," I offered.

Spears drove ahead. De Gaulle and I followed, and as soon as de Gaulle had slid his tall frame past the glass entrance door to the hotel we looked around for a place to sleep. To the right of the hall was the old-fashioned salon, reached by steps lined by statues of seminaked ladies. We sat down on the red plush, Empire-style chairs while de Gaulle explained more fully to Spears why he felt he must go to London immediately. He not only wanted to continue to fight—and that would be impossible in France—but he wanted above all to broadcast to Frenchmen, to appeal for continued resistance before the defeatists broadcast *their* message. De Gaulle's only chance was to reach Mérignac airfield, which could soon be in Weygand's hands, and fly to Britain in Churchill's aircraft.

Finally, after de Gaulle prepared to bed down in a small salon, on the largest sofa he could find to accommodate his lanky legs, it was agreed that we would all prepare to leave the Hôtel Montré at seven the following morning.

Sleep was out of the question for hours. The excitement of being an eyewitness to history kept my mind so alert I could think of nothing except the prospect of the following day. If I *did* manage to help de Gaulle to escape, how the hell would I ever be able to get the story out? And *could* de Gaulle escape? I hoped so, I admired him greatly, though whether he could do anything from Britain, already girding itself for possible invasion by the Germans, was a different matter. Thoughts kept crowding in, and for some reason my mind flew back to the time when de Gaulle had quoted to me a maxim from some Chinese general he admired. That had been positive advice. But now I was niggled by another piece of Chinese advice, a Taoist pearl of wisdom, "Of all the thirty-six alternatives to war, running away is the best." What a way to think about a man like de Gaulle! But I couldn't put the phrase out of my mind until at last I fell into a troubled sleep. I awoke earlier to go and fetch the morning edition of *Le Journal,* which had continued publication in Bordeaux. I took it, with a roll and some coffee, to de Gaulle and let him see the headlines himself:

PÉTAIN À LA TÊTE DU GOUVERNEMENT,
PAUL REYNAUD A DÉMISSIONÉ

"He tried his best," was all de Gaulle said, then added with his usual irony, "He might have succeeded but for that woman."

Within a few minutes, with me driving, Spears next to me, de Gaulle half crouching, sitting sideways in the back seat, we set off. We did not take the direct route to the airfield. Still convinced that Weygand planned to arrest him, de Gaulle was determined to disguise his flight in case any officials saw him and reported back. He seemed afraid that the French commandant at the airfield might have already received orders to prevent him flying to Britain.

We stopped first at the Ministry of War, where de Gaulle, without leaving his seat, made a great show of arranging a number of appointments for the rest of the day. While he made plans, I kept the motor running just in case we had to make a dash for it.

We enacted a similar drama at another building housing some War Ministry personnel. Only then did de Gaulle agree to make for the airfield, which we reached just before 9:00 A.M. As the car turned on to the bomb-pitted apron in front of the control room we all looked round in disgust. It was not a scene of pillage or destruction that made us angry; the airfield was filled with hundreds of aircraft packed wing to wing—and none of them was apparently preparing to take off for North Africa.

Now we had to find the solitary British plane, and our task was made more difficult because we could hardly manipulate the car through the tightly packed lines of aircraft. Yet we needed the car because de Gaulle had piled in a lot of luggage. At last I found it. There was an agonizing delay while the luggage was stowed. All seemed ready, but then the pilot insisted that de Gaulle's heavy trunk, filled with papers, should be lashed in case they ran into bumpy weather. This was easier said than done, for there was nothing to tie it up with. One of the aircrew ran off to find some rope; it took another precious ten minutes.

Still worried that he might be stopped if anyone saw him get in first, de Gaulle insisted on playing one last scene. When the luggage was stowed and the propellers turning, Spears jumped into the aircraft. I followed him while de Gaulle, pretending to wave farewell, stood by the plane. At the last second, at the very moment when the chocks were pulled from under the wheels, de Gaulle leaned forward as though for a final handshake. Then as we jumped out de Gaulle clambered aboard. The pilot revved up the engines and roared along the runway. Within a few minutes the tiny plane was over the sea and heading for Britain.

For me, that was the end of the fight for France. What followed was anticlimax, including the armistice terms and the eventual partition of the country to give Pétain a government in Vichy. In the here and now—a matter of hours—I had to make an urgent decision. I was sitting on one of the hottest stories any newspaperman had ever had—I had helped de Gaulle to *escape*. But de Gaulle had told me that Churchill not only approved of the French setting up some sort of Free French movement but that he wanted to broadcast to France the day after he arrived in England. And that—however important to history—would kill my story stone dead unless I could print the details of his flight beforehand. I had to file this day.

I could almost feel the sharp intake of excitement, the

electricity of achievement at the prospect of the challenge, the hunger of my own ego. This was an exclusive account of a major historical event, one in which—did I even dare to say this?—I had played a minor role by helping de Gaulle on his way. It might well rank as one of the supreme moments of my life as a journalist—and a signpost to my future.

But how would I achieve this? With the new government thirsting for de Gaulle's blood, I knew that no cable office in France would ever transmit my story without higher authority. The makeshift American embassy couldn't help, simply because they had given an undertaking to cable only messages passed by the censor. And though Reynaud had helped me once, he could not help me now.

It was 10:00 A.M. Spears got a lift back to Bordeaux in the car which had brought the aircrew to Mérignac. I stayed—for the moment, all manner of wild ideas crossing my mind. Could I rent a speedboat at the mouth of the Gironde and make for the Spanish coast by sea? If only I could charter an aircraft! Impossible of course. I discarded them—discard is perhaps too strong a word. It suggests a choice, and in fact I had none.

Except one. With the time difference between Washington and France, I did not need to file a story before midnight. That gave me twelve hours, even longer. Why not drive to Spain and phone my story directly from there? It was barely a hundred miles, I had the last of my gas in the champagne bottles. I also had a fair supply of dollars as well as plenty of French currency. And I had a Spanish visa.

It was the only way. And since there was no hope of filing from France, I would be no worse off if I failed to reach Spain.

I crossed the bridge at Hendaye at 7:00 P.M., my eyes tired from peering through the dirty, fly-specked windshield. The motor was burning hot from hours of stopping and starting. On the whole, though, the trip was much easier than the earlier one down to Tours—simply because

halfway along the crowded roads the French police turned
everyone back who didn't have the necessary visa. I had to
queue before we reached the police, but after that I had a
straight run into the checkpoint at the frontier, and then I
was only thirty miles or so from San Sebastián, the nearest
large town in Spain.

I made my way to the biggest hotel, the Reina Christina,
booked a room, then walked up to the concierge. In nine
cases out of ten the concierge is the man who can achieve
the impossible—especially if you flash a few dollar bills
around. But when I told him I wanted to call Washington—
and for around twenty minutes without being disturbed—
even he looked dumbfounded.

"Look," I said desperately. "I know it *can* be done if
someone like you really tries. I know the connections are
always difficult, but can't you have a word with the girl
who operates the switchboard? I'll pay in dollars, and I'll
tell you what, concierge—if you can get me through to
Washington, I'll give you a couple of hundred bucks and
you can tell your girl behind the switchboard that I'll give
her an extra hundred for herself. Is that fair?"

Dollars still talked—especially in miserably impover-
ished Spain. I booked a person-to-person call to Schill
Scotter, the editor, and when I finally got through, two
hours later, he gave almost a yelp of surprise.

"Where the hell are you?"

"San Sebastián, Spain. This morning I helped de Gaulle
to escape. Absolutely exclusive."

"Jesus! I'll get you through to dictation."

"I'm frightened of getting cut off. And anyway I haven't
written the story yet. I haven't had time."

"Don't worry," Schill acted swiftly. I'd never met the editor, but I could tell that he was a man of action. "My secretary's right here. I'm listening in on the extension. Just
start telling her the story in your own words, and we'll lick
any little problems into shape when you've finished."

I spoke for fifteen minutes. "You'll have to polish it," I
said, voice croaking with the effort of talking.

"Terrific!" he cried. "We'll have a brand new slant on

the whole war. Jesus! Is this going to make your name forever."

It sounds crazy—even indecent weighed against the tragedy of France—but I was a newspaperman and I couldn't help feeling a kind of excited glow which only someone in the newspaper business can understand; not only *getting* a scoop—but the even more difficult business of getting the news out when everyone else wanted to hide it. The greatest story in the world has no real value to a newspaperman if you can't get it to your editor.

The concierge had entered into the spirit of the "adventure" and was delighted that I had succeeded. I paid him and his assistant off—and by the time I had settled for the phone call, I had only a few dollars left in my pocket, though I had plenty of French currency, which the hotel would have to accept.

However, the enthusiasm of the concierge made me want to try another "adventure." I was in a neutral country. Why couldn't I try to phone Sonia at her father's home in Rome?

"Why not?" said the concierge, still excited by what we had done. But also making it clear that he could expect further remuneration for any new service he could render me.

"I'm running short of dollars," I said. "Are francs possible?"

"I regret, sir," he spread out his hands in apology.

"But I have no more dollars."

He hesitated, thinking. "This is not a matter for the Spanish authorities," he said. "For them I can exchange French francs and put the call to Italy on your bill, sir, but—well, I am not supposed to do this, sir, you must understand. I'll risk my neck. The new regime in Spain—" he didn't need to elaborate. He wanted a bribe—and he didn't favor French francs, which might be worthless in twenty-four hours.

Finally he explained, "You see, sir, we are all so poor, especially here in the north—many dead—and although I look as though I have a good job, we can only make both ends meet—if monsieur has perhaps a *very* small piece of jewelry I could sell for him, or a gold coin perhaps?"

"I don't wear jewelry," I forgot the irony of my reply. "No rings. And in this weather—but wait—" I had a sudden thought.

I hadn't even been to my room yet, the overnight bag was still in the front hall. And I remembered that I *did* have some jewelry. When Sonia and I set off from Paris, I was wearing the shirt with her cuff links in it.

Her cuff links. Solid gold with four small emeralds, one in the center of each link. The ones Sonia had given me for my birthday, and which I had promised her I would never, never lose.

I had promised. But now, what were the true values we faced in the blue-carpeted entrance of the Hotel Reina Christina? What was more important—a pair of cuff links she or I could replace when peace came, or five minutes of spoken words at a moment in our lives when both of us were beset with anxiety about our immediate future? If a pair of cuff links—wrapped in a promise—could give us the opportunity to tell each of us that we were safe at this climax to the war, surely the price was cheap. And the cuff links *could* be replaced. If we kept them, those words of love and encouragement would *never* be spoken.

There was no choice really. I gave him the number of Sonia's parents' house in Rome. "Person to person," I said, "to the Countess de Feo. And no connection, no pay."

"I will make the connection," he eyed the cuff links greedily. "There may be a delay, so may I suggest that you take the call in your room."

The call came through at two o'clock in the morning. Her words, her voice, her love distorted by distance, the seas separating us, the neutrals from enemies, but still, it was her voice.

"My darling," she cried, "where are you?"

"In *Spain!*"

I told her I was returning to France the following morning, and in the faint voice that somehow seemed washed by the waves that separated us, she told me that she was leaving soon for Rolle. Everything had been fixed up, and if I could go there, she would be waiting for me.

"I'll try," I promised.

"Give me a couple of weeks and I'll be in Switzerland."

"Still love me?" It was a stupid question, but suddenly after all the talking to Washington, I couldn't think of anything new to say.

"Never so much as now. Oh, darling, thank you for phoning. I've been so worried—and now just hearing you, I feel safe and secure. And, darling, I've seen Francesco and he's told me—" At that moment the phone clicked and we were cut off. I rattled the ancient instrument. God! how infuriating. Told me what? Yes or no? Yes to a new life? Together? I banged the instrument in desperation, but I never got the call reconnected.

30

IN THE MONTHS FOLLOWING THE ARMISTICE, it was as though I lived in two countries, the difference was so marked between country life in Douzy and city life in Paris, the hub of occupied France. Several factors enabled me to spend so much time away from Paris. First, there was a dearth of news from Paris. Britain, with the possibility of an invasion, then the blitz, soon replaced France as a news center. Then I was able to travel fairly regularly between Paris and Douzy because the Germans, with typical thoroughness, had improved the telephone system so that not only Oregon could phone me but at times even Washington was able to reach me on my direct line. Finally, now that the war was over, Tommy Tomlinson had put his uniform in mothballs and was in Paris waiting for transport back to America, where he had been appointed foreign editor of the *Globe.* So he was at a loose end—and this could provide me with an extra insurance against being caught away from Paris if a major news story developed.

So I got into the habit of visiting Douzy almost weekly, not only because there I felt less lonely without Sonia, but because I had this feeling that I could give the troubled family—Papa, Grandma, Anna, Guy, and Olivia—a kind of moral support.

Though outwardly unchanged, nothing could disguise the difference in spirit. Our neutral enclave had been invested with the sinister overtones of a prison without bars. There might be no barbed wire, no probing searchlights on

461

squat watchtowers, but once outside our own land, the Germans were everywhere. It had been like this ever since the armistice was signed, when the town crier stood on the village square at Douzy and gave a roll on the drum to summon the villagers.

"*Avis!*" he had cried, the signal for doors to fly open, shutters to be thrown back, windows to be pushed open.

"Today, June twenty-sixth," announced the town crier sonorously, "is a day of national mourning. At eleven everyone will gather at the war memorial. A one-minute silence will unite the nation's homage to the glorious dead of 1914 to 1918, and those no less glorious of 1939 to 1940."

The people dispersed, they had fifteen minutes to change into black, which, as most of them were peasants, meant their Sunday-best clothes.

The next day the swastika flew over the ugly square tower of Douzy church. Signs appeared everywhere. Each empty house bore the warning "Anyone found in an abandoned habitation will be considered a looter and will be liable to capital punishment."

Every night German soldiers policed the winding narrow streets of Douzy to enforce the blackout. When a chink of light showed in the Café des Sports, the first that Monsieur Roland heard was the blast of a whistle. Roland had no idea he was in trouble, until three minutes later—the official time allowed—when a German shot all the glass out of his windows.

"It wasn't the shot that frightened me," Roland moaned later, "but the fact that it took three months to get the panes of glass to mend the window."

Not far from Douzy, at a large field where the corn had been reduced to stubble, fifteen thousand French soldiers spent a miserable three weeks behind barbed wire, with no real shelter and very little food. On my next visit to Douzy they had vanished; I could only hope that with peace they had been sent home, but I never found out what happened to them.

Germans from country areas even tried to help "fellow peasants" in particular as the time for the *vendange* approached. Douzy certainly needed help for the harvesting of the grapes, for there was no way we could expect the usual transit harvesters to travel from the coal mines of Lorraine to Douzy and other champagne vineyards as they had done in the past. And these men and women were experienced by tradition.

"It looks as though we'll have to rely on inexperienced volunteers," said Papa. *"Very* disturbing."

Then one day a German sergeant arrived on a dusty gray motorcycle. His name was Sergeant Bischwihr—a typical Alsace name. According to Papa the man said, "Yes, sir, I come from across the border beyond Colmar." He was with a unit, he explained, which included many men who worked in the vineyards.

"We are about twenty," he said in passable French, "and if you wish, sir, we would like to help out with the harvest. We are bored here—there is nothing to do. Our commandant has given his approval." At first Papa thought it was a great idea.

"He was all for it," said Guy when recounting what had happened, "and to be frank, so was I. I was getting more involved with the vineyard, and the leader seemed a decent enough chap, a vigneron like us. It wasn't *his* fault he'd been dragged into a war any more than poor old Willi's."

"And I have to admit, yes, I *do,*" said Papa, "that the soil—er—brings all people *together.*"

During this brief moment when the German was politely standing twiddling his field cap, fully expecting to be thanked for his offer of help, Olivia walked in. With an almost rueful grin, rather like a boy caught doing something he knows he shouldn't, Guy told me, "She went as white as a sheet, and as soon as she heard the German discussing the prospect of work, she stormed out of the room. I dashed after her, she shouted—yes, shouted, I never heard anything like it—that if just one German worked in the vineyards, she was leaving Douzy forever and would never come back. Phew, Larry! She was tough. And outraged. But that was nothing to what happened next."

Grandma, it transpired, had come into the hall during the brief shouting match in the salon next to the living room. When she opened the door, Olivia burst into tears and cried, "The Germans are in the next room!"

I could imagine the set of Grandma's jaw. And the look of astonishment on the face of the quiet German as she walked in wearing her cycling "uniform" of slacks, green jacket, broad belt, and felt hat—the uniform which was the trademark of La Châtelaine. Guy followed her in, watched, listened, as in her haughtiest voice, Grandma cried to my father, "Who is this creature?"

"A German soldier who—"

"I can see he is a German. But what is he doing soiling this Aubusson carpet?"

The German began to flush, first pink, then slowly turning to puce. "My boots are clean, frau—and I'd thank you to mind your manners."

"He only wanted to help with the *vendange*," Papa tried to explain.

"Don't worry, old woman," the German replied. "If that's all the thanks I get for helping people in a country that's rotten to the core—"

"You may leave my house," said Grandma without losing her dignity. "I would rather lose the entire harvest then let one *Boche* touch one grape on our vines."

"I've heard of you," sneered the German, and how astonishing it was to see the way quiet people can be transformed by anger, aroused by circumstances. "They call you La Châtelaine. As far as I'm concerned you're *une vieille chatte.*"

When Guy told me of the confrontation I said to him laughingly, "She's sure got a temper! Olivia, I mean."

"Doesn't show often," Guy laughed too. "Normally she's very quiet, almost placid."

I wondered, thinking back to the night in the apartment. Did a woman become placid—or unplacid, if that was the word?—because of the influence of her partner? Olivia hadn't been placid when rioting near the Châtelet or in bed afterward. But Guy had settled down to a quiet easy-going life—after the one moment when he gained his demand—and perhaps, like a good wife or lover, Olivia had accommodated her life to Guy's. She couldn't always have been placid by nature. Nor for that matter could Guy. After all, he had gone to bed with Mlle. Lisette, with disastrous results, and yet, didn't he ever want to know what had happened to the child? His child! It seemed as though to Guy it had never existed. And Guy didn't invite confidences. He was never affable when asked leading questions, he just smiled vaguely and made no reply. I tried him now with one.

"She's a great girl," I said. "Do you and Olivia ever plan to—well, get married? You've been together for a helluva long time."

"Never given the matter any thought," he replied. "I suppose if Olivia got bad-tempered and started demanding her 'rights'—or whatever you call them—I'd have to start thinking. Don't know *what* I'd do. But I have a feeling that Olivia might not want to marry *me.*"

Anna came in just as Guy, still in the same vein, asked me, "And what about you and Sonia?"

"Never mind us—you have bigger problems," I turned to Anna. "What are *your* plans?"

"I don't care," she said. "I've decided to stay—and in a way I'm much more worried about Papa. He's working himself into the grave trying to help the French to produce champagne—all for the damn Germans to swill down."

"But what exactly is he doing?" I asked.

Guy shrugged his shoulders. "I dunno. But the commander of the German garrison in Reims and the German champagne führer seem to agree with everything that Papa wants. I suppose it's because Papa keeps production up—and keeps all unrest quiet."

Though I didn't really understand what Papa was doing, I couldn't keep asking, "Is it right for an American—or a Frenchman—to encourage the French to work harder?"

* * *

Some weeks after this I was again visiting Douzy, and this time I was actually there when a German officer arrived and asked to speak to Papa. Though he looked presentable and polite, with none of the swagger which films of Nazi parades had led us to believe was normal, I still found it hard to be civil.

"I'm the son of the house," I said. "My father has just gone out for a walk." I felt a sudden anger at his presence —nothing to do with the poor German, but because I knew that the moment Aubergine had seen the Nazi flag on the car at the bottom of the drive, she must have rushed to warn Anna to stay in the stable. It was so damn demeaning—for Anna to have to hide in our own house.

"May I wait, Herr Astell?" he asked politely.

I couldn't say no, but left him in the uncomfortable salon until Papa arrived a quarter of an hour later. He, too, always panicked on the rare occasions when we were visited by Germans. "There's always the feeling at the back of my mind," he confessed once, "that they've found out about Anna and come to fetch her away."

This time, however, the visit had nothing to do with Anna. The officer, a Captain Deschuer, had come on a very different matter.

"I have been asked by Major Kissling, the commander in Reims, to request"—he hesitated, politely trying to make an order sound more like a request—"that the pyramid at Douzy be closed forthwith and placed under a German guard."

My father jumped up. I'd never seen him so suddenly angry.

"Close Douzy Pyramid! What on earth for? This is American property, I would remind you!"

"I'm sorry, sir, please do not be alarmed," the officer looked more terrified than he looked a symbol of German might. "There is a very good reason."

"It is American property, there can be no good reason, and I refuse to listen to one. I shall telephone to Major Kissling immediately."

"Perhaps, Papa," I tried to soothe him, "we should find out."

"Why, captain?"

"I have the papers here, Herr Astell. Four men were arrested two nights ago in the cellars of Douzy Pyramid. They were Frenchmen who were discovered manufacturing explosives. I regret, Herr Astell, but there is no doubt about it."

"Who are they?"

"I do not know. They are now in jail. The pyramid is too difficult to guard, Herr Astell. If it is locked up, you will be saved much inconvenience."

"And my stocks of champagne! Really, captain, my *champagne.*"

"It will be sealed and remain untouched," the officer promised. "The commander has told me he's given you his word."

In fact the idea of closing off the potential hideout for the few Frenchmen did make sense. Many men were beginning to form a kind of resistance in country areas. Anyone could get lost in those tunnels of Douzy and make all the explosives they wanted without being discovered. But it was a sudden twist to the conversation that made me open my eyes.

"I was planning to use our pyramid to increase production," my father protested—to my astonishment. "It has been arranged with Major Kissling."

"The major regrets," said the captain, "and suggests you might like to do the extra work in the pyramid at Rilly."

"What's all this about?" I asked.

"It's nothing, nothing really. Our pyramid seemed a good place to store champagne when production increased. Really—the Germans are—" my father hesitated to use the word *stupid.*

"Like any army we are bogged down in red tape, Herr Astell. I apologize. But please do understand that the cellars in the pyramid at Rilly are smaller, safer, and next to the village, so that the danger of"—he coughed again—"unauthorized entry is minimal."

He was right. Douzy was a huge pyramid in comparison with Rilly—and who wanted a deep cavern like that just to make champagne for the Germans? It was a showplace rather than a going concern.

The Douzy Pyramid lay between our house and the main railway line linking Reims and Epernay, close to the point at Rilly station where it entered the tunnel under the Montagne de Champagne. Rilly Pyramid lay on the other side of the railway. Each pyramid was so close to the tunnel that they even had underground passages, formed many years ago, leading to platforms on either side of the tunnel, in the days when the champagne was pushed from the cellar to the railway and loaded up by the end of the tunnel fifty yards distant. But the passages had been closed for years.

Some weeks later two curious events happened in quick succession. First the Germans blocked the southern end of the Rilly tunnel. Not at Rilly village, but at the southern end, where it emerged in the sunlight before traveling on the last lap from Reims to Epernay. The entire south face of the exit—exit, that is, if you were traveling southward—was blown up and left a mass of debris. It seemed to be the height of folly. Trains would now have to take a slow circuitous route between the two most important towns in the area. And anyway, if the Germans had blown up the southern end of the tunnel, why not the north end as well?

Two weeks later on a bright moonlit night, a small force of RAF planes flew straight to a pinpoint they had obviously marked exactly on their charts. There they unloaded every bomb in their planes—all of them on the sleepy little village of Rilly. It seemed crazy, even more so when they returned three times to bomb the village again.

"I did have faith in the RAF"—Guy summed up bitterly what everyone thought—"but they must be completely mad to bomb an unimportant village like Rilly."

Not for a long time did it occur to me that the Germans

had deliberately left the north end of the tunnel open, and
that the RAF had been trying unsuccessfully to close the
tunnel by bombing it—obviously to seal it off, but for what?
The pyramids? The tunnel itself? It didn't seem to make
sense.

Then the German army picked up Olivia. I was virtually
alone in the house when it happened. Anna was upstairs,
Papa was in the Rilly cellars, Grandma was out in the
vineyards, while Guy and Olivia had cycled across the valley road to take some eggs from the Home Farm to the
Misses B and B, who still lived in their small cottage on
part of our land.

I had seen Guy and Olivia set off on their bikes—Olivia,
as you might expect, sitting upright and steady, Guy wobbling a bit and laughing as he hit a rut and nearly knocked
into her. I was thinking, How ironic that Grandma's insistence on cycling everywhere for all these years should now
be copied by all of us. We cycled all over the vineyards,
conserving our gas for longer journeys, even though we
had our secret stocks.

Anna almost never went out—which was why she was
upstairs; she was intelligent enough to realize that it was
dangerous even to go into the village of Douzy, especially
as the end of the war had been followed by dozens of sinister promulgations. It was now an offense punishable by
the death penalty to harbor a German refugee—and Anna
was being harbored. I don't think the Germans would have
dared to arrest the other members of the family, all of
them neutral Americans, for hiding a German relative—
but they would certainly arrest Anna. She knew that.

I also had twinges of apprehension when Olivia went
out. She didn't go far, and never into Reims, but she made
regular trips in the countryside. Apart from anything else,
some of the vineyards were quite a distance from our
home. In theory there was no real danger because we had
our own ID cards (and for the family, American passports).
She was "accredited" to the neutral Astells, and though
the countryside was at times crawling with Germans from

a large camp in the hills behind the B and B cottage, where they had a firing range, they didn't seem to interfere. On the other hand, by now—the autumn of 1940—both the German and French attitude to Jews in France was hardening. Many shops displayed signs OUT OF BOUNDS TO JEWS. Anyone asking for a job now had to swear on oath that he or she wasn't a Jew or a Freemason. Olivia, who didn't look particularly Jewish, had never registered as a Jew. Papa had declared firmly, "She's a member of our family. That's the end of it. Her race has nothing to do with anybody, *really.*"

He was right, but we all prayed that it would never come to a showdown.

It did—half an hour or so after she and Guy had left on their bikes. I was in the courtyard when Aubergine fluttered out crying, "Please, sir, Monsieur Guy is on the telephone. He says it's very urgent."

I had no sense of premonition—not really, just the niggling fear that was always present these days at the mention of the word *urgent.* Grabbing the phone, I said, "What's the problem?"

"It's Guy here. Where the hell have you been?"

"I am allowed to go for a walk," I said.

"Cut out the crap, Larry," Guy's voice suddenly warned me that he was teetering on the edge of panic.

"Sorry. What's the trouble?"

"Olivia's gone!"

"What do you mean—*gone?* Where are you?"

"Near the Grand Champagne," he mentioned the name of the large hotel half way up the hillside. "They've taken Olivia away."

"Taken her?"

"For God's sake, do something—"

"But who took her?"

"The fucking Germans, who do you think? They just walked in—and grabbed her and took her away."

"But they can't—"

"There's a damn war on, Larry—and she's Jewish. They even knew her name—who she was!"

"That's impossible."

"It's happened."

"Stay put. I'll come over. It'll only take me a few minutes. Any Germans around?"

"Not too many, that's what makes the whole thing so goddamn mysterious."

"But what exactly *happened?*"

"We decided after we'd dropped the eggs to go and have a drink at the Grand Champagne. A German officer came in—he was expecting us. Or it seemed like that. He was very polite—saluted, heels clicking and all that crap. He didn't even look at my passport closely. All he said was, 'I advise you, Herr Astell, to stay indoors for the moment.' "

"He knew your name?" According to Guy, the German officer turned to Olivia and said, not quite so politely, "Are you Fräulein Jacobsen?"

Then he told her she was wanted for questioning. He clapped his hands, soldiers approached. Some of the hotel staff were peering from behind half-open doors like rabbits, mesmerized. Olivia, it seemed, was suddenly grabbed by two of the German soldiers. She tore her arms free and stood there. Guy, as he told me later, rushed up to put an arm round her shoulder. The German soldiers looked at the officer, who nodded.

"You would be wise to observe your American neutrality, Herr Astell," said the officer.

"Tell your damn goons to take their hands off this girl," shouted Guy, "then we'll talk." The "goons" hesitated.

"The girl is not under arrest," said the officer, obviously trying to prevent a fight with a neutral. "She is only being detained for routine questioning."

"Well, you can detain her another time," shouted Guy. "She's under my protection now—and I know my rights. I'm an American citizen."

The officer, Guy remembers, gave another almost imperceptible nod. Three soldiers grabbed Guy from the back, pinning his arms back from the shoulders until he could feel the pain that almost dislocated his joints. He kicked and struggled to free himself, screaming to Olivia to run for it—an instinctive scream, he knew in his heart there was no way of escape.

Held by the viselike grip of three burly German soldiers, oblivious to Guy's kicks as he struggled to twist himself free, the two other soldiers grabbed Olivia and marched her outside the hotel. Guy could see her being bundled into a large gray truck with flapping canvas roof and sides. A group of soldiers was already sitting in the back and started laughing and shouting as she all but fell inside.

"As soon as she had gone," said Guy, "the soldiers freed my arms, but by then the truck had gone."

I wasted no time on further questions.

"Stay where you are at the Grand Champagne," I suggested. "I'll be round in ten minutes in the Citroën." I set off on the winding road up the hill under which the Rilly tunnel stood. There was something sinister about the whole affair, dozens of unanswered questions. How had the Germans picked Olivia out? There must be dozens of Jewish girls in the Champagne region, but they had even known her *name*. Why should the mighty Wehrmacht send an officer to one specific hotel to meet one neutral American whom they greeted by name, then take away his Jewish girl friend? And what worried me too was the thought that if they could do this to Olivia—know all about her—might not Anna be the next in line for arrest?

The road was virtually free—by which I mean I was stopped only at one checkpoint, where a polite officer saluted me when I showed my pass and waved me on. Then, as the Citroën climbed the hairpin bends leading to the hotel, I had a sudden thought. I would telephone Papa and tell him what had happened—but not from the hotel, there might still be a German sentry around, and I didn't want to look for trouble. Much better to stop first at the cottage where the Misses B and B lived, though Papa had tried to persuade them that they must leave Champagne and return to their apartment in Paris.

I stopped the car outside their trim white cottage, which the Misses B and B had furnished as though they had gone to painstaking trouble to provide a place which exactly reflected their characters. The cottage itself was small and old, and the gate creaked as I pushed it open and strode down the small, crazy paving path with its carefully tended flowers on either side—geraniums with borders of bright blue lobelia—and behind that windows framed in roses. The interior was hidden by white curtains. I was convinced that the living room would have an old-fashioned barometer and—yes!—there was a rocking chair, which I had also expected. It was very clean, and there was the unmistakable odor which goes with sachets of lavender in every drawer.

"I just wanted to use your phone," I asked Miss B, "do you mind?"

"Of course, Larry, you know where it is."

Local calls were much easier now, and I got through to Papa in the new headquarters of the German-run Champagne Bureau at Rilly. Without preamble I told him what had happened to Olivia, adding, "I'm on my way to the Grand Champagne now. As far as I can see, Guy's very lucky he didn't get beaten up."

"There *must* be a mistake," Papa was horrified. "Must be, *yes*. I will go and see Gaertner right away—and the German officer Major Kissling. I have met with him several times. He will help if he can. Yes he *must.*"

As I begged Papa to hurry, he cried, "I'm going right now to see Major Kissling at the Hôtel de Ville. And as you're at the cottage, don't you think you should warn the—er—ladies to return to Paris. Yes, *really*, it's very silly for them to live alone in that small cottage."

Before leaving I said to the Misses B and B, "There's been trouble. Olivia has been arrested by the police."

"Oh dear," said one of them, "she and Guy didn't seem to be in any trouble just a short time ago."

"Well she is—and *you* might be in trouble one day. I don't want to frighten you, but I really think you should prepare to go to Paris."

"Oh, we couldn't do *that*, we couldn't leave the garden," said Miss Brewer, nodding, "not until we've decided to go for good. But," with a smile, "we do keep a couple of suit-cases packed ready."

"You may need them." I was anxious to get away, to see Guy, but there was no way you could ever shorten conver-sation with either of the Misses B and B.

"The only trouble," said Miss Barron, "is that I can't close my suitcase."

"Let me help you," I said desperately. "Then I *must* go."

"It's in here," she said.

Closing Miss Barron's suitcase wasn't difficult. She had left some clothes hanging out. I helped to tuck them in. On top of the dresser was an open American passport with a schoolboyish face staring out. It was poor Jean-Pierre.

"Poor boy," Miss Barron sighed. "Such a short life, and he was so much in love with Anna."

"He never had much chance there," Miss Brewer picked up the passport, eyes bright with unshed tears, as she kissed the photo.

At the gate I paused, remembering the comment that hadn't properly registered. "You say you *saw* Guy and Olivia."

They nodded. "They said they were going to the hotel for a drink."

The thought that anyone had warned the Germans about Olivia was preposterous, so it was almost idly that I asked, as I jumped into my car, "Did you have any other visitors?"

"Only Mlle. Lisette," Miss Barron said. "She often drops in to see us, you know. Her cottage is only a quarter of a mile from us, on your father's property."

I suddenly went ice cold, almost trembling.

"She just missed Guy and Olivia," said Miss Brewer brightly, nodding in emphasis. "They were just leaving, but I know Mademoiselle saw them because she asked where they were going."

Pressing the starter ready to make for the Grand Cham-pagne, I suddenly realized that my forehead was covered in sweat. I could feel a tiny twitch in the corner of my left eye, a trembling like a tiny tic, as awful, impossible thoughts came tracking through my mind. It was too wicked for words—and yet, suddenly on the hillside, looking down on the valley in the sun, I *knew*. I had the deep-rooted conviction that Mlle. Lisette had informed on Olivia.

Was it possible, I asked myself, that our ex-nanny harbored such an intense hatred for our family that she had denounced Olivia to the Germans? It seemed inconceivable, but we weren't in our world any longer, we were in Hitler's world, where it was considered honorable for a son to betray his father, for a daughter to inform on her loving mother. And there were plenty of French who hated Jews.

I decided it was better not to voice my suspicions to Guy, not at this moment anyway, for when I reached the hotel I found him in a terrible state of anger, nerves, a tinge of fear, I couldn't be sure what.

"There's probably a perfectly logical reason for it," I tried to reassure him, lying.

I explained that I had arranged for Papa to phone *me* at the Grand Champagne when he had news.

"But in the meantime," I knew I was being idiotic to advise him, "just relax."

"Relax! God! These god-damn Germans actually grabbed me—that's virtually an arrest. I'm going to the embassy to complain."

"Let's see what Papa says first."

"Papa! Come off it, Larry. Papa can't do a thing. He couldn't even let us keep the Douzy Pyramid open when it was closed for no reason. He's too busy looking after champagne, there's nothing he could do for us—or for Olivia."

But Guy was wrong, completely wrong. Fifteen minutes later Papa was on the phone to me at the hotel, and almost with an air of disbelief I heard him say, "It was a mistake. I've been to Major Kissling and Herr Gaertner. Olivia is waiting at the Hôtel de Ville. You must go and see the major personally and sign for her release. I am very angry at what has happened. Yes, *very*."

"But that's fantastic, Papa!"

After a moment's hesitation he said, "You'd better not

take Guy. He can be very hot-tempered, and after what he's been through—"

So Guy cycled home, and when I reached the Town Hall Olivia was waiting on the steps for me and I drove straight back to Douzy. She was remarkably calm and poised. She told me that she had not been ill-treated in any way but had just been taken in for questioning.

"Thanks to your father, I'm all right," she said calmly, but then, almost fatalistically, she added the chilling thought, "I might not be so lucky the next time. Or Anna too."

"Why Anna?" I asked.

"One of the things they asked me," said Olivia, "was a long string of questions about Anna. They got nothing out of me, but they asked about her all the time."

What puzzled me above everything else was the power that Papa wielded. For there was no doubt that he had intervened and secured Olivia's release. To get a Jewish girl who had been arrested out of the hands of the Germans! It was unheard of. And I also began to wonder, not for the first time, why it had been so comparatively easy to keep Anna in Douzy. Surely if the Germans were anxious to trace a missing national who they believed was in the area, they could have overruled our neutral objections? The occasional German visits of inquiry seemed almost too casual, they were put on for show. It all seemed curious.

Papa was vague in his answers. Only once was he really firm.

"Watch your step, all of you," he said. "Do nothing to provoke the Germans. I've managed to insist on our neutral rights so far, but one false move—one act of provocation—and you could let the Gestapo in. And once *they're* in, then none of us can do anything."

Papa never talked much about his work, but by chance I met someone in the champagne business who had to sit next to me in Boulingrin's because it was so crowded.

"Remember that your father is the president of the syndicate dealing with the Germans," he said. "And the Germans respect him."

"They must do," I said dryly. "But do the French respect him too?"

"The French! Your father's a hero to the French. He's saving hundreds of lives by producing work that *he* has persuaded the Germans to undertake—to construct a series of new cellars linked to each other round the Rilly Pyramid."

"But if the Germans are going to use these cellars, surely my father shouldn't be helping them?" I asked. "Isn't it aiding the enemy?"

"They'll never use them," said my colleague. "There are hundreds of miles of cellars in Champagne. Who wants any more? I tell you, your father is playing it brilliantly. He's got the Germans eating out of his hand—and employing Frenchmen who'd otherwise be sent to labor camps."

It was certainly true, I thought, that Papa's influence had saved Olivia. But now there was Anna—and this worried me even more. I didn't like the way the Germans had questioned Olivia about my sister. Whatever else I did, I must stop the Germans arresting her or—even finding out where she was living.

I suppose it was on this day that I decided there was only one way of trying to get Anna to safety. I must ask Sonia to help. I couldn't phone, I couldn't telegraph, but surely if I went to see her in Switzerland, explained everything, she would be able to pull diplomatic strings.

I decided to return to Paris the next day and then take the first available train to Lausanne. I knew there was a massive delay in railway travel, but I had to get to Switzerland as soon as possible.

31

QUITE APART FROM HELPING ANNA, the prospect of seeing Sonia, of putting my arms around her, of kissing her, of taking her to bed filled me with an intense longing and excitement. At times over the past months I would think of her with a physical desire I could hardly control; and at other moments a mental longing would engulf me, the subtle joy of good times remembered, incidents returning like snapshots—Sonia laughing, Sonia angry, Sonia wistful.

Now though, it was different. There was war, separation, the absurd twist that made us into enemies while still remaining lovers and—friends. Separation was a way of life to millions of people who like us had been torn apart by war. Yet none of this mattered because the growing pains of youth, with their jealousies and torment, had ended; I knew now with a certainty that I would love her forever, and equally important, I knew that she loved me and would forever too. It was strange, thinking back, to realize how we had altered. I had in a modest way succeeded in my chosen profession and that had changed me; but she—twisting this way and that to free herself from the unwelcome parental chains—she had *suffered,* mentally if not physically; now though, it was only a question of waiting, and after the years apart I could face the future.

On the Tuesday Guy rang through to say that a German officer had made yet another routine call to inquire if there was any news of "the missing Frau Frankel."

The shiver of apprehension, as Guy told me on the

phone, emphasizing the urgent need to contact Sonia, gave me a spasm of guilt because I was thinking of us rather than what she could do to help my own sister.

Were the Germans baiting Anna? Did they *know* that Anna was at Douzy, hidden in the stables as soon as anyone saw a German car approach? I couldn't believe it, and yet, why would the Germans bother about one unimportant missing German national—unless the apparently innocent requests masked hidden threats?

I had to get her out of the country because, without realizing it, she needed our help to escape from her own devils. And Sonia presented the only chance. After all, Italy and Germany were allies. Sonia moved in diplomatic circles. Couldn't she persuade someone in Rome to plead her cause to the Germans? Wasn't she—or Francesco—very close to Ciano? Surely one of them could pull strings in high places.

"Maybe Sonia," said Oregon, "but don't you think it's asking quite a lot for her husband to help? After all, you are in love with Francesco's wife."

"Well, Sonia, then," I said defensively. Everyone knew about Sonia and me, but when someone put it into words it always embarrassed me.

I couldn't, of course, warn Sonia. What a hell it was having no international telephones, no cables, no way of contacting each other quickly. But I could see how matters might be arranged. I felt sure that she would be in Rolle now. I would try to take a day off in Switzerland. I could see no dangers in leaving the office. Not only was Oregon there to file on my behalf, but Tommy Tomlinson was still in Paris, hanging around, still waiting for transport back to America. He might have to stay in Paris for weeks before leaving for Portugal, where he hoped to book passage on a neutral ship.

Once I had booked a seat on the train to Switzerland— there were none available for six days—I felt relieved. There was no reason why I shouldn't be in Sonia's arms in a week.

A week! Then I would have to return. I wasn't apprehensive, even though the Germans had allowed no more neutral correspondents into France. But those of us who were already accredited faced no problems—providing we didn't misbehave. There had been no instances of anyone having his press permit revoked.

All the same, I checked with the Ministry of Information, telling the official that I was due for a vacation and wanted to spend it in Switzerland. He examined my papers, checked my dossier, and agreed that I was perfectly entitled to come and go as I wished.

Apart from the danger facing Anna—and the overwhelming desire to see Sonia—I needed a change anyway, for I was heartily sick of Paris. Douzy, with its German troops everywhere, was bad enough, but Paris, with its hypocrisy, was rotten.

In the months following the armistice and the creation of the Vichy government in unoccupied France a profound change had gripped Paris. It was the metamorphosis from apprehension to acceptance.

"It's not a *willing* acceptance of defeat," said Oregon, "but before the war Paris was a nervous, anxious, and downright scared city. Like someone waiting to have all his teeth pulled out. Well, now they've got their dentures and it's turned out not to be so bad."

It was true. The city was more tranquil now than it had been for years.

"Nine out of ten people still hate the Germans," one French friend confided, "but we've got to make the best of a bad job because there's damn little we can do about them. So we have the best time we can and ignore the Germans."

In a way I could sympathize. Even André Gide said after the fall of France, "To come to terms with yesterday's enemy is not cowardice, but wisdom."

Certainly life, though tougher physically, was more relaxed. The Germans had been ordered to maintain a polite presence and cause no problems. There were obviously many hardships, often because everything had to be paid for in occupation marks, which could be changed only at the official rate of twenty francs to the mark. Just before the war, however, the rate had hovered around four francs to the mark. It soon became clear that with this artificial rate of exchange, France was being stripped of sugar, tobacco, coal, clothing, all paid for in occupation marks—and that meant a polite form of looting.

"I like the French description of Germans who pay in occupation marks," chuckled Oregon. "They call them *doryphores.*"

It was one of those catchwords which immediately became used by everyone, for the *doryphore* is a potato beetle which strips the leaves from the fields, leaving the plants dying and the farmers with no crops.

The discomfort was accentuated in other ways. Most of the cars had disappeared. Hundreds had been commandeered by the Germans, though as a neutral my Citroën was safe—even if at times it was difficult to get gas, until I could refill my tank at Douzy. Taxis had virtually vanished. Some ran on gas cylinders, others on contraptions filled with charcoal. But the most popular "taxi" was a Western imitation of an Eastern rickshaw—a kind of wheelchair pulled by a tandem bicycle. At the stations—still crowded with refugees—men had developed a new enterprise: carrying luggage. For forty francs they would carry your trunk. For eighty they would take a cabin trunk, hauling it in an ancient soapbox fitted with two old baby-carriage wheels.

Food was very scarce in Paris. The rations were soon reduced to the barest minimum—twelve ounces of bread a day for people who normally nibbled their *baguettes* even on the way home from the baker's. There was only about twelve ounces of meat a week. Most Parisians were reduced to smoking tobacco concocted from Jerusalem artichokes, nettle leaves, or even lime flowers.

Many of the food shops I had patronized for years—the little shops with stalls in the rue Jacob, the rue de l'Université, and so on—had closed. I noticed that when I did find a shop open, I was one of the very few men patronizing it. Paris had become a woman's city, and time after time I heard the same whispered question, "Heard any news of him?" and almost always it was answered with a shake of the head.

Yet despite the deprivations, the capital was filled with dozens of oases of plenty—and I found this sickening. You could still find all the caviar you wanted at Petrossian's, all the food you could eat at Maxim's, which was by now being run by Herr Horcher, a renowned Berlin restaurateur. The flabby-jowled Albert, however, was still headwaiter, bowing and scraping, though now to Göring instead of to the Astells. All the great couture houses quickly reopened—Lelong, Dior, Balenciaga, Coco Chanel (who made doubly sure of her comforts by becoming the mistress of a high-ranking German officer). Writers and painters carried on as usual—Paul Valéry continued to lecture, Simenon continued to write, Cocteau even advised writers in an article that autumn, "Seize your chance, it's here!"

Famous painters, like Braque, Vlaminck, and Picasso, continued to paint, famous singers, like Yves Montand and Maurice Chevalier, continued to sing. Even the most exclusive brothel in Paris, the "One Two Two"—which theoretically did not permit German clients—was booming, according to Fabienne Jamet, its madame, who admitted cheerfully, "I have never been so happy."

On the other hand, for me there was little work, for there was little news likely to interest American readers. As one French friend said to me, "Killing time is more difficult than killing Germans."

After all, correspondents did need a change of scene, something new to write about, and though there weren't many neutral countries left, there were always stories to be picked up in Switzerland, Spain, Portugal, even Sweden —if you could get there. A new dateline meant a change of pace as well as a welcome break; and our press card allowed us to go to neutral countries and then reenter France without formality. I could hardly wait to get away.

Then the blow fell. It came in a circular from Otto Abetz,

now back in Paris as German ambassador. The warning
was blunt. No foreign correspondents leaving France
would have the automatic right to reenter the country.
"This is not a threat to muzzle the press," explained Abetz
in his signed letter, "but rather a precaution to prevent
correspondents making a quick trip to a neutral country in
order to file material that has not been censored by the
Germans."

It was an old trick, and I could see the reasoning behind
the edict. Especially when the circular added, "The Ministry of Information has no wish to be hard or obstructive.
Anyone who is in good standing has nothing to be afraid of
from the Third Reich." For most correspondents it would
still be possible to get reentry permits, even before leaving
France for a trip abroad.

I had to apply of course—and with Abetz behind this new
move, I wondered whether I would be considered "a correspondent in good standing." I soon discovered the truth
when I made a routine application to the Ministry of Information for an exit permit to visit Switzerland for a week's
vacation, with the understanding that I would return to
my job in Paris as soon as the trip was over.

"There's nothing to stop you leaving France," said the
official, "but permission to return to France if you leave
the country is not granted. If you leave the country, your
press card is annulled."

"But why?"

"We are not required to give reasons," said the official,
insolently throwing my card back on the desk.

"But it's unfair—I haven't done anything wrong. What's
the *reason?*"

"No reasons need to be given." He closed his book with a
bang and after what damn nearly amounted to a sneer ignored me. "If you wish, you can apply to the ambassador's
office."

I knew there could be no successful appeal—not from
Abetz of all people. If I once crossed the frontier to see
Sonia, it would be as though a portcullis had clanged down
behind me.

"We should take it up at the highest level in Washington," said Oregon. "It's monstrous." Then he added, "But why *not* try a direct appeal to Abetz first? I know he hates you—but it's just possible that he doesn't know about what's happening."

I didn't believe this for a moment. At the same time though, knowing the grudge which Abetz did bear against me, I had the feeling that if I applied for an interview he would get a curious satisfaction in watching my reaction. That's exactly what happened.

Sitting at a large desk on which was a picture of Hitler, Abetz was in no mood for small talk. Gone were the pleasantries about trips to the Fatherland, which he had promised me years previously.

"I'm very busy, Astell," he fiddled with a paper knife and had deliberately dropped the "Herr."

"I just wanted to know, Mr. Ambassador," I tried to be polite, "why I can't have a reentry permit."

"Shall we say that this is a privilege reserved for friends of the Third Reich."

"But that's grossly unfair! I am a friend—I am neutral."

"All who are not involved in war are neutral, but," his voice was silky, "some men are less neutral than others. You come into that category."

"That's your final word?"

"It is. Except for one more thing," he put down the paper knife and stared at me with those unblinking, flinty blue eyes which—so long ago it seemed—had scared the hell out of me.

"You asked to go to Switzerland. Alas, perhaps you didn't know, but for the moment your—well, *mistress* I suppose is the right word—is in Rome."

I must have looked startled. "Ah! So you didn't know? Of course not, how could you? We in Germany are better informed than you Americans. I hear that the beautiful *contessa* is neglecting her husband—"

My nerves grated at the cold, supercilious sneer, the insult, compounded by his almost feline gestures, but I kept silent, raging inwardly.

"No, my dear Astell, not for you. Distance, a cynic once told me, makes the heart grow fonder—of someone else. The *contessa*'s regular consort these days is Count Ciano."

And as I choked back the words that I fought not to shout, he added superciliously, "Quite a step up from a newspaperman."

I knew he was lying, of course, but still, I could feel the prick of tears—brought on by anger. Memory plucked at my last encounter with this bastard. I wanted to smash his face in and dammit I *could have done* easily, knocked the stuffing out of that inflated windbag! But the price would have been too tough—for all of us, the family, Sonia, never mind me. I would have gone straight to jail.

"I know how you feel," Abetz almost chuckled as I reached the door. "You'd love to throw the chair at me, wouldn't you? I don't advise it."

With my hand on the knob, I shouted, "Thanks for the help. Remember my last word to you? I'll refresh your memory—*Gefundenshite!*"

"And the same to you," Abetz said softly. "I'll remember that stupid word of yours when we run down your sister —as we surely will do one day. I'm waiting for the moment."

Now I began to panic. I sensed danger ahead, and I knew now I would never be issued with a French pass if I left the country and hoped to return. So it was impossible to go— for if I did go, what would happen to my job? I could hardly expect the *Globe* to let me stay on as their correspondent in Switzerland just because my married girl friend lived there. And quite apart from that, the prospect of leaving the family was unthinkable.

I tried to thrash out the problem with Tommy Tomlinson, leaving nothing out. Especially I emphasized the danger to which Anna and Olivia could be subjected. I had, I told him, finally persuaded them that they must be pre-

pared to part. Olivia herself had told Anna that she would
be mad not to leave France.

"Since you can't get out," said Tommy finally, "I'll go as
your messenger. Makes no difference to me whether I stay
on here until there's a ship available to get back to the
States. I could go to Switzerland—and wait there until I
get the call to go to the port from which I'm sailing."

My heart leaped. I had, almost without realizing it,
hoped for just this to happen.

"She might not be there yet—but she will be soon. Would
you really do this? Don't you agree with me that it's time
we got Anna out?"

"I do. I know that in a way Anna's still American, but
this shit Abetz is gunning for her—or perhaps for you. The
sooner she's out of France and then stateside, the better.
The obvious thing is for me to fill Sonia in with all the details, and then she can travel to France. That shouldn't
present any problems. She's got a diplomatic passport."

"I'll never forget this, Tommy."

"Anna should have bolted months ago. As I see it, when
Sonia gets to Douzy she'll be able to sort things out, make
plans, then go back to Rome and start the ball rolling."

I heard no direct news of Tommy for two weeks, though I
did get a signal from Washington that he had arrived.
Then at eleven one morning the phone rang in the rue du
Sentier and a voice I didn't recognize asked, "Signore Astell, *per favore?*"

"That's me. Who is it speaking?"

"The Italian embassy has just been reopened a week
ago. I have a message for you, sir. I am to let you know that
the Countess de Feo will be visiting Paris the day after tomorrow."

"You know the time? Where she will stay?"

"I am sorry, sir. That is all I have been told in the message. *Buon giorno, signore.*"

Sonia arrived the following Tuesday and was met by a
diplomatic car which took her straight to the rue du

Sentier. I was in my office, sitting on the edge of the desk
talking to Oregon, when she rushed past the door, gave
him a dazzling smile, and without a word threw her arms
round me, hugging me, kissing me, opening her mouth
slightly, crying *"Baciami! Stringimi!"* and only after I had
kissed and hugged her did she gasp, "Sorry, Uncle Oregon!
Oh, darling, I've waited so long for this moment!"

She had never looked more radiant. I caught a glimpse
of gray and pink—her favorite autumn clothes, a Prince of
Wales check jacket and skirt, with the ruffles of a pink
blouse peeping out, framing her neck. I held her away from
me to see her better, the black crocodile shoes, the matching bag, the long, slim legs in sheer silk stockings—getting
increasingly hard to find.

When I had caught my breath, and Oregon had thoughtfully made an exit, I asked her, "Where are you staying?"

"Nowhere. I mean I haven't got a room. I thought—how
about the family flat?"

I shook my head. I was still holding her, running one
hand through the silky black hair, and when I pressed her
close to me, I could feel the giving in her breasts and asked
laughingly, "Still no bra?" She had never worn one.

She shook her head. Her eyes were bright with tears, but
they were signals of happiness renewed.

"Where then?"

"The rue de l'Université. The family flat has been commandeered by the Germans."

"Our apartment! Monsieur Coquelicot! I couldn't ask for
more."

"It's a bit cold at night," I warned her.

"We'll spend all the time in bed keeping warm, making
petites chaises." I had almost forgotten the old French
phrase, used so many times so long ago when we cuddled
each other, the front of one circled round the back of the
other.

"I know we've got to get to Douzy right away," said
Sonia, "and I've already started planning to help Anna,
but, Monsieur Coquelicot, can't we just have this one night
alone—in the old flat—and is Marcel's still running?"

"Of course." My voice was husky. "We'll go home now. We'll do anything you want, anything you say, *anything* to make you happy. And tomorrow we'll go to Douzy."

I held her hand, lacing her long, beautiful fingers in mine. On one finger blazed the engagement ring I had given her when we first hoped to get married.

"Come on, darling," I said, "let's go home!"

I had wondered if distance, war, the last sight of her leaving in the bus would make any difference to our lovemaking. We *had* changed, both of us, we must have done. And yet I need not have worried.

On the way to the flat she told me that Francesco had agreed to an annulment. He had, she said almost shyly, even wished us well, and I wondered if the shyness would persist as we entered our tiny flat again. I wondered whether yesterday's impulsive love, with an ending which we had never been able to forsee, a live-for-today love would change now that we were, so to speak, "engaged," "settled down," secure at least in the knowledge that however long we might have to wait in order to be free, we would one day marry.

I needn't have worried about any shyness, any modesty. She slid off her gray skirt, then her stockings, standing only in her slip—beautiful blue satin, covered with the finest lace.

"Scratch my back!" she whispered as I slid off her slip, and as she stood there naked I scratched her gently between the shoulder blades, my hand slowly scratching downward.

"Don't catch cold," I whispered. "Come into bed." Her feet *were* cold, and as we lay facing each other, kissing, I warmed her feet with mine, pressing them together until, still cold, she bent her legs and cuddled up to me, putting her feet between my legs, rubbing against the insides of my thighs until the cold had vanished. And at the same time kissing, stroking gently, while I aroused her.

"Don't touch *me*," I entreated her. "Or it'll be all over before we start."

"Never mind," she twisted round, facing me, kissed the edge of my ear, then closed her lips on mine, and she was kissing me, biting me, and I was doing the same with a kind of wild frenzy and disregard for anything else in the world. In that moment nothing mattered, not even the actual joy of making love, for we never had time—not that time—to make love properly. We were kissing, fingers and arms grabbing for each other, legs entwined with lost love regained. I gasped, "I can't wait, I just can't," and she cried, "Me too. Do it now!" But I couldn't find her, she was moving with an ecstasy which she couldn't stop, she just couldn't lie still. I tried, but I couldn't. With every movement the rhythm accelerated, her mouth searching for mine, until before I could enter her she gave a gasping cry of, "Oh, Larry!" A cry of pain or pleasure—I couldn't tell which—and one last movement was all I needed so that, before we could actually make real love, both of us suddenly went lax and drained.

"It'll never happen again as long as we live and as long as we love each other," she lay back in bed. "Do you realize that we didn't even make love!"

"Well—we did—in a way."

"We *thought* of each other, but without actually doing anything. It was just all the love locked inside us."

She lit a cigarette, lying back in bed, her head as she used to do in the old days on my right shoulder, one breast crushed against my chest.

"I know I'll never feel anything like it again. It was like," she searched for words, "like an explosion because I didn't *want* it to happen, I wanted you inside me, but there was no power on earth that could have stopped me moving. It was overwhelming, *piercing*—I wanted to scream—I knew I was coming, that I was robbing you, but I couldn't stop, darling, it was beyond me. And then, O God, as I stopped, feeling as though my insides were pulling out of me, I felt the sudden heat of you pouring over me, I knew it was all right."

* * *

There was still an hour or so before dinner, and we opened a bottle of Astell while Sonia outlined how she would try to help Anna. Everything had of course been explained by Tommy—and Sonia felt sure she could help. But she did need to collect all the documentation, the details of Anna's life, as soon as we reached Douzy—things like birth certificate, marriage certificate, American passport numbers, and so on.

"Once I've got something to go on," she said, "I'll get her out before the Germans get her, even if I have to go and see Mussolini personally!"

"Or Ciano?"

"Maybe."

"But since you know him"—I wasn't really jealous—"I hear that he's become a regular dinner date of yours."

"Who on earth told you that?"

"Our friend Abetz."

"Darling Larry, you don't have to be jealous. Galeazzo —yes, that's Ciano's name—is a compulsive womanizer. I *do* have dinner with him occasionally—but no more than that. He's repulsive."

The real problem, as she explained, was that under new decrees Italians were forbidden to export money out of Italy without express permission for each separate journey. This was the sort of thing that applied to almost every country at war. "And I have to get permission from the Valuta Estera—that's the foreign exchange control—because I don't want the Italians to know I've got money already in Switzerland. Otherwise the Fascists might sieze it. Of course I *use* my Swiss money, but I have to make a pretense by obeying the Italian rules and keeping up appearances. And it's virtually impossible to get an export license from the Valuta Estera unless someone pulls strings."

"Like Ciano?"

"Exactly. Not personally, but he orders someone to deal with it for me. But there's another reason, darling. By being friendly to Ciano—no, no, not *too* friendly"—she kissed me—"I may be able to make use of him after I've learned more about Anna. He's a shortcut to power, he's Mussolini's son-in-law, he could get Anna out like that," she snapped her fingers, "if someone could persuade him."

I *wasn't* jealous—I told her—but I caught myself wondering what price a shit like Ciano would demand for the safety of my sister. Wouldn't be cheap, that was for sure.

We decided to have a scratch dinner in the flat. Sonia and Tommy between them had brought half a suitcase filled with food from neutral Switzerland: huge steaks, even some *morilles*—the most wonderful mushrooms in the world—butter, cooking oil, slabs of chocolate, even a two pound chunk of *grana*, the name by which Parmesan is known when it is still so fresh it would be a crime to grate it. When we opened the second bottle of champagne, after she had cooked dinner, we toasted first each other and then, "To Anna and a safe journey." After that we went to bed.

It must have been nearly midnight when there was a banging at the door outside, just below my window.

"It can't be the Germans?" Sonia woke up terrified.

"Hope not. Wait a second—I'll peep out of the window."

No, it was not a German—nor the police. I opened one of the windows to try to get a closer look.

"Good God!" I cried, "it's Oregon! What the hell does he want?" thinking a major story had suddenly broken, and Oregon wanted me to go to the office.

"I couldn't get you on the phone," he shouted. "I've been trying to get through for a couple of hours."

I rang the bell which opened the outside front door and then opened the tiny door to our poppy-colored little flat.

As Oregon walked into the tiny hall I thought I was looking at a ghost. I was horrified. The normally twinkling eyes were dulled, hardly seeing me, the ruddy complexion was gray as ashes, even the fringe of white hair below his bald head was looking an off white or gray.

"What the hell is it?" I whispered. "What's happened?"

"What *is* it, Uncle Oregon?" Sonia had slipped one of my overcoats over her thin nightie.

"Oh! Both of you!" he cried in terrible anguish. "I have to tell you, and yet I daren't. Douzy got through to me at the office when they couldn't get through to you at home."

At the word Douzy I felt suddenly ice cold, knowing instinctively that everything we had feared had come to pass.

"The Germans?" I could feel anger—and fear—swamp the room.

He nodded. "Worse, Larry. It took six hours for your father to get through on the phone to the office."

"*Worse?*"

"The Gestapo. They've arrested Anna and Olivia—both of them."

32

PAINFULLY I PIECED TOGETHER A PICTURE of what had happened, drawing on the memories and experiences of all who were there, then trying to sort out in my mind the relevant facts, put them in a coherent, composite form.

Papa was working in the Rilly Pyramid when Guy, looking out from the window of the observatory, saw Germans at the bottom of the two-mile drive, beyond the tip of the dell. It was mid-afternoon. All previous visits by the Germans had been limited to a car or even a gray motorcycle coming up the drive on some obviously unimportant mission. But this time there were three cars, all black Citroëns with yellow wheels, making their way slowly toward the château. And everyone knew by now what those yellow wheels signified—the Gestapo.

Before anything else Guy shouted, "Anna! The Germans are here! A whole convoy!" Then he ran upstairs to get a better view.

Aubergine was in the living room, and Guy told her to run to fetch Anna and tell Olivia to remain upstairs. They all knew what to do. No one was *really* afraid, the family felt that Papa had some influence whereby the Astells would not be harassed providing they behaved and observed their strict neutrality. Even so, at the first sign of any German, Anna always made her way to the "suite," as she called it, the room arranged over the onetime stables on the opposite side of the courtyard, facing the large double front doors of the château.

The German convoy crunched into the courtyard. Doors opened, slammed. And Guy, who had crossed the landing and was overlooking the courtyard, saw several men looking like army privates. They wore field gray uniforms and carried rifles, through they weren't wearing helmets. But then one of the soldiers sprang to attention, as the third car stopped, and saluted briskly. From each side of the backseat a man climbed out. One look warned Guy that there would be trouble. The one nearest to the house was wearing a peaked cap, jackboots, and breeches, a black leather overcoat with the swastika armband, black gloves and—even though the sun was not shining—that most sinister of all trademarks of the Gestapo, dark glasses.

Out of the other door a man in gray uniform emerged— the official uniform, with its insignia of the Waffen SS, the dreaded elite detachments of the Schutzstaffel—the SS— the army's corps dealing mostly with special police duties. Sometimes the SS and the Gestapo worked together, sometimes they were deadly rivals.

Guy peered down from behind the curtains. At the bottom of the stairs he could hear Aubergine panting with fear—though she couldn't have been more frightened than Guy was. Jean, the butler, appeared at the front door even before anyone pulled the old-fashioned bell. The open window made it easy to hear as Jean nervously stuttered a few remarks. Then in a loud voice the SS man said, "I am Sturmbannführer Rascher of the Waffen SS. I wish to speak to your master or mistress."

"They are both out," stammered Jean, terrified out of his wits. "Monsieur is in the cellars and La Châtelaine," he instinctively used Grandma's nickname, "is out in the vineyards."

The SS man—his rank was the equivalent of a major— looked at the Gestapo man, who slowly pulled off both his black gloves, studied his fingernails, and said only three words in a tone that sent a shiver of fear through Guy's veins.

"Where's the Jewess?"

Stumbling for words, Jean replied, "I don't know. I know—"

Without a split-second warning the Gestapo man, with one swift movement, slapped his black gloves across Jean's face. The old butler almost fell, but with a cry Aubergine ran out to the door and caught him. With a handkerchief pulled out of a sleeve she wiped away a small trickle of blood.

At that moment a voice roared from the far end of the courtyard. It was Grandma, who had entered by the small gate leading from the back to the vineyard and the Home Farm. Looking every inch La Châtelaine, she stalked up to the Gestapo officer, a formidable, even frightening figure in her long green cloak, and raised her stick as though about to hit him over the head. Two German soldiers rushed in and seized the stick. Grandma looked the black-coated man up and down scornfully and then, quite unafraid, said to him, "You German pig! How dare you hit an old man?"

"If you were not an American, I would hit you," the man replied silkily. "On the other hand, why should I bother with an old cow like you, dressed up to look like a lamp shade."

Grandma looked as though she would explode. The soldiers stood alert—not threatening, but ready to act if Grandma provoked the Germans. Villagers—attracted as always when bad news travels fast—gathered by the back gate, including old Pagniez, who was the father of both Aubergine and Gaston, Madame Robert from the Home Farm, and half a dozen others.

The SS major clicked his heels and said almost politely, "We have orders to detain Fräulein Jacobsen. She is liable to punishment for not registering as a Jewess. I must ask you to send for her—or my man will fetch her."

Scorning to reply at first, Grandma took out her own handkerchief and said to Jean, "Go inside and clean up your face."

All this happened in a few seconds, long before Guy had even had time to think of running downstairs. Guy's own fear was that Anna would boil over with anger and run down the stable steps into the courtyard. Before anything could happen, Grandma walked with dignity to the front entrance, stood on the steps, and said firmly, "This is American property and you are not going in—unless you kill me." And to the Gestapo man, she added, "Not even you, you—*petit crotte! Merde.*"

The SS man whispered to the Gestapo man, who said in an almost cheerful voice, yet the tone was that of a man suggesting that he was enjoying a sinister joke, "If the laws of neutrality don't permit us to enter, we must try other methods."

As this was happening Olivia had run across the second floor of the house and joined Guy, whispering, "I'd better go. There'll be trouble if I don't."

"Don't be a fool," Guy whispered. "Not while Grandma is here. They're bluffing. They *can't* come into this house. If you *go,* it'll be all over. Grandma might be able to beat them."

No one, however, realized what the Gestapo would do next. The man snapped his fingers. A soldier brought a megaphone. The Gestapo man said silkily, "Fräulein Jacobsen is wanted for questioning. This is her last chance to come out of the house where she has no right to be. I would remind you that the house might be neutral, but the *land* of France is now under total German authority."

As Olivia started to run down, Guy grabbed her, clamped a hand over her mouth to stifle a cry. "Hold it!" he hissed. "Hold it—and hope."

The Gestapo man waited a minute—certainly no longer —then walked across to the wicker gate leading to the fields at the rear of the courtyard. He pointed.

"You!" he cried. "Who are you?"

"Pagniez, sir." Gaston's father fumbled with his old cap, terrified out of the normal stolid reaction of old age to a lifetime of security.

"Come here!" commanded the Gestapo man. A terrified Pagniez slowly advanced, each step a sinister crunch. From upstairs Guy prepared to run down and, as he told

Olivia, "I must do *something*—though God knows what I can do!"

As everyone watched fascinated, Guy almost tumbled down the stairs. Unceremoniously he pulled Grandma off the front steps and inside the house. "Get inside, Grandma!" he shouted. "This is no place for you."

She was so astounded at being ordered around that she obeyed. The Gestapo man turned to Guy.

"Who are you?" he asked insolently.

"Guy Astell."

"What do you want?"

Pagniez made to move away to the knot of onlookers, which had grown. The Gestapo man shouted, "Stay where you are until I give you permission to move."

"You ask who I am," said Guy, adding with a courage which he admitted he didn't feel, "but who are you? What gives you the right to come barging into a private home and hit an old man?"

"We are German. That is enough. My name is Hoess." He held out a hand—almost as though to taunt Guy.

"No thanks," muttered Guy.

"As you please."

"Then get out of here. This is our home. What do you want anyway?" Guy, knowing perfectly well that the Gestapo were after Olivia, could only try to stall, hoping that Papa might return early—a forlorn hope. Guy knew that Papa never returned early from the office.

"There's a cold breeze," said Hoess. "May I step inside to discuss this matter?"

"Non, jamais!" screamed Grandma from inside the door.

"What do you want?" asked Guy.

"The Jewish girl."

"She's under my father's protection as a worker. Major Kissling has agreed."

"Mr. Astell," said Hoess, still smoothly, "I am in authority. The Jewish girl should have registered by now. She hasn't. She has broken the law. Therefore I am taking her in for questioning—whether you like it or not."

"You're not stepping inside this house. You have no right," said Guy.

"Germany respects the law. And we have no wish to antagonize Americans, who are not our enemies. But the girl has *broken* the law—she is Jewish. And Germany has won the war. Therefore she will come in for questioning. I will demonstrate how. But first—and for the last time—send the Jewess out of the house."

Guy stubbornly shook his head.

"It's your fault," said Hoess almost regretfully, and he suddenly barked out some orders. As Guy tried to intercept, two guards stood in front of him. It was madness, he remembers thinking, this was a scene out of Dante's *Inferno,* a scene etched in his memory—the silky, sinister figure in shining black leather, the black Citroën, poor old Pagniez wringing his hands, looking to Guy for protection and help, Aubergine sniffling, Grandma inside the door bursting to come out and hit someone, while above and still hidden, Olivia must have been standing behind the window, and opposite, in the stables, the hidden figure of Anna watching. And all this set against the white archway leading to the park, the dell, the orchard, the vineyards, every stick and stone of it a haven of peace and love and gentleness into which this black-coated monster had suddenly intruded. During the few seconds when Hoess was talking, Guy, perhaps for the first time in his life, took a look at him—tall, a wisp of nondescript mouse-colored hair behind his cap with its shiny peak, his cold gray eyes, an aquiline nose, not hooked, but narrow with flared nostrils above thin, supercilious lips.

"We'll use this old man to teach the Jews a lesson," said Hoess.

As two soldiers all but gripped Guy from advancing, two more grabbed old Pagniez. What happened then happened so fast it was all over before anyone could prevent it. Pagniez had no chance to struggle, and for the first moment Guy was convinced the old man was going to be shot.

"Don't worry," sneered Hoess. "He's not worth shooting —not for a Jewish bitch. This'll flush her out."

The two soldiers dragged Pagniez across the gravel toward the stable door, above which Anna was hiding. Guy
stood, two soldiers barring his way with crossed rifles.
While Hoess stood barely a couple of yards away, Grandma
stood behind the double front doors of the château. Still
nobody realized what was going to happen. There was
no suggestion of shooting—even the crossed rifles held
against Guy were being used more as a "fence" to prevent
him charging forward. The two Gestapo men who held
Pagniez knew exactly what to do. They forced the old man
against the stable door, which opened inward. Hoess almost languidly uttered one sentence, "The right hand."

Even then nobody realized how the Gestapo men were
going to set "an example." A guard gripped Pagniez's
hand by the wrist, another moved forward to help. They
told him to spread out his hands, fingertips together, almost as though they were going to fingerprint him.

The third man opened the wooden door—inward as
usual. Wide open. Two men gripped Pagniez's right wrist
and hand and pulled him round the edge of the door, then
with a quick movement forced his fingers into the opening
made between the wooden door frame and the door itself
when it was open. Despite his struggle two Gestapo men
held Pagniez's fingers between the gap of the wall and the
hinge formed by the door. Before anyone could see what
was happening, a third man inside the ground floor of the
stables opened the door to its widest, then with all his force
slammed it closed. There was one terrible scream as all
hell erupted. Everything seemed to happen in seconds.
Guy caught a glimpse of the mangled bloody fingertips opposite as Pagniez slumped to the ground. So, with a
scream, did Aubergine. All caution forgotten, Guy charged
the sentries aside, and wresting one rifle he tried to hit
Hoess. He almost missed, but as Guy fell over he at least
managed to hit Hoess full on the thin, bony nose. Another
soldier hit Guy over the head. He remembered a glimpse of
Olivia walking scornfully out of the front door into the
courtyard. But what horrified Guy in the split second before he passed out was the terrible cry of anger and despair

from Anna, running from the stable door and shouting, beating the Gestapo man's chest with her fists—all she had—and shouting like a madman, "Let her go! Let her go, you bastards."

She was flailing her arms wildly. A soldier grabbed her, and then Guy passed out. Luckily for him, though he didn't realize it at the moment, he fell forward on the steps of the house, halfway through the door, where Jean and Grandma pulled him inside. That probably saved Guy from arrest, for he was on neutral ground once he was inside the house.

The others by the back gate could all see, even hear, what happened next. Olivia was handcuffed without ceremony and pushed into the back of a car. Pagniez was left on the ground screaming with pain, tended ineffectually by Aubergine until Madame Robert dashed across the courtyard to help.

It was Madame Robert, the farmer's wife at the Home Farm, who, being more composed than the others, saw a soldier grab Anna from behind and pinion her arms behind her. Somehow Anna managed to lean forward and spit full in the face of the Gestapo man.

For one second Hoess was so astonished he did nothing. Then, with Anna helpless, he hit her across the face with all the strength in his right hand.

"You will pay for this as long as you live," he said softly, and then, with Anna still held tight, he used all his force to tear open the front of her clothes, her blouse, her bra, leaving her breasts naked. He touched them and then shouted, "Let's see the rest."

Anna tried to kick. She never had a chance. Other men gripped her by the ankles. Hoess tore the band round her skirt till it broke, then ripped open the front, leaving her clad only in panties. He ripped them off too, almost with a grin, then riffled one hand through her blond pubic hairs.

"This is an unexpected bonus," he said. "Herr Abetz has been looking for you."

Almost crying with anger, and oblivious to the weal across her face, or the fact that she was standing naked,

Anna screamed, "I am an American citizen. Take your dirty hands off me."

"Silence!" said Hoess. "You know perfectly well, Frau Frankel, that the Reich never—but never—acknowledges the right of a German to change her nationality just to suit herself. You became a German when you married. You stay one until you die. And before long, you will be *hoping* to die."

That was the moment Guy came round—just in time to see his sister naked except for torn silk stockings and shoes. As he screamed and tried to rush out of the door, Hoess said brutally to him, "Better stay where you are, sonny boy, safe in your house. Because if I ever catch you outside this building, God help you. Meanwhile I'm going to enjoy your sister. Yes, I'm going to—what do you Americans call it?—I'm going to lay her. And I think I might try the Jewess as well."

Guy didn't need a psychologist to know that the girls had fallen into the hands of a monster. Like hundreds of his kind, Hoess's warped pleasure lay in finding sexual satisfaction through violence.

Between them, distraught vignerons and women like Madame Robert managed to get La Châtelaine to bed. Even her immense powers of resistance had—for the moment—been shattered by what she had seen, what had happened in front of her. That and the awful agony of wondering what would happen to the girls now. Two hefty men carried her upstairs. She was conscious, but her brain was not working quite properly, she was moaning. There was a skim of froth on her lips, she was muttering French, but the words were unintelligible. Someone gave her a brandy. Guy decided that before anything else he must phone a doctor—even before phoning Papa. Pagniez's right hand was crushed, the bones little more than fragments in a bloody, fleshy pulp. Grandma needed medical help too. Everyone was suffering from shock.

Above everything else Guy dreaded phoning Papa. Trying later to rationalize what he had done, he realized he had phoned the doctor, then Paris, until finally he got through, and only then did he have the courage to know that he could no longer evade telling Papa. And Guy knew, too, that he had to go and see Papa at Rilly himself and break the news to him, man to man.

"It was the worst of all my life," Guy confessed when finally Sonia and I arrived at Douzy. "Papa went deathly pale, he kind of crumpled up. He actually seemed to shrink, to bow under some awful weight. It's a moment I never want to see again as long as I live."

Douzy was like a haunted house by the time we arrived. We had been unable to leave before dawn because of the curfew and didn't reach Douzy until just before lunch. In a selfish way I was grateful for our delay in arriving because it spared us from the initial agonizing shock of that terrible afternoon. By the next day everyone had calmed down, and despair, though never absent, had in part given way to some kind of positive feeling, a desire for action, however ineffective any action could possibly be.

First Papa telephoned Bullitt in Paris, who promised to help—though warning him that it would take time. Papa went to see Major Kissling, the commandant in Reims. But though he was sympathetic and said he would try to find out what had happened, it was, as he admitted to Papa, almost impossible to find out the secrets of the Gestapo.

"Had it been an army problem, I could have helped," he told Papa. "But the Gestapo makes its own laws."

The fundamental problem which faced us was simply that Anna and Olivia had vanished completely. On that afternoon they had been there in the château. From the moment they had been forced—with poor Anna stripped naked—into the black Citroën, they might as well have ceased to exist—a terrible prospect which I refused to consider, but which I couldn't altogether banish from my own haunted thoughts.

We tried everything. Major Kissling gave Papa the address of the Gestapo headquarters in Reims, a dingy building in the rue de Venise, near the old so-called port which served the canal—and in whose waters, it was already ru-

mored, many corpses had been thrown. I went there—
thinking that as I hadn't been involved in the scene, and
that I also had a press card, I might be able to see them,
but I couldn't even get past the sentry at the door.

Poor Papa was heartbroken by the news. Over and over
he repeated the same sentence "I told you not to rock the
boat!" Sometimes he added a curious remark, "I have no
power with the Gestapo," as though to affirm that he *did*
have power with the Wehrmacht. Guy, too, was at his wits'
end—and he had not only lost a sister and a girl friend, he
was now a marked man.

For four days, while we explored every possibility of
finding the girls, Guy wandered round the house like a tormented soul. He didn't shave, he hardly ate, though he
knocked down more than his share of whiskey. Without
knowing what course of action to take, Guy had assumed
that, for the time being anyway, he would be safe if he remained in the château, which was neutral. I felt uneasy.
This arrangement was too simple for a rat like Hoess. That
kind of man didn't just accept a public humiliation and do
nothing about it.

Sure enough, on the fourth day, Papa returned home
from Rilly early, and highly agitated. "Major Kissling has
told me unofficially that the Gestapo have persuaded the
French to take out a warrant for Guy's arrest. When the
paperwork is done they'll probably arrest him. It could be
tomorrow."

"You've got to get out fast," I warned Guy. "You can't
come back to Douzy until the war's over."

"But Papa?" Guy was tormented. "Yes, I'm scared, but I
can't leave Papa. And I might be able to help to find the
girls."

"Don't be a fool," said Grandma almost harshly. "You
must leave now." And to Papa she said, more kindly than I
had ever her talk for a long time, "Don't worry, *mon fils.* I
know you feel bad, but you must have patience. Patience
and planning. You and I and Larry are neutral," she told
my father, "so we can plan. But Guy is a wanted man—and
if he's going to help us, he must be free. Out of France if

necessary. Perhaps, who knows, to make contact with Sonia."

Sonia was also a tower of strength.

"It may take months to find Anna." Sonia wasn't forgetting Olivia, it was only that Anna had been brought up with her, was her oldest friend. "And I don't know how to go about it—but I will. I swear it. And don't look so sad, my beloved," she stroked my cheeks gently, "I know the agony which you're going through. But I, too, am sure she's alive."

"And Olivia?" asked Guy harshly.

"I'm sure we can find her too," said Sonia, "but it's a different problem. Anna is a German or an American citizen. Olivia is French—and Jewish. It must be dealt with by different departments. But you know I'll do all I can, Guy."

In many ways Sonia emerged as the most authoritative voice in the agonizing days that followed—partly of course because she was the only one who might be able to exercise power to secure the girls' release. Grandma could give moral support, but her help was limited to making threatening noises. Sonia was *practical,* but she did say to me, alone in our old bedroom, "I think I ought to get out of Douzy quickly."

I must have looked baffled.

"Darling, I *am*—in theory—an ally of the Germans who took away the girls. If I'm found here—collaborating so to speak with the other side—oh, darling Larry, it's so awful, but if the Gestapo did find me, it would spoil all my chances for getting help in the future."

"But why should they care?" I added bitterly, "They've got what they wanted, the girls."

"No, they haven't got all they wanted," replied Sonia, "they want Guy. Remember what happened—a high-ranking Gestapo officer has been publicly insulted in front of other Germans. The Gestapo will never stand for that. Never."

"But Douzy *is* neutral. You can't get away from that."

"You can. He could be arrested by the ordinary police on an assault charge. And then handed over to the Gestapo.

And Guy must escape quickly. If he once gets into the hands of the Gestapo—after what he's done to them— Larry, I would rather he was dead. I mean it."

Guy came into the room just in time to catch the last part of the sentence and asked, "What's this about me escaping quickly?"

"Sonia's right," I said. "They're out to get you—and being defiant isn't enough. They're in the box seat."

"I give the Germans twenty-four hours to do the paperwork—and then get official permission to have you arrested by the French," said Sonia.

"But I *am* an American!"

"That's precisely the reason for the paperwork. Normally the Gestapo or SS just bash a door down and grab you. But you're neutral. So they're going to make a formal charge through the French."

"When I tell the court—"

"Please, Guy. Don't be so naive. You've seen what they've done to the girls—taken them by force, God knows where. You talk about a court! You'll *never* have a trial. You'd just vanish."

"But if I run away, what about Anna and Olivia? I can't just leave them."

"It's your only chance," I insisted. "If you can get out, escape to Switzerland or wherever, at least you can keep on fighting somehow, getting some action from the government perhaps. But if you're in some stinking prison—"

"Maybe you're right."

"Of course he's right," Grandma had walked into the room. "I'm not going to have a grandson of mine ordered around by those—those *scum.* Understand?"

"There are army patrols by the gates at the bottom of the drive," said Sonia. "You can't just walk out."

"My God! I've got it!" I cried suddenly. "If we act quickly you can get out now—it's your only chance, your last chance before they come to arrest you."

It was the urgency facing us that stimulated me to find a simple solution. We all knew it would be hopeless if Guy just tried to walk out through the main gates. He would have been arrested in a moment. But I said to Guy now, "I think I've found a way."

"How?" he seemed doubtful.

"The Misses B and B are leaving for Paris today. It's all been planned with Papa. They'll take you along."

"Holy cow! You must be mad!" cried Guy. "Those two twittering old maids—are you *trying* to land me in jail?"

"Trust me," I said. Even Sonia looked doubtful.

"But if we're stopped," Guy objected, "if there was a confrontation, they'd just go into a dead faint."

"They're tougher than you think. And you won't be stopped. Listen. I'll explain!"

33

The idea had come to me because I had insisted that the
Misses B and B must get away from their lonely cottage in
the vineyard. They had finally agreed, and the date had
been fixed in advance for one particular reason: understandably the old ladies were frightened of driving all the
way through German-held territory to Paris in their ancient Renault.

Papa had therefore asked Major Kissling to issue them
with specially franked passes, dated for the day they had
chosen. These were, after all, two elderly American ladies,
and they were neutral, so there was nothing unusual in a
request for them to have a safe conduct. Their route had
been chosen, command posts had been alerted to expect
them and to look after them; Kissling had apparently done
this willingly, at a time when the German high command
was doing everything it could to create an atmosphere of
goodwill between America and Germany.

Indeed, vast sums had been spent on propaganda to
make the Americans believe that Hitler's quarrel was
only with Europe. Oregon himself had once told me, as we
puzzled over the way Papa treated the Germans, that a desire to create goodwill toward neutral America was a
major factor contributing to Papa's success; that and the
fact that the Germans were delighted with the increased
production of champagne.

"That's why the Krauts are treating the Misses B and B
as sort of VIPs," I explained. "It's a kind of propaganda ex-

ercise. I'll bet the Germans even arrange to take their photos and distribute them to the press. And some'll probably find their way into the *Chicago Tribune.*"

"But, hell," cried Guy impatiently, "how do I come into the act? They and their worn-out jalopy?" I could see that Guy was rattled, the shock of what had happened to the girls overtaken now by a very real fear—fear combined with an urgent desire for revenge. Guy knew now that if he didn't escape from Hoess, he would never see either of the girls again.

The plan was simple, and it depended entirely on the Misses B and B's Renault, an old model which had not been produced for years. It was an odd machine, considered very snappy in its day, but I was convinced that as it was so outmoded, no German stopping a couple of sedate elderly American ladies would realize that every Renault made in 1931 contained a "secret" compartment.

There was the normal small trunk opening from the rear—and unless anyone stripped the car down, this appeared to be all the luggage space there was. But the Renault of that vintage had a second luggage compartment behind the backseat. If you pulled the back of the bench seat away, it revealed a narrow space in which the spare wheel was housed, together with the jack and other tools. It was narrow, a tight fit, but it might be possible to hide a man in it provided no one sat on the back seat.

I had told the Misses B and B earlier when discussing the route and the passes not to call at the château, really because I thought it more sensible for them not to while (as I thought at the time) Anna was there. But their route down the Mont de Champagne came past the Home Farm before it joined the main road to Paris. I had told the ladies to stop at the farm and pick up a supply of food—eggs, butter, fresh bread, and *saucisse*—which Madame Robert would prepare for them.

"I can't see any problems," I told Guy. "The most important thing is for you to stay alive—to help all of us, wherever you escape to. Alive you may be able to do *something.* Dead or in prison you don't have a chance."

Getting Guy to the Home Farm presented no problem.
The ochre lanes bisecting the vineyards, leading from the
rear of the château, were hidden from any but the most
vigilant German soldiers who might be patrolling the
main entrance to the drive.

"I'll come down as far as the Home Farm," I suggested,
"then return to Douzy and pick up Sonia. Then, after the
Renault has gone ahead, Sonia and I will drive to Paris in
my Citroën. No problems there. We'll drive slowly, follow
you in case of trouble. I don't see what I could do if there *is*
any trouble, but," with an attempt at a smile, "we'll give
you moral support."

"Do you think they'll take us—the Misses B and B?"
asked Guy. "Christ! I'm bloody scared myself, but what
about those two old maids?"

"They'll go along," I promised him. "Remember poor
Jean-Pierre. Those two old girls are not the only ones who
have a debt to settle with the Germans."

Not for the first time I felt that behind the twitterings of
two old maids there was a longing to be loved by us all, perhaps born of a fear that one of them must die before the
other. Even as I was talking to Guy, I was thinking of the
dinner at Douzy when one of the old ladies had talked
about the guinea fowls, and the awful prospect that faced
birds and beasts when dying alone. One of us had thought
then of them as guinea fowls, doomed to die in loneliness.

But behind every man and woman is a second character—one which isn't needed perhaps except in dire peril,
just as a frail old lady can sometimes draw on a greater
store of hidden strength than some stronger woman in the
ultimate crisis of a loved one's death.

Now, for the first time perhaps, the death of Jean-Pierre
had stiffened characters that hadn't needed stiffening beforehand. I was sure that at the prospect of action they
would change, as though they would suddenly produce a
surprise present, kept hidden all these years.

Guy and I both reached the Home Farm unseen and settled down to wait until we heard the warning sound of
their old rattletrap. It arrived around three o'clock, and of

course the ladies were totally unaware of what we hoped they would do. As quickly as I could I outlined the dangers and the plan.

"Guy is a wanted man," I felt I had to warn them. "If you're caught hiding him, you could both go to jail."

It was almost comical really—or would have been had it not been so tragic. The two elderly ladies looked at each other, nodded, and then Miss Barron said almost briskly, "Well, the sooner we start the better. I don't like driving after dark. My eyes, you know."

"I could drive," Miss Brewer offered, nodding with hope.

"Now, Millie, you know you can't tell left from right," adding by way of explanation, "she has a small wart on her left arm. That's the only way she knows left from right."

In a corner of the farmyard we pulled out the backseat and took out all the tools and the spare wheel.

"We'll have to risk a puncture," I rolled the tire out into the yard.

At first I didn't think we could squeeze Guy into the hidden compartment. It was such a tight fit that he had to take off his shoes. By saving that extra inch or two he could just manage to lie on his back, head on a cushion, knees bent, bracing his stockinged feet against the far side of the car. It was going to be a rough ride, and if any official—French or German—by chance pulled away the back cushion of the rear seat, he would arrest the man on sight. With four days of stubble on his chin, Guy looked every inch a wanted man on the run.

"But if there's any real trouble," I said before the Misses B and B set off, "Sonia and I will be driving behind you, and Sonia will create a diversion. I don't know how or if"—I shrugged my shoulders—"but after all, she *is* a friendly ally of the Germans—and the wife of a diplomat. The Germans love kowtowing to authority, titles and all that."

I wanted to give the Renault a good start because Miss Barron drove slowly and I thought I would look conspicuous—suspicious even—if I dawdled on the main road lead-

ing to Paris, but I planned to catch up to them before we
reached Château-Thierry. It wasn't big as big towns go,
but a German garrison was stationed nearby at Condé-en-
Brie, and what little traffic passed through Château-
Thierry would automatically be stopped for identification.

By the time we reached the checkpoint I was perhaps a
hundred yards behind the old ladies and there were no cars
in between us—in fact there was virtually no traffic other
than German cars and trucks. As we reached the town by
the rue l'Hermitte, large signs blocked off the through
road and forced us to drive along the rue de Fere, next to
the château in its beautiful old grounds. A German military policeman held up a red disk on a short stick—how
long it seemed since I had first seen those disks when the
Germans marched into Paris!—and I drew up a few yards
behind the Renault, heart quaking, as one German officer
saluted and asked the old ladies to show their papers.

Gripping Sonia's hand, I had a sudden irreverent
thought: what would happen if Guy suddenly sneezed! A
soldier opened the trunk in the back, gave the suitcases a
cursory look, nodded; the officer saluted, still politely, and
within a couple of minutes the two innocent elderly ladies
received a signal to drive on.

We were equally quick. A one-way detour took us slightly out of our way, but then we were driving along the north
bank of the river Marne, then forked right to join the road
which I knew led to La Ferté and straight on to Paris, only
fifty or sixty miles away.

All went well for the next twenty miles or so. Both cars
passed two smaller checkpoints without problems. We
must have been just about halfway to Paris when we
passed through Meaux. The checkpoint was on the far side
of town, giving us the opportunity to drive slowly behind
the Renault. This time there was a barrier across the road.
It consisted of a striped pole, weighted at one end, so that it
could swing up and down, like those you sometimes see at
frontier posts.

A few yards behind the Renault I watched as a German
officer saluted, and then with a gesture of the hand or-

dered the two women out. At the same time a man in
German soldier's fatigue overalls—not unlike those of a
mechanic—started examining the wheels, opened up the
uniquely shaped hood to examine the engine. A third man
took a look at the interior, even taking out and examining
the rubber mat beneath the foot pedals, before taking a
look at the contents of the glove compartment.

I began to feel the sweat on the palms of my hands. Sonia
clutched my right arm more tightly than before.

"Wait a minute longer," she whispered.

At that moment the officer examined the documents
signed by Major Kissling and with an arrogant gesture,
which seemed to indicate that it was of no value as he was
in charge, threw the piece of paper back onto the front seat
of the car.

"I don't like him," I whispered.

In front of us the officer barked an order to a soldier. The
soldier opened the back of the trunk. Only a thin slip of
plywood separated the suitcases from the doubled-up figure of Guy squeezed behind the cushions. You could have
heard a man breathing behind it. For a moment the soldier
poked round the interior of the small compartment, and
then he took out the hamper. With a gesture of triumph he
opened it, eyes wide with greed at the display of food.

"Look here, Herr Captain!" he cried. "A real storehouse.
The *marché noir.*"

The captain bustled over, barked to the Misses B and B,
"Where did you get this food?"

The Misses B and B fumbled for words.

As I watched the sweat started to trickle down the back
of my neck. The captain shouted, "If there's all this in the
back, there's bound to be more hidden. Strip the car. Take
out the seats."

O God! I thought, there's no way out now.

Suddenly I was desperately afraid. I felt I could hardly
hold in the contents of my bowels, and I felt ashamed. Was
it anything to be ashamed of though? Surely not.

The captain asked again, "Where did you get this food? I
demand to know! You may be neutral Americans, but

when you deal in the French black market you are robbing
German soldiers of their rightful rations."

"It's from a friend," said Miss Barron faintly, looking
desperately at us in the car, for I had told her that we had
planned a diversion. But we had to wait until the very last
second.

It came when Sonia stepped out of the car. I had always
admired the way she could act the part of a diplomat's
wife, and she now turned in a performance that could
never have been bettered.

"Herr Captain!" she called imperiously to the officer. "A
word with you please!"

He looked the apoplectic type, the fussy, arrogant,
jumped-up kind of man who wore his officer status like a
uniform that didn't fit very well. I could see, even by his
gestures, that being an officer was giving him a pleasure
by exercising power over people who couldn't answer back.

For a moment he looked as though he would splutter
with rage, but then—perhaps with an eye on the vision of
beauty which suddenly appeared before him—he softened
visibly, but still growled, "Can't you see I'm busy, Frau?"

"Herr Captain, why am I being delayed?"

And as he spluttered, Sonia added, "Here is my diplomatic permit to travel. I am the wife of the Count de Feo,
one of the chief assistants on the staff of Il Duce."

His eyes popped out at the mention of Mussolini's title,
and with a pathetic attempt to air his spurious Italian, he
cried, *"Signora Contessa! Mille scuse!"*

"An American is giving me a lift to Paris," she said, less
imperiously.

"Please—you can pass, signora. It is my pleasure."

Slimy little creep, I thought, listening. The perfect ass-
licker.

"And the car in front?" asked Sonia.

"Black-market goods," he said pompously. "I am going
to confiscate the lot after I have searched the car."

I could hear every word, even sense the hidden menace. I
licked my lips—dry as a bone. There was no saliva there for

my parched throat. I knew the signs. I was scared stiff—for the Misses B and B and for Guy as much as for myself.

"I don't think so, Herr Captain," said Sonia. "Mr. Astell—you know his champagne by repute of course—gave the ladies in the car ahead of us some produce from his farm. They are rather—" she whispered something and he smiled conspiratorily.

"Ah! I understand, signora. Perhaps we must be understanding to older ladies. One moment, signora."

The peppery self-important captain barked an order. I didn't understand it, but then, with a show of ingratiating gallantry that made my sweat turn to bile, he said, "Of course, signora. If it has been legally acquired I will allow the women to proceed."

He shouted another order.

"Zu befehl, Herr Kapitän," a soldier shouted back. The officer stiffened into a salute, and one of the soldiers put the basket of food back into the car. The captain aired his Italian once more—with a final, *"Buon viaggio, signora."*

We drove straight into Paris without further incident. By prior agreement we had agreed to part as soon as we reached the city proper. The Misses B and B—and Guy— made for the apartment they shared in a modern building in the rue Balny-d'Avricourt round the corner from the Arc de Triomphe. I dropped Sonia at the embassy, knowing that she must leave for Rome as soon as possible.

"But not before tomorrow," I pleaded at the gates. "I know every minute counts, but please, one more night."

"I'll try," she promised. "It does depend on the trains— when I can get a seat."

"And I must go back to the office," I looked at my watch. "Give me a ring later—and I'll fit in with anything you can fix."

"Stringimi!" she cried, "give the embassy staff a treat!"

I did hug her, not caring for anyone else in the world. The Italian word itself excited me, pronounced with the soft *g* the way she murmured *"strinjimi."*

"See you later, beloved."

As usual there was little news at the office—except the personal news about the girls, which I recounted in detail to Oregon.

"It's terrible," he sighed. "And it's the lack of information that's worst of all. It seems incredible that people— Americans dammit—can just disappear, vanish without a trace." Then his irrepressible sense of humor showed through as he chuckled, "I'd have given a year's pay to see Grandma trying to hit the Gestapo shit with her walking stick."

I couldn't help smiling. "Or the moment he said that she looked like a lamp shade!"

"Poor Grandma," Oregon never called her mother, "she never did have much of a dress sense. Odd! I thought all Frenchwomen knew about clothes instinctively."

It was a tiny effort to make each other smile, but neither of us could dispel the ever-recurring emptiness of not knowing. Where, oh where, had those monsters taken my precious sister, Anna, where, oh where, was Guy's Olivia? Had I been able to kill that bastard Hoess to gain their freedom, I would have willingly done it. Whatever the cost. But I couldn't even *see* him. And the girls—my mind kept dwelling on the terrible stories I had already heard of men and women deported to labor camps. I'd already heard rumors of vast concentration camps—one at a place called Dachau—where Jews were being killed by the thousands. Some said they were gassed, others that they were kept as slaves until they could no longer work. Anna was a German-American would surely merit better treatment—but Olivia was different. For all we knew, she was at this very moment being tortured by sadists like Hoess and others.

Not for the first time I thought too of Mlle. Lisette, that evil woman! I *knew* that she had betrayed Olivia—and I thanked God that I hadn't told Guy of my suspicions. But by betraying Olivia she had, even if indirectly, betrayed my own sister, the baby which Mlle. Lisette had brought up, handled in her cot, cuddled in the nursery, helped with her first steps as a toddler. True she had not deliberately betrayed Anna, but this vile woman would have to bear the responsibility for the rest of her life.

"Where are they?" I asked for the fiftieth time. "Where are they?"

"Sounds damned stupid advice," said Oregon, "but our only hope of finding them depends on Sonia—one of our enemies." I hoped it would be a prophetic remark—like knowing that before long another of our enemies would be helping in the search for the girls.

My thoughts were so depressed, so deep, that the jangle of the phone made me jump in my seat. For half a second I nursed the wild hope that the girls might have been freed. Instead, a cold impersonal voice, with a strong Teutonic accent, asked, "Herr Astell?"

"Who is it?" My dashed hopes turned to ice as he replied, "The SS. You are the brother of Herr Guy Astell?"

"I am."

"The French police have issued a warrant for your brother's arrest, but the Gestapo in Reims inform me that he is not there."

"Well," masking my fear with bluster, "what the hell am I supposed to do? Don't you know this is a newspaper office? It's our deadline time. I'm busy."

"I advise you not to be angry—or attempt to terminate this conversation," the voice sounded as silkily offensive as that of Hoess. "Your brother has escaped."

"Bully for him!" I shouted into the receiver.

"Fortunately for you, you do not appear to have been implicated. We have checked at the roadblocks you passed." Then at the next words the fear leaped inside me. "But I notice that your old friend Madamoiselle Barron and her companion have also left today. Do you know where they are?"

"Of course I don't," I lied.

"No matter," he said. "We have the address of their apartment near the Etoile. And," sarcastically, "thank you for your cooperation."

I felt as though my heart had been encased in ice. I could feel it pounding as I told Oregon what had happened.

"We must warn the Misses B and B, there's no place to hide a mouse in their tiny apartment. But maybe Guy can do something—run for it—Chirst! If they catch Guy too we might as well all give ourselves up."

"I'll phone from Yvette's," Oregon made for the elevator. "I'm sure your phone is tapped."

He was back in five minutes. "Got through right away. They're fantastic, those two. They just told me not to worry, they'd arrange everything."

What's more, they did. But as the Misses B and Be recounted the story to me later, it must have been touch and go.

Outside their apartment in the rue Balny-d'Avricourt they had waited until the street was empty, after which they had parted from the Renault. Then the two women went in first to make sure the elevator was on the ground floor. Guy followed, and Miss Barron pressed the sixth-floor button. She remembered that "the elevator took long enough to reach the top of the Empire State Building," before finally it did stop at the sixth floor. The three hurried inside, and Miss Barron threw herself against the door, pushed the safety bolt in a state approaching panic, then tottered toward a chair and sat down.

The other lady seemed to have stronger nerves. She actually remembers that she laughed happily and said, "Who would believe us if we told the Germans that we had smuggled a wanted man past hundreds of guards into Paris and into our apartment?"

It was shortly after this that Oregon managed to telephone them a warning—and it was just in time.

The Misses B and B and Guy were sitting in the living room, with its large leather-backed divan and gay warm colors, when the doorbell rang.

Miss Barron bundled Guy into her bedroom and whispered, "Quick! Take off your clothes and jump into bed. Pretend you are ill. Leave the talking to me."

More than once Guy had reminded Miss Barron of Jean-Pierre, who had been killed shortly after the outbreak of the war and who had in fact been buried at the Père Lachaise cemetery. Jean-Pierre's photograph was on the dresser, and she remembers, "I couldn't help noticing again how much this picture of Jean-Pierre reminded me of poor Guy, now waiting for the Gestapo."

Guy was in bed in seconds. Miss Barron tied a towel round his head—just as she heard Miss Brewer call out, "Where are you, dear? This gentleman wants to see your room." As Miss Barron walked out into the living room, it seemed to her that the piercing glance of the Gestapo agent bored right through her. Two plainclothesmen stood in the doorway. Miss Barron opened the bedroom door for the Gestapo man saying, "You'll have to excuse the mess. We have a patient who is quite ill with intestinal flu. I hope you won't have to disturb him too much."

As the German walked into the big bedroom, she said in what she hoped was a soothing voice, "It's all right, Jean-Pierre, don't try to talk." And turning to the agent added, "This is Jean-Pierre."

"His papers, please," the German asked.

She had kept all Jean-Pierre's papers in a red wallet, which I remembered seeing when she had helped me to close her emergency suitcase. And now she took out his American passport, which she had left on top of the other clothes. The Gestapo man flicked through the papers casually, while Miss Barron thanked God for Guy's unshaven face and also for the fact that the passport, issued some years' back, carried a picture taken when Jean-Pierre was nearer Guy's age.

It seemed to satisfy the German, for he walked back into the living room, asked Miss Barron a few noncommittal questions, and left. Within seconds the two women heard the peal of the next-door bell and then the pale-faced, unshaven face of Guy appeared—in his underclothes, a towel tied round his head.

"Where is Guy now?" I asked when she told me the story.

"I don't know. But not in France. He has his own

friends, and he planned to leave for the unoccupied zone or
for Spain. But I don't know how or where—we thought it
better *not* to know in case the awful Gestapo men took us
to prison and tried to make us tell what we didn't know!"
Miss Barron smiled while Miss Brewer nodded. "But we do
know that he escaped."

"You do? How?"

"Guy had promised he would let me know. The phone
rang and a French voice just said, *'C'est bon.'* Then the unknown voice rang off. It was a code we had arranged."

"You're very brave, both of you," I kissed them gently,
thinking back once again to the twittering concern of the
two old ladies for the guinea fowls.

34

FOR MONTHS we had had no news of either Olivia or Anna. Poor Sonia had tried everything—but she was powerless because she had no starting point from which she could work. Had she known the destination to which one or both of the girls had been sent—a prison, a work camp—she could have tried to do something. But the girls had vanished from the face of the earth. Every attempt to see Hoess of the Gestapo had been brusquely refused. The SS had also refused to meet me. There were no records—none available anyway—for anyone to study, to give anyone a reference point. They might by now both be dead; in fact I was more and more beginning to believe they had been murdered, though a faint spark of hope refused to be dimmed.

And then in the spring of 1941 I learned that Anna was alive—from one of the men I hated and despised most in the world, Otto Abetz.

I had finally requested his office for an appointment; I was determined to apologize and beg for help, for as ambassador to France, he could surely request details from the Gestapo. But I realized that blustering demands would get me nowhere with a man who was very close to Hitler, and that my only hope of succeeding lay in being polite, even servile.

It was a difficult confrontation, for me certainly. As I was ushered into the imposing embassy building in the rue de Grenelle, still with the photo of Hitler on the big polished desk in his study, Abetz looked at me coldly, the periwinkle-blue eyes staring with hostility, but at least he motioned me to sit down in the leather armchair facing him on the opposite side of the desk.

"Well?" he asked coldly.

I swallowed—God! how I hated that man and all he had done to us—and said, with as much politeness as I could muster, "Mr. Ambassador, I know that we don't particularly like each other, but," I hesitated, "well, that's no reason for bad manners. And I've come to apologize. I'm sorry, Herr Abetz. You are an ambassador, and I am a neutral, and I should at least—well, respect the rank and be polite."

His entire face changed, breaking into a smile. It was astounding. It was not a smile of victory, but (or so it seemed) a smile generous to a defeated opponent, an all-is-forgiven kind of smile, though I knew that for me the work was yet to come; I had to beg abjectly for news of my sister.

"My dear Astell," he said, "forget it. I hate to see two—well, intelligent—men fighting over nothing."

Thwarting my marriage to Sonia was hardly "nothing." Neither was the murder of the two Italians years ago. But I let the remark pass.

He rang the bell and gave an order to a man in livery.

"Let's drink a glass of champagne," he said as the man appeared with tray, glasses, ice, and a bottle, which he proceeded to open.

"I'm afraid it's not Astell," apologized Abetz. "But as you know, my boss, Herr von Ribbentrop, the foreign minister, used to be a champagne salesman for Pommery, and he won't let us have any other brand in any of our embassies. He is loyal to his old life, *nein?*"

I looked at him. Young—still in his thirties—his fresh complexioned cheeks looked even healthier than they had ever done, and after a drink I was less hesitant about approaching the subject of Anna. With a swallow, I said, "I wonder if I could ask you a favor, Herr Ambassador?"

"Ask away!" he said magnanimously.

"It's about my sister."

"Your sister? You mean Frau Frankel?"

I nodded. "She was taken away by the Gestapo some weeks ago. We haven't heard a word from her. Since she's done nothing—"

He hesitated, and I was aware of the tiniest touch of cunning as he said, "I had no idea she was missing."

It was a lie, I could feel it in my bones, the split second of hesitation neatly covered up. "I knew," he added, "that she had been told to return to Germany, but—missing! I don't believe it."

"Well—we haven't heard a word," I said bitterly, "not a word. Even the American embassy can't help. The Gestapo picked her up, and for all I know she's dead."

"No, no, I'm sure she's not," he assured me, and this time I *did* believe him. It was queer, one moment scenting a lie, the next moment sensing the truth. With a mounting excitement I suddenly realized that perhaps Abetz actually knew where Anna was, what had happened to her. The way he had emphasized, "I'm *sure* she's not." He *was* sure. I couldn't explain my feelings but I was convinced that this time Abetz was telling the truth.

"Leave it to me," he rose out of his chair, a polite signal that my time was up. "I'll make inquiries—I promise you. Right away. And I'll let you know. Please don't worry. I'm sure your sister is alive."

As I got up, heart tingling with hope, lightened as though I had thrown away a millstone, he came round the edge of the desk and held out a hand.

It was the second time I had shaken hands with him, and I remembered how on the first occasion in the Ritz Hotel I had been ashamed of myself for lacking the moral fiber to refuse the handshake. This time, though, it was different. I still hated his guts, but I needed him—and politeness had paid off this time better than aggression the previous time.

Sure enough I received a summons to the embassy within a week.

"Good news!" he cried almost jovially. "I'm afraid I can't give away information that might be of military importance, but I am glad to assure you that your sister is well."

"Where is she?" I asked, excitement rising.

"She's working—serving the Third Reich. And for that reason I can't say where she is."

"But why not?"

"Please be reasonable, Astell. You must realize that I've gone to a great deal of trouble on your behalf—not the kind of work, either, that an ambassador—" he left the rest of the sentence unsaid.

"I'm grateful, very grateful, sir. Don't think I'm not. It's only that—"

"I know, I know. You must be very worried. I understand your anxiety—and your father's."

"She's not in jail?"

"Of course not," he almost laughed. "You have my word on it. I told you she's working—with some German officers, and in a very worthwhile job. But military secrets are—well—you understand."

"She's happy?"

"She has realized where her duty lies. She's performing a very useful service."

"What's she doing—her actual work, I mean?"

"That I can't say."

"Can I write to her?" I asked. "Or can my father?"

"I don't see why not. But not directly. On the other hand, if you let me have letters for her, I can see no reason why I shouldn't arrange for them to be delivered to your sister."

"And letters from her?"

"That's a military problem, I'm afraid. I'll try, but Germans aren't really allowed to write abroad, as you know, except to a military post office."

I did know that. But at least Anna was alive! Where, we did not know. But at least Abetz, in return for a groveling apology, had tried his best, and I was convinced that he was sure Anna was alive. For the first time since we had met I felt a little more disposed to him as I rushed to telephone Papa with the good news.

That piece of good news had helped to make a new man of my father. But in the spring of 1941 he had more good news. One day, unannounced, Gaston just walked into Douzy and reported for work.

"Well, *really*, this is *most* unusual," exclaimed a delighted Papa. "I thought you were in North Africa."

It transpired that with the armistice, soldiers who had sick or dependent relatives had the opportunity from time to time to return to civilian life. Gaston, by ill chance, came into that category because his father, old Pagniez, had been so brutally tortured by Hoess of the Gestapo that he was too crippled to work. Gaston, therefore, was able to argue that he was needed to help his family on the land. It took months for the papers to be processed, but finally he returned home. He looked leaner, even tougher than I had remembered him when he was our family chauffeur. His fair hair had been cut short, he was tanned, the face had more resolution to it than in the past. From my father's point of view his arrival was a blessing. We were short-handed, Gaston had been born and bred in the vineyards and soon took the place of Guy.

Grandma was also delighted to see him, though she issued a stern warning when first they met. She was still as ramrod straight as ever, she still looked "like a scarecrow," as someone once said, but she ran the vineyards like the professional she was.

"And I'm also a professional hater of Germans," she declared when Gaston reported for duty. "And I always will be. On the other hand, we need men—men who will work as well as hate the Germans. But don't let what happened to your father make you so bitter that your anger will run away with you. Don't do anything that could get you into trouble. Wait—and the moment for retribution will come."

"I am proud to be working again for La Châtelaine," said Gaston a trifle theatrically. "And one day I am going to kill Hoess. But I am not going to hang for it, madame. I shall wait."

Later on as we talked he said to me with a smile, "She's pure *sauce tartare,* La Châtelaine. And it does one good to see someone hate the Germans as much as she does."

"I was sorry about your father," I said awkwardly—

partly because I *was* sorry, but also because I could never
be sure whether Gaston knew that I knew about Mama.

"I know," he said. "I suppose we can all be thankful that
he's alive. And that your sister's alive too, it was wonderful to learn that. When I think of poor Miss Jacobsen—"

It was strange how, after months of inactivity, when
nothing seemed to have happened, everything was bustle
and movement. Soon after Gaston arrived, two unexpected
letters reached us from America. One was for me, one was
for Papa. Both had been sent to Paris in the diplomatic
pouch. It was the first news for months, even though in
theory letters could be posted in America and delivered in
France. The only thing was—they never arrived. We knew
that Mama had written many times, but somewhere along
the line letters just disappeared.

I didn't read all of Mama's letter to Papa, only the bits
he wanted me to read. But it was enough to confirm that
she had written regularly and that it was Tommy Tomlinson who had arranged for them to be sent via the bag. She
asked after us, she was desperate for news of Anna, but
what did astonish me was the information that Guy had
actually met her in New York.

Guy in America! I not only felt a surge of relief but a
shaft of envy. Life was so depressing in France. Sonia was
so far away. Douzy was so empty and sad that suddenly I
found myself envying Guy, imagining him strolling along
Fifth Avenue in the special crisp spring weather. In her
letter Mama simply wrote, "Guy visited New York for a
few days and came to see me, but said he was just passing
through and wasn't sure where he was going. How very
odd!"

I was astounded. We had been able to let Mama know all
the latest family news through Sonia, who wrote regularly
from Switzerland, from one neutral country to another—
but the relief that Guy was safe after months when we
hadn't heard a word from him was tinged also with speculation. What was he up to? Where was he going? I got my
first hint from Tommy Tomlinson, for my second letter

came from him. As a journalist, he was not only accustomed to writing factual letters, but he didn't like leaving loose ends. So he wrote (without mentioning Guy's name) that "our friend has already left for Spain and then intends to look up old friends with whom he's lost touch"—the inference being that those "old friends" could be only Anna and Olivia—which in turn meant that Guy must be planning to return to France, where there was a warrant out for his arrest. He must be crazy!

There was also a long, typed screed from Tommy giving me the latest news from Sonia, who could, of course, write openly. Again, just in case the diplomatic bag was mislaid, Tommy had called her Poppy—not a bad *nom de guerre* bearing in mind my name Monsieur Coquelicot.

She had, she confessed, got nowhere. She had met the leaders in the Fascist party. "I have even been out for dinner several times with Count Ciano," she wrote to Tommy and said that Ciano had personally promised to do anything he could, but that she must have a starting point. Once she knew what had happened to the girls, where they were, then the rest—as she put it—would only be a matter of asking Ciano to help. And then, as she wrote to Tommy, "I'll do everything I can."

I hated that phrase, "I'll do anything I can." I wasn't jealous—dammit, I had no right to be—but Ciano was known as a double-dyed shit who invariably demanded payment for all favors granted. And I knew that he expected payment to be made in a horizontal position.

Poor Sonia, I thought, wasn't it ironic that half her young and beautiful life had been torn apart by a ruthless man who had needed her help to save him from jail—in that case her father; and now here she was again, history repeating itself, forced to beg help from another ruthless man to save someone else from jail—in this case my sister.

Tommy had also visited Mama in her new apartment on his first visit to New York, and he wrote, "Your mother has never looked more beautiful—or younger. Seems incredible, but despite the problems you all face, she's taken on a new lease of life. Don't misunderstand me. About the rest of the family she's doing everything she can to help—pulling strings in high places and so on—but it's not what she *does,* it's the bevy of young men I met who surrounded her on the two visits I made to New York! Without making an effort she attracts men like flies round a honey pot. Honey's the word! She's a real beauty. America sure agrees with her."

Rereading the letter I had a sudden picture of Mama—and of course the photo of her and Gaston. How infuriating really that a picture which had nothing to do with me, had never been part of my business, had caused nobody any harm, should refuse to be forgotten. That each time I saw Mama, I saw him. And now—a bevy of young men surrounding Mama. Did that mean a new young man in her life? Papa forgotten? Or at best ignored, Mama still searching for youth, if once removed? I would have laughed off any such suspicions but for the fact that Tommy was not a man who weighed words lightly. I had the feeling that he had penned the lines thoughtfully, paying as much attention to what was written between them as in the lines themselves.

All in all, the letter that I had opened with such anticipated excitement left a sour taste when I put it back in the envelope. Guy behaving like an idiot by planning to return to France. As though we didn't face enough troubles! Mama enjoying herself! The insensitivity of it seemed somehow to be in bad taste, unworthy of her, though of course she could not spend the rest of our war knitting socks in New York.

And then there was beloved Sonia. I trusted her, I adored her, and at long last I had the sure feeling that one day we would be married. But who is strong enough to marshal wild thoughts? Of course my thoughts were wild, she would never do anything that would harm our love. And yet the nagging thought persisted: Sonia loved us—Anna as well as me. Given the opportunity to save Anna, what price would she be prepared to pay?

* * *

At least with spring on the way Papa had less time to
dwell on the fate of Anna, for though Grandma's work in
the vineyard was less arduous at that time of the year, this
was the moment when Papa came into his own, during the
process of the *cuvée*.

It gave a curious sense of permanence to realize that
though Champagne was now ruled by different masters,
nothing had really changed since Dom Pérignon found out
how to put the bubbles into white wine. And now the Germans queued as avidly as the French had done to hear and
see the mysteries of the *cuvée* explained, only now of
course, the audiences were hand picked. They included officers and men from the region opposite Alsace who were
experts at producing white wine, and there was therefore
no rancor on these occasions. The processes leading up to
the *cuvée* were magical, depending on the whims, taste,
and knowledge of one man, in the case of Astell champagne, of Papa. It was an individual achievement as personal as painting a picture, for he could literally change
the taste of the grapes he had grown.

I visited Douzy as often as I could that spring, for Papa
needed all the help—moral and physical—that I could offer
him. Gaston was invaluable of course; I never realized how
much the family depended on him, a wry situation, I reflected, thinking of the photo, long torn up, of Gaston and
Mama looking so happy. Gaston wasn't an expert in the
celliers, but he had been born and bred in the vineyards,
and his general knowledge and aptitude were considerable. And my father, who had always liked him, soon began to use him as a replacement for Guy.

On this day a score of officers had assembled in the
cellier, the large area of outhouses, including the big wine-
press, above ground, at the far end of the Home Farm, and
from which there were passages leading to underground
cellars, even all the way to the most famous cellar of all,
the Douzy Pyramid, now blocked off by the Germans until
the end of the war.

Papa had several stock speeches which he used to explain highly technical terms, and though he tried his best

now, the enjoyment of similar past occasions in the days before Anna disappeared were sadly lacking. He tried of course. He introduced his *chef de cave* and other experienced men—and as I looked at the German officers, for all the world like a group of interested businessmen, I found myself thinking, Is it *possible* these men could treat Anna as they have done?

But of course they weren't to blame. It was almost unfair to think ill of them, to compare the polite Major Kissling, whom I was watching, with the evil Hoess (who of course wouldn't have been allowed in the building).

"This is the moment, yes the real *moment*," said Papa indulgently, "when we can watch the profit emerge out of thin air by adding the bubbles which come for free."

There was a polite titter from the captive audience. "Since the *vendange*, the grape juice has been stored in forty-four-gallon casks over there," he pointed to an adjacent building, "and considering that we like to store our champagne in cellars at a steady temperature of ten degrees all year round, it may seem odd that we have just finished boiling the juice."

Boiling was the technical term used during the winter, when the casks were stored above ground—in the *celliers* as apart from the *caves*—and maintained at a constant temperature of nearly twenty degrees centrigrade, causing the first fermentation, usually ending in the spring.

"After the turn of the year the *cellier* windows are opened," explained Papa, "the heat is turned off, and the cold causes a precipitation which throws off the impurities, so that we have been able to draw off the clear wine. Now we come to the preparation for the *cuvée.*"

It was a complicated business, but simplified it meant what Papa called "composing" a champagne to his taste. As always each cask which the Germans watched had been labeled with the name of its special vineyard. The twenty or so wines from different vineyards were now married to produce a balanced individual wine, as nearly as possible similar to that of previous years.

"People like champagne to taste the same every Christ-

mas," explained Papa, "and how we achieve that—our own
formula—is our most seriously guarded secret."

"You haven't mixed in any black grapes?" asked one
knowledgeable German.

Papa shook his head. "We will for some blends, but here
we're blending our specialty—we're very proud of our
blanc de blancs, and for that we use only white grapes,
even if they come from different vineyards. And now I
have to add the bubbles."

The remark was always greeted with another ripple of
polite laughter, though in fact the only additives consisted
of a small quantity of cane sugar and fermenting agents.

"Now we bottle it," explained Papa, "and put it to rest
in deep cellars—but of course it's not ready to drink for at
least a year, even many years if we decide to keep it."

During this period, he explained, the fermenting agents
would react slowly on the sugar, causing a second fermentation. The sugar was transformed into alcohol and car-
bonic gas, which was imprisoned in each bottle. "And
that's why"—he picked up an empty champagne bottle and
put his hand into the hollow at its base—"champagne bottles are never flat at the bottom. They have to be strength-
ened like this or the fermenting bubbles would blow the
bottom off every bottle."

I always had the feeling on these conducted tours—and
God! how many thousands I had been to as a kid—that
many of the people thought the champagne would now be
ready to drink. But the incredible fact is that every bottle,
after it was aged, would have to be opened once more. Before this the bottles had been stored, neck tilted downward, during which a second fermentation had formed, a
deposit which had to be cleared from the neck of the bottle.

"This is called *dégorgement*," explained Papa. "It's a
highly skilled operation. A man has to remove the sediment by withdrawing the cork, wasting as little of the
froth and wine as possible, then topping the bottle up with
a few drops of reserve wine and sugar. I'm told that someone is inventing a process in which the sediment in the
neck can be instantly frozen and automatically taken out

in seconds before the bottle is recorked and held in place with a wire cage. That'll be a wonderful improvement—if it ever comes."

After the morning "lecture" Major Kissling—who I had to admit was very civilized, very polite, and very helpful—asked if he could take a look at the Rilly Pyramid. Papa was delighted.

"Come along too, Larry," he urged me, and I felt that he really wanted me to come, needed me.

"Sure," I agreed. "I won't guarantee that I'll like it after our pyramid, but—"

"I'm sorry about that," said Major Kissling to me, "but you know, Mr. Astell, the trouble is that if the"—he hesitated—"the wrong authorities arrest people suspected of anti-German activity, then often we can't even discover what has happened to them. By closing Douzy, I have tried to protect your father from trouble. If, for instance, any resistance elements use Douzy, it would embarrass your father." That was very true—and thoughtful.

We walked toward Rilly Pyramid. To get there we had to pass through Rilly—once a picturesque village with its trim station under the lee of the Mont de Champagne, where the tunnel started, but now disfigured by different mountains—gray, dusty hillocks of rubble pockmarked with the skeletal outlines of once-beautiful houses, sticking out like rotten teeth.

"All this," I said bitterly, picking my way through the debris, "is the result of *British* bombing by the RAF."

"They are crazy," Major Kissling agreed. "The war is over. We are at peace."

I wasn't so sure of *that,* but even so, each time I visited Rilly I became more and more angry at the futility of the RAF bombing raids on a small, unimportant village which could not possibly have any strategic value.

The Rilly Pyramid was much smaller than ours, but of much the same structure: a tall, narrow, white underground pyramid, with steps and small terraces or balconies hewn into the white chalk. Chains and pulleys hoisted up wine from the ground floor to the cellar passages above, some of them visible on the sides, like black holes because of the lack of light. "Too much light is bad for storing champagne," my father was always fond of explaining.

The place seemed busy. Some men were trundling cases, the contents of which I could not see. Rilly *did* produce an excellent local wine, but not in any quantity, and of nothing like the same standard as ours, and I had always assumed that the pyramid was never really used for practical purposes as it was in Douzy. But everything seemed very busy. Yet what was everyone *doing?* I watched from a balcony as Papa pointed out to Major Kissling one large hole, darker and bigger than the rest, perhaps fifty feet from the apex of the pyramid, where the small rectangular light shone from the sky above. Steps led up to the hole in the wall. Papa was explaining, "That's an old passage which leads directly to the railway line, almost at the beginning of the tunnel."

"But it's not used?" asked the major.

Papa shook his head. "Not for years and years—and the same thing applies to the Douzy Pyramid. Someone had an idea years ago that they might be able to take advantage—yes, *advantage* is the word, I think—of the proximity of the railway to both pyramids, and load champagne straight onto goods trains from this tunnel and the one like it at Douzy."

"But nothing came of it?" asked Kissling.

Papa shook his head again. "Not worth it. We had by then installed trucks, rather like small streetcars, running on rails directly to our headquarters. Both tunnels were blocked up near the railway—except for small emergency exit doors."

On one side of the Rilly Pyramid gangs of men were actually hewing new passages to link up with other cellars, some perhaps half a mile away. It seemed crazy. There were around fifty pyramids on the outskirts of Reims alone, to say nothing of hundreds of miles of cellars. And with the biggest champagne drinkers in the world cut off from supplies, there seemed no point in digging out new corridors or new cellars. I almost blurted out as much, but then Major Kissling, watching the workers, said enthusiastically, "Excellent, Herr Astell! Thank you for the tour." He clicked his heels and smiled to me politely, but didn't offer a hand to be shaken, realizing perhaps that he didn't want to risk rebuff.

"But *why,* Papa?" I asked when he had gone. "It seems ridiculous."

"Don't worry," Papa said testily. "You don't understand. My job is to look after the French—and keep the Germans quiet."

I didn't like to argue. I wasn't sure that efforts to keep the French happy *should* be made if the price was making the Germans happier. Wasn't it more honest to make the Germans *less* happy? Gaston, for instance, was already talking—still in a vague way—of starting up a kind of resistance movement. Preliminary plans had been formed. He talked vaguely about blowing up bridges and derailing trains later on.

"One day the people of France will rise up and fight against the Germans," he insisted. "De Gaulle has given us the lead. And in the south—where the Maquis is already operating—the French have formed teams to rescue British fliers, get them home via Spain. And at the same time, to make life hell for the German occupation forces."

"And you plan to do the same?" We were walking around the lake quietly on a cold day, the grass stiff with rime, but the sky a blue canopy above.

"One day—but not yet. We're not strong enough. And anyway your father is doing his bit to help the French."

"But not by blowing up buildings?" I laughed.

"You don't realize, but by using the Germans he's got the same objectives as we have. The week before last your father actually saved three men whose deportation orders had been signed and processed. They were due to leave the next day for some terrible camp. Instead they're now working in the Rilly Pyramid. Your father arranged it. He's a hero."

That *was* good news—and yet, unfair thoughts niggled

me. Papa was no collaborationist of course, yet would *any* German in authority—even an apparently agreeable man like Kissling—would *anyone* let a Franco-American champagne shipper cancel deportation orders, dig unnecessary tunnels, without asking for *something* in return? The Germans didn't operate that way. They were too tough.

"I can see your point of view," said Gaston, "but it's got one flaw. The Germans are *not* asking for anything in return except more champagne for the Germans to guzzle."

It was some time after this when, for no reason I can explain, I suddenly revealed for the first time to anyone my feelings about Mlle. Lisette. Thinking it over, I *do* know why I spoke about her. I had cycled up to the cottage once used by the Misses B and B (now settled in Paris) on a routine check to see that the building had not been vandalized or occupied by the Germans, who were always threatening to seize empty houses. From the hills above I could hear the sound of firing from the hidden range where Germans practiced pistol shooting.

Cycling down the hill toward the hotel where Olivia had first been arrested, I saw Mlle. Lisette in the garden of her neighboring cottage. I hadn't set eyes on her since that day, and for a moment I thought of marching into her garden and confronting her—with violence if necessary to extráct a confession—but stopped myself in time. That would do no good. Indeed if she had admitted anything and I had beat her up, I would be the next Astell in trouble, and that was the last thing I wanted, especially as I couldn't be *sure* she had informed against Olivia.

Perhaps this was why I told Gaston, to unburden my soul of suspicion.

"It was all too pat, the way the Germans seized her that day," I explained. "I can never prove that Lisette did it— but how else could the Germans have found out about her—and been there just at the very moment when Olivia was there?"

"Thank God you didn't do anything—it's much more important to keep suspicious people around as possible con-

tacts in the future. You understand? I don't say you will
ever need Mlle. Lisette, but if she was out of circulation,
she could *never* help. If she's around, she *might* be able to.
There's one sure thing—you can never get a confession
from a dead man."

"You make it sound very—well, technical."

Gaston hesitated. "In a way, you being neutral, I
shouldn't tell you, but I don't see why I should hold anything back from you. I came back from Africa with a lot of
troops who were specially trained just outside Switzerland
in sabotage and so on. The day will come when we will
form a real French Resistance, Not in this sleepy village
perhaps, but somewhere. It's too early yet—just as it would
be too early to confront Mlle. Lisette. But some of us are
laying the foundations for the future. And keeping tabs on
the Lisettes of this world will help. They might be much
more useful alive in the future than dead now."

"Be careful," I warned him. "And of course, I haven't
heard a word you've said."

"I'll make a few inquiries though, all the same," Gaston
promised me. "Not me personally, others." And then, as I
was about to go, he asked me an odd question.

"Does La Châtelaine have any suspicions about Lisette?"

Grandma! I was astounded—also in a way at the use of
her nickname again. "Good Lord, no. What on earth made
you think she'd possibly know?"

"Just a question. La Châtelaine gets around much more
than you think."

Around the end of April I was sitting in the conservatory, with its commanding view of the dell stretching to
the entrance gates in the distance, when I saw a car draw
up. Someone leaned out and spoke to the sentry. I saw the
sentry salute, then the car drove toward the house.

It was a black Citroën.

"It must be the Gestapo," I cried to Grandma, who was
sitting with me, cutting up pieces of old material to stitch

into a patchwork quilt, just as Mama used to do before she left for America.

Grandma got up angrily.

"Are you sure? Don't let him in, whoever he is. No German has any right to come into our house. Be firm, Larry."

"I will, I promise," she had no need to persuade me.

"They are vultures, the lot of them. Where's your father?"

"At Rilly."

"Be firm. I'm going upstairs—I just can't even bear to set eyes on any of them."

Halfway up the drive I saw the telltale yellow wheels of the Citroën. It *was* the Gestapo. I only hoped—for the sake of all of us—that it wasn't Hoess, because I don't think I could have kept my hands from his throat. Yet violence could only lead to arrest—and one more Astell out of circulation. On the other hand, they couldn't arrest me for words spoken in my own home, for refusing them admittance. And I didn't need La Châtelaine to urge me on.

I called for Jean. It was pitiful to see how the war had aged him. He was years younger than Grandma, but it wasn't rheumatic legs or rheumy eyes that painted him with age, it was the spirit. The war had knocked the stuffing out of him—perhaps for him encapsulated in that terrible few minutes when Hoess had tortured Pagniez and "Mademoiselle Anna" had been arrested.

"Whatever you do, Jean," I ordered him, "don't allow any of the Gestapo into this house."

"But, sir, if they use force—" he began.

"That's different. I don't expect you to knock him down." Jean joined me in an attempt at a smile. "But—if anyone asks to speak to me, tell them to wait outside while you come to see me. And close the door. You know, Jean, there's not much I can do to help people like you—but at least we'll show who's the boss in our own home."

I could hear the car rumbling along the drive, past Grandma's cutting bed, until it finally crunched to a stop on the gravel terrace. By then, of course, I couldn't see if it were Hoess. I heard voices, an indistinct blur, then Jean came in. Despite his clean white jacket, the small silver salver he carried almost as a badge of office, he looked more agitated than I had ever seen him.

"Good God, man, you look as though you've seen a ghost!" I was vaguely irritated because he didn't look afraid, more astounded. "Is it the Gestapo?"

He nodded.

"You kept them out?"

"There's only one man, sir, alone."

"Don't let him in. Keep the bastard waiting. I'll see him outside."

"But, sir," at first Jean couldn't force the words out, then he blurted, "it's no ordinary Gestapo man, sir. It's—you'll never believe this, sir—it's Monsieur Willi, Miss Anna's husband."

I, too, must have looked as though I had seen a ghost, for Jean said tentatively, "Are you all right, monsieur? Shall I—?"

Willi! *Willi* of all people! The man I had last seen with his face smashed in, telling me he was going to join the German army. The *army*—yes, that was one way out of the mess he was in. But the Gestapo, the scum of Germany—the same force of brutes who had taken away my sister, Willi's wife.

"By Christ!" I said savagely to myself as I strode to the door, "you've got a lot of nerve—you've got a hell of a lot to answer for. You! The *Gestapo!*"

I wrenched open the door with almost a shout of anger, "You!" I shouted again. "How dare you show your face in that uniform?"

Willi looked terrified, different from the sophisticated German engineer ordering meals at Maxim's in Paris. At the sight of my glowering face, his own was stamped with apprehension.

"How dare you come here?" I asked again. "Have you heard about Anna? Your wife! Vanished! My God, Papa was right to warn Anna against marrying a German. You damn swine." I looked at him with loathing. "If you've got business," I snarled, "let's get it over with. Otherwise get the hell off our property."

"It's not what you think," he began.

"You want to see your wife?"

He nodded eagerly.

"Well, you can't—because she's either in jail or she's dead," I said brutally. "Taken by the Gestapo—your lot! And since then not a trace of her anywhere."

For a moment he stood there, almost rocking with the suddenness of knowledge.

"So there, you shit," I stormed. "Get out!"

"It isn't what it seems."

"I know you had to be a soldier," I said bitterly, "but *this*—this hideous uniform."

"But will you listen—?"

"No, I won't. I know that damn black uniform. I've got nothing to say to you."

"Let me *explain!*"

"Just answer me one question. Are you—or are you not—in the Gestapo?"

After a long pause, Willi answered with one word: "Yes."

"Then get off my fucking ground."

"Listen!" he shouted. "Goddammit, you listen to me for once."

His voice was so angry—and, if that's the word, *sincere* with anger—that I stopped shouting.

"You remember the promise you made when I was beaten up in Düsseldorf? You promised then to believe me when I told you that I was not a free agent and that anything I did you had to believe in me. You *promised.* I believed you, I came all the way to see you, and instead I find you are a liar. You're the one to be ashamed."

Suddenly, embarrassingly, Willi stood there just outside the front door and burst into tears. Huge sobs racked his body as he stuttered, "I'm sorry."

"Better come in," I said gruffly. I couldn't ignore that hideous uniform, but somewhere at the back of my mind was the thought that maybe—only maybe—I'd jumped to the wrong conclusion. Though how could I? Not only the uniform, but he had *admitted* being in the Gestapo.

"Sorry about this," he wiped his face as he walked into the living room.

I got him a stiff drink. He downed it at one gulp. I had a drink too, I felt I needed it.

"I hoped that Anna would be in America by now," he said when he was able to speak a little more quietly. "I've lost everything in the world worth living for, but I risked everything to come here because—it was foolish of me, I see that now—I thought I could count on *one* friend!"

I felt awful—yet what else could I say?

"But, Christ, Willi! Your lot have tortured one poor devil in Douzy, you've abducted Anna and Olivia—you can hardly expect me to welcome you with open arms."

He shook his head. "I'll go," he said slowly, a broken man.

"Then why are you here?"

"To help."

"You, help!" I cried bitterly. "How can the Gestapo help, for Christ's sake, Willi!"

A sudden voice stilled my anger.

"Let Willi explain before you condemn him," Grandma had walked into the room. She must have been listening.

"But Grandma! He's a German!" as though that explained everything.

"I know. But I think Willi has suffered a lot and—well, tell me what happened, Willi, then we'll see."

She stood there, and I was at first puzzled by her ready acceptance of *any* hated German. But when I looked at her inquiringly while I was pouring out another drink for Willi, she just said briefly, as though in an aside that explained everything, "We need all the help we can get— even from the enemy."

Willi's story was quickly told. He had at first joined the army as he said he would, but his only thoughts were to find Anna. Or at least to get news of her. The army offered no chance, and he was on the point of being sent to the eastern front in Russia when he learned that the SS was asking for volunteers with specialized knowledge of languages and geography in France.

"They were recruiting experts for occupied France in various regions, to enforce civil government," he explained. "I was the perfect choice for this area. We've been stationed in several places, but now I'm at Châlons-sur-Marne, less than twenty miles away from Douzy. I didn't dare to drive over before, but today I was able to get a car. I wanted to find out—and, Larry, believe me—to help, to do *anything*. Half Germany is disillusioned with Hitler, the war, now the Russians, we *know* it's a hopeless cause now the invasion of England has failed."

"I'm sorry, Willi," I apologized.

"It was understandable. The German people don't have a very good image these days. Tell me—do you know the man who arrested Anna and Olivia?"

"His name is Hoess. He's stationed at Reims."

"I'll kill him!" burst out Willi. "I know all about him. He's a sadist."

"Don't be a fool," I said. "He knows the name Frankel. He'd realize who you are right away."

"I'm still going to kill him."

"You're going to do nothing of the sort," said La Châtelaine in her own special bossy voice. "Are you with us—or neutral?"

"With you?" Willi looked from me to Grandma.

"Yes—will you help?" She sounded almost impatient. "I don't expect you to start killing Germans for us, but all information is useful, and if you have any—"

"I'll do what I can," Willi promised. "It won't be much. I can't get involved. It might ruin everything—there are spies spying on other spies in the Gestapo."

"All the more reason to stop telling us you're going to kill Hoess," said La Châtelaine acidly. "If you kill Hoess, you might destroy the one man who can tell us where Anna has got to. Get your priorities right, young man. The time for killing Germans will come later."

With that she stalked out, every inch La Châtelaine.

35

FOR SOME WEEKS I had been undecided what tactics to employ about a major piece I was anxious to write for the *Globe*, but which I knew I could not file from France, not even under my own name. I wanted to write the truth about the hypocrisy among many Frenchmen, living comfortably in occupied Paris. I'd been thinking about women like Coco Chanel, who had a German lover, and many other French men and women who seemed to—well, at least not to suffer under the occupation.

Stories like the one I had in mind don't boil up overnight, but gradually in the mind, and mine, I think, was born partly because of the difference between city and rural life—the different standards between Paris and Douzy.

Country life in Douzy might be uneventful, even gloomy, with only Grandma and Papa as companions most of the time, but at least the air smelled clean, and I *felt* clean, whereas Paris depressed me—and always I had the feeling that whatever you were doing, you had to watch yourself because someone else was watching you.

One day I saw a man in a shabby suit sit down at the Flore and order *"Café crème, s'il vous plaît."*

There was nothing to mark him out from his fellows. He was nondescript, the kind of man turned out by the thousand, seemingly mass-produced for large cities, to live lonely, friendless lives, living each day as they lived yesterday and tomorrow. Yet at his request the waiter looked at him suspiciously, and within seconds two plainclothes

Germans who had heard him give the order demanded to see his papers. Eventually they took him away—and roughly. I never discovered what happened to an apparently innocent man, but the waiter explained *why*. "Those men were Gestapo in civilian clothes," he spat in disgust, "and the minute they heard him ask for a *café crème* they were suspicious that he might be a spy. There hasn't been a drop of milk in a café for months. Everyone knows that *café crème* is unobtainable."

This is what I wanted to write about, the way in which every move was dictated by fear, while collaborators thrived on the miseries of others.

Even if they weren't arresting people, the Germans became more ill mannered. The early veneer of politeness had rubbed off. In the Métro German soldiers often entered by the exit stairs, pushing civilians aside. Places in trains were desperately hard to find, yet dozens were reserved for the army, the half-empty compartments bearing stickers on the windows NUR FÜR WEHRMACHT.

In contrast to the spit and polish of the Germans, most Parisians looked dowdy. The hat had given way to the bandeau. Stockings had vanished. Girls painted their legs, even down to the black line of the nonexistent seam at the back. The first wooden soles were appearing. Bottles of liquid saccharin had replaced sugar in ersatz coffee. The bread was now a dirty gray—and you were lucky to get any. In place of the renowned French *confiture,* you could now buy only what was derisively called "approximate jam."

And always it was the Jews above everyone else who lived in fear, especially since the anti-Jewish police—known as the *police des questions juives*—was established to enforce new legislation under which thousands of Jewish refugees who had acquired French citizenship were liable to have it rescinded.

Many Jews had been hidden by friends, just as we had hidden Olivia; I knew of at least one who had been hidden by Sylvia Beach at her bookshop, Shakespeare and Company. I hadn't seen her for several weeks so I decided to pick her brains and ask for specific instances about life in

Paris which I would then incorporate in my article, to be
written under a false name of course. I had gone on the
spur of the moment, but I walked into a real-life drama.

An arrogant Prussian-type officer was having an argument with her. He obviously wanted to buy one particular
book from Sylvia, who equally firmly was refusing to let
him have it. Sylvia was an even-tempered woman, but now
she had dug her heels in and said, "I'm sorry, this is my
last copy, and I don't want to sell it."

The book was James Joyce's *Finnegan's Wake.*

"I demand to buy it. That's what a bookshop is for, isn't
it? You sell books?" asked the German angrily.

To ease the tension I cried cheerfully, "Hello, Sylvia! All
going well?"

The German looked me up and down with the kind of in-
solence that only Germans can put into a stare—especially
when they are victorious.

"I warn you, Fräulein," he ignored me, "that you will
sell me that book."

"I won't!" she shook her head.

"Very well," he shouted angrily. "We'll see. I'll be back
tomorrow with a squad of soldiers and I'll have your bookshop closed down!" He stomped out.

Sylvia looked at me. "He means it," she whispered.

"He does," I agreed. "The Germans have the power to
close down any foreign bookstore. Any excuse will serve."

"He's not getting *Finnegan's Wake,*" she cried. "In fact
I'm fed up with even having to serve these bastards. I'm
going to close down. I've turned fifty and I've had enough."

I knew she had already talked about closing the shop;
there had been too many Germans like this last one. "I *am*
going to close it down—I'm not going to let *them* close it
down. Come on! Let's go to work, Larry."

We did. We had several hours start—and my car. And
friends. Before nightfall we had removed all the books,
taken them into hiding, and knocked down all the shelving. We couldn't carry the wood away, but the crowd which
gathered round the shop, intrigued by our activity, was delighted to take away shelving, no doubt hoarding it for the

winter's fires. Sylvia gave away all the furniture. Finally, early the following morning, I tracked down Fernandez, the Spaniard who had papered the poppies all over the walls of the rue de l'Université, and he painted out the name Shakespeare and Company. By the time the furious officer arrived the next day with four armed soldiers, the most famous foreign bookshop in Paris had simply ceased to exist.

These were the happenings I wanted to write about, but obviously such a story could never be written from Paris. It would not only be censored, but I would probably be kicked out of Paris. My best plan was to file the story under another name from neutral Switzerland—which would have the added bonus of allowing me to see Sonia.

Once I had decided to go, the question was *how?* I couldn't leave France legally, for I would get no reentry permit. So the simplest way would be for me to smuggle my way across the border into Switzerland and then file from there. I decided to tell Oregon what I had in mind.

Wise old bird, he spotted at once the factor I hadn't mentioned and with apparent innocence said to me, "Great idea. But dangerous. If you really want to safeguard your name for the *Globe,* much better to let me go. I'm only a messenger. Unless of course," with a twinkle in his eye, "you're thinking of popping into Rolle to see a certain young lady."

"Okay!" I sighed, for a trip to see Sonia had of course been in my mind all the time. "I can't fool you, Uncle Oregon. I should have known better."

"Actually," he said seriously, "I *would* have gone as a messenger because I think you *do* run a danger of being discovered—but honestly, I'm too old to climb mountains and hide in woods."

"I do want to see her," I admitted. "I'm dying to see her again, Oregon. But honestly, I've got a great story to tell, and I'm even willing to sacrifice my by-line. I can't do more than that."

"You can't write it—and then carry it with you," he said. I shook my head. "That would be too dangerous, I agree

with you. I can remember everything—and I'll write it in
Switzerland and send it through our Bern office."

"But what if you're caught? I mean, if you're an American correspondent, you have every right to travel about
France—but you can't leave the country and get back."

"It's absolutely essential there's no suspicion that I've left
the country. The way I plan to go is to get a new identity card
with a French name on it and smuggle my way into Switzerland. After all, if I cross the frontier at—say—Divonne, overlooking the lake, I'll only have to cover five miles or so to get
to Rolle, and I'll lie up there, get our man in Bern to come
and meet me, and hand him the copy. Then after I've said
good-bye to Sonia, I'll go back—as a Frenchman."

"But getting a French identity card might be difficult,"
said Oregon.

I shook my head. "It's easy. I know a chap who turns
them out by the dozen. Very smart. I'm not in a rush to go
to Switzerland, but I want to be prepared, and I'm going to
start the ball rolling right away."

In fact my plan, though ingenious, took a little time.
Through a friend I spent a morning at the faculty of the
Sorbonne and started leafing through the register of en-
rollments. When I found one of about my age, I wrote down
his name, Henri Vasson, and the department in the Seine-
et-Oise where he had been born. This happened to be at
Pontoise. Then I wrote under the name of Vasson to the
local records office at Pontoise, giving details of my birthday, the clinic where my birth had been registered, and so
on, asking for a copy of my lost birth certificate, saying I
needed it because I had mislaid my identity card.

The copy of the certificate was duly delivered in a matter
of days, then all I needed were a couple of friendly witnesses, after which the nearest police station issued me
with a genuine duplicate identity card, though this one
was decorated with my own photograph and even my own
fingerprints, and of course the name Henri Vasson.

"Here you are," I showed it to Oregon when it finally arrived. "It's a funny feeling—like being given a present of a
new life."

"For God's sake, hide it until you need to use it," said Oregon quite sharply for him.

"I will," I promised him, never realizing how valuable that card would become before long, that a journey planned almost as an escapade to land a story with a derring-do dateline, to thumb my nose at the French, would result in a desperate bid to help in the rescue of Anna.

I had no idea when I returned to Douzy on my next visit that I would hear the first rumors of Anna's fate. They were only rumors, there was no confirmation, and I didn't hear about them at first. But they came eventually from Gaston.

Gaston had now assumed the role of Grandma's right-hand man in the vineyard. She was as active as ever herself, cycling indefatigably from one vineyard to another, a straight-backed figure recognizable from a distance. Grandma liked Gaston, I could tell that, not only by the way she spoke about him whenever we were at home. I found a touch of cynical amusement in the way my mother and now my grandmother both liked him.

"He's dependable, that's what it is," said Grandma.

"I quite agree, yes, I *do,*" said Papa. "Without doubt he's learned very quickly and he's an admirable—yes, *admirable*—replacement for—" But poor Papa, he couldn't bring himself to utter any of our names, not even the word *Guy,* whom at least we believed to be safe. Absence really had made Papa's heart grow fonder. Perhaps it had this effect on everyone? I remembered the rows when Olivia had moved in—and, not without a touch of bitterness, the row when Sonia moved out. One law for Guy, another law for me. Still, as I looked at Papa, older, worn by sadness, spooning his soup carefully, sometimes finding it difficult to bring spoon to mouth without spilling a few drops, I knew that my thoughts were unfair. What had outraged Papa years ago was that I had betrayed the trust which he had placed in Sonia. With Olivia there was nothing to betray. Guy had demanded, she had moved in. After a few weeks she had become part of the family.

"I'm so glad *you* like him," I said to Grandma.

She had lost none of her asperity, which I often think she assumed as a cloak to indicate her sense of authority, to mask any feeling of age and consequent fatigue.

"Of course I like him," she all but snorted. "He hates the Germans as well as being a vigneron." Grandma's priorities were intriguing. Hatred before skill!

I noticed something else about Grandma. She accepted Papa's work as necessary and useful in helping the French, but I had the feeling that as far as she herself was concerned, she would be happier in a more active role, a more anti-German role.

"If I was younger," she said at dinner one night, "I'd go south like a shot and join the Maquis." So it was still hatred before skill! She had just finished saying this when, almost without a second's pause, she turned to the butler and said, "Jean, this chicken is vile. Tastes like old string warmed up."

Jean muttered apologies. I heard a whispered "I'll tell Madame Robert, but there's no feeding stuff left." Poor Jean! It wasn't his fault, he wasn't the cook, and no one could produce first-class feeding stuff for the animals when the Germans grabbed everything. We were darned lucky that we could kill a pig or wring the neck of a chicken or turkey or duck whenever we felt like it.

"You're a little bit hard on poor Jean, yes, *hard*," said Papa when the butler had left the room.

"Fiddlesticks! Keeps everyone on their toes! A bit of complaining doesn't do any harm. Doesn't make any difference whom you complain to, the message always filters through." Then, returning to the subject before the interruption, she said, "Yes, I would like to have joined the Maquis! Maybe later—perhaps if we start up here—who knows?"

"Really, you are a *neutral*," said Papa almost severely. "You mustn't entertain, yes, *entertain*, such thoughts really!"

"I'm no more neutral—than a—" Grandma started witheringly but couldn't think of the right word so rose from the table almost glowering.

"She's very headstrong," Papa sighed. "I hope she doesn't do anything foolish, you know, *headstrong.*"

"Headstrong! Papa, that's the last word you could use to describe Grandma!"

"She's La Patronne. She likes the title and feels the need to live up to it. She's a *leader* in the area, yes, more than I ever was, and she *could* do something rash. I'm sure if she'd had a gun in her hand, she'd have shot that Gestapo man on that terrible day."

"Who wouldn't, but thank God she didn't."

"Me too," said my father. "I hear rumors about Frenchmen starting to form groups to fight the Germans—a sort of Resistance. If your Grandma gets involved in that sort of thing, our last hopes of ever finding the girls—" he still couldn't bear to use Anna's name and left the sentence unfinished.

I mentioned Grandma's "rashness" to Gaston next time we met, saying I hoped she wouldn't become involved.

"No danger of that—not yet," he said. "There's nothing to get involved about. But she's a wonderful old lady—and who knows, one day America might be in the war."

"Think so?"

"It's not inconceivable. Though less likely now that Britain has won the blitz and the German invasion of England has failed. Pretty good stuff. I wish I'd been able to get to Britain and fight with the Free French."

"You might do more valuable work here." Gaston had already confided to me that he and his friends were completing a dossier of all German activity—and rumors of fifth columnists.

"The Germans can't control Europe forever," he said. "But it will be a terrible struggle to get them out, even though they have now invaded Russia. The only way the French people can help is to collect every scrap of information about the Germans. One day it will all be of value."

"But events—conditions—they could change?"

"Well, we'll have to keep our information up-to-date. We can't do anything now, but one day"—he was speaking al-

most dreamily—"we'll use the British and the Free French
and send in saboteurs—parachute them down into the
dozens of hidden valleys in Champagne. The Germans can
never patrol them all."

It was about two weeks later that Gaston came up to me,
looked round, and said, "I've got something extremely important to tell you. Can you meet me in the orchard—say
five o'clock?"

"Sure. But remember that as a neutral, I can do more for
you than if you drag me in—"

"Don't worry. Promise."

I had, at first, hesitated, making the excuse about neutrality because a horrible thought had passed through my
mind. If Gaston wanted to see me so urgently—and alone
—what could he possibly want to see me about—except perhaps Mama? Had he heard from her? No, that was impossible. Or had Papa found out? No, that was also impossible.
But what else could it be? Anyway, I decided to go and
have a word with him.

Instead of making my way directly down the dell to the
orchard to meet him, I walked along the back paths leading to and past the Home Farm. The country always gave
me a sense of permanence lacking in Paris itself. The
house, with its walls of hand-shaped stones three to four
feet thick, had stood for centuries, and war or no war, the
open sheds in the yards were still being used to dry corn-
cobs for the pigs and cows. One of the farm lads was walking a horse to the nearest blacksmith near Rilly. The nine
cows were ready to be milked, and though food was scarce
by our normal standards, we were almost self-sufficient.

"I've wrapped up some *saucisse* and ham for you to take
back to Paris," said Madame Robert, adding the question
everyone asked, "Any news yet?"

I turned to say hello to old Pagniez, who hailed me with
a greeting, and I thought then that even with the crushed
and crippled right hand, he had come to terms with life
much better than if he had been a town dweller. He was an
old man, stooped after a life bent over the vines, but he

never complained. I shook his left hand and crossed the bottom of the dell toward the rhododendron bushes where I had first overheard Guy and Lisette quarreling, and then went through the wicker gate into the orchard. I was suddenly stabbed by the painful memory of the day I upended Sonia in the tall hayseed grass, and the intriguing look she gave me when, without warning, as I held her up by the ankles, she let her skirt fall down almost over her face. It wasn't a painful memory, of course, more a beautiful one, but thinking of that moment, when our love for each other can be said to have really started, I actually felt a short stab of pain in the chest. Then Gaston appeared, and the past visions flew away.

I had never seen him so ill at ease, metaphorically shuffling his feet as we stood in the long grass. The secrecy of the meeting made me wonder again if he wanted to talk about Mama. Well, I wasn't going to stand for *that*.

"You didn't suggest this talk because you want to go for a walk," I said lightly, swiping at some weeds with "Willi's" malacca stick.

"No, no. But it's very hard to tell you, very hard indeed. But I have to. I didn't like to talk to you about this until I was ninety percent sure."

"Well, for Christ's sake, come on! What's all the bull about?"

But then of course, I couldn't have had the faintest idea of the bombshell that was going to burst upon my head.

Finally he asked, "Did you know that in the rue Christina, just off the boulevard de Pommery—about halfway between the cathedral and the town hall—the Germans have established a brothel for German troops and officers?"

I had heard rumors—terrible ones. The Germans had not only rounded up every known streetwalker, they had imported some from Paris and also forced dozens of local girls, many of them Jewish, presenting them with an alternative: either work in the brothel or face a firing squad or deportation. The desire to cling to human life was so strong that though some girls were shot, many had en-

tered the bordello. Even so, as Gaston stood there, the
truth never entered my head.

"The brothel is in two sections," explained Gaston.
"One for officers. One for other ranks."

"What are you trying to tell me?"

For a moment Gaston hesitated, obviously scared to tell
me, and *then* I knew what he was trying to say.

"We don't know who she is," he said, "we can't even be
certain our information isn't just a rumor, but we've had
seven different reports from contacts who have never even
met each other—they all confirm that there's an American
girl being forced to work in the—" he didn't like to use the
word *bordello,* "in the *maison de plaisir,*" adding, "the one
reserved for officers only."

At first I was so stunned I couldn't believe it. I couldn't
because I didn't want to, I refused to. When Gaston told me
I couldn't at first assimilate the shock, perhaps because he
had attempted to soften the blow by saying, "It's not certain of course." Rather like a doctor who tells a relative,
"She's very, very ill" when in fact the patient is already
dead. But when the full impact hit me I couldn't say even a
word to Gaston. I left him there, stumbling back to the
dell, hardly seeing the grass, eyes brimming with tears.
For in a way, death would have been easier to bear. The finality of death can help to blot out the past. It *is* past.
Death is final. You know where you are. But now, as I
stumbled up toward the house, I suddenly thought, What's
she doing, my sister, Anna? What's she doing at this very
minute while I'm alive and free? Try as I might I couldn't
eradicate a picture from my mind. Anna on her back, legs
spread-eagled, and a man grunting on top of her, a German
pig. Oh, my darling Anna! I can do nothing—nothing to
help you, nothing to save you. If only you had died! One
filthy picture chased another, one evil thought chased the
last one. Poor Anna, how many times a day did she have to
do this? How many men queued up every day to take her?
If only she had died! For a moment I couldn't go on. I'm not
the one suffering, I thought, and yet my legs felt like jelly,

and suddenly I retched and all my guts seemed to spew out of my mouth, some of the sick caught where the nose and throat meet when you are violently ill, so that as I blew my nose out came the last remnants of vomit.

I knew it was true. I had at first forced myself to believe the whole thing was an exaggeration—a case of mistaken identity perhaps—but suddenly a picture from the immediate past flashed before my eyes telling me it was true, that poor Anna was being subjected to a systematic; degrading torture as brutal in its way as the pain meted out to other victims shackled in the cells.

I was thinking of the friendliness of Otto Abetz when he assured me that Anna was alive, of his smile as he said, "She is serving the Third Reich."

The words had been deliberately chosen, of that I was certain. And one day, I vowed, I would revenge myself on him.

The most awful emotion was the loneliness of my knowledge. I couldn't share it. I couldn't tell Papa—unless I believed he could help to free her. He would go berserk, kill somebody, or curl up and die, if not in fact, in spirit, a husk of the man who had raised our happy family. I couldn't just burst in and tell Grandma, saying, "Your granddaughter is working in a brothel."

She could have borne the blow better than my father—better than me for that matter—but what good would it do to worry an old lady in her seventies? I think I would have told Papa had I not shared the secret with Gaston. Though there was a certain irony in sharing the secret with the man who had once been Mother's lover.

But there was another reason why I didn't tell the family. We didn't know for sure. True, there were no records of any missing blonde American girls in the Champagne area, but the unknown blonde in the bordello might have been brought in from anywhere—if, that is, there *was* a blonde American girl in the *maison de plaisir.* So far we had only unconfirmed reports. Even so, dozens of wild thoughts raced through my mind. I had a map of the underground passages linking our cellars with others. I knew the address, I could pinpoint almost the exact spot directly underneath the buildings in the rue Christina. But the chalk passage would be, perhaps, fifty feet under the street level, and there was no way I could dynamite my way up. I didn't want to blow up Anna when trying to rescue her.

In my heart I was already aware of two facts: I had to be sure it *was* Anna in the brothel, and then I would have to get to see Sonia as quickly as possible and beg her to help. Over and over again she had promised that if she could only find out *where* Anna was, she could pull the necessary strings and obtain her release. I believed her. But I didn't want to bring Sonia into this until we were absolutely certain, if only because Sonia might not be able to exert her influence a second time if we made a mistake at the first attempt.

I determined to tell Oregon as soon as I reached Paris, but first I went to see the outside of the bordello. It wasn't just morbid curiosity—far from it. I wanted to be sure of the geography, I wanted to *feel* the agony of propinquity, however nauseating, however revolting.

The brothel consisted of a group of several large houses, each distinctively painted with yellow doors. They lay almost under the shadow of the cathedral, each door for different soldiers, who were lined up outside. Their sex life was organized according to rank. Officers stood in line outside a two-story house on the right side of the street. That would be the place where Anna was. The next house was besieged by sergeant majors, recognizable by the narrow silver stripes on their collars. The drill sergeants, with stars on their epaulets, stood at the foot of the stairs leading to an old half-dilapidated house. Privates and corporals waited outside the other houses.

As I watched them, like cattle waiting to be fed, I thought of the filth and degradation to which man sank, and I thought too—though I tried to banish the thought— that she was in there, that she might be ill, she might have a disease—anything. An old military saying kept running through my thoughts as I stood in the street, "A soldier's pay, a soldier's risks."

From the ground-level room I could hear the sound of

music blaring. Now and then one of the closed windows on the first or second floor would open, and a girl would lean out and scream. Gaston told me later that sex could be bought for between twenty and fifty occupation marks.

Large signs along the street read MEMBERS OF THE GERMAN ARMED FORCES ARE PERMITTED TO ENTER THIS STREET ONLY BETWEEN 6 A.M. AND IO P.M.

I don't quite know when I first realized that there was only one way to find out about Anna. Since the bordello was reserved for officers only, I would never be allowed to patronize it. But I *did* know of one German officer—and so the macabre, ghoulish thought persisted. Willi had promised to keep in touch—he was as desperate as I for news— and on his next visit to Douzy I would have to put it to him: Willi was the only man who could find out if the girl in the bordello was Anna. I hadn't worked out the details, but the scheme—if Willi would agree, *had* to agree—was so crazy that we could get away with it. And once we knew that it was Anna, once we had names, places, dates, then I could use my false identity card to rush to Switzerland and Sonia could move into action.

Willi didn't visit Douzy very often, it was too risky. Though to the enemy the Gestapo exuded an aura of being all-powerful, it had its own rigid code of discipline, including geographical areas of operation. Nobody trespassed on another officer's preserves without risking embarrassing questions. It was almost as though even poaching for torture victims was frowned upon. So, as Willi was stationed at Châlons-sur-Marne, each journey to Douzy posed a hazard. He was always accompanied by a Gestapo driver—and every member of the Gestapo was as eager to spy on his colleagues as on the enemy. Consequently Willi's visits to Douzy had to appear important, with, whenever possible, a different driver each time. He tried to visit Douzy about once every five or six weeks. When he arrived the next time he didn't have the faintest idea of what to expect.

I myself was almost afraid to tell him, when two weeks later I heard the sound of a car rounding the drive and saw the swastika fluttering on the black Citroën, it was Willi. I poured out a drink for him.

"Any news from your end?" I asked.

He shook his head. "And your side?" For a split second I hesitated—it was a terrible moment to tell him what I suspected had happened—but he pounced on that split second with the speed of a panther, and also, I though wryly, with the expert training of a professional interrogator. He jumped up, grabbed my shoulders.

"Was ist?" he shouted almost hoarsely. "What do you know?"

"Take your hands off me, Willi," angrily I thrust his shoulders away. "I'm not being bashed around by your lot."

"I am sorry. I feel—"

"I'm sorry too, Willi. But don't shout. You don't want the Gestapo driver outside to hear you."

"But what?" he demanded. *"Gott in Himmel!* I can tell you have news. Why are you torturing me?"

Torture! Willi's unconscious irony was lost in the rush of thoughts.

"Sit down," I said. "For Chrissake, *sit down.* At least do as I ask you in *my* house."

He sat down, almost glowering. He took off his jacket, tie, collar. "You are trying to inform me she is dead," he used an old-fashioned phrase.

I shook my head—wondering guiltily if death wouldn't be a better fate than the terrible alternative.

"This is only a rumor, Willi," I just didn't know how to begin, "so don't count on it. Don't get all heated up. It's possible that Anna is here—in Reims."

"But where?" he shouted. "You speak in a riddle, in a roundabout way."

"It's a roundabout story," I said shortly, and then as calmly as I could, I told him everything, no holds barred.

His face seemed to crumple into a thousand creases, and then without warning he burst into a spasm of terrible sobbing—just as he had done the last time, as though they would tear out his guts, almost animal cries, so loud that Jean came in alarmed.

"It's all right," I told Jean. "I'll give Monsieur Frankel another brandy."

"My *Liebchen, my Liebchen,*" he cried, holding his face to his arms, rocking backward and forward and groaning in this terrible way. "My beautiful, innocent, lovely *Liebchen.* My Anna—why did they do this to you? Why did they make you a *Mädchen für alles.*" I knew the German phrase, a girl for all purposes.

"They did it to your wife—the Germans," I said, because I thought it would bring him down to earth, "but don't forget, Willi, that the Gestapo also did it to my sister."

He looked at me, incongruous in his shirt without jacket or tie, as though trying to disguise the uniform. Tears stained his ruddy face. Now, confronted with the terrible news of how the Gestapo had treated his own wife, Willi looked at the jacket, crumpled, lying on the floor, with loathing—the symbol of brutishness, of bestiality, of torture, of degradation inflicted by one human being on another, and often for no other reason than to satisfy a sadist's whim.

"Does anyone know?" instinctively Willi lowered his voice as though to hide the shame.

I shook my head.

"Not even your father?"

"No, no. I said nothing to him. After all it may not even be true."

"You know it's true. Yes?" I hesitated again, then repeated, "All I can say is that several independent reports confirm that there *is* a blond girl with an American accent working—working *there.*"

"Where is it?" he asked in a flat, dull voice.

I told him—explaining where the rue Christina was, how to recognize the group of houses with yellow doors, though I couldn't keep the bitterness out of my voice when I added, "Though it's easy to find—there's always a queue outside."

Willi held his head in his hands again as though trying in vain to blot out the picture of all life behind those doors.

"I can't even *begin* to imagine it," he groaned. He was

begging me for comfort. Again I couldn't help thinking—
however swiftly passing—how ironic it was to find a member of the mighty Gestapo begging a neutral civilian for
help, for advice, for—and I knew this as I looked at Willi—
for forgiveness, not for what *he* had done, but as a measure
of the contrition he felt on behalf of all the beasts.

Of course, I thought as I watched him, it wasn't all Willi's fault. One fault lay in the happy-go-lucky way we had
all blithely swayed our parents away from their own instincts of fear, had persuaded them to let Willi marry
Anna, against all their doubts. We were to blame. Yet who
could have known? What right had any of us to interfere in
the destiny of others—especially when none of us knew
where that destiny was leading.

"What are we going to do?" All the fight had gone from
Willi. In his white shirt without its collar, the brass stud
sticking out of the old-fashioned neckband, the face sagging with despair, he could in peacetime have passed for
some scruffy down-and-out asking for a job. That's just
what he looked like.

The master race! How much simpler brutality was when
you were dealing with ciphers, not friends. I stole another
look at Willi. Yes, he was broken. Yet it was the fate of his
wife that must have been a factor in persuading a "good"
German to become an enemy of the Third Reich. But what
had he been like before that? Had Willi ever tortured a victim with the same indifference that Hoess had tortured
poor old Jacques Pagniez? Had Willi ever torn off a woman's fingernails just because she was a Jewess? Or inserted
electric bulbs in a girl's vagina as part of a routine way of
getting more information?

Of course it was unfair of me to think that of Willie. He
couldn't have behaved like that. The German forces were
full of men who never wielded any weapon more lethal
than a typewriter.

"Do you think if I went to see the Gestapo in Reims,"
asked Willi, "they might release her in my custody?" It
was a forlorn hope, one he knew to be doomed before I
shook my head.

"If they trace you back to her," I warned him, "you'll be in serious trouble. And besides we don't *know*. Above everything else we must *know*, we must be certain we're not making a mistake."

"Then what?" he asked helplessly.

"I have a plan," I said slowly. "It'll work—but only if you keep cool." Jean brought in another bottle of cold Perrier. "Better have another brandy and soda," I urged him. "The plan is based on several factors. But Willi—remember this is *my sister* just as much as she's your wife. And if you think that as a German you can get her out of this damn place, you've got another think coming."

"I'll do anything I can," he promised.

"I'm sure you will. Because Willi—better get this straight —you'll do *exactly* what I say because if anything goes wrong I wouldn't hesitate to kill a German—even one particular German—to get Anna free."

"I know, I know. But remember I too hate the Nazis."

"I hope so. But I remember the day at Douzy—sitting in this very room—when you said the Nazis didn't count! Your lot brought the Nazis into power, Willi, so cut out the crap. Though I believe you hate them now. Better late than never. I believe I've found a way I might be able to get Anna out."

"I'll do anything," he begged me again. And I believed him. I saw him look nervously at his watch. Rightly, he was afraid of staying too long at a place where, as he had told the driver, he was making a cursory inspection— presumably on some nonexistent orders.

"You'll have to go?"

"Five minutes. Can you tell me—now, quickly. I cannot get her out, *nein?* Not possible. Nor you, Larry. So who?"

I hesitated, almost for effect.

"Sonia!" I said softly.

"Sonia!"

"Who better? She's an ally of the Germans. She's the wife of a high-ranking Italian diplomat. I understand that even Mussolini himself admires her—when his mistress, Clara Petacci, isn't around."

I explained as quickly as I could how Sonia might be able to help—once we were all sure that Anna was in the rue Christina.

"For there's one other problem," I said. "We can't send Sonia out on a wild goose chase. We can't set a complicated plan in motion unless we're a hundred percent sure the girl behind the yellow door *is* Anna. And that's where you come in," I added as Willi started to put on his collar and tie and shake the creases out of his uniform. "That's the moment when you're going to have to keep cool. If you don't, you lose your head."

Willi was so numb with despair, shock, anguish that he looked at me, mouth open, as though he hadn't the faintest idea what I was talking about.

"If I can help," he mumbled finally.

"Willi," I said gently, "we must have a positive identification of Anna before we drag Sonia into this. I can't help. You're the only one who can make sure if she's there."

"But how?" he asked almost stupidly.

"You've got to go to the bordello in the rue Christina, pay your money, queue up with the other officers, and insist on having the blonde," I said almost brutally.

For a moment I thought he was going to throw up—literally to vomit. His face went a sickly color, he leaned forward, he started to retch again. In a panic I looked round for a vase or a cachepot, but as the wave of nausea passed he shouted, "I couldn't do it."

"You will," I said, adding with deliberate brutality, "don't be such a fucking coward. It's the only way, and you owe it to us."

"I couldn't, I couldn't."

"You will. This is my sister! And at the rate Anna is being used, she probably won't last much longer. If you want to see her alive—"

"Mein Gott," he groaned. "If only I was dead, how easy."

"How easy it would be for you. To let her spend the rest of her life in a whorehouse. Yes, damn easy—for you. You're gutless."

"I'm sorry. But even if I do this thing, will she ever be the same again? How can she be?"

"I don't give a shit about that. That's a problem for the future. First things first. Identification—then I'll contact Sonia in Rolle. Sonia will have no problems traveling to France. But you come first. And remember," my voice hardened again, "quite apart from what *you* want, I want my *sister* back. If you love Anna, then you'll go through with this. You'll just have to go to the brothel and confront her. It's the only chance you'll ever have of saving her."

So it was arranged. We couldn't fix on a definite date for Willi to visit the house with the yellow door; he couldn't just walk out of Gestapo headquarters in Châlons-sur-Marne without making arrangements. But he did promise to go as soon as possible and then let me know if it was Anna.

"You'll be on your own," I said, "and the most critical moment of all will be when you go into her room. She probably won't have the faintest idea it's you—or that you know her. That's bad enough for any woman—going whoring and then finding it's her own husband."

"I could hold my hand over my face?"

"I don't give a damn what you do. Because even this isn't the most important moment. If I know Anna, the moment she's going to scream—to lose all her control, irrespective of what might happen to her—will be the moment of *double* shock. First when she recognizes you, second when she sees the Gestapo uniform. It's enough to make any woman go mad."

Willi looked at me helplessly.

"Somehow you've got to stop that first scream, Willi—but it must be with your first words. *Your very first words.* Even if you have to grab her mouth for a few seconds, tell her before anything else, 'I've come from Larry. Help is on the way.' Once you get that message across, even if she doesn't believe it at first, even if she's about to vomit, *you've got to stop that first scream.*"

36

IT WAS THREE WEEKS before Willi was able to manufacture an adequate excuse to get away from Châlons-sur-Marne and spend the day at Reims. He had taken care to have a different driver and called in at Douzy for five minutes.

"I go this afternoon to the rue Christina," he said dully, his precise Germanic English failing to mask his obvious distress—and fear.

"You'll call in on the way back?"

"Of course," he nodded. What would happen, I wondered, at the moment of meeting—if they met, that is. How could *anyone* suppress a shriek of despair at the sight of him? There he was, hateful black uniform, the sharply angled peaked cap, the death's head emblem, the exaggerated cut of his tightly fitting breeches, even the equally exaggerated shine on the polished jackboots. He looked every inch a sadist.

"It is the uniform," he apologized, seeing me look at him, "if I want to make certain of demanding the blond girl, then I must *look* like the Gestapo officer—you know, I am used to being obeyed. I must give this impression. We go now. Do not think this will be easy for me."

"I know that, Willi. I understand. But it's the only way."

For the benefit of the driver, Willi marched out of the front door, all but shouting, "These papers must be found, you understand! I am going to Reims on business, I will come back. You may be neutral, but everything must be ready, understand?"

"But I'm not sure—" playing my part.

"No excuses!" shouted Willi as the driver jumped round to open the back door, and I heard him mutter, *"Dummkopf!"* That was at 11:30 A.M. I settled down to wait.

It *was* Anna. I had never doubted it, though Willi did not return to Douzy until nearly four that afternoon. As the driver rushed round the car to open the door for Willi, he stumbled out, and I thought he was going to die on the spot—or at least faint. But somehow, dragging out the last reserves of his strength, he shouted, "The papers? *Ich habe es eilig!"*

I realized that Willi was saying, for the benefit of the driver, that he was in a hurry. He had told the driver to wait, muttering, *"Bitte warten Sie hier ein paar Minuten."* As he stumbled to the front door, Willi whispered, "It's her, *mein Liebchen.* For God's sake, get me a drink."

I even had to help him to the sofa. I poured out a stiff brandy—neat. He downed it in a gulp and held out the glass for a refill. I could see the flush slowly spreading across the deadly pallor of a man who has seen a ghost—as, in a way, I suppose Willi had. He undid his collar in a fight to ease his breathing, and now that I knew it was Anna, I didn't rush him. As we had another drink, and I waited with a patience I certainly didn't feel, thinking of the time we had met in Düsseldorf, when I had opened the front door to look upon the bleeding pulp of Willi's smashed-in face, I knew that this was far worse for him. For now he had been beaten mentally. At first it was impossible to force a word out of him. He was half sobbing, face at times buried in his hands. Finally he became composed enough to give me a coherent account of what had happened.

He had, he said, told his driver where he was going, and why, telling him to report for duty in three hours at the officers' car pool near the cathedral. Then he walked to the rue Christina, panicking at the prospect of seeing Anna, though it never entered his head that there would be much delay. He was astounded to find the rue Christina crammed

with Germans—laughing soldiers queuing in front of one
house, NCOs at another, a couple of dozen officers at a
third yellow door. From the man in front of him, who was a
regular officer, Willi learned that each man was allowed
thirty minutes with a girl. It cost fifty occupation francs,
payable at the desk.

Forcing himself to pretense of conviviality, Willi asked
the other man, "Can you pick and choose?"

"Of course. There is a sitting room, and once you are inside, then if you want a special girl, you can't be kept waiting more than half an hour can you? I have a favorite.
Many do. We have a nice waiting room, some champagne,
it is very civilized."

Civilized! Willi almost retched at the thought of it, but
somehow he managed to keep up the appearance that he
was enjoying the outing and asked, "They tell me there's a
blond American in there?" He jerked his head to the yellow door.

"I hear there is. Can't say I've ever seen her. Too frustrated, the Americans. Don't know a thing about the art of
pleasing a man. Now a French whore—she *does.*"

They queued for an hour before the officer ahead and
Willi were allowed through the door. Behind them the
queue in the street had grown—there must have been fifty
officers alone standing in line for sex.

"There are only twelve girls, all hand picked," confided
the young officer. "I'm going to wait for Olga. I've been
with her several times. I always bring her a bar of chocolate or something as a present."

The house had in fact once been a small residential hotel
before the Wehrmacht took it over, and the reception room
looked unchanged, with a lady in black wearing glasses,
behind a desk. She looked up at Willi and asked, "Any particular one?"

"The blonde, please—the American blonde."

"She's busy, half an hour if you don't mind waiting. A
bottle of champagne?"

The champagne was obviously one of the perks of the
madam, and a girl assistant led the way to a sitting room,

where half a dozen officers, awaiting their particular choices, sat talking and drinking. It was like the front parlor of a middle-class home, almost impossible to imagine what lay upstairs, behind the secret doors. Everything bore the stamp of mediocre respectability—the antimacassar, the potted green shrubs, the leaves brown at the tips, the round table in the center covered with a crochet lace cloth on which stood several empty bottles. Leather chairs were grouped round the wall so that men could stretch their legs. On second thought it didn't look to Willi like the front parlor of a home. It looked more like the waiting room of a provincial dentist.

Most of all Willi was dreading the moment when the girl, who was obviously the madam's assistant, would beckon him to enter. He was terrified because he knew that at the first sight of the uniform Anna—or whoever she might be—would stiffen with revulsion. Even while Willi was waiting, he noticed that, as the only Gestapo man in the room, the banter among fellow officers awaiting their turn did not include him. Virtually all German regular army officers—many brought up with a strict code of tradition—looked upon the Gestapo officers as pariahs.

Worse, Willi did not have the faintest idea what to expect when he walked into the room. Ordinarily a man visiting a brothel wasn't unduly concerned, he just took everything as it came, but to Willi the unknown drama assumed an importance bordering on panic. Would she be on the bed? Would she greet him? Would she be dressed or wearing a dressing gown? And above everything else, would she scream?

He decided that he must try at first to hide his face, turn in sideways, take off his hat in the hope that he could shield his face and so stop her from crying out with fear. But how?

Two or three officers left the room, each one summoned by the madam's assistant, who told them which numbered door was theirs at the top of the stairs. Suddenly the girl approached Willi and tapped his shoulder. Willi almost jumped out of his skin.

"Number nine, m'sieu," she pointed the way, and Willi felt his skin crawl, though his forehead was suddenly bathed in sweat. He climbed the stairs, opened the door marked 9 at the far end of the corridor. He caught a glimpse of a bidet and wash basin, a brass bedstead with a pink woolen coverlet and two pillows, together with the back view of a woman in a pink dressing gown. Though he had planned to clap a hand over her mouth to stop an instinctive cry, she was too far away. Hiding his face as best he could with his ugly, shining peaked cap, he coughed and then said his first words, very quietly, knowing that if it *wasn't* Anna the words would mean nothing.

"Larry has sent me," he said very quietly.

She spun round, hand to mouth in her shock, suppressing her own scream. "Larry!"

At first she apparently didn't realize that it was Willi, for she cried, "Oh my God! my God!" and then she saw him and barely whispered, "You! What are you doing here? The Gestapo?"

Willi had to rush her, not give her time to think, pretend. He couldn't tell *all* the truth.

"Larry sent me to help."

"But the Gestapo?"

"No, no. Forget this uniform. It's a disguise," Willi urged her, the words tumbling out. "Larry found out where you are. He sent me to let you know. Sonia is going to help you."

"Is it really you? Willi? In this hateful uniform?"

"I had to put it on to get in here," he lied. "You will be free soon. Sonia has promised."

Terrified, she looked at the door, put her fingers to her lips, whispered, "Speak softly, tell me, are you all right?"

She fell into his arms, sobbing, "Get me out, for God's sake get me out of this terrible place. You're not one of them are you?"

"No," he lied again, "I will get you out *Liebchen*. I promise." He led her to the bed, sitting down beside her.

"Don't look at me," she whispered to Willi. And when Willi did, she covered her face with her hands again. "No, please! I feel so old—and tired—and so dirty. Oh Willi I'm so tired. I just want to die, to end it all I'm so miserable."

"Listen *Liebchen,*" he said. "It is hard to tell you this, to think of what is happening to you—but *please,* one woman at Gestapo headquarters had her nails pulled out one each day. Ten days of screaming hell. Another had electric light bulbs pushed inside her. Be brave Anna. Yours is a filthy torture of a different kind, but it will be over soon. Larry has made the promise. And we will get you away, to Switzerland to live."

She looked at him almost with wonder. "Is it really you? Am I *really* going to be saved? Are you sure? How can you tell?" The questions tumbled out as though she still couldn't believe what she was seeing and hearing.

Willi nodded. "It's taken all this time to find out where you were," he explained. "I'll tell you about it all later. Meanwhile this nightmare is nearly over."

"I can never get over this, it's a nightmare," she said. "Never! I wish I had been tortured to death, but this is a human hell. Twenty times a day—with pigs!"

Willi looked at her face; the bloom of youth had gone and he knew she was right, it had gone forever, replaced by ugly lines etched on a gray face, a map of despair.

"Never mind my face!" she cried suddenly. "Look at this!" With a sudden angry gesture she tore away her dressing gown so that Willi could see her stomach, thighs, and blond pubic hair. And surrounding it the mottled yellow and purple of bruises.

"They don't even know when they're hurting me," with a sudden defensive gesture she closed her dressing gown, "but they're often in such a rush they force their way inside me. Yes," in a melancholy voice loaded with tears, "up to twenty times a day. With three days off once a month when I have the curse."

"I can't tell you any more," Willi finally said to me. "I can't *remember* any more. I was in a daze all through the time I was there."

"But she realizes—well, that there's hope?"

"I'm sure she does. I'm only hoping that she understands. She's very, very tired."

"Poor Anna. She must be suffering like hell." My first ice-cold fury had been followed by utter dejection, a sense of shared degradation for a sister I had once seen laughing and gay.

"I'm going to leave for Switzerland tonight" I told Willi suddenly. "Right away. I'm going now. You see, Willi, it's still going to take time. There's no way I can explain this on the phone to Sonia—even if I could get through to Sonia, which I can't. And if I did, the phone might be tapped. And the most important thing of all, Willi—for God's sake, not a word. One leak and we're done."

"How do you mean?"

"There's one good reason for not phoning. If Hoess ever gets a hint that we're on the track of Anna, she'll be whisked out of the rue Christina before we can do anything. And then—even if they put her in a house in the next town, in the next street, even—she'd be lost again. So, Willi, do me a favor. However you feel, don't go back to the rue Christina. Don't fall into the trap of trying to see Anna again, just to cheer her up. Wait till I come back, I'll be back in less than a week, then come to see me first, and I'll tell you all my plans—Sonia's plans. *Then* you can go to see her and tell her what to expect. But until then—you promise?"

At first he looked horrified. I think he had planned to try to see Anna regularly—maybe twice a week, I don't know. "But you can't," I urged him, *"anything* can arouse suspicion—you yourself said that the Gestapo spies on its own members. It must be dangerous going off from one headquarters to visit another where you're not supposed to be. It was okay when we *had* to do it—but don't give anyone the slightest chance to find out. *You* of all people know how the Gestapo works!"

"You're right," he admitted. "When do you expect to be back? You said in one week?"

"Maybe four or five days. I'll stay one night to tell Sonia, and then I'll return as soon as I can."

"I'll come to Douzy in a week or ten days."

"Do that," I said, and as an afterthought, for everything else had been driven out of my mind, I asked, "Did you hear any news about Olivia?"

He nodded. "She was also in the rue Christina, but then an extraordinary thing happened. Hoess sent for her. Apparently he decided to keep her as his—well, for himself. So now she lives in his house. Anna told me that much, but she wasn't sure of the details."

"He's next on the list," I said savagely. "If we can find a way to get Anna out, then we'll find a way to deal with Hoess later."

The journey across France to within a few miles of the Swiss border presented no serious problems because I planned to hide my false French identity card and travel legally in France as a neutral American journalist investigating conditions in occupied France. But I didn't dare to cross the border *legally* on my American passport in case I was caught, or even if a check might be made with head office in Paris. If that happened I would be prohibited from returning to France. So I decided to swap identities as I approached Divonne, the nearest town to the frontier, because if I should be caught, then as a Frenchman I might be able to bluff my way out of an argument with the French.

I decided to drive straight south from Reims through Châlons-sur-Marne, the cut across to Troyes and on to Dijon, after which the main road branched left and led to Dole, instead of missing Switzerland if I had gone straight on to the south coast of France. I decided on the route for two reasons: I knew it well, and at a time when the Germans had removed virtually all signposts, and it was impossible to buy maps, this was a major factor, apart from the fact that if I had taken the northern route through Vesoul, crossing the frontier near Belfort, I would have had to spend at least two days crossing Switzerland itself—an added hazard as I had no papers permitting me to stay there.

On the other hand, Divonne was almost within sight of Nyon on Lake Leman in Switzerland, and Nyon was barely seven miles from Rolle. In fact by not going into Nyon I could reduce the distance considerably by taking the shortcut along the mountain roads.

I also had a contact in Divonne, thanks to Gaston, to whom I had explained my plan.

"Divonne can be tricky," he advised me. "But about two miles out of the town—and that means away from the border post, but nearer the lake—there's an old inn called the Bois Jolie. I stayed there after leaving North Africa. You remember our training? Well, it included two days in Switzerland, getting initiated. I had a wonderful holiday there too. As for Madame Gavroche, who's the boss of the inn, she'll help if she can. There's a regular traffic across the border. But be careful—it's pretty rough going, through wooded country."

"You think she won't be suspicious if I ask for her?"

"You'll have switched nationalities by then," Gaston asked me. "She's very pro-French. You'll like her."

"And I can mention you by name?"

He nodded.

"She might have forgotten you," I laughed.

"She won't," he said with a cryptic smile.

It turned out to be almost as simple as that. I was stopped several times at German checkpoints, and I'm quite sure that each time details of my passport, identity card, car registration papers, and so on were noted and sent back via local headquarters to some vague central authority. But I was doing no wrong, so I didn't care. As long as I had gas, and that was stored in champagne magnum bottles as usual, and as long as I stayed in France on legitimate business, no one really had any right to stop me except in a military area. Even the champagne bottles filled with gas had a legitimate look to them, for the labels bore my name. And I did keep a dozen bottles of nonvintage to offer occasionally when I wanted to smooth the ruffled feelings of any official in a bad temper. The difference in the size of bottles made doubly sure that nobody would get a dose of gas by mistake.

I had to stop now and again to try to find a bite to eat, and I retraced my steps to two places where I had once spent such happy hours. I passed one night in the old mill near Dijon, where, greatly daring, I had checked in with Sonia when she was seventeen, and when I reached the frontier town of Pontarlier on the second day I stopped for a beer at the same western-style bar in the main street, before passing through the ancient gates of the city walls and plunging into the dark caverns of the thickly wooded, twisting roads of the Jura Mountains.

I found the hotel which Gaston had told me about without any trouble, after hiding my American passport and "becoming" a Frenchman. And there was quite a surprise when I reached the Bois Jolie and asked Madame Gavroche if she could put me up for the night.

I don't know what I had expected—I suppose my mental pictures hovered between two extremes: on the one hand, a buxom, motherly type who would make me welcome; on the other hand, the vinegary, spinster type all dressed in black with rimless glasses tied to a cord, and a sharp eye on the cash register. In fact Madame Gavroche was neither of these. The building was unpretentious and could have done with a lick of paint, but it was attractive in a village sort of way, and I made my way to the small entrance hall with its inevitable polished reception counter and row of a dozen keys on hooks behind an extremely pretty woman who stood waiting at the desk. Tentatively I asked her, "Can I please speak with Madame Gavroche?"

She smiled, showing beautiful teeth. A touch of hidden amusement made her eyes twinkle.

"C'est moi-même, monsieur."

"You, madame! *Pardon!*" Confused I added, "I expected someone—well, a little older perhaps."

"Everyone does," she laughed. "I'll have to try and grow older more quickly." And then in a more businesslike tone she asked, "What can I do for you, sir?"

"I wondered if you had a room for the night. And a garage for my car perhaps."

She shook her head. "I'm sorry, sir, we're full up."

I looked at the row of keys dangling on the wooden rack, as though to say, "You don't *look* full up."

"No rooms available," she said more firmly. "I'm sorry, sir."

"So am I," I said slowly. "Because I have a message from a friend of yours."

"Who is he?" for the first time she looked interested.

"Gaston. He said you would remember him."

"Gaston!" she almost blushed. "How is he? Is he well? He's not being foolish—on dangerous missions? Oh, Gaston! Come inside, monsieur, I think I can offer you a cup of *real* coffee—not this ersatz. We get supplies sometimes from across the frontier. Please do come in!"

She showed me into what I suppose would be called the parlor, very comfortable, and looking prettier than ever, she cried, "Tell me more—about Gaston and your name if I may ask?"

"Henri Vasson."

"Monsieur Vasson. Ah! Gaston. *Quel homme!* He didn't stay long training in the mountains—two weeks maybe, then," a little shyly, "he took me for two days to Switzerland in Geneva. In the middle of the war, it was a very pleasing interlude."

I had no doubt it was! A pleasant change from Mama! Younger too. I suppose I must have looked puzzled at her youth, for she explained gently, "My husband was killed in the first two weeks of June. A year ago. I can hardly believe it. We had been married for six years, and we bought this place with his savings. Since then I've helped anyone I can—anyone who hates the *Boche!*"

"I do," I said. "The Gestapo have taken my sister."

"If I can help?"

"I have a very good friend—I hope to marry her one day—and she lives in Rolle. I want to go and see her. That's all."

"Of course. I understand." I caught a look—regret? I

thought that for a moment she eyed me rather wistfully, thinking perhaps of a substitute for Gaston, but I am sure I was flattering myself.

"And the room?"

"Of course. I always say no first—because we have to fill in *fiches* for the police, and I am always afraid unless I trust someone."

Later she took me up to the loft under the roof, steeply sloping to guard against the winter snow. From there I had a perfect view of Lake Leman, shining like a gray slate on which you could have drawn with a pencil. She pointed out Nyon in the distance. It looked ridiculously close. "Rolle is over there," she pointed to the left. "You see, you don't have to go to Nyon at all to get to Rolle. You can bear left, walk across the side of the hills, and then eventually you'll see the town hall of Rolle below you. It's the next town after Nyon."

In some detail she explained the topography. The town of Divonne, with its customs post, was away to the right—out of sight. Below us were thick woods, which lay spread out like a carpet in front of me. The belt of trees, she told me, was two miles deep and I had to get through them, but they were only a few hundred yards wide. Even so, I must on no account try to make my way across open ground. I could see the woods in front of me, though the tip at the far end—the bottom end near the frontier—was hidden.

"But be careful," she warned me again, "the vineyards you see *before* the bottom of the trees, on either side of the belt of woods, they are in France. And though the actual border is only a barbed-wire fence at the bottom of the woods, if you stray outside that woodland in order to try to get across quicker, the area is still busy with police. And remember, this is still occupied France, we're just inside the demarcation line. Many of the police work directly under German supervision. That's why I didn't want to tell at first. Be very, very careful. Sometimes Germans come on patrol with the French police. And if you try to cross the vineyards or open ground and you are spotted—and the countryside is pretty bare at this time of year—you only get one warning. Then they shoot. It's not fair to blame the French entirely," she shrugged her shoulders. *"They* would be shot if they didn't uphold the German orders."

It was very clear. She arranged for me to leave the car locked in a shed attached to the house, and I took away the ignition keys and gave them to her for safekeeping. I went upstairs to rest and came down around five o'clock to get something to eat. As usual they ate better in the country than in the towns, and I had a half-bottle of very palatable local wine to wash down a ham sandwich. Half a dozen people had by now gravitated to the pub's inevitable bar, the zinc top being wiped clean by another girl, whom I hadn't seen before. I fell into conversation with some of the men— well, I didn't *fall* into conversation, they seemed so anxious to talk to a new face that they pushed me into the talking. But it was all very harmless and it helped to pass the time. It also allayed suspicion, and since I had to wait until ten o'clock at night when the moon was up before setting off for the woods, I played a few hands of piquet with three of the men. One man, called André, left early, and two of the others, called Louis and Valéry, stayed on, and we drank our share of rough red wine, though I was careful not to overdo it, and at nine thirty I announced that I was going to bed.

I went upstairs, took a flashlight and my malacca cane-cum-sword-stick, not so much as a weapon of protection—I would have been terrified had I been forced to use it—but I thought I might need it to feel my way in a dark wood, in much the same way as a blind man tests the way ahead when walking. The thick foliage would probably be impenetrable even though there was a moon.

Madame Gavroche's last words as she handed me a packet of sandwiches were, *"Do* be careful of the police. We've had a couple looking around. But I think they've gone. But *do* be careful, I beseech you."

Then I set off. Following her instructions, I walked about a couple of hundred yards along the roadside and then entered the wood, plunging from the moonlight into the thick darkness of the forest. Thank God for the shape of the forest! If it had been square, I don't think I could have ever found my way out of it. But because it was long and narrow, I knew that if I strayed too far to the left or right I would see the lightness of the sky through thinning trees. It gave me an added sense of security—and I needed it, for it had never entered my head that the undergrowth would be so dense, and at times almost impossible. Thank God for my malacca cane! By waving it in a semicircle ahead of me I could make slow progress. And every now and again, I switched on my flashlight, literally for a second.

What really infuriated me was the *nature* of the undergrowth. It seemed to consist entirely of thorn bushes, gorse perhaps, holly maybe, but every now and again the sounds of the forest would be broken by another sound—that of tearing, ripping cloth as I stumbled against a bush tougher and higher than the others. There was only a glimmer of light from the moon shining directly down, and my eyes did become more accustomed to the darkness, but it was tough going all the same.

The only trouble—apart from my torn clothes—was that without warning I suddenly sank over my ankles into some sludge—a shallow pond. My feet were covered. Worse, in the effort of getting out, I fell, covering the bottom half of my trousers with filth and losing one shoe. That I *had* to find—for even if I reached the frontier, there was no way I could walk seven or eight miles to Rolle with only one shoe.

Cautiously I switched on my flashlight and managed to retrieve the filthy shoe. I had to pour the mud and water out before I could put it on, squelching ooze out as I walked. Then I pushed ahead.

To this day I can never be sure of the exact moment when I realized I was being followed. The thickness of the forest at first muffled the sound, or perhaps I didn't *want* to hear it, was afraid to. But then I heard a twig snap. It was definite. No doubt about it. Then an eerie silence, though *not* a silence, a semisilence broken by the sound of

panting, of heavy breathing, the sound a dog makes when
it has been running. Only this was no dog, otherwise it
would have smelled me, approached me, friend or foe.

I reckoned I must be fairly near the frontier by now as I
had been forging ahead slowly for two hours. Now I had to
get out quickly. I knew that once I was over the frontier,
the French police would be powerless, and only the Swiss
could touch me—if, that is, they were there, which was un-
likely. I knew that once over the frontier, I could find
Rolle. For there would be signposts again to help me. Even
the name of the house on a wooden board, THREE CIRCLES
FARM.

But that was ahead.

Behind me the breathing grew nearer—and I suddenly
realized there was more than one man. I had to run for it.
But I couldn't. No man could run in this tangle. I was
young and fit—and I did manage to increase my pace, reck-
oning that if the *flics* gave chase in the dark I would be less
encumbered, could probably outpace them. But why didn't
they shout? Why didn't they order me to halt? I had no
time to think. On my credit side I had youth and the fact
that they didn't know exactly where I was, or where I was
making for. On the debit side was the fact that they must
be familiar with the terrain.

So I crashed ahead, an unknown in a wilderness, all
sound confined by the darkness, making no attempt at silence. Searchlights stabbed the night, went out. Then I
heard French curses, *"Halte!" "Merde!" "A gauche!"*

And then in French, "Don't kill him."

The last gave me a mite of consolation—at least they
weren't going to shoot me. And thank God they didn't have
any tracker dogs.

Cursing, I almost fell into a gorse bush, the prickly
needles tearing at my clothes again. The backlash of taller
branches whipped savage scratches across my face and
forehead. Suddenly I could taste blood—my blood—
superficial, but still blood. Panting I scrambled headlong,
oblivious to the tears in my clothes, the ripping of cloth I
could feel. Once or twice resolution almost gave out. But

always a picture of Anna was there to goad me on as, gasping for breath, I tried to cover the last few yards of hell.

What worried me most of all was that I might be running off my track. I knew the wood was narrow, but still, I was afraid I might turn full circle, back in the same gorse bush. Then I would never reach my target of freedom.

It was panic, of course. Reason told me that I was in the right place, but even so I was almost exhausted when two circles of light blazed at me and a voice shouted again, "Halt or I fire!" They couldn't have been more than twenty feet away. I kept still, hoping the undergrowth, the bushes, the thick leaves of the evergreens would hide me. Then the man spoke again, but this time in a hoarse whisper to his colleague.

"Il est là, Louis. J'en suis sûr!"

At the sound of the name the penny dropped. Louis! Christ! All this time I had assumed that the police were searching for me; the alternative had never entered my head. But Louis! Suddenly I realized that this was no police matter, I was up against a couple of thugs whom I had met in the bar and who had lain in wait for me, presumably to rob me.

Fury—at my own stupidity as much as at the two bastards—pumped in the adrenaline. By God! I wasn't going to let a couple of thugs beat me; how many others, perhaps even more helpless, had been robbed by them as they were on the point of gaining freedom?

Well, I had one weapon they didn't expect. And it could be frightening. I realized now that I mustn't run anymore. I must wait for them. I hadn't dared to wait and provoke the police; for an attack on the police would be flashed across the frontier in no time. But a couple of amateur Al Capones was a different matter. I was scared, yes, but they would never be in a position to press charges if I hurt them.

I waited. They switched on their searchlights, on and off, searching, only the nearness of the breathing telling me they were getting close to a tree behind which I was crouching. I had never in my life used my sword stick, and my heart was pumping with fear, but I did know the cardinal advantage of the weapon: you didn't *unsheathe* it if defending yourself, you used it first as a stick, which a couple of hoods could grasp, imagining they would wrest it from you—especially two to one.

That is what happened now. I couldn't see either of them, but I knew one at least—probably both—had reached the other side of the tree.

At that moment, praying it was the right second, I shrieked, screaming an unearthly sound—merely for effect—then switched on my flashlight with my left hand, and as it showed up Louis I slashed his face with all my might—*but with my stick.* It must have been a terrifying blow. A scream of rage erupted and at the same moment Valéry, the other man, plunged toward me—to save Louis, to attack me. Louis almost fell with the force of the blow, and I prepared to strike again.

"Oh, no, you don't, you bastard," growled Valéry, who, warding off the second blow, seized the stick with both hands.

That was his mistake. He thought the stick was a stick, that with his powerful arms he could wrench it from me and then I would be helpless. He did wrench it from me—but with a difference.

With all his might he pulled, cursing me, ready to kill me—and then fell over as the sheath of the sword came away in his hands. Louis was screaming with pain. I didn't have to worry about him—not for the moment—but I charged on top of Valéry and didn't wait for threats. You can be killed if you threaten instead of act. Standing on top of Valéry, one foot digging into his crotch—and that was deliberate, I enjoyed that—I snarled at him, "Now, you sonofabitch, it's my turn!" With that, and without waiting for one second, I thrust the sword stick as deep as I could into his right shoulder.

I felt it go in—oddly enough, for a first time swordsman, it gave me a curious immediate sensation. "That's like a rubber ball that's sealed itself up," I remember thinking.

As I pulled out the blade I looked for the stick and found

it. Valéry screamed, not only with pain but with fury, "You could have killed me!"

"I still can," I said. "And if you try to fuck me up any more, I will. *Salauds!*"

The other man was bleeding more badly. I hadn't used the sword on him, but the force of the slash had split open his right cheek—there was a huge, wide, bloody gash that would leave a scar for life, stretching from forehead to chin.

"You'd better go and see a doctor," I said, "you and your mate."

I found the edge of the woods ten minutes later; I was almost out, not only with fatigue—but with reaction. I was trembling all over. My legs buckled at the knees. But it seemed a different world when I emerged from the trees, so thick they had blotted out the moonlight. It was like being presented with a new pair of eyes.

The actual frontier post was a couple of miles away at Divonne, but here I was faced with only a barbed wire fence near the edge of the woods. For one moment I was scared that it might be electrified, but I had to take a chance and clamber over it, ripping once more my sports jacket. I knew—apart from the map—that it was downhill all the way until I reached the lake. And from the point where I had emerged from the woods, I had to travel left, but at least after the horrors of the wood I felt at home in vineyards, more like my usual friendly territory. It was like treading the paths of my life. All I had to do was walk and be sure nobody saw me.

It was by now one in the morning. I had to cover the seven or eight miles to Rolle before daylight—earlier even than that, before the first farm workers were astir. If *anyone* saw me in my present state, he would call the police before touching me, for I looked like a scarecrow. My clothes hung in ribbons, my shoes were filthy, my face was torn and bleeding. I was in no mood to be seen by *anyone*.

The lake below, shimmering in the moonlight, offered the perfect guide. All I had to do was walk parallel to it, leaving Nyon behind. I was very tired, but Madame Gavroche had given me some sandwiches and an apple, which I chewed as I trudged along.

It was nearly half past four when I saw the outline of Rolle—the nearest town after Nyon—picked out in the moonlight of the lake. I had to skirt several small villages—all of them signposted of course, but with street lamps blazing so that I gave them a wide berth. I also had to be very careful of dogs that kept barking when I approached any habitation. I started climbing downward, I made out a signpost for Rolle, barely half a mile distant.

I found the little road at quarter to five. There was only one house on the left, as I peered ahead at the outline of the railway bridge; so I knew exactly where I was. I pushed open the five-barred gate and suddenly found myself in the courtyard, where I knew there would be the sound of running water from an old horse trough fed by a spring. There it was.

Almost trembling with fatigue of a kind I had never believed possible, I pushed open the gate, switching on my flashlight. The trough, used in the old days for watering the horses, tinkled from some pump.

I just managed to reach the front door and started to pull the bell and bang on it. I heard a voice, angry at being awakened, Sonia's voice, then lights, then a man's voice, another woman shouting, then a figure coming out in the cold onto a first-floor balcony. It was Sonia who shouted, "Who are you? What do you want?"

I just managed to croak, "Sonia! Sonia darling, it's me!"

I heard a shriek, "Larry!" but I had passed out before she had time to open the front door.

37

I MUST HAVE TAKEN a bigger bashing in the forest than I realized, for when I woke up, feeling new pajamas, clean
sheets, feeling *clean,* in a four-poster bed draped in white
at the corners, I held out my arms to Sonia, and before uttering any other words, I demanded hoarsely, "I heard a
man's voice—who is it? Does he live here? Did he carry me
upstairs?"

"Yes, he did—and that's a fine way to greet me!" she realized the strain under which I was still suffering. "I do believe you're jealous!"

"I am!" I blurted out. "Who is he?"

"I'll ask him to come in. But first—let me kiss you, with
your poor, torn face. Be careful, my darling. But your lips
are all right. There! My beloved Larry, here in *our* home."
Then she opened the door, and with a touch of laughter in
her voice called, "You can come in for two minutes to say
good morning to the invalid."

I heard the vague clatter of footsteps on the stone
staircase—had a sudden half-conscious remembrance of a
sweeping, circular stone staircase—and then a man appeared in the doorway. He had fair hair, but most of his
face was hidden in a bushy, reddish-blond beard. I screwed
up my eyes, the better to see him, but I couldn't focus properly. Then he spoke, and voices are sometimes easier to
recognize than faces.

"What the hell have you been up to?" he asked cheerfully, looking at my scratched face.

"Guy!"

"None other! See you for breakfast if you're up to it. Meanwhile I'll leave you two lovebirds together."

"What's he doing here?" I asked weakly when we were alone.

"It's a long story. But—in a few words—he's in and out of France using false French papers—organizing a Resistance group—and then when he needs to he comes back to Switzerland—as an honest American neutral. In fact he's attached to the Red Cross in Bern. But don't worry about that now, darling; I'll explain later. Much more important first—you haven't even told me you love me."

"I'll prove it after breakfast," I put my arms round her and said teasingly when she had put her hands on my chest. "You wait! Monsieur Coquelicot is still waiting for you."

"Always, I hope, always," she was suddenly serious as she kissed me again. "I haven't had the chance to tell you yet, but though it's going to take time, the annulment is on the way. Francesco has done wonderfully. I don't know how long it'll take, but things are on the move. We are cutting through the red tape."

After breakfast, sitting round the old square table in the dining room-cum-entrance hall, I outlined everything that had happened. I told them about Mlle. Lisette. Sonia and Guy listened horrified, for I spared them nothing. It was too terrible even to imagine, to realize that it was actually happening, this very day, this very minute. Sonia was not crying audibly, but her face was streaked with tears. For there was no way anyone could soften a blow like this, no way to minimize it, no way to skirt round the truth; the wicked things that other men were doing to those we loved was there—was happening *now*. Innocence snared by sadistic monsters like Hoess.

Sonia proposed to take immediate action. "If you're going to return to France," she said firmly, "I'll go straight to Rome. Tomorrow. Ciano has promised me he'll do everything he can."

As she explained, she had already broached the subject

to Ciano, the foreign minister. "He's not my favorite character," she confessed, "but I've had dinner with him a few times, and he does have the power to ask favors—after all he *is* Mussolini's son-in-law—and now that I have the precise details of where Anna is—after all, considering he's the number two, he's not asking for a great deal."

"I only hope the price that he demands isn't going to be too much," I said half jokingly.

"No price is too high to get Anna," Sonia was serious. "But I think I can handle him. He's a smarmy brute—he's a great one for ogling and pawing you—but I think I can handle him."

I knew that Sonia, who really and truly loved Anna like a sister, almost more than a sister, perhaps, because of us, was thinking how every day counted. She said to me, "If I can get her out of that hell one day earlier, then I'll save her—" She didn't have to end the sentence, she was thinking, If I can save a day—that's twenty times less she'll have to do it.

We didn't have to say that, but it was always in our thoughts—the number, the pictures that came to us and couldn't be stamped out, that refused to be wiped off the slate of our imagination.

And there was Olivia too. We tended to forget that she, too, had spent several weeks in the bordello before being transferred to Hoess's house—and what happened there, I shuddered to think. Guy and I went for a walk immediately after our breakfast conference, while Sonia drove the few miles to Lausanne to make sure of her train ticket and reservation for a sleeper to Rome. She was also, she said, going to send a message to Ciano that she would be arriving, while at the same time the *Globe* man in Bern was setting off for Rolle to meet us that evening so that I could hand him the story for Washington.

"Before we decide on what we *can* do to help Olivia," I said to Guy, "it might be a good idea to tell me what you're doing already. What's this about your French nationality?"

He told me as we walked round the small garden. In

brief, he had become an unpaid assistant to the Red Cross, who was always looking for volunteers. Apart from providing it with invaluable information, this gave him a kind of cover to use Switzerland as a base while in fact helping to organize Resistance groups inside France. He was ideal for the job, for like all of us Guy really was more at home speaking French than English, and he had acquired French papers, a new nationality, everything.

He also told me how he came to grow a beard. "Apart from the fact that it's a good disguise," he said almost with a grin, "I actually started a beard when I escaped in the car with the Misses B and B and—and then, like Topsy, it just growed and growed!"

"But what do you do exactly?"

Guy's activities were very different from the kind of work which men like Gaston undertook, for Gaston was basically planning for the future in that part of France directly under German rule. Guy, on the other hand, worked in unoccupied France, passing the frontier near the southwest tip of Lake Leman. He was helping to organize escape routes and active Resistance circuits inside the demarcation line—all of them were code names which didn't mean anything to me, of course, and which of course he never mentioned until years later when he talked about the "Autogiro" circuit near Dole and the "Spruce" and "Pimento" circuits near Lyon. What he did in actual fact he never told me at the time, but it was obvious that he was crossing into Switzerland in order to return and pass on vital information to the Red Cross.

"Now," he said, "I'm going to switch plans because of Olivia. I don't know how yet, but we've got to get Olivia out. I can't do anything more for Anna. That's up to Sonia. But we might be able to use Willi to help out again. What do you think?"

"Perhaps, but one thing at a time," I cautioned him. "Let's be certain we get Anna out of France first. God knows how Sonia's going to pull that one off."

"That sonofabitch Ciano will do it for her," Guy said savagely. "God! He's a double-dyed shit. He rings her up regularly—oh, yes, he's mad about her—and she has to go to Italy now and again anyway to get her permit or whatever it is renewed. He insists on it."

"I don't like it," I said. "The thought—"

"Forget it," Guy had grown more aggressive; perhaps the nature of his work was making him tougher, more abrasive.

"You can't *forget* like that. Any more than I can forget what Lisette's done."

"You have to," he said roughly. "I hope Sonia will be able to handle Ciano—but if you want Anna back—well, let's hope she can feed him on promises."

"I'll drink to that."

"So will I," he said soberly. "One thing I've learned from a lot of very brave women I've met since I joined the Resistance—the women pay, they really do. But you must never ask them questions. That way you'll never know what price they *have* to pay in order to save you!"

"But if you can rescue Olivia? Won't you want to know?"

"I would never ask her, never, never," said Guy. "That way at least I will give Olivia a little present—her private self-respect."

"And what are your plans for Olivia?"

Guy had obviously been thinking a great deal. "One thing is certain—I've got to get back to Reims."

"There's a price on your head there—and don't forget that Hoess has a long memory."

"They'll never recognize me behind all this fuzz," he laughed and stroked his beard. "In fact I might come along with you."

"Not a hope!" I said flatly, "and you know it. As soon as I get over the border, I'm an American—and I'm not giving a lift to anyone."

"I suppose you're right. It was okay when I went with the Misses B and B. God! that seems a long time ago. I'll never forget that moment when the Gestapo men came into the room and I pretended to be Jean-Pierre. They were tough, those two. Are they still all right?"

I nodded. "Still living in Paris—and firmly determined to stick to their neutral status."

"They might not be neutral that long," said Guy.

"Roosevelt would never get us into a war."

"I wasn't thinking of that," said Guy. "There's a helluva lot of funny business going on in the Far East. Japan is getting uppity. We've cut off her oil and the Japs are making threatening noises."

"They may *threaten,* but they can't fight *America*—the very thought is ridiculous!"

"I guess so. But there are a lot of double-dyed bastards. And they seem to have a passion for committing suicide. You know—hari-kari. Maybe they'd like to do it on a nationwide scale—Tom, Dick and Harry Kari—if you can see the joke."

"By the way," I asked almost as an afterthought, "you saw Mama in New York? How was she?"

"Don't ask me," Guy almost groaned. "Honestly, she never moves without a retinue of men."

"Well, it's not *her* fault she's so attractive," I laughed.

"It *is* her fault. She's the instigator. She's man mad."

"Nothing serious?" I was thinking of poor Papa, all alone, so sad in Douzy.

"If you mean marriage—no!"

"But—?" I left the question unasked.

"Jig-a-jig—sure," Guy nodded vigorously. "Making up for lost time I'd say. The big city life after the country blues."

I was almost tempted to tell Guy about Gaston but thought better of it.

"Mind you, she's discreet—at least the bed part of it," said Guy. "She's just having a whale of a time. As I say, making up for lost time. I have the feeling," he was obviously thinking of Douzy, "that Papa was never a great performer in bed. Takes after me. Whereas Mama takes after you, you old ram."

How odd it was to hear Guy say that about himself—an echo of a remark made years ago by Olivia.

"I hope she'll be happy," I said, "and come back when this damn war's over."

"She'll be back," said Guy cheerfully. "She'll probably be so fed up with men, anything for a quiet life."

Sonia arrived back at the farm before lunch, and we walked round the small grounds, so quiet, so gentle—God! what a wonderful feeling not to have a German at your back.

Three Circles Farm was beautiful. It was long and low and white, with shutters folded back, set back from the house so that no one using the lane could overlook it. The stone horse trough which I had seen in shadow during the night matched the house perfectly; the water gurgled and spilled into it from the pipe, and above it like a gigantic umbrella were the bare branches of an enormous plane tree. Behind it the courtyard with its circle of tubs, empty now of flowers, shielded a dozen or so fruit trees set in knee-high grass and bordering them, and behind them, but without a fence, was a large wheatfield. It was secluded but not isolated, and clumps of big trees hid the nearest house about four hundred yards away.

"What I really like about it," I said to Sonia, "is that it's not a chalet, it's not a house, it's an old *farmhouse*. Why did you call it Three Circles Farm?" I asked.

"I didn't," holding my hand she walked to the gate and looked out across the vineyards sweeping up the hillside. "I inherited the name. All I know is that it used to belong to a journalist and he christened it. Why I've no idea. But since *you're* a journalist, I thought we should stick to the name. Anyway in Switzerland it's very complicated changing a name."

She gave me a squeeze, we turned round and looked again at the long, low house, and she whispered, "I have a dream sometimes that you'll come and live here—that this will be *our* home when we're married. It's so peaceful. Even the fact that the Swiss are pretty dull and that life is boring doesn't matter—it's so regulated, so safe, so *secure*. You feel you don't have to lock your doors at night."

"But you did lock yours last night," I teased her.

"Habit," she confessed. "Just old habits left over from France and Italy." Sonia had booked to leave the following night on the express for Rome, while Guy, around the same time, would drive me through to Nyon to the point where I would cross the frontier.

"But you *will* be careful, Sonia, won't you? Don't think I don't realize what you're doing—and that our only hope for poor Anna is you—but, darling, *do* be careful."

"I will, I promise you. I can handle all this."

She had planned all the outlines of what she would do. She would go to see Ciano—"I'm having dinner with him the night I arrive in Rome"—then she added, with a pratical sense, that once the request to the Foreign Ministry for Anna's release as a favor was *official*, Ciano would contact the Italian embassy in Paris and they would relay messages to me. "It's far easier than us trying to get in touch on the telephone, which is virtually impossible," she said.

"How it's going to work, I don't know," I said.

"I've told Ciano that Anna was born American, made a disastrous marriage, her husband has vanished, and I want her to come to Switzerland, and then, if she wishes, to go off to America. Just keep your fingers crossed, darling."

"And you keep your legs crossed," I said with a touch of vulgarity I immediately regretted.

"That wasn't necessary," she said quietly. "You forget something. I've been yours since that first day near Dijon. I'm going to be yours forever—when we marry and our children arrive, I'll still be yours—so don't worry, whatever happens."

That afternoon I typed out the story—after all that was the original reason for my visit to Rolle—and the *Globe* man in Bern passed by the farm and then spent the night in Lausanne. I found it almost impossible to adjust to the tempo of *peace*. The casual way in which, when I had handed over my copy, and we had sipped a glass or two of *fendant* Swiss wine, he picked up the telephone, and calmly ordered a taxi to take him to Lausanne. *Ordered* a taxi! And it *came!* Why! I hadn't seen a proper taxi in Paris for two years. And I had forgotten the shabbiness of life in Paris, worn almost as a badge of courage to begin with, but by now a lack of new clothes so commonplace that no one noticed the shabbiness anymore. Not until now when I saw the difference, watching Sonia's housekeeper, a middle-aged lady, very pleasant, very quiet, no doubt not that rich, but still wearing good clothes and new leather shoes, even new stockings. Everything looked so *new.* Everything in France looked so *old.*

Toward the evening Sonia suggested, "Rolle is dead by now. Let's go for a walk—just down the main street."

"You're sure it's safe?"

She nodded. "Only for a few minutes."

The streetlights were on, in itself a wondrous sight, and down by the fountain, where our small lane met the main street, was the same old café where we had first had a *cappuccino.* I had forgotten the name, but there it was—unchanged from the day when we sat down there, and then dashed out to the MG and I kissed her near the lake. The café was still open, almost empty, and the window filled with delicious pastries. "Shall we go in for a coffee—for old time's sake?" I asked.

She nodded and we went inside. A girl served us—obviously not the same girl as on that first day, but with the same singsong Vaudois accent. We drank coffee, ate a huge cake, and after that we walked arm in arm to the square by the lake where I had parked the MG under the peeling plane trees so long ago.

"It seems like yesterday," I sighed. "So peaceful—no hassle, no enemies, no Germans."

She stood facing me, tiptoeing to kiss me, arms round my neck and said, "I'll always love you—always, Larry. But I just couldn't love you any more than I do at this moment. Let's go to bed and pretend we're married before tomorrow comes—and the real world with all its problems."

38

In MID-NOVEMBER the Italian embassy official phoned me at the rue du Sentier. It was the same man who once before had relayed information.

"Signore Astell," he said, "I have a message for you. La Contessa de Feo says she will be arriving on Thursday and that everything has been arranged to pick up the parcel."

Thursday! Two days away. *The parcel!* That could only mean Anna. My heart started thumping with excitement, though I knew—indeed Sonia had warned me—that I must be most careful to play only a passive role. I could do nothing but await events—await Sonia's "orders" in fact, for only she knew what had been planned. And too, during the brief stay in Rolle, she had impressed one other thing on me: the need for secrecy.

"A few days this way or that may make all the difference to Anna," she had said then, "but the others—your father, Uncle Oregon, Grandma—an extra day of waiting won't make any difference because they're not expecting any news at the moment. If they were to get excited *beforehand*—well, I'd be scared they might give something away. And the stakes are so high we can't afford to take even the slightest risk."

This was the advice she had given me in Rolle, and I was glad of it now because on the Wednesday a heavily bearded "Frenchman" who gave the name of "Guy Marchand" turned up at the office and asked for me.

It was Guy, of course. He had arrived after a series of

hair-raising adventures, traveling through unoccupied France and then into Paris, breathing fire. He wanted to make straight for Douzy and then—at least this is what he said—quickly strangle Mlle. Lisette.

"And ruin everything?" I asked. "We keep Lisette on ice for just as long as we need her. You know that better than I do—after all, you're a professional. And then"—I shrugged my shoulders—"she's all yours."

"What's happened to Sonia?" he asked. "And plans for getting Anna out?"

"Nothing really dramatic," that was both a lie and the truth. "We're in Sonia's hands."

"And that bastard Ciano?"

"You don't have to remind me," I said coldly.

"Sorry."

"Well, do me a favor. *Don't* go to Douzy right now. You're safer in a big city. Let me sound out plans with Gaston—for your approval of course. And I think you're right, Guy, Willi could help us. After all, if we get Anna out, Willi owes us one more favor. And he'll make it. In fact he's told me he'd like to defect, cross the border into Spain or Switzerland and give himself up."

"He'd be interned, wouldn't he?"

"Yeah. But at least he'd stay alive. I've got a plan formulating. It includes Willi. And if he'll help you to get Olivia out, then we could help him to get across the frontier. But wait, Guy, till I give you the word. And for Chrissake remember—for the moment *most* of the Astell family have kept their lives neutrally clean. Except you. You're on the list. So don't get caught or you'll be no damn good to anyone."

"Okay," he promised. "I've got my own contacts here. I'll tell you what—I'll be back in four days. How's that? You outline a plan and then we'll crack this goddamn thing wide open."

"Four days." I was relieved—above all that he obviously didn't have the faintest suspicion that Sonia was about to arrive in Paris. It seemed a bit mean not to tell my own brother good news about our own sister, but Sonia was right—a couple days more of ignorance couldn't make any difference to him.

I didn't feel really guilty about withholding the truth from Guy. But I *did* feel guilty about not telling Oregon, for we had a mutual trust which, oddly enough, was shared by none of the rest of the family, not to the same extent. I think it was because we shared the common denominator of being newspapermen. It was a link in which every secret had always been shared. All except this one.

Sonia arrived around 10:00 A.M., the time I knew the train from Switzerland was normally due, and I reached the office early because I had the feeling that she would follow the same routine as she had done the last time, being met by an embassy car and driven straight to my office.

She did exactly that. I was peering out of my office window on the second floor when I saw the car draw up, with a green, red, and white flag on the hood. My heart missed a beat as I saw her step out, slim, desirable. Even the way she climbed out of the low Italian car had an elegance about it, the way somehow both feet seemed to land on the pavement at the same time without showing a lot of leg; the way she shook out her black hair, the glance at her watch, her orders to the embassy chauffeur, all given with a warm smile. I heard the shuddering elevator groan its way toward the second floor, and I waited to open the trellised iron gate as it seemed to hesitate before stopping with a jerk. Then she was in my arms, on the landing, before gently pushing me away, again shaking out her shiny blue-black hair, and said, "Let me get my breath back! Oh, Larry, it's wonderful to see you again. But—"

"But nothing!" I led the way into my office. "I must look at you."

"Larry—we don't have much time!"

"Not even for looking?" I said jokingly. I could sense the tautness in her voice, almost as though she had made an effort to embrace me. Though that, of course, was nonsense. She must be tired after a night in the train.

"Sorry," I said, for after all there was one reason above all others for her being in Paris—Anna. Even my presence was incidental to that.

"It's all arranged," she sat down on my office sofa. Then she said in that same rather strained voice, "But there are several conditions. The first is that I'll become entirely responsible for Anna while she's on French soil—in other words till we get her to Switzerland."

"But that's all right. We can spend a night or two at Douzy—poor Anna, after what's—"

"Poor Anna!" she was almost mocking. "You make it sound as though she's getting over a dose of flu. Really! You men are stupid."

"But what do you mean? Are you trying to tell me something?"

"Of course not. How could I know? But my God, Larry, you don't expect her to be the same girl who was arrested in Douzy, do you? She could be—well—ill."

I had considered that. I was not quite as stupid as Sonia thought, but I had always tried to pretend—except in my innermost thoughts—that this kind of problem didn't exist and I had thought that way for one reason only: the less we dwelt on the terrors of the future, the more we *pretended* to act normally, the less danger of all of us becoming morbid. That was one reason why I hadn't told Papa where Anna was.

"I'm not quite a fool," I muttered shortly, all thoughts of a romantic meeting dashed under the cold shower of reason.

"I know, but," with a sigh, "it's been a great strain for me too."

I looked at her. She *looked* tired—beaten in a way, like she had looked once before when her father had said we couldn't marry. There must be an added emotion that made her so different this morning. People of our age didn't get tired just because of a few missed hours of sleep on a train. Had the "great strain" really been brought about by one night's jolting train journey? Or anxiety, while waiting for the news to come through? Or had it something to do with Ciano? Almost harshly I said, "We're all under a strain. But yours—was it—?" I was on the point of asking her, when I remembered Guy's remark about never asking a woman what price she has paid. Instead I said, swallowing hard, tormenting myself with ugly pictures, "I know, but we're going to save Anna—thanks to you. What are the plans?"

She hesitated before saying in a flat sort of way, all the emotion drained out of her, "You and I are going to fetch her—now, in half an hour. And then," she hesitated, "we take her to Switzerland tonight."

"Tonight!" I shouted.

"There's nothing any of us can do about it," she said wearily. "And please, Larry, don't shout. I've got a blinding headache. The authority to release her has come through. But it's a condition that she leaves with me tonight. Don't blame me for things like this. The train reservations have been booked by other people. I've even arranged to have a special set of papers issued for her."

"But tonight! It's criminal! She needs rest. Dammit, she *is* my sister—and what about Papa? Doesn't he want to see his own daughter? Shouldn't he?"

"He shouldn't—not right away, and you know it. It would be too painful. You've done your share. So has Willi. Nobody could have rescued Anna unless you had found out where she was—but after that, there's nothing you can do. Once you had located her, you needed me to help. Well, I've done it—but," she added bitterly, "I've had to fight—remember the Germans are the bosses now; the Italians play second fiddle. A lot of Italian pressure had to be brought to get Anna out. And getting her out is the only thing that matters. We could never demand conditions. Good God, Larry! What do *conditions* matter?"

"So what's the story?" I asked dully.

"Anna is to be handed over to me at the Hôtel de Ville in Reims between three and four this afternoon. I'll have to sign for her as a sort of legal guardian while she's on French soil."

"And what about the others?"

"You come with me."

"Why me especially? Why not Papa?"

She passed a hand across her forehead wearily and explained, trying to be patient, "Because I had to make all the decisions on the spot without consulting any of you. I had no choices. I'm taking responsibility, but the German authorities demanded the presence of one member of the family to sign a declaration that she *is* Anna Frankel, or Anna Astell."

"I see. And then?"

"Nothing, Larry dear, try to understand. In a way it's not *me* you're talking to, I'm just a messenger from the Italian government. There's no time—not even any *desire* —to kiss each other and swear undying love. This isn't the time or place. We're sure about our love anyway—or I wouldn't be here, would I?"

"No, I do understand. But—"

"First I need a wash," she interrupted me almost deliberately, as though to prevent me arguing. But that was my imagination. "Can I use your 'gentleman's' place, please?"

I nodded. She had used it before, the time she waited to greet me with a room full of poppies; and there was no one around on the second floor at this time of day. "I'll stand guard!" I laughed. She went in. There was a toilet and a wash basin, and it was always clean and always with fresh towels.

"I'll put on a new face," she said, "and have as good a wash as I can."

During the quarter of an hour I was thinking—jumbled thoughts tumbling one over the other—above all of Anna. Soon she would be free. But what would she be like? She would be changed—but how? I was thinking back to the fun weekends when she used to sneak away to the Crillon with Willi—and Willi was somewhere around now, without even knowing that his wife, my sister, Papa's daughter, was about to be freed from the terrible trap into which she had fallen. Yet in a way I was almost afraid of the meeting that lay ahead—in case—well, what *would* she be like? She couldn't be normal, I couldn't expect her to be af-

ter the horrors she had passed through. For a moment I almost wondered whether it wouldn't be better to let Sonia
take Anna back alone. But no, that would be a coward's
way out. Even if no one else in the family could see her for
the moment, at least I should, to show her that we were all
together in this.

Sonia agreed when she returned to the office, and
Charles had brought up some ersatz coffee from Madame
Yvette's bistro downstairs. "You're her favorite brother.
She'll look to you for—well—moral support, I suppose
you'd call it."

"And Papa?"

"You forget one thing," Sonia reminded me. "*You* may
have problems crossing frontiers, but that's only because
you *choose* to be a newspaperman who's unpopular with
the Germans. But your father is a true neutral, a real neutral. He's respected—by all sides. He can travel to Switzerland to see Anna whenever he wants—next week, if you
like. And stay at Rolle."

"But why not today? At Douzy? On the way home?" I
asked.

"No risks, Larry—not until we get her out of the country. I never trust men like Abetz—God knows," she still
sounded bitter, "we realize how wicked *he* is—and don't
forget, this is an *official* diplomatic visit by me, as an
emissary of the Italian government. The orders for release,
the details, everything I have in my handbag," she held it
up, "are here—but there are copies in the embassy. This is
official. Even a visit to your office has been noted here.
And the itinerary is in the embassy's hands as well as in
mine. I have to drive back from Douzy after Anna is
handed over and stay inside the embassy until it's time for
the train to leave."

"But that means—" I began to see that, incredibly, I
would never have her alone.

"There's no other way. You can imagine that the driver
of the embassy car has been specially chosen."

"But to come all this way, darling—and never even to
see you alone. To talk to each other."

"I came for Anna," she said simply. "Nothing else matters. These few moments are the only ones we'll have
alone—this time."

"Well, dammit," I said almost savagely, "I'll come back
the same way as I did the other time—through the woods."

"I hope you will, I hope so with all my heart, when all
this is over," suddenly gentler, lips trembling, eyes bright
with tears. "But on the next trip don't scratch your face,
like you did before."

For a moment I clung to her, not kissing but holding
each other in our arms, then she said, "We must go. And be
careful in the car. What we talk about I mean. And no
holding hands."

The journey to Reims was utterly miserable. We sat like
a couple of strangers in the backseat, talking inanities,
while I let my mind wander around phrases she had used
like "when all this is over," and the reference to Ciano. I
thought, too, of the innuendos which Abetz had made,
which even Guy had hinted at. Yes, a journey to rescue my
sister, a journey that should have been an occasion for joy,
for the pealing of bells, proceeded with the glum silence of
a funeral procession.

We didn't even stop for lunch—in a way a good thing, for
there was no such thing as a good lunch in a bistro anymore. However, Sonia had packed a picnic lunch, which
she had put in the car at the station and now proceeded to
open.

"Some for us," she said as she unwrapped the square
parcels of tissue and grease-proof paper, "and some for
Anna if she wants it."

There was an assortment of Swiss food easy to eat in the
car—even though it was a raw November day; some salami
and other *charcuterie* and a *tarte de blette*, a kind of quiche
made of Swiss chard with cheese and eggs. There was a
huge chunk of Emmenthal, the best Swiss cheese. "With
the best holes in them," Sonia said, laughingly for once.
And there was some late fruit from the Rhone Valley, together with two bottles of good Swiss wine, a *fendant*,

which fizzes very gently because, as Papa had once told me, it is bottled without being separated from its yeasty sediment.

I did drink my share of wine—I loved it for a change—but I could hardly eat a bite, neither could Sonia. The tension was too oppressive, not only the anxiety but in a curious way a kind of apprehension of the confrontation to come. Would Anna and I fall into each others arms, would we kiss? Would she cry? Would I? How *do* you prepare to say hello to one you love but have not seen since she passed through the valley of the damned?

When the moment *did* arrive it proved to be almost an anticlimax. I helped to direct the chauffeur, telling him where to turn left off the Paris road when we reached the boulevard Louis Roederer, leading to the place de la République. From there it was only a few yards along the right fork of the rue de Mars, named after the famous Roman gate.

"You'd better come inside too," Sonia whispered instinctively as we stopped outside the steps of the Hôtel de Ville, where Sonia had been told that Anna would be ready. I followed her up the steps. A French policeman stood at the door, but so did a German soldier—at the other side, as though sharing responsibility for law and order. Seeing the chauffeur and the Italian flag on the right bumper, to say nothing of the Corps Diplomatique plate at the rear, the German soldier stepped forward, saluted smartly, and said, "You are expected, madame."

Once inside the main entrance he beckoned us to an anteroom, looking as if it hadn't been dusted for a year. A man who seemed like a clerk was introduced to Sonia, "This is Herr Weiss. He is dealing with your problem."

Dr. Weiss didn't seem very enthused. He motioned Sonia to a hard chair opposite his cheap desk—he ignored me completely—asked Sonia to show him her papers, read them, finally turned to me and asked, "Are you the relative?"

"I am," I said.

"The lady is outside. Will you please identify her?" I must have looked puzzled.

"Through the window behind you," said Weiss in a tired voice. I walked to the end of the room, which overlooked the main entrance lobby through which she had come. And there she was, Anna—sitting straight up on a hard chair. I didn't have time to study her face—perhaps I was frightened to look too closely—I returned and said, "That's my sister."

"Sign here, please." He might have been asking me to put my signature on a new driving license. "This is your sworn declaration in front of me that this is your sister. You understand? It is a formality, for our records. And," turning to Sonia, he offered her some papers, "here is the safe conduct from Reims to Lausanne, countersigned by the SS. That will be all."

And that *was* all. Even Sonia had turned pale with the anticipation of the moment. The clerklike Weiss left through a different door after a curt "Good afternoon." I held Sonia's arm—more for support than a gesture of love—and we walked out into the large entrance hall.

Anna still sat on the chair, as though rooted to it—or was she afraid to move without permission? Sonia ran across the room, arms outstretched, and only then did Anna get up. She said nothing—nothing I could hear—as Sonia put her arms round her, and then Anna was looking at me, full in the eyes, and I kissed the cheek of her gray, lined face below its stringy hair and said nothing. She let her arms fall on my shoulder, smiled at me, a tired smile, and kissed me back.

"Let Sonia help you to the car," I said gently. There wasn't much to say really. The girls sat in the backseat. I got in front, next to the driver. Halfway there Anna began to ask one or two questions. "How is Papa?" I told her Papa was well, and when she asked, "Does he know where I am—was?" I replied, "No, Anna, I didn't tell him. He doesn't know yet that you're free."

"And Guy?"

"He's fine," and with an attempt at humor, "he's grown a huge beard."

I turned my head to look at her in the rear seat—a damned uncomfortable way to talk to anyone for a long time; but perhaps it was just as well. I didn't want to give her the impression I was examining her. But at the mention of Guy's beard, she did manage a wan smile. "I'm so glad," though I didn't quite know what she meant by that remark. But then she didn't say much. It was an awful journey back to Paris, a trip fearful in Anna's total resignation, mental exhaustion, acceptance. Looking back, I find it hard to analyze the emotions, not that I could have expected to know what those emotions were, except that I could *see* them in the gray, tired face whose very silence was more eloquent than any words. I caught myself thinking, halfway along that interminable, cold November drive, I hope to God I never have to make a trip like this again as long as I live.

The thought was immediately followed by one of selfishness, of guilt—how shameful to be thinking like this, how wicked of me to be so selfish. But the trouble is that you can't harness thoughts, you can't make them do what you want. And of course there *was* one other reason I felt the way I did. I shouldn't really have been in the car, I realize that now. Brother I might be, but I was unwanted at this reunion, and understandably so. A man was the last repository for a girl's confidence, confessions, at a moment like this. I realized that I would actually have *helped* Anna to overcome the initial shock of freedom had I greeted her in Reims and then let the two girls drive back alone to Paris, with promises that I would come down to see them. Instead I was here, inhibiting any chance that they might talk to each other, give way to their emotions. Well, I thought, we would be back in Paris by six o'clock and they would have all the evening in the embassy, and then all the night in the train, to talk to each other.

Once or twice she did speak, especially as we reached the outskirts of Paris. I hadn't been thinking of the route, but as we reached the porte de Pantin I suddenly realized that

I wasn't being invited to the embassy anyway. Normally when we drove to our flat on the Left Bank—and the Italian Embassy was also on the Left Bank—we came in by the porte de Vincennes, and then passed the place de la Nation, along the boulevard Diderot, past the Gare d'Austerlitz. I could almost drive it blindfolded.

But now, after entering by the porte de Pantin, we drove along the avenue Jean-Jaurès, and the rue La Fayette, where Anna, suddenly sparked by memories, cried, "Oh! There's the Galerie La Fayette." We made our way along the rue Haussmann, then to the Opéra—and then, with hardly a moment to say good-bye, Sonia had ordered the car to stop along the Grands Boulevards at the corner of the rue du Sentier.

"It's better this way," Sonia's voice wasn't meant for argument, "and for everyone. And you'll come to see us as soon as you can, won't you?"

"I promise."

"Give my love to Papa," said Anna. "And please come soon."

Sonia stepped out of the car to have a word with me in private.

"No kissing," she whispered. "Except on the cheek. The driver's looking. And don't be angry, darling. Anna's in a state of absolute shock. Believe me, this is the best way. It's our only hope of bringing Anna back to normal. And don't tell anyone until the embassy phones you tomorrow confirming that we're on Swiss soil."

There was nothing left for me to say. I waved to Anna, she waved back, and as Sonia prepared to get back into the car she whispered, "And remember, all this business has upset me too, you know, but it hasn't stopped me from loving you. Please don't *you* stop loving *me.*"

The telephone message arrived two days later. It was simple. After identifying myself verbally, the same man from the Italian embassy announced on the phone in the same deadpan voice, "Monsieur le Comte de Feo has asked

me to pass on a message? sir. Madame and her friend have
arrived in Switzerland."

I had known it would be all right. The arrangements,
backed by officialdom, were too watertight to admit of error, but even so, I startled Oregon in the next room by
shouting, "Whoopee!" And as he came in, looking almost
Pickwickian with his fringe of white hair, his twinkling
eyes, he was even more startled.

I had committed the sin, usually indulged in by victorious racing drivers, of uncorking a bottle of Astell and,
thumb in neck, was shaking it until, just as Oregon opened
the door, I pulled out my thumb and a fountain of froth and
bubbles shot out in a shower, spraying the entire room.

"What the hell?" cried Oregon. "Your father would be
furious," for it was considered very ill mannered even to
make a "pop" when uncorking champagne. "What's happened? You've been appointed editor of the *Globe*, or
what?"

I shook my head.

"Well—we haven't won the war—not yet."

"We *have* won our greatest victory of the war—Anna's
safe. I've just heard that she's in Switzerland—with
Sonia."

"Anna! I can't believe it. But how? When?" Almost fer-
vently Oregon lit one Gauloises from the stub of the last,
brushing the ash off his jacket lapels. "Sit down!" and
laughing with happiness he almost shouted, "You may be
the boss around here, but remember—I taught you all you
know!"

"Oh, Oregon!" I did sit down and poured out a glass of
the remaining champagne. "I'm so happy. Poor Anna. I
was sworn to secrecy until she was actually safe in Switzerland—safe from that bastard Abetz. And no one can
touch her now. So I couldn't even hint. But now I must
take a day off and go and tell Papa. He'll be overjoyed."

I knew I merited a day or two of leave because by now
the piece I had written on life in France, and filed from
Switzerland, had been published, causing one helluva row
in France. The *Globe* had been officially proscribed by

Vichy France—not that it ever arrived there. It was not so much the Germans who were angry, more the French. The French police, who couldn't take any serious action without consulting the Germans, came to see me, studied my papers, asked me where I had been around the time the article was printed. I had a perfect alibi—inasmuch as I had never left France—not officially. But the article was not only a major scoop about conditions under the Germans in France, it bore the stamp of my writing, which by now had, I realized, its own character, as clear to an expert analyst as my signature. Only this story had appeared under the name of our Bern correspondent. And so long as I kept out of trouble, and the identity of Henri Vasson was never discovered, the French and Germans in Paris could think what the hell they liked. All I had to do was say, "Of course I never wrote it! It's unthinkable." My only regret was that I could never see the copy of the newspaper. I did get news of it from Jim Parks, the consul, who had remained in Paris as part of the skeleton staff now that Admiral Leahy had been appointed U.S. ambassador to the Vichy government. Parks didn't get copies of American newspapers, but the office did get a daily digest of what the American press was saying, and the "Bern story" figured prominently, so at least I knew it had caused a stir.

On the Sunday I drove to Douzy—just for one night, arriving very late. After breakfast I told Papa and Grandma. To spare their feelings I had never revealed the truth about Anna, only that we couldn't trace the prison where she was being held. But by substituting *prison* for *brothel* I didn't have to get involved in too many lies, and I stuck to the story that she had been arrested and put in jail. I didn't want Papa in particular ever to learn the truth. It would haunt him for the rest of his life. So all I said was that Anna had been held in detention without trial and that we had discovered where she was. Apart from that, everything I said was true—I explained that Sonia had arranged for Anna's release, how she had done it, the conditions which had been imposed, even the need for secrecy.

After the first shock had passed, the near tears, Papa said, "I think we should go to mass, yes, yes, even *you*, Larry." And as an afterthought, he added, "This is a moment of great *rejoicing*, yes, that's the word, *rejoicing*, so let us ask the congregation to join us in a glass after lunch."

It sounded a little complicated to me—for how could you ask all the people at church? You couldn't expect the good father to announce it from the pulpit. But I needn't have worried. I was so out of touch it never occurred to me that Douzy's congregation would have shrunk to a handful of people. Apart from anything else the cold of this November —without any heating of any sort in this old stone church— kept them away. Papa warned me of that, yet the idea of a "welcome home" party for the absent Anna *was* a good idea, for everyone knew she had vanished, and this was the simplest way of telling everyone that she was alive, and well and safe.

"Go to the Café des Sports before the service," suggested Grandma when Papa had gone to his study. "Monsieur Roland will pass the word along. Thank God this nightmare is over." And then, with a secret look at me, she asked, "Did her husband help? Willi?"

"Yes, Grandma, he did. But he doesn't know yet that Anna is safe. He told me that he wants to try and escape to Switzerland—to defect, is that the word?"

"Best thing in the world," she grunted. "One less German to fight. Good or bad, one less. Come on, let's walk to church."

She set off at a brisk pace, a wonderful old lady for her age, still upright, tall and angular, severe looking. For church she wore a hat which helped to hide her thinning gray hair, only allowing a few wisps to peep out. She walked as she cycled, always with determination, with purpose, just as she walked now, straight back with long strides, as though to save shoe leather.

It was wonderful to sense the happiness that suffused the faces of all our villagers after church. Almost all were connected in one way or another with our family. When

Papa asked for silence and announced his standard introduction to *any* speech, "I don't propose to make a long speech," he actually didn't this time. "I just want all our friends here, all of us suffering under a cruel war, to share in our happiness—yes, our *happiness*—at what has happened."

He didn't of course *announce* that Anna was free, the word had spread through the village in a matter of minutes, but it was touching to see men and women like old Pagniez and Madame Robert hold up their glasses and cry, *"Bonne chance*, Mademoiselle Anna!" and "Bravo, Miss Anna." I didn't hear one person toast "Madame Frankel," but it wasn't done deliberately. If Anna had married a dozen times, the people of Douzy would always call her "Miss Anna."

39

As the party was about to end, Gaston, who had been there, whispered to me, "Did you know that M'sieu Guy, the so-called Guy Marchand, is here?"

"Already?" I nearly spluttered in my drink. "He *did* say he was coming in four days—I suppose that *was* four days ago."

"He's come to discuss plans to rescue Olivia. Now that your sister—it was wonderful what you all did."

"But Olivia?"

"Well, I agree with Guy Marchand. Apart from the fact that a friend of your family is involved—Miss Jacobsen, I mean—I think it's time some of us in the Resistance showed the stuff we're made of. Marchand has been telling me what he's been doing near Lyon. We're just beginners here."

"How do you propose to set about it, Gaston? I mean, you can't just raid Gestapo headquarters and abduct Hoess and whisk Olivia away."

"Not quite," he gave a wry smile. "But we might do the next best thing. We might lure Hoess away from Gestapo headquarters and *then* abduct him."

"Be careful," I warned Gaston. "I'm all for *anything* we can do, but Marchand—he's a very brave man, but he's a daredevil."

"We need a daredevil. Guy's all right," said Gaston.

Guy! They're on first-name terms, I thought. But then they *were* members of the same army of the night. Half humorously I asked, "Isn't it a bit unwise calling him Guy?"

"Not Guy as in Guy Fawkes. Guy as in a Gee. And it's Guy Marchand. No, it's not dangerous."

"No more dangerous than calling—"

"Calling you Larry? No," he shook his head. "In a way, after what you've done, you're one of us whether you like it or not. We have no ranks, only Christian names in our groups."

And that is how, without any fuss, I was in a way "accepted" by the Resistance—if only as a passive member. And now equally without any fuss, Gaston started quite naturally to call me Larry. His next remark, however, startled and shook me.

"We've been having preliminary thoughts on how to go about it. I'd like your advice. Do you think we can trust Willi Frankel of the Gestapo?"

I gaped again, not at the idea, and asked angrily, "What the hell do you know about Willi Frankel?"

He had the grace to look a little uncomfortable, and finally, dragging the words out, he said, "You'd better ask La Châtelaine."

"La Châtelaine! I damn well will."

At first I was furious—and I remembered feeling the same anger years previously when Olivia first came into our lives; it had to do with "the family"—the Astells didn't like "outsiders" discussing the family. But when I confronted Grandma with Gaston's statement, she became almost angry with me for being angry with him.

"Be more intelligent!" she snorted. "There's a war on, remember?"

"Not ours."

"Nonsense! *You* think it's important to write your articles for the *Globe*. Maybe it is. But, my boy, life has changed since you and Oregon started playing with words. It's changed, do you hear?" she asked almost fiercely. "We've reached a stage in history when the sword is now mightier than the pen—and the sooner people help with the sword the better."

"But, Grandma, I think you've been unfair. And as Americans—we *are* neutral."

"Fiddlesticks! To pretend otherwise is stupidity. And I can't abide stupid people. As for Willi, without his help we would never have freed Anna, and you know it. He proved that he was capable of keeping calm in a crisis."

A dozen questions leaped to my mind. Why should Grandma decide so firmly? Had she and Willi met?

"I've met Willi twice," she said, adding a trifle ironically, "after all, you don't *live* here, Larry. We *do* have visitors when you're busy in Paris."

Of course I could hardly expect Willi to send me a cable telling me when he was going to pay a visit to Douzy, but somehow I was irritated.

"So I arranged for him and Gaston to meet," said Grandma.

"Was that wise?"

"Of course it was," with the return of her old fire, "otherwise I wouldn't have done it. And perhaps now you realize we have a German agent working for us in the Resistance."

Again I looked at her, this time aghast. Grandma was over seventy. "What on earth do you mean—'us in the Resistance'?" I asked.

Almost with a smirk, she replied, "Let's just say that I'm an *ex officio* member. If I can help, I mean to. Till the last German is kicked out of France."

Thinking it over on the drive back to Paris, I wondered if all this plotting and secrecy were worthwhile—or whether Grandma, Gaston, Guy, all the others whom I didn't know, were really of any importance in the scheme of war—leaving out Anna, that is, and of course Olivia. But the plans to blow up railway lines? Were they really of any value, or were they an extension of irresponsibility, like the stuff we used to read about in schoolboy magazines? I didn't see how a handful of Resistance men and women, however brave, could take on the might of Germany, could even be of any account. What did it matter, really, blowing up a bridge or a tunnel? After all, the RAF had tried to blow up the Rilly tunnel and had only killed some innocent Civilians instead. And if the Resistance did blow up a train, then what about the fear of reprisals? We had already heard terrible stories from central France, where whole families had been executed—children as well as grandmothers—as reprisals for killing a couple of German soldiers. But could such an act of violence ever influence the war sufficiently to cause the deaths of innocent children?

Driving alone toward Paris—this time taking the road through La Ferté that would lead to the Left Bank—I hated the idea of being thought a cynic, I *wanted* to believe in heroes, and after all, having obtained the release of Anna, I was inwardly excited at the prospect of helping Olivia to escape.

"Well," said Gaston the next time I met him, which was during the last week in November, "we're going to—what's the word they use in American movies?—we're going to spring Olivia next week. But remember, there's only one way we can do it. It will involve tortures—and then cold-blooded killing. So there will be reprisals when the Gestapo discovers what we've done—and who we've killed."

"Hoess?"

"Absolutely. Apart from Olivia, who to be frank I only know as a member of your family, I haven't forgotten what Hoess did to my father."

"I understand—but if you hardly know Olivia, it seems a little extreme."

"It's not my idea. It's Guy's. He wants her freed. And he's an experienced senior member of the Resistance. I know he operates mainly in Vichy France and I don't come under his orders, but he is experienced. He knows what he's doing and he can help."

"Where is Guy now?"

"He's still at Douzy, staying in a safe house."

"Where?" I persisted.

"He's not far away. As I say, in a safe place."

"But where?"

Reluctantly Gaston finally admitted, "He's been staying with my father. But now we've arranged a local place to meet secretly if we have to pass on messages or hide."

"But where?" I repeated. "Or would you rather not tell me?"

"Well, yes, I think I can. You'd have to go there sooner or later if we need your help. It's in Douzy church. Up near the belfry there's a tiny room we've turned into a place where you can sleep—only a straw mattress but it's safe so long as we can get food in."

I had to admire Guy, roughing it in the belfry of a cold church. Of course he couldn't have gone to stay at Douzy, for he would be on the wanted list as long as there were Germans in France. Still, it was one thing to do what he had previously done—slip over the border, however dangerous, and then return to the comfort and safety of Switzerland. But this—this living like a hunted animal, it must take a lot of guts. Either he loved Olivia very much, or he had seized on her release as a focal point, a challenge he had to meet.

"I hope Grandma won't be dragged into any of this?"

Gaston was truly horrified. "You *must* think I'm a wicked bastard," he said. "All she does is relay messages— verbal messages—to and from Willi Frankel whenever they meet. Of course La Châtelaine will never become involved—any more than she did when, as she told me at a meeting, she was the only one who saw the value of Frankel, of how he could be useful."

"A meeting?" My amazement never stopped. "You mean to say La Châtelaine is not involved, yet you're having secret meetings—about a man in the Gestapo?"

"It wasn't a meeting really. She sent for me. I had no option."

"But a *meeting?*"

"It was in the vineyards," and, with a shrug, "La Châtelaine does—well—tend to *give* orders. And as you know, there's an enormous amount of work to be done in the vineyards in November and December—turning over the earth, covering the stocks, protecting them against frost, banking up the soil, fertilizing, replacing worked-out soil. It's a heavy program, and our talks started when La Châtelaine came and worked alongside me." Gaston looked at me almost pleadingly, "I couldn't do *anything*—you must know that. La Châtelaine is—what's the word?—unique. She decides, everyone else obeys."

I couldn't help but grin. "You're right there," I said, "she really laid into me the other day—more or less told me I was wasting my time writing. So, I would like to say hello to Guy. And offer to help if I can. After all, I do have a really good neutral cover."

"I'll tell Guy, of course he'll want to see you. But as for helping," Gaston sounded doubtful, "all the plans are laid now, everything's prepared."

However, I did meet Guy, but not in Douzy. When I returned to Paris he left a message for me at the rue du Sentier, asking me if I would meet him at the Deux Magots.

"I didn't know you were back in Paris," I said. "You could have phoned me at the office."

"I didn't dare to. The phone might be tapped."

"I'm sure it is," I agreed. "What are you doing here? I thought—?"

"I came to reassure you. *Garçon!* Two beers please." He sipped it. "Tastes like weasel pee," he said disgustedly. "Ah! For a pint of good Swiss Feltschlossen."

Finally he came to the plan. "Grandma knows nothing about what we're going to do," he said first to reassure me. "And I hope that we'll be able to go it alone; but we need someone as a backup—in case things don't go as smoothly as we hope they will."

"And what are those plans? Am I allowed to know?"

"You shouldn't," Guy almost grinned, and then without stopping the laugh, said in a loud voice, "God! It's late! I must be going!" As we both fumbled with money to pay, he whispered, "Don't look round, but we're being watched. See you at the Boule Blanche this time tomorrow and then—" with a touch of irony he added in a whisper, "I'll tell all."

The Boule Blanche was round the corner, just off the rue Jacob, and the next day at four o'clock Guy was waiting for me.

"Sorry I had to rush off yesterday," he explained. "I can smell the Gestapo a mile away. And they always get suspicious if they see two men talking earnestly at the same table for too long."

The first thing that Guy and Gaston had learned was that Mlle. Lisette had not betrayed just one woman when Olivia was denounced. She was a regular traitor, working with the Gestapo for money.

"My first thought was to kill her right out," Guy admitted. "But that's a stupid thing to do. Never kill anyone you might need to use."

Where had I heard that advice before?

"But how do you *know?*" I asked. "You can't be sure, I mean you can't know what goes on in Gestapo headquarters?"

"No, but Lisette is too scared—and too useful—to risk *visiting* the Gestapo. They come to see her. Even Hoess pays her regular visits, presumably to collect information. And Gaston has virtual proof of five people who have mysteriously disappeared—and who were known to Lisette. She's one of dozens of French bastards who believe Germany has won and are backing the right horse—or what they think is the right horse."

"Still—how can you trap her? And get Olivia out—for after all, Olivia is the main object of the exercise."

"Of course."

This in brief was the plan. It was almost the end of November by now, and on the following Friday—that would be the fifth of December—Guy and Gaston planned to make the bid for Olivia's freedom. Willi apparently was due to visit Douzy on the Thursday evening—the Thursday before the plan went into operation.

"Yes, we've had to make this one a firm date for Willi," said Guy.

"But how do you know Willi can keep the date?" I asked.

"Don't worry, Willi will keep it," said Guy, "we know he will because this is going to be his last trip. After that he's going to try and get to Switzerland, and give himself up."

According to the arrangements Willi would drop off his driver at Reims on the Thursday evening, giving him a three-day pass to Paris—it was a rare privilege to be allowed to stay overnight in Paris—and then Willi would make for Douzy.

"Why on Thursday evening?" I asked.

"We need two cars and time to rearrange Willi's Gestapo car a bit," said Guy. "I hope you don't mind, but we plan to take off the license plates from your old MG and use them. That should get us through."

I gulped. I didn't expect to use the MG for a long time, but she *was* my pride and joy, even though she was in the garage. But Gaston had promised to get a replacement set of license plates. Once Willi reached Douzy on the Thursday, Gaston would take away his Gestapo car, change the license plates, and paint out the yellow wheels—the dreaded Gestapo trademark—so that the car could be used to escape to Switzerland.

"That's fine in theory. But you've skipped one important part of the story," I objected.

"You mean—how we're going to get Olivia out," Guy smiled.

I nodded.

"Let me outline our plans," he said. "Someone in the Resistance would make sure on the Friday that Hoess was in Gestapo headquarters. Then Gaston and Guy would drive an old tractor up to Lisette's old cottage at the end of the same lane as the cottage once used by the Misses B and B. Gaston on a tractor would excite no comment."

"But wouldn't she recognize you?"

"Doesn't matter," said Guy. "She won't know it, but she'll be in serious trouble before the day's out."

Once in the house, a quarter of a mile from the B and B house, Lisette would be forced to write to Hoess. "We'll have to persuade her to write that letter," said Guy unemotionally, "but we know how to do it."

"And then?"

"Lisette would be forced to write a note to Hoess saying she had important news that couldn't wait. She's done that before," said Guy bitterly, "and if it's hot news, Hoess always comes. After all, *she* can't be seen at Gestapo HQ, and it's only a couple of miles drive up the hill for him."

Guy realized that Hoess would never come alone to such a lone spot. But Gaston's Resistance fighters would have half a dozen hit men hiding in the woods round the cottage. They had arms stolen from the Germans.

"It sounds damned dangerous," I said.

"It is. But you've got to understand one thing, Larry. The fact that I want Olivia freed is of course important, but the others—they want something bigger: to prove themselves, to stage a major coup, to kill a Gestapo man who is hated all over the area. Why, even Willi Frankel says he's a swine."

"Where *does* Willi come in?" I asked. I could understand the fledglings of the Resistance wanting to prove their mettle.

That was the second stage. Once Hoess had been trapped into coming to Lisette's cottage, he too would be subjected to what Guy called "persuasion." He would be forced to write a letter to the house where he lived in the rue St. Julien, where Olivia also lived as a prisoner.

Hoess in theory would say in the letter that he wanted Olivia sent to see him under Gestapo guard. And Willi, in his own Gestapo uniform, would arrive in his own car to the rue St. Julien. It would look perfectly normal—one Gestapo officer bearing a letter from another, ordering a prisoner to be sent to him.

"But Hoess will never agree. Never. And what about noise? What about the soldiers outside?" I asked.

"Hoess *will* agree. You wait. And there'll be no noise."

"You might be able to force Lisette to give in, but Hoess isn't the sort to crack early, quickly, is he?"

"Not easily. But we'll have to *make* him crack. And we know how to do it."

"And then?"

"Once we get Olivia out, she'll be driven back to Lisette's cottage. But she'll stay in the car at the bottom of the lane. Willi will run up to the cottage to tell us she's free, and also to help if needed—disposing of the bodies, or whatever. Yes, of course we'll have to kill them both."

His matter of fact statement not only sent a shiver down my spine, it made me realize how Guy had changed, what a hell of a life he had been living—proving that his particular sword was far mightier than my own particular pen. He was *saving* men and women, he was *killing* enemies. Once the couple had been killed, Willi would go out to tell any waiting SS men that they could return to barracks. He would be in Gestapo uniform of course, and it would seem quite natural for him to tell their sergeant that he was driving Hoess back home. Once the SS had gone, everyone would make for the belfry at Douzy church, where peasant clothes for Willi would be waiting, together with food and anything else needed for the journey to Switzerland. Guy, Willi, and Olivia planned to set off for Switzerland immediately.

"Only one thing is missing," I said with a touch of irony. "Where do I come in?"

"Not very heroic," admitted Guy. "But we don't want *your* identity known to the Gestapo—to those who start panicking when they find out that Hoess has been murdered. There'll be hell to pay. But there's one thing you can do. While we're changing in the church, you can drive Willi's car to our secret gas pump in Douzy and fill her up. We need all the gas we can get."

"And Gaston?" I asked.

"He doesn't want to go to Switzerland. I can understand. After all, he works in *this* sector," said Guy.

"But won't there be a danger that he'll be traced—seen?"

"I don't see why," Guy shook his head. "All witnesses will be dead—and *they* won't be able to tell any tales. It's important that Gaston does try to keep out of this—not be discovered. And of course the same thing applies to you, Larry. It's important that you keep out of this, as a neutral, as a newspaperman, and it applies to Papa too."

That was all—and to be frank I didn't like it. The plan seemed too pat, too easy. But it was their plan and they were the professionals.

40

Guy planned to reach the cottage around nine o'clock on the Friday morning. If all went well, Olivia could be freed in a few hours, leaving several hours of daylight to drive as near to the Swiss frontier as possible. If anyone in the party ran into trouble, they would take the road or the railway. Somehow they would move southward. It all seemed very hit-and-miss to me, but then I suppose this sort of operation always would be.

The first real snag came on the Thursday. Aubergine asked me very politely if I could go to see Gaston, who was working in the vineyard. It was perfectly normal for him to be there when he had nothing else to do. To any outsider my presence there seemed perfectly innocent, and my presence there was reinforced in the eyes of anybody who might be suspicious by the presence of Grandma, bossing everyone, walking with long strides along the lanes of bare stalks, shouting an order here, giving an instruction there, eyes missing nothing. All in all it was a perfect picture of a law-abiding neutral vineyard at work—and a perfect cover for meeting, passing plans, arranging secret rendezvous.

"We've hit a snag," Gaston bent over and from a container replaced some "sour" soil with fresh while I helped, squatting down.

"What's the trouble?"

"I've just been tipped off that Lisette's cottage is fitted with an alarm. The Gestapo calls it a *Notknopf*—a panic button."

Gaston explained in detail that about fifty French informers whom the Germans thought worth protecting had
been linked up with Gestapo headquarters by an alarm
system which was doubly dangerous, according to Gaston's informant, because it wasn't a shrill alarm inside a
house—the kind of alarm that would scare off people—but
a silent alarm which, without the knowledge of the in-
truder, would alert Gestapo headquarters so that anyone
suspicious could be caught red-handed.

"We had planned to send Guy in first. He might be suspicious, but at least he could argue with Lisette, saying
anything he wanted as—well, as an old friend. Even if she
was suspicious, there'd be nothing she could do about it
once Guy got past the front door."

"But now?"

"I understand these panic buttons, as the Gestapo calls
them, are always hidden near the point of entry—obviously they would be, so that if anyone *does* panic, he or she
can press the button without anyone knowing. That would
have to be the reaction of Lisette if she suddenly saw Guy,
who she must know is wanted by the Gestapo on charges of
assaulting Hoess. Their last words were filled with hate
—or so he told me. She's a woman who must live in fear—
all informers do. So she'd take no chances."

"So? Will you go?"

"I could, I suppose," said Gaston, "but I'm the only one
who can manage the tractor. It's got to be turned around,
prepared, ready for the escape before there's any alarm."

"What about Willi?"

"He won't be there—not to begin with."

"So what?"

Gaston lifted his eyes from the chalky soil, which he had
been patting round the roots of the vines, and his eyes
stared straight into mine.

"You'd be perfect," he said almost with a twitch of humor.

"Me! But you said my value rested on being really
neutral—"

"I know, I know, and we still don't want to involve you.

But this is our only chance to get Olivia out. Willi has burned his bridges. He'll never be able to operate again. Guy's waiting for you in my father's cottage. He's gone there for some food. Go and see him if you can find a better way of solving the problem."

In fact Guy could offer no other solution. Old Pagniez had gone off to the Home Farm, and we sat in the tiny kitchen of his thick stone cottage, trying to keep warm with a fire made of bits of wood hauled down from the hillside. I wasn't that worried about getting involved, of taking a chance, except to protect Papa's reputation and the work he was doing for the French. And if Lisette was going to be killed anyway, I wouldn't be taking that much of a chance. After the fight in the woods, I didn't feel as squeamish as I had felt before—or thought I didn't. But even so, I didn't relish the prospect of actually killing a woman—even a bitch like Lisette—in cold blood.

"You don't have to do it," urged Guy. "The way I see it, you're the only Astell—except for Grandma and Papa—who isn't connected in any way with the Germans. You don't have to creep up to the cottage. You don't have to hide. You can drive up openly in our Citroën, give a toot so as not to frighten Lisette, and when she peers through the window, she won't have the faintest idea what you have in mind."

"And what *will* I have in mind?"

"Not killing! That's for sure. We want her alive. But you are the only one who can talk to her at the front door, tell her any story you like—why not say Grandma is ill and could Lisette help? I'm sure she'll say no, but you can *beg* her for help. Then ask if you can talk it over, invite yourself inside, worm your way in—*get past the panic button*, then grab her. We'll follow. Then you can go home and leave us to clean up the mess."

"You know I'll do anything I can." Funnily enough, though I hated the woman—after all, she, however indirectly, was responsible for Anna's being arrested—at that moment I was thinking of something very different: I'll do it, yes, but God, I must be careful not to jeopardize my job

on the *Globe!* Not for the money, not because I was afraid of
starving or being fired—that was a consideration which
never entered the head of any Astell—but because I didn't
want to let people down in Washington. Then of course my
mind pictured Anna and Olivia. And every other thought
vanished, only hatred remaining. Well, perhaps hatred
and revenge.

Though I drove up the Mont de Champagne, outwardly
calm, I was quaking inside—not with fear, I had nothing
really to be frightened about, except letting down the
others. I was nervous because I knew that everything depended on my ability to get past the intriguing but invisible panic button.

I wanted to make some noise, draw attention to the fact
that I was not making a secretive excursion; so I called in
first at the old house to which the Misses B and B had
never returned since they left with Guy hidden behind the
backseat. All pretty gardens look at their worst in winter,
but the "B and B" garden looked worse than most, for it
had lost its neat and tidy trademark. The grass in the
small patch of lawn had not been mown since the previous
summer. The trim flower beds were overgrown with weeds;
the hanging basket over the door, once filled with geraniums and lobelia, looked as though it should be thrown
away.

The "B and B" house—like Lisette's—belonged to the
Astell estate, of course, and had been built originally by
Grandma's father to house workers; but over the years
they had tended to congregate near Douzy, forming a village. We had, however, a perfect right to check on houses
on our land, and as I drove slowly on toward Lisette's home
at the end of the lane I heard the steady clop-clop of a farm
horse with a young plowman called Fresnay sitting sideways on its broad back, legs dangling over the side.

I stopped the car. The knowledgeable old cart horse
stopped instinctively, and I was delighted, for I knew I was
in earshot of Lisette's house.

"Haven't seen you for a long time," I shouted—deliberately loud.

"No. Whoa! I suppose with your work in Paris, Monsieur Larry, you're too busy."

"Well," I laughed. "There's not much good news to write about these days." I kept young Fresnay talking as long as I could—in the hope that Lisette would be curious enough to see what was going on. Sure enough, she did eventually open the front door to her house at the bottom of the lane. I left the car where it was and walked toward her.

"Good morning, Mlle. Lisette," I instinctively used her nursery title as I added, "I was on my way to see you to ask for help."

"I don't see what you can possibly want with me," she replied coldly, no doubt remembering the terrible scene when we had kicked her out of the house after learning what had happened between her and Guy. She didn't sound *too* aggressive, and I smothered a temptation to say, Well, you are living free in one of the Astell houses! You might try to be polite!

She could never be polite, this bitter old maid, now a paid informer, the woman who had, however inadvertently, been responsible for poor Anna being arrested—arrested and worse. I had to swallow hard to produce a hypocritical smile and say, "I know we've all had our problems, but did you know that Grandma is very ill?"

"La Châtelaine?"

I nodded. "She needs someone to help her."

Standing by the front door—and was the panic button just behind that door?—she said abruptly, "I'm sorry. I'm busy. And anyway—"

"Anyway what, mademoiselle?"

"How do I know your grandmother would *want* me?"

Was she weakening? I didn't believe it. She was stalling. Perhaps she didn't want to set foot in our house. Or? Perhaps I was wrong. I decided to test her.

"I think you're wrong," I forced a smile. "Perhaps. I certainly hope you'll come—and after all," with a laugh,

"Papa is the one who counts. He's the one who pays the bills. And he's asked you to come."

The inference was, I hoped, clear, though without a scrap of truth in it—a veiled suggestion that if she didn't help a family "friend" in a desperate hour of need, Papa was quite capable of cutting off the modest allowance he paid regularly as "conscience money" to the Crédit Lyonnais. I *knew* that Papa would never be a party to blackmail—not unless he knew the truth about Anna. What I was trying to do was persuade *Lisette* to ask *me* in, so I wouldn't have to say, Can I come in? I wanted to make sure she was completely off her guard, I wanted her to take the initiative, I wanted her to feel that perhaps she ought to help; anything so that I could get her into the middle of the house, away from any hidden alarms, which must be near the door.

"I *am* busy, teaching part time at school. I expect you know. But maybe I could—I don't know—manage once or twice a week. What's the matter with La Châtelaine?"

I looked suitably sad and lied through my teeth. "We're afraid it's cancer," I said, crossing my fingers for poor Grandma, who had never looked fitter for her age.

"Oh dear," Lisette's face fell. "I *am* sorry. I never had any quarrel with La Châtelaine."

"And there's no one to help," I said desperately. "Not a soul except Madame Robert."

"That one! She can't do anything except bake bread!" And then, so suddenly it took me by surprise, "Come in. Let me look at my book and see what time I have free."

I walked in—thinking as I did so, how life can twist you round. Here was this plain middle-aged woman, hair like gray string, the classical nanny, and for that matter, the classical virgin, yet once, long ago, she and Guy had tumbled into bed and then hate had warped her mind and she turned into the most degrading kind of human being—the informer, the traitor, sending people to their deaths—or worse.

"That's very kind of you," I said, once inside, "it's a very pretty room you have here."

"Thank you," she leaned over her kneehole escritoire, halfway in the living room, along an inside wall. "My papers are always in such a mess. Ah here!"

As she bent forward, presumably to find her diary, I realized that this was my chance, perhaps my only one. It was safe now, she was well past the front door. As I sprang forward from behind and grabbed her throat, my thumbs on the back of her neck, my fingers squeezing into her windpipe, she cried out once, then scrabbled with her hands for the bureau, pushing the chair out of the way as she struggled, then sinking down to her knees so that I all but lost my grip. I had to keep her quiet, to stop the screams by pressing on her windpipe, and in those first seconds it seemed to me that she was not only trying to pull herself away from me, but, gasping and panting, was trying to do something else. After the first instinctive wrench with her hands on my wrists, those hands of hers were outstretched toward the desk, on her knees, below the top of the desk.

Grabbing a defenseless woman by the throat wasn't as easy as it sounds, as I had expected it to be. She was grunting, foaming at the mouth, and all the time kicking, arms flailing, so that I had my work cut out to hold on. She managed to grab the side of the kneehole desk, in order I thought (if I thought at all) to get leverage to push me off, but it wasn't that. Even as her breathing turned to more ugly gasps, as her face turned almost puce, she still instinctively fought, fingers outstretched, not to loosen my grip so much, not to fight me. Her fingers were searching for a different solution, they were moving around, as though anxious to grab something, to press up against it.

"Christ Almighty!" I yelled instinctively, suddenly realizing as I pulled her away from the old French kneehole desk that she was searching for her panic button—it must be there, not at the door. I let go of her throat. She gasped, but she wasn't out, and she crawled like an animal toward the kneehole.

"No you don't, you bitch!" I cried, and as she almost reached the desk, fingers outstretched, I picked up the nearest chair and hit her across the head. She dropped like a sack.

Trembling all over with the sudden surge of relief, I pulled down the curtains to tie her up. But where the hell were the scissors, where was the handy piece of rope or whatever which always seemed so convenient in the movies. I threw the curtains aside. She would be out for another minute or two I guessed, so I dashed into the kitchen and grabbed two dish towels and a carving knife. Ripping one cloth in two, I managed, however roughly, to tie her wrists behind her back—hard and tight, this was no time for niceties. With the other half of the dishcloth I tied her arms above the elbows as a double protection. I ripped the other dishcloth and tied up her legs, again tightly. Then with the carving knife I finally managed to cut up some of the thick curtain material and tie it round her mouth, biting into the corners, to form a gag. Just in time. She was beginning to move, to gurgle and gasp.

Then, only then, I spared a few seconds to leave the writhing, grunting figure and examine the desk. There was the button, almost invisible, there could be no doubt of it. It was on the inside of the kneehole, so unobtrusive that if she had needed help she could even summon the alarm by sitting at her desk and operating it with her right knee. And no one would know except at Gestapo headquarters.

The others would be here at any moment, but as I waited I was amazed to discover what a lot of damage Mlle. Lisette had done—to me, merely in defending herself. My legs and arms were bruised where she had slammed her pointed heels into my shins. One trouser leg was torn, buttons had been ripped off my sports jacket, even off my shirt.

Four or five minutes later I heard the growl of the tractor arriving. I opened the door—to show there was no danger—as I saw Guy at the foot of the lane. He jumped off as planned, while Gaston started to turn round the cumbersome old machine.

"You've got her?"

I nodded, "Yeah. She's tied up."

"Great. Where's the button—by the door?"

"No—under the kneehole of the desk."

As Guy followed her into the room, Mlle. Lisette had somehow managed to slide off the sofa where I had left her tied up and was wriggling like a worm along the floor—in the direction of the desk.

"Stop her!" I cried. "She might be able to press the button by lifting both her feet."

I would have hesitated, I suppose. Guy raced across the tiny living room and without hesitation hit Mlle. Lisette with a clenched fist on the side of the face. The force of the blow turned her over. For a second I was appalled. I knew I had fought to *control* her, but to hit a defenseless woman in the face—and so savagely! I'd never seen anything like it.

"Don't be so fucking squeamish." Guy pulled Lisette by the feet into the middle of the floor as she moaned, as the blood soaked into the gag in her mouth. "Every time you are, just think how many times Anna was raped—because of her."

"I know. It was the shock." I was thinking how curious it was, the almost grim pleasure I had got from beating the two hoodlums in the forest not so long ago. They were only robbers. But Lisette was a million times more wicked. A woman beyond redemption. And yet I had been shocked. For the moment, anyway.

"I know what your instincts are," said Guy gruffly, "but believe me, that business about the female of the species— well, they may not be *more* deadly than the male, but in war, they're equal. And you've got to treat them as equals. The enemy, I mean." Adding kindly, "You'd better go now, Larry. You've done your job better than anyone else could have been expected to do it. You've got the first stage over with by capturing Lisette. But what you've seen so far is kid stuff to what's going to follow."

"No. I'll stay." I had my own sudden thoughts of Anna and Olivia.

"Please yourself—only one thing, Larry. You may be the boss of the family, the eldest son sort of thing, but I've been doing this—extorting confessions—for over a year. It's not pretty work—especially with women—but honestly, I reck-on.our teams in Vichy France, where Laval *encourages* traitors to betray France, I reckon we've saved hundreds of lives. So what I do, I'm doing to save those that are going to *live*. Kill the ones who are trying to kill *them*—you get my meaning?"

He leaned over, turned Lisette round with his shoe, and as she opened her eyes he hauled her up to a sitting posi-tion in an armchair and looked at her frightened, almost glassy but open eyes and said, "Remember me? Guy—behind this beard. Yes, it's me. Now you can cooperate with us or be hurt. The choice is yours." Then, leaning closer, he said, "I'll take this gag out of your mouth if you promise not to scream. If you *do* scream, you'll be kicked in the face again. And you'd better realize that I mean it. If you prom-ise not to cry out, nod."

She nodded her head furiously.

"We'll try you—but watch your step. Untie it, Larry, will you. No, just loosen it, so that it hangs round her neck. That way we can pull it back if we have to."

She nodded more furiously. I loosened the gag, caught sight of the bleeding where the corners of her lips had been cut. She seemed to choke, drawing in huge gasps of breath, panting like an animal, until finally she gasped, "You'll pay for this. You'll never get away with it. Stop it at once, I tell you."

It was extraordinary how instinctively, with the return of her breath, she had become our nanny again, almost telling us kids how to behave.

"We want you to write a letter," said Guy, ignoring her.

I could see for a moment her eyes light up—or at least a glimmer of excitement came over the film of pain from which she was suffering. She obviously thought that she would have to go to the desk.

"No, not the desk," said Guy, "Larry found out where the panic button is, so you can forget it."

She seemed to sag with despair. "What letter?" she asked, frightened by the hate in Guy's voice. "I can't write anything unless you untie my wrists. You're hurting me. Larry, undo them."

It was a command! An order from the nursery!

"What letter?" she asked again.

"Telling Standartenführer Hoess of the Gestapo to come and pay you a visit."

"I don't know who you're talking about. Get me a handkerchief to wipe my face, please."

"Yes, you do know. Hoess comes here regularly—to collect information."

"I'll write no letters to anyone."

At that moment Gaston appeared.

"You'll be sorry about this, Gaston," she cried when she saw him. "*Very* sorry. I'll have you reported for this," she added viciously.

Ignoring her, Gaston said, "There's something wrong with the tractor. It goes in fits and starts so I've managed to get it to the bottom of the hill. That's why I've been so long. When I saw that Larry's car was still here I thought that maybe we could use it—that or Willi's, when he arrives—instead of the tractor."

"Good," said Guy briskly, "good. Now, Mlle. Lisette, you will write a letter to the Standartenführer," Guy had carefully used the proper rank for the Gestapo equivalent of a colonel, "telling him you've got some vital information and want to see him urgently."

"You're crazy!" she gasped. "Even if I wanted to, you'd never get away with it."

"Why not?"

"You *are* a fool. Even if I wrote your ridiculous letter, who would believe it?"

"The Gestapo. Don't you worry."

She was gasping for breath, and I could see that her neck was hurting.

"We've very little time," said Guy. "And I don't want to hurt you, but—"

She seemed to sag again, yet she still had a curl of hatred and disbelief to her cut lips, perhaps knowing that the manners she had instilled into the Astell boys from birth would prohibit Guy from hitting her again.

"We've all changed—since you betrayed Olivia and Anna."

"I did nothing! It wasn't me," she cried, not with defiance now, but a kind of whimper. "It was all an accident."

"And do you know what happened to Anna?" Guy didn't wait for an answer. He told her—brutally, no details spared. "*You* were responsible for that. *You,* and now its our turn. Will you write the letter?"

She shook her head. "I can't. I don't know what—"

"What if she doesn't write it?" I began to think the whole plan might not work.

"She will. I've seen this sort a dozen times. Cowards at heart," said Guy.

"What are you going to do?" I asked.

"Watch—or rather don't watch if you'd rather not. It won't take long."

He took a copy of the *Echo Reimois,* rolled it up, and then with the carving knife that I had used to tear the curtains, he ripped open her skirt.

"Stop it!" she cried. "Stop being so disgusting. You wouldn't dare."

"No, I'm not going to do *that.*" He tore off her skirt, her slip, panting with exertion, leaving her in a pair of pink panties. "I'm going to light a fire between your legs."

As he put a match to the rolled up paper and barely touched her thighs, she screamed. Guy shouted to Gaston, "Put the gag over her mouth." Then to me, "Larry! Take your car and hide it behind the end of the lane, we don't want anyone to see it. Willi should arrive any moment in his car."

Mlle. Lisette didn't hold out for long—thank God I didn't see what happened. What fascinated me about my single involvement with someone being tortured was the relief that if they talked, their life would be spared. If Mlle. Lisette wasn't killed, she would eventually denounce us—so how could she escape death? Surely she must realize that death was inevitable, not so much to mete out justice as to safeguard ourselves. Yet each time she had passed out, each time Guy dashed a pail of water in her face and she revived, moaning with pain, she had, as he told me, *believed* what he had promised her—despite the brutality, the pain. Each time he leaned over and said, "You see we mean business. All you have to do is write the letter—it's Hoess we want, not you. Once we've got Hoess, we'll leave you alone if you give us your word to forget all this." And she believed it! She believed such obvious lies.

"They all do," said Guy almost sadly when she had finally written the note. "The only thing that matters to all of them is the instinct with which everyone is born—the desire to cling to life. They *want* to believe they're going to live, so they are confident that they will."

"It beats me," I looked at the pitiful bundle of the woman who had brought up the young Astell family.

"And when I started out on this lark—after I decided to join the Resistance and the Red Cross—some of us went to a lecture by a psychiatrist. He explained another fundamental truth—the way pain distorts your thoughts. It makes you believe what you otherwise couldn't believe."

I didn't understand.

"Well, Mlle. Lisette is an example. If she was behaving rationally, she'd know that this is the primary cause of what happened to the girls. But through what this man called the three P's—pain, persuasion, and promises—it's been quite easy to *make* Mlle. Lisette really believe that Hoess is the guilty man, that the girls would have been arrested anyway, that her betrayal was incidental—or even accidental. Therefore she feels she has a right to be allowed to live. At least in her mind. Whereas we know that exactly the opposite happened—Mlle. Lisette is really the guilty party. Hoess is just an agent—a sadist no doubt, but an agent."

I had heard the sound of Gaston driving in my car. Then I heard another car arrive.

"That'll be Willi."

It was. And it was the first time I had seen him since he

learned that Anna was safe. He thanked me effusively, until Guy cut him short—kindly but firmly.

"If we're going to make a getaway by lunch"—he took an approving look at Willi's neatly pressed Gestapo uniform—"every minute counts. Now, here's the letter from Mlle. Lisette. You drive directly to Gestapo headquarters. When the SS salutes, hand in the letter and rev up the Citroën before he has a chance to ask who you are. The letter will fetch Hoess, don't worry about it, I'm sure it will."

Willi read the letter: "Dear Standartenführer Hoess, This is a very urgent request. I must see you. Guy Astell is back in Reims, and I think I know where he is, but I'm told he is leaving tomorrow." She signed, as she said she always did, "L."

"That should fetch him," said Guy. "Stroke of genius on my part to name myself. I know he hates my guts."

Looking round uneasily before he left, Willi asked, "Where's the girl?"

"In the kitchen. Bound and gagged. Now comes the second stage. Though we've persuaded Lisette fairly easily to write to Hoess,he's going to be a much tougher proposition when he gets here. We've got to get *him* to write a letter for you, Willi, to take to his house in the rue St. Julien asking to deliver up Olivia."

I heard the sound of Willi setting off down the hill. Soon Gaston arrived back on foot.

"With luck Hoess will be here in an hour," Guy looked at his watch. "But being the Gestapo he's bound to suspect a trap. He certainly won't come alone. The men in position?"

Gaston nodded. It intrigued me, the way in which I, as an amateur in this "business," watched the professionals at work. Gaston was not a real mature professional killer of Germans yet, but still, he was dedicated and he shared with Guy a kind of clinical approach to the whole business of outwitting the Germans. It was intriguing. Nobody, for instance, could have hated the Germans more than Grandma, nobody could have called more loudly for the last German on French soil to be killed, but she cried with the fervor of an elderly Joan of Arc, or a member of the Crusades ridding the country of the infidel. Gaston and Guy were more cold-blooded, as though soldiers who were not permitted to give way to their emotions. Too disciplined. They, too, wanted to kill the last German in France, but as executioners, not as religious maniacs. The change in Guy's character was enormous. He had grown a couple of metaphorical inches in mental stature. Nothing illustrated it more than his remark when Gaston returned from the kitchen, where he had been checking on Mlle. Lisette's bindings, and warned Guy that he would be surprised if the woman wasn't on the point of dying.

"Save us a lot of trouble if she does," Guy shrugged his shoulders. Then he asked Gaston again, "All the men in position?"

Gaston nodded. "Seven men, all armed, in the surrounding woods."

"Good. As I said, I can't see Hoess arriving by himself. He's a suspicious sonofabitch. He'll have a bodyguard. So long as your men don't panic and kill Hoess. And don't shoot too soon. Or we'll never get Olivia out. Odd isn't it," he said to no one in particular with an almost philosophical detachment, "how much easier it is to kill people than to capture them alive."

Willi arrived back, leaving his Citroën behind the turn of the lane, away from the direction that would be taken by the Gestapo cars, so that unless they backtracked, there was no reason why they should find it.

"All okay?" asked Guy.

"I do everything I was able to do," said Willi in his rather stilted English. "I give in the letter, then say my mission is very urgent and leave quickly. Now I am ready for the next letter when she comes."

That, as Guy had said, would be a tougher proposition, and now we all had to wait. I carried no arms—I could have asked for a gun I suppose, but honestly I didn't know how to handle one in a crisis. But both Guy and Gaston carried guns. Guy, a Luger P 08, stolen from the SS, and Gaston, a Walther PPK, a brute of a German pistol, also stolen.

"We won't have to use them, I hope," Guy reassured me. "But it gives you a feeling of confidence—and without sounding morbid, I like to keep one up the spout for myself, in case. I've seen the torturers at work. I've no desire to be one of the victims, whose only prayer is for a merciful death, which the Germans never permit."

"Do I know the men outside?" I asked Gaston.

"Perhaps. Every one I'd trust with my life. They're armed with whatever they could get—shotguns, one with a twenty-two rifle, one with a Luger taken from a German corpse. But they have the great advantage of surprise. *If* the worst comes to the worst, they could, from the cover of the trees, pick off the bodyguards one by one without any trouble."

"I'm not worried," said Guy, and he explained what he meant. First of all there was a training camp about a mile above the hill, where new German arrivals trained for occupation duties. "It's a very different kind of war for them," he said. "Fighting battles is one thing, being an occupying power is rather different. They undergo an intensive training course up there." With a nod in the general direction of the camp, which no cilivians had ever seen, Guy added, "They train them in the use of pistols instead of guns, they are also training for ambushes rather than straightforward attack. And I've often heard shooting on a rifle range. Anyway, it won't come to shooting."

But it did. For all of us had made one major miscalculation. An hour and a quarter after Willi had left to deliver the message to Hoess, we heard the sound of a car coming up the hill. No, it sounded like two cars.

"They're Citroëns," whispered Gaston, "I can read the sound of motors just like a book."

41

WITH FOUR OR FIVE MEN to a car, the two Citroëns coming up toward the cottage meant a force of possibly ten men. That didn't worry Guy as we prepared for their arrival, the three of us hidden inside the house. Gaston was in the kitchen in case anybody started checking in the back, while Guy and I waited at first from behind the curtains of the upstairs front bedroom, where we could see what was happening.

From there I had a bird's-eye view as the two black Citroëns arrived. A driver from the leading car jumped out and saluted like a robot, as one man alighted and whispered an order. The SS man saluted again, barking out, *"Jawohl,* Standartenführer."

"That's Hoess," whispered Guy as he ran downstairs to hide behind the front door. I saw the other Germans tumble out of both cars, eight men in all. They took up their positions, virtually surrounding the little cottage. All were armed, each one almost caressing his ugly-looking weapon, which I knew was deadly: a Schmeisser machine pistol. One man, a sergeant in the SS, walked up the pathway, covering Hoess as he advanced.

I had assumed—we had all assumed—that Hoess would knock to let Mlle. Lisette know that he was there and then perhaps slip inside, thinking she hadn't heard him. It would be a natural reaction. She lived alone, there was no phone in an isolated cottage. After all, he was well guarded, he had no real need to fear a trap. But he didn't knock. Instead he called out, a low voice, "Mlle. Lisette. *Her ist Hoess*. Where are you? *Ich habe es eilig.*" Meaning that he was in a hurry. Still he shouted again for Mlle. Lisette and refused to enter the house.

Instead Hoess drew his Luger. From the upstairs room I could see that he was really suspicious. He barked out orders; I could hear in the cold-carrying air the sinister sound of magazine clips being snapped into automatic weapons. Slowly, machine pistols at the hip, the German troops advanced. They were now in a tight ring almost round the house. Hoess stood his ground. But it was obviously he wasn't going to enter the house.

I couldn't see, of course, what was happening inside the house, but I *did* realize that if the French Resistance was going to pick off the Germans, they would have to act quickly. Yet they mustn't kill Hoess.

At that moment there was a diversion. Because I could hear everything, I could easily imagine what was happening. In a desperate attempt to break the deadlock, Willi, despite the drawn gun of Hoess, opened the front door and shouted, *"Standartenführer Hoess? Heil Hitler!"*

Hoess, still gripping his Luger, let his arm fall downward and—presumably seeing the junior status of a man he didn't know—shouted angrily, "What the hell are you doing here? Who are you?"

"I am Obersturmführer Brandt, sir," Willi gave the SS equivalent of a first lieutenant's rank, adding urgently, "Fräulein Lisette has been taken ill. I am a friend."

"A friend!" shouted Hoess scornfully. "Since when does the Gestapo become friends of traitors? There's something funny going on. Explain yourself, Obersturmführer. *Was ist los?*" I knew that Willi was playing for time—and was fast running out of that time.

"Es hat einen unfall gegeben!" he cried.

"I can see there's been an accident, you *dummkopf,*" roared Hoess. "Right! Turn round. I'll find out later what the hell you are doing in my territory. Now," he stabbed his gun into Willi's back, "I'll follow you. You take me to

Mlle. Lisette. And if there's any monkey business—you won't know what's hit you!"

Even I could appreciate that two things were vital: if Hoess saw the bound and gagged body of Mlle. Lisette, now on the kitchen floor, he would take no chances, but would shoot Willi on the spot. And without Willi as a messenger, there was no way to approach Hoess's house and save Olivia. Secondly, if we saved Willi by killing Hoess, we would also fail—for there would be no one to write a letter of authority demanding Olivia's release. So we needed *both* men alive. But how?

Guy made a decision—it was the only way. As Hoess passed through the door, gun stuck into Willi's back, the SS sergeant who had been guarding him fell behind him, following.

At that moment, in the split second before the inevitable discovery, Guy, from behind the door, shouted to divert Hoess's attention. As the Gestapo man wheeled round, drew up his firing arm, Guy got in the first shot, hitting him on the right side, smashing the gun out of his hand as the arm spurted blood. Hoess screamed with rage, Willi dropped on his knees unbalancing Hoess, causing him to fall so that Willi could hit him.

He did—over the head, with the butt of his gun. All this I learned later, so that I could imagine the scene. Then, as the NCO behind Hoess dashed in to save his master, both men seemed to fire at each other simultaneously. Only one man screamed though. And luckily it was Guy who screamed, "They've got me!" I say "luckily" because the other man couldn't scream. Guy had shot him through the head, whereas the NCO had only winged Guy, a nasty flesh wound just below the thigh, though we didn't realize how bad it was at the moment.

Now all hell seemed to erupt as the house—every single corner of it—was sprayed with automatic fire. Glass smashed, there was the sound of air as bullets whammed past, as the Germans prepared to assault the cottage. But the Resistance men, shielded by the trees, were able to weed them out in seconds, for though the SS had sur-

rounded the *house,* the Resistance had surrounded the
SS—and by the very nature of the attack, the SS had their
backs to the Resistance. Not one of them had the time to
turn round and return the Resistance fire or enter the
house. They were too busy to look both ways at once. I was
safe upstairs. Willi was safe. The only other casualty was
Gaston, hit in one arm, but not badly. And Mlle. Lisette. A
stray bullet through the kitchen window had perhaps mercifully robbed one of us from assuming the role of executioner.

As Guy shouted to me, I clambered downstairs, Willi
and I tying Hoess to a dining-room chair, each arm to one
chair, each leg to a chair leg. Guy was in severe pain, I
could see that, and losing blood, but we managed to find a
first-aid kit from the back of the Citroën, once we realized
that all the Germans were killed. "That needs stitching," I
said.

"Not a hope," grunted Guy. "Not until I get to Switzerland."

"You'll never be able to drive."

Outside it was like a battlefield. But with an extraordinary methodical discipline, the Resistance fighters were
stripping the German bodies outside of everything they
might need—not only precious machine pistols, ammuni-
tion, but even uniforms in case they needed them for
disguise. Then they dragged the bodies in their underclothes into the forest.

"Now," said Guy savagely as he faced Hoess, "we'll deal
with you."

The German's face was drained of color. His right arm
was covered in blood. Even so he sneered at Guy, "You amateur bungler. Do you think an overgrown schoolboy like
you can take on a member of the Gestapo? What do you
want?"

"The girl in your house. Olivia Jacobsen."

"Ah! The Jewess! Ah! I see."

"No, you don't," shouted Guy and slapped him across
the face.

"That's the second time you've done that," said Hoess.

"I didn't recognize you behind that stupid beard. You'll pay for that. Do you think you can intimidate me, as you have presumably intimidated that wretched woman who betrayed your family?"

"You will write a letter to your home asking for someone in authority to hand over Miss Jacobsen to the Obersturm-führer here, and then—"

"And then you'll kill me?" He actually laughed. "Do you really think I'm a fool to let this," with a withering look at Willi, "this despicable traitor to the Führer take a letter that I *write?* And sign my death warrant. You must be mad! And do you think I'm afraid that you might engage in a little torture? Try it, my friend. Just try it. You need quick results, eh? Otherwise someone's going to realize that something's wrong. And then you'll have to kill me!"

"I wasn't thinking of killing you," said Guy, almost with an air of apology.

"Very considerate. So! You are not going to kill me, eh? You fool!" It was extraordinary really, the hauteur, the disdain with which he, as our prisoner, regarded the rest of us.

"Willi," cried Guy. "I think as a German you had better leave the room." Willi went obediently through to the kitchen—I think he had a feeling of guilt at the sight of Hoess. He wanted to help us, but he also had a loyalty to the German people, and anyway he was obviously mixed up, so it was much better for him not to be present. Gaston came in. I listened to the threats made by Guy—and looked at my watch.

"You, Hoess," said Guy, "are the lowest of the low. Our sister—"

"She betrayed Germany!"

"No betrayal deserves that kind of revenge. You tortured her in a way that will affect her mind for the rest of her life."

"Well—kill me," said Hoess. "I'm not afraid to die. And as for torture—try it. You fool. I am a *German.*"

"There is no torture bestial enough to avenge our family," said Guy.

"You think," he wriggled instinctively in his bonds to make himself more comfortable, if possible, "you really think that a German officer—*Heil Hitler!*—is afraid? What do you plan? To pull out a few fingernails?"

"No, that's one of your favorite methods, no doubt."

"It works with the weak—but not with the strong. And I am strong."

"You may change your mind because—though I'm not a sadist, like you are, Hoess—I know two things. I have a picture of my beautiful sister before you wrecked her life. And of Olivia. And secondly I know that *you're* not as feeble as Mlle. Lisette, who is dead, of course. We know that you can resist torture—you've been trained to it. And I don't think you *are* afraid of death."

"Your assessment is correct." Hoess didn't even seem to be aware of his bleeding arm, the blood now dried. He still managed to convey a touch of irony, even sarcasm.

"And we know that in hundreds of German camps, tortured prisoners are begging only for one thing—for death, for release," continued Guy remorselessly. "And you won't give it to them, will you?"

"Go on, you don't have much time left before the alarm goes off."

"Plenty of time yet, Hoess. Despite what you have done to my sister and Miss Jacobsen, I'm prepared to be more merciful. I'm prepared to give you my word of honor that if you ask me to, I will shoot you."

He looked at Guy as though he were an idiot. "Schoolboys!" he spluttered. "Are you mad? Germans don't ask to die. They don't ask anything except to serve the Führer."

"You will."

For the first time a flicker of unease passed across Hoess's strained face. I was as puzzled as he was, for I hadn't the faintest idea what was coming next.

"You will write a letter to the Obersturmführer, and he will take it to the rue St. Julien and ask Miss Jacobsen to come and join you here. Once we knew she's free, you have my word I'll shoot you."

"And otherwise?"

For a moment—but only for a moment—Guy hesitated, then in a dead level voice he said, "We shall blind you."

The words were like a cold douche, as though draining the room of every sound except one lonesome bird outside. I couldn't believe it! Blind a man! Guy wouldn't dare—I wouldn't even dare to *look*.

"Yes, we shall blind you," said Guy quietly. "With this," he picked up a paper knife from the desk. "Remember what you did to my sister and Miss Jacobsen?" he added softly.

"You wouldn't dare."

"I have a debt to repay—and a girl to be freed. Why shouldn't I dare? I don't want to do any of this. But I have had to find a way of making sure that I can give you the ultimate gift—*you* begging *me* to kill you. When you're blind, if you don't crack by then, we'll break both your elbows. Then we'll make sure you're rescued by the Gestapo. You'll be a shell—valueless—but they'll look after you, try to help you, an old blind man with crippled arms for the rest of your life."

"You'd never dare. Anyway, Americans don't behave like that."

"American sisters don't get treated like whores. It's true we don't behave like this. But you've got Olivia Jacobsen, and I'm going to get her back—or you're going to live as a blind man with crippled arms for the rest of your life. If Olivia wasn't a prisoner I would be merciful and shoot you. But she *is* a prisoner in your home, and so I'm going to make sure you don't die—until she's free, then I'll be merciful."

Guy turned to me. "Larry! Go and wait in your car. Tell Willi to wait in his, and as soon as we finish off our—well, our business—I'll give Willi a shout to pick up the letter and set off."

It was Guy's way of getting rid of me, and I was glad to obey "orders" for I knew it had to be done—even though I was beset with confusing thoughts. You know, the sort of things, is it *ever* right to stoop to the level of a man you despise? Isn't a man demeaning himself by so doing? And yet

there was poor Olivia being demeaned by this warped
monster who could, it seemed, obtain sexual gratification
only from the excesses of cruelty. And could we so easily
forget Anna? None of us had seen her since the escape, but
we were all haunted by the possibility that she would
never *really* recover. And it would have been simple for
Hoess to send her to an ordinary jail; instead, and no doubt
to infuriate the Astells and teach them a lesson, he had
consigned her to a bordello.

I was thinking thus when a scream pierced the still
winter air. A terrifying wail of anguish. I had never heard
a sound like it in my life. I was almost sick on the spot. A
moment or two later another scream tore into the silence,
but this time it was a blubbery, muffled scream of someone
on the edge of fainting or whatever it was. Gaston rushed
to the front door and shouted, "Willi! Come here!"

Instinctively—morbid curiosity—I ran along to the door,
almost bumping into Willi.

"He's agreed," panted Guy, and that was all he said before *he* fainted. I just managed to keep on my feet. All this
had taken perhaps ten or fifteen minutes while we were
outside in the car waiting. Now on the chair, moaning, was
the wreck of the once proud Hoess. I had never seen a blind
man before, the black, bloody holes out of which presumably the eyes had been torn out. Blood was seeping slowly
down both cheeks, but Hoess was coming round and
shouting, "You promised to kill me, you promised! Your
word as a gentleman!"

I tried to bring Guy back to consciousness, pouring some
water over him. Even Gaston looked as gray as the wood
ash in the grate, the face incredibly older—for the moment
anyway.

"You tell him what to write," Gaston said to Willi. "In
German. Not at the desk. It's still got the panic button. In
the dining room—where he can sit at the table and you can
guide his writing."

The fight had gone out of Hoess. I don't think he could
ever have believed that normal, "simple" Americans
would behave like this. I *couldn't* have done it. I admit it

frankly. I was nauseated, I felt like throwing up, but Hoess hadn't realized that Guy was not only motivated by a desire to get Olivia free but had been working with the Resistance for a year, had known from *firsthand* experience the terrible tortures that the Germans and the Vichy French inflicted. Guy had known from experience that no "normal" torture would break Hoess, that he *was* a soldier, that he was unafraid of death. But Guy, having seen the victims who had been forced to stay alive, denied the promise of death after repeated tortures, sometimes for months —Guy knew that the only way to beat Hoess was to promise him an end to the living death we *could* inflict on him.

The letter took some time to write. Willi had to make four attempts, and Hoess was by no means in control of himself for he couldn't see, he couldn't find the edge of the paper. He was blubbering, whimpering with pain, but even Gaston, who looked as though he would pass out any moment, whispered to me, "God! The man has got guts!"

"You will shoot him?" I asked.

Gaston nodded. "I hate what we've done, but when I think what they did to your sister—it's nothing compared to that, is it?" He was almost apologizing, trying to excuse the brutality of it all, to erase it from his mind. "Isn't it ironic," he continued as we waited for the letter, "that the world only begs to stay alive—yet here we have a man who is begging to die."

Guy was better now, lying back on the sofa, panting a bit, and with a hell of a lot of blood seeping through the bandage which we had taken from the first-aid kit in the German car. Gaston was much better. The bullet had just sliced the flesh on the left arm, he wasn't in any pain.

Willi came through with the letter. "The writing is not good for a German, it is very shaky," he admitted, "but the signature, she is firm. Please look!"

We all examined the letter. It was just good enough. "Right," said Guy, "off you go. Call back here with Olivia and then—"

As Willi put on his ugly, shiny peaked cap and ran out of the house to drive to Reims, he cried, *"Bis bald,"* and I echoed, "See you soon." At that moment I heard something move in the next room. It was that bastard Hoess. By God, he was like a worm you cut in half but which still goes on moving. Do the Germans never give up hope? Blind, he was feeling his way along the side of the wall, trying to find the desk.

"The panic button!" I screamed, throwing myself across the blind man just as he had reached the side of the wall. Even as he fell, screaming with pain and fury, he was scrabbling with his left hand, trying to find the button as I pushed him away and tied up what was left of him.

The rescue of Olivia took place without a hitch, according to both Willi and Olivia. Smart and trim in the uniform of a Gestapo officer, there was no reason for the servant or soldier—presumably an officer's orderly—to doubt the authenticity of a letter asking for Olivia to report to the Standarteführer. It was the sort of thing that could happen to a prisoner at any time.

When I ran out at the sound of the Citroën, leaving Guy waiting on the sofa, I could see that Olivia was still afraid. All the honeyed words in the world couldn't hide the evil uniform of the man who was driving her, all the lies and deceit which it normally covered.

But then I cried, "Olivia!" and she jumped out of the car and ran toward me, half crying, trying to smile through tears.

"We got you out!" I cried. "Let me look at you."

"No, no. Please don't look. And thank you, Larry. I didn't recognize Willi at first and then I thought—"

"Guy's waiting for you—here in the cottage," I said gently.

"He's here?"

"Yes, he's lying down. He's been hit—but not badly."

As we walked toward the house, I stole a look at her. She was wan, tired, still suffering mentally from what had happened to her, but even so—and taking everything into account—she didn't look as bad, as gray, as taut, as I would have expected. It did occur to me, a fleeting thought, that however terrible her life had been, she had perhaps not suffered as much as Anna had, who had just had to serve every customer she was offered. Olivia was in the hands of a bestial brute, but in a sense, living in his home, she was in the position of a married woman who is forced to copulate with a man she loathes and despises. But only one—and there is a limit to the endurance of even the vilest pig of a man.

As we almost reached the door, shouting, "Olivia's here, Guy!" a shot sounded inside the house. That would be Hoess.

"Wait here," I said to Olivia and ran forward, almost forgetting her.

"That was Gaston," said Guy. "I kept my word. We'll throw both the bodies in the cellars underneath the trapdoor of the kitchen floor. With luck they may not be discovered for months."

At that moment another shot rang out—this time outside.

For a moment I thought we had been ambushed—I had visions of being surrounded by the Germans who had come to the rescue of Hoess. Instinctively we all ducked—until Guy cried, "God Almighty! It's Willi."

Guy could barely walk as Olivia ran to the door, helped him back into the room. I raced to the back of the garden. Willi was sprawled there along the shrubs, his gun in his hand, not quite dead, eyes glazed but fluttering.

"Willi, you idiot," I cried, not realizing how little time he had left.

"Is best," he gasped. "I do what I can for the Astells, yes?"

"Don't talk like that, Willi," I felt the tears stinging my eyes. "Oh, Willi! We were going to get you away."

"Can never be the same with Anna," he tried to smile. "No future for me—a good past, yes?" Gathering his breath as though for a huge effort, he gave a genuine smile and cried out, just before he died, "We had good times dancing at Maxim's, Larry, yes? Remember? Give my love to Anna."

42

EVERYTHING WAS CHANGED NOW. We had no time to waste, ironically, no time to think even of Olivia. Poor Willi was dead and there was no time to mourn his fate.

First things first: before anything else we had to get rid of Willi's body. It seemed unceremonious, but he had to be lowered—a little more reverently if we could—into the cellar below the kitchen trapdoor together with the other bodies.

We did this. Then Gaston, despite his wounded arm, had to make for Pagniez's house—his father's house, of course. He drove Willi's car, taking with him Guy, who had to be helped into the seat next to him. But now what? Guy had planned to drive Olivia and Willi to Switzerland. Now, however, there was no Willi—and Guy couldn't possibly drive, certainly not until he had received proper attention and been bandaged up. And he might not be in a fit state to drive, even then.

I didn't want to go to Switzerland. I had driven to Douzy to help, to do everything I could to free Olivia, but I had a job to do, the *Globe* to serve, and after I had done all that was expected of me, I wanted to return to Paris as fast as possible. Not a soul knew of my involvement with Hoess and the rest of the dead men. I had taken care not to contact Papa on this trip—no one knew I was here—but within a very short time the Germans would be looking for the missing men, trying to find out what had happened. I wanted my alibi established—Paris.

I drove Olivia to Pagniez's cottage. "But I'm only staying a second," I said abruptly. "I don't want my Citroën to be seen." We had originally planned to hide Olivia in the belfry at Douzy church until Guy was ready to leave, but of course there was no way Guy could climb the belfry steps unless at least two of us helped him up.

"I've got to get back," declared Guy. "I've a job to do in Vichy France. But I can't drive you, Olivia. I just can't. Can you, Gaston?"

"If I have to," he hesitated. "I'll do anything I can to help, but I don't want to spoil *my* cover. I'm regarded in the Douzy area as an honest vigneron, working for La Châtelaine. It's a vital role I play—if I'm caught driving a car a hundred miles from Douzy, an ordinary worker in the fields, how can I be expected to answer any questions at a roadblock? I may never be able to return to Douzy, and then I lose half my value."

"You're right. I'll have to stay for the time being. Hide up—perhaps here. I think I could make the steps to the belfry," said Guy. "You'll want to stay here in your father's cottage, won't you?"

Gaston nodded. "If I can."

"I'll make it easier," said Olivia, sitting down, hands cupped round a big bowl of hot, ersatz coffee. She looked up and said slowly, "I want to stay in Douzy."

"But you're crazy!" I said.

"Is Guy crazy, helping like he does? After all, he's neutral. Are you crazy, fighting for me?"

"Come on, Olivia," I tried to convince her. "That's different. We all love you—and we're going to look after you."

"I'm not going." I knew from the past how stubborn—no, stubborn is too ugly a word—how determined Olivia could be. "Thank you all for everything you have done. I feel new, cleansed—and grateful in a way you'll never be able to understand."

"Well in that case, repay us by getting to Switzerland," said Guy, twisting his leg round in a search for comfort.

"No," she sipped her coffee, then put down the earthenware colored bowl, "no. I want to repay what you've done—

and get my revenge for what the Germans have done to my people. I want to fight—here."

"We need trained men and women," said Gaston shortly.

"Then train me!" retorted Olivia.

We might have argued for hours, and I wanted to leave because it really did mean a great deal to me to preserve my job, to get back to Paris. Apart from anything else, I admired Guy and felt that if *he* could actively fight the Germans, possibly I could be useful in a more—well, more passive role, using the perfect cover of a neutral newspaperman. And I wanted to help. We had beat the might of the German army. We had proved they were not infallible! What was it the Misses B and B had said? Words to the effect that "two old ladies have smuggled a wanted man through the German lines!" Of course I wanted to help! But I was a newspaperman, and as far as I was concerned *my* pen was more mighty than La Châtelaine's sword. I could be useful tipping off people, doing anything they wanted without actually fighting. Not that I was afraid. But this was the thing I was best at. And yet—I couldn't leave Guy here. Apart from anything else, he would eventually need medical attention. And there was bound to be one helluva fuss soon. You can't have Gestapo men suddenly vanishing and not have an intensive manhunt. Guy had to leave.

"Well," I said, though I couldn't hide my reluctance, "I'd better take you to Switzerland. But I think we'll go in my car. It's safer. I've got my set of French papers anyway."

"I can't let you do that," said Olivia. "I want to stay, but I'll drive Guy down to Switzerland if you like. You remember *I* was the chauffeur of the Hisp! Then I'll drive the car back to Douzy."

"A Jewish girl, on her own in France! You'll be asking for trouble at the first checkpoint!"

"I'll go," said Gaston.

In the end, the matter was settled by a development which nobody envisaged. Looking through the front window, Gaston saw the figure of a man cycling, shoulders hunched forward, pedaling hard, up the incline to his cottage. "That's Pinot," said Gaston. "I wonder what he wants. He's one of us—but he'd never come here unless the matter was urgent."

The man, whom I recognized vaguely as a farmer's son, almost tumbled off his bike as he arrived. He took one look at me and gasped, "Monsieur Larry! Go quick! The Gestapo are after you!"

"Me! They don't even know I'm here!"

"They do. You must go. Don't go to Douzy."

"What on earth are you talking about?" asked Gaston.

"Look!" The man pulled the bottom of his jacket up over his shoulders. I realized that despite the cold he wore no shirt or vest. His back was raw red.

"They picked up half a dozen of us, I don't know what happened, why, but I heard that a lot of Gestapo men had been killed. They beat me, I couldn't say anything because I didn't *know* anything. In the end they threw me out. But one of them, Fresnay, did talk after they had torn out two of his nails."

"Fresnay? Who is he?" I asked.

"He mentioned you, Monsieur Larry. Said you'd been talking to him this morning near Lisette's cottage—it didn't seem harmful, but the second one of them heard your name—"

Of course! I had forgotten Fresnay, the farmer's boy on horseback. Probably he hadn't the faintest idea that he had done me any harm. And as he was tortured, he had mentioned my name.

That was that.

"Now it's all changed," said Gaston. "I'll be able to repaint the Gestapo car—don't worry about that. But you, Larry—bolt for it. Now. Not in ten minutes, not in five minutes, get off now—for Switzerland I suppose. We'll get a doctor to fix up Guy."

"I can't. The *Globe*—"

"Damn the *Globe*," cried Guy. "I'll have to stay now. I'll get to the church belfry, don't worry about me. It's too risky, you coming with me. This is a completely new ball

game. Your neutral image has been split wide open. You'd
better get the hell out of here—out of France—before the
Gestapo grab you. I can imagine that nothing would give
Abetz more pleasure than taking you inside. And there are
plenty more men where Hoess came from."

Almost in a daze, I agreed. It's hard to explain how, in
the midst of a near panic, after a morning in which I had
actually seen a man who had been deliberately blinded,
how Willi had said good-bye with his last breath—how all
this tumult had raged in a few hours, and yet all I could
think of was the *Globe*. You're a stupid bastard to care so
much, I said to myself. Ten minutes later I was on my way
to the south.

As I set off, making for the secondary roads round Dijon
and then Dole, I wasn't sure which "identity" I should use.
If—as seemed certain—I had even been seen in the vicinity
of the gun battle, I would certainly be wanted for questioning. For one moment, before I set off, I wondered whether
running away was wise; it would certainly be taken as an
admission of guilt. Yet I knew I had to run for it. Once they
found the bodies, then that Olivia had been freed—and the
other bodies in the woods, the two empty Gestapo cars; no,
it was too big a risk to be ignored. I would be implicated,
and I didn't relish the Gestapo methods of extracting confessions.

I decided to go "French." With my papers as Henri
Vasson and my profession as a champagne salesman, it did
not seem likely that anyone would have the number of the
car—the most common make in France. I didn't even know
whether it would be possible for the German authorities to
flash messages giving my name and American passport
details by radio all over France. After all, Reims was a
local Gestapo office. But I couldn't take that chance, for
Guy was right—Abetz might take a hand, seeking a personal revenge. I hadn't seen him since Anna was freed, but
he couldn't have relished our victory.

I wondered when I would see Oregon again—to say nothing of Papa and Grandma, who, now that I was cutting my

links with France, seemed much warmer and more friendly than when she was bossing us around! Gaston had promised to explain carefully that I had left Paris, and to pass
on the news to Papa. It would soon be around Reims, anyway. Talking to myself as I drove along, I was thinking, I
know I won't see the family again until the war is over,
and that looks as if it's dragging on forever.

Then I thought, *know!* How easy to use that word. I
thought I knew we would be parted until the end of the
war, but nobody knows the future; or the sudden machina-
tions of war than can reunite people unexpectedly, as Willi
and I had been reunited before his death. But in my heart,
I *knew*—and that included Olivia too.

As I bowled along, meeting no problems along the
straight, poplar-edged roads, I was thinking how well she
had behaved when she had been freed. No tears, no recrim-
inations, just a dedicated determination to go in and fight.
She was built that way. Wasted on poor Guy, I thought
wryly; but in another way, I knew that they would make
good companions if nothing else when they got married.
There I go again, I laughed to myself, *know!* I didn't know
anything. Certainly I didn't know if those two would ever
get married—or if I should ever see them again. Know!

I knew—and this time I really *knew,* or thought I did—
that if I made for the Bois Jolie and sought help from Madame Gavroche, I would have to go through the woods
again, though I imagined that the two toughs I had beaten
up wouldn't yet be fit enough to plot revenge. In fact there
was something else I didn't know.

It was like coming "home," to reach the warm country
atmosphere of the Bois Jolie with the lake in front of me in
the moonlight—in another country—and to find a warm
log fire in the sitting room, for the night was cold and miserable, a typical early December wet day, a touch of snow
on the Juras, otherwise rain.

Madame Gavroche welcomed me with open arms—and
some rough bread, much better than the bread of the
north, and with a bowl of homemade soup, filled with

chunks of parsnips, one of my favorite vegetables. I realized I had hardly eaten since dawn.

"Going over again?" That was her way of saying, "Are
you crossing the frontier?"

I nodded, busy dunking bread into the thick, hot soup.

"Well, you won't have any trouble this time—with, well,
you know, the two men. The police moved them out of the
area. The *gendarmerie* were furious. There are a great
number of policemen here who try to help—if they *can.*"
She poured out more wine from a *pichet.*

"Thank God. Even so, I'm dreading the trip through the
woods."

"You have to go that way? Through the woods, I mean?"
she asked the question guardedly, as if trying to encourage
me to ask *her* questions, for then she added slyly, "It's a
pity you're not an American."

"Would that be easy?"

"Straightforward."

"You guessed?"

"I thought from the way you behaved. English perhaps,
but the English are fighting, so they *have* to hide more.
Such brave boys! But you didn't *have* to hide. So why can't
you cross the frontier normally?"

"Well, Gaston and I—we had a bit of a fight this morning. Killed a lot of men."

"Gaston is safe?"

"Yes. But I was identified after someone had been tortured."

"Salauds!"

"So I daren't go by the normal frontier, in case I'm on a
wanted list." She poured herself out another glass of wine,
and one out for me. *"Santé."* She touched the rim of her
glass with mine. "Let me find out if they are looking for
you."

"From the Germans?"

"No, no, not the bastards. Quite often they leave the
frontier post to be checked by the French. And every day
they issue what they call the 'prohibited list.' People on it
are stopped. But not if the right police can help us. It only

applies to foreigners, of course. There's *no* way a Frenchman can cross the frontier legally."

"Even so, it seems risky to me," I said doubtfully.

"Safe as houses—at the right time. And also, if you're going to stay some time in Switzerland, surely it's much better to enter legally? The last time you went you only stayed for a night or two, but if you plan to stay longer, and they pick you up without the proper stamp at the frontier, that could mean trouble for you."

I had thought of that but had decided to take the risk of being picked up, and if my papers were not in order, I would bluff it out with my press card, American passport, and if necessary a diplomatic push from Sonia.

"The Swiss are getting tougher. But what time is it?" She looked at her watch. "Seven o'clock. The frontier closes at nine. And le Capitaine Dumont of the immigration service will be in charge of the frontier tonight. He's an old friend of ours. How you say—very close?" She smiled engagingly, really a very pretty, lonely widow. "When he's on duty, he always comes here for supper at seven thirty. Then at eight o'clock he goes back, and the German officer slips into town for a bite of food. The captain says the food is better here. And as he has an eye on me, *and*"—she paused, "when I tell him you're an American, he will let me see the 'prohibited list.' And if you're not on it, I'll introduce you, and you can both go to the frontier together. Or perhaps follow just afterward to give the German officer time to go for his supper."

Captain Dumont turned out to be a genial, vaguely anti-German, middle-aged man, who obviously had an eye on Madame Gavroche and would do anything to help.

"The French are the masters of the blind eye," he exercised his rather cryptic English. "No see, no action."

I didn't like to be too pushy, and I was still a little afraid that it was all too easy, but the immigration officer and Madame Gavroche studied official lists together, and though she now knew that I was an American, and my

American name, she hadn't told the officer, so she went through the list carefully.

"Eh bien," she said finally. *"Pas de problème."*

And there wasn't. Before driving to Divonne I unloaded Madame Gavroche a few bottles, to be hidden for safekeeping if I was refused permission to leave, but a present for her if she didn't hear from me by midnight. They consisted of four magnums of precious gas, and the five bottles of the still-remaining Astell.

"I don't want to be caught by the Swiss trying to smuggle in my own champagne," I laughed.

Then letting Captain Dumont cycle ahead in the rain and dark, I followed him so as to arrive at quarter to nine.

There was no German officer at the post, though two German soldiers had been left on guard. Dumont behaved as though he had never seen me before, an obviously intelligent ploy in front of witnesses, and rather grandly asked for my passport, examined it, and then stamped it, adding a prefunctory, "We also look after the customs, to save money. Have you anything to declare?"

I shook my head. "Nothing, monsieur."

On the other side of the road, barely fifty yards away, I could see the gray and green uniforms of the Swiss, and I was glad I had got rid of the champagne and gas, for they searched the car thoroughly, even checking on the chassis number on the engine in case it had been stolen. No problems, because my *carnet* and *triptyque* were in order, and I had nothing to hide. I had even left my false French papers at the Bois Jolie.

And this time I arrived at Three Circles Farm in style, tooting as I opened the five-barred white gate and drove in, and two minutes later I was inside the house, my arms wrapped round Sonia.

43

IT WAS THE PEACE, the feeling of relief, of safety, that was so wonderful after all the events of that terrible day. As soon as I had washed, cleaned up a bit, and swilled my eyes with cold water, I had to tell Sonia everything that had happened. We sat down in the living room, and I recounted how Olivia had been freed, Guy wounded, and how I had become involved—and identified by the Germans. I left out the most gory details of the torture.

"Does that mean you can't go back to France?" Sonia asked eagerly. "That you'll be staying?"

"For some time, I suppose. I'll have to phone the *Globe* after I've got my breath back—and after we've spent a little time together. God! How I've missed you. But," with a sudden thought, "where's Anna? I must see her."

"She's not here."

"I don't understand."

"Don't panic, but she's in a superior sort of clinic just outside Lausanne."

"Clinic!" I knew the French used the word *clinic* more than we do to denote a more elegant kind of hospital, but the way she said it, slowly, started a rush of terrible anxiety pounding into my head.

"Clinic! You don't mean—well"—I could only think of the French words—*"Un asile d'aliénés."*

"An asylum! Darling, of course not," her genuine laugh was like throwing a great fear out of the house. "No, my dear, she's exhausted—and she's *not* normal. She won't be for weeks. But you'll go and see her tomorrow, we'll go together. And now let me look at you."

She held me away from her in the way she often did, hands on my shoulders, looking at me critically before she said, "You look gray with fatigue!" She rippled her hands through my thick blond hair. "But you haven't started going bald!"

"I'm surprised," I laughed, "after all I've been through."

"Poor Larry. And you *have* lost a lot of weight."

"A bit," I nodded.

"And those patches of red on your cheeks," she touched the two spots.

"Fatigue—and fear," I laughed again. "The two *F's*— they'll disappear right away."

The housekeeper, whom I remembered as being so well dressed—her good quality shoes somehow stuck in my memory—came in to ask if there was anything monsieur needed.

"I've had some supper, thanks," I said. "But I *could* drink some really good coffee."

I'd almost forgotten what the taste of genuine coffee was like, for though we received a small ration from the U. S. embassy in Paris, it was of a new kind, already prepared. Here, now, in Switzerland, I could smell the coffee before it arrived—and hear the old lady grinding the beans in the kitchen. What luxury! What peace! and soon there would be crisp sheets and the warm, naked, loving body of Sonia next to mine.

During the night I had a terrible nightmare, I dreamed that I had to push—shovel would be a better word—the bodies of Hoess and Lisette down the trapdoor hole into the cellar below, and as I did so I turned over the dead man's body and the corpse was that of Guy, with two sightless, bloody holes where the eyes whould have been. And the body of the girl had a creamy white complexion and the eyes filled with fear—in the face of Olivia.

I must have moaned, for Sonia turned me over, then put on the bedside light. I was drenched with sweat; pillows, pajamas, even the sheets were wet through. She got up, rubbed me down, and then I left off my pajamas and wrapped myself in the bathrobe of thin toweling and moved to her side of the bed, which was still dry.

I must have overslept, physically exhausted. When in the morning I peeped out at the courtyard with the horse trough and the huge umbrella of a plane tree, and the stumps of the vineyard beyond, the world was covered with snow. I must have fallen asleep again, and when next I woke it was to see her standing there in her dressing gown, holding a tray.

"Breakfast, monsieur," she cried, then put the tray down carefully and leaned across the quilt, whispering, *"my* monsieur—for all time, forever now."

I ate every scrap of breakfast—the grapefruit, the bacon and eggs, the croissant and black cherry jam, and, perhaps best of all, three cups of *real* coffee—and then I said with a pretense of sternness, "If I *am* your monsieur, you are my madame, and so, madame, I order you to enter my bed."

She laughed, her face lighting with pure happiness and relief; I don't remember Sonia ever looking more beautiful, eyes shining with the joy that comes from the knowledge that whatever the price we had paid, we had succeeded. She put the tray down on the floor, turned the key in the door lock, took off her dressing gown, and then, by the side of the bed, pulled her blue nightie over the top of her head and slid under the covers—and without any words necessary, she was in the warmth of my arms and I was in the warmth of her body.

Long after—or so it seemed—she kissed me gently and whispered, "I've got to go shopping at Lausanne, and then we'll go and see Anna. Is that all right with you?"

We drove to Lausanne quietly, the lake on our right, the vineyards hugging every inch of hillside on our left.

"I'll park the car here in the place St. François," Sonia said. "Then we'll walk down the hill and buy our provisions for the weekend."

The "hill" consisted of the narrow, winding chéneau de

Bourg, and it really was narrow, for *chéneau* literally translated means "gutter."

After two years of war I gazed in wonder at the shops of either side of the narrow street. Habit had made me forget the variety of cooked meats, the mounds of pâté, the pink ham, the darker tongues, the even darker *viande de Grisons.* A dozen different salamis lined one counter, together with the larger white and pink Italian mortadella. Next door a butcher displayed joints of beef, decked out to look attractive enough to pop straight into the oven, together with chops and fat chickens. It was the hunting season, so there were saddles of venison ready for the kitchen.

I wasn't being greedy, looking at those shops with wide-open eyes, smelling the nearby bakery with a dozen different kinds of bread. It was my instinctive reaction to the plight—not mine, I was luckier—of millions of Frenchmen who for months had been grateful for a few turnips or fish heads as a staple diet.

Of course there was more to it than that. Plenty was a sign of peace, but it could also be a sign of conquest—or, for that matter, an undeclared war between unfair poverty and wealth; but here in Lausanne it was the breath of freedom, the lack of an instinctive need to look over a shoulder. I would have to make up my mind what to do soon, I thought; but until I did, I was at peace, with no wish to reenter the nightmare world from which I had just escaped.

Shopping over, Sonia drove me in her little Fiat, with Swiss license plates, to the Cecilia Clinic on a hillside above Morges, a lakeside town, little more than a village really, midway between Lausanne and Rolle.

I had, without realizing it, been prolonging the shopping expedition partly because I was dreading the meeting with Anna. I wanted to see her—of course I did—and yet I was nervous, afraid perhaps that I would be disagreeably shocked by what I saw, that Sonia had been hiding the real truth from me.

After all, my sister in a hospital! I know she had suffered, but "a clinic" did smack of something worse than shock, a period of rehabilitation. The word *clinic* held a vaguely sinister note, and my first impressions did little to allay my apprehension—the smell of antiseptic, even the floor polish, the bustling, efficient nurses, so busy with the patients that they seemed to have no time for the relatives of patients.

A sister nodded to Sonia at her office on the second floor; the sister obviously knew Sonia and preceded us toward a room, peeped through a small window, and said, "That's all right, countess. She's presentable. A bit sleepy, but—" she smiled and shrugged her shoulders.

The sleep, I learned later, was drug-induced, as the doctors quietly kept her sedated during a period of nightmares, often violent and resulting in screams that would have awakened anyone if the room hadn't been soundproofed.

She was half asleep when we walked in on tiptoe, but almost as soon as I leaned over the bed she opened her eyes, they met mine, and, though hardly awake, she recognized me and smiled and held out her fingers. I couldn't make out what she said, something on the lines of "Wonderful to be home!" and then she faded away into sleep again, her hand still clutching mine, locked to it.

I remained with her for an hour or so, and once or twice the semiconsciousness was interrupted by open eyes, recognition, smiles of joy, mumbled words.

"It's all over now," I whispered. "We're here to protect you. For ever and ever. The nightmare's finished."

She smiled and closed her eyes in sleep.

"She's much better," said the sister, when she decided we had stayed long enough," but we mustn't tire her." Later that day Sonia told me, in outline, the problems which the doctors had faced, the reason for helping Anna to sleep as much as possible. It was not only the nightmares but the fears when she was awake. At first the sight of even the most inoffensive doctor in his white coat sent her screaming with rage, the violence spilling out when she jumped from bed and tried to attack any man. And she was very strong. One male hospital orderly was severely bitten when Anna dug her teeth into his arm as she was being lifted. Two received bruises.

"The only way to keep poor Anna quiet," confessed Sonia. "The specialist—you will meet him—has given me his word that there's nothing *really* wrong with Anna. No real mental disturbance, though she's not," she hesitated, "not *really* normal yet. You can't expect her to be."

"Poor Anna," I said as we walked along the corridor to the stairs and the outside world, "poor Anna. If only I could do something."

She pressed my arm, linked hers with mine. "You may not realize it, Larry, but Anna's taken a gigantic step forward today."

I must have looked astonished.

"You are the first man to see her alone in the room. We'd planned it in advance with the doctor. But he was so frightened of violence that he agreed to your visit only if he was outside, with two male nurses to overpower her if she attacked you."

"And she didn't."

"No, she didn't," Sonia smiled happily. "She took one look at you and I could see the Astell love darting between the two of you. And when she woke up again too."

"Was it as bad as that?"

"It was never *bad*," she walked toward the parking space and offered to let me drive but I shook my head. "Never bad. I was impressed by this doctor from the moment I met him. It was never hopeless. But lengthy." Sonia started up the Fiat and crunched in the gears professionally before backing out. "But it's all different now. She obviously believed when she first came to Switzerland that every man was trying to rape her. I think you've speeded up the improvement by months just because she trusts you. She'll be all right, you see. Go and visit her every day until she associates you with love—and not hate."

"I will," I promised.

That Saturday we went for a walk—and that in itself

was a symbol of our freedom. We drove for dinner to a small inn at a village called St. Saphorin, where the owner bottled his own white wine, and we had the most famous of all Geneva dishes, *filets de perches,* small fish caught that morning in the lake and sautéed in butter with *pomme frites* such as I had never tasted since oil became virtually unobtainable in France. We washed it down with local wine followed by espresso and a glass each of kirsch.

On the Sunday, after I had visited the clinic again, I had the feeling before dinner that Sonia wanted to talk to me—and seriously. The living room was warm, white walled, with sofas on either side of the large fireplace with its logs, sometimes crackling, sometimes hissing as tongues of blue flame settled down to a more normal color.

I was drinking a Scotch and cold water. We were not great whiskey drinkers at home, but we did enjoy it from time to time, and Oregon—ah! where was Oregon?—had always drunk his favorite called Old Rarity, which in the old days was delivered to Douzy by the case. It came in gray and green stone jars and looked as good as it tasted. I had found a couple of bottles in Lausanne and was sipping it gratefully, left arm around Sonia's shoulders, her head resting on my shoulder.

"Bliss," she said, "that's the only word to describe it. Bliss. Does it ever have to end?"

"Meaning?"

"Well, I mean"—she sat up, turning slightly to look me in the face—"for a country that isn't at war, you've not done badly. You've written nasty things about Hitler, you've nearly been killed, you've saved two innocent girls from—" she shuddered. "I'm very proud of you, darling, but isn't enough enough?"

"I must contact the *Globe.* I've phoned our man in Bern, passing them your phone number so that Washington can phone me here."

"But what can they—or you—do?"

"I don't know," adding laughingly, "I wonder what would happen if they sent me to Rome!"

"Oh, no! Then I'd have to leave Rolle."

"Well, if I don't stay in Europe, we'd be worse off. I might be sent to, say Argentina or China, then we'd *never* meet."

"Why go anywhere?" she hesitated. "Why not stay here? You have money in America—and I have all the money we need here—from, well Paraguay, if you want the truth. You've done your share in this war. It isn't *your* war. Let the other people fight it."

"What about people like Guy?"

"Guy *chooses* this way of life. In a way he enjoys it. At least I think he does. In a way—it's nasty to say this, but you know what I mean—he's trying to compensate with action what you've achieved by thinking. Now you're the opposite."

"I say!" I protested. "What about my fight in the woods on my last trip here? No action!"

"I still say *you* are not an action man. Have you ever thought *why* you got involved in fighting—and killing now? Not to win the war, Larry. For you the pen *is* mightier than the sword. No, you only get involved in fighting to save your women! Me, Anna, and then you felt you had to help Guy get Olivia out. And look where it's landed you."

I knew what she was driving at. I *wasn't* the bull-headed type, I hated fighting really, and yet, I had a niggling feeling that even a neutral couldn't just walk out on a tortured world because it wasn't his problem. It would be like walking past, pretending not to notice some bully beating up a woman. You couldn't just leave people to rot.

And I was thinking not only of myself, but of Sonia as well. How could both of us spend years hiding in a way from the truth, shirking it? Wouldn't it be impossible to live that way, after all that had happened, all that would happen in the days to come? I loved her, that went without saying, but with each year—and each new experience of work or war—I felt the need to go on. Looking at her, silent for the moment, I wondered, Am I pompous? I *had* changed. In the past I had been happy with each day we had loved together; all I had asked of life then was that the next day be as happy. But now—I needed more, with her of course, but more.

"I don't want to be a hero," I protested, "but I can't just sit around enjoying the view of Lake Leman for the rest of the war."

I knew that in a sense Sonia was fighting for us *both*, for our future together, especially when she said, "Couldn't you write a book? Surely after what you've seen and done, and with your name splashed all over American newspapers—well, nobody has written a good book yet on how France lost the war. And what life is like in France under the Germans. The material you sent from Switzerland the last time you were here was terrific."

That was an idea that *did* tempt me. Like almost any newspapermen I had toyed with the idea of writing a book—we all wanted to write "our book," and I had wonderful raw material, though I faced one snag; there was no way I could complete any extra research I might need without talking to French friends. Though, sitting there in the living room sipping Scotch before dinner, it did occur to me that as a neutral in search of a book, I might be able to visit England and talk to de Gaulle. It was a thought, anyway.

"I don't know," I sighed, "it's so damn confusing."

"Don't worry now"—she took a sip of cool white wine—"we'll work something out," adding almost ruefully, "Life has a habit of working things out for you, whatever you decide yourself. Especially in these days."

It was a casually uttered prophecy uncanny in its accuracy—and the speed with which it was fulfilled. We were sitting drinking coffee after dinner on that Sunday evening when I switched on the BBC to listen to the latest reports of the siege of Leningrad, now in its third month. I listened with only part of my mind—until I exclaimed, "Jesus Christ!" I sprang up suddenly, switched the radio to full blast, spilling my hot coffee over my only suit. For the impersonal BBC announcer, after warning listeners to stand by for important news, announced in a calm voice,

"This morning units of the Japanese navy and air force attacked Pearl Harbor without warning."

"Good God!" I cried again.

"It's not possible," said Sonia. I waved her to silence, listening as the announcer filled in the details. The attack
had taken place in Honolulu that morning—the evening of
the same day here in Switzerland—by more than three
hundred and fifty torpedo bombers and Zero fighters from
six Japanese carriers. The *Arizona* had exploded after a direct hit, four other battleships were sunk, half a dozen
more damaged, nearly two hundred American aircraft had
been destroyed.

"They must be mad!" I switched off at the end of the bul-
letin. "They must be absolutely crazy. They may have
sunk half the American navy, but the Japs just *can't* take
on the United States. It's a preposterous thought."

"It's terrible," she cried.

"It's war—now it really *is* a world war. Everyone's in it.
All of us."

"Us?" she echoed. "What's it going to mean to us?" she
asked in a very small, sad voice.

I hesitated. "I don't know. But it looks as though you're
right. Events *have* had a hand in shaping our destinies." I
sighed because I knew from the moment of the broadcast
what I would have to do, though I did not tell her until
much later in the evening. Then very quietly I said, "I'll
have to go back to America and join up."

"You can't," she said dully. "I know how you feel, but—"

"There aren't any buts. The fact that I could get out of
the fighting—by being, say, a war correspondent in the Pa-
cific—well, that only makes it more important that I *do*
join up of my own free will."

"But, my own Larry," she was almost crying, "this will
make us—enemies."

"I know. But only our countries!"

"It's so wicked, Larry. So unfair. At least until now, we
weren't enemies."

"We're not now, darling. Not really. The damn Japanese! Now they're in, we'll have to fight—Europe as well as Asia. And that includes me."

"But why? Why *try* to become a hero? If they order you to, that's one thing. But you don't have to volunteer—to fight me, and that's what it means."

"Sonia, don't be angry if I say something that's going to hurt you. You know I love you, you know I adore you. But like it or not, the Fascists in Italy are in their way as bad as the Nazis in Germany. Not as powerful, but as bad. You know this in your heart. And if the Germans can torture Anna because some sonofabitch squealed on her, the Fascists can do exactly the same to you. Without warning. That's what I'm fighting for, darling. You!"

I said it that night, and a month later when I got the chance to fly to Portugal, where a boatload of Americans was being evacuated for the States, I said it again, lying in bed, kissing her, promising her eternal love, peace on earth, an end to war.

"That is what I am fighting for, Sonia," I said on that last night. "You're the love of my life—and I'm going to fight to *free* you, so that we can marry and have children in a land of peace. When I join the U.S. Army, I won't be fighting to win the *war*. I'll be fighting to win *you*."

Part Four

1942–1944

44

PERHAPS IT WASN'T SURPRISING really, the change I found in Mama when I arrived in America. Vague remarks by Tommy Tomlinson had prepared me. Early in the spring of 1942 I arrived on a Swedish freighter at Pier 86 in New York City, without having been able to warn anyone of my arrival.

All the shipping schedules, passenger manifests, and so on were secret in case of U-boat attack. So I checked in at the St. Regis on East Fifty-fifth Street, and the first thing I did was to wallow in a hot bath, then have an old fashioned in the Old King Cole bar, before dinner in the Oak Room. I knew I had arrived in America when I heard the waiter, laden wth a tray of food, hold out one plate and bellow to the diners at a nearby table, "And who gets the frogs' legs?"

Mama lived only a block or two away, across Madison and Park at the corner of Fifty-fifth Street and Lexington. I phoned her in advance at her apartment, and when, before lunch the following day, I reached the fourteenth floor where she had a corner flat overlooking Fifty-fifth and back toward Third Avenue, she was waiting at the door at the end of the corridor with open arms.

"I was listening for the elevator to stop," she hugged and kissed me. "Larry, you look *thin.*"

"And you look stunning!" I laughed.

She did. Still under fifty, with good legs, she was beautifully dressed. Her hair was still a natural blond, which had never been rinsed in bleach. Her nails were long and painted pink, her teeth small and white, and after another look I summed her up with another laugh, "What a dishy blonde!"

She obviously liked the compliment. But what I *didn't* say, but felt, was that she glowed with a kind of inner satisfaction. Yes, that was it. She wore the same look of happiness blended with contentment which used to suffuse Sonia when we were able to translate our love into physical terms. I knew that look of Sonia's well, and it gave me an odd sensation, seeing it reflected in my own mother's face.

She was bursting to learn all the family news, especially about Anna, and I told her everything—everything, that is, except what had *really* happened to Anna and Oliva. As far as Mama was concerned, they had just been "wrongfully imprisoned."

As we talked, I looked around the apartment, very attractive, the front door opening directly onto an L-shaped room, the far end furnished with a glass-topped table leading directly to a kitchen.

"It's just what I need," Mama showed me around, "handy for the Fifth Avenue shops. I didn't really need two bedrooms and bathrooms, but it was the only one I could get. And I *did* hope that at one stage Anna might come and join me."

"I know," I admitted. "But in a way I think she's better off with Sonia. They always have been close and—"

"And how is Sonia?" asked my mother gently. "Still in love?"

I nodded. "Francesco's trying to get their marriage annulled; it's a long, dreary business, but apparently he has a lot of influence and it'll come through eventually."

"And then—at long last?"

"Yes. We'll get married. I've always wanted to. But this damn war—I can't see it ending for years."

"With America so strong?"

"I know. But the physical problem of actually invading huge countries like France—to say nothing of Japan.

There aren't enough men in the world to kill all those Germans and Japs. We will never be able to knock them out."

"And what are you going to do?"

"I'm going to join up. There's no nonsense about being heroic. I just feel that I might be useful if I can get into some sort of, oh, some sort of undercover job or something like that."

She didn't really want to talk about the war; naturally all the conversation revolved around the family, the latest news, what had happened to Papa—and to everyone at Douzy.

"It seems like a different world," she pulled open a kind of bureau, revealing a selection of bottles and glasses. "I've already got the ice prepared," she said. "Are you going to take me for lunch? Shall I mix a drink? A martini? Or something else American?"

I don't know why, I had the impression Mama was making small talk. She never mixed drinks at home. She never asked what we wanted. She was nervous.

"Here, let me do it," I started to stir the gin with its few drops of Noilly Prat. "And what about the '21' for lunch?"

She prattled on for the hour or so before lunch, bombarding me with questions, but all the time I had the feeling that though she certainly wanted to know everything there was to know about the family, she was carefully avoiding another subject. Surely after all that had happened, the life so different, it couldn't still be Gaston?

It wasn't—because I asked her; not brutally, but firmly; not to upset her, but more to put her mind at rest. It came out naturally when I asked, "Shall we have a quiet dinner tonight before I leave for Washington tomorrow to see the *Globe* people and then see about volunteering for active service?"

"Oh, darling," she did seem sorry. "I know you couldn't let me have advance warning that you were coming. I realize that, but I do have another date for dinner. Such dreary old people. But—"

"Like the—what was their name?" I asked slyly.

"Who?"

"Don't you remember? When you were in Paris and I asked you out for dinner, you said you were dining with these people, but later I discovered quite by chance that they weren't even in France at the time."

She looked at me and murmured, "I must have got mixed up. I don't remember."

"Mama! I adore you," I laughed, "but you've turned quite pink! You don't fib very well. If it's any consolation, I know who you had dinner with that night."

"Now, Larry!" she tried her "mothering" tone.

"It's past history. And," airily, "I opened the attaché case that was saved from the *Athenia* before anyone else— and I threw away the incriminating evidence."

"Oh, Larry! You did." She was bright red now.

"I did," I said. "Did you know that Gaston is back in France? He's number two to La Châtelaine."

Impetuously my mother took another sip of her martini and laid her hand on mine. "It was just a—"

"I know, of course," I said. "And I never let on to Gaston that I knew."

"It's strange you should know," she said finally, after I had poured her another drink, "but Gaston helped me— yes, a lot. I was so depressed, so lonely, so *bored.*"

"With Papa?" I hope I didn't sound reproving, but I did feel slightly embarrassed.

"Not *with* Papa! What an awful thing to say, Larry! But with *life*—and"—she was talking frankly but a little sadly, though I realized that she was aching to talk to me—"I suppose that does include Papa in a way. I don't mean that in a nasty way. I didn't realize until Gaston—and that happened all by accident you know—I never intended—but until then, I never realized what I had been missing. I shouldn't talk to you like this. Your own mother! But I can't help it. Your father gets so involved, he's no time for me—or didn't have. For any woman. I'm not being nasty. He's a man's man. But I—well, you must understand— after you and Sonia—I used to be so envious, so jealous of your happiness."

"And are you happy now?"

She hesitated. "You can never be entirely happy in a situation like mine—the family split up—by war I mean," she
added hastily.

"But still?" I persisted.

"I've achieved a kind of happiness," she admitted guardedly.

"Which means you have a boy friend?" I wasn't sure
whether she would be irritated or treat my remark as a
joke.

She made no reply. She didn't have to. No mask could
have disguised her face—that of a woman in the midst of a
love affair.

I went to Washington the next day to tell the *Globe* that
I wanted to volunteer for the army, and they understood,
but when I asked Tommy Tomlinson, now firmly established as our foreign editor in Washington, whom I should
approach to find out if there was any outfit that worked
with the Underground or clandestine forces—so that I
could put my knowledge of French to good use—nobody
seemed to know, and in fact it was Mama of all people who
put me in touch with just the right man after I had returned to New York.

I had already firmly established in my mind that I
wanted to do something different from the ordinary run of
things—partly due to something that Guy had said in a
casual conversation months previously, when I had tried
to pump him about his work. "Sure, my job is clandestine,"
he said, and this was *before* Pearl Harbor. "But who do you
think's paying for it all?"

"The Red Cross?"

"You must be crazy! The Red Cross is *neutral.* The
Americans—they're the ones who are paying. We may not
be at war, but we know where our sympathies lie. I'm
working underground for an American military outfit."

It transpired that almost as soon as Roosevelt appointed
his old friend Admiral William Leahy as ambassador to
Vichy, FDR made it clear that he expected Leahy to gather
secret information which could be passed on to the British.

In turn, Colonel Robert Schow became military attaché to Admiral Leahy. His job, said Guy, was to keep in close touch with the Resistance. Though I did not learn this until much later, Guy passed his information to Schow.

Even before the war Roosevelt had set up an agency to organize propaganda and espionage under the umbrella of the COI, the letters standing for Coordinator of Information.

I didn't know much about it, but this was the kind of outfit I wanted to join—not a stick-in-the-mud job where my knowledge of French would probably lead me to a dead-end desk as a translator of leaflets to be scattered over France.

And that's what I might have been had it not been for Mama, of all people.

"Come to the apartment next Tuesday," she said, "some friends of mine are coming in for drinks. One of them you must know by repute. Bill Donovan. Bob Sherwood, the playwright, is coming too."

I didn't know either of them—though I did know that Donovan was a legend from the last war, a millionaire Wall Street lawyer known to his cronies as Colonel "Wild Bill" Donovan. Nor had I ever met Robert Sherwood, but as it happened we had corresponded. Years previously I had seen a movie of Sherwood's play *The Petrified Forest,* and as I was unable to get the book of the play in France, I had written to Sherwood. He immediately sent me a copy in which he had written on the flyleaf some very complimentary things about my writing.

Bob Sherwood, who was the boss of the COI, arrived first, and couldn't have been more agreeable. He was tall, loose-limbed, handsome, reminded me in a way of Jimmy Stewart, the actor, and spent most of his time these days in Washington. He read the *Globe,* and he remembered our correspondence. Then Donovan arrived, a stocky, gray-haired man who exuded power and imagination. If Sherwood was the titular head of the COI, Donovan worked for that section of the organization devoted specifically to intelligence and underground activities.

I was intrigued at the way they—and the other guests—

adored my mother. I thought back to the way she had entertained Vance, the owner of the *Globe,* and his wife on their first trip to France so long ago, and the easy way she had made everyone feel at home and wanted. Here, reflecting again as I watched the others relax, I realized what a flair she had for being an ideal hostess, full of fun, easy, unfussy.

"You're very lucky to meet both Bob and Bill," said an amused Mama when we were all talking. "I'm sure they can fix you up with any kind of uniform you want!"

I was not quite sure at first that I would be interested. They gave me the impression of being planners—and I didn't want to be an assistant to a planner. In the end, incredibly, *each* one of them offered me a job! Not, I am sure, because of favoritism, but more because of the timing; for what I didn't know then was that I had entered the scene—enacted really in Mama's flat—just at the very moment when Sherwood and Donovan were deciding to divide up their "empire."

"The president has decided that shortly—in July—I'll run a new department called the OWI," explained Sherwood, "the Office of War Information. We'll be handling propaganda. I plan to set up our own radio station called the 'Voice of America,' to serve all Europe. You're exactly the kind of man we're looking for. Knowledgeable of the countries—fluent in French—you're a cinch for us. Consider yourself booked for the duration."

I felt almost embarrassed by this flattery. I might be a bilingual newspaperman, but still I was not trained in propaganda. However my reaction was nothing to the blush I could feel on my cheeks when Bill Donovan said, with a glint of amusement in those piercing eyes of his, "Just a minute, Bob. You've got no right to go taking my boy just like that!"

It was said in fun, but then Donovan explained—and I began to tingle with excitement. For Sherwood's OWI was one thing, but Donovan was setting up something very, very different—an entirely separate organization, the OSS—the Office of Strategic Services.

"And I'll be the boss of the dirty-tricks department," said Donovan. "On the ground, in the ditches, the front, or wherever," he added. "Volunteers only. And they'll be trained by the British SOE, the Special Operations Executive. It's concerned with intelligence organization for Resistance and sabotage in occupied countries. It's headed by a Britisher who used to be a boss of Fords in France."

I was very impressed with the prospect of working for the OSS—if I could wait until it was established. But Donovan made it clear that the OSS wasn't even formed yet, and that very few Americans were allowed to work with the SOE in England.

"There's no problem if you're right at the top," said Donovan. "The SOE is the most professional bunch of men I've ever met in my life. And you've got to be professional to stay alive in their kind of business."

Donovan knew what he was talking about. As far back as March 1941 he had, he told me, been taken round some of the SOE training establishments in England, from where the first intelligence agents had already been sent by parachute into France.

That settled it. Because the OSS was not even formed, it took several months before I gained my commission. I was posted to G_2, Military Intelligence. I underwent preliminary training at Fort Benning and half a dozen military bases in America, and was then posted to London on attachment to the British "for special duties." I sailed from New York in a blacked-out *Queen Mary*, one of the sixteen thousand troops on the world's most prestigious liner, now converted into a troopship in which the same beds or berths were used for eight-hour shifts, leading to the boast, "Our beds never get cold."

It had never entered my head that any training of human beings could be so exhausting. I had heard naturally of the rigorous preparation that goes into the making of an American marine, but this was different. A "civilian" job—in a way that was what I was being trained for. And somehow I had rather expected to receive a course con-

cerned mainly with formal problems; identities, methods
of transmission, code names, perhaps elementary training
in the use of weapons. I had not envisaged a commando-
type physical training program that left me exhausted
physically and mentally.

At first I was utterly miserable. There were no other
Americans training with me. There was no way I could
write a letter to anyone in France. And of course from the
moment America entered the war even Mama in New
York had no way of contacting my father or Grandma. The
only guarded letters Mama could write were to Sonia in
neutral Switzerland. England, being much deeper into the
war, and struggling at this stage to stay alive after heroic
resistance, could offer no sort of fun for anyone. The only
way I could write after I landed in England was through
the army post office. And this would be forwarded eventually to Mama in New York. Other than that I had virtually
ceased to exist.

From Liverpool I was first sent to be interviewed in
London, my acceptance approved for F section of the
SOE—F for France—then I was told that I would have the
rank of major, which had been my rank in America,
though it would not be announced formally. And there was
one simple order in addition to this: "We would like you to
grow a beard, starting this morning," and seeing my look
of surprise the spokesman added, "It's quite understandable, really. We expect to be sending you over to France.
You might as well have a little elementary disguise in case
someone you know runs into you. It's not likely, but it's a
sensible precaution—and it's about the only thing in this
war that costs nothing."

Then I took a slow, cold train in streaming rain to
Guildford, from where a bumpy truck transported me to an
old English country house called Wanborough Manor. In-
quisitive locals had been told that it was a commando
training course—and it might just as well have been, for
the PT, as the British called physical training, was designed to toughen me up.

We started with "square bashing," carrying twenty

pound packs. We were bombed with flour sacks from nearby rooftops, and if we were hit, we were ordered by tough British army sergeants to clean up our uniforms and be on parade in twenty minutes looking spotless. The hotter the weather, the heavier the clothes we were forced to wear. From time to time exhausted men keeled over, fainting; I almost did myself half a dozen times. Anyone who fell had a bucket of cold water dashed over him by a soldier who was screaming, "Defend yourself! Otherwise you're dead!"

It was a rigorous kill-or-cure-regime, and when I thought I got over the worst I was sent on a paramilitary training course in another country house near Arisaig, on the wild west coast of Inverness. Security was tight. There were few roads, and because the Admiralty had some nearby naval bases, the entire area was restricted anyway. It was the perfect place to train for a new life in a world I had never dreamed of entering—a very different world from that of the ordinary soldier whose instilled discipline taught him to obey every single order without question. I was taught to think, act, kill on my own initiative, once the original order had been given.

In Inverness I was taught everything that I might have to know—how to kill silently, with a knife, by strangling, by pistol—using British, French, and German weapons, in case we captured any. On one occasion two of us were sent off for four days without a penny in our pockets or a scrap of food and told to reach a point eighty miles away in those four days. We had to beg or steal food, if necessary, robbing lonely cottages—without being discovered. I thought I had done very well considering all the problems and was rather pleased with myself as I flopped down on my bunk. Two hours later, after the shortest sleep ever, when my vision was blurred with tiredness, I was called out by a screaming sergeant major for pistol target practice at man-sized moving targets ranged behind the wall of the house. The fact that it was pelting with rain didn't make sighting the targets any easier, but as the instructor put it,

"None of you'll ever be a shot until you can shoot straight
by instinct out of your pocket or lying on your back in bed."

We used a fearsome but exciting murder weapon, a silencer pistol with a long, thick barrel full of baffles. It even
had luminous sights when we set off for night firing practice.

The only language spoken throughout the course was
French—even in the unarmed combat which we practiced
daily, even during demolitions when we blew up old buildings using PE, plastic explosives, because PE was considered safer than anything else. It would not detonate even if
hit by a bullet. A detonator embedded in it was essential.
It was so soft that one night a trainee ate some—mistaking
it for chocolate—and lived.

When I was considered expert enough, small parties
were told to report to SOE's F section in a small house in
Harley Street. It was one of those typical, long, narrow (to
American eyes anyway) streets lined with dignified Victo-
rian houses, most of them bearing the highly polished
brass plates of doctors or dentists. There I was received by
a British lady in the Women's Auxiliary Air Force, the
WAAF. A neatly uniformed flight lieutenant, Joyce Brock,
seemed to handle all the details, and told me that I had
passed all my examinations and would be told when to report for examinations.

My first three "trips" to occupied France were brief,
dangerous and yet in a curious way uneventful. I was
dropped twice by parachute on northern France, helped
local Resistance groups to be re-formed, took them canisters of arms, and returned across the Channel by fishing
boat. The third time I was sent both ways by fishing boat,
landing at Le Touquet, and making my way inland to report to a local Resistance group.

I loved the work. I hope that doesn't sound pompous. I
was never in any *real* danger, though there were moments
of disquiet. But every mission I undertook was, I knew,
preparing me for what I hoped would be the "big one" on
home territory. For I had more and more been receiving

hints that something big was brewing in the Champagne area. And that I might be sent there. I hadn't the faintest idea what *was* excercising people's mind in Champagne, but if there was trouble, it would seem natural for me to be sent. Apart from anything else, SOE *was* a professional outfit and I would obviously have a head start if I knew the geography of the area. And I was anxious for action, like a runner who has been trained for one race of his life and has now reached his peak of training. I was ready—now, this minute.

My instictive belief that I would be sent to an area I knew was increased when I was asked specific questions about my family. Was my sister still in Switzerland? Where was my brother? Did my grandmother still live in the château at Douzy? And my father? I answered as best I could, and certainly the heads of F section seemed to know all the good work that Papa was doing.

Early in 1944 I was ordered to visit Harley Street to report in the first instance to WAAF officer Brock.

"You're to meet Major Turbeville," she said briskly, "for a preliminary discussion. Then you'll receive a detailed briefing. After that, if all goes well, we'll give you your orders and then—I imagine you're anxious to be off!"

"I can hardly wait," I admitted.

"I know," she sympathized. "You get all steamed up and then—nothing happens. There's always a good reason for it."

"But *any action?*" I started.

A phone rang. She listened, said "Certainly, sir." Then she turned to me. "The major will see you. You can go into his office now, room eleven."

I was tingling with excitement. It was hard to explain the sensation bordering on relief at the prospect of *doing* something big, however dangerous it might be.

Major Turbeville seemed a pleasant, middle-aged man —he might have been a commercial traveler or the owner of a small prosperous factory. It was hard to say. And it was equally hard to determine whether he was French or English, since he had greeted me in impeccable English, after which every word was spoken in French. The *name* seemed to be vaguely French. But I had long since learned never to ask questions of *anyone* in SOE. If you were a member of this elite and highly secret force, you were in business to *answer* questions—until you took over in the territory to which you had been assigned.

"I expect you've been wondering about your next assignment," began Turbeville. "And hoping it will be in part of France where you can capitalize on your local knowledge. Well, I'll put you out of your misery—we *do* plan to send you to the Reims area. But not for three months. And because we need your specialized knowledge of the area, we don't want to send you on any other mission of—well, risk."

"Champagne is wonderful!" I cried. "But three months! Why do I have to wait that long? If you've got a job earmarked for me, why not now?"

Turbeville sighed. " 'Fraid not, but don't blame me. It's a question of waiting for the exact moment when we're ready to launch the second front. Yes, of course we know it's coming, but the job waiting for you is so big that it must be timed almost to the hour; don't worry, we're keeping it for you, but it's supremely important not to act too quickly. Could ruin everything."

"What the hell will I do while I'm waiting?"

Guardedly Turbeville said, "Somebody's got to do their share of paperwork. What about three months on a desk job? Change of pace."

"Oh, no!" I groaned.

"Could be interesting," Turbeville seemed to be enjoying a kind of private joke. "And it's only three months." As he noticed my look of dejection he added, as though musing to himself, "After all, you've got the rank. People do have to go on leave."

"You're not going to make me an instructor!" It was the hidden fear of everyone in SOE.

"Good Lord, no!" I hardly knew Turbeville, so I was totally unprepared for his next remarks. "No," he repeated. "But we do have a couple of problems. The first is how to keep you occupied for three months. The second is that the OSS has asked if we can replace a man who's gone on sick leave—needs three months off. An American. Washington knows all about your future plans, and they thought it might be a good idea if you could help out. And in three months you'll be all set for Champagne."

"I suppose I'll have to," I could hardly conceal my disappointment. "Where?"

"As an assistant military attaché," said Turbeville, "with a little undercover work. We'll lend you to the Americans for three months."

"Where?" I repeated.

"Bern," said Turbeville blandly. "Or as you Americans would say, 'Bern, Switzerland.'"

45

It was more than two years since I had said good-bye to Sonia, and I was thinking of that farewell in Rolle as my car bowled along the wide, sunny road southward from Bern, past fields hazy with heat, the spotted, lazily chewing cows looking as though they had been scrubbed each day, and the country chalets, red and white flags everywhere. Soon after I skirted Fribourg, I was dropping down to the lakeside where I reached Lausanne, then Morges, past the clinic where Anna had stayed to recuperate. A few minutes later I was approaching Rolle, the old castle on the left, then, almost opposite the cake shop, I saw the fountain on the main street. It was decked with petunias. I swung right up the country lane, under the bridge, and there, swinging gently over the white gate, was a wooden sign THREE CIRCLES FARM. I caught a glimpse of the low white house, heard the soft splash of water from the drinking trough, almost hidden under the canopy of the plane tree, as I drove through the open gate, hooting.

There was a rush to open the front door, cries of excitement as the two girls ran out to greet me—Sonia, to me unchanged as she threw her arms around me, and Anna, more reserved perhaps, a little plumper, but with a smile and a kiss and—like Sonia—bubbling with excitement.

I carried my overnight bag into the house, up the old stone stairs and along the corridor to the end room, where we had spent our last night together—the same four-poster bed on the raised dais, the same flimsy white curtains at each corner.

"Oh, Larry! It's been so long," she said when we were alone. She stood on tiptoe to reach me. "Just forget everything and kiss me—then later we'll sit down together just like an old married couple and fill in the years apart."

"You mean—we're bored with each other?" I teased her.

"Ass!" How long it was since she and Anna used to regard *ass* as their favorite word. "If you show one sign of boredom in bed, I'll know you've got a new girl!" And, typically female, she asked suspiciously, "Have you? Honestly?"

I shook my head. "Not me. I've never wanted to. Must be something wrong with my hormones or genes—undersexed. The British have a saying that all us Americans are oversexed and overpaid."

"The British? You were in England?"

I nodded. "Two years in England, with trips—well, you can guess where."

"You never told me." There was a hint of reproach.

"I couldn't, darling," and trying to joke about it, for there were no secrets between us, "Imagine if I'd written you a postcard—you an enemy!—saying that I was off to France at the weekend."

"All these long years of separation." Her eyes looked troubled and glistened with unshed tears. "And I've been thankful you were safe in America—and all the time—"

"If I'd written to you, darling, the censors would have thrown the letter away."

"It must have been terribly dangerous."

I smiled and kissed her, "Don't worry. I'm *fine*. I'm thriving!"

"For how long?" she asked almost bitterly.

"Forever. With you. And now this—a bonus—plucked out of the war, thrown into peace—I don't know how to behave! Weren't you surprised when the embassy in Bern let you know I was coming?"

"I thought it was a dream," she said simply, while I looked out of the bedroom window. It was warm, with the dappled evening sunlight moving across the ceiling of the room each time puffs of cloud chased the sun away. Once in bed, we lay in each other's arms, just as we had always done, naked, enjoying the joys of anticipation, yet our lovemaking, after the long absence, was quiet, in a way more beautiful, tender, just as happy yet without the savage desire which in the past had sometimes made the physical act into a frantic fight.

"Do you think we're growing old?" I asked afterward. "Loving quietly like this?"

"Not old. Mature. We've changed, Larry. Not only you—but me and Italy."

"I know," I said. "All the suffering we see around us, it's helped to change both of us. And the hell that's going to break out soon."

"Hell?"

"It's no secret," I said. "The Allies are going to launch an invasion of Europe; they'll have to. Otherwise the war would go on forever. Like stalemate in a chess game."

"When?"

"I haven't the faintest idea. But they can't delay it much longer. I'm not telling you military secrets. I don't *know* any details, but that doesn't mean that everyone in England—and France and Germany—knows that an invasion is being planned. So I'm not talking out of turn."

I explained to her that though I could tell her that I had been smuggled into Europe, I wasn't really breaking secrets, so long as I didn't say what I was doing. Each trip had been a separate secret—but it was a secret I didn't know about until each operation started. Nobody could betray me before I left—only if I was denounced by a traitor pretending to work with the Resistance.

"I shouldn't be telling you *anything*. But even if you were an Italian spy and told the enemy that Major Astell was a spy operating in France, it wouldn't make any difference. Nobody would know where I was going, when, what I was called. My name changes on every visit. I must hand it to the British, they produce a watertight way of protecting their men—and they do anything to rescue any of us who get into trouble."

I knew I had changed, but Sonia had changed too—because Italy had changed; it now hardly existed as an entity, but had reverted to the warring factions of barely a hundred years previously, when a city like Florence had been an enemy of a republic like Venice.

"Ciano was murdered early this year, wasn't he?" I asked.

She nodded. "In January. Poor Galeazzo! He was pretty awful, but he *did* help us, because when he saw that the Italians were on the point of surrender Ciano very smartly had himself appointed ambassador to the Vatican. And it was then that he helped Francesco push forward his plan for an annulment. It's odd, isn't it—that you never met Ciano, yet he was not only responsible for getting Anna her freedom but will enable you in the end to marry me by getting my marriage annulled."

I let the remark pass. Any retort would have been barbed, for Ciano never gave anything for nothing, and I always felt angry and jealous at the mention of his name.

Instead I asked, "We in Britain knew nothing really of what happened, where you all stand today. Can you fill me in? Give me a picture."

"I don't really know myself, except that by the end of 1942—after the Italian defeats, especially in North Africa—anti-Fascists set up a committee of different parties in Turin. All northern Italy—from big firms like Fiat—went on strike. Thank God I wasn't there."

"The luckiest thing you ever did in your life was to get a permanent residence in Switzerland," I said. "But you still haven't explained how in the middle of a war you could just manage to get rid of a dictator as powerful as Mussolini."

"I do know that Francesco played a part in searching for a peaceful way out of the war. In July last year—and believe me, to all of us in Italy 1943 will be a year never to be forgotten—it was decided to get rid of Mussolini."

What fascinated me, as I listened to Sonia's explanation, was that anyone as powerful as Mussolini could *ever* be kicked out—short of being assassinated, that is. But of course we in Britain—and no doubt America—couldn't possibly imagine the utter lack of morale and fighting spirit that must have followed the catastrophic defeats inflicted on the Italian armed forces.

On July 24, 1943, Mussolini—just back from a meeting with Hitler—was confronted by his Italian opponents, the Grand Council. Count Dino Grandi, former ambassador to London, invited the king to assume command of the armed forces and exercise his constitutional powers. Grandi told Mussolini to his face, "You believe you have the devotion of the people. You lost it the day you tied Italy to Germany." That afternoon, when Mussolini's resignation was accepted, King Victor Emmanuel told him, "You are the most hated man in Italy."

I still didn't know what happened then. According to Sonia, Mussolini was bundled out of the meeting in an ambulance and driven to Ponzo, where he was held in custody. Marshal Pietro Badoglio formed a new government. She only discovered what *really* happened through Francesco, before he quietly slipped out of the scene.

"The next forty-five days leading to the armistice was a mixture of farce and tragedy," explained Sonia. It seems that Badoglio was one of the most monstrous double-crossers in recent history. After all, he had led the campaign against Ethiopia; now he dissolved the Fascist party. But he kept on pro-German soldiers and officers and promised Ribbentrop there would be no change in Italian foreign policy. At the same time Badoglio was negotiating with Eisenhower. In the end, according to Sonia, he lost all credibility, and Hitler lost patience and sent in German troops, who crossed the Alps. And when the Allied troops landed in Italy, Badoglio surrendered to them. This left southern Italy as a government under Badoglio. But in the north German glider troops had freed Mussolini, who immediately reformed his Fascist party. Apparently there followed a chaotic winter with Italy under three masters—

Badoglio working for the Allies in the south, Mussolini hoping for the re-emergence of power in the north, and the Germans in control of large sections where, in effect, they were the occupying power.

"It was soon after this," said Sonia, "early this year, that Ciano was captured by the Germans and handed over to Mussolini. He put Ciano on trial in Verona and had him shot for treason."

"And what happened to Francesco?"

"He was arrested with Ciano—I do know that—and sentenced to death, but he and several others escaped. I'm very worried about him. I had one message saying that he was safe a few months ago. I know we can talk as though he's just a good friend—he never has been any more than that—but the truth is, he's vanished."

"Killed? You can't just vanish."

"You *can,*" she said sadly. "I don't think he is dead. If Mussolini had kept him prisoner when Ciano was murdered, he would certainly have been included in the trial at Verona. But I saw a list of everyone who had been tried. Francesco wasn't among them."

"Perhaps he's in hiding."

"I hope so. He knows I'm here. He's always kept in touch."

But now, as she explained, Italy was in such disorder that nobody knew where anyone was. And, as she added with a wry smile, that also concerned her annulment, which had almost come through before Ciano was arrested.

"But now," she shrugged, suddenly despondent, "just as our freedom is in sight, Italy's in such a mess that we may never be able to trace the papers. I may even be free by now—or next month—and then we could be married. But for all I know, we'll never find out."

That evening, forgetting that back in London you went to endless trouble and bribery to acquire an occasional bottle of scotch, here in Rolle a bottle of my favorite Old Rarity awaited me, and we sat talking before dinner.

I was delighted to see how normally Anna behaved. She was eager to be told everything she could about my life, though I had warned Sonia not to share the information about myself with anyone—not Anna, not even Guy if he happened to come down to Rolle, as he did occasionally. So to Anna I talked about my "desk job"; and I did say that I had been to Britain—almost every American had been there or in North Africa—but I didn't enlighten her about the secret nature of my work. It was a natural caution, I suppose. I knew that by rights I should not have told a single soul about my work, but then—I justified myself—Sonia and I were a single soul.

We had so much to talk about that there seemed no end, or rather so many loose ends that we didn't have time—or else were unable—to tie them up. Guy, for instance, had the previous month been to Rolle for a day, but no one had heard a word from him since.

"I think he feels more at home when he's in France than he does in Switzerland. He's bored here." It was Anna who spoke. She didn't talk a great deal, but she had an uncanny habit of striking any verbal nail right in the middle. I could just imagine how boring Guy *would* find Switzerland—whereas to me, perhaps as a change from action, or simply because Sonia was there, I began to feel more and more as though I never wanted to leave the country.

We all had our worries, of course. Anna was concerned about Papa. No one had had any news for months; on the three brief and highly secret trips I had made to France, I just hadn't dared to telephone my father. But I was able to quiet some of Anna's fears—our fears—by asking the embassy in Bern if they could find out anything from the U.S. embassy in Vichy. And a few days later I received a signal from Vichy which read laconically, "Subject under investigation is alive and kicking."

One thing was puzzling: Anna's complete lack of interest in our mother. Mama's letters to me in London, always addressed "C/O the Army Post Office" were noncommittal, perhaps because she knew they would be censored by the military. But she did write more openly to Sonia, possibly because letters to neutral countries were censored by civilians.

"As far as I'm concerned," I laughed when discussing the censorship problem with Anna and Sonia, "I'm sure Mama thinks that if my letters are censored by the U.S. Army they'll probably be deliberately handled by my closest friends, who are snooping to see what I've got to say. She just won't believe that censorship is an impersonal affair."

To Sonia, and thus to Anna, Mama had even confided that she was thinking—only thinking, she underlined the word three times—that she might not return to Douzy after the war. She didn't write openly about divorce, but she sometimes hinted at separation, that she was in love with someone in New York.

"She'll *never* come back to poor Papa," said Anna bitterly. "She having too good a time." Sitting there, in the long living room with its two sofas, one on either side of the fireplace, filled now with beautiful dried flowers, what would Anna say, I wondered, if she knew about Mama and Gaston!

The three months of early 1944 slipped past in perfect bliss. I could never quite fathom the underlying reason why we seemed happier in that period than ever before, excepting the first year of innocence. Was it the years of separation? Perhaps the forced parting was a test: if you failed, your love split up, as Mama's seemed in danger of doing; if (without trying that is) you succeeded, then the bonds of love were more strongly bound together than ever before. That's how it seemed to me anyway, in those three months during which I went to the office at Bern with very little work to do and drove off at lunchtime each Friday to Rolle, returning on the Monday morning. And on two occasions Sonia spent the week at Bern in the apartment which I had taken over from the man who was on sick leave.

"We're just like an old married couple," said Sonia happily, "all we want is Marcel's and dinner in the rue Jacob."

"Ah! That's asking too much. We'll have to wait for that. Meanwhile," with a laugh, "you'll have all the Swiss cheese you can swallow." It was said as a joke, because I had fallen in love with Swiss regional cheese dishes—an appetite sharpened by the knowledge that as soon as I returned to England I'd be lucky to get one thin slice a week of what the British called "mousetrap cheese."

"When I go back to England," I laughed again, "I'll take all my luggage allowance in cheese."

"Don't talk about leaving," she kissed me. We were back in the living room at Rolle, and Anna had gone to bed. "Let's hang on to what we've got. So much is changing—so many *people* are changing."

It was true. What a long time since Willi had shot himself—and what a long time before *that* since Reynaud had congratulated Anna and Willi the day they were married in white at Douzy church. Now Willi was gone and Anna—she *tried* to be cheerful, but I felt there was a block somewhere. And Mama—what was she doing, whose arms were embracing her now? And Guy—where was Guy? Certainly not thinking of that terrible day when Olivia had offered to leave. Where was Olivia now? Probably still in France—if, that is, she was still alive. And above all, Papa? Working so hard to try to help the French. Sometimes I missed him very much, sitting there at home in Douzy, making his "Well *really!*" pronouncements or "I must *say,* that's a little bit *too* much!" Or setting off on his "one way" walks, reaching the local bistro, then waiting for Gaston to arrive in the Hisp.

If we had been worried from time to time about Papa, I could understand that Sonia must be worried about Francesco. After all, even though a husband in name only, he was close to her. And then news of him came from a startling—and totally unexpected—source. At first I couldn't believe my eyes. On the last day of the second week we spent together in Bern, Sonia and I were walking hand in hand through the main street, with its gaily colored, elaborate fountains, arcades in streets jutting off,

and Bern's famous sixteenth-century clock on the Gate
Tower. We stopped to watch its figures striking the hour
under the shadow of the beautiful old-fashioned gabled
houses, when a voice in cultured French said, "Good morning, countess—and good morning, Herr Astell."

I spun round. I knew that enemy voice anywhere.

"And," it added silkily, "so pleased to see two people so
much in love after all these years."

"Herr Abetz!" I blurted out. "What are *you* doing here?"

As Sonia clutched my arm and said "Good day," Abetz
said, "Well, Mr. Astell, I am an ambassador if you don't
mind, and I have the right to visit our embassy in Bern if I
feel like a change!"

"Of course," I muttered.

"More to the point," he added as we stood in the warm
sunshine under the clock tower, "if it's not an impertinent
question, what are *you* doing here? I thought all you young
Americans were in khaki helping to save the British from
defeat."

"I'm attached to the embassy here for a few months," I
said shortly.

"Ah! One of us! Welcome to the club—even if you *are*
only a temporary member." Then, as I was wondering how
to get away from a man I hated, he added two things,
"Strange, running into you both—because," with a nod to
Sonia, "I have news of your husband."

"Francesco?"

"Ah! I see you remember his name—well," looking
straight at our linked arms, "he seems to be your husband
only in—er—name."

"Where is Francesco?" asked Sonia almost hoarsely.
"Please! We're all very worried—no news—"

"He's safe—for the moment. And I'm trying to help him.
But I'm afraid," again that silky voice, the deprecating
shrug of the shoulders under the pink face, ice-blue eyes,
the reddish-blond hair, "you Italians are giving us in Germany a great deal of trouble. So *volatile.*"

I squeezed Sonia's arm to stop her from getting angry. It
was true that the Germans despised the Italians, but I

didn't want to be dragged into a battle of words. He would tell us all he wanted to when he felt like it. But there was no need to give him the satisfaction of letting Sonia beg for news.

And in the end, what he told us was simple but reassuring. Francesco, unable to get into Switzerland, let alone telephone Sonia, had been in danger of arrest ever since Ciano had been arrested. He had managed to escape to Lisbon with the help of Abetz. "After all, we worked together in Germany and in France," said Abetz, "it was the least I could do as one gentleman to another."

I let the first "gentleman" pass without comment. "And I regret to say that there's a price on your husband's head—as a very high-up member of Ciano's staff," said Abetz. "Mussolini wanted him first—and almost had him shot. Now the anti-Fascisti want him dead or alive. Stupid people. I arranged for him to be issued with the necessary papers—for a new life if you like—and he's waiting now for transport to Argentina. Yes, there are more than a million Italians living in that country, and most Argentines are a pretty rotten lot, so any man like your husband is bound to succeed. Buenos Aires is, I am told, a paradise. Francesco will fit in there perfectly. A very elegant figure, especially as he will be able to keep his title once he's arrived in South America."

"Well, thank God he's safe," said Sonia, who almost had to drag out the words, though she did sound immensely relieved.

"This war," Abetz waved an airy hand, "will soon be over—when we've won it."

"How can you ever *think* that?" I retorted. "You can *never* win the war against America and Britain."

"My dear Astell," he said, "once the British and Americans start to invade France—if they are stupid enough to commit suicide—the Allied losses will be so appalling that in a few months the Third Reich and America will arrange a negotiated peace. And then we can join up to get rid of the Communists. You wait and see. *Auf Wiedersehen!*"

* * *

"He's mad," I said to Sonia when he had gone. "Stark, raving mad. Do the Germans really believe all that balls? Germany and America as allies! With the British, I suppose, an occupied island!"

"He's *cottolengo!*" she echoed.

"Yes, he does come from a madhouse, and I'm sorry for the poor deluded Germans."

"And the poor deluded Italians," added Sonia.

"Yes—it's not their fault," I said. "Hitler and Mussolini intoxicated people. When they spoke, their words meant more than bread. When they thundered on about conquest and splendor, everyone believed them—including, it seems, Abetz."

That was our last complete week in what we eventually called nostalgically "the Swiss interlude." We didn't see Abetz again, and when I drove Sonia to Rolle on the Friday, I left my usual weekend address and phone number at the embassy. It was our eleventh weekend together so I knew that peace—for us—was running out. But I was unprepared for the news that awaited me at Rolle on the Friday evening: an urgent request, left with Anna, to telephone the embassy as soon as possible.

I called the duty officer the moment I entered the house.

"Thank God you arrived in time," he said. "I've a message for you. There's apparently a plane leaving Zurich tomorrow morning at five A.M.—and you've got to be on it, to catch a connection from Lisbon to London."

In a way it was better that way. I dreaded long partings, our life together over the years seemed to have been so brutally interrupted so many times that it was less painful to have a quick farewell imposed on us by others.

"Don't worry," I said during that last dinner in the old farmhouse dining room. "Despite what Mr. Abetz says, I reckon I'll be back by the end of the summer. And free too!"

"Don't tempt providence by saying things like that," begged Sonia.

"I won't," I laughed, and then, thinking of the imminent parting, I asked, a little troubled, "What about Anna?"

"Don't worry," Sonia reassured me. "She's getting better every day. She'll stay with me as long as she likes. You know how close Anna and I have been all our lives. And she reminds me of you."

"But the future?"

"After the war—who knows, she might go to America. Your mother has already suggested it. We'll see. The most important thing is for her to relax—and there's no better place than Switzerland for that."

As she was speaking, Anna came into the room. "I forgot to tell you," she said to Sonia, "but there are a dozen letters that arrived while you were away. I left them on the desk in the sitting room."

"Bills, I'm sure," laughed Sonia, but one of them at least was not a bill. I saw Sonia handle the envelope, saw its thick square shape, rather like an envelope concerning an official invitation.

Sonia, I could tell, knew who had sent it. And I could sense her mounting excitement as she ripped open the envelope, then read the contents. When she turned to me her eyes were swimming.

"It's from my lawyer in the Vatican," she cried. "It's come through! The annulment! It's been granted! Oh, darling! The lawyer says there'll be a short delay until the official documents arrive by registered post, but then—well—" she turned to me, eyes brimming with tears of happiness.

"And then," I said gently, "then *nothing* will stop you being called Sonia Astell for the rest of your life."

46

THE SUMMONS FROM F SECTION came the day after I arrived back in England. I could tell from the tone of Turbeville's voice when he called me on the phone that this was a call to action. I felt a flutter of excitement—I actually felt the pounding of my heart like a hammer—when I was ushered into his modest office in Harley Street.

"Have a good time in Bern?" he asked by way of starting the conversation.

"Very enjoyable," I replied. "And not too much work."

"Plenty of time to visit Rolle," he almost chuckled, and seeing my embarrassment, added, "Don't worry, Astell, we're all human. And I'm told she's absolutely stunning. And that you're going to get married after the war. Wonderful."

"Spies spying on spies!" I said angrily.

"Not at all," he replied coldly. "Just perfectly routine checks."

I knew he was right. Everyone checked everyone else in our job—and having a girl in Switzerland wasn't a secret. In fact it had been hinted to me when I reached Bern that I'd been offered a busman's holiday among friends. Still, being told about it so bluntly, I felt a little naked.

"Don't worry," Turbeville said more kindly. "Make yourself comfortable," he led me to a couple of deep leather armchairs. "And to put you out of your misery—you'll be leaving right away."

The hammering of excitement increased with every word he spoke.

"It's tricky—very dangerous. And—don't panic—it involves your own home, the Château de Douzy."

"What on earth do you mean?"

"That's why we chose you. You *know* it; but it may be too close to you. So close that at first we ruled you out for the operation."

I felt a sudden surge of anger but managed to contain it.

"Yes, we did have the feeling that personal problems might interfere with the logic of the task you have to perform. But we decided you were big enough to overcome this. The local Resistance is very good in the Reims area." I had a sudden flashback to that last day in France, so long ago it seemed, and wondered what had happened to Gaston—and for that matter to Olivia.

"It might help, Major Astell, if you paid attention," said Turbeville mildly.

"I'm sorry—but the shock of what you've told me—and I was friends with one or two of the Resistance people."

"I know," he said not unkindly. "Who knows—you may run across some more of your friends soon," adding like a cold shower, "those who weren't killed as reprisals after the death of Hoess. Now," rather abruptly, "I'd like to ask you a few questions about your local territory. What do you know about the village of Rilly?"

I told him all I did know—that the Germans had blocked the southern end of the tunnel, that the RAF had bombed it inefficiently, adding, "My belief is that the Germans are using the tunnel as a sort of a storehouse."

"Right. Storing what?"

"I have no idea."

"I'll come to that later," said Turbeville. "Now, what about the Douzy Pyramid—your family pyramid, right?"

I nodded, explained that the Germans had closed the pyramid long before Pearl Harbor.

"You're sure it's closed?"

"Absolutely, I mean—it *was* closed when I last saw it. There's only one real way into Douzy, and that's through the main entrance, cut into the side of the hill—it was all boarded up when I last saw it."

"What about the back entrance through the *celliers*— the underground passages through the farm near the château?"

"They were boarded up too. Of course it might have been opened up by the Germans—I wouldn't know."

"No, they haven't opened it up. I don't know whether you are aware of this, but the Château de Douzy was requisitioned by the Germans—that means your family home. It's now an officers' mess."

I was staggered. I should have thought of it, of course— obviously Douzy was now German-held property. But the damn Germans strutting around our house! "I wonder—" I began.

"Your grandmother is still running the vineyards," Turbeville anticipated my question. "Because of her age—and her French birth—she's not been interned. She's living in the cottage that you used to rent to a couple of old ladies."

The Misses B and B! So Grandma was living there.

"And my father?"

"He's fine. Helping the French." And then, obviously enjoying a moment of quiet drama, he added in an elaborately casual tone, "In fact I had lunch with your father at Berlinguet's three weeks ago!"

"You *what?*"

"I thought that would amuse you."

"But you—"

Perhaps inadvertently I had thought of him as an armchair officer, and he added even more dryly, "When we are on to a critical operation, the chief believes in checking the preliminary steps *sur place.* Your father is well. He's been allowed freedom to continue his work, using his French passport."

"I don't suppose—I haven't seen him since before Pearl Harbor."

"I couldn't say anything, of course. I went on business. But I told one of our local Resistance executives to tip your father off—after I had returned to England. Just to say you were well and living in America."

I knew I shouldn't ask questions, but I couldn't refrain from this one: "How did you manage to meet my father?"

"Easy," replied Turbeville. "Before the war I used to manufacture bottles in my factory outside Lyon. I went to see if I could get your father to persuade the Germans to give us a permit to increase production of bottles for champagne. And now," once again he switched abruptly, "to business. You are right. The Rilly tunnel is by now used as a vast storehouse. But as far as the Douzy Pyramid is concerned, you are wrong. It has never—I repeat never—been closed."

"Before Pearl Harbor it was," I said.

"Not even then," Turbeville shook his head. "It *looked* closed. It was *meant* to look closed. But there is a third entrance to both the Rilly and Douzy pyramids. Or there was until it was bricked up."

"Of course! Hardly an entrance, more an exit."

"Yes, you've got it," agreed Turbeville. "In the old days corridors led from the Douzy and Rilly pyramids straight to loading platforms inside the railway tunnel. The original idea, as you know, was to ship champagne straight into the railway. But the idea never came to anything."

"But they were never used," I said. "And surely they were all bricked up years ago?"

"Right. We believe the Rilly exit to the tunnel is still bricked up. So your father couldn't even get into the tunnel if he wanted to. On the other hand, we've been told that the Douzy wall blocking the way into the tunnel has been knocked down. It's now the entrance to the pyramid and can of course be used secretly by the Germans because nobody can get into the tunnel except German personnel. In fact we believe the Douzy Pyramid is being used as a huge secret laboratory."

"I don't believe it!" I cried.

"That's why you're going to Reims. To find out if it *is* true."

I asked Turbeville what he *thought* was hidden.

"We're fairly sure that the tunnel is being used to store components for V-2 rockets, even completed rockets. It's an ideal place. It can't be bombed, we know that in Germany tunnels are being prepared in an old potassium mine at Bleicherode, ten miles or so from the Kohnstein Mountains. Some of them go five hundred feet below the surface. The main objective is to prepare sites for V-2 rockets that can't be bombed if the Allies start a second front. The Rilly tunnel fits the bill perfectly. High-level photo reconnaissance shows that they're planning to store a liquid oxygen plant as well as other detailed material."

"But isn't Rilly too far from the coast?"

"It doesn't really matter." As Turbeville explained, the V-2 needed no sophisticated site works, unlike the V-1, which required a distinctive ski ramp to launch it and which was easily identified by Allied aerial photography. A V-2 needed only road access to flat ground, with a metal or concrete slab for the launching pad. It was invisible from the air, and V-2s could be launched by mobile teams capable of setting up a V-2, arming and refueling it, and then firing it, all within four hours.

He explained in some detail the mechanics of the V-2s, and then I asked him, "What about the secret work that's supposed to be going on inside Douzy? What does that consist of?"

He hesitated and his voice was suddenly invested with an entirely new edge of gravity. "It's dynamite. No, it's worse than dynamite." Turbeville hesitated again and said, "I want to put one question to you before I tell you any more—off the record: knowing that your family and friends may be involved in the Reims area—especially if there are reprisals—you can opt to be sent somewhere else on another mission. We need you in France, but you don't have to be sent to Douzy—for I'm afraid everything may center on the pyramid, your pyramid. I'm not sure, but if our fears are correct—"

"You should know me better than that!" I said almost harshly.

"I do. I knew your answer before I asked the question,

but we have an understanding in F section. If we send anyone—especially a Frenchman—behind the lines to organize sabotage, which means automatic reprisals in his own area—among his old friends—we feel it our duty to point that out before he agrees to undertake the mission."

"I understand. But what's so special about Douzy?"

"I think you'd better have a word with one of our tame boffins," said Turbeville. "He's waiting outside to see you." Boffin—a slang word for what the Americans called an egghead—was one of dozens of English words introduced during the war. This one was a gray-haired Doctor Chisholm, who had a sense of humor. He started by saying, almost jovially, "I'm going to ask you a question to which I know you won't be able to give me any answer."

He roared with laughter, and I couldn't help smiling, though I hadn't the faintest idea what he was talking about.

"Ever heard of isopropylmethyl phosphoro-fluoridate?"

He had such an impish look that I was almost tempted to ask, How do you spell it?

"Don't worry," he almost choked with laughter at his own sense of fun, "we'll use its more common name. Sarin. Ever hear of *that?*" I shook my head.

"At this stage I'll just say that sarin is the deadliest chemical killer the world has ever known. One-fiftieth of one drop of concentrated sarin will kill a man in sixty seconds. And our information is that Hitler is manufacturing sarin—in your pyramid at Douzy."

A long unmeasurable span of silence seemed to kill the air I was breathing as the two of us faced each other across the bare wooden desk. It was the sort of silence that lasted perhaps a minute, perhaps a lifetime, for I was not thinking of clouds of death sprayed from the skies, of hateful Germans, of the beastliness of war, I was thinking simply, with an agony I couldn't put into words, of—my father.

I found it hard to concentrate, and finally Dr. Chisholm said, not unkindly, "It must be a blow to you—your own estate, your home. But, remember, we don't know for certain. So let's take heart. First things first."

He paused, then added, "This may all be a rumor, but we've got to know. And unless things change, the mission for which we would like to send you will fall into three parts—the easiest one will be to check on the contents of the tunnel—are there any V-2s there? Second, you've got to find out if the Germans are manufacturing sarin in Douzy. And third, and *only if you're absolutely certain*, and only after specific instructions from London, you'll have to"—he hesitated—"neutralize the plant. Even if it means blowing up, or sealing up forever, the pyramid."

My brain was racing overtime. The problems of finding out didn't worry me—well, they would have done so except for the one overwhelming thought that haunted me, Papa. Did he know? Was he aware of the monstrous evil in the next pyramid? If what Chisholm said was true, it would have to be blown up. And even if my father didn't know—and I knew in my heart that he couldn't know—what would happen if I was ordered to blow up Douzy? For, though the entrances to Douzy and Rilly pyramids were apart at the apex, the bases of both pyramids were adjacent by the very nature of the Roman excavations and construction. The holes were tiny at the top but huge at the bottom, and as they both came inward toward each other, they met. If I had to blow up Douzy, the explosion would certainly blow up Rilly as well. Unless I could warn my father? But no, that sort of private consideration was against all the rules of SOE. The very factor which, according to Turbeville had made SOE hesitate before choosing me for the mission. But perhaps it would never come to that.

"This sarin," I said to Dr. Chisholm finally, "are the Germans really making it?"

"A German chemist—I'll let you read all the details later on—discovered tabun, an earlier nerve gas, in 1936, and then he discovered sarin while he was engaged in further research. It's interesting to know that the German plant, which is situated on the river Oder, where some sarin is now being manufactured, is ten stories high. It seems that apparently the height is needed to start the process at the top end of the building so that the mixture goes downward through miles and miles of pipes by gravitation until the product comes out on the ground floor. I mention that because it's an interesting added reason for using a pyramid a hundred feet tall like Douzy. It's also important, of course, because Douzy is so much safer. All the dangerous work is being done underground in virtually bombproof surroundings. Sarin is so deadly that they can't risk having the plant bombed. So—almost by accident—General Hermann Ochsner, the head of the Nazi chemical division, thought of the champagne cellars. It seems he had visited them before the war—they're bombproof, invisible to air reconnaissance, in fact perfect."

"But why Douzy? Why not Rilly?"

Turbeville, who was listening to the conversation, sighed. "Let me make it clear that there has never been a word uttered against your father. He *has* saved scores of lives—but you must appreciate that all this is a blind. The Germans wish to make the entire area more—what's the word I'm looking for?—*content,* so that no one will stir up any trouble. There is an understanding officer in charge. He keeps up very good relations with the champagne producers—and that means work for all the people in the area. Your father is honest, loyal, and would be horrified if he knew what is really happening. But the entire operation—allowing your father the liberty he has achieved to increase production—is a plot to lull the people of the area into a sense of false security."

I had often wondered as much. Poor Papa! So honest, as Turbeville had said. Such a—such a *gentleman,* never in his wildest dreams imagining that *anyone* would be capable of such madness, such deceit, even in warfare.

"This German general—Ochsner?" I asked. "Does he really have any power?"

"He does," said Dr. Chisholm, "and we have a copy of a secret memorandum which Ochsner drafted for Hitler as far back as 1939 in which he cited several reasons why Germany should use chemical warfare, as he put it in the memorandum, 'in the coming European war.' Here. Read this, it's a copy of the Ochsner report."

He handed it to me and I read, "Thanks to the unique position which our chemical industry enjoys in the world, we are in a position to achieve and hold our lead over all countries—if we show the necessary determination." But it was the last reason that made me suddenly break out into a cold sweat.

"We must never forget that the importance of terror in the civilian population," wrote Ochsner, "the impact of the air force using chemicals in fairly substantial quantities against the enemy hinterland, in particular against industrial concentration and large cities, could have a very great effect on morale. There is no doubt that a city like London would be plunged into a state of unbearable turmoil which would bring enormous pressure to bear on the enemy government."

I looked at Dr. Chisholm, handing him back the piece of paper. I found my hand was shaking.

"Is it really as bad as that?" I asked.

He nodded. "Tabun and sarin are colorless, they have virtually no smell, and microscopic quantities can kill thousands in under a minute."

"How?"

"They're absorbed through the skin or the lungs. They work very simply—by blocking an enzyme in the body which controls the movement of muscles. Death results almost immediately."

"I should explain," added Turbeville, "that our information—which is admittedly very sketchy in parts—leads us to believe that it's possible the V-2s hidden in the Rilly tunnel are being fitted with special warheads which could carry chemical gases. We've heard—no proof yet—that German scientists have discovered how to detonate warheads hundreds of feet above the ground. If that happened over, let's say London, you'd have clouds of invisible, odorless sarin over the capital. It would virtually kill the entire population of London. And then of course, Britain would have to ask for peace—simply because a new and terrifying

dimension would have been added to conventional warfare. One against which there would be absolutely no defense. It's as though America suddenly realized the dream
on which she's been working for ten years—we know what
that is—to split the atom and contain it in a bomb. Imagine
one atom bomb destroying an entire city—the other side
would *have* to give in."

Dr. Chisholm handed over a buff folder. "I know the
technicalities won't mean much to you," he said, "but
glance through this memorandum on sarin. I think it's the
sort of information you'll be able to digest more easily in
print than if I tried to explain it. I'll leave you now, but
please read it before you leave this room."

The folder was marked "Top Secret," and I sat there,
trying to understand the fearsome details.

"Don't worry about remembering anything," said Chisholm. "When you get your real orders, we'll go through
this all again—a dozen times if necessary. This is just background. Ring this," he indicated a bell on the table, "when
you're through, and I'll collect it. I'm afraid you'll have to
be locked in while you read it."

The document was not very long, typed on foolscap paper
and divided into sections. I settled down to try to absorb
the details. The first part read:

DEVELOPMENT AND PROPERTIES OF SARIN AS MANUFACTURED IN GERMANY

Sarin is the trade name given to isopropylmethyl
phosphoro-fluoridate which was first discovered by
Dr. Gebhardt Schrader of IG Farbenindustrie in
Leverkusen, Germany, during the same time that
tabun, the name for ethyldimethylamido-phosphoro-
cyanidate, was being manufactured. (Cases of tabun
incidentally when shipped to storage places early in
the war were always labelled 'Trilon,' a popular German soap.)

Sarin, however, is difficult to manufacture, but is
more deadly than any of the other chemical agents de-

veloped by Germany. The lethal dose is one milligram—that is to say one-fiftieth of one drop. It works with devastating speed, acting on key enzyme. This enzyme is called acetylcholinesterase, commonly known as 'acat.' This enzyme in the body controls muscular activity.

CAUSE OF DEATH

The body includes millions of junctions in the nervous system in which the chemical acetylcholine (which is body produced) sends out automatic nerve signals of which we are unaware. If the nerve signals overreact, the body automatically counterbalances the danger of releasing acetylcholinesterase, thus neutralising the dangers of acetylcholine.

If a minute particle of sarin enters the body through the skin or lungs, it immediately stops the production of acetylcholinestrerase, causing the body to lose control. The muscles begin to vibrate, which in turn is followed almost immediately by paralysis. The involuntary muscles, which normally help to regulate blood vessels and internal organs, no longer function properly.

The pupils of the eyes constrict, the heart slows, the bladder and alimentary canal are also constricted. The penis invariably stiffens into an erection. Death follows within sixty seconds, whether the poison enters the body by injection, is absorbed through the skin, or is inhaled. Insofar as it is possible to label a cause of death, it is generally caused by asphyxia following paralysis of the muscles of the respiratory system.

LAUNCHING METHOD

Almost everything we know is subject to confirmation so far as launching methods are concerned and is the result of information supplied to us by undercover agents and a study of RAF PRU (photographic recon-

naissance unit). It is believed that warheads have
been specially constructed for use with V-2 rockets
which can now be aimed with a large degree of accuracy to fall within a rectangle sixteen miles by
thirteen miles at a target 183 miles from the launching site. The V-2 can be assembled and launched
within four hours, and if the preparatory work is done
by night, the cumbersome machinery would not be
seen by PRU. By day, if aircraft are in the vicinity, it
is comparatively easy to take action because, though
the V-2s can be assembled and fired quickly, each one
needs a large convoy of ancillary machinery (see
below). The V-2 is a short name for the second *vergel-
tungswaffe* (Vengance) weapon but is always known
to the German army as the A-4. It is Mark IV in the
series of 'A' rockets developed by the German scien-
tist von Braun. It weighs approximately 13.6 tons at
launch, carries a warhead that can be loaded with one
ton of HE or else with small quantities of sarin. It is
estimated that the rocket motor, using liquid oxygen
and alcohol, would burn for seventy seconds.

One of the reasons that leads us to suppose that the
rockets are being stored in the Rilly tunnel is that
PRU show an increasing amount of specialised vehicle
traffic in the vicinity. For, even though it may be possible to mount and fire a rocket in four hours, an enormous convoy is required. For each battery there are
three special tractors, each carrying a rocket, and
drawn by a half-track, which also carries the firing
crew. Three tankers, up to sixty feet long, are required—one for alcohol, one for liquid oxygen, one for
auxiliary fuel. In addition there must be a generator
truck for electric power and a firing-control truck, as
well as staff cars for officers.

The standard warhead fuse operates by an electrical
contact system which allows the warhead to explode
three feet below the ground before detonation. We understand that for use with sarin the Germans are ex-
perimenting with a new proximity fuse which would

release gas seven hundred feet above ground. Information suggests that the Germans are endeavouring to modify the Zünder 19 (fuse 19) designed originally for a two-hundred-and-fifty-kilogram bomb with a burst height of around 115 yards.

PRODUCTION LOCALITIES

A statement by Albert Speer, Hitler's Minister of Production, a copy of which has reached London, reads as follows: 'I know from various associates that they are discussing the question of using our two new combat gases, tabun and sarin. They believe these gases would be of particular efficacy and they have in fact produced the most frightful results. For the manufacture of this gas we have about three factories all of which are undamaged.'

We also have unconfirmed information however that sarin is being manufactured in France, where General Ochsner, as a result of his visit to the Champagne region, decided the caverns or deep cellars surrounding the area would be an ideal bombproof site. The deepest underground chalk cave in this area is situated at the village of Douzy, just south of Reims, and we understand that old disused tunnels link the underground pyramid with the bombproof tunnel outside the neighbouring village of Rilly.

Earlier information of the manufacturing processes in Dyhernfurth on the river Oder near Breslau, based on information reaching us from German-Jewish chemists fleeing from Germany, says that a maze of piping is required before the original raw material can be transformed into the finished product.

Aerial photographs taken in the Champagne region by PRU indicate the import of a large quantity of steel drums, usually eight feet long and two feet wide. In the judgment of those evaluating the photographs, these drums are three-quarter-inch steel. They are painted silver, with a paint which is known to erode in the case of a phosphate leak.

Other PRU evidence gives clear indications of the matériel being shipped for use with rockets.

CONCLUSIONS

All the evidence points to the manufacture and/or storage of sarin liquid in one or more chalk pyramids south of Reims. Before any decisions can be made as to the bombing or sealing up of the storage spaces, it is suggested that an agent be sent to the area to penetrate the above-mentioned pyramid and advise, after which SOE HQ can determine what action should be taken.

As I closed the buff folder I sat back, hand stretched out to ring the bell, then paused. Jumbled thoughts, fears, danced round my brain, all in the end revolving not so much round the diabolical witches' brew being manufactured in Douzy Pyramid—though that was fearful enough—but the more selfish, more terrifying worry of the part played by my father. Oh, yes, it was innocent enough, it was laudable, no danger on that score. But the secret thought that *all* of us had been hoodwinked by the Germans was something I found impossible to believe. The smooth Major Kissling and his explanation that Douzy Pyramid had been closed to save my gullible father from any embarrassment! All false, all lies, to cover up the fact that probably it had never been closed at all. The Germans had entered through the old, long-forgotten bricked-up passage linking the pyramid with the Rilly tunnel. To the world Douzy was closed—and there was evidence of that in barred and shuttered gates at the grandiose front entrance, while the original Roman apex entrance, long since covered with a thick plate of glass, the size of a dining-room table, was covered and surrounded with German barbed wire and even, so the warnings read, land mines near the vicinity.

I knew that my father was a patriot, he would rather die than betray France, the country he really loved above all others. He had a curious innocence—which made him unsuspecting of anything devious. He took *everyone* at his or her face value. He had found Major Kissling a "gentleman," and when Kissling suggested closing the pyramid, my father had agreed because he genuinely believed that Kissling had closed it to protect my father and the family from embarrassment. It was the same with my father's attitude to the workers in Rilly. He was saving lives! Major Kissling was a humanitarian—this, I could see, was how my father's thoughts were running—one of hundreds of Germans forced to fight for Hitler, but doing his best to alleviate any suffering. Maybe Kissling was innocent! Maybe he *didn't* know what was going on in the tunnel under the pyramid, maybe the German army's chemical warfare division kept its secrets away from the "ordinary" German officers. And maybe there was nothing in the Douzy Pyramid after all.

Waiting to press the bell, I remembered the time when I had voiced my doubts on Papa's work to Gaston. He had laughed in my face. He had actually told me that after the war the French would erect a statue to my father for all the wonderful work he had done to save Frenchmen.

Maybe it was all nonsense! Wouldn't that be wonderful, like a huge weight which had been crushing my shoulders suddenly being taken away by a miracle. But as I pressed the bell, heard the key turn in the lock, and Turbeville walked in and picked up the file, I knew it was all true.

47

"RIGHT," SAID MAJOR TURBEVILLE BRISKLY, "here are your latest orders. Your fourth mission, eh? Well, you leave in four days."

It was now the beginning of May 1944, and he handed me a copy of the official orders. It was headed "Operation Instruction F103a." Under that I read, "Operation: Pedlar; field name: Johnnie; name on papers: Jean Vivier."

Pedlar was, I knew, the code name of the circuit operating around Reims. Until a few months previously the circuit in the area had been *Professor,* I do not know why it had been changed. Its nearest "neighbor" was *Silversmith,* the circuit operating between Reims and Châlons-sur-Marne. So that meant that I was going "home" at last!

"I don't need you to tell me that things are on the move," said Turbeville. "It's any day now."

He was, of course, referring to the invasion plans for Europe. Everything pointed to massive action in the near future. "And then," added Turbeville, "if our suspicions are right, Hitler, who's absolutely mad, may well decide to bring the world down with him. You know, like Wotan at Valhalla, to kill not only his enemies, but his own people. Because there's increasing evidence that Hitler's now convinced the German people have let him down and deserve to be punished."

"Thanks for the cheerful news," I tried to match Turbeville's dry sense of humor. "Who's coming with me as radio op?"

Normally an agent such as myself traveled with a radio operator, for though I had learned the groundwork of Morse, and how to operate a set if I had to, the sending of ciphered messages was so vital—and usually had nothing to do with the operation—that it tended to be treated separately. And it was a rule of SOE that though the agent had full responsibility in the field, the WT operator, as he was known, was allowed a great deal of latitude because of the high risk of discovery when he was tapping a message on the air. My eye caught a paragraph headed "Notes for Liaison with WT Security." "The WT operator assigned to you will be under your command and will take his instructions from you, but he will be the ultimate judge as regards technicalities and security."

I had practiced WT with several operators—some of them back in England after a spell in occupied territory, others new to the job and ready to set off on their first mission. I liked to know who my WT operator was. So much depended on his character.

"Who's coming with me?" I repeated the question almost casually.

"She's already there—waiting for you."

"She!"

Turbeville nodded. "She's very good, a French woman, but remember—keep your messages short—shorter than ever now. When the balloon goes up, it's going to be hell for everyone. You blokes *do* bear charmed lives—in comparison with WT operators. With the sophisticated methods of tracking down transmissions by direction finders, the average life expectancy of a radio operator in the field is now just under seven months."

"I hope she's good!"

"She's the best. Code name Portia. She'd better be good. Your information could make all the difference to the outcome of the war—if it's what we think it is."

Turbeville had a mass of instructions for me. First of all, he wanted me to take with me a new radio set. The one in the Champagne area was giving trouble, and SOE had perfected a new later set. Agents had no speech radios, but

SOE's new machine was the shortwave Morse transceiv-
er—a combined transmitter and receiver, B Mark II, which
weighed thirty pounds and was fitted in a suitcase two feet
long. The signal was weak and needed seventy feet of aerial, which didn't have to be fixed. It could trail along the
ground—providing it wasn't seen. The frequency it worked
on was determined by removable crystals, small enough to
lie in the palm of the hand. Every operator needed at least
two to vary the frequencies, but they were delicate and
easily broken.

"So take care of it," Turbeville begged me, and using the
nickname by which all radio operators were known, added,
"The pianist is looking forward to getting her new toy."

There were other details to be worked out. My cover as
Jean Vivier, code name Johnnie, was as a vigneron, a disguise I could "wear" without even trying. The SOE wardrobe department, in a warehouse behind Lords cricket
ground, fitted me out with peasant's clothes. All this was
fairly simple. So were the basic orders—to identify the contents of the tunnel and the pyramid. No problem there. I
was given the sum of two hundred thousand francs, and
with it a prim warning. "Please account for all expendi-
tures when possible."

As usual I was also given the code name of the operator
who would help me locally. Each operator in charge of
major missions worked with one of the leaders of the Resistance in his particular area. Often the man—or woman—
would work with him. All that Turbeville told me was that
my contact—who would contact *me*—was code named Hamlet.

Codes and passwords were vital, for they had to be mem-
orized, and if you forgot the magic words, you would never
be able to make contact. Some codes, or false names and
addresses, were needed in case something went wrong
with an operation. I was supposed to be met by Hamlet,
but if he didn't turn up, if the French "reception committee" failed to keep the rendezvous, then I had to telephone
a Madame Ronson, at 205 rue de France in Reims, and
give the password, which was based on a simple inversion,

so that I could be sure the coast was clear in a "safe house." I would ask Madame Ronson if I could come and see her. If she replied, "By all means, do come," that would be a warning *not* to come, as the Germans would be either in her house or in the vicinity. If, on the other hand, she said, "It's not really convenient," that meant it was safe to come round.

SOE had spent a great deal of time devising types of passwords that were not too difficult for uneducated people to remember and use; and experience had shown that the inversion system was the safest.

"As you're working in the vicinity—and even with the beard you may be recognized—you face an added danger. Yet you're the only man in the world who has any chance of getting into Douzy and finding out what's happened. But you *are* known. One of the problems you'll face," all this from Turbeville, "is knowing who your real friends are. I mean fellow members of the Resistance. Your number two, Hamlet, will give you the latest general recognition passwords. At the moment the one we use in Pedlar is *'Où peut-on trouver de l'essence à briquet?'* and the correct answer to this request for lighter fuel is *'Du carbonant, vous voulez dire?'* "

As far as my messages to London were concerned, I would code them all myself before passing them on to Portia. Earlier the commonest cipher had been based on a line from a poem chosen by the agent, so he or she was certain to remember it. But now I was issued with a "onetime pad." This was a pad of ultrathin silk slips on which columns of random letters and figures were printed. I would use them in the order they were on the pad and burn each one after use. There was only one duplicate—at SOE in London.

"The onetime pad is useful for another reason," said Turbeville in his occasionally cynical tone, "there's no way your radio operator can decode it under torture, and what's more, once you've burned the silk slip, you can't decode it either, whatever the torture. Damned clever, these boffins."

Among other problems which I had to memorize was the address of a *cachette*. If I ran into serious trouble, I was to go to the *cachette* in a safe house in Paris and tell London by means of a guarded postcard sent to a name and address in Lisbon. "And remember, the French spell it different-ly—*Lisbonne*—so if we get a card from you in Lisbon," ex-plained Turbeville, "you will be contacted at the *cachette* and we can then try to get you out of the country. But we hope it won't come to that."

When I had been told that I would be picked up by car and taken to an airfield "somewhere in England," I said almost without thinking, "I hope you pack up the radio well. It would be a tragedy if I parachuted in and then we broke the radio after a bad landing."

"You're not parachuting in," said Tuberville blandly. "Didn't I tell you? God! I must have forgotten. You're going in by Lysander, that's a light monoplane that can land on a sixpence. Here's your exact destination. It's a grass field near a tiny village called Trois Puits, just south of Reims. It's easily picked out because a small river called the Rouillat crosses the main road just south of Reims. It's moderately hilly country, with small valleys where the pi-lot will be able to land without any trouble. The Lysand-er—as usual—will be on the ground for a maximum of two minutes before taking off. They don't like to waste time."

"I know the place well," I said.

"By the way," said Turbeville when discussing last-minute details, "What about your next of kin?" With a suitable look of apology, for he couldn't quite conceal his cynicism, Turbeville added, "I know it won't be necessary of course, but on every op I have to put the same question."

"It's a bit difficult," I hesitated. "I do have a mother."

"Are mothers difficult?"

I shook my head. "My fiancée lives in Switzerland. I *would* like her to know I'm—well, in the land of the liv-ing."

"That can be managed. A monthly message from your old friends in the British embassy in Bern. Fill in the pa-

pers here," he handed me a form, "and," with a touch of
mockery, "don't worry about phony excuses to hide the
fact that she's an Italian."

"You knew?"

"Of course. We *try* to know everything. And why do you
think we gave you a free holiday in Switzerland?"

I had flown familiarization missions over England in
Lysanders several times, and I was delighted—or should I
say relieved?—that I was being landed rather than parachuted into France. The captain of the aircraft was the
same squadron leader, a man called Dobson, who had
taken me on the previous short trips.

We made our way to an airfield, which bore no name,
but which I guessed was at West Malling in Kent, where
we had a final briefing. The Lysander was a small, sturdy,
single-engined, high-winged monoplane with a cruising
speed of about one hundred sixty-five miles an hour, and if
fitted with an extra tank, it could fly to Champagne and
back and land in five or six hundred yards of grass or clo-
ver.

I was flying alone with the pilot, and at 11:00 P.M., when
the moon was full and we prepared to depart, I was given
the best meal I had ever eaten in England—bacon and eggs
and fried bread; at the last minute a Scotland Yard detec-
tive gave me a friendly search to check that I didn't have
any "incriminating" documents—such as laundry tickets,
spare dollars, odd bus tickets or whatever. As usual all my
English money and a few odds and ends such as keys were
put in an envelope and labeled with my name, then sealed
in front of me. Only then was I given the final items of
equipment. First my money so it could be worn round the
waist in a special money belt, which I put on before I put
my clothes back after the search. Then a syringe of mor-
phia, a compass disguised as a button, a .45 Browning, a
switchblade, and finally my L pill—which would end my
life in less than a minute if I fell into the hands of the Gestapo.

"All set?" asked the briefing officer.

"Fine by me," I agreed.

The heaviest luggage—the radio—was packed under the front seat nearest the center of gravity of the plane, which only weighed less than five tons. My suitcase was strapped onto a shelf behind the backseat. I was placing it and other packages below the shelf—it seemed easier that way— when Dobson, who was supervising everything from his maps to his gas gauge, said, "Better put it back on the shelf, old boy. Anything stowed underneath has a tendency to slide down the tail of the fuselage when we climb— and we don't want to waste time on the ground when we get there and you're crawling inside looking for something."

There were two other heavy packages. "Machine guns for the lads," explained Dobson briefly.

We crossed the enemy coast at eight thousand feet, with nothing but a little desultory flak to interrupt the steady drone of the single motor. The coast of France lay below, etched as clearly as a pictorial map. Through my intercom Dobson shouted, "Calais!" and pointed to a large black smudge on the right—a big city. I was not in the Lysander to map read—a highly technical job depending on a man's ability to translate the lie of streams, railways, and roads from a map to the limited visibility of a place far below, where people were trying to shoot me down.

I had been too excited to experience any sensation of fear during the flight—and during previous flights—but once we approached the target area I began to feel a little differently. As we crossed into "home country" Dobson yelled, "About fifteen minutes." He opened up a flask of hot coffee, handed me some from a tin mug.

"Watch out for the recognition signals," he shouted. "Tonight it's the letter R. It should be repeated three times. Don't get mixed up with the ground landing lights." He waited for a few minutes and then suddenly shouted, "There it is!" I had never seen the tiny pinpoint of light, a dot, a larger dash, another dot. Then blackness before the message was repeated.

"We're ready to land," he returned the signal out of the

side of the plane. "As soon as they see our signal, they'll switch on the landing lights."

Only three landing lights were needed for a Lysander pickup. They were arranged in the form of an upside down *L* or, to put it another way, the top and left-hand sides of a square. I could see the "top line"—indicated simply by two tiny flashlights; this was the "crossbar" at the upwind end, so that we would land on the field facing this line.

But where from? What side of this two-lamp line was the end of the field? We had to know which direction to make our approach, otherwise we wouldn't be flying into the wind as we had to.

"Okay!" cried Dobson, pointing out the faint twinkle of a third light. This was the suggested actual "start" of the airfield, the landing point on the "strip." There was no strip really, of course, just the field, but the Lysander was easy to handle, easy to land slowly, and with the two flash-lights marking the "bar" at the end of the field, Dobson knew he could land on any part of it just before he reached the twin lights. Preferably near the third light, which in a sense was the "control tower" of the operation.

There was no problem. We bumped down within fifty yards of the pickup flash. The other two faint lights disappeared—until Dobson was ready to fly again, then the markers would indicate the lie of the land—and the direction of the wind for takeoff.

The night was warm and smelled good, and as I tumbled out, the pilot shouted above the sound of the propeller, "Cheerio! Good hunting!" and without a moment's hesitation he lumbered round, made his way to the far end of the field, then as he revved up the small single engine, he seemed to rush past me, balance and wobble for a few minutes in the night air, and then start to climb and vanish until I was alone.

Suddenly I shivered—half cold, half frightened. I had been told to remain where the plane had actually landed because of the heavy packages, including the radio and my deliberately cheap cardboard case, kept closed with an old piece of rope containing my spare clothes as a vigneron. Anyway, I couldn't possibly haul everything to the edge of the field, where I would have had a spurious feeling of being safer.

I was not alone. Soon I could hear whispers, then *smell* a horse, hear the rumblings of old wheels, the pinpoint of light had vanished. A dark figure lumbered up, said, "You're Johnnie? Jean Vivier? Good. Come with me. Here, let me carry this," he knew which was the suitcase radio, for he said—and I could almost feel the grin in his face— "Our pianist can hardly wait to play with her new toy." He had a young laugh, was obviously enjoying himself.

With the familiarity of one used to handling heavy loads he picked up the packages of guns and put them in an old farm cart, which I had hardly seen in the dark. It was very dark, but the moon eerily etched in the scene at certain times, as he said, "Delivery is a dangerous business." Another man arrived, a dark shadow, shook hands but said nothing, and then led the horse away. "They'll be looked after, but it's better if we split—so that if one lot gets caught, the other might be lucky."

As we crouched, half loping toward the corner of the field, hugging my suitcase, I reflected suddenly that I didn't know who in hell the man was: I had been taught to memorize passwords, but when I said, "You haven't identified yourself. Where's Hamlet?" he just laughed cheerfully and said, "I'm taking you to him. I go under the name of Oscar. Don't worry. I'm not a German. I was one of the men who helped to surround Lisette's house when we killed the Gestapo man. That was a night! Here, this way. It's a two-mile walk. Yes, I know who you are. I work for Moët et Chandon."

So much for security! So much for secret passwords, double-checking! A moment later, as we almost reached the gate, I got another shock. Near the corner two figures converged from the far end of the field. Both were women. Both were cycling over the grass. Even the dark could not mask something familiar about one of them. As I made out the figures in the moonlight, wobbling across the rough field, I knew that figure, nothing could disguise it, as she cycled past the gate in the distance and into the nearest lane, and then was gone.

"Yes," admitted Oscar with a laugh, "I thought you'd recognize her. No one on earth can disguise La Châtelaine. She and Hamlet's sister run our airfield. It's her field, she goes up and lights the lights when a drop is expected."

I might have known it! Nothing could stop La Châtelaine from fighting the Germans. Not even age. Even so it was damned stupid for anyone to allow an old woman like that to come out in the middle of the night and play at soldiers. I wondered if Papa knew. I was sure he didn't.

No one had told me the identity of Hamlet, but even in London I had guessed—and hoped—that it might be Gaston. Now, due to careless talk on the part of my "reception committee," I was virtually certain, for Oscar had said that Hamlet's sister was La Châtelaine's "assistant" at the airfield. And La Châtelaine didn't encourage strangers to work with her; she would automatically choose someone from the family—and who better than Aubergine, Gaston's sister, or Hamlet's sister? The need for security had been drilled into me so remorselessly at SOE that I was appalled at the casual way the man had leaked the secret.

The "safe house" was in old Pagniez's cottage—and I had expected it. Oscar tapped a signal on the heavy oak door. It was instantly opened, and though the room inside was dark and I could see nothing for a moment, I knew it was Gaston. We threw our arms round each other. Oscar slid away. Gaston closed the door and switched on the single light bulb. Though thinner, he looked just the same, so did the living room of his father's cottage.

As he brought out a bottle of *marc*, I asked, "How long is it, Gaston?"

"Must be eighteen months. *That* was a day to remember, when we all said good-bye."

"As long as that?"

"Even longer."

"See my father?" I asked.

"Often. He's doing a fine job as usual in the Rilly Pyramid. But he keeps himself to himself."

"And what about La Châtelaine?" I tossed back the tiny drink in one gulp and held out my glass for another. "I couldn't believe my eyes. I hope she didn't see me."

"I'll tell you all about it later. And don't blame me!"

"And your father?" I changed the subject. "He must be getting on now."

"He's dead," said Gaston briefly. "Nearly a year ago. Old age—and he never really got over the shock of that terrible day at Douzy."

"I'm sorry," I said awkwardly.

"It's a long time ago now," Gaston sighed. "And a lot more people have died since then. Yes, it's getting on for two years. You'll find a lot of changes have taken place. We heard vague rumors about you—nothing tangible— that you were in America."

"I was," I stretched my legs and leaned back in the worn old chair. "Did my preliminary training there."

"And now?"

"It's a long story. Let's sleep on it."

In fact SOE had instructed me not to reveal *all* my suspicions, but to work with Hamlet step by step. First things first. And that meant a check on the tunnel without even discussing the next step—not to learn the *contents* of the Douzy Pyramid, but to check first on whether or not it was being used.

"You're sure this is a safe house?" I asked.

"Absolutely. As far as the Germans are concerned, I'm a veteran who became a respected vigneron. There's nothing—absolutely nothing—to link me with the activities of Hamlet. In fact since that day I've never really *done* anything of any importance. We've been told to lie low—I don't know why, but they're orders. That and answering radio questions from London."

"And the house?" again I persisted. "You're sure it's safe?"

"The Germans occasionally pop in for a drink, but most of them are Alsatians, and many of them worked in the

German vineyards across the border before the war, so in a way they're understanding and never suspicious."

"And if they do come? Any searches?"

"No. Never. But just in case, there *is* a loft. I'll show you where later on."

"And my cover? Jean Vivier?"

"Perfect—because Jean Vivier exists—yes, he's alive and well—"

"And—"

"In England." Gaston almost grinned. "Vivier is Free French, and he's been staying with me as a vigneron for six months. He's been registered, probably had his identity card checked. Even had a beard like you. Now he's joined de Gaulle's staff in London, but nobody on the register here knows he's even left the area. So *you* are Jean Vivier. You can use his room, work on the land—when you need to. I more or less run the vineyards when La Châtelaine isn't here."

"And La Châtelaine? That does worry me, Gaston. She's an old lady. I'd have thought you'd have tried to keep her out of this sort of thing. I was horrified when I saw that old figure wobbling around on a bicycle."

Gaston's voice was almost sharp. "You *thought*. Since when did La Châtelaine allow her workers to *think*? She *acts*. She held us all to ransom. Yes, she *forced* us to let her join the Resistance."

I asked how, and it was a story quickly told. The indefatigable Grandma had, it seems, casually mentioned her frustrations to Madame Robert at the Home Farm, saying she wished she could do something to help beat the Germans. Madame Robert told Gaston. And there was a way that Grandma could help. By allowing the Resistance to use a lonely field beyond the vineyard as a secret airstrip. Grandma owned the field, it was true, but the Resistance didn't want to use it without her permission in case of discovery by the Germans. So when she asked if she could help, it seemed a perfect way to solve the problem.

"Of course La Châtelaine jumped at the idea," said Gaston. "But dammit! She made conditions! It was her land, she said, so it would be her airfield, and we could use it if we let her run it. Well," Gaston almost grinned, "you can't argue with La Châtelaine. So we got an airfield—and a ground staff! Couldn't ask for a better team. And your grandmother looks ten years younger."

The questions were tumbling over each other as I sought to fill in the gaps of lost years. "And the Germans are using the château," I said. "I did hear that."

Gaston nodded again. "They just marched in one day, nearly a year ago it must have been, and took the place over as an officers' mess."

"And La Châtelaine lives in the old Misses B and B house?"

"Yes," said Gaston. "She was furious at the time. But in a way it's better. Jean, the old butler, has been forced to work for the Germans, but that means he can keep an eye on the place. La Châtelaine doesn't have the labor needed to keep up a place like the château. So she's better off living quietly with one maid—Aubergine, as you call her."

"It seems so awful—life so disrupted, poor Grandma and your father—so damn terrible, this war."

"And it's lasting so long!" Gaston sighed.

"It might start moving a bit quicker soon," I said. "And maybe we can help to make it shorter still."

"Your mission?"

"Yes. But let's give Hamlet and Johnnie a few hours off! Let's pretend we're Gaston and Larry—until we've finished off this bottle. And tomorrow we'll get to work."

We stayed up half the night just talking—about the good old days, the happiness that was Douzy, poor Willi, Anna, Sonia, Mama (carefully!), and how it had all started, the war, and then the terrible things that had happened to the family. Since this was like a twenty-four-hour leave pass, we were talking about real people, so there was no way I could ignore Olivia—and no way in which I could force Gaston to lie if I asked how she was. So I had to go straight to the point.

"I know we said we wouldn't talk business tonight," I

smiled, "but how's Portia? No, I've already guessed—a woman. It must be Olivia."

He shrugged his shoulders, "No point in denying it. You'll know the moment you hand her a message for transmission. She's the best in France. Takes the craziest risks—or did until I ordered her—yes, *ordered* her—to take life more easily."

"I'd like to see her as soon as I could. Is her safe house a secret?"

"It's supposed to be. Because she's a Jewess—involved in a murder case—there's no way she can ever go out, even leave the place where she lives."

"Christ! What a life!"

"Well, she does go for walks at night. And often I join her. But she's got to be kept hidden—and its selfish, I know, but in a way the more she's hidden, the safer the signal."

"But *where?*"

"In the belfry at Douzy church. You remember? It's not only safe, it has the advantage that she can trail her aerial down the side, just pay it out like a fishing line and then, when she's transmitted, pull it in."

"But to *live* there!"

"I've begged her to go. I even contacted London to suggest they might fly her out—but nothing doing—she just won't budge."

"I'd love to see her soon," I said.

"Of course. It's all so long ago that sometimes I forget that in a way she was part of your family."

But that was true. It gave me a peculiar feeling to think that Olivia was barely half a mile away from the place I was sitting—and there was no way that I could ever go to see her unless it was behind the back of the enemy.

The next morning we started work in the vineyards. It was the best cover—the simplest way of being able to exchange information without exciting any curiosity, especially from the occasional German patrols which I was told passed our way from time to time. There was plenty to do in the vineyards at this time of year, in high summer the soil not only had to be harrowed, the vines were receiving their second trimming, a careful, tricky operation to reduce foliage just where it would allow more sunlight to filter into the clusters of grapes.

"No chance of any of our neighbors recognizing me?" I asked.

"Eventually you're bound to be seen. But not yet. Apart from the beard, some of the civilians are new, we're so short of workers anyway there's rarely more than two or three men to a plot of land. So I can arrange that we work together and make plans as we talk."

Bending over side by side, I explained to Gaston my "stage one" orders. Someone had to penetrate the Rilly tunnel and discover what the Germans were storing there. Or rather confirm my suspicions.

"London's certain the Germans are keeping components for V-2s there—or even completed rockets. It's up to us to find out before any action is taken."

Gaston listened, but I found it hard to concentrate on what we were talking about. It was not only the beautiful summer sun that made me feel great after English weather, it was the feeling I was *home,* working in our own vineyards, that opposite as I looked up I could see the stark outline of Douzy church—the church where the entire family had been christened, had gone to first communion. It gave me a singular feeling to be living here—and yet not living here. It was Monsieur Jean Vivier who was squatting down where I was working, it wasn't me.

"It won't be easy," Gaston interrupted my thoughts. "We've thought once or twice of taking a look—there must be something suspicious about that RAF bombing—even though it was ineffectual. But getting past the German guard—and the gates into the tunnel—it needs a bit of thought."

"London's anxious to know quickly," I said. "They've got other jobs lined up after this one."

"Won't be easy," he repeated. "We'll talk about it tonight."

His voice was interrupted by a roar of anger. La Châtelaine, bicycle thrown down at the corner of the field,
charged toward us shouting, *"Merde! Crétins! Imbéciles!"*

"That's ruined it," whispered Gaston as he stood up.
"But keep calm."

"What the devil do you think you're doing, tearing off
all those leaves," shouted La Châtelaine furiously to the
bearded man, whose eyes were still on the ground. "Don't
you know how to prune vines." And with added anger at
my downcast eyes, she shouted, "Get up, man, when I
speak to you. Look at that!" I *had* done a poor job of the second trimming, and there was nothing to do now but stand
up. Despite the beard, there could be no way a woman
couldn't recognize her own grandson. *"Idiot!"* she cried—
and stopped dead, eyes narrowing at recognition.

"You remember Jean Vivier?" said Gaston tactfully as a
few other workers in nearby vineyards stopped to listen to
the tirade.

I must hand it to La Châtelaine. She took what seemed
to be a deep breath and then pointing downward shouted,
"Look! Like this!" She dropped to her knees, those nimble
fingers of hers stroking the vines. There was the beginning
of a tear—the first I think I can ever remember seeing from
her weather-beaten face—as she said, "God bless you,
Larry," then straightening up, as she cried to Gaston in a
voice loud enough for everyone in the vicinity to hear, "I'd
fire this dolt on the spot if you weren't so shorthanded! For
God's sake, get your workers to learn their business properly."

Then she stalked away, without a glance backward, to
the corner of the field. I had a picture of her, her long green
skirt, small hat, picking up her old bike and setting off for
the next vineyard.

"She's still wearing all her jewelry," I said to Gaston,
"just the same!"

"What poise!" said Gaston. "She'd have made a fortune
on the stage."

48

I DID NOT SEE OLIVIA for four days, though Gaston arranged
to deliver a coded message telling London the day after my
arrival that I had landed safely. But this was a "courtesy"
visit. Normally most radio operators landed with the
agent whose messages they would transmit, so they knew
each other, however slightly. I hadn't met my operator—
not officially anyway. And as the whole success of our plan
would be nullified if she didn't get the message through to
base, everything in the end depended on her.

And, in a different way, I was rather like a reporter on
the *Globe*. I was thinking of that wild dash from Bordeaux
to file my story in San Sebastián. Even the greatest scoop
would be valueless if I couldn't get it home. And this could
be one of the greatest scoops of my life. And I was thinking,
too, of a chance remark made by someone at SOE in
London. It kept echoing through my mind, "The average
life expectancy of a radio operator is under seven months."

I made my way to the church, walking, an old hoe across
my left shoulder, like any scruffy, bearded vigneron on the
way home after a day's work. A hundred yards from the
church, a workman stood by the edge of the ochre path,
leaning on his rake as though resting from hard work. He
wiped his forehead. He was certainly a lookout for anyone
suspicious or otherwise.

"Good afternoon," I said, one workman greeting another, "is that the village of Douzy over there?" This was a
simple inversion password. I *knew* that this was Douzy.

Everyone in the area knew that. If the workman nodded agreement, that meant he was not a member of the Resistance. No suggestion that he was a potential enemy, but he wasn't a "watchman." However, the man replied—with Douzy in full view—"But no! Douzy's straight down the hill!"

He had completed the password. I could trust him. We shook hands, as the French do on the slightest pretext, and then I whispered, "You're sure the coast is clear at the church? And the belfry?"

"Clean as a whistle," he replied. "The good Father has gone to the village—he always does, every evening, he asks no questions, just goes, visiting the people, sometimes stopping for a *vin rouge* at the Café des Sports. He's a good sort. Doesn't necessarily want to get involved, but he thinks we use the church for secret meetings. He's no idea about," he hesitated, "the pianist."

He was inclined to be talkative, but I put him off as politely as I could, with a "See you again soon, I hope." Then I walked to the church—which we had been ordered as kids to attend every Sunday with Mlle. Lisette, where we had been washed and scrubbed for our communions. I pushed open the heavy door leading directly to the nave of the rather ugly church. Even in summer the church had a feeling of cold, it seemed vaguely inhospitable, it offered nothing of the warm welcome one felt a church should offer. But perhaps, I thought, as my boots rang on the flagstones, the lack of a congregation gave it a cold, unlived-in atmosphere.

The staircase to the belfry was concealed behind the door near the back of the modest choir stalls. It was not deliberately hidden, it was such an ugly narrow staircase, and in such bad repair, that years previously a separation wall with a door had been built to hide the rear section of the church. Because the stairs were dangerous—unless you watched out for the ones to miss—the door was always locked. The key was kept on a lintel above. Anyone wanting to use the stairs would warn Olivia, who also had a key, by giving the Beethoven signal—three sharp knocks, followed by a pause and one which somehow seemed longer, the unmistakable "V for Victory" signal.

I heard a faint reply, not far above, and only then unlocked the door to the musty, dirty stairway and started to climb up.

"Hamlet?" asked a soft voice.

"Portia?" I whispered.

Then I was at the top of the stairs and giving her a big bear hug to celebrate our reunion after the best part of two years.

She was very changed. Nothing could hide the beautiful soft eyes, not the size, not the shape, but even though they sparkled a welcome as I reached the wooden floor of the belfry, her eyes had a certain wariness. They reminded me of the eyes of a cat, always on the lookout for the unexpected. Yet, despite a certain shyness, those same eyes were filled with pleasure—after all, wasn't I the one who had "officially" welcomed Olivia as a member of the family? She was one of us, always would be—what was left of the family, now sadly scattered.

"You look healthy and younger than ever," she laughed.

"You too," I scrambled off the top rung and sat down on a wooden chair, one of three which had somehow reached the rooftop aerie.

"Oh, no," she said sadly. *"You* look marvelous, but me, *no!* I'm a very old lady now—in experience anyway—and no longer a very pretty one."

Though nothing would ever be able to iron out the wrinkles that lined her, I was even more shocked to see that her hair had gone completely gray. The fact that it looked unkempt, even dirty, couldn't be helped. But *gray!* Neither could the lines be helped. But what had happened to the beautiful creamy pallor we had all so admired in Olivia? Her skin was as gray as her hair.

"I know," instinctively she patted her hair when she realized I was looking at her, "the only place I can wash is in the bathroom behind the vestry," adding with a laugh more like her old self, "the water's very cold in winter, and though Gaston does his best to keep me supplied with soap, we run out at times."

"You're really a prisoner here." I felt awful watching her.

"I am," she admitted frankly, "but it has to be like this for several reasons. After I took the WT training in Morse, I had to find a safe place where the chances of a radio detector were minimal. The power of the WT transmitter is so bad that it must have an aerial—even a trailing aerial. What better place than to hang it out over the edge of the belfry when I'm on the air? Obviously the height helps to give me better reception as well."

"But you *live* here, Olivia. What about eating and—?"

"The boys bring in more than I can eat. And there's always a bottle of wine to spare. And a thermos of soup. There's a toilet at the bottom of the stairs next to the vestry. It's not too bad—"

A sudden thought struck me. "The bell? The sound must break your eardrums."

"There is no bell. The Germans melted it down for scrap. Otherwise I couldn't have stayed here."

I looked round as she poured out a glass of wine. "Douzy *blanc,*" she promised me. The belfry was perhaps ten feet square, with the steps coming up through a hole in one corner. There were three wooden chairs, a camp bed, blankets, pillows. For washing, an old-fashioned jug or pitcher stood in a basin. There was a bucket on the floor below the rudimentary dressing table. "One of the boys brings up a new pitcher of water every day, and I throw the dirty water out of the window," my eye caught an old-fashioned chamber pot below the bed. "At night I can go down," she laughed, "but I daren't in the daytime, so if I need to—" she shrugged her shoulders.

"And that?" I pointed to the machine pistol hanging on the wall. "Where did you get *that?*"

"You don't remember? It's one of the machine pistols the boys took when they shot all the SS men at Lisette's—or rather you did. They took everything, remember? Uniforms, guns, SS caps—everything! My Schmeisser machine pistol is my last line of defense. Nobody can get up to my place. *Nobody.* I can shoot down every single man who tries to get up. They'd have to burn the place down to get me out."

Later, when it came to dispatching the message, she was intensely professional. "The new piano is a joy," she cried as she opened the narrow window by the bed and paid out her aerial down the side of the church wall. She inserted the right crystals to get the correct frequency and then, when she had made contact, tapped out the short message I had sent in code, waited for the acknowledgment or instructions. Then when London signed off, she pulled up the aerial, twisting the wire round her left hand like a ball of wool, then tucked it into the appropriate place in the corner of the set. "That's that until the next transmission," she said and closed down the dowdy-looking suitcase.

"It's a rough life," I said to her.

"It is. But, Larry—if my message can help to get one more German killed, preferably slowly, then I feel the same sense of achievement of anyone who's been successful."

As I prepared to climb down the rickety stairs I said, "I'll be back in a couple of days. Maybe I'll come at night and we can go out for a walk, for a breath of air," adding with a laugh, "take a walk round the churchyard!"

"That would be very nice," she said quietly.

I reached up to kiss her cheeks—a purely familial kiss, the kind to celebrate a reunion. Nothing more than that. To my surprise she skillfully moved the cheek away.

"I'm sorry," I didn't quite know what to say or do.

"Don't be sorry. I'm not much for kissing anyone. Maybe when we're all free again—and I've got my looks back again," she said bitterly.

"That's all right," I said awkwardly. "But your beauty is inside you, Olivia. It's got nothing to do with whether or not you had your hair waved. You're Olivia—the one and only Olivia. Remember?"

"Am I? Do I?" her voice was forlorn.

* * *

We spent many hours discussing how best to get into the
Rilly tunnel. At first, without involving anyone in direct
consultation, Gaston talked over possibilities with individual members of the Resistance. Many were French civilian
workers who had access to the general area of the tunnel
entrance, which was near Rilly railway station. In the old
days the train service linking Reims with Epernay had entered the tunnel a few yards after leaving Rilly station.
But after the Germans blocked the tunnel, the trains had
been forced to use a slow train which meandered through a
dozen villages before linking up with the main train and
then going on to Epernay. The junction from the main line
to this branch line was actually in Rilly station. But one
thing I did learn. Every now and then, trains manned by
Germans drove into Rilly itself—and stopped there. It
seemed absurd for a train to puff its way all the distance
from Germany to Rilly—and then, after unloading, to return to the Fatherland. Ridiculous, unless the train was
transporting vital materials to a place like Rilly, where
nothing ever happened. From time to time the Resistance
gleaned snippets of information.

These glimpses made more sense to me than they did to
the villagers, for I was able to interpret scattered information because London had told me what to look for. In the
end I would still have to get *into* the tunnel to see for myself, but it was important to know that some of the trains
arriving from Germany included double-length flatbed
trucks. The machines on them were under wraps, and the
imagination of the locals was limited to the possibilities of
large field guns. I thought differently. And when some in-
quisitive Resistant discovered that one train was carrying
three huge transformers, the Resistants did not have the
faintest idea what they might be used for. I knew that
mobile transformers were needed to take any rockets to
possible launching pads. There were other snippets of information that I was able to piece together, like parts of a
jigsaw puzzle. One *cheminot*—the French railway workers
were among the forefront of the Resistance movement—
counted one German-goods train arriving at Rilly and

then counted it when, five days later, it left on the branch
line. It was eight double-length wagons shorter. They had
just vanished. Of course they hadn't really vanished. Despite RAF bombing, the tracks of the main railway line
still continued into the mouth of the tunnel. Obviously the
flatbed railway wagons had been shunted inside the
mouth of the tunnel, which was guarded by a twenty-four-
hour sentry patrol behind specially built, grilled iron gates
twenty feet tall, with only a small doorway in the grill
through which Germans could enter on production of special passes.

There was another intriguing point. Nobody could hide
the arrival by road of three convoys of extra-long Mercedes
trucks, huge eight-wheelers, which arrived near Rilly and
were promptly driven into a nearby field and wrapped in
tarpaulin—as though they were never going to be used. I
knew from London briefings that however quickly a V-2
could be fired, it needed a large convoy of ancillary
equipment—containers of liquid oxygen, transformers,
and so on. It seemed clear to me, in view of London's suspicions, that all this apparently unrelated movement of
matériel indicated V-2s—either for assembly or to be
stored. I asked one or two *cheminots* if Europe's railway
system included any simple method of being able to transfer extremely heavy unwieldy loads from goods trains to
road haulage. Apparently it was a fairly simple operation
provided you had the right machinery. Specially constructed chassis trucks only a few inches lower than railway trucks could be backed up against a train and the
machinery could be transferred to the lower level by a system of rollers. The truck would then drive off to a parking
lot, fully laden, and the empty railway wagons shunted to
a siding.

Yet how could I ever get into the tunnel? And stay there
for, say, twenty minutes? For though I had told Gaston
only that I wanted to check on the contents of the tunnel
and its state of readiness, it was also vital to find out if the
old, never-used subway linking the railway tunnel with
the Douzy Pyramid had been reopened by the Germans, as

London suggested. That subway was large enough to have
accommodated in the old days a primitive kind of tram on
which the champagne could be pushed in bulk from the
pyramid to the railway siding inside the tunnel. The idea
had come to nothing, but the linking subway still existed,
and I wanted, if I could get into the Rilly tunnel, to see if a
way had been opened up by the Germans to get into the
pyramid when ostensibly it was closed.

But how to get into the tunnel? I asked Gaston to arrange for me to meet one of the leading *cheminot* Resistance men whose work was a legend. His code name
was Drax and he was only twenty-two, but he had helped
to derail several trains. He had even organized one
head-on collision between two trains on the Paris-Lille
line. One was filled with German troops on the way to
the channel ports, the other with Panzers destined for
the Russian front. Drax "arranged" for the switches to
be manipulated and over a hundred and fifty Germans
were killed.

He was a likable young man with a frank face, almost
innocent. He looked as though he'd never shaved, as remotely different from a professional train wrecker as a
killer from a bank clerk.

"I'm just ready to create a big bang!" he said. "I don't
want to get out of training."

Expertly he rolled a cigarette, running the thin edge of
the paper along his lips, and then asked me, "Can you wait
five days?"

"As long as you like—up to a point. But why five days?" I
asked.

"We've got a German train due here on May thirty-
first—that's a Wednesday. Don't ask me how we found out,
it's too complicated, but basically the Germans have to
give advance warning to the French railways of a German-
goods train coming through, simply because everything
has to be sorted out and preparations made in case some of
the tracks are on different gauges. It's not as complicated
as it sounds, but it takes a lot of time to prepare. And the
Germans have to tell us what to expect. Otherwise they'd

have to run all the railways themselves, and they couldn't possibly do that."

"And this train's a big one?" I asked.

He nodded, picking a piece of loose tobacco from the tip of his tongue. "I saw a copy of the manifest—forty-two double-length flatbeds. And—this is interesting—a wagon-lit for the big shots, led by a general no less, on a tour of inspection. Named something like Hocher."

"General Hermann Ochsner?"

"That's the man. You know him?"

"Not personally. But I know all about him. He *is* a big shot." I didn't bother to tell him, or anyone else, that he was the head of Hitler's chemical corps.

"But if you could blow that train up!"

"I will, if you give the orders."

"You think you could?"

"Drax can do anything," said Gaston. "But there's always one thing that has to be weighed up—is it worth it? In terms of reprisals, deaths, and so on to us?"

"If Drax can blow up the train at Rilly and cause enough commotion to give me the chance to get into the tunnel—yes, I hate to think of the reprisals, but I have to say one thing to you, Hamlet—and you, Drax—it must be obvious to you that I'm onto a very big thing. It may sound pompous, but it's a sort of action which, if I can be successful, could make all the difference to the outcome of the war. It could shorten it, it could do anything. I'll put it as high as that."

"That's good enough for me," said Drax, rolling another cigarette. "What about you, Gaston?"

"I'm with you—if—"

"If we can get into the tunnel?" I finished his question.

Gaston nodded. "The Germans are not fools—and they don't scare easily. They *might* think that we detailed the Ochsner train just because it's an attack on a big shot, but *some* Germans would begin to wonder if it's a trap to draw attention from those guarding the tunnel. We could get the disturbance going—in theory anyway—

but still we don't know how to get into the tunnel during the panic."

I was puzzling the problem in my mind, when I had a curious feeling that I *knew* there was a way to solve it, to get into the tunnel, but somehow I had missed the way. It was as though someone had dropped a hint and I had thrust it aside unthinkingly.

We discussed whether in the pause it would be possible for any one of us to scale the iron gates.

"Impossible!" said Gaston. "Forget it."

"But the small inner gate is open?"

"Always—but with a heavy guard. It's open because technicians keep on going in and out. But security is watertight."

We even wondered whether it would be possible to climb to the top of the Rilly Mountain—which was more of a thickly wooded hill, anyway—and some of us could drop the others by a rope.

"It's too far. And you'd be seen—a sniper could pick you off as easily as batting a fly on a wall."

Still, I was plagued by the fact that there *was* a way—and I knew it, or *ought* to know it. Somewhere a link was missing. I sat there smoking and drinking with Drax and Gaston.

"You've got a gun, of course?" asked Drax.

"A forty-five," I nodded. "Not the biggest in the world but—"

"Not as big as Olivia's machine pistol," laughed Gaston. "One of those we pinched—"

"I've got it!" I cried. "Olivia!"

Gaston looked baffled.

"No! I'm not going to involve *her!* But it's what she *said.*" What *had* she said when she was showing me the machine pistol? Thinking back to the days when we had freed her, she had almost laughingly said, "They took everything, remember? Uniforms, guns—"

"Where are the SS uniforms?" I asked Gaston almost hoarsely. "The ones we stripped from the bodies that day?"

Gaston looked doubtful.

"They were distributed to other circuits and used several times. One British POW reached the coast in one of those uniforms."

I felt a great letdown. "You haven't got any left?"

He shook his head. I suddenly realized, of course, that it was a long time since we had stolen those uniforms and a lot of things had happened—and yet I also realized that wearing German uniforms offered the best chance we would ever get to enter the tunnel: wait for the derailment at the station, almost in the center of Rilly, and then in the terrible smashup, Gaston and I, dressed in SS uniforms, could shout to the guards at the iron grill, "Help! Come quickly!" or something like that. In SS uniforms nobody would dare to question *anyone.* I could picture it. All the Germans would be terrified—a high-ranking officer ambushed, perhaps even killed, forty or fifty wagons derailed, smashed up—in uniform we could almost *walk* into the tunnel!

And now, dammit, I thought despondently, I had remembered the SS uniforms, but I had forgotten that we had acquired them nearly two years ago, and no Frenchman was going to keep German uniforms in a drawer as a souvenir.

"Shit!" I said it in English. "Shit and shit. I thought I'd found a way out."

"That means *merde, non?*" asked a sympathetic Gaston. "I know how you feel."

"Anyway, it's too late now, we must think of a new plan."

Drax hadn't been following the conversation, no doubt because it referred to previous actions which Gaston and I had taken together.

"You want some uniforms, is that what you mean?" he asked.

"It was an idea."

"Maybe I can help."

"You've got some uniforms?" I asked incredulously.

"Not military uniforms. But maybe better. I've got a different idea—but basically it's the same. The *cheminots* killed four German railway workers on our last derail-

ment. A driver and some guards. We could use their uniforms."

I must have looked doubtful.

"No, wait," he explained. "Rilly station, where we're
going to blow up the train, is barely two hundred yards
from the entrance of the tunnel. Am I right?"

I nodded.

"Well, we'll make *two* explosions. One halfway along
the train, a second five minutes later, when all hell's
broken loose, in the *front* section of the train. Not too
far front, but when that goes up, and everyone's panicking, I'll be dressed as a German engineer, you two as
guards or whatever we can find for you. At the critical
moment—remember we're only two hundred yards from
the tunnel entrance—the engineer will either get out of
his cab or I'll come in and kick him out. You jump in.
Then, with the power of the locomotive—tough enough
to carry over forty fully laden wagons—I'll pull the
engine to full steam ahead. The engine should have
enough force to tear itself away from the wrecked car-
riages near it—for a while. I'll be screaming that I can't
stop the engine. I don't know much German, but enough
to know how to shout out that I'm scared. It'll look just
as though it's a runaway engine. And before anyone realizes what's happening, it'll be on the rails heading
straight for the grilled iron gates. It'll smash right
through them. That'll be a nasty moment—maybe we
can jump off in time. Then I'll bolt for it—I'll vanish.
You two can get into the tunnel, throw away the jackets
if you don't want to be recognized—you can get away
with German-issue trousers for a while—and take a
quick look round, and then," he shrugged his shoulders,
"it's up to you to make yourselves scarce. How's that for
an idea?"

I stood in awe of this remarkable young man with his
baby face, whose prowess as a saboteur had spread across
all Europe.

"There's no flaw anywhere," I said softly. "Thanks, my
friend." In actual fact I used the word *copain,* which means

you are closer than a friend; in English you might say "a pal."

"It's going to be exciting," he said with a laugh.

"It's all set then," I looked around for confirmation. "I'm going to report to London, then all we have to do is wait—until May thirty-first."

49

Two days before the train was due, when Drax was deciding where to lay explosive charges, two of the Resistance *cheminots* were caught by the Germans and never seen again. No one knew what had happened, why or how they had been caught, because they were hustled off to jail. But Drax did know they had been checking on locations for him. The Resistants had been posing as members of one of the innumerable repair gangs needed to keep the tracks in good repair. So many were needed that Frenchmen had to be employed from time to time. For some reason they had been suspected. Immediately, all French workers were cleared from the tracks for several miles north of Rilly and replaced by German army engineers checking against possible sabotage.

"Explosives are out," said Drax, anger at the hitch in his plans darkening his baby face. "We'll have to derail instead."

I must have looked puzzled. We were meeting as usual in Gaston's house.

"We did it on the Paris-Lille train. We'll switch points outside Douzy." He explained more simply by spreading out a large-scale map of the type used by professional railway men. It showed no roads, but took note of signal posts, points, dangerous curves where speed had to be reduced, it even showed the location of sidings, and of course the secondary line used since the tunnel was blocked.

"And there are two points of importance," Drax pointed

to his map. "The train will automatically slow down as it
approaches Rilly—after all, it *is* the end of a long journey.
But once it gets the green signal at the Rilly signal box before the station, it will carry on slowly. The points are always kept in the same position—so that every southbound
train automatically goes round the mouth of the tunnel.
The only exceptions occur when wagons have to be shunted into the tunnel. Then the points are switched over."

Drax's alternative scheme was simple. Resistants would
overpower the signalmen in their box after dark, set the
Rilly signal at red—in those days unexplained delays were
always occurring—and when the engine driver stopped
and leaned out of the cab, he, too, would be overpowered.
At that moment—before anyone on the train had time to
wonder what was happening—the signal would turn back
to green. Drax would take the place of the engineer. As the
train blew steam and started to move, the signalman
would switch the points over and the train would go
straight past Rilly station and carry on until it smashed
into the gates at the mouth of the tunnel.

"It's the same ending we planned—only the methods
have had to be changed. But in actual fact it's simpler this
way. Better make sure your gun works. You'll be needing
it. Gaston, what plans are you making for a getaway?"

Gaston explained that Oscar—he was the young man
who had met me the night I had landed in France—would
spend the evening at the Café Moderne at the edge of Rilly,
ostensibly drinking, with his horse and cart waiting outside.

I was thinking about what Drax had said—I might need
my gun. I had never shot a man in cold blood—I wasn't
even present when Guy had shot Hoess—but my training
as a potential killer had been so thorough that I knew that
I would never be interested in feeling pity for the men at
the receiving end of my American .45 automatic Browning, known as the M1911A1. It was often used in prefer-
ence to revolvers because saboteurs preferred it. It was not
only less bulky than the old-fashioned "six-shooter"—but

it was flatter, about nine inches overall length, and could be fitted with a silencer whereas the revolver couldn't.

I oiled it carefully, pushed the catch to eject the magazine, loaded it with a clip of seven bullets, then pushed the magazine into the butt until it clicked, after which I pulled back the slide with the left hand, which compressed the spring and cocked the weapon ready for use. Then I put on the safety catch and fitted the silencer, basically a set of flanged "sleeves" which fitted over the barrel, lengthening it. The .45 could only be fitted with the Welrod silencer, or in more technical terms, the Mark 1 hand firing device.

The moment to reveal the tunnel's secrets had arrived. Preparing the Browning, loading the magazine, had helped me to overcome the tension of the long wait. I hated anxious preparations, but now anxiety was replaced by a new emotion. I grasped Gaston's hand and said, "I'm ready!" Any dread of danger now was a shared one. I suddenly felt younger—how absurd I thought!—but I did, razor sharp with anticipation. The preliminaries were over, thank God. The job was on.

Almost on the point of leaving I explained again to Gaston the importance of accuracy if or when we got into the tunnel. I had to drill the facts into him, even though with his knowledge of mechanics he would be able to observe anything with a more technical view than I could.

"I know I'm a bore, but it is vital to remember the technical details, to be able to recognize a V-2 rocket *instantly.* We may have less than a minute inside the tunnel—that's if we ever *do* get in. Or get out! And we daren't make a mistake. That's why I'm asking you to come along with me. In case one of us can't get away, the other can radio London."

Details of the rocket had been drilled into me even before the RAF bombed its first site at Peenemünde. What we expected to find was a monster of a rocket, forty-six feet long, five feet in diameter, and weighing around fourteen tons, able to be fired from a mobile launching pad, at a speed faster than sound, so that it would in theory reach

London from the Channel coast and explode in less than six minutes.

"It's a terrifying thought," I said to Gaston.

By 11:00 P.M.—with the train due at 11:30—Drax, Gaston, and I were hidden under some of the tarpaulins covering trucks in the big field used as a parking lot outside the station. We wore our ill-fitting German railway uniforms. My .45 with its silencer seemed bulky. I also felt for my switchblade. We had to wait until the very last minute before overpowering the three men in the signal box—two German operators and one soldier as a guard. But we knew exactly what to do when the moment did arrive.

And it would all have to be over in five minutes—not a second longer. At 11:25 we slithered silently across the grass of the parking lot until we reached the edge of the railway and the signal box. It was lit up, we could hear talking and laughing from inside, for it was a warm night and the door was open at the top of the steps.

Drax had to go first because he was the only one who spoke a little German. But it was important that I go second—for I had a specific job to do as I was the only man with a silencer on his gun, so that when the first surprise turned to suspicion, I could handle the soldier, for he would probably be the only man who was armed.

Heart pounding, I followed Drax up the wooden steps to the signal box, flooded with light. At the one moment in my life when I craved darkness, obscurity, I was bathed in light as bright as stage footlights. It was intriguing how, in moments of tension—and in this moment I knew I would soon have to kill a man I had never seen—odd thoughts chased across my mind. It wasn't fear, it wasn't the prospect of being an executioner. Breathless with fear, heart constricted, I found myself thinking, that damn man Turbeville never told me I might have to work under arc lamps!

Drax appeared in the doorway, cried in his passable German, *"Guten Abend!* I've been told to report for the return journey!" The German uniform gave the three men in the glass cabin a second of spurious confidence that all was well, as I heard in the distance the sound of the approaching train. I could see outside, on the darkness of the track, the bright light of the signal showing green, like a green halo along the track.

The second of hesitation was enough. The German soldier, suspicious, started to say, "You're a bit early, aren't you? The train hasn't arrived. What's the password for tonight?" He half-leveled his tommy gun, not sure what to think. I gave him no chance to think. Standing behind Drax I shot the German straight in the face—higher than I had expected. I had aimed for the heart, but I had forgotten the upward kick. I heard the hiss of my gun with its baffles to silence the noise, then sound and vision became fused as though the hiss had come from the German, whose face seemed to splash out in scarlet as though someone had hurled a tin of red paint across the room, covering the wall.

One signal operator started to scream, but it was stillborn as I wheeled round and shot him in the back before the sound left the signal box. The third man I covered. He was terrified. His mouth was slack with fear, and he started blubbering and begging for mercy. Then suddenly, standing there, he put his right hand to the back of his trousers. He wasn't reaching for a gun. He had just emptied his bowels and was suddenly embarrassed.

Gaston stood at the top of the steps; the rhythmic puff of the approaching train was growing louder.

"Where's the lever that operates the points switch?" rapped Drax.

The man hesitated. He moved to the stack of old-fashioned levers with a curious ungainly walk, as though ashamed, as though trying to stop the contents of his trousers from seeping out over his shoes. "And the signal—switch it to red!" shouted Drax. "Come on! Unless you want to be shot too!"

I took in the scene. The soldier's head had almost been blown off; half of it remained on his neck. The bleeding had slowed down, and I could actually see inside his head, where it had been blown off, leaving a cross section. The

German signalman had died more cleanly, one hole through the back. I had remembered the upward kick of the .45 and allowed for it. He had slumped into the side of the instrument panel, almost sitting on the floor, eyes open and staring, not even a trace of blood showing through the dark green jacket.

The terrified man pointed to a lever.

"Pull it!" shouted Drax. "Or you'll get the same treatment." The man hesitated. Drax pulled a knife. "Pull it, damn you!"

"Yes, sir," gasped the man. "This one!"

With a savage jerk Drax pulled the lever himself. It was extraordinary, as though the stage had suddenly changed its spotlight. The vague greenish tinge up the line gave way suddenly to a reddish glow.

"Now!" cried Drax. "The points!" He knew there could be only one alternative point on the track ahead so there was only one lever to be pulled to switch over the points. Drax tugged away.

"Onto the train!" he cried. "The two of us," he said to me. "Come on!"

"And Gaston?"

"You wait here," to Gaston. "When the train comes to a halt, there might be a bit more fighting, but you've got your gun with a silencer, Johnnie," he used my code name. "We'll take care of the driver and his assistant—one way or another. Then I'll flash a light to you, Gaston—watch out for it."

"And then?" I asked.

"Then Gaston will pull the signal back to green. We'll start the train. We'll go slow, we can't even get to fifteen miles an hour by the time we go through the station. You can jump on, Gaston."

As Drax started to run down the steps he turned to Gaston and, with a look at the terrified man, said, "You know what to do."

We ran along the side of the track. The chug-chug of the train had turned into a louder, more impatient noise, but almost as we reached the red signal we heard the rhythm slow down. There was a squeal of brakes and the great black shadow groaned, the wheels seemed to cry almost plaintively, and then with a hiss, the engine stopped by the bright red signal light. I heard the engineer shout out, asking what the hell had happened, and Drax, with his limited German cried, *"Es hat einen unfall gageben!"*

"What kind of an accident?"

"This way!" cried Drax, as though making off.

In a matter of seconds, but swearing furiously, the driver climbed down the rung of iron steps. As he tried to peer into Drax's face, ignoring me—I was only a fireman —he turned his back to me. From point-blank range I shot him through the back of the neck. He never knew what ended his life as he slumped on the track without a sound. I heard nothing but the swoosh, but the shot was so close I could smell the singeing, the burning of his hair.

"What the hell's happened?" asked the driver's assistant.

For a moment I caught sight of his face, a kid of perhaps eighteen, round-faced under a mop of blond hair, a "bowl" haircut. But they were sometimes the most fanatic, these blond German super-Aryans. This was no time to threaten, but to kill. As he saw my automatic he started to argue, beg, but if I had argued he might have killed me. As it was I cut him off forever before anyone had a chance to cut me off.

All the same I felt slightly sick at the thought that in the space of two or three minutes I had abruptly ended the life of four unknown men who had probably never done any of us any harm.

"Vous êtes vraiment professionnel!" From an admiring Drax, that was high praise indeed as he blinked the light in the direction of the signal box.

"Come on," climbing up the steps, "we've got no time to waste."

Gaston had seen the flashlight and changed the signal back to green. He was running toward us. With professional skill Drax pulled the complicated levers inside the engine cab, and the great beast, straining to pull its mas-

sive load from a standing start, grunted and heaved and
squealed, almost like a living animal, with a hiss of steam
and groaning of effort. As it increased speed, Gaston
jumped on the bottom rung and hauled himself up, gasping, "Made it!"

"Great!" cried Drax. "Now that you're on—prepare to
jump—or we'll all be killed." It was an eerie sight, unfor-
gettable. To the right of the engine was Rilly station, a few
chinks of light in the waiting room peeping out from a
badly arranged blackout. Some people stood on the platform—soldiers, engineers, guards, I suppose. Suddenly
they realized that something was wrong. I could hear it
from the shouts, and what I couldn't hear I could see—
gesticulations, raised arms, shouts. They must have realized that something was wrong—that the slowly moving
train should have gone right automatically, taking the
fork that led past the main railway and round the side of
the mountain. I could hear the screams, almost drowning
the roar and hiss inside the cab of the engine. Then as the
train didn't stop, the screams increased in harshness, fear,
the edge of pandemonium. I could hear this. But all I could
see was the black outline of the mountain looming in front
of me and the ring of lights in its center—the inside of the
tunnel—as the monster grunted on relentlessly toward catastrophe.

As the lights inside the tunnel increased, Drax shouted
above the din, "Ready to jump! You got three seconds.
Then we jump."

Without warning, in front of us, I suddenly saw the huge
bars of the twenty-foot iron gates. Gaston and I jumped to
the left—hurling ourselves out as far as we could in case
the engine toppled over. Drax jumped to the right.

I felt a vague stab of pain as I hit something—a stone
perhaps, a girder, I never discovered what. Then everything else—my own pain, my fear—was engulfed in a great
roaring, grinding of metal on metal, with escaping steam,
with the cries of men on every side, with screams of panic
or pain. The engine was too tough to fall over—Drax had
known that. But as it hit the gates, and then I opened the

eyes I had instinctively closed when jumping, I saw it: a terrifying, almost human, dragon gushing steam from its "nostrils," the engine not flat anymore; having smashed and twisted the huge gates, it had come to rest with its front wheels in a grotesque position, raised like a praying mantis.

"All right?" I shouted to Gaston. He patted my shoulder and a crowd raced along toward us. Back on the train itself I could hear and vaguely see the doors of sleeping cars open, people clamber down. It didn't look as if anyone had received more than a severe shaking, the train had been going too slowly. But there was a helluva lot of shouting. Anxious hands helped to lift me up, to see if I was hurt. They all spoke German, any French villagers had obviously not been allowed so near the tunnel. I took refuge in what they would expect—a sense of shock, bewilderment, a lot of head nodding. My uniform helped. I was treated with respect. I stumbled to my feet. So did Gaston. I knew just enough German to shout, "Explosion! Beware!"

Realizing that I was an "experienced"—if slightly bemused—engineer or assistant, they opened a way for me to clamber over the twisted girders and make my way to the front of the engine, beckoning Gaston to follow me. I had one objective—and one word left in my vocabulary. Clambering over the wrecked girders of the gates until I was standing right at the entrance to the tunnel—stretching ahead, all its lights blazing—I shouted, trying to make myself heard above the hissing, *"Aus!"* and I prayed to God that it *did* mean "Out!" My voice rang with a simulated mixture of authority and fear, and I hoped that my gestures looked like those of an expert on the verge of panic, urging everyone to escape while there was still time. I didn't realize it until later, but when falling I had cut my head—only a slight graze, but enough to give me a convincing and heroic trickle of blood.

Men from inside the tunnel scrambled across the twisted metal in their anxiety to run. I think almost everyone in the world has a horror of being buried alive, and perhaps they thought that a violent explosion—if the engine blew up in the mouth of the tunnel—might bring about a rock fall that would block the tunnel forever. Anyway, they bolted.

From inside the tunnel I saw a couple of men silhouetted against the arc lights and started to wave to them, and then as though impatient with a couple of idiots who did not realize the danger, I ran along the inside of the tunnel, warning them to get out. The uniform helped. I was, to the onlookers, still dazed with shock, but I was the only man around who *knew* the dangers. Drax had told me that there was little likelihood of the engine blowing up, but the soldiers and German civilian workers didn't know that. In any event most of them had drawn back fifty yards or so. Several German sentries had not escaped before the crash. Their bodies lay strewn across the tangled wreckage as though pinned there, arms and legs outstretched and twisted like some grotesque display of butterflies.

Two sentries who hadn't been hurt shouted incomprehensible words as Gaston and I started to climb into the actual tunnel.

"Nein, nein!" one cried. *"Verboten!"*

"Aus, aus!" I pointed to the figures in the distance.

One German ran out of the tunnel to force the crowd to keep away. He tried to push them back. The other soldier hesitated. I thought the uniform had won—but he still said, *"Verboten!"*

I had to get into the tunnel now. In a matter of minutes someone would stumble on the bodies by the signal box. Even apart from that, no doubt some officials clearly suspected sabotage, it had hardly needed the proof that would soon confirm suspicion. There was a hell of a lot of noise. Not only from men shouting, but from others trying to force open doors that had jammed. Two of the flatbed trucks just behind the engine had overturned—a gigantic piece of machinery which I didn't recognize lay smashed by the side of the track. Apart from the bodies, a dozen or so men—and, I noticed, two women—were receiving medical treatment. One man had a leg crushed and was screaming, still trapped by fallen masonry.

Finally I realized the only way to get rid of the sentry was to beg him to come with us. Luckily the din was so terrific it was easier to pretend to shout and not be heard. So, as I mouthed noiseless sounds, I beckoned him to join me. That—and my uniform—satisfied his doubts. All the same he carried a submachine gun—power, authority, prestige, death.

Almost gratefully, it seemed, he followed me as I loped in, still shouting, for effect, *"Aus! aus!"*

I don't suppose I had been in Rilly tunnel since I was a child and then I had only peered into it from the subway that linked the tunnel with the pyramid before it was blocked up. What astonished me was the filth on the walls. Most chalk passages in Champagne retained some of the whiteness, and in some places like the pyramids they give the effect of a blinding whiteness. But over the years, hundreds, thousands of trains had puffed their way through the tunnel, belching filthy smoke, which had long since covered the walls with a black deposit, absent from the miles of corridors underneath Reims, where the air suffered no such pollution.

We were running along the left-hand side of the tunnel, along the two lines of track, when I was suddenly faced with the huge bulk of a rocket. There was no doubt about it. I didn't need my technical training to see it at a glance. I must, without thinking, have hesitated as I looked at it, for the soldier jerked up his submachine gun and shouted, *"Verboten!"*

"Ja, ja!" I cried, but Gaston as well as I knew we couldn't keep up the deception, based on a vocabulary limited to two or three words, much longer. Gaston was walking behind me and knew what to do. As I stumbled forward, suddenly realizing that the figures ahead had mysteriously vanished, that the tunnel as far as I could see was empty, put his left arm around the neck of the guard, jerked it back, and, at the same time as the German cursed and struggled, plunged his knife straight into the man's back, just between the shoulder blades. As the man sagged—I wasn't sure if he was dead—Gaston gave a sharp

jerk back, and I heard the man's neck crack as it snapped.
Gaston grabbed the German's machine gun and whispered, "Seen enough?"

"No. Not yet!" I was taking in every detail I could
remember—not only four V-2s assembled on flatbeds and
ready to be towed out to be fired, but also generators, massive lumps of machinery which I didn't understand, obviously crates of spares. The awesome sight was staggering.
The entrance to the tunnel might have been only a few
yards away, but the noise, fearsome pandemonium of the
crash, the twisted heap of metal had been exchanged as
abruptly as though an operator had inserted a new slide to
illustrate a lecture. For the noisy evidence of chaos had
been substituted for the silent evidence of a secret engineering machine shop.

Only one thing puzzled me. Where was everyone? The
tunnel was deserted. I could understand that those near
the mouth of the tunnel most have emerged—to help, out of
curiosity, fear, for a dozen reasons—but I had seen shadow
figures farther back. Where were they? They had vanished. They couldn't be *hiding*. Who from? What for? It
didn't make sense. And therefore they had left the tunnel
by another exit.

"And there's only one way they could have gone," I
whispered to Gaston. "Into Douzy Pyramid. You go back—
in case I run into trouble. I'm going in to see. But it's imperative that you get away, just in case I can't get out.
Then you can contact London and tell them there are four
V-2s."

It had to be done that way because in my bones I had always believed what London had told me—that the way into
Douzy Pyramid, which to the outside world was closed, lay
through the subway connecting it to the railway tunnel.

I knew that the entrance from the tunnel to the subway
had long since been bricked up, but it would have been
easy to knock it down, open up the subway—and provide a
secret entrance to Douzy Pyramid.

"I'll hang on for a bit longer," Gaston whispered.

"Please—go. As they say in the movies, 'That's an order.'

Your going is a routine precaution, but absolutely vital—to keep the boys in London informed if I'm delayed.
Nothing's going to happen, but that's the way it is."

"I hope you'll be okay. But if it's an order—" he squeezed
my shoulder. How crazily life changed! I thought. Once a
kid with whom I played, then Father's driver, then my
mother's lover, now my closest friend. He slid away
quietly.

I wanted one thing: confirmation that the old bricked-up
subway linking the pyramid with the tunnel had been
opened—and what lay before it. I crept toward it carefully
under the arc lamps, which were swinging directly overhead on wires. When the subway had been built, we had
also erected a narrow platform in order to lower champagne directly onto the railway—grandiose plans that had
never been used.

I climbed up the platform—and there, as I had known all
along, was the subway. Open. The brickwork had been
knocked down, the subway opened by the German.

One thought struck me. Rilly had also built a subway
like ours linking their pyramid with the tunnel. It had
been sealed off at the same time. Had the Germans opened
that subway? If so, not even a moron could fail to see what
was happening in the tunnel. Somebody would have been
curious enough to investigate. And my father was in
charge of operations in the Rilly Pyramid. I began to
sweat—at the thought that just a few yards away my own
father, who did not even know I was in France, worked
every day; did he know what was happening on the other
side of the brick wall in the tunnel? I had to find out. I had
to make sure that the tunnel was closed off. A monster V-2
on a flatbed blocked any view. But I crawled under the
wheels, wriggling along the track. Then, by lying on my
stomach, I could peer at the opposite wall, hoping, praying,
that one look would be enough. It was. A jet-black soot encrusted every inch of bricks undisturbed for years since the
entrance to both subways had been bricked up. At least
there was no way my father could know what the Germans

were doing in Rilly tunnel. Or for that matter in Douzy Pyramid.

Innocent or naive, he was quietly getting on with his job of helping—and to be fair, saving—Frenchmen, without the faintest suspicion that anything so close to him was unusual, that he was being duped, all but cosseted by the Germans with a few tidbits in the way of saved French lives.

I crawled backward to the lighted hole in the wall, until my feet touched the small raised platform. Then I was able to slither sideways. I *had* to go into the subway for a look. I knew that I had accomplished stage one. I had identified the V-2s, would be able to report on a mass of machinery which was obviously ancillary matériel to be used for launching. So, in theory, I should chase Gaston, try to escape in the dislocation. For all this action—the penetration of the tunnel, the killing of the soldiers, had taken only minutes. I had no doubt that back at the entrance to the tunnel, the scene, with the dead and wounded, the danger of explosion, the hissing of steam, would be one of uproar. If I threw away my railway man's uniform, I could probably escape, trousers unnoticed, and reach the Café Moderne.

Yet I couldn't do it. I might never again have such a golden opportunity to examine the pyramid. I wouldn't wait—the subway wasn't very long—but what if I could already report back that it was being used? Suspicions though weren't enough for Turbeville, I had to report what I saw with my own eyes. Not the details, just a picture, just proof that it *was* being used, when the Germans had gone to such lengths to let the local people—my own father included—believe it was closed and would remain empty until the end of the war.

The old streetcar lines still existed in the subway though the light inside was not as bright as in the tunnel proper, so I almost fell over the line. I held on to the damp brick of the wall. The wall paler, lighter, uncontaminated by soot; I could smell the slightly sour smell of champagne cellars, just as I had when a child.

I felt my way along the wall carefully. The subway was perhaps a hundred feet long, possibly a little longer. As I approached the pyramid, the semicircle of light at the far end grew into a startling bright, white light, of an intensity that I had never before seen.

And then I was there, huddled against the damp well, staring out at the scene which my reason told me *must* be our Douzy Pyramid, but which the same reason told me could not be the same place, it was so completely unrecognizable. It *had* to be Douzy, yes, it *had* to be, but it *couldn't* be. Yet it *was*. The white walls of the past and present were the only common factor. As for the rest of this new world I gazed on, I might as well have been on Mars. The dim light so necessary for storing champagne had been replaced by blinding arc lamps so bright you couldn't look directly into one. That was not all. The eerie drama of Douzy had lain not only in whiteness, but in the strange emptiness of its echoing, pointed vaults. Now, not only had the dim light been replaced by vivid lighting, so had the emptiness vanished. In its place I saw a vision of some future planet, of terrifying platforms and tubes, that filled the pyramid almost from its apex to the ground far below. It not only looked like some insane magician's cave, but like a giant's Erector set. And in the middle, rising from the floor as I watched, a modern elevator whined upward, high above my head, carrying two men and—my memory jogged by training in London—a long silver-colored tube. What had the document Chisholm gave me said? Something like "The steel canisters are painted with a special silver coating which changes color if any of the gas escapes." Without any question I was looking at one of the canisters which the RAF had photographed aboveground, and which Chisholm had warned me about. And what else could that canister contain but sarin?

Almost mesmerized, I tried to take in the jungle of tubular scaffolding linking platforms, to combat the feeling that this really was a den for stirring a witches' brew or a kind of alchemist's laboratory where Dr. Jekyll and Mr. Hyde might have worked.

Suddenly I shivered with fear. I felt rather than saw the
presence of another man watching me and wheeled round,
automatic flashing up, firing without stopping to think. I
hadn't *seen* anything. And it all happened before I *did* see
anything, long before I was able to adjust from staring into
the blinding light of the pyramid into the gloom of the subway behind me—perhaps two seconds, which is a lifetime
or a flash of lightning, a compound of time. An arm with
something in it, an extension of metal, a gun perhaps,
swiped across the side of my face tearing it open, and as I
screamed, the unknown assailant struck again, this time
aiming for the back of my skull. I ducked.

Dimly, automatically, I could hear my old sergeant
major in the SOE training camp at Arisaig say in his Scottish accent, "It's easy to learn how to fight if you fight
dirty." I slid to one side as I felt the assailant's breath, and
then, almost blinded by blood, I hit him, a short punch like
a piston, straight into his kidneys. As he half fell my knee
drove into his testicles. He still wasn't out, but neither was
I. I knew that if I was caught by someone who had seen my
inspection of Douzy, I would be tortured for years. If it
came to that, I must grab my L pill. But I wasn't caught
yet, though neither was he defeated. When he tried to hit
me again across my face, I slipped deliberately on the
damp chalk subway, then as I fell against him, I jabbed the
fingers of my right hand into his eyes. The sergeant major
had taught me that trick too, long after Guy had deliberately blinded Hoess.

No man could stand that pain without instinctively
moving his hands to protect himself. As I felt my fingers go
into the softness of the eye, he screamed and raised his
hands. I reckoned I had perhaps thirty seconds to get out of
the tunnel before he raised the alarm—if he was able to. I
didn't wait to find out. Without a moment's hesitation I
jumped on the man's face as he fell. Heavy peasant's hob-
nailed boots splintered bone, teeth, jaw, skin, what was
left of his eyes.

Then, wiping the blood from my face, I staggered,
crouching along the subway to the tunnel. Once at the en-

trance I hoped I could pass as a man who had been injured in the derailment. I never quite lost consciousness, but I never quite knew what happened. I reached the exit to the tunnel, struggling to stop my body from leaving my brain, which wanted to stand in mute defiance of what my body wanted to do. To help keep myself moving I grabbed anything I could, including shards of razor-sharp glass, which my bloodied eyes couldn't see.

I never knew until later that, in the brief moments before the attack, Gaston had been waiting outside, lost in the panic of the crowds surrounding the wrecked train, dozens of men still searching for bodies or trying to extricate screaming wounded trapped by the giant gates. Somehow Gaston had wiped my face and helped me away. Dimly I remember being dragged by the feet. Nor did I learn until later that Gaston had carried me like a sack to the outskirts of Rilly to the Café Moderne. Oscar seemed to have vanished, but the horse and trap were outside, and Gaston dumped me in it, covered me with straw, and I knew nothing until I woke up. Three days later.

50

SO FAR AS TIME WAS CONCERNED, I lost two weeks of my life, recovering slowly from the injuries I received in the subway. Drifting in and out of consciousness, I had no idea of the momentous news that the Allies had landed in Europe during the first week of June. I did not even know where I was. I had assumed I would seek refuge in Gaston's house, but only later I learned that after the train crash his house was being watched. So instead, Gaston took me to another safe house—an extraordinary old mill standing on the ridge of a small rise not far from Verzenay. In the First World War the Germans had constructed a concrete blockhouse on the ground floor of the mill, from which they could direct machine-gun fire over a wide area. After the war the blockhouse had been virtually closed, but the mill still operated. It was about eight or ten miles from Douzy— far enough away not to excite German anger at the "outrage" at Rilly. But the miller was an active member of the Resistance, and the mill had the advantage that a fugitive could be hidden high up, providing he could make the stairs.

My most urgent need was for medical attention, but my most urgent fear was that I would be found in the hue and cry that followed the derailment of the train. This was the second time in two years that the Resistance had struck savagely against the Germans—first the murder and obvious torture of Hoess and his bodyguards, all killed; and now a fullscale attack on a train, carried out with all the

hallmarks of professional expertise. We couldn't tell just
what the Germans were thinking, but General Ochsner,
who had escaped injury, must have realized that the thorough preparations to derail the train at an "unknown" village smacked of secret knowledge on the part of the
Resistance or agents sent to France by the Allied high
command. The exploits of the SOE were already legend-
ary, and the murders by the signal box and in the cab of
the engine all had the stamp of the professional.

The reprisals were swift and savage. Without any trial
ten men and women were publicly shot outside the small
Hôtel de Ville at Rilly. Others, uncounted, were indiscriminately snatched from innocence and dispatched, like cattle being rounded up, to concentration camps.

The indiscriminate slaughter was a classic German
method of waging war through terror. It was hard for the
local people to derive any consolation from the knowledge
that they were suffering for what might look like an act of
bravado in derailing the train. How could they ever realize
that the casualties among civilians in Rilly was a modest
price to pay for preventing the enemy use of sarin, which
could exterminate entire cities?

Many Resistants—and they must have included men
like my father—faced a terrible moral dilemma when
weighing Resistance killings against the revenge taken by
the Germans. I myself found some refuge from twinges of
conscience in the anonymity of the innocent victims. But
once I knew the identity of a victim—once I could picture
his or her face—everything changed. Six days after we had
escaped, when I was just emerging from a kind of delirium,
I heard that Oscar had been tortured, then executed.

Poor Oscar! Twenty years old and so full of life. In a way,
I suppose, every death in war is the same—the brutal ending of a life. But it somehow seemed more wicked, more innocent when it happened to a young man rather than an
old one. The old had lived, had been through a life, and had
something to remember in the last moments of death. But
youngsters—what did they know about living? Men like
poor Jean-Pierre, who had been cut off before his life had

really started. With his bashful schoolboy crush on Anna, his life had been limited to a couple of blushes. It was the same with Oscar, laughing as he cried, "I love this life! I'm living for the first time." Lying in the stifling heat of my old mill hideout, wounded—not seriously though in some pain—I caught myself thinking of him and in my half-dreams mixing his face with that of Sonia, of all the life that Sonia had given to me, while poor Oscar had never known his "Sonia" and an experience which truly meant that life had been worth living. Even at thirty-two, even when I felt afraid, I could not really complain, whatever happened to me. But remembering the cheerful way Oscar had hidden the canisters of arms in the old farm cart the night when I landed, laughing on his way to the edge of the field, he had simply ceased to live before being given a chance to start to live.

This I learned, lying in the comparative safety of the mill, everything shrouded in fine white dust, the silence of the countryside broken by the grinding stone wheels of the mill itself or the sound of horses and carts as, presumably, sacks of flour were loaded up.

Gaston kept me fed with the latest news via London or on a battery radio, which we had hidden in the mill. The news of the Europe-wide advances was the finest tonic I could have been given. The fighting was tough, but the bridgehead in Europe had been securely established. Fascinated, I listened to the details—those which were released: more than a thousand warships taking part, four thousand landing craft, more than eighty-three thousand British and Canadian troops, another seventy thousand Americans.

"It's incredible!" that was all I could say to Gaston—until I got a message from London on June 17 saying that the first V-1 rockets had landed on London four days previously, and that in the following twenty-four hours the Germans had launched two hundred and forty-four V-1s.

Then I got the message I had really been waiting for. It read: "It may soon be time to strike. Are you OK? Please acknowledge."

I wasn't really "okay" but I wasn't going to be left out of the biggest climax of my SOE career. "Ready for action" I signalled back via Olivia and received in return a laconic "Stand by."

A local Reims doctor who was in the Resistance had come to visit me on his bicycle twice a week, usually at night. His name was Claude Benoit, and on the first evening he had to stitch me up without any anesthetic. To stop me jerking with the sudden pain as I hovered between agony and merciful oblivion, Gaston held my arms, while Dr. Benoit said, as though I were a child, "There, there! Only three more and you'll look as beautiful as new!" He put in eleven stitches. Luckily my jaw, though badly bruised, hadn't been broken, but two back teeth had been smashed and would have to be extracted, though a visit to the dentist would have to wait.

At first my nose was so large I could never stop seeing it in front of my eyes. It had been slightly broken—a hairline fracture—but Dr. Benoit assured me it would give me no permanent catarrh.

I wouldn't admit it at first, but what really hastened my cure, especially the gash across my face and the cuts from broken glass, was Dr. Benoit's insistence on using an "old wives" medicine, one familiar to every single vigneron living in Champagne. It consisted of a rather unpleasant kind of fungus or mold which seemed to appear on the slightly damp chalk walls of every cellar. On each visit Dr. Benoit smeared every cut with it, every gash. Only years later did I realize the fungus was a pure form of penicillin.

By the middle of July I was walking again and receiving regular coded messages from London, mostly concerned with scientific procedures to be followed when the time came to blow up Douzy. I knew that SOE had charts of most of the underground cellars—not only in Reims but places like the sewers of Paris—and they were anxious that I should understand where exactly to place any explosive charges in order to collapse the walls above in the pyramid. As Dr. Chisholm had said in London, the only safe way to neutralize sarin is to bury it alive—forever. This meant collapsing the pyramid. SOE was explaining the technical details.

By now it was clear that SOE regarded my evidence as "proof" that Douzy must be "neutralized"—a favorite word at SOE, but though the liberation of Europe was proceeding magnificently, it had not yet reached the point where Hitler would despair. The operation had to be timed exactly—by others who knew more than I did. Only one worry nagged me through the period of waiting. What was going to happen to my father when I faced the moment for action? Sometimes at night, tossing on my straw mattress after a supper of thin, watery, and often cold soup, I would dream of my father—wild dreams, that he was executed by the Germans, that in the tangled skein of the nightmare world he had taken my place and was secretly plotting against the Germans. Sometimes I woke up sweating—with weakness as much as the stifling heat of the blockhouse. I was praying that he would denounce the Germans, but I knew that my naive father wouldn't have the faintest inkling of what was really happening under his nose, next to the office where he was working. Yet there was no way I could tell him. No warning.

"I don't know what the hell to do," I sighed to Gaston. "It's the height of damn irony. Here's my own father, convinced he's *helping* the French, when in fact he's helping the Germans—in his own pyramid, in Douzy. And here am I planning to blow it all sky-high. And neither of us—my father or me—knows the other is in the Reims area. We each believe that what we're doing is right. There's no communication, and we're both heading for Christ knows what."

By now I appeared more like my old self, or at any rate like Jean Vivier. I was able to help in the mill and also to work in the Douzy vineyards a couple of days a week, for Vivier's papers were in order, so that I was even able to exchange the occasional word with La Châtelaine when working. Gaston had, of course, warned her right at the

start that on no account must she communicate with my
father. It wasn't that we distrusted him, but even Gaston
was now beginning to realize that though my father's *inten-
tions* were strictly honorable, they were not turning out to
be as heroic as Gaston had at first thought.

I was working in the vineyards, harrowing some hard
soil round the roots of the vines, when simultaneously I
saw the shadow and felt the presence of Grandma looking
down on me. She pointed to some vines, asked an aggressive question, even moved behind Gaston to show him
something, and then, amid the disguise of her words and
actions—always in case of collaborators—she suddenly
hissed in my ear, "I've got a message from Olivia. London
says you've got to keep clear of Douzy."

"What on earth do you mean?" I was almost angry at
the way La Châtelaine was—as usual—giving me orders.
"Why haven't I got the message through the usual channels?"

"Because Douzy church is under suspicion. Germans are
searching the church regularly. Gaston, you ought to get
out right away. And someone has to find a way of getting
Olivia out."

I dropped my hoe in confusion. Grandma had the wit to
shout, "Clumsy fool! You almost snapped the root of that
vine."

"What do you mean? Olivia is really in danger?"

"I don't know." Quickly, squatting as though showing
me how to do better work, she said, "I've arranged to find
out. No one questions me. The Germans all know me—they
know who I am."

With an angry toss of her head for the benefit of other
workers, Grandma disappeared. She had hardly left the
vineyard and cycled away out of sight when I saw a small
armored vehicle appear at the far end of the field. Three
German soldiers jumped out, brandishing submachine
guns. I saw gesticulations, then one of the vignerons
pointed in our direction. We were some distance away.

"I'm running for it," I gasped. "I daren't risk being questioned. And until this scar on my face is healed—" Gaston

realized as well as I that anyone who had been wounded
was *always* suspect when the Germans arrested them.

"Run along the ditch at the back," he whispered urgently, "then to the woods. Better make for Verzenay. It's
not Reims, but it's easy to get lost, even in a small town.
I'll find you through the bookshop."

We both knew the address of the "cut-out" bookshop at
Verzenay, a system which helped to eliminate betrayal by
traitors or even by loyal men and women who had revealed
secrets under torture.

"Look after yourself, Gaston," I panted.

"You too," he started to run in the opposite direction. At
the far end of the vineyard was a large ditch, which had
been dug many years previously to mark the boundary between our vines and those of Mumm. But it had been constructed by someone with a passion for English gardens,
and so the ditch was similar to an English ha-ha contriv-
ance, invented by the British landscape gardeners in the
nineteenth century to keep out cows without disfiguring
the view by unsightly fences. In fact, because of the slight
dip in the hillside, it was impossible for the German soldiers, even though they were only two fields away, to know
there was a ditch at all, it was so cunningly disguised.

As I ran, crouching toward a belt of woodland, I heard
the stutter of machine-gun fire and warning shots. They
couldn't see me. I stumbled on. Gaston had vanished. The
ditch led straight as an arrow to the woods—a small copse
really, not a real wood. I was sure I could make it, and
then—if hidden for only minutes—I could set off in a new
direction.

Certainly it was no longer safe to return to either the
mill or Gaston's house or the vineyard. Once you saw a
couple of German soldiers asking to point you out, it meant
that you and the place where you lived were under surveil-
lance. And with the traces of facial wounds difficult to explain away, I had no doubt that the Germans would ask a
great many questions—and not very politely.

I decided to make for Verzenay. It would not take long to
reach, especially if I could steal a bicycle. And it was un-

likely that the entire German army had been alerted just
to question Jean Vivier. At Verzenay both Gaston and I
had the address of the safe house, and the password. And I
had to be doubly careful, now that I had received the news
that the operation was going to be undertaken soon. Apart
from any personal consideration, it meant that I had to
take the greatest possible care not to fall into enemy hands
before we cut off Germany's supplies of sarin. I knew that
the actual go-ahead message, giving me an approximate
date for action, would depend on when the Allies reached
the critical point at which Hitler would be faced with the
need to try the gambler's last throw—to force Britain to capitulate by the use of a new and terrible weapon, at which
moment he could magnanimously offer a "just" peace
to the Americans. Now that critical point was almost
reached.

I was wondering how best to steal an old bicycle, then
hide in the ditch and wait for dark, when burst after burst
of machine-gun fire tore into the still afternoon. The noise
was horrific and couldn't have been more than a mile
away, one rat-a-tat running into another, so that it
sounded as though a hundred men had opened fire. I had
no idea what had happened. Because I was in the ditch the
noise seemed to come first from one direction, then another. Crouching, I stumbled to the point where the ditch
ended at the small copse. Cautiously I peered over, almost
expecting bullets to send up spurts of dirt as I was spotted.
But I had been forgotten, the attack was somewhere else.
But where? I had lost my bearings, but the copse was small
and once I had crashed—all thought of silence forgotten—
through the tangled thicket and brambles, I knew where
the German attack was being launched.

A dozen men with machine guns had surrounded the
church at Douzy and were firing indiscriminately—but always pointing to the sky, to the belfry on the top of the
squat church tower. At Olivia! She must have been
discovered—or betrayed. One or the other, it didn't matter
now, she was trapped—trapped at the top of a flight of rick-

ety steps so narrow she had once boasted that with her machine pistol, no one would ever be able to take her alive.

My first thought was that I—and Gaston, who must be
somewhere around—*must* save her, not only because she
was Olivia, but because, with the training that had been
drilled and forced into me, I must protect the wireless operator who, until I made alternative arrangements, was my
only way of keeping in contact with London—at a vital moment.

I had my .45, but I was too far away to risk using it. I had
to get closer. It was strange, but even as I crept nearer I
could sense the beginning of panic in the Germans. The
shooting became more sporadic. I suddenly realized they
were taking casualties. I saw two bodies being pulled out
of the church. Then a single shot from inside, followed by a
scream—a man's scream. Olivia was still at the top of the
belfry, shooting anyone who tried to mount the stairs.

Hiding in the undergrowth not a hundred yards behind
the church, I could see four or five Germans in the churchyard. There might be others inside the church. Then on the
road beyond the opposite side of the churchyard, I saw Gaston. He was walking unconcerned toward the lane that led
to the village, almost as though he was making for the
Café des Sports to slake his thirst with a Slavia at the end
of a hard day's work.

A crowd of men and women on the fringe of the village
watched uncertainly, attracted by the noise of heavy firing. A German who was near warned them to return to
their homes, and most scuttled away after he had fired a
burst above their heads.

Gaston seemed not to notice what was going on. The soldier ran toward him, shouting to him to follow the others,
to go away, gesticulating with his submachine gun. Gaston pretended not to understand, even made a gesture with
his right hand as though going for a drink, then pointed to
the Café des Sports in the village. The Germans waved
him on. I had no idea what Gaston would do—or what I
would do.

Then suddenly, before I even *saw* what had happened, I

smelled it. The smell of burning in the church. Almost immediately I saw the first greedy tongues of flames. Gaston must have had the same instantaneous reaction as I. But he was closer to the nearest German, and as I drew my automatic and ran crouching toward the churchyard from one direction, I caught a glimpse of Gaston, who had been playing the part of a village idiot in front of the German next to him; Gaston suddenly changed, sprang forward, hurled himself at the unsuspecting German, and as they fell together, Gaston grabbed the German's tommy gun and holding the barrel hit the German across the head with the metal butt. Gaston had no time to deal with the German. Gaston grabbed the gun. Dead or alive nothing mattered in those desperate moments except one thing: to save Olivia before the flames burned down the ancient, tinder-dry steps to the belfry.

The flames had so far been contained. Perhaps it was the heavy stonework of the old church. At least there were no huge scarlet tongues of flame leaping out of the church windows or roof, nor yet the sound of crackling, that most ominous telltale sign of fire. But smoke billowed from everywhere, and it could be only minutes before the entire church—or the wood inside the heavy stone walls—became a raging inferno. And then there would be no hope for Olivia.

I reached the churchyard first, shot once into the back of a German who never saw me, he was so entranced gazing at the smoke. Almost immediately Gaston seemed to change, ignoring all danger, every vestige of prudence, crying almost like a man demented. I don't suppose I actually had the time to realize at that moment that I had never seen Gaston behave like this before. Legs apart, the German machine gun at his hip, he stood there spraying the three or four remaining Germans until not one was left alive.

Inside we both started choking, but the choir at the back of the church, though filled with smoke, wasn't crackling, and Gaston shouted, "Olivia! Come down! It's safe!" The first flames were beginning to lick their way round the feet of the twisting worn steps.

"You can handle this," I shouted to Gaston. "I'm going to drag the bodies in from outside. If the church burns down, it might all be put down as an accident if the bodies are inside. At least *we* won't be blamed."

I saw Gaston start to climb the steps, but at first he was impeded by the bodies of men who had fallen to Olivia's Schmeisser. He pushed them down with his feet. I dashed out, escaping for a few moments from the acrid smoke, retching as I pulled all the bodies in by their heels and laid them in the nave. After I'd pulled the last one in, I dashed across to the choir stalls and the belfry steps. The wooden floor had long since gone, the broken steps had almost gone, enveloped in the beginnings of flames. I heard Gaston cry out above me to Olivia to be careful in case the steps gave way. She came round the corner of the steps, eyes red, face blackened.

"You'll have to jump for it," cried Gaston. "Larry will catch you when you fall."

"No, this first!" cried Olivia. *"No, no, this first!"* and with only one word she shouted, "Catch!" and threw the radio in its suitcase into my arms. Only when I had safely caught it did she accept the help from Gaston, halfway up the steps. The last four or five steps were well afire by now, but Gaston lowered her down, and as she jumped I broke her fall and we both landed together on the floor of the nave.

Gaston jumped next. Almost at the same moment the roof of the nave collapsed and the flames, as though angry at being robbed, moved inward, turning the choir into a furnace.

"Christ! That was just in time," Gaston gasped. "Is all the evidence inside the church?"

I nodded. "You all right, Olivia?"

"Yes," she gasped. "But some air—I'm choking. And I've got a message for you." Surrounded by the flat gravestones we gasped and drew in huge mouthfuls of air until our lungs would hold no more.

"Look at that!" Gaston showed me the bottom of his trousers. They had actually caught afire as he jumped.

Still finding it difficult to speak, Olivia answered Gaston, "Just give me a moment, darling, to get my breath back."

Something in the tone of her voice—the use of the word *darling,* an unsuspected gentleness—made me look at her and then at Gaston.

Olivia was lying on her back, still breathing hard, as though the air were rationed, as though the supply might be cut off at any moment.

"I wasn't going to tell you," said Gaston awkwardly when he saw me looking at him. "Until we could all celebrate—the three of us. But Olivia and I hope to get married when all this business is over."

"Gaston! Congratulations! I'm so glad. And for you, Olivia. So happy. Oh! Really happy."

A small patch of grass edged the graveyard, and we lay on it ready to move as soon as we could get our breath back.

"A minute more, then we must run for it," Gaston warned us. But I was looking at the flames and the smoke and thinking how long Douzy church had been part of our lives, long before we had even thought that one day we would be killing people inside it.

"Let's go." We were still retching, but I turned to Olivia and said, "Didn't you mention something about a message?"

Olivia nodded, getting off the ground with difficulty. "I lost the text in the scramble to escape. Sorry," she apologized. "But I can remember the text as it was in plain language. It just said, 'Neutralize objective urgentest.'"

51

NOW WE HAD TO IMPLEMENT THE PLAN within hours, not days. Our method of contact had been arranged, but getting to Verzenay didn't prove easy because for two days the countryside was filled with avenging Germans—and at the same time the sultry August weather suddenly erupted into the most violent thunderstorms that locals in the area could remember. As far as I was concerned, it meant that I spent two nights soaked to the skin in ditches, often flooded. I had nothing to eat for three days, except for some fruit and on one occasion the remnants of a loaf which I stole from a farmyard kitchen.

On the fourth day I made my way, the most bedraggled, scruffy peasant in Verzenay, and stopped at the bookshop run by Monsieur Dufy—no relation of the painter.

He looked me up and down—until I asked him if he had a copy of a first edition of Alexander Dumas.

"I'm afraid not, sir," he said, ignoring my wet and dirty trousers, "but I'm told that one has arrived at the whole-salers."

Dufy's bookstore, in the rue de Tremoille, was a cut-out rendezvous. No one knew who passed on a message or to whom. It was used not only to contact people—in this case, the reply meant that Gaston had arrived—but for WT messages to be handed to operators. The cut-out acted as a double guard against betrayal. So many good men, loyal Frenchmen, eager Britons, brave Poles, had volunteered to help France, only to be betrayed by traitors, so that

765

when they knocked at a "safe house" they were greeted by members of the Gestapo. Dufy's bookstore helped to stop this. By the use of simple codes, intelligible to anyone who didn't even know them, hundreds of men had been fore-warned. Dufy needed only to say in answer to a query about Alexander Dumas, "Sorry, I'm afraid the supply has dried up." You were then warned.

Now that I knew Gaston had arrived, I made my way to the safe house. And there I was given some dry clothes, a bowl of soup—and the chance to find out from Gaston what was happening.

"And Olivia's all right," said Gaston. "She's staying with La Châtelaine."

"I'm so glad about you two," I said a little awkwardly.

"We all forget," said Gaston, "that I've been looking af-ter Olivia—virtually a prisoner—for two years. You're bound to feel something for each other." Adding with his infectious grin, "After all, she's only human—and most of the time I've been the only man available."

What a significant choice of words! "I have been the only man available." For there must have been a time long ago when Mama, looking hungrily at Gaston, had harbored the same thought in the same village, He is the only man who is available. And how ironic that Gaston should fall in love with a wonderful, intelligent, and loyal girl—but still a girl with whom both my brother and myself had been to bed. It was, I thought wryly, just one happy family.

For two days Gaston and I shared a room in Verzenay. The bookstore was our lifeline to London, for we used it as the cut-out station between ourselves and Olivia. Olivia, of course, could never appear personally—she was high on the Nazi wanted list as a "Jewish murderess"—nor was it possible, or wise, for either of us to make regular trips to the B and B house to check on messages when the circuit with London was opened at regular, predetermined hours. So La Châtelaine stepped into the breach. It was natural really, a kind of evolution in her progressive and bloodthirsty determination to kill as many Germans as she could.

There were very few messages for London, for when I acknowledged the "go-ahead" signal I told London I would observe radio silence until after the action had been taken. That, however, wouldn't stop London sending any urgent messages to me, so a daily check had to be made. This was La Châtelaine's job. In her trap she paid regular visits to Dufy's bookstore, on her way (deliberately) to the Boulingrin, because she had always gone there and everyone knew she had always gone there. Late in the day I would ask politely, but regularly, if Monsieur Dufy had received any copies of Alexander Dumas first editions. If he had, he beamed and handed me a message, which I read and destroyed. If he said that no books had arrived, then I knew that there had been no word from London.

When I explained to Gaston the full gravity of the stakes we were playing for, and that somehow we had to neutralize the stocks of sarin, we both thought at first that the only way to enter the pyramids would be through the old blocked-up entrance from the *cellier,* the above-ground workshops and presses behind the Home Farm. The Germans had not only covered the main entrance to the pyramid with barbed wire, they had also bricked up one particular gallery leading from the *cellier* directly to the pyramid. Obviously underground passages branched off in several directions to different cellars, only the one leading to the pyramid had been blocked off.

Fortunately none of the Germans who locked up this entrance had the faintest idea that not far away the Astells had bricked up another cellar—more than a tunnel, an entire wall, to hide the Hisp and its precious stocks of gasoline. I knew that the wall which Papa had built was thin and could be easily smashed open. But behind it tunnels led out to dozens of cellars and passages, and I felt sure that if we could quickly break into the hidden cache of gas, we might eventually be able to find our way into the pyramid.

The *cellier* was never guarded. The Germans didn't have

a large enough garrison in the Champagne area to guard every entrance to every cellar. It was a physical impossibility. And besides, Champagne was "at peace" with enemies living as harmoniously as possible. Yet the plans presented many difficulties—and the need for action was growing more urgent, especially after I received a message at Dufy's bookstore, which was terse and to the point: "Informatively Pétain arrested. Resistance uprising in Paris now control all main buildings. De Gaulle enters Cherbourg 20th. When are you ready?"

I burned the message, but only after reading its contents to Gaston, who whistled, "They really want their pint of blood!"

"This time it's really death or glory!" I replied as cheerfully as I could. "But with a time limit."

Certainly I hoped we had found the simplest of all ways to reach the pyramid; but I felt that first we should check.

"And there's only one person who knows every passage leading to every cellar," I said to Gaston. "It's La Châtelaine. We've got to meet her."

"Isn't it dangerous?"

"It's necessary," I insisted. "We'd look damn stupid if we got into the Hisp cellar and found it led nowhere."

"I still say it's risky."

"It's the only way," I said. "La Châtelaine is involved now, like it or not. And she's in the most powerful position a secret agent could be in—the boss, respected, feared, even by the Germans. Her word is law. If we break into the Hisp cellar and she wants to cover up the hole in the wall which we make to get in by stacking up some empty barrels—or even putting the bricks back—nobody would dare ask her why, let alone argue with her."

"That's true," agreed Gaston. "I'll make the arrangements to meet her."

Using the cut-out at Dufy's bookstore, we met the following day in the village house at Verzenay, where we had taken refuge. I explained that I must get into the Douzy Pyramid. "And please don't ask me why, Grandma," I said

as firmly as possible. "It's top secret. And London has ordered me in."

I told her about the bricked-up wall hiding the cellar
where the car had been hidden together with gas on the
outbreak of war.

"Well, that's news to me," she almost chuckled. "I always supposed the Germans had stolen the Hisp, taken it
away or something."

She thought for a long time.

"You see," I was instinctively trying to persuade her,
"that once inside the Hisp cellar, we could use plastic explosives to break into any tunnel leading to the pyramid.
The noise would be muffled. But it's vital to choose the
right place for the explosion among the honeycomb of tunnels. That's where you can help."

"I'm sorry, Larry," she said finally, "but it's impossible.
I know the cellars where the Hisp was hidden. They lead
down to a dead end. There's no way through. You can take
my word for it."

I must have looked crestfallen.

"Don't worry," she said. "There's a much easier way
into the pyramid. I could show you right away how to get
in."

"But how?" I found it hard to believe.

"Did you know that when my father was alive there had
been an explosion in one of the neighboring pyramids?"
asked Grandma. "No one ever discovered the reason why,
but ten people died simply because there was no way any
of them could get out. My father's immediate reaction was
to make sure a similar tragedy could never happen in his
pyramid. So he built what the sailors in submarines call
an escape hatch."

"But, Grandma, I never heard of it!" I exclaimed. "I
never knew it existed."

"There's no reason why you should. It's been forgotten,
it was built before you were born. There's never been another explosion in any of the pyramids in the Champagne
area, and there probably never will be. We found out later
that the original tragedy had been caused not by an acci-

dent, but because someone with a grudge—a crank—had
blown up the pyramid on purpose. But your great-grandfather took no chances and decided to build an escape
hatch."

She explained the details, unknown, fascinating, all taking place many, many years previously. In effect the hatch
consisted of a narrow, sloping shaft with iron rungs fixed
into the side chalk walls from a point on the Rilly Mountain. It ran right down to the base of the Douzy Pyramid,
almost to the point where it was adjacent to the Rilly Pyramid. The shaft contained an exit so that people could escape from the base, and another exit at the halfway mark
near the subway leading to the tunnel.

"But I've never seen the exits—or heard of them. Have
you, Gaston?" He shook his head.

"And anyway," I continued, "how could anyone have
constructed such a shaft years ago, when there was no
modern machinery?"

"They dug down on a slope," said Grandma. "And
though I've never been down, I'm told that when the work
started the chalk was pulled up from the beginning of the
shaft by what the Americans call banana sledges."

According to Grandma, the excavations would, when
they reached a certain stage, branch outward—just like
the Romans' did, but on a much smaller scale, and the engineers constructed small cellars into which they piled the
chalk they were excavating from the shaft, so that they
never really had to carry the load of chalk which they were
digging out any great distance. And sometimes, it seemed,
they actually came across old disused cellars or galleries,
opened them up, and used them to get rid of the chalk they
were digging out.

It seemed, too, that though the escape hatch had impressed my great-grandfather and his cronies, it was valueless, not only because there was no likelihood of any
explosion, but, as Grandma explained tartly, "The general
opinion has always been that anyone trapped at the foot of
Douzy would have died of a heart attack trying to climb

about a hundred and fifty rungs of the ladder fixed into the side of the shaft."

"What I don't understand," I repeated to Grandma, "is why I never *saw* anything."

"I think I could find the entrance and show it to you. It's on the hillside. It must be about halfway between Douzy and Rilly. It must be overgrown, of course, and it might take a bit of finding."

"But I never saw any exits *inside* the pyramid."

My great-grandfather, it appeared, didn't like the exit to be too obvious. He knew where it was, but both exits from inside the pyramid—one at the foot of the pyramid, the other in the subway leading up to the tunnel—were invisible from inside. They could be broken down by pushing. Either inside or outside the shaft.

This news opened up an entirely new avenue of planning, after learning that it was impossible to enter the pyramid through the Hisp cellar. Providing we could find the shaft entrance on the Rilly Mountain, we might be able to reach both the railway tunnel and the base of the pyramid. To Gaston I called it a miracle because I was so staggered that none of us had even heard of the escape hatch. Looking back, it is understandable. No one remembered it any more. It had never figured in any of our plans, our discussions, our talks. The entrance itself wasn't really on Douzy land, but on the hillside above the Rilly tunnel. It must have sloped down toward the base of both pyramids at quite an angle. I don't suppose anyone had given the long-forgotten—and highly impractical—escape hatch a single thought since before we were born. And now that old Pagniez was dead, La Châtelaine was probably the only person who would be able to find it.

Finally, sitting at the village house at Verzenay, La Châtelaine asked one question in, for her, a very quiet voice, "What about your father?"

I explained as best I could—and without telling her what was hidden in the Douzy Pyramid—that we had two objectives: the Rilly tunnel had to be blown up with PE, using delayed-action fuses to give us time to escape. The pyramid needed a different treatment, details of which had previously been carefully explained to me—even with diagrams produced in London. For we did not want to blow *up* Douzy Pyramid, we wanted to blow it *down*. It was no good blowing up the pyramid and in the process releasing all the dangerous sarin. The warheads for the V-2s were stocked in the Pyramid—with his mechanic's eyes Gaston had confirmed immediately that the rockets were not primed in the tunnel—as London had originally explained.

Our task was to prepare a series of explosions which would cause the walls of the pyramid to collapse inward and bury the lethal contents. According to the explosives experts in London, the simplest method was to mine the walls round the base of the pyramid so that they would dislodge huge blocks of chalk and weaken any overhang. Carefully placed PE charges, halfway up the pyramid, could also be used. The explosives experts in SOE, who superintended my crash course, had insisted that the shock of detonations would dislodge huge quantities of overhang. Five thousand tons of chalk would probably bury the secrets of sarin forever. The only explosion factor that I *didn't* need to learn was that the explosions laid at the base, where both pyramids were adjacent, would surely dislodge the chalk at the base of the Rilly side of the pyramid as well. What if those detonations dislodged huge lumps of chalk high up the Rilly Pyramid, and it, too, started to fall and crumble inward?

Grandma certainly realized vaguely the dangers of what we planned to do, for once again she asked me, "What about your father?"

Most of the Rilly Mountain, as the glorified hill through which the tunnel ran was known, consisted of rough, untended "mountain land," too difficult for farmers to reach; nor was the soil good. A few clumps of trees clothed the uneven landscape, together with acres of scrub and gorse, bright yellow in June, but now just a mass of sharp, prickly bushes. A few narrow paths crisscrossed the countryside, produced by repeated tread over the decades by walkers. It was not very pretty, too rough, too neglected, and even the Germans found it too boring to police it with any regularity.

Early the following morning, Grandma cycled to the foot of Rilly Mountain and climbed a quarter of the way up, so as not to be seen arriving there with us. Her energy was amazing. Dressed in a long skirt, thinner than usual because of the heat, and a pair of stout shoes, and a bandeau holding her wispy gray hair in place, her heaviest items of "clothing" consisted of gold bangles round her skinny, pockmarked wrists, gold chains hanging from her scrawny neck, half a dozen rings—one a magnificent diamond solitaire—on her bony fingers.

Slowly, knees bent as we climbed, we followed the forgotten footpaths up the modest hillside. We met no one— nor had we expected to. Peasants did not as a rule waste their time on land they do not use profitably. And with waist-high scrub or gorse and the occasional clumps of trees, together with the angle of the ground, it was virtually impossible to be overseen by anyone except by an airplane from above.

Gaston had brought with him two implements only—a crowbar and a heavy hammer, which we carried, together with two powerful English-made flashlights, standard SOE issue. I had complete faith that Grandma—a walking geographer in her own area—would find the place, but I was not so sure that it would be quite as easy to force open any entry into an underground shaft that hadn't been used for fifty years or more. So it proved to be. The entrance took some finding, simply because it lay beneath a mass of tangled undergrowth. Too late I realized I should have brought a spade or hoe, but we hacked away with the crowbar until we had dislodged the main roots, tearing them out with our hands. Finally we cleared away the circle of cast iron. I could read part of the raised inscription, presumably the name of the maker, *"Etablissement Gerard et*

Fils," but the date of the manufacture and the address of the maker were undecipherable.

"It's going to take hours to force this open," I said after a quick examination. "It's jammed solid. We can do it, but—"

"Yes, I know," said Grandma. "But I'll have to leave you here. I must go to the *cellier* and then to Douzy to see if there are any messages. Here," she pulled out a paper bag from her capacious pockets, "some cheese from the Home Farm. I'll check tomorrow at Dufy's to see what's happened."

Her last words as she set off down the hill were, "Remember your father. Better give it some thought."

When she had gone, and we sat down and ate the cheese, Gaston laughed, his mouth full, and said, "La Châtelaine is wonderful! She's quite determined to run the whole show."

It took us four hours of back-breaking work to undo the manhole cover. It had rusted solid into the rim of the escape hatch and we faced two alternatives: to return to Verzenay and organize, through the Resistance, tools more suited to our task, and even possibly a blow-torch if we could find one, or else alternatively just to hack away, taking hours to do the job ourselves. We chose the latter way and stayed where we were. I didn't want to go down the hill unless I had to. Though we were moderately safe when working in the vineyard, I always felt a stab of fear if I was anywhere unusual—in other words walking down the Rilly Mountain. The catastrophe of Rilly had rocked the Germans in the entire area—and when it was followed by the disastrous fire at Douzy church, the Germans became even more nervy and even more savage in their determination to find out who had been responsible—and why. So any "simple" French peasant walking near Rilly—even on the hill above—might be brusquely told to produce his papers, and count himself lucky if he didn't end up being arrested for questioning. So the fewer unnecessary journeys, the better.

* * *

Finally we got the manhole cover freed of rust and dirt.
It lay on the supporting rim, but it took the two of us all
our strength to open. (It occurred to me that if, in the event
of an explosion, workers climbed the shaft only to find at
the top that they hadn't got the strength to push open the
manhole cover they'd never have escaped anyway. That
must have been an oversight on the part of my great-
grandfather!)

"We'll leave the cover slightly off center, when we climb
down." Even Gaston was panting with the effort of hauling it away.

"When *I* go down," I corrected him. "I am trying it out
first—and alone. God knows whether the iron rungs will
hold in the chalk or what I'll find. And," with a smile. "I
might need you to get me out."

Gaston knew better than to waste energy on argument.
In the Resistance internal squabbling, jockeying for power, especially among rival political factions, caused untold
delays, sometimes resulting in death through negligence
or, worse, betrayal. One of the strengths of SOE was its
clearly stated power to lead. When organizing Resistance
groups, or helping to arm them, any local Resistants who
believed they knew better (but had no idea of the long-term
planning behind specific incidents) would be discarded
quickly; and if disloyalty were proved, they just
vanished—equally quickly.

"I'm going in for a look-see," I explained. "I want to discover if there's any way I can tell from inside the shaft
when we reach the subway leading to the Rilly tunnel.
Somehow we'll have to break into the tunnel when the
time comes—probably on the way *back* from the base, but
God knows how."

The first rung was barely two feet above the lip of the
shaft, and I stepped on it gingerly, half expecting that with
rust and old age it might fall out of the side of the shaft,
which was very narrow at the entrance. The rung held
without the slightest looseness. I slowly climbed down. I
was in a slanting position, face to the rungs. It was inky
black. The circle of light above me grew smaller with each

fumbling, faltering downward step. I couldn't help reflecting that really great-grandpa had been responsible for a remarkable engineering achievement. I knew that this must be a copy of the many French escape shafts used for emergency in coal mines. But they had been made with all the money, expertise, and engineering paraphernalia of huge government organizations. For one man to sink a shaft like this was a remarkable—if unnecessary—achievement.

The darkness was inpenetrable. Not one speck of light—reflected, direct, even imagined—showed beyond the pinprick far above. I had my flashlight—and the SOE had copied the German practice by devising flashlights like the German ones, with a specially designed clip; mine could be fixed either onto a belt or onto the top of a pair of trousers or even the outside of a breast pocket. This meant that I could use both hands on the rung above. The narrowness of the shaft had another advantage. As climbers do when climbing a narrow rock "staircase," the shaft was in places narrow enough for me to use my back. It was useful now to rest my arms, for I was employing muscles in a new way, so that on the upward climb I would have even more need of a backrest.

I had not been worried by the physical effort required, I knew that SOE had trained me to a pitch of physical fitness I had never known before in my life—even after the beating I had received. But I had not reckoned on one thing: the foul air inside. There had been no fresh air in that shaft for decades, and I gagged and retched with every step I took down. I was breathing used-up air, and at times I had to struggle not to vomit.

I kept careful count of the steps and after I had gone down fifty-eight steps, I nearly jumped out of my skin—and I would have done had there been room in the narrow, airless, chalky shaft. For suddenly, without warning, I heard voices. Two Germans were talking, laughing, so loudly that for the first impossible moment of fear I thought they were in the shaft below me. Of course it couldn't be. Then I realized on the fifty-eighth rung I had reached the subway.

That must be it. There could be no other explanation. The two Germans must be in the subway, separated from me, from the shaft, by a wall no thicker than a piece of three-ply wood.

It was obviously disguised. I wondered why in the first place the precautions had been taken. Perhaps great-grandpa didn't want anyone using the subway to the tunnel—to know that, in effect, the shaft provided a secret *entrance* into the pyramid. The existence of the shaft must have been a nine days' wonder when it was first built, and no doubt there were plenty of daredevil youngsters anxious to explore it.

The garrulous Germans kept talking, loud enough for me to hear some words distinctly, though I hadn't the faintest idea what they were talking about. The voices seemed to come from all around me; no sense of sound direction, not even up or down. They were like reverberating echoes sometimes used in the movies to create an eerie effect.

I was so scared I rested without moving a muscle, hardly daring to breathe. In fact I could actually hear one of them give a sudden cough and then spit. If I could hear *them* talking so clearly, what the hell would happen if *I* sneezed or coughed? The conversation seemed to last an age and I began to feel nausea, an urgent desire to vomit; then an attack of cramp in the calf of one leg almost made me scream. All I could do was move the ankle in an up-and-down motion, then press hard with my instep on the rung of the step below me. But the illusion of nearness—not an illusion really, but I felt as though I were separated by a sheet of glass—was so overpowering that I experienced a sense of danger even just by pressing the sole of my foot against the iron bar.

Finally the voices grew less raucous. I heard the sound of footsteps moving away. They must be walking along the subway toward the Rilly tunnel—or perhaps in the other direction, into the pyramid proper. I waited a few more minutes—or seconds, I hadn't the faintest idea—then pulled my flashlight, which had been switched off, from my belt, and leaning my back against the shaft to take the strain, I shone the light on the side of the shaft. There was nothing in front of course, for the rungs could be embedded only in the solid material facing me. But where had the voices come from?

Almost panicking, I realized that the weak wall—the wall containing the "secret" exit—must be behind me, the one I was leaning against. With a sudden surge of fear I was terrified that if I pressed too hard, I would fall into the subway. Instinctively I held myself flat against the rungs. It was impossible to turn myself round, the shaft was too tight a fit.

I did manage to half twist round, but I was so frightened of dropping my flashlight that before I did so, I clipped it again on to my belt. If that fell to the bottom of the shaft, I would not only be sightless, but the noise would be bound to raise an alarm.

Finally, by holding on the rung with one hand and switching the flashlight round to pinpoint sections of the wall, I was able to make out some dusty, dirty thin lines— obviously invisible unless you were looking specially for them.

Very, very gently I pressed the wall. It gave slightly. Nothing to worry about—unless I was rough—but I knew then that this small section of the shaft, the exit from and into the subway, wasn't chalk at all. It had been made, I guessed, of thin wood, plastered over on the other side so that the join would be invisible.

The first thing I did now was to identify the crack so that each of us could spot the place immediately when we returned. I didn't want to spend precious seconds in this fetid atmosphere looking for it—especially as I knew that the next time we would be festooned with PE and fuses, to say nothing of guns and grenades. I would have been grateful for anything—a piece of chalk to give an "X marks the spot" identification. But I hadn't any. I tried to rub away the dust, but it was so thickly encrusted that it would have taken a chisel to scrape a mark. Finally I did the simplest thing of all. I tied my handkerchief to the nearest rung. Then I started to climb down to the bottom.

52

WE DECIDED TO BLOW UP the tunnel and the Douzy Pyramid around 1:15 P.M. on August 24. By then I was fighting fit again—and I needed to be, for the "trial run" down the shaft had taught me that I would need every ounce of my strength. I let London know, in code, using my silk pad.

I knew just what I would have to do after kicking our way into both the tunnel and the pyramid. I was sure that we could *get in* fairly easily by pushing the weak section of the wall away, but I didn't want to rush in, firing at random, yet being a standing target for any Germans who would certainly be armed with submachine guns. No; wearing gas masks as we pushed in, we would roll in canisters of tear gas, which Gaston had saved from previous raids. Two would go into the gallery, joining the pyramid with the tunnel, while I descended to the base, broke open the false wall, and rolled in three more. The Resistance had been collecting German tear gas for months.

Instinct—or training—told me that a sudden outbreak of gas—any gas—in a lethal store of sarin would cause instant panic.

"What I *plan,*" I explained to Gaston, "is to fall down as I break in, roll or hurl the first canisters, crying in German, 'Gas! Sarin gas leaking!' or something like that, then pretend to faint. It'll panic even the strongest nerve—especially among troops who know that the Germans are on the run and that gas is stored in the pyramid."

"And me?"

"When you break into the gallery door, you do the same thing—throw one canister, crying, 'Gas leak!' and run like hell, as though trying to escape the gas, to the Rilly tunnel. Then you open up another canister. It'll start a panic. I'm certain of it. After all, everyone working at Douzy and in the tunnel must know the danger they run of a leak from a lethal gas."

We would have our gas masks of course—the French had issued them at the start of the war. And that, I argued, would also help, in the first panic, to make us less noticeable.

"But surely the people working on dangerous gases in Douzy will be issued with gas masks?"

"They will, I agree," I replied. "But we've chosen to start the attack at midday—quarter past one—because we know that the main body of methodically minded Germans in the tunnel go for lunch at one o'clock, leaving temporary guards on duty. Remember three things, Gaston—their instinct, even as they grab their gas masks, will be to climb upward, away from the clouds of gas hugging the floor. Second, I'll be so damn quick—and so damn scared—that I'll lay those charges before they know what's happening, and then be away as they're already climbing up the stairs to escape. And three—most important—no one is going to believe that *anyone* can push open the wall of the pyramid. It's like," I hesitated, searching for the right metaphor, "like pushing down the walls of Jericho."

Our preliminary plans were simple. Gas masks presented no problem. We both had "borrowed" Schmeisser machine pistols, which we had stolen from the Germans, and our automatics. We each carried a couple of grenades, our PE and denotators in separate haversacks—old French army issue, everyone used them since the end of the war.

The plastic explosives were harmless—until the detonator was inserted and primed. We would each insert the detonators, with a "pencil" time fuse set for thirty minutes, at the very last minute before bursting in and rolling the canisters into the room. I reckoned that, with the fuse set beforehand, I could be inside the pyramid, stick in four lots of PE, and be out and start climbing up the shaft in about three minutes.

Even though Gaston, stopping at the gallery, would be in position before me, he would synchronize his attack with mine so that all the clouds of tear gas would seep into all areas at the same time.

We would both have our flashlights, and Gaston would carry a coil of rope, wound round one shoulder like a mountaineer. "In case one of us needs to help the other if anything goes wrong," I explained.

I gave my last instructions personally to Grandma at our final meeting before we left for the hill. "There'll be no problems," I assured her. "But I'll need to get a message away urgently—from the top of Rilly hill. Do you think you can make it, Grandma? Then collect it?"

"Of course," she snorted, as though to say, "How dare you." Then she added, "So you are going down?"

For the first time I could remember her voice held doubts. I had noticed slight traces before, the old angry authority was being subdued. Not that I minded. La Châtelaine had for so long been "a character" that maybe a few doubts would mellow her! Or perhaps she was just getting tired and older.

"I must," I said to her. "A great deal depends on it."

"I don't understand why you have to do this," she said. "And it's not my place to ask. But Douzy Pyramid is a *part* of us—part of our lives."

"But, Grandma," I tried to explain, "in one way you're right, but in another you're wrong. You talk about 'our lives'—but they're *not* our lives, they haven't been for years. They belong to the Germans—all of us do."

"Never!" she cried, with a flash of her old spirit.

"Soon it'll be all over," I said gently. "But you're the one who always said that we had to kill every German we could. Well—"

"It all seems so senseless. Here, give me a *marc,*" she asked for her favorite drink. "I can hardly remember the times when all of us were so happy," she said bitterly. "And now, what happens?" She held out her blue-veined

hands for the small glass of fiery drink. "Anna, living in
Switzerland. Your mother in America. And where's Guy?"

"He's all right. Sonia saw him not long ago. He's fine.
He's working with the Resistance near the Swiss border."

"And Sonia? Fancy Sonia. Like one of the family—and
now an enemy."

"Not for long," I promised her.

"And your father?" Looking at me suspiciously, "Tell
me—is he involved in this? Your father?"

"No, no, Grandma. I promise you. That's the reason why
I've never let him even know I'm in France—I don't want
him to be involved." It was true, though I didn't think it
necessary to tell Grandma that I had been *ordered* by
London not to let my father know that I was in the area. Or
that I was worried about the danger of blowing up Rilly as
well as Douzy.

With an almost uncanny touch of suspicion, La Châtelaine said slowly, "So long as nothing happens to your
father—he's a very precious man. And a very loyal Frenchman. And don't forget that he's my son as well as your father."

As she left, after making arrangements to meet on the
mountain, I had the uncomfortable feeling that she wasn't
just expressing a hope, she was warning me obliquely
where the responsibility would lie in the event of any tragedy.

Everything went according to plan. We reached the top
of the hill early in the morning and waited in the scrub until after midday, when laboriously we started to pull the
rusted, old manhole cover aside. Before we were ready to
climb down, we tore out a few big branches of gorse and
small branches of trees to try, as we balanced just inside
the shaft, to cover up as much of the hole as we could. We
weren't very successful, though we did manage to pull
across some of the larger broken branches. Anyway, we expected to be back on the hill without much delay.

I climbed down first. Because of the slope it was comparatively easy, though the stinking air still made me gag

with every step I took. But with our faces to the rungs, I experienced none of the tension I would have felt had I been climbing vertically downward for such a long stretch of ladder. Every step could have been missed so much more easily if it had been vertical. And I would have gone hurtling down into the black unknown pit below.

I went first, mainly because I would be able to feel, with my hands, the rung on which I had tied a handkerchief to mark the entrance to the gallery leading to the Rilly tunnel. And of course I had to go farther down than Gaston, so it was obvious I would go down first to be able to point to him above me where to break in when the right time came.

When I did feel the handkerchief, I reached one arm above me and gently tugged Gaston's trouser leg. He knew then that silence was imperative, for we were separated from the Germans by a false wall, almost paper thin. I climbed a couple more rungs. Then, holding on to one rung with my right hand, I was able to shine the light onto the dusty, chalky surface of the shaft and indicate the rough outline of the false exit. Gaston gave the thumbs-up signal. He could see it clearly, and he knew just what to do—give me time to get to the bottom of the shaft, set the timed pencil fuses embedded in the PE, and then wait for our synchronized watches to read one fifteen, when the main body of Germans would have left the pyramid for their lunch.

I knew I could get the timing exactly right, for I had asked London to parachute (with other supplies) some standard RAF-issue chromium-plated Rolex watches, the kind RAF navigators used when they had to reach a specific target a thousand miles distant and were permitted only a fifteen-second discrepancy in their ETA—estimated time of arrival.

Worse even than the heat on the descent was the stench of stale air, so foul that it took all our efforts not to vomit. So far, of course, we had not worn our gas masks, but I began to wonder if we wouldn't be better off wearing them and at least breathing filtered air.

Leaving Gaston to await the synchronized time, I made my way down to the base. I had my two grenades, my PE ready when I reached the bottom. The time pencils, with their delayed action fuses, were ingenious, and they came in various "sizes"—or rather "time zones." Mine were half-hour fuses, timed to blow up the PE thirty minutes after they were inserted and primed. They were light and easy to handle. By the light of my flashlight I checked on the time: 1:04. It was the moment to insert the time pencils. Each one consisted of thin wire sticking out of a small tube. In my last few minutes I stuck one wire deep into each of the pieces of PE. At this stage the fuse was still "safe." At the very last moment before I thrust open the "door" and rolled out the cans of gas, I would squeeze each tube on the fuse. This forced out acid, which would burn its way along the thin wire until it dissolved—I hoped in exactly thirty minutes, when the charge would blow up.

As I stuck the wires in, I knew it was a sticky moment. I had to either hold or handle, at the same moment, four clumps of explosive, primed to blow up, two grenades, three canisters of gas, and a flashlight, so that I could see—among other things—where to burst into the pyramid.

By 1:14 I was wearing my gas mask and all was set, flashlight hanging by my pocket. The lumps of PE were cradled in my left arm. I carried one canister of tear gas in my right hand, two more in my haversack. I suddenly thought, with a slightly sick feeling, Goddammit! This is *our* pyramid. Belongs to us! I hope to Christ I don't end my days in here.

Then I charged in.

The phony door gave way like rotten matchwood. After all, it was nearly a hundred years old. I had—for safety's sake—smashed it open with my bottom; it was safer than the other way round. I was always terrified that the PE would go off if I messed around with it too much. As the door gave, I swiveled round, pulled the pin out of the canister of tear gas, and immediately the gas seeped out. I screamed, holding my mouth open for a second, *"Gas! Sarin!"* It was the only German I knew. Then I pulled my gas mask over my face and fell down as though I were dy-

ing, but I fell down, very, very gingerly, still grabbing the
PE.

The effect was electric. I had known it would be; even in
London, SOE had regarded the actual blowing up of the
pyramid as comparatively easy and nothing to worry
about in the panic. They had been much more concerned
with how I would get into it. Well, I'd done *that.*

Even I, though, was astounded. Screams, shouts, filled
the air. I couldn't tell what the hell anyone was saying, but
I could *see* that the lunchtime skeleton staff was gripped
by a total panic; some were not carrying their gas masks—
like so many of us in the war who regarded them as unnecessary encumbrances. Without hesitation, but still
screaming, *"Gas! Gas!"* I rolled open another can, then,
still on my back, I hurled the third can as far as I could into
the middle of the ground area. Up the steps a panic-
stricken group of twenty or thirty men was trying to
scramble to safety. In the center of the pyramid was the elevator, specially constructed and made of steel, and which
at first had reminded me of a huge Erector set. I caught
only a glimpse of those scrambling to safety because I now
had to stick the PE where it would do most harm. SOE had
explained how to place it in cracks where it would weaken
the lower sides of the pyramid, forcing the walls above to
crumble inward through lack of support.

I reckoned I could spare sixty seconds—perhaps two minutes at the most. The base of the pyramid had miraculously become half empty. I found one group trying to
escape into the steel elevator, which the Germans had installed. It was not supposed to take men, but machinery.
However gas was everywhere, and a thick spreading cloud
of it was engulfing the few men left on the floor area. I ran
across to the other side of the base to spread the PE around
the entire area, and as I was running back and passing the
elevator, a German shouted at me.

For a moment, hardly able to see through my gas mask,
I almost shot the vague shadow half hidden in the mist.
But then I realized that I was stumbling, that he was try-
ing to help me get into the elevator, that he must have mis-

taken me for a German. I could do only one thing. With a groan and muffled shout of *"Sarin!"* I slid to the ground as though dying. It was enough. The German forced his way into the elevator and left me for dead.

No one could see me. I knew though that I must not let the elevator ascend, for—gas or no gas—it would lead to the gallery and escape via the tunnel.

And even though Gaston must have used gas in the gallery, I couldn't risk the other men escaping from inside the pyramid. As I reached the false door, perhaps twenty feet from the elevator, I grabbed one of my two grenades and pulled the pin with my teeth. Then I hurled it with all my strength straight at the strange-looking open-steel construction of the elevator. I barely managed to duck behind the foot of the escape hatch—the other side of the wall—before the elevator seemed to erupt in an almighty crash. A blinding flash lit up my narrow entrance, mingled with screams and groans and curses. I daren't spare even a second to look. Apart from the urgency I was not an explosives expert. All I knew was that the acid was burning into the fuse of the explosives, and if the walls of the pyramid collapsed, so too would the base of our escape hatch. I was afraid that the explosion in the elevator might set off a chain reaction that would blow up the PE as well—before it was due to be exploded.

Somehow I reached the halfway stage of the upward climb. Panting, almost invisible in the haze of gas, Gaston grabbed me under the arms and helped me onto the solid ground of the opening next to the gallery, which Gaston had forced open—as easily, I could see, as I had done below. He had already set the fuses for the V-2s and was back at the escape hatch. As I joined him, ready to clamber up, two Germans in gas masks arrived. Gaston shot them both.

"There're more on the steps coming up inside the pyramid," I shouted, though I wasn't sure whether he could hear me.

He must have done, for he cried, "We can't wait for long!"

"Leave it to me," I was retching with the fetid air. I

rolled my last grenade down the chalky steps, on the other
side I saw a German standing on the ledge opposite—the
very ledge where Papa used to invite guests to see the wonder that was Douzy, the very ledge where I had first met
Willi. I saw the German hesitate and pull out a gun.
He never had time to use it. Gaston shot him with his
Schmeisser, and I saw the man tumble over the edge and
into the tangled mass of wreckage of the elevator below.

"Let's go!" I shouted. "Time's short!"

"All laid?" asked Gaston.

"Everything. Four explosives at the base," and looking
at the luminous hands of my watch, I added, "twenty minutes until the bang."

"Same here," said Gaston. "Let's get out of this place before it collapses."

"Okay in the tunnel?"

"Sure," said Gaston, who was able to take his gas mask
off as soon as we got up a couple of steps. He was breathing
heavily, and he too was retching. "Two charges under each
of the four V-2s, one extra near the first rocket. Then I
laid three charges just inside the half-platform, to bring
down the sides of the pyramid above us."

I had actually put my foot on a rung of the ladder to start
the last ascent up to the hilltop. My hands had actually
gripped the rung above me, when I stopped.

"Come on!" cried Gaston desperately. "We've only got
nineteen minutes left."

"I can't!" I opened the mouth of the gas mask for a second and gasped, "You go on, Gaston—go on. I've got a job to
do."

"Your father?"

I nodded, short of words, short of breath. I stood there,
then holding my breath, eyes closed tightly, just for the
moment. I pressed my face to the cool, damp walls of the
gallery as though to rid myself of the hideous gas and
the equally hideous dilemma.

"For Christ's sake, put it on," Gaston must have thought
I had lost my reason. I hadn't—I pulled my mask on before

I opened my eyes. But I knew that this was no longer a simple matter of our survival.

"You go," I shouted hoarsely. "I'm going to warn my father. I *have* to. I'll follow you up."

"How?" shouted Gaston. "How can you?"

It was difficult to shout clearly through the mask, even though I could sense that the gas was beginning to thin out.

"This!" I held out my last small piece of PE. "The wall to the Rilly Pyramid."

Gaston would know what I meant. In the old days a gallery had connected Rilly Pyramid with the Rilly tunnel—just like our gallery. And though the entrance linking the Rilly tunnel to the pyramid had been blocked up by the Germans, it would be only the thickness of a brick, even of plaster. One tiny explosion would blow a hole in it without any problem.

"I'm coming with you," Gaston's muffled voice shouted. "But for Chrissake, let's make it quick—I'm so scared I've just pissed in my pants."

We couldn't waste a second—not even in argument. Nor did I want to tell Gaston to make his way up the shaft—because I knew he would refuse.

We ran along the gallery, every step sounding hollow on the damp chalk, with the occasional clink as boots struck the old streetcar lines. The inside of the tunnel, arc lamps still lit, like giant eyes suspended from the ceiling, over the low-lying clouds of gas, made an eerie backdrop.

"Careful of the PE," warned Gaston. "Go between the rockets." He wriggled ahead. The tunnel was eerily deserted. But I knew that before the explosions were timed to go off, the first panic would subside and men with gas masks would return to investigate.

On the other side of the giant V-2s, opposite the gallery leading to Douzy, I could see the bricked-up entrance to the Rilly gallery. I started to fumble with my plastic explosive—no danger until I had inserted a pencil fuse—when Gaston seemed to emerge from nowhere like a shadow, wielding a huge hammer.

"This is quicker!" he shouted, voice deadened and stifled by the mask, then swung the hammer into the center of the brick wall. Only it wasn't brick. It was ordinary lath and plaster. I wouldn't have believed it. It had been erected as a real "show wall" to keep the French from prying into the Rilly tunnel.

"Wait," my dampened voice sounded odd. Then to save time I just hurled myself ass first into the lath and plaster wall and almost fell into the gallery.

Time, I knew, was running out. I didn't have to look at my watch to know that we had perhaps fifteen minutes left before Douzy and the tunnel were blown up. At least the air on the other side of the gaping hole through which I had fallen must be purer, fresher. And there had been no gas there. I pulled the mask upward, leaving it over my forehead so that I could pull it over my face quickly and, switching on my flashlight, stumbled forward toward a circle of light at the far end of the gallery. I heard Gaston clumping after me. Even though this gallery had been unused for two or three years, the air there tasted like nectar after the gas mask. I shook my head to welcome the air.

As I reached the circle of light, the end of the tunnel, the platform—just like ours—looking down on the floor of the pyramid, a startled German soldier barred my way, terrified by my appearance from nowhere, my gas mask worn like a hat. With a guttural cry he began to shout, *"Was ist—?"*

I had no time—not even five seconds—to spare. I hit him across the chest with my German machine pistol, grabbed him as he stumbled, and hurled him over the railings of the platform, to lie sprawled out on the floor below.

The cries from fifty people or more gave way to silence as I stood by the railings of the platform, arms apread out and upward like a prophet or a messiah, and shouted in French, "Everyone run for it! Run like hell! Go now! The pyramid is going to be blown up!"

I heard a shot from the ground. A bullet whizzed past me, but I shouted again, "Run! You will all die if you don't. You have ten minutes!" The seconds it took to throw the man overboard, to cry a warning, took effect before I had a chance to look for my father. I had to find him.

I had no need to. He found *me*—without knowing who I was. Completely fearless—for after all, I had just thrown a man to his death—my father grabbed me by the shoulders, wheeled me round, and shouted angrily, "What the hell do you mean by bursting into my office!"

He must have had his desk behind the balcony where I had been confronted by the German, and he tore at the strange bearded interloper, livid with fury. "What the devil—?"

Human reaction is difficult to measure. I was so concerned with warning my father—and the people, some of whom were beginning to stream up the stairs to safety— that all I did at first was to beg him, "Be quick. You have only ten minutes." With my own life hanging by a few minutes, it never entered my head that he wouldn't recognize me, that I would have to identify myself.

"We're blowing the Douzy Pyramid up in ten minutes!"

"How dare you?" he peered at me, beginning to realize, his mouth open with astonishment.

"Yes, it's Larry!"

"My God!" he whispered. "What are you doing here?"

"I've been living here for months. *Please,* Papa, please, leave now! We're blowing up Douzy in a matter of minutes," I looked at my watch, "eleven minutes exactly. Nothing can stop it. The explosives are all laid. The fuses are working. It'll blow up. Rilly as well."

"But why are you here? Dressed as a peasant? And you— that's Gaston, isn't it?"

"Yes, sir," the words slipped out involuntarily.

"That gun!" he seemed stupefied. "Are you in the army?"

"Yes, but that doesn't matter, Father. I joined up in America, I've been trained in Britain. I was landed in France to blow up Douzy—so get out—*now*—"

"But why? We've had such good relations—"

"It's all a blind. All *this*, Father!" With a sweep I indicated the Rilly Pyramid. "You've been kept quiet—anesthetized if you like—to stop you finding out what's been going on in Douzy!"

"But," still bewildered, "Douzy's been closed for years."

"It *hasn't*, Papa." I couldn't help adding bitterly, "Thanks to the policy of keeping everyone happy, the Germans have been able to divert suspicion from anything that's happening in Douzy."

"But what? Why blow it?"

"You never thought to check?"

"Why should I? Check what?"

"It's *your* pyramid, Papa. The Germans hoodwinked you by—"

"Nine minutes to go!" cried Gaston.

"But *what?*" cried my father.

"Douzy has enough stocks of chemical German gas to destroy London—and enough rockets in the tunnel at Rilly to see that they can *get* delivered to London. Now, Father, will you go?" And turning to the edge of the gallery, I shouted, "Run, everyone—you've only got a few minutes left before this place goes up in smoke." My father had turned whiter than the chalk walls around him. He looked at me uncomprehendingly. His face had aged, not by wrinkles but by the realization of truth.

"What have I done?" he asked hoarsely. "Why didn't you warn me, tell me?"

"I couldn't. Everything I was doing was too secret. I was under orders. Run for it, Papa. I can't come out with you." I knew that all workmen at Rilly wore identification tags and somebody like myself would never pass the main gate—especially as nothing had happened yet. To all intents and purposes the exit and entrance into both pyramids were perfectly normal. "I'll make my own way," I explained.

"What have I done? My God, what have I done?" He asked over and over again. "If I'm to blame," his face crumpled almost into tears. "You could have warned me," he cried.

"I couldn't."

"You could."

"Eight minutes," said Gaston. "Come on."

Then in a split second I grabbed my father's shoulder, and in the old French way, I kissed him on the cheeks and cried, "Good luck, Papa! Run. Now. Run as you've never run before."

I might have been kissing a statue. He looked at me—through me—as though he didn't recognize me, didn't *want* to recognize me, as though I was an unwelcome interloper, the bearer of bad news. As I crouched and started off to run toward the tunnel, across it, then up the steps in the shaft, I looked back at him. He was standing there, refusing to budge, just moaning over and over again, "What have I done? What have I done?"

"Seven minutes! We'll just make it if we run like hell!"

Once near the end of the Rilly gallery we put on gas masks and then squirmed underneath the V-2s and into the second gallery. As we crossed the tunnel I saw four men in gas masks run toward me. Because I was also in a gas mask, they didn't know who I was. Gaston gave them one burst and we ran on.

"You first!" I shouted to Gaston, and he didn't have the strength to argue either.

I had no time to take a last look into Douzy Pyramid, no time even to give more than a fleeting thought to the times we had spent there. For no reason I remembered the visit of Vance, the owner of the *Globe*. Why have I thought of him, I wondered, my immediate horizon bounded by the feet of the panting Gaston climbing above me. I heard him shout, "Safe to take off our masks!" And of course the tear gas was below us by now. I pulled mine off, dropping it as I did so. The flashlight gave me a welcome light, and then far up—hidden at first because the steps were on a slanting shaft—I saw the welcome circle of distant light.

Neither of us could talk, we were exhausted—by retching as much as by climbing. Then ten or fifteen rungs from the top I almost fell. The rung ahead of me, on which I depended to haul my feet up from below, parted in my hands. I started to fall right down the shaft, arms and legs scrambling for a rung to grasp. To try to use my back to gain a purchase. My flashlight was wrenched from its hook. I lost my grip on my Schmeisser, it clattered below as it hit rung after rung.

"Gaston!" I screamed as a red-hot pain shot through my left arm and shoulder. Until then he didn't even realize what had happened.

I must have had barely three minutes left to live. And the pain shot through my arm so that I could hardly bend it.

"Gaston!" I cried again, but he was already clattering down the iron rungs until he was directly above me.

"Twisted my shoulder and arm! Lost my light. Shine yours down and I think I can make it."

To be honest, I wasn't sure I could. I had fallen five rungs and was badly bruised. It's true that as we neared the end of the shaft the air was a little better, and that made breathing easier, but it required enormous physical strength to pull myself up with only one arm.

"Here," said Gaston, "hang on to this." He threw down his length of rope, one end tied round his waist, then said, "Can you tie the other end round your waist? Then I can help to take the strain."

It was impossible with one arm—and however much I wanted to, I just couldn't use the left arm and shoulder.

"You'd better get up top," I said. "We can't have more than one minute left."

"Shut up," he said. Holding on with one hand, he hauled the other end of the rope up, made a loop, then cried, "Try and get it over your shoulders and under your arms. Then I'll help to pull you up."

Somehow I managed to wriggle the loop underneath my armpits. "Good," he cried. "Now let's try it."

Laboriously I used one hand. Certainly Gaston was taking most of the weight so that I was able to make slow, if agonizingly painful, progress.

"But we'll never make it," I gasped.

We didn't—but we didn't die.

When we were ten rungs from the top, the whole of Rilly Mountain seemed to tremble. Deep, deep below us was a terrible thunder. Then the earth shuddered as though in an earthquake, so that all around us was a temporary feeling of impotence. Another clap of thunder—much nearer this time—was heralded with more violent shuddering; flakes of the side walls disintegrated, and though nothing happened above me, I could hear the noise of falling rocks below us. One of the rungs above me suddenly loosened. I yelled to Gaston, "It's all coming out!" As he helped to pull me up, the rungs below me gave way, fell to the ground with an ugly ringing noise as they hit each rung below. Worse, I was left dangling, held only by one arm and Gaston's lifeline. Trying to synchronize our movements, he yelled, "Try to move with me! Now! Up!"

Slowly, with agonizing pain, one useless arm and shoulder dangling beside me, I pushed with my feet against the opposite wall of the shaft so that I was able to make one superhuman effort and put my feet onto the rung above the one that had given way.

Again I had to repeat the twisting maneuver in order to raise myself just one rung at a time. And always I could hear vague rumblings of rocks below, falling into the shaft; once I vomited—from bad air or fear, I don't know which. I suddenly felt as though I was going to keel over; I grabbed the rungs with my one good arm as though my hand were welded to the iron step.

The moment passed. Miraculously I made one more step up the ladder, though it didn't reach the top of the shaft— but Gaston's bulk was still above me, making all the difference. The air had changed too. It was as though I had, at one given moment, managed to surface when drowning and found my head above water. The separation of bad air and good air was as clearly divisible as water from air.

After that everything seemed easier. Not only was the air purer, the shaft was narrower so that I was able to use my back more and more against the rungs, and this helped me to take the strain. Finally Gaston scrambled out of the hole, grabbed the rope, and hauled me up and onto dry land.

"We made it, thanks to you," we both lay gasping on the mountaintop.

"How's the shoulder?" He lit two cigarettes, one for me.

"Hell—but not broken. God, I was scared in that damn shaft."

"Me too!"

"What do you think happened?"

"There was an explosion, all right," said Gaston. "No doubt about that. When I felt that first shudder I thought we were both going to slide down."

"I believe it's the slant in the safety shaft that saved us from being blown up," I said, and engineering experts later proved this theory to be correct. Because the shaft was slanting from the top of Rilly Mountain, it meant that the nearer we got to the top of the shaft, the farther away we were from the Douzy Pyramid.

"But what about the Rilly tunnel?"

"That's different. We've blown the *contents* up, not collapsed the tunnel. Which you couldn't have done anyway."

"How's your shoulder?" he asked again.

"Absolutely hell," I repeated.

"More work for Dr. Benoit," he sighed with mock despair. "You certainly keep him busy."

The shoulder wasn't a bad injury. It might have been a collar bone dislocated, I couldn't tell.

"I'll make some sort of sling to keep it tight to the chest," said Gaston. "That'll save the pain."

We had no means of telling what had happened apart from the sound of the explosion. I said to Gaston, "Hope my father got away."

"I hope so."

"You sound doubtful."

"I don't know," he hesitated. "I had an awful feeling as we rushed off that he didn't *want* to leave."

"Funny—I thought that too. O God! what a damn awful life this is!"

We never did get back to the base of the mountain. Well, not until four days later.

* * *

I had arranged with La Châtelaine—in her role as cou-
rier for Olivia's messages—to climb the hill if she could, or
else send another member of the Resistance, at 3:00 P.M.,
for it was essential that I let London know as soon as possible. Yet both of us were afraid to go down the hill too
quickly in case we were challenged. Though the hilltop at
Rilly seemed quiet enough on that warm August afternoon, we knew that all hell must have been let loose
among the Germans down below if the V-2s and Rilly had
been blown up.

Yet on the surface nothing had apparently happened.
Unlike the derailment at Rilly station or the fire at the
church, both of which had produced chaos visible to all, the
violent explosions in the pyramid and the tunnel had been
shrouded in secrecy. Many Germans might well have
thought they had been caused by gas. Those who had escaped from Rilly would soon be spreading rumors all over
the area. Yet even to them everything on the surface
seemed tranquil. It was so quiet that even Gaston and I
found it difficult to recapture the seconds—those few fearful seconds—when we were all but trapped in the shaft.
The earth had literally trembled at that moment.

"But we're out now!" still filling our lungs with deep
breaths as though to make up for lost time. And it was thus
that La Châtelaine found us.

Even she was puffing when she strode over the brow of
the hill, barely a quarter of an hour behind the rendezvous
time. Of course she didn't know what had happened. She
had no idea of the magnitude of the operation we had been
told to undertake. Nor could she yet know whether my father had escaped or perished or was even involved. How
could she? Escape from what? Possibly she didn't even
know that an explosion had taken place—or why.

"But all I can say is that something big has happened,"
she sat down on a patch of scrub, surrounded by bramble
and gorse, a remarkable figure to look at, heavy boots
peeping out of her "working" corduroy trousers. And her
green felt hat, hiding wispy hair; *and* a cabochon star-
sapphire ring the size of a pigeon's egg.

"I don't know what's happened, but the Germans are running round in circles as though the bottom's dropped out of their world. They're arresting anyone they can find."

"Any news of Papa?" I ventured.

"Oh, they won't arrest *him,*" said Grandma firmly. "But you two—I knew since the day you landed in our field that you'd be engaged in a big project, apart from the train, and I'm proud of you both. But," with an almost severe glare, as though to act the part she had always been determined to play, she added, "but don't spoil everything by getting caught." Then looking at my bad shoulder, she asked almost gruffly, "Hurt yourself?"

"I twisted my shoulder. It's okay—nothing broken—but it hurts like hell."

"Look after yourself," was her gruff way of expressing her fondness for me. "And you'll want something to eat. Here!" She opened a brown khaki haversack, often used by women to carry their gas masks. "I've brought some sandwiches. A couple of *baguettes,* straight from the Home Farm, and a couple of bottles of red wine. I'll take the message to Olivia right away. Will you promise me one thing, Larry—and you, Gaston—to stay here, in hiding, till I come to fetch you, till we know it's safe?"

"Unless I get orders from London," I promised her, "I will."

"That's understood then. *Bon! A bientôt!*"

"Let me know if," I hesitated, "you have any news of Papa."

She looked at me suspiciously, but finally refrained from questioning me, just said quietly, "I will."

With that Grandma strode down the hill and out of sight. Purposely I had not given her a written message to transmit. I *knew* that behind the apparent quiet, the Germans must be going frantic—and that was just the time to pick up all the Frenchmen and search them. So I told her the message verbally—it was safer that way. And it was only two words anyway—"Mission accomplished." She would remember that.

When we saw her sturdy figure disappear below the rim of the hill, we opened the wine, drinking from the bottle. It was extraordinary, really, how now that it was all over, I was suddenly hungry and the earth smelled good as I seized a *baguette*. In the heat of high afternoon birds were darting among the bushes, even some wasps came buzzing suspiciously close to us. It was as though the war below were being enacted on another planet. Here we were at peace—having a picnic, just as Sonia and I had planned on that day when we drove from Rolle.

We stayed on the mountain for four days and nights. My shoulder gave me hell, but there was no way I could get to a doctor. On the other hand, I was able to rest it. We made a rough sling out of a length of the rope, wrapped the part where the arm would lie in an old pullover, then pulled the sling tight so that my shoulder couldn't move. There was no break, of that I was sure, and the best cure for a sprain or a bad twist or even a dislocation was not to use the injured limb at all.

For four days we had no news. We had hoped that by venturing to the edge of the hill overlooking Rilly and the entrance to the tunnel, we might be able to see something of what was happening, but it didn't work out that way. It wasn't as though we could look down the face of a cliffside. Rilly sloped down from the top of the hill, and it was covered with scrub, trees which effectively blocked any view, even of the village itself. Had we climbed halfway down it might have been possible, but with my bad shoulder—and the danger of a nationwide search—that was too risky, especially as curiosity would have been our only motive.

It was cold at night, but we did the only thing possible—made quilts of dried brushwood. Anyway both of us were used to sleeping rough. Nothing could have been worse that the days I spent sleeping in a Scottish ditch. And though we weren't exactly living off the fat of the land, Grandma had provided enough bread and ham to last us a few days. We were a little short of wine. But that was our own fault—after Grandma had gone down the hill, we had

drunk a bottle between us to celebrate. We felt we deserved it.

Around three thirty on what I now know to be the fourth
day on the hill, we ate the last of the bread and ham and
drank the last of the wine. We were not quite sure of the
date; Gaston said it was August 27. I thought it was the
twenty-eighth, but it was by no means certain, for the days
and nights on the mountain seemed to fuse into one long
day. Sometimes—out of boredom or exhaustion?—we slept
in the afternoons. Sometimes we stayed awake with cold
during the night. The measurement of time had in a few
hours been eroded so that we could only guess what day it
was. Our situation was made more bizarre because we
were blanketed in complete silence. We might have expected the sound of distant gunfire, even rifle shots. Nothing!

Then on this day we did hear distant sounds, nothing we
could distinguish, but far below, sounds masked by trees
as well as distance. Then we heard shouting and noise as
though the Germans were rounding up hostages or taking
prisoners for work camps. It was impossible to identify the
sound, it was so vague.

There was nothing vague about the next sound though.
We had been straining our ears in vain, even behind
bushes and trees where we had made our rough shelter,
when my breath seemed to stop as our own silence was
broken by a sinister, unexpected sound—that of feet approaching: big feet, men's feet, more than one man, feet
crackling on dry wood just behind the trees. Then the most
frightening sound of all—German guttural accents, *"Ja!
Das ist sehr gut!"* and phrases I couldn't understand. Gaston had silently picked up his stolen German machine pistol. I had dropped mine in the shaft, but I still had my .45
and loaded it with a full clip of bullets, plus one in the
breech. I slipped back the safety catch and froze behind a
tree. Maybe they would pass us by unnoticed. I saw ahead
of them—and us—our empty wine bottles, our litter, some
paper. It wouldn't mean anything to them—at least I

hoped it wouldn't. I couldn't tell how many Germans there were, but if they spotted us, well, we would kill as many as we could before they killed one or both of us.

What, I wondered, had brought this patrol up to the top of the normally uninhabited Rilly Mountain? Why so suddenly, so unexpectedly? Frozen immobile, there was nothing to do but wait. I was suddenly thinking, Fancy doing all this, achieving all this, only to end up on the wrong side of a damn German machine gun.

In my imagination the stamp of approaching footsteps sounded like death knells, as my twisted shoulder, imprisoned in one position, became knotted with a cramp brought on by fear. I'm a prisoner of fear, I thought for no reason, shivering as the mountainside was suddenly invaded by aliens, bent on killing us. My right hand still gripped my automatic, but for a moment panic struck, as I realized that my right hand was also locked with cramp; locked in a grip nothing could pry open, frozen to one position. I couldn't say anything. Pleading eyes turned to Gaston, eyes looking to him, then to my right hand. He saw. Without moving his feet, cradling his machine pistol in one arm as carefully as a baby, he quietly prized open my fingers. The pain was excruciating—but he did open the fingers, gently. The only thing neither of us thought of was that the hand, bereft of its clasping fingers, was for a few seconds as useless as a dummy's. Without warning my snub-nosed automatic crashed onto the brushwood. *Crash* may sound like a big word for a small steel implement, but it sounded like an almighty crash—to the Germans too. I heard a hoarse cry, *"Was ist das?"* and then as I could imagine German submachine guns going up to the "ready" position to fire, Gaston opened up at the unseen target behind the woods. Figures—how many? What arms? Hidden on the other side of the screen of trees. I waited for the sound of anguished wounded, the reply of massive German firepower which could butcher us, the unseen target behind the trees. It didn't come. Instead, as I was thinking that Gaston had missed them, as I managed to bend down and—cramp forgotten—pick up my automatic, there was a cry totally unexpected.

"Kamerad!" shouted voices, and one in French added, "We have no guns!"

"It's a trap!" I whispered. "It *must* be!"

"Don't worry," Gaston pushed a new magazine into his Schmeisser. "One move out of those bastards and I'll fire."

"Kamerad!" cried the Germans, and then as we waited behind the trees, our position identified to them by the pattern of Gaston's firing, I saw a sight I never thought I would see. Through the trees five Germans approached, arms and hands held high, shrieking as though in unison, *"Kamerad! Kamerad!"*

"They're not fooling," I whispered to Gaston.

I stepped out into the open, motioned them with my automatic to keep their hands up.

"You check that they've got no guns, Gaston, and watch it—there's still five of them to two of us."

Yes, despite my instinct for preservation, I knew immediately that they meant no harm. They couldn't be deserters—the Germans *never* deserted. Yet why the hell were they shouting *"Kamerad!"*—and unarmed? They would never get away with it.

An unexpected thought trickled into a brain dulled by the pain and inactivity during the four empty days and nights. *What had happened during those last four days and nights?* In the world? In France? At Rilly? Our last radio news had told us that de Gaulle had landed in France, that the Resistance had taken over the main government offices in Paris. Could it be that the Allies had already taken Paris? It's so hard, when you have been apparently losing a war for so long, to believe *any* good news. I dismissed the idea. It was impossible to have reached Paris so quickly. Yet *why* were these Germans wandering around a lonely mountain, unarmed, surrendering? Suddenly the truth snapped into a lethargic brain.

"Anyone speak French?" I demanded, signaling to the men to lower their arms.

"Oui, monsieur," said one eagerly.

"What's happened? Why this—this *'Kamerad'?"*

He looked at me in astonishment.

"But, sir—you didn't know?"

"Know *what,* for God's sake?"

"Your American General Patton has marched into Reims. This morning. The fighting in this sector is over."

I couldn't believe it, Gaston looked open-mouthed.

"And that's not all, sir," the German was eager to tell us everything, "two days ago de Gaulle entered Paris. In Italy the Allies have taken Florence—and Mussolini has been executed."

"But the war—that's still going on? Germany is still fighting?"

"Yes, sir," he said eagerly. "But I speak for everyone of hundreds of German troops in this area who have already been sent east in case the Americans arrive. We don't want to be sent to the Russian front—so, will you accept our surrender? *Please, sir!"*

All at once I couldn't stop laughing. Nervous reaction, I suppose, to the hell of that trip to blow up Douzy. They laughed too. With relief. They, like us, had been through hell. One of them offered us a piece of sausage—as a sort of peace offering.

I did want to ask one question: "Did anything happen in Rilly? In the pyramid?"

"Many dead," answered the German soberly, almost guiltily. "I don't know what happened, but the tunnel has been blown up, I do know that. And I heard that the pyramid at Douzy—I'm not sure, I always thought it was empty—but there was an explosion there too. At least that was what I heard."

For a few moments we all looked at each other, enemies, yes, still—hell, young men sent by others to kill us all while someone at the end of a Morse transmitter was telling us to kill them.

"Monsieur Gaston Pagniez will accept your surrender," I said, pointing gravely to Gaston. "Now, if you say it's safe, we can go down the hill."

There was, however, one more visitor to the top of Rilly

Mountain. She came into view a section at a time, because the last few steps of the path she had taken were steep, so that Olivia's face appeared first, then her blouse, then a dark colored skirt, legs, finally shoes.

As she waved, ignoring the Germans, Gaston ran forward to greet her, and he took her in his arms and kissed her gently. I wondered at that moment how long it would be before I could take my beloved Sonia into my arms and crush her with love.

The Germans stood huddled together, as though gaining strength from each other, as I kissed Olivia on both cheeks and said, smiling, "How does it feel to be free? To walk outside?"

"Wonderful," she said. But there was no smile in her voice.

"Is Grandma all right?"

"She is," still the grave warning tone in her voice, "but she didn't feel up to the task of coming to see you—"

"Task?"

"Yes, Larry dear." Olivia was never one to spar with words, she was too forthright. "Your father—perhaps you've already guessed—and we sometimes forget you know, he was La Châtelaine's son. He died very bravely. We only heard yesterday."

I sighed. He *was* my father, but distance, time, events, war had in a curious way separated us, made him a stranger to me. I don't mean that cruelly: we both loved each other as much as we had always done; but it was almost as though I were being told bad news of a distant relative I hardly knew. It was unfair of me to think thus, but in those first moments it was perhaps better; at least it helped to exorcise any of the guilt I felt at having helped to cause his death.

And to exorcise too the last few seconds of our only meeting since Pearl Harbor—the look of anguish in his face when I confronted him, the near sob in his voice when he cried, "What have I done?"

"We know any of the details?" I asked heavily.

"Most of the men escaped from the Rilly Pyramid. And

they all said the same thing: that your father—in a way my father too, he was so wonderful to me—he refused to move until the others had gone first. The last few were too late, it seems. About a dozen men, your father and his close friends, were there when the pyramid blew up at the base. Apparently it wasn't a very big explosion, but it rocked the sides and the whole thing fell inward."

"Thanks, Olivia, for coming to tell me. Did poor Grandma take it very badly?"

"Yes. We forget she's an old lady. She's been sustained in a way by all this excitement—it's pumped adrenaline into her day after day—but now, it's virtually over. She's still in the Misses B and B house"—without thinking she used our own description of that much-loved cottage—"and Aubergine is with her. La Châtelaine is spending a few days in bed, but she'll be all right when she gets over the shock."

"I'll go to see her as soon as I can. But first of all I must get into Reims and check in with the colonel in command of the U.S. unit."

"I thought—SOE?—" asked Gaston.

"That's true," I said. "But as Americans—and as a last hope in case I was caught—I was also attached to Com Z, the American communications section. I must get a lift there as soon as I can and report in."

"I'll come with you," said Gaston. And awkwardly he added, "I'm so sorry about your father. He was such a fine man, Larry. I don't know what to say."

"Thanks," I sighed. "There's nothing anyone can say. It had to be, I suppose, something else to live with. Let's go." And sadly, if victoriously, we made our way down the hillside, a strange assorted party: a Frenchman—the man who had been my chauffeur and my mother's lover, a wonderful Jewish girl betrayed by another Frenchwoman, a handful of Germans, and an American.

"It takes all sorts to fight a war," I said, but I said it to myself.

53

REIMS WAS LIKE A NEW WORLD, one we had forgotten, the dreary twilight world of subdued people, hardly daring to speak, every guarded word or furtive action couched in fear. The French had for so long been oppressed, *suppressed,* that at first they had been almost afraid to shout their joy, even talk aloud. Then, as we reached the capital of Champagne and handed over our prisoners to an American patrol, the bubble burst.

The Germans had gone! Run away! The tricolor flew everywhere, appearing so quickly it was almost as though the flags and bunting had been kept hidden by men and women of faith and hope, to be brought out when the nightmare was over.

At first I felt almost ill at ease as Gaston and I walked along the streets toward the market place behind the boulevard Lundy. Some pretty girls rushed forward with flowers, and when one tried to kiss me I drew back, suddenly aware that I hadn't brushed my teeth for four days. I am sure I looked filthy, but so did many people after a day's honest toil. The difference was that I *felt* dirty.

We went into a small bar and ordered two draft beers. After the waiter had sliced off the froth with his wooden slat, we both drank the half-pint in one gulp. It was so cold, so beautifully tangy and sharp, that we both smacked our lips at the same time—loudly.

The barman looked up, laughed at the sound, and said, "Tastes good, eh?"

"Nectar!" I cried, and the words broke the spell of reserve. The barman hadn't noticed that I looked dirty, that I smelled, that my beard was untrimmed.

"Come on," I cried to Gaston. "I'm going to shave off my beard. You could do with a shave too."

We both went into a small barbershop and I felt a new man when we emerged.

"Let's see if we can get a square meal at the Boulingrin."

"Like this?" Gaston might have shaved, but he still looked dubiously at our old clothes. We hadn't been able to change *them.*

"Sure. The Astells regard it as our local bistro."

"I'm not an Astell."

"You are now." I put an arm on his shoulder. "In all but name—just as much a member of the family as Olivia has always been. Come on."

Monsieur Leleu was delighted to see us and, perfect gentleman that he was, found a table for us with a whispered, "Steaks—beautiful ones—for you both? With *pommes frites?*"

As we nodded, he added, "I was so sorry to hear about your father. So many fine men and women have died for our country. But it's good to see *you* back—and alive."

Sitting at our corner table, a dish of *pommes frites* dusted with salt in front of us, we tucked into a couple of the largest steaks I had seen for years.

"Not bad, eh?" I looked at Gaston.

He laughed. "I'd forgotten about steaks. I'd forgotten what they looked like, never mind what they tasted like."

We washed the meal down with a bottle of Bouzy *rouge,* hard to find these days.

"I kept it specially for old friends," said Leleu. "Just a few bottles," and later, "No, no, Monsieur Astell. I wouldn't hear of it. This is on the house—to celebrate!"

As I thanked Monsieur Leleu, he apoligized for not having any good coffee, so we skipped the ersatz substitute and were starting on large glasses of the finest *marc de champagne* when suddenly I heard a yell, "Larry! Larry!"

I almost knocked down the small square table with its red-and-white-checked cloth as I tried to swivel round. I knew that voice anywhere.

"Uncle Oregon!"

And there he was, not only my uncle, but my mentor, the man who had founded the *Paris American,* who had given me my first job as a junior reporter, who had guided my footsteps from there to the *Globe.*

Gaston dragged a chair from the nearest table. Oregon looked as though he would prefer to sit down—and for that matter, so did we. After all, we *had* spent four days and nights on a mountaintop.

"I'd no idea you were here," I said. "I heard a couple of years ago from Mama in New York that you'd been interned in Fresnes, and that you'd managed to get one letter through to New York. After that, not a word. It's wonderful to see you. And looking so fit—"

He wasn't that fit really. The twinkle in his eyes was still there, but dulled. The halo of curly white hair had thinned down and what was left was more straggly than curly. And he had lost a great deal of weight.

"But you're still a chain-smoker," I laughed.

"Started the day I was released. The Resistance took us to Paris, I only stopped to buy some Gauloises, then I bummed a lift here as soon as it was safe. Yes, I will have a *marc,*" he said as Monsieur Leleu produced the bottle. "Tell me—how did *you* get back here so quickly?"

"It's a long story," I laughed. "Actually, I've been here for weeks. I'm in the U.S. Army. I joined up after Pearl Harbor."

He must have looked puzzled, for he asked, "Odd sort of uniform you're wearing—farmer's clothes!"

"Let's just say I'm on leave. I'll tell you the whole story one day soon."

"And the *Globe?*"

"Not a word since I joined up. Have you seen Grandma?"

"Have I! I had a job finding her, but I tracked her down. Larry, I hear she's been running an airfield for the Resistance."

I nodded. "But how is she now?"

He lit another cigarette, stubbed the first one out on the ashtray. "Very depressed, as you can imagine. She must have taken a hard knock when she heard about your father—especially as she hadn't the faintest idea whether or not *I* was alive."

"But you are," I cried. "And what do you plan to do next? Take over the running of the vineyards?"

"Me a vigneron!" His face crinkled into that special twinkling smile I remembered so well. "Never! I'd make a mess of it. Besides, La Châtelaine tells me that Gaston here has been running the vineyards better than any of us ever did."

Gaston was hardly the blushing type, but he *did* look pleased and said, "Thank you," as we poured out a final glass.

"Well," I asked, "what *are* you going to do?"

He looked at me with genuine astonishment.

"I'm off to Paris of course—to reopen the *Paris American*. What else? It'll sell like hotcakes to the American troops," adding with a twinkle, "Want to rejoin the old firm?"

I shook my head, and replied, "Thanks for the offer, but before anything else, I've got some unfinished business to attend to."

"Such as?"

"Getting married. Remember a young lady called Sonia?"

"Ah! Darling Sonia. But she is married." It was more of a statement than a question.

"Annulled. It's an old Vatican trick—if you've got enough money. We're free—both of us. As soon as I get permission from the army brass, I'm off to spend my leave in Switzerland and get married."

"Bully for you! Your father—" He paused, suddenly embarrassed at the unthinking use of the word, then hurried on, "Well, I've always thought that when you two were caught in what must have been very delectable *flagrante delicto,* you should have been allowed to marry. It's always a pity when parents stand in the way of young love."

"And do you remember Olivia?"

"Of course. That beautiful creamy complexion. Is she all right?"

"She certainly is. She's been working in the Resistance as a radio operator. She's getting married soon."

"Seems to be catching."

"To Gaston."

"Well, I never," Oregon sounded really surprised. "I thought, well, what about Guy?"

I explained the ways that all our lives had been divided. It was the first time that Oregon knew of Guy's activities or that Anna had been living in Switzerland with Sonia.

Just before Oregon got up to leave, he said, "I'll be staying here for two or three days. But what about *your* future? Now that your father has died, will *you* be taking over the business?"

"I don't think so. In theory my job on the *Globe* has been kept on for me—but I've also got an idea for a book. I can't really decide anything until I've seen Sonia, had time to think things out."

Oregon said, "Maybe Guy would like the job?"

"Working with Gaston's wife? Come off it, Uncle!"

"Hadn't thought of that."

"I was only joking," I explained. "In fact Guy's married to the secret service. His immediate boss in Switzerland, Allen Dulles, has been doing undercover work—brilliant man, lots of guts, and Guy has been working with him."

"But that's going to stop now."

"It seems that Allen Dulles—who has a brother, Foster—is being tipped to head a new organization, hasn't even got a name yet, though it might be called the CIA—stands for Central Intelligence Agency. Guy's been offered a big job with Dulles. He loves that line of business."

"Isn't it sad," Oregon said, "our beautiful, wonderful Douzy—and nobody really wants it."

"That does include you," I couldn't help saying.

"I know. I was the first. Ah, well! Where are you staying?"

"Nowhere. We've been living rough. Probably I'll spend a couple of nights in the BOQ."

"What on earth's that?"

"Bachelor Officers Quarters."

"Why does everything have to be in initials?"

"It's habit," I laughed. "And after the BOQ," I added, "it's Switzerland."

"So that"—though he looked older, Oregon's eyes were still twinkling and he still had his infectious laughter—"so that you can finally make an honest woman of Sonia."

Later that day, after Gaston went to meet Olivia, I stopped an American MP—military policeman—who looked twice at my disheveled, unkempt appearance, until I used the magic formula "Department QJ," the code name used for both the OSS and the SOE men reporting after finishing a project. It gave them the highest priority and came under Com Z, which ran the communications network.

The officer who greeted me was a Colonel Nolan, and before anything else he offered me my first cup of real American coffee for months. He provided me with a selection of uniforms, the toothbrush I so badly needed, the warmest of baths in which to lie soaking, and he had obviously heard of my name, for after I had cleaned up he announced, "I've been told to give you all the help I can."

I appreciated that. He was surprised to learn that, though American, I actually lived near Reims, and he very kindly drove me to see our home. On the way I asked him how I could go about getting some leave after I had been debriefed. After all, though Germany was still fighting, virtually all of France had now been liberated. Nolan promised me that he would be able to fix me up with a trip to Paris or even back to New York. He was a little dubious when I said that I just wanted to drive a car to Switzerland to meet the girl I was going to marry.

"Switzerland! Hold up, major," he said. "I'd have no

problem lending you a car to go to Paris, but, hell—I don't
know whether I'm *permitted* to send army property into a
neutral country. And then there's the problem of gas."

"Don't worry, colonal," I said. "I've got all the gas I
need—and my own car. We hid it before the Germans took
over."

"Well, that makes a difference. Two weeks long enough?
I've already received leave notice for about a dozen guys in
QJ—orders to grant it immediately they report in."

"You can't make it three weeks?"

"I guess so. But be back on time," adding, "Don't let's
forget, major, that though France has virtually been liberated, there's going to be some tough fighting before the
war's over. There're several million Nazis going to fight to
protect Germany itself."

"Don't worry," I promised Nolan, "I'll be back."

Our Château de Douzy was a shambles. I was horrified,
almost sick, as I took the colonel on a "conducted tour" of
the lovely old place. The German vandals who had been
billeted there had behaved like pigs. "Officers and gentlemen—in theory," I commented bitterly to Nolan, who immediately ordered a patrol of men to be sent from Reims to
help clear up the mess. Plates and glasses had been
smashed. Remnants of old food had been strewn in the living room, on the floor, even on the chairs, and of course
there were empty champagne bottles by the dozen.

When Nolan discovered that my family actually produced their own champagne as a way of earning a living—
"And a famous champagne too," he added—I had to open a
couple of bottles and, despite the ghost of Papa haunting
the house, welcome the colonel in the traditional manner.

"Astell champagne," he tasted it reverently. "I never
thought—"

"*Pardon,* monsieur," the voice was quavering as Jean,
the old butler, who had materialized from nowhere, offered
the colonel more champagne and then, when I embraced
him, promptly burst into tears. I remembered that Jean
had remained at the château when the Germans comman-

deered it—a sensible move, at least it meant he had been
able to keep an eye on the place. But a sudden reunion, the
relief, the death of my father a few days previously, and
then the sight of me in uniform—it had all been too much
for the old man.

Tearfully—but still professionally—he opened another
bottle, then Madame Robert, the farmer's wife from the
Home Farm, arrived carrying two hams. Soon Monsieur
Roland, the *patron* of the Café des Sports in the village,
came to pay his respects, and after that, so it seemed, almost the entire village streamed in. Gaston and Olivia
turned up. Everyone was excited at the thought of their
newfound freedom—nothing could dim that—yet while
Colonel Nolan stood smiling and drinking amid the "foreign" throng of villagers, Roland tapped on the glass with
a pencil for silence and then, in a polite but muted toast,
cried, "To *Messieurs Astell—père, frère, et fils.*"

Father, brother, and son!

They were welcoming me back, of course. But they were
also paying their last respects to Papa, with a mention too
for Oregon. Colonel Nolan, who could barely stop showing
his admiration for the house, even in its filthy state, was
standing in the conservatory, where the geraniums still
bloomed, climbing up the back wall.

"Lovely, isn't it?" I pointed toward the dell and, below
it, the orchard.

"Breathtaking!" Then he saw on the other side of the horizon a pile of blackened masonry, the sharp edges of ruins
jutting out like decayed teeth.

"Douzy church," I said, "and you see that girl over
there?" I pointed her out. "She's a French girl who suffered terribly at the hands of the Gestapo, but do you
know, she escaped, we helped her, and then she spent *two
years* hidden in the belfry of the church, sending radio
messages to SOE in London. That's *real* bravery. Finally,
the Germans set fire to the church to try and burn her
out."

Nolan looked at Olivia with admiration. Then his eye

caught a movement halfway up the dell. "There's an old gal cycling toward us," he said. "Another villager?"

"Only one woman in Champagne cycles like that," I answered, amused. "That's my grandmother. She's quite a character, and known all over the Champagne area as La Châtelaine. She's around eighty, she cycles everywhere; and everyone, including the Germans, is terrified of her."

"She does look a little," politely, "unusual."

"She is, she's a hundred percent French. My grandfather, who died long ago, was American, but it's always been Grandma who runs the show."

"Are *you* frightened of her?" asked Nolan with a laugh.

"Terrified!" I laughed back. "Or was. She's beginning to mellow a bit, and though I haven't seen her since my father died, I imagine she took it hard."

A few minutes later La Châtelaine arrived and, after leaning her ancient bike against the stable doors, marched in followed by Aubergine. The colonel stared in wonder when I introduced her to him. She was dressed in her corduroy trousers, her usual green felt hat, and on her blouse she boasted an enormous emerald brooch. Her knotted, gnarled fingers were covered with rings.

As she kissed me, I said gently, "I'm so sorry, Grandma, so sorry—"

"I know, Larry," she was more emotional than I had even seen her. "It's war. It's horrible. But he died bravely—my son died a hero—and you have a father you can be proud of. At least that's something."

"My respects, ma'am," Colonel Nolan, who had a pleasant smile, took her hand, "and I'm arranging for my boys to come and clean up your place."

"Thank you, colonel. *Sales Boches!* I want to get the smell of Germans out of the house." And to me she added, "I'm very selfish, Larry. I know how you must be feeling."

"I understand, Grandma," I didn't want to elaborate on the events which had taken place at Douzy and Rilly. They would soon be buried with honors in legend. "You know what Oregon said? That if all Frenchmen had been as loyal as Papa, France would never have lost the war."

I turned to Colonal Nolan and said, "You did promise me I could go on leave if I provided my own transport?"

"Sure. You'll have to be debriefed, but that won't take long, will it?"

I didn't think so. Department QJ would handle it, but I did ask if there was any chance of getting a phone call through from the military switchboard at Reims to Switzerland, and Nolan didn't seem to think there would be any problem.

I made a suggestion: I would return with him right away to Reims, make my report to QJ, then phone through to Rolle. "And tomorrow," I said, "I'm going to show you the sight of a lifetime—if you can spare an hour or two. We're going to have an official unveiling of the Hisp."

"Hisp?"

"Short for Hispano-Suiza, the finest car of its make in the world when it was built. More than a car. A twelve-cylinder battleship. Then we'll have lunch." I turned to Jean, "Can you and Madame Robert prepare a scratch meal?"

"Easily, sir," Jean said eagerly. "And if we knock down the wall before lunch, I could get some of the thirty-three vintage."

"You have to knock down a wall to get at it?" Nolan was baffled.

"It's the finest vintage since the early twenties—and my father not only walled up and hid his favorite car, he walled up ten thousand bottles of thirty-three to stop the Germans drinking it. They never discovered where it was. We'll crack some bottles tomorrow."

That evening—it was still Monday, the twenty-eighth, the day Reims was liberated—I spoke to Sonia, asking my very first question, "Have the annulment documents finally come through?"

"Yes, they have. Are you all right? I've been so worried."

"It's all over, Sonia. It's all over."

"When shall I see you? I wouldn't be allowed to visit France—not now. But you? I can hardly wait."

"On Thursday," I promised. "Tomorrow I'm going to get the Hisp from the cellars. I'll have to give Gaston the day after that to tune it up. And then, darling Sonia, at dawn on Thursday morning, I'll be on my way. And, tell me—how long will it take us to get married? The formalities, the paperwork?"

"I'll be round at the Town Hall in Rolle tomorrow morning, first thing," her voice was not only laughing, it was singing with happiness. "Oh, darling, is it *really* over—is it really possible, is it *true* that at long last—?"

"It is. And soon I'll be introducing you to all our friends—and this time forever—as Mrs. Larry Astell."

The re-emergence of the Hisp from its hiding place had all the overtones of pomp usually associated with the launching of a ship. A score of villagers arrived at 10:00 A.M. and were offered free champagne—though not the thirty-three vintage. With Gaston in charge, one bottle of non-vintage was ceremoniously hurled at the wall my father had built. It smashed against it in a shower of froth. Then Gaston and three or four helpers armed with sledge hammers started to break down the wall.

When there was a hole large enough to scramble through, Jean crept in with a torch to find the thirty-three and emerged with a couple of bottles. Soon the wall—hated symbol of Nazi domination—had been demolished, and the Hisp stood like a ghost wrapped in dust sheets.

We tore the covering off. Some dust had slipped in through the years, that was inevitable, but even so the black monster with its silver fittings would need only a feather brush and a little polish to restore it to its former magnificence.

"Quite an automobile," said the colonel.

"She is. And she does a hundred miles an hour. By tomorrow night Gaston will have it tuned to perfection. He's worked on that car since he was a boy."

* * *

We drank quite a few bottles of the thirty-three, more than we had intended to, because La Châtelaine joined Colonel Nolan for lunch, together with Oregon, who was leaving the following day for Paris. Then Gaston and Olivia arrived, after he had interrupted work on the Hisp. I was delighted when Grandma invited Gaston to lunch, asking Nolan, "I believe you've met. Gaston is the head of our vineyard production." How Gaston had changed his life since the time when he used to tinker with cars, or drive Papa—and Mama—in his chauffeur's uniform. I could not have asked for a better friend, a more staunch comrade. He deserved everything—including Olivia, already changing for the better. Nothing would ever erase the wrinkles caused by suffering, nothing could obliterate the memories, but at least she had had her hair waved, touched up, and her nails manicured. She was, in short, a woman again. I raised my glass to her in a silent toast. A wonderful girl.

Then I drank again—to Anna. Sonia had told me on the phone that she had virtually recovered—enough to be planning a trip to America as soon as she would be allowed. Wonderful news! I wasn't all that sure how my very much changed mama would get on with her daughter, but the fact that Anna was well enough to want to travel meant that the terrible scars had all but healed.

As the meal ended, Grandma drank a toast to her son, then turned to me, glass raised, and said, "All of us here send our love to Sonia. It's like a bridal party. But it's more than that. We're saying farewell to the France we knew, for we know it can never be the same again. So off you go, and get married. And God speed you. But come back—come back soon. We need you. We need all the friends we can muster to help to rebuild our new France all over again."

Within a few hours I was on my way to meet Sonia. It was a warm, sunny day, the streets of country villages were lined with flags. The elegant black and silver car purred along silently with hardly more than an engine whisper. Sometimes in a village street men and women turned and clapped at the sight of her, so rare to see the emblem of luxury in war-torn France.

I stopped at the roadside to drink some wine and eat some *baguettes* which Madame Robert had packed for me, then set off again toward Dole. Nearly there! And in the warm sunshine I was thinking not only of the meeting with Sonia in only a few hours, but the very first time I had driven to Rolle—then in my beloved MG—and of that journey back and how everything had started when we lay in love in a bed of golden corn flecked with red poppies.

How much had happened since then! Not only war, but life itself—those first entrancing months in the rue de l'Université when I worked all day in the rue de Sentier, learning to be a newspaperman, then danced or made love all night till the first streaks of dawn touched the Champs-Elysées as we walked home. And then the arrival of Sonia's father, Signore Riccardi, and his friendship with the sinister Otto Abetz, of the way they used their hidden powers to murder two Italians, and later to force Sonia to leave France. And then her marriage to Francesco—but that didn't stop us loving each other, even that. It even led us to the mad journey through roads chocked with traffic in a vain bid to help Sonia escape before France fell—until I lost her after the air raid.

Then war—with Mama almost drowned in the *Athenia*—and the saving of her attaché case, with its telltale photo of Mama and Gaston. I would never tell him that I knew about them. It was after that, after I stumbled into the flat in Germany to find Willi beaten up, almost dying, it was after that, when the worst of all terrible tortures happened to the Astells. Anna and Olivia were captured by the Gestapo, and suffered the fate of the damned until, with the help of Sonia, we rescued them.

Now it was all over. I couldn't remember the number of men Gaston and I had killed in cold blood—face-to-face killings, not the impersonal load of death dropped by a bomber pilot. I would never remember. I only wanted to forget it all.

I drove carefully through the twisting streets of Dole,

and headed for the Juras and Pontarlier. That was where we had stopped on the first journey, stopping at the "frontier" town for a glass of beer, then tearing off to find the cornfield.

That was what I wanted to remember. The war had been an interlude, fought by others. Life had really started—for me anyway—on that first trip to Rolle, and now, after all the agonies that life and fate had laid before us, like tests to be surmounted on the road to happiness, we had come full circle.

Once again—a day later, a year later, a lifetime later?—I was driving through the sunshine to the lakeside at Switzerland to meet a beautiful girl. The same beautiful girl, dressed in pink on that day so long ago, the only girl I had ever loved and ever would.